**"Promises, promises." Rafe laughed, taking her
hand again.**

That was all she had to give, Dana thought. Promises.
Promises he might not want, once he knew everything.

She was setting herself up for a fall. There was no getting
away from it. She had to face the fact that a reckoning was
coming. It was just a matter of time.

Time, the one thing she needed. The one thing she didn't
have.

Dana had to tell him about the baby, and yet something
within her kept crying out, "More, just a little more."

The problem with wanting more was that it was endless.

Just like her craving for Rafe.

Please address questions and book requests to:
Silhouette Reader Service
U.S.: 3010 Walden Ave., P.O. Box 1325, Buffalo, NY 14269
Canada: P.O. Box 609, Fort Erie, Ont. L2A 5X3

MARIE FERRARELLA

In The Family Way

Published by Silhouette Books

America's Publisher of Contemporary Romance

SILHOUETTE BOOKS

IN THE FAMILY WAY

Copyright © 1998 by Marie Rydzynski-Ferrarella

ISBN 0-373-48364-3

This edition published by arrangement with Harlequin Books S.A.

® and TM are trademarks of Harlequin Books S.A., used under
license. Trademarks indicated with ® are registered in the United States
Patent and Trademark Office, the Canadian Trade Marks Office and in
other countries.

Printed in U.S.A.

To
my family,
for making me crazy
and
for making me feel needed and loved

MARIE FERRARELLA

sold her first contemporary romance to Silhouette Books
fifteen years ago and has recently been named to Silhouette's
exclusive Five Star Club, having sold more than five million
copies of her books. Her romances are beloved by fans
worldwide and have been translated into Spanish, Italian,
German, Russian, Polish, Japanese and Korean. In 1998,
she celebrates the publication of her seventy-fifth novel for
Silhouette Books. Having earned a master's degree in
Shakespearean comedy, her writing is distinguished by
humor and realistic dialogue. Marie Ferrarella describes
herself as the tired mother of two overenergetic children
and the contented wife of one wonderful man. This RITA
Award-winning author is thrilled to be following her dream
of writing full-time.

Chapter 1

"I'm what?"

Dana Morrow gripped the armrests of the chair she was sitting in, as if that would somehow negate what her doctor, her friend, was telling her. Her voice, suddenly thin and high, vibrated in the small office.

Shock was something Dr. Sheila Pollack had never expected to see on Dana's face. It took a little getting used to. As did, she supposed, her news.

"Pregnant," Sheila repeated. "With child. In the family way." A fond smile curved her lips, an unconscious response to the news she'd just delivered. To Sheila, there was nothing more sacred, more wonderful, than the creation of life between two people in love. But then, she was one of the lucky ones. She had Slade, and that tended to color her view of things. "There's a little human being forming and growing within you even as we speak."

For a moment, Dana felt as if she'd just received the salvo that would finally sink the ship she'd been trying so desperately to keep afloat. Sheila had to be wrong.

"That's impossible. There has to be some mistake." Dana passed her hand along her belly. There was no change to be felt there. Nothing was different than it had been from last week, last month, last year. Except that, for the last few days, her morning ritual included communing with the toilet bowl while poised before it on her knees. But that didn't mean she was pregnant. She was just coming down with the flu. People with the flu threw up all the time.

The look in her eyes willed Sheila to retract her words. "I can't be pregnant."

Dana *was* in shock, Sheila realized. Sympathy nudged its way forward. "I'm afraid that you are. All the signs are positive."

Sheila had started out her professional morning two hours earlier than usual, delivering a healthy baby boy who'd decided to make his debut three weeks before his due date. It was while she'd been rushing to get ready to leave that she'd heard her houseguest trying to muffle the sounds of retching. She'd ordered Dana to the office for an exam, fitting her in before her first appointment. As a result, there was now a roomful of women waiting for her.

She rounded the desk, took the chair beside Dana and placed her arm around the younger woman's shoulders. For a brief moment, the clock turned back twenty-three years. She was in the Morrow home, baby-sitting Dana and her younger sister, Megan, while Mr. Morrow was off to some new place in the limelight, enmeshed in yet another high profile murder case, and Mrs. Morrow was quietly looking for validation at the bottom of a bottle she thought no one knew she kept.

Five years separated her from Dana. Twenty-three years ago, the gap had felt like a wide chasm. Now there was no difference between them. Except that Sheila was happy, and Dana, it was apparent from the moment the younger woman had turned up on her doorstep yesterday morning, Mollie in tow, was not.

Why was it that some people were never allowed their share of happiness? Sheila wondered. God knew Dana had both earned and deserved it. "I take it this isn't a welcome turn of events."

A welcome turn of events? Dana thought. It might have been, once, when she and Steven had first gotten together. Then she'd believed in the possibility of love. Now she knew better. It had taken her a while, but she had finally learned.

Numb, she could only shake her head in response.

"No chance of this bringing about a reconciliation?" Sheila looked at her hopefully. Dana had been pretty vague about what had brought her back to Bedford, only that she'd left the man she was living with.

Dana could feel her mind scrambling around, like a tiny mouse looking for a way out of the maze before it died there. A baby. Oh God, this was terrible, really terrible. The timing couldn't have been worse than if it had been wished on her as a curse.

Struggling for composure even as she felt herself sinking, Dana shook her head. "More chance of Megan walking in through that door, telling me she's here for Mollie."

Just one damn thing on top of another and another, Dana thought, her anger rising. Anger had always been her edge. It kept her from slipping under, from being shredded by the talons of despair. The way her mother eventually had been. No one needed to know that beneath the anger, the bravado, was the small child from long ago who still hurt.

Sheila hugged Dana to her, wishing there was something she could do. But there wasn't, other than to be there for her friend. "Have I told you how very sorry I was to hear about Megan and her husband?"

Dana drew back to look at Sheila. "You don't have to say anything, Sheila. I saw it in your eyes when Mollie and I descended on you yesterday like the plague."

Sheila frowned at the description. They were friends. More than friends. Almost sisters. Sisters were not beholden to one another. They were just there, to act as buffers whenever necessary.

"You didn't descend," she corrected, then added pointedly, "locusts descend."

The faint outline of a smile lifted a corner of Dana's mouth. She'd gone to Sheila rather than to the place school records had once cited as her home because she'd needed to see the sight of an understanding face almost more than she'd needed to breathe. And because Sheila would accept her without asking for any explanations, any excuses. Unlike her father.

"Like I said—"

Sheila didn't want Dana's gratitude, just her well-being. "You're welcome at my house, Dana, you and Mollie," she said in the no-nonsense tone that her husband teased her about. "For as long as you want to stay."

"I want to stay forever." The tired smile widened just a little. "However, Slade might have different ideas."

"Slade and I think very much alike." His kindness was one of the qualities that endeared him to her so much. "Besides, being around Mollie is good practice for him. Rebecca isn't going to be a toddler forever. He might as well see what he's in for a few years down the line."

Dana was tempted, just for a second, to take Sheila up on her hospitality. But that would be hiding from the world, and Dana had never allowed herself to be a coward. Once begun, it would be a hard habit to break.

"Thanks, but I really can't hide out at your place forever." Dana looked at her abdomen. How could she be pregnant? Why now, of all times? Now, when she'd left her position at the law firm, her apartment, and abandoned her things? Everything except for a few of Mollie's belongings and the box of photographs she treasured. The box of photographs she'd always meant to place into an album someday.

The box that held visual evidence of the very best pieces of her life.

Frustration welled inside her. It just wasn't fair.

Damn it, anyway. Damn Steven for making me believe. Damn me for believing.

She pressed the heel of her hand hard against her stomach,

as if to rub the tiny seed out, erasing it. Silly thought, she upbraided herself.

"Seems like I can't hide at all." Dana caught her lower lip between her teeth, afraid that her voice would break.

"It's okay to cry," Sheila whispered soothingly.

"I'm not going to cry," Dana answered quietly as the numbness continued to pour through her, anesthetizing everything in its path. "I'm just not sure I can breathe very well at the moment."

Been there, done that, Sheila thought. "If it helps any, I felt the same way you did when I found out I was pregnant."

Dana looked at Sheila. She couldn't remotely picture Sheila being as devastated as she felt right at this moment. If anyone had ever been born to be a mother, it was Sheila. Sheila adored babies.

So did she. She just didn't want to have one right now, Dana thought miserably.

Sheila saw the look of disbelief in Dana's eyes. "Don't forget, Slade wasn't in my life anymore by the time I realized I was carrying his child. He was overseas, dodging bullets and writing headlines. I thought having a baby, *raising* a baby, was going to be something I was going to go through alone." She remembered how much she'd resisted loving him when he returned—and how futile that had been. "Until he showed up, like the cavalry."

That might have been true for Sheila, but Dana didn't live in a fairy-tale world.

"Steven isn't the cavalry." Her voice was flat, stripped of feelings. "He'd be something the cavalry would be saving me from." That, too, she had learned the hard way. Steven had changed the way he seemed to be—kind, funny, thoughtful—to the man he really was. Self-centered and egotistical, and impossible to live with. It had taken Mollie's coming to live with her to realize the truth.

She saw the look on Sheila's face. Ever the optimist, Sheila was going to try to find something good to say about a man she'd never met. That was just Sheila's way. To forage for

the positive. But there was nothing positive to say about
Steven. Not anymore.

Once she'd thought otherwise. Steven had entered her life
like a song. No, like a poem, Dana amended.

She'd almost forgotten about that. Steven used to write the
loveliest poems to her. He'd create them while she sat and
listened. His words had vibrated with such feeling. Such love.

It was the poems that had convinced her. Convinced her
she'd finally found someone to love. Someone who really
loved her in return, the way George had loved her sister.

Not everyone was destined to have love in their lives, she
thought cynically. She was living proof of that.

Sorrow yawned before her, its jaws wide and sharp, threatening to swallow her up. Just for a moment, Dana felt completely helpless.

"Oh, Sheila, if there was ever a time not to be pregnant,
this is it."

Concern overwhelmed Sheila. She'd never seen Dana like
this. Yesterday, when Dana had come to her, she'd seemed
no different than the girl she'd always known. A little older,
to be sure, but there was still an air of strength about her, still
a hint of laughter in her eyes. Today, she was the portrait of
a troubled woman.

"What are you going to do?" The offer of support was
silent but understood.

"You mean besides throw up?" Dana mustered a ghost of
a smile. "I don't know. Be numb, I guess, at least for a
while."

Pregnant.

The word echoed in Dana's brain, mocking her. She still
couldn't bring herself to believe it. She'd been so careful.
"Sheila, how could this have happened?"

"My guess is the usual way." Sympathy and humor filled
her eyes. "Didn't anyone ever tell you about the birds and
the bees?"

Dana laughed shortly. "Yes, but in my case, the bird was
practicing birth control."

Rising, Sheila pushed her hands deep into the pockets of her lab coat. A baby's arrival should be something to look forward to, not despair of. She couldn't think of anything sadder than not to want the child you were blessed with. "Nothing's foolproof."

"Emphasis on the word fool."

Sheila studied Dana's face. "Are you talking about him or you?"

"Me." She raised her chin, a sliver of defiance wedging its way in. "For ever having gotten mixed up with him."

That was more like it, Sheila thought. For a moment there, she'd been afraid that Dana was going to break down. "From what you wrote me, he was quite charming."

"Yes, he was." But in Steven's case, charming was merely camouflage for shallow. "In the beginning," Dana qualified. "He actually wrote poetry to me. We started out like poetry and wound up like a limerick, the kind that leaves a bad taste in your mouth."

She should have left earlier, Dana thought, annoyed with herself. Left when the first signs had begun to show. When the romance had begun to unravel. Cut her losses and go. If she had, at least she wouldn't be in this predicament.

Dana needed something to get her mind off this, off everything, Sheila thought. There was so much that was resting on her slim shoulders these days. Custody of her orphaned niece, a failed relationship, uprooting her life and an as-yet-untried reconciliation with a father who, in Sheila's estimation, most saints would have had trouble with. With the pregnancy on top of that, a weaker person would be coming unglued.

"Listen, why don't the three of us go out tonight? Pilar can stay with the kids." Her housekeeper was excellent with children. "Slade just wrapped up an investigative series he was working on, and if the stork's willing to cooperate, I don't have anyone due to deliver for another few weeks. I could use the break."

But it wasn't Sheila who needed the break, and they both knew it. Dana appreciated the gesture but shook her head.

"I don't like leaving Mollie alone for more than an hour or so at the moment. She hasn't been well." Mollie was all that was making life worthwhile for her these days. It had been Mollie she was thinking of when she finally made the break from Steven. Mollie, so young to already have been touched by the darker side of life, needed the opportunity to laugh, to play, to be a normal little girl. To grow up into a happy young woman. Mollie wouldn't have gotten her chance if Dana had remained with Steven.

Sheila frowned, trying to remember. Had she missed something? The little girl had seemed pale but otherwise all right to her. "I didn't notice—"

"She's run-down, listless, coughing. It may just be a run-of-the-mill cold, but I don't think so. Maybe it's even psychological." All she knew was that she'd watched Mollie's spirit and her health decline a little with each week that passed. "Losing her parents like that, and then coming to live with me—with us," she amended, thinking of Steven, "it's unsettling for someone her age. And Steven didn't make it very easy on her." She left it at that. There was no need to go into detail.

But that had been the last straw, what had finally sent her on her way. The way Steven had behaved toward Mollie. As if she was an intrusion into his life, something to be pushed out of the way and then ignored like a piece of offending furniture. Dana had seen herself and her father all over again. Except that her father had never been that direct. For the most part, when he was around at all, her father had ignored her and Megan completely.

When he did acknowledge their existence, it was to criticize. Nothing they did was ever good enough for him. He'd wanted more from them. Always more. Meggie had gone out of her way to give it to him. Dana had simply gone.

Sheila wondered how much of Mollie's problem was real and how much Dana might be imagining, transferring her grief to the child. "I forget, how long has she been with you?"

It seemed like forever. And only yesterday. "Straight out of the hospital." Dana didn't need to pause to calculate the length of time. It was engraved in her brain. Mollie had come to live with her after the fatal accident that had taken Megan and George. "Six months." Mollie had been like a broken sparrow in need of so much attention, so much love, just to heal. And Steven had become jealous of the time she'd devoted to the little girl. Time, he claimed, that was stolen from him.

That was when Dana had finally wiped the cobwebs from her eyes. She'd taken off with Mollie while he was at work, sparing herself the grief of yet another nasty, drawn-out argument. By the time he'd realized she wasn't at work, she and Mollie had been on the road for eight hours.

Sheila began to edge to the door, acutely aware of just how far behind schedule she'd fallen. She paused for one last word of assurance.

"I can take a look at Mollie when I get home tonight, if you like. But if you're really worried, I can recommend an excellent pediatrician. His patients love him, and his patients' parents think the man walks on water."

The analogy succeeded in bringing a smile to Dana's lips. "Does he?"

Sheila gave Rafael Saldana her unqualified seal of approval. "Pretty much. He's really terrific. I did my residency with him, and there's no one I'd rather entrust my baby to than Rafe."

"Rebecca has a pediatrician?"

"Yes." Sheila rested her hand on the doorknob. "Why is that so surprising?"

Dana shrugged. "I just thought a doctor wouldn't need to send members of her family to another doctor unless there was something drastically wrong and she needed a specialist."

"No, but she does need to admit she's human and not all-knowing," Sheila pointed out. "Rafe's idea of recreational reading is to immerse himself in the latest AMA findings in pediatric care. He's really dedicated. Like I said, he's the best." She opened the door. The soft murmur of voices from the reception area floated to her. Time to get rolling or she would be here straight through the evening. "I'll have Lisa arrange an appointment. Do you want to take Mollie to him this afternoon?"

The sooner the better. The coughing episodes were getting worse. Dana smiled her appreciation.

"I'd feel better knowing there's nothing wrong with Mollie. Then all I'll have to come to grips with is the news you just laid on me." She blew out a breath. "That, and making peace with my father."

Sheila knew why Dana had chosen to return to Bedford after all this time rather than settle somewhere else. She'd been the one to write to her friend, telling Dana of her father's recent stroke. Sheila didn't envy the road Dana had before her. "Remember, you're welcome to stay with us for as long as you'd like."

Dana knew the invitation was tendered in earnest, and part of her wanted to accept, to pull the covers over her head and hide from the world. For just a little while.

But she really didn't have that luxury. Time, for all she knew, might be running out for her father.

"I came back to mend fences, Sheila. Before…before there's no one to mend fences with." Meggie's sudden death had made Dana acutely aware of just how tenuous life was. And how much more so for a man past middle age and in deteriorating health.

Sheila squeezed her hand. "That's not an easy row to hoe, Dana."

There was no reason to pretend with Sheila. Sheila had pretty much been privy to it all. Their parents had been friends since before either one of them was born, and the two had grown up together.

"No, all rocks and hard ground," Dana agreed. But that wasn't a cause for pity—it was just the way things were. "But he is my father and, except for Mollie, all the family I have.

It's not right to let things stay the way they are.'' She glanced
at her stomach and the offending resident there. "Of course,
this isn't going to make things any easier."

Sheila didn't hesitate. "Don't tell him yet."

Dana laughed for the first time that day. She had no intention of mentioning her pregnancy to Paul Morrow until other
things were resolved between them. And perhaps not even
then. She knew that finding the words to tell him would be
next to impossible. An unwed pregnancy was far from unusual these days, but it wouldn't fly with her father and his
particular code of morals.

"I might not even tell him until after the baby goes to
college."

"If anyone can pull that off, you can." Sheila laid a hand
on her shoulder. She really had to get to work, but she hated
to see her friend in such distress. "You going to be all right?"
She felt Dana's shoulders stiffen beneath her hand.

"Yeah. You know me, Sheila, I thrive on challenges and
rough times." But it would be nice, just once, to have things
go smoothly, at least for a little while.

She supposed maybe she was asking for too much.

Sheila saw Lisa motioning to her from the hall. "I'll have
Lisa make that appointment," she promised.

Dana nodded. Well, one thing down, four million to go,
she thought, leaving Sheila's office. None of which she was
looking forward to.

It was five o'clock when Dana walked into Dr. Rafael Saldana's office. The appointment had been almost impossible
to get. Dr. Saldana was every bit as popular as Sheila claimed.
Dana had stood beside Lisa as the nurse argued with the
woman on the other end of the line that, while this was not
an emergency, Dr. Pollack would regard it as a personal favor
as well as a professional courtesy if Dr. Saldana could somehow squeeze Mollie Aliprantis into his busy schedule. Today.
The woman had finally—reluctantly—agreed to the end of

the day, but not without putting Lisa on hold and consulting with the doctor.

The waiting room was empty. It looked like the aftermath of a war. An army of toys was scattered throughout the room, covering the floor and the table that was usually reserved for magazines in other offices. Dana was surprised at how many toys, most in fairly good condition, there were. How many and how varied. The doctor she and Meggie used to go to had had exactly five children's books to occupy his patients' attention. She knew, because she'd read them all until she could recite them from memory.

Dana supposed this was a good sign. At least Dr. Saldana knew children liked to play more than they like to sit still and read.

As the door closed behind them, she could feel Mollie's hand tighten on hers. The little girl was almost clinging to her. Wide, deep blue eyes looked around the room slowly. Apprehensively. Mollie didn't like anything new. Even leaving Dallas had been difficult for her.

"Why are we here, Aunt Dana?" If she could have managed it, Mollie would have melted into Dana's body. She clearly didn't want to be here.

Dana ran her hand over the silky blond curls. Hair so fine, it felt like a light mist against her fingertips. "To see the doctor, pet."

Mollie's chin trembled. "I don't like doctors."

"I know you don't, sweetie."

She had little reason to, Dana thought. Doctors meant hospitals, and hospitals were synonymous with death to the girl.

"But he's going to make you feel better, Mol." Ignoring the reception desk for the moment, Dana steered Mollie toward a huge Barbie playhouse, its accessories spread out on the floor.

Here was one doll who knew how to live, Dana mused. At least here, in the world of make-believe, opulence was synonymous with happiness.

"Will I have to go to the hospital?" Fear framed each word.

"No, honey. No hospital. I promise." She fervently hoped it was a promise she could keep. But Mollie didn't need to hear a debate about necessity or circumstance. She needed someone to make the monsters go away. "He's just going to make you feel better." *I hope,* she added silently. "Sit here for a second, baby. I'm going to announce you."

"Like a princess?" Mollie asked brightly.

Cinderella was one of Mollie's favorite stories. Dana must have read the ballroom scene to her several hundred times. Mollie liked to pretend she was Cinderella, who in turn was pretending to be a princess. Dana could readily identify with that.

"Like a princess." Dana turned toward the reception desk, her face growing somber. She hoped Dr. Saldana was half as good as Sheila thought. "Dana Morrow here, with Mollie Aliprantis," she told the young nurse at the window crisply. "Dr. Pollack's office called earlier today to make the appointment," she added when the woman looked at her blankly.

The woman came to life and reached for a clipboard. She attached several sheets to it, passing them to Dana over the counter. "Of course. If you'd just fill out these forms…"

Dana loathed paperwork, and a quick glance told her that most of the required information she didn't know or thought irrelevant. Dana waved the clipboard at the woman.

"I'm not sure I *can* fill these out." Surprise registered on the nurse's face. "We've just moved here from Dallas, and her medical records haven't caught up with us yet," Dana explained. "I don't have a permanent address or a job yet."

I do, however, have a baby on the way, she thought with a touch of bitterness she couldn't suppress. The receptionist was staring at her, dumbfounded. Obviously no one had ever objected to filling out the forms before.

"And there's no health insurance. I'll be paying by charge card."

The nurse worked her lower lip, continuing to look uncertain. "Alice—" she turned in her chair to face the back "—this lady doesn't want to fill out the forms."

An older woman with a kindly face came up behind the nurse. Dana reiterated what she had just said, emphasizing that she was paying for the visit. That was all the paperwork was for, to ensure payment, she thought.

The woman named Alice moved the clipboard toward Dana, a sympathetic smile on her lips and in her eyes. "Why don't you just fill in what you can? Patient's history, that sort of thing."

She was talking to her as if she was mentally impaired, Dana thought with a frustrated sigh. She glanced at the form, scanning it. She didn't have the answers to most of the questions. But she would, she promised herself. In time. However, that time wasn't now.

"I don't know her history." She heard the edge in her voice and was unable to stop it. "I'm her aunt. Her legal guardian," she added when she saw the two women exchange looks. Out of the corner of her eye, she saw Mollie solemnly watching her. For her sake, Dana softened her tone. "Look, I haven't gotten everything sorted out yet." She indicated the questionnaire, struggling with a temper that had already been pushed too far today. "She's not feeling well. If the doctor could just take a look at her for five minutes, that's all I need."

Not true, a small voice within her said. *I need a lot more than that. I need a miracle or two.*

"Is there a problem?" a deep voice asked from inside the office.

Ah, the doctor who walked on water, Dana thought. Maybe he was given to listening to reason. At least, since she was here, it was worth a try.

Hands splayed against the counter, Dana leaned over as far as she could, her head turned toward the sound of the voice.

"None," she informed him, "if I can just dispense with the paperwork."

Drawn by the suppressed anger he heard in the woman's

voice, Rafe Saldana walked into the reception area. ''Doesn't seem like such a difficult request to me.''

Looking up, Dana took a step back, startled. The gentle voice belonged to a giant of a man.

Chapter 2

Accustomed to making quick assessments, Dana scrutinized the man in the white tunic before her. With hands like that, he looked as if he would be right at home as a lumberjack, felling trees the old-fashioned way. And given his large, broad frame, he would have been considered a godsend on moving day. Everything about him pointed to a man who would be more comfortable handling large, bulky things. Definitely a physical man.

This was Sheila's pediatrician?

It took an effort to picture those hands holding a tiny baby, much less handling one gently.

Suddenly, Mollie was at her side, grabbing her hand. Dana's hand tightened on Mollie's, concerned that the man might frighten the little girl by his very stature.

Mollie moved closer to her, pressing her face against her leg. As if being close could somehow magically protect her from everything that threatened to harm her in this scary new place.

Rafe was accustomed to these first meetings. He knew all

about the fears that went along with them. He vividly remembered his first visit to Dr. Saunders. He'd been so terrified, he'd hidden under one of the chairs in the waiting room and refused to come out until the doctor had coaxed him with a candy bar and a promise that he could examine all the instruments. If he didn't miss his guess, he'd been around the same age this new patient was.

Smiling, Rafe squatted to the little girl's level and addressed the side of woman's leg where Mollie was hiding. "You must be Mollie."

Ever so slowly, Mollie peered around Dana's leg to look at him. Her eyes solemnly fixed on his face, she nodded in response. With her heart fluttering hard in her chest, she popped her thumb into her mouth. Her daddy had told her that big girls didn't do that, but right now, it made her feel better.

Rafe put out his hand to her as if she were the exact same age he was. "How do you do, Mollie? I'm Dr. Rafe." He waited, his hand extended.

After a beat, Mollie hesitantly drew her thumb out of her mouth and slipped her small, slightly damp hand into his. She watched with wavering anxiety as it was swallowed up, covered by his large, tanned fingers. His hand felt strong as he shook hers. Strong, but nice.

Rafe glanced toward the woman behind the child and saw the quizzical look on her face. "Rafe is a lot easier for a small tongue to manage than Saldana." His eyes returned to Mollie. "Isn't it, Mollie?"

She liked being talked to as if she was a grown-up. Aunt Dana talked to her like that. And so did the nice lady and man they were staying with. Not like Steven. He didn't talk to her at all. He just mumbled and grunted at her, like he didn't want to say anything. She knew he didn't like her.

"Uh-huh."

Rafe rose slowly, in order not to startle her. When he gained his feet, he was still holding her hand. "Why don't we go into the examining room?'' He glanced behind him. "Your mom can come along, too, if she'd like.''

Mollie shook her head. Her voice was barely audible when she said, "My mom can't come. She's gone to heaven.''

"I'm sorry to hear that, Mollie.'' Rafe looked at Dana for an explanation.

Rather than go into detail and distress Mollie further, Dana told him, "I'm her aunt. And her legal guardian,'' she added, to forestall any concerns he might have about her right to bring Mollie in to see him. After all, this was the day and age of malpractice suits. Dana had few illusions left, and fewer about doctors. Most were more concerned about covering their tails than they were about treating their patients. Sheila was in a class by herself, but this person holding Mollie's hand wasn't Sheila. This was someone she didn't know.

Sheila's recommendation carried weight, but Dana still reserved the right to form her own opinion of the man. Right now, he was guilty until proven innocent. She'd learned that it was the safest approach to take. There was usually a lot less grief that way.

Too bad she hadn't learned that lesson earlier.

Dr. Saldana nodded, apparently taking her explanation in stride.

Leading the way, he took them into the first examining room. It was small, but its orientation allowed the afternoon sun to bounce playfully along the walls, making the room appear breezy and bright. Three of the walls were light yellow, but it was the fourth that caught her attention. There was a mural covering it, depicting a scene where children and baby animals freely mingled, playing with joyful abandon.

Mollie was staring at it, her attention temporarily drawn away from the nervous anticipation the visit to the doctor had created. Dana wondered if that was just an accident, or intentional on the doctor's part. Looking at him again, she had a feeling he wasn't the type who allowed things to happen by accident.

"Nice wall,'' Dana commented.

Rafe glanced at it. At times, he forgot that it was there. He'd put in over three weeks creating this one and the ones in the other two exam rooms, working nights and whenever he had a free bit of time.

"Thanks. But I don't think I got the colt's hooves quite right." He'd tried six times before he'd finally given up. Most of his patients would never notice, anyway. It was the total effect that he'd been after. Only the perfectionist in him had egged him on to try to improve on what he'd done.

Dana's brows came together as she studied the mural more closely. Was he serious or just seeing how gullible she was?

Glancing over her shoulder, she pinned him with a look that forbade him to lie. "You did this?"

He nodded. To him, it was no big deal. The ability to put brush to canvas had always been with him. Something he'd inherited from his mother.

"Painting relaxes me. I don't get much of a chance to do it anymore."

Or at all, if he was being truthful. Life had become one hell of a toboggan ride this last year. He hadn't taken more than a day off at a time in eighteen months. There was too much to do, and his practice continued to grow. He had trouble saying no when it involved children.

Like now. He smiled at his newest patient and was rewarded with a timid half-smile in return. Nothing better, he thought. The smile of a child was priceless and innocent. Unlike its adult counterpart.

Hands on either side of Mollie's waist, Rafe lifted her onto the examining table. It vaguely registered that he had textbooks that felt heavier than she did.

"Now then," he began in his kindest voice, looking straight into her eyes, "how old are you, Mollie?" Mollie held up five fingers. "I see." He nodded solemnly, taking in the information. "And what seems to be the problem?"

Mollie wiggled a little, blossoming in response to his tone. "I cough."

"I see." He looked properly serious. "Is it a big cough or

a little cough?'' He let the question sink in before continuing. ''Is it a cough that comes a lot?''

Mollie paused, thinking. ''A lot.''

Forcing a cough, she gave him her best demonstration. It sounded suspiciously as if she was having trouble clearing her throat.

But Rafe nodded as if impressed by what he'd heard. He took his stethoscope from around his neck and placed the ends to his ears. ''Well, let's just see what it sounds like inside you.''

Her eyes on the instrument, Mollie scrambled back on the table, moving so quickly she nearly tumbled off. Rafe grabbed the side of her overalls, catching her just in time. Dana's hands were right on top of his, less than half a heart-beat behind.

She dropped her hands to her side. ''Mollie, be careful.''

But Mollie's attention was riveted on Rafe. The fear was back, stronger than before. She'd lain in a hospital bed, her arms held down, funny long tubes running through them. She was afraid he would take her back there.

''Are you going to open me up?'' Her voice trembled. So did she.

He resisted the impulse to hug her to him until the fear had been blotted out. Instead, one hand on her shoulder to hold her still, Rafe calmly explained what he was about to do.

''We don't have to open you up, Mollie. I just listen with this.'' He tapped the stethoscope, then took it off for her to examine. He suspected that, like him, she appreciated know-ing the enemy. It made things less frightening and mysterious. ''Ever see one of these?''

''She's been in the hospital,'' Dana cut in, wishing he would hurry up.

She was feeling incredibly tired all of a sudden. Fatigue had come like a huge, smothering blanket, dropping out of nowhere and oppressing her. All she could think of doing was going to Sheila's and crawling into bed once Mollie was taken care of. She vaguely recalled hearing that pregnancy did that to you in the early stages. Wiped you out without notice. Another reason to resent her condition.

Having momentarily allayed Mollie's fears, Rafe laid the stethoscope to her chest and prompted her to breathe. "When was she in the hospital?" he wanted to know.

"Six months ago," Dana answered tersely.

Was that anger in her voice? Why? He hadn't asked her anything particularly difficult or private. If he was going to treat Mollie, these were things he had to know.

Rafe turned Mollie around, pressing the stethoscope to her back, telling her to breathe again. "Why? What was she in for?"

Dana watched Mollie's face. The little girl was too involved with what the doctor was doing to pay attention to the conversation. Good.

"She was in a car accident," Dana said softly. "She had cuts, internal bruising and a broken wrist."

The same accident, Rafe surmised from the woman's tone, that had robbed the little girl of her mother. He wondered where the child's father was, and whether he took an active part in his daughter's life.

"Sound like quite an ordeal. I guess that makes you an expert," he said to Mollie. "You know, this little thing can pick up your heartbeat." Taking the stethoscope off, he angled the earpiece so that Mollie could listen to her own heart. The wonder that spread over her face tickled him. "How does that sound?"

Mollie wrinkled her nose. "Funny." She wasn't sure if she was being teased or not. Aunt Dana's friend Slade teased her, but he laughed when he did it. "Is that really me?"

"That's really you," he assured her. He coaxed the stethoscope from her fingers and hung it carefully in its place on a rack. "And that funny little noise you just heard is a very comforting sound for everyone who loves you."

"There's just Aunt Dana," Mollie solemnly told him, as if it was a secret. "And my grandpa," she remembered. Mollie leaned forward, lowering her voice. "Except that he doesn't really love me."

Rafe studied her face, trying to discern whether the little girl was being fanciful or telling the truth. And just what that might mean to Mollie's general well-being. He was always on the alert for cases of abuse. To him, there was no more heinous crime than the willful abuse of a child.

"Are you sure? I can't see anyone not loving a pretty little girl like you." Since she didn't launch into an immediate litany of what she took to be her grandfather's offense, or pull back into her shell, both indications of trouble, he decided that perhaps he was just overreacting. "Maybe you should give him another chance."

Mollie willingly agreed. "Okay." She looked at Dana for backup.

Dana had no intention of getting into a personal conversation with Mollie in front of a stranger, even if he was a pediatrician who was thought to walk on water. Since Mollie had never met her grandfather, Dana assumed that Mollie's statement could be traced to something the little girl had overheard her parents discussing. It went without saying that neither Megan nor George would ever have said anything remotely as harsh to Mollie directly.

In any case, none of this was any of the doctor's business.

"So, can you tell what's wrong with her?" Dana pressed, redirecting the conversation.

"When did this cough start?" As he spoke, Rafe continued with his examination. Mollie watched in fascination as her knee jerked in response to the little rubber hammer.

Dana paused, trying to think. Her mind felt as if it was sinking into a fog. "Two weeks ago."

He set the hammer down, picked up another instrument and examined Mollie's eyes. "Describe it."

"It's a cough," she answered shortly.

He glanced at her, apparently unfazed by her tone. "Hacking? Dry? Wet? Intermittent or continuous? Adjectives are very usefully when I play doctor."

She blew out a breath, knowing she had no right to be impatient. He was doing her a favor. It was just that this sudden wave of exhaustion was making her irritable.

"Dry, intermittent. For the past few days it's sounded as if it's getting worse." Dana edged closer to him, as if she could somehow see what he saw if only she stood close enough. "What does she have?" she asked again.

"The good news is that she doesn't seem to have the flu that's making the rounds." About every fourth child he'd seen in the last few days had a case of it, and half of those were severe. The beds at the hospital were filling up quickly.

Having carefully examined each nostril, he shut off the light and laid the instrument on a metal tray. "From what I can see, Mollie has URI—an upper respiratory infection. Don't worry, that sounds a lot worse than it is." He skimmed the tip of his finger down Mollie's small nose. "I'll write you a prescription, and she'll be fine in no time."

Dana was sure he was wrong. There had to be more to it than that. "And that's it?"

Rafe nodded. He heard the outer door closing. That meant the others had gone home for the day. Time for him to wrap this up, too. "Is she allergic to any medications?"

"Not that I know of."

He picked up his pad and wrote out a prescription for Amoxicillin. There wasn't a child born who didn't like the bubble-gum taste of the pink liquid. He tore the sheet off and handed it to Mollie's aunt.

"This should take care of any lingering infection. One teaspoon, three times a day. Keep it in the refrigerator, and make sure she finishes the bottle. If there's any problem, call me. I'll be happy to see her." Then, because he couldn't resist, he tousled Mollie's hair. "But more than likely, there won't be any need to. This dazzling young lady's going to be just fine."

Which was more, he thought, than he could say about her aunt. The woman's face was definitely pale, and her eyes looked glassy. "Are you all right?"

She probably looked like hell. God knew she felt like it. Embarrassed, impatient and exhausted, Dana waved away his question and gathered Mollie in her arms, taking her off the table. This was all the medicine she needed, she thought, right here in her arms.

"I'm fine," Dana murmured. "Just adjusting to a different time zone, that's all."

Walking her into the hall, he shut off the light behind him. "You're not from around here?"

She'd been born not ten miles from the medical building they were standing in. At the very hospital Dr. Saldana was affiliated with. The one where Sheila worked. "I am, but not recently."

He'd thought he'd detected a tiny trace of an accent, but it wasn't strong enough for him to pinpoint. "Where *are* you from? Recently."

She answered before the thought there was no reason for him to ask or to know occurred to her. "Dallas." And if she never went back, that was fine with her. Because Dallas meant Steven.

Setting Mollie on the floor, Dana took her hand and went to the receptionist's desk.

But there was no one sitting there. There was no one in the office at all. Surprised, she turned to look at the doctor. "Do I pay you?"

It was late, and he would be damned if he was going to start messing with Alice's system at this hour. The woman had everything coded and locked up. She was a jewel when it came to running the office, but she did have her idiosyncrasies. Being deemed indispensable was one of them, and the way she accomplished that was having a system that would have taken the CIA five days to crack.

Rafe raised a shoulder and let it drop carelessly. "It's on the house." It was a lot simpler that way. He knew there was no file set up on Mollie, so there was nowhere to make an initial payment notation. Besides, he'd only spent a few minutes with her.

Maybe she was being unduly sensitive, Dana thought, but she had her pride. She wasn't about to accept charity from a stranger. "I can pay."

Obviously he'd struck a nerve. "I'm sure you can." Rafe indicated the computer. "But Alice has a program running on that thing that defies logic, and after a long day, I don't feel like fooling around with it." It was off, and there was no way he was going to turn it on. He'd learned the hard way that it responded only to her password. Technology was wonderful, as long as someone else's fingers were on the keyboard. "I owe Sheila a favor. Tell her this makes us square."

It didn't square anything, Dana thought. It was Sheila he owed the favor to, not her. She took out her wallet and extracted a plastic card. She offered it to him. "Can't you just take a charge card?"

Stubborn, he thought. It wasn't a quality he normally admired unless coupled with gaining a lifelong goal or beating the odds and getting well. For the most part, it was irritating.

Very gingerly, he pushed the card toward her with the tips of his fingers.

"I can *take* it, but there isn't much I can *do* with it. Her desk's locked." He jiggled the drawer to show her. It remained shut. "If my writing off this visit somehow offends your sense of dignity or self-esteem, you can pay Alice the next time you come."

She wasn't sure if she liked his attitude. He was a little too flippant for her taste. Doctors were supposed to be somber, capable and not opinionated.

"The next time?" she repeated. Her eyes narrowed as she read more into the remark than he'd intended. "Does Mollie need a more thorough workup?"

"No, but she does need a regular pediatrician." He assumed she didn't have one or Sheila would have mentioned it. "I take it that you and Mollie are staying in the area?"

There were no options open to her right now, and even if there were, there was a responsibility to face. That precluded leaving anytime soon.

"Yes, we are."

He placed his hand on the small of her back to usher her toward the door. She jumped as if he'd touched her with a hot poker. Wondering what that was about, he silently indicated the door, then walked beside her when she finally moved.

"Good, then I'll look forward to seeing you again." The words were addressed to Mollie, whose shy smile had broadened. "Here, let me get that for you," he offered just as Dana reached for the doorknob. The door tended to stick.

"That's all right, we can see ourselves out." Turning the knob, she felt resistance. Dana braced herself and pulled, refusing to ask for help after she had just turned it down. "Thank you," she told him formally before she walked out.

Mollie waved, then grasped her aunt's hand.

"Stubborn." The door closed with the firm snap of a lock slipping into place. Rafe shook his head. "Definitely got a burr under her saddle."

Well, that was her problem. He had other things that needed his attention. Specifically, seven patients under the age of eleven with the flu, waiting for him to make his rounds at the hospital. And Timmie.

He thought of the small boy. Timmie didn't have the flu. Rafe only wished he did. He didn't know what was wrong with the six-year-old, and he was growing progressively worse. The boy was far too young to spend his days in a hospital bed. But he needed more help than Rafe could give him. Timmie needed a specialist.

And maybe a miracle or two along the way.

Too bad he wasn't in the business of making them.

He was never going to get used to it, Rafe thought. He would never truly make peace with the fact that he couldn't cure every patient who came to him. Despite the fact that he had lost his wife, Debra, during his second year of residency, he still believed deep down that he could keep all his patients well if he tried hard enough. It was his mother's optimism and his father's silent but nonetheless strong reinforcement of it that had forged the way he thought, the way he approached his life and his work.

It didn't matter who took the credit or the blame, Rafe mused. He was what he was. A man who refused to give up even in the face of defeat. Timmie was going to get well. He'd promised the boy.

Rafe went to the telephone. Maybe he would give Jim Reilly a call. His former medical school roommate was associated with the pediatric wing of the Mayo Clinic these days. No harm in approaching him for some unofficial help. What mattered was curing Timmie and licking this thing that was slowly weakening him.

He did a quick calculation on the time difference. It was late back east. Jim undoubtedly wasn't in his office now, but Rafe had several numbers he could try. Jim had to be at one of them.

Rafe sat down, stretching his legs out beneath the desk his parents had had custom-built for him. It was a gift delivered the week before he'd opened his doors for the first time.

As if they hadn't already given him more than any son could hope for.

Sighing, Rafe pulled the phone over and began tapping out the first number. It looked like it was going to be another long evening.

Sheila arrived at her house fifteen minutes after Dana and Mollie returned from their visit to the doctor. Throwing her jacket in the general direction of an antique coatrack, she announced that she had only come home to check on Slade and Rebecca before dashing to the hospital. En route home, she'd answered her cell phone, only to hear that Mrs. Masterson's twins had decided to put in an early appearance.

Mr. Masterson was on his way to the hospital with his wife. He'd sounded as if he was about to come apart when he called. She sincerely hoped he would get a grip on himself long enough to arrive at Harris Memorial in one piece.

After kissing Slade and peeking in on Rebecca, who was

sound asleep in her crib, Sheila quickly turned her attention to Dana.

She stopped to pick up one of her housekeeper's sandwiches. Pilar threw in everything but the kitchen sink. It was just what Sheila needed right now, energy on rye.

"So..." She eyed Dana as she threw the thick sandwich into a paper sack. "What did you think of him?"

Dana shrugged. She didn't want to be too critical. After all, the man was a friend of Sheila's. "He was nice to Mollie. He put her at ease." And that was the most important thing.

There was something in Dana's tone that indicated she was less than thrilled with Rafe. Sheila had expected a more positive response. Everyone else she'd sent to Rafe raved about him. "Didn't I tell you he was terrific?"

Dana's exhaustion had passed. Restless now, she felt like going for a long walk. Instead, she accompanied Sheila to the living room. She saw no point in lying. They were too close for that. But she did try to play up the positive, though there was something about him that rubbed her the wrong way.

"I wouldn't go that far. I wasn't there long enough to label him terrific. But the fact that he didn't terrify Mollie is a definite point in his favor. He has a nice manner when it comes to children."

And women, Sheila thought. Although Dana seemed to be immune to it. Her friend had lost some of her sparkle, some of her energy. It wasn't all due to the pregnancy or even the news that she was pregnant. This was not the same person she'd known. Dana seemed to have been born with a streetwise edge to her, but it had always been tempered, balanced out by her positive approach to life. Somewhere along the line, Steven or someone else had snuffed out the light that was Dana.

For now, Sheila kept her thoughts to herself. "What did he say was wrong with her?"

"An upper respiratory infection."

Sheila nodded. "Very common. Probably prescribed Amoxicillin, right?"

"Right." Dana looked at Mollie, dubious. "I don't know...."

Sheila knew that look, had seen it reflected at her in the mirror despite all the training she'd had. "Know," she echoed. "I'm sure he's right." She slipped an arm around Dana's shoulders, pulling her close. "Welcome to motherhood, Dana," Sheila teased. "If it's not one worry, it's another."

Dana was quickly learning that. Learning, too, that maybe she wasn't equipped for this. There was no way she would give up Mollie, but the baby who was growing within her...well, she didn't know that child yet. Maybe she should start thinking about giving it up for adoption. It would be the simpler thing to do.

"How do women stand it?" she wanted to know.

Ah, Sheila thought, the eternal question. Luckily, the answer was just as eternal.

"Because, my dear, squeezed in between the emergencies, the tantrums and the sleepless nights are the little slices of heaven that are absolutely priceless. Judging from your expression, you already know what I mean."

Dana laughed softly. "Yeah, I know what you mean."

Caring for Mollie these past few months had made her feel more fulfilled than she had in years. It centered her and gave her a purpose. She couldn't think just of herself anymore. There was someone else who was directly affected by everything she did, everything she said.

It was a very sobering experience.

And one, she knew, she wouldn't have traded for the world. Because having Mollie depend on her made her feel that she was equal to anything, including beginning a new life.

And trying to make amends with an old one, she suddenly thought, an image of her father in her mind.

Before it was too late.

Chapter 3

Rafe ran his hand along the back of his neck, slowly kneading the muscles beneath his mop of damp, black hair. It didn't do any good. The muscles were hours past being stiff and were in all probability on their way to becoming permanently fused into a rigid state.

It felt as if he'd spent every minute of the past three days when he wasn't at his office leaning over the railings of hospital beds and cribs, assuring his small patients—those who could understand him—and their worried parents that all would be well in a few days.

Was it his imagination, or had the annual flu season shifted its timetable to appear earlier and stay longer the past few years? It felt as if he'd been through this endless whirlwind of patients and hospital beds only a couple of months ago. As of late this afternoon, the pediatric wing at Harris Memorial was almost filled to capacity. The latest outbreak went under the whimsical identifying marker of the Singapore flu, although as far as he knew its origins were far less exotic.

Closing his eyes, Rafe took a deep breath and then exhaled

slowly. Maybe, if he stood very still, no one would notice him for five minutes. That was all he asked, just five minutes. It seemed to be his quota of rest time these days.

"Buy you a soda, sailor?"

Rafe opened his eyes and smiled before he saw her, recognizing the voice. He eyed the can of pop in her hand. "I could use more than a soda, Sheila."

"Sorry, I'm a married woman. You'll have to see someone else about that. Maybe Kate." Exhausted, Sheila leaned against the wall beside Rafe, her trim figure all but hidden beneath the green surgical livery. The mask she'd worn only ten minutes ago was dangling about her neck like a limp badge of courage. It had been a tough delivery, but it was over, and she could finally relax.

Until the next frantic call.

She peered at the tall man beside her. Rafe looked tired. Bone tired. Because they were friends, she asked, "*Have* you seen Kate lately?"

It had been more than four years since his wife had died. She'd hoped that when he started seeing one of the hospital's research biologists, Kate Mulligan, just before Christmas last year, that meant he was taking his heart out of the deep freeze. But Kate's willingness notwithstanding, the relationship didn't seem to be destined for the altar. There was something missing in Rafe's eyes whenever Kate's name came up. Something she'd seen when he had been married to Debra.

A bemused smile lifted his mouth as he gave her question due consideration.

"Actually, I don't think I've even seen the sun lately." Or, at least, he hadn't paid attention to it. Between the flu, stray patients and Timmie's mysterious ailment, he was too preoccupied to pay attention to anything.

Sheila popped the top of her can. A gentle fizz emerged, then retreated.

"It hasn't changed," she assured him, taking a long, deep drink. She offered the can to Rafe, but he passed. "Still round, still yellow. Except at sunset." She sighed, remembering the first time she had been with her husband. It had been at sunset. On the beach. He hadn't been her husband then. "I really need to see a sunset again. With Slade."

Rafe heard the longing in her voice and understood. The kind of hours they kept could be brutal. It was the price they paid for making a difference. When he wasn't falling on his face with exhaustion, like now, he figured it was worth it.

"Then you should have become a dermatologist. No one calls a dermatologist in the middle of the night to deliver an eight-pound boil." It was well past midnight. Never enough time, he thought. Rafe looked at the woman he'd interned with. It had pleased him beyond words when he had discovered that the same hospital had accepted them both once residency had become nothing more than an ugly, grueling memory. "So, what brings you to my neck of the woods? The nursery window is in the other direction."

She had heard him paged over the loudspeaker earlier in the evening and come looking for him straight out of the delivery room, hoping he was still on the premises. "I came to get you."

"Me?" Rafe straightened, the doctor in him taking over. "Why?"

"I thought you might want to examine your newest patient."

He thought of the small child with the wide eyes who'd come to see him after hours. And the pale-looking woman who had hovered protectively over her. Had he missed something during his examination?

"Mollie's here?"

Completely absorbed by the last delivery, she'd forgotten about sending Mollie to him. Chagrined, Sheila shook her head. "No, even newer than that. By the way, thanks for seeing Mollie on such short notice. Dana's an old friend, and she seemed pretty worried. I thought a pediatrician would set her mind at ease better than I could, and we all know you're the best."

Rafe ignored her last comment. Compliments only tended

to embarrass him. Instead, he recalled the woman who had been in his office earlier and the air of edgy distrust she'd exuded.

"She didn't seem all that friendly to me," he observed.

"That would make her the first." Though he seemed oblivious to it, he'd been the object of lustful comments since the day he'd arrived at the hospital. "Frankly, I don't know how you manage to keep from being yanked into the linen closet with a fair amount of regularity."

They shared the kind of relationship that was reminiscent of siblings, he and Sheila. There were times when he found talking to her immensely comforting. Other times, it was just entertaining. This was both. "Maybe I'm too large to fit."

She grinned. "Ah, you underestimate how resourceful a determined woman can be. I think you manage to avoid women having their way with you because you're oblivious to their very blatant attentions."

Rafe shrugged carelessly. He'd had his one all-consuming relationship. As far as he was concerned, that was enough for him. What he shared with Kate was a mutual interest in a variety of areas—and the luxury of being thought off the market by everyone else. It spared him embarrassing entanglements he had no time or desire for. And he did enjoy Kate's company—when their schedules permitted getting together.

Right now, he was having trouble mustering the strength to put one foot in front of the other.

Rafe turned to Sheila. "This newer patient you want me to see, does he or she have a name?"

The question made her laugh. Rafe raised a brow, waiting. If there was a joke, he could certainly stand to be let in on it. His conversation with Jim Reilly about Timmie had done little to help clear up the mystery surrounding the boy's progressively deteriorating condition.

"Only a last one," Sheila told him. "The parents were still arguing about what name to put down—or, actually, names, they had twins—when I left the delivery room. They were hoping for girls."

"And they got two boys." Murphy's Law.

Rafe smiled. He had to admit he would have been rooting for a girl if he was the one awaiting an arrival. Girls were less trouble than boys. At least, that was what his mother had always sworn. But then, he mused, she'd only had him and Gabe to go by. There were times when they were growing up that Lizzie Borden would have been less trouble than they were.

The smile turned into a grin. That, too, had come from his mother.

Sheila nodded. "Six pounds three ounces, and six, one."

"Ouch." Wincing, he let out a low whistle of appreciation. "Doesn't sound like Mama had an easy time of it."

That was definitely putting it mildly. Mrs. Arthur Masterson had not been reticent in her expression of anguish and pain, nor in her thoughts about her husband's future chances of ever laying a hand on her again, in or out of their bedroom. The nurses were going to be talking about this delivery for weeks.

"She certainly didn't. My ears are going to be ringing for a month. I'm surprised you didn't hear her." She took another sip. The bubbles were fading. "I would have laid odds that all of Newport Beach heard her sometime during the past six hours."

Rafe had spent the past half hour with a sick little girl and her worried parents. Nothing had occupied his mind at the time but making them feel at ease. Allison Adray's mother was a hypochondriac who saw the handwriting of God on the wall when only smudge marks were evident to the eye. It had taken a great deal of patience to explain that Allison only had the flu and not something far more fatal, despite what it seemed like to her mother.

He wished he could say the same thing to Timmie's parents.

For a moment, he debated sharing his burden with Sheila. When they had interned together, they'd acted as each other's buffer. Sheila had been there for him, as much as anyone could be, when his wife had died. But Sheila had her own concerns. She didn't need to hear about his. Somehow, he would find a way to work things out.

Rafe shrugged casually. "Sometimes I get lucky."

Sheila thought of the way the nurses talked about Rafe. As if he was a Greek god who regularly walked amid the mortals. Every one of them wanted her chance to touch immortality, she thought with a smile.

"I'm sure you could if you wanted to." She laughed softly when he gave her a bewildered look. "Come on, I'll introduce you to Baby Boy Masterson—One and Two. Maybe, if they get desperate enough, his parents will name one of them after you."

With the ease of a longtime friend, Rafe let himself be led off. "I could live with that."

"You're sure you want to do this so soon?"

Concern etched itself on Sheila's face as she stood regarding Dana. She'd come into Dana's room this morning to find that her friend was getting ready to see her father. Though she had been the one who had written to Dana about her father's stroke and failing condition, she was having second thoughts. Dana had had so much grief in her life these last few months, and Sheila wanted to spare her the confrontation she feared lay ahead for as long as possible.

Sheila laid a hand on Dana's arm. "You know you're welcome to stay here."

Because Mollie was still asleep, despite the fact that it was close to nine in the morning, Dana drew Sheila into the hall before answering.

"If you say that one more time, I'm going to have it embroidered on a pillow and plopped on your sofa in front of the fireplace."

She saw the protest rising to Sheila's lips. In a way, Dana thought, she was very lucky. Some people went their whole lives without finding a friend like Sheila. She knew Sheila meant what she said. Sheila and Slade would let her remain here for as long as she needed to. But she'd always prided herself on being able to stand on her own two feet. It was time she found them again.

Dana took both of her friend's hands in hers. "Sheila, you're a wonderful friend, and I appreciate everything you've done for me—"

Sheila didn't want her gratitude. She wanted Dana's peace of mind. She'd talked it all out with Slade the night after Dana and Mollie had arrived, and it was all right with him if the invitation was open-ended. His generosity of spirit was one of the reasons she loved him so much. With all her heart, she wished Dana could find someone like Slade.

"What everything?" Sheila wanted to know. "It's not as if I built the bed single-handedly." A hint of a smile played on her lips. "I had help. Seriously, the bedroom was just standing there, empty. No reason it shouldn't have someone in it." She touched Dana's cheek. Sheila knew stubbornness when she saw it, and she was seeing it now. "A very special someone."

Special. When had she ever heard that word applied to her? Only once. But Steven was known for his short attention span. And it had been a lie, anyway. "Thanks, I needed that."

Sheila looked into her eyes, searching for the bravado, the steel underpinnings, she knew had to be there somewhere. They needed to be coaxed into evidence again. "You don't need me to tell you that you're special, Dana. You already know that."

It was what Dana had believed once, but that had been hubris. Like her father, she supposed. And if that was the case, she deserved to have been shot down.

"Okay," Dana said, "maybe I just needed to hear it." Sheila meant well, and she wasn't about to pay back her hospitality by arguing with her. "It doesn't make facing my father after all these years any easier, but it does help knowing that everyone doesn't see me the way he does, as completely lacking in every area." Her father hadn't attended Megan and George's funeral. To Dana, that had been the ultimate insult.

Yet here she was, trying to ignore it. Trying to ignore years of bad feelings.

Sheila thought of Paul Morrow. She'd grown up with misconceptions about her own parents because of a communication gap. Could the same be true of Dana and her father?

"Dana, I know it's hard to accept." Very slowly, Sheila tested the ground she was crossing before continuing. Dana's face remained impassive. "But maybe your father just has trouble expressing how he feels. Some men do, you know, even in our generation. And he's from the last generation, the one that dictates a man can't cry, can't let his feelings show."

That all sounded very nice, and Dana had no doubt that in some cases, for some men, it was true. But not her father. She knew better. The only thing that meant anything to her father was found within the arena of the courtroom.

"He never had any trouble expressing his displeasure." She heard a noise coming from the bedroom and peeked in. Mollie was still asleep. Probably having a dream. She hoped it wouldn't turn into one of her nightmares. "No, I think the only thing my father had—and *has*—trouble with is that God didn't give him children he felt were worth his while. I suspect he wanted sons who were exact replicas of him. Clones."

Dana pressed her lips together before she said anything more. If she wasn't careful, she was going to talk herself right out of doing what she felt she had to do. She'd returned to Bedford, rather than going somewhere else, for a reason, and she couldn't allow old wounds to get in the way.

Resigned, determined, Dana turned toward the stairs and headed down. Standing here talking about the past wasn't going to help her with the present.

Sheila was right behind her.

"Even so, I've got to go see him." Dana directed the words over her shoulder. "When he's gone, I don't want some kernel of guilt suddenly popping open inside me years down the line, telling me I should have tried to mend the break that's between us. It'll be too late then. I want to know that at least I did my part. If he doesn't want to do his—and he won't," she interjected before Sheila could offer her any platitudes to the contrary, "well, then that will be that, won't it? But at least my conscience will be clear."

"Parents have a way of surprising you," Sheila observed.

Hers had. She sincerely hoped that Paul Morrow would, too. Time had a way of mellowing people, making them see their mistakes. She doubted that anything in the world could have made Dana agree to be in the same room with her father five years ago, much less initiate the encounter. If Dana could mellow, why couldn't her father?

Dana shook her head. She held no such hope. "Not mine. If there were any surprises, they came out of the box years ago." She looked up the stairs and wondered if she should take Mollie with her after all. She didn't like leaving the little girl, although the idea of exposing her to what might go on between her and her father appealed to Dana even less. She bit her lip, debating. "Pilar's okay with watching Mollie until I get back?"

At least here Sheila could set Dana's mind at ease. "Are you kidding? Pilar's the original earth mother. I don't know what I'd do without her." The woman's cooking abilities left a little to be desired, but the way she cared for Rebecca more than made up for that. Sheila had no reservations about leaving her child or anyone else's with Pilar.

A high-pitched noise suddenly wedged its way into the conversation, throbbing rhythmically as it demanded immediate attention. Angling the pager she wore on her belt, Sheila looked at it with resignation. It took her a moment to associate a name with the number she saw.

"Mrs. Gaetano." She silenced the pager. According to her records, Faye Gaetano wasn't due for another two weeks, but the woman had looked ripe enough to pop on her visit last Monday. "This is going to play havoc with my office hours again."

"Another early baby?" Even as she asked, Dana was conscious of the child she was carrying. The one who had no place in her life but was there anyway.

Sheila went to the nearest telephone and picked up the receiver as she sighed. "My third this month. Must be something in the air."

Ambivalent feelings tugged at Dana, adding to the stress she was trying to manage. "Just how cold was it here last winter?"

"Obviously too cold. Business is booming, you should only pardon the expression." Sheila began dialing, then stopped when Dana opened the front door. "Will I see you when I get back?" she asked hopefully. If things went as badly between Dana and her father as Dana anticipated, Sheila was afraid she might pick Mollie up and leave without a word to anyone. That was the way it had happened last time—after a row with her father, Dana had disappeared.

"Count on it."

Sheila replaced the receiver. Mrs. Gaetano had waited this long, she could wait another minute. She surprised Dana by crossing to her and kissing her cheek. Then, moving back, Sheila used her thumb to rub away the slight trace of pink she'd branded Dana with. "Good luck."

Dana managed a smile. "Thanks. I have a feeling I'll need it."

She almost turned back twice, once halfway to her father's estate and once as she pulled up the massive driveway where she and Megan had played when they were children.

Before life had caught up to them.

But she didn't turn back. She forced herself on. In the driveway, she shut off the engine, then pocketed the key. She supposed her determination to see this through gave her something in common with her father. To her recollection, he had never backed away from a fight. On the contrary, he relished fights and the attention they garnered. He was never more alive than when he was defending a client. It seemed to her that for the price of a retainer, her father felt he owed his client far more than he owed his family.

Maybe her mother would have done better retaining him instead of marrying him.

Dana neither relished confrontations nor craved the attention, but she refused to back away. At least, she refused to back away anymore. She'd run from this house once, when life had gotten so intolerable she couldn't endure it any longer.

That had obviously been a mistake.

She was through running. Through running from her past, from her father. From everything. She was making her stand. Forging a present so that there could be a future.

This was for Mollie as much as for herself. And, she thought with a sigh, for her father. She supposed that she owed him something in return for the creature comforts she'd enjoyed while growing up. God knew she'd never lacked for anything material.

A bitter smile twisted her lips. She would have traded it all if, just for the space of one hour, she had felt as if her father loved her. Loved her not as an extension of his shadow, a bearer of the Morrow name, but as herself. As Dana.

But love was the one thing Paul Morrow couldn't dispense, because he couldn't buy it, and he had none of his own to give.

It had started raining when she'd left Sheila's, and rain followed her to her father's house. Somehow, that seemed appropriate.

Leaving her car in the center of the driveway, Dana got out and shut the door firmly. It amused her that her battered little white car looked so incongruous standing here, where only expensive cars had always been parked. The clients and associates who passed through the doors of Paul Morrow's estate were all upper crust or, barring that, at least well-moneyed. Chieftains of the corporate world, movie stars, celebrities from all walks of life, her father had rubbed elbows with them all, waiting for his next splashy trial, his next encounter with the media and fame.

As a child, she'd been awed by the parade of people. But,

relegated to the sidelines, deprived of the attention she sought from her father, watching her mother grow more and more remote as she sank deeper into anesthetizing alcohol, she'd soon tired of the circus, eventually growing to resent it.

But she hadn't come here to dwell on that or rehash past offenses. She'd come to see a father who was ailing. A father whose time left on earth might very well be finite. He'd had a stroke and been diagnosed with Parkinson's. While neither had defeated him, they certainly had limited him.

There was a time, she remembered, a very long time ago, when she'd thought Paul Morrow was invincible. She had no doubt that he'd thought the same thing.

Surprise.

Squaring her shoulders and turning up her collar against the fine mist, she went to meet the man she hadn't seen in eight years.

The queasiness that rippled from her stomach as she approached the towering double doors caught her off guard and nearly stopped her in her tracks.

"How about that—your unborn grandchild is afraid of you and he doesn't even know you," she murmured cynically under her breath. "It won't be any different when he does."

To know him is to fear him, wasn't that something one of his opponents had said? At the time it hadn't been applicable only to his adversaries in court, but to his family, as well. Her father had moods when they cowered and ran for cover.

And through it all, her mother had gone on loving him until the day she died. Dana couldn't understand it.

Had to be something there, she decided. Her mother, once a promising nurse practitioner who had given it all up to be Mrs. Paul S. Morrow, hadn't been a fool. Except for loving the wrong man.

Taking a deep breath, Dana rang the bell. The chimes sounded like hushed cathedral bells. She supposed her father had thought that appropriate. *You are now entering sacred ground.*

There was no answer. Dana counted to ten as slowly as

she could, then moved to ring the doorbell again. Before she could, the door swung open.

Esther.

The face of the tall, thin woman standing on the other side of the threshold transformed from politely reserved to joyous in the space of a breath as she recognized the visitor.

The housekeeper took a step forward, blocking the doorway with her body even though her employer was nowhere near this part of the house. She vividly remembered their parting.

"Miss Dana, is that you?"

God, but it was good to see her, good to see a familiar face and feel welcomed. She could feel herself smiling with relief.

"Yes, it's me. How've you been, Esther?"

Very little fazed Esther Cooper. It was one of the reasons she'd remained employed so long in the Morrow household, while others had come and gone. Paul Morrow valued people who knew how to control their emotions and hold their tongues.

But there were tears on Esther's lashes.

"Come in out of the rain, child." Dispensing with decorum, Esther threw her arms around the woman she had raised from a small child. The hug was warm and intense, as if she was convincing herself that Dana was actually there. She'd worried about her over the years, wondering where she was and what she was doing. And if she was well.

Standing back, she took full measure of the younger woman. Some of the wild rebellion was gone from her eyes, and she looked weary. This was no longer the go-to-hell teenager who had stormed out the door so many years ago.

"You look so thin, I hardly recognized you."

Dana laughed quietly, struggling with emotion she wasn't prepared for. "You should talk. If you didn't have rocks in your pockets, you would have blown away during one of the Santanas long ago. Those winds from the desert can get pretty mean."

Esther sniffed. "Tame stuff after what I've been through

over all these years.'' The hushed whisper was all she could manage at the moment. She pressed her lips together, drinking in the sight of Dana. "I thought I'd never see you again.''

"That goes double for me. I know that's what my father hoped.'' Dana felt her courage flagging and clutched at it. She'd come this far—she had to see it through. "Is he here, Esther?''

She couldn't help it. Part of Dana hoped that he wasn't here but at the office, the place she'd always thought of as his real home. Despite his failing health, or maybe because of it, she knew he would continue going to the office, continue taking cases, damning people if they cut him any slack because he was ill. Even so, on another plane, she knew he would use his illness, just as he used everything else, as a tool to help him win. It cast unconscious sympathy on his side.

Esther nodded. "He's getting a late start today. It's been a bad week for him.''

Dana didn't want to think about what that meant. It was easier to seek refuge in cynicism. She'd learned the art of doing that at the knee of a master. "Time away from the courtroom and the TV cameras always was.''

She looked around. It surprised her how little everything had changed. But then, had she really expected it to? The house had been decorated for the sole purpose of impressing whoever stepped through these doors. Why should anything change? The criteria hadn't.

Dana waited for a wave of nostalgia, of something, to hit her. She waited in vain. There were no warm feelings waiting for her here. This had ceased to be a home a long time ago, becoming instead an ornate mausoleum where she and her sister had felt more like prisoners than daughters. Wealthy, pampered prisoners, but prisoners nonetheless. Prisoners of her father's fame, of his expectations, of his moods.

"I've come to see him, Esther.''

If she was surprised, Esther gave no indication. Instead,

she inclined her head, ever the accommodating servant. "Shall I announce you?"

And give him time to prepare? No, she didn't think so. "I think I'd rather do that myself. For once, I'd like to catch him off guard. Which room?"

"He's in the downstairs den."

"How appropriate."

Telling herself he couldn't hurt her anymore, Dana went to face the man the newspapers had once dubbed "the lion of the courtroom."

Chapter 4

His back was to her as she entered the room. Even so, she could feel the old reaction coming over her. A pinching sensation in the pit of her stomach that threatened to slice it in half. It was too late in the day for morning sickness. This was Paul Morrow sickness. She had certainly lived through enough bouts to recognize it.

For a moment, because it was so artfully constructed, she didn't realize he was sitting in a wheelchair. Amid the jumble of nerves that had accompanied her in the drive over here, she'd somehow managed to forget that her father had lost the use of his legs. The stroke, not the disease, had done that to him, robbed him of the ability to stride across the courtroom. Spending his days in a wheelchair was a blow to his pride and to the self-image he'd so carefully constructed.

She wondered who he'd taken that out on. Probably everyone. And, just as probably, it was an ongoing thing. Her father didn't suffer what he took to be indignities and insults in silence.

He might have lost the use of his legs, but not his mind

and not his caustic tongue. Sheila had passed that along in her letter, too, but she needn't have bothered. Dana would have made book on it. As long as there was a breath left in him, her father wouldn't surrender, not to an opponent and not to a disease. She had no doubt that he practiced law harder than ever because he had something to prove to the world.

And maybe, she thought, to himself, though she knew her father would have scathingly chastised anyone who even remotely suggested that might be the case. Because that would point to a character flaw, and everyone knew he didn't have any.

Dana dragged a hand through her damp hair. For a second, she toyed with the idea of leaving before he turned around. But then she realized it was already too late.

He was sitting by a window, a book open on his lap. She could see her reflection in the glass. If she could see it, so could he.

Why hadn't he acknowledged her presence?

Why? she mocked herself. Because he was waiting for her to say the first word, to humbly genuflect before him and pay the great man homage. If he'd been prone to wearing jewelry, he would have wanted her to kiss his ring.

Dana wondered what he would say if he knew that she would gladly have done all of that once if he would only have paid the least bit of attention to his role as her father. If he had only tried to make them a family instead of occupants of a battlefield.

She hadn't wanted a great man, she'd only wanted her father. She'd gotten neither.

Slowly she drew a deep breath, bracing herself. No use lamenting over things that weren't and things that couldn't be.

She stared at the back of his head. He'd gotten gray since she'd seen him. His hair was the color of forged steel. Still thick and lush, it went with the image.

Tired of the waiting game, she met his eyes in the reflection. "Hello, Father."

Only then did he slowly turn the chair. Dana was stunned at how gaunt his face had become. She hadn't realized that, seeing only his reflection. All the more apt to frighten the opposition, she thought.

That would be his response to it. Everything was always aimed toward his goal—wiping out the opposition. Being the most famous defense lawyer of his time.

The sharp blue eyes took slow, full measure of her. There wasn't even so much as a hint of surprise or pleasure. No emotion at all. It was what she'd expected, wasn't it?

"What are you doing here?"

His voice still brought a chill to her. But she could withstand it. She'd gone to hell and back and knew that he was only a minor player in the game. Dana looked at the drops of rain gathered around her shoes.

"Dripping on your carpet, it would appear."

He nodded almost imperceptibly. "You always did make a mess no matter where you went."

He still knew how to aim straight for the heart. Dana thought she'd learned how to control her temper, but confronted with the supreme test, she failed.

Her anger swept over her, cold and galvanizing. "That's it? After eight years, that's all you have to say to me?"

The painfully thin shoulders rustled beneath the jacket of his hand-tailored suit. "I don't know. I haven't had long enough to prepare. Why don't you come back in another eight and I'll see if I can do better?"

Well, she'd certainly left herself open for that, hadn't she? She must have been crazy, having charitable feelings toward her father.

"I don't know what I was thinking of, coming here." Dana turned on her heel, determined to make it out the door in minimum time. "Goodbye."

She was almost there when she heard him ask, "You have a place to stay?"

The question froze her in her tracks. Concern about her welfare? Her comfort? Where had that come from? She turned to see if he was joking. His expression gave nothing away. As usual.

She chose not to tell him that she was staying with Sheila. She wouldn't be, soon enough. "I'll find someplace."

His eyes narrowed, twin lasers meant to cut through to the truth. "That wasn't the question."

He didn't frighten her anymore, she realized. Whether it was the wheelchair or the fact that she was older, she wasn't sure, but it didn't matter. She wasn't afraid of him anymore. She could hear that tone of voice and not cringe.

Dana took a step toward him. "Stop badgering the witness, Counselor."

If he was a storm cloud, there would be lightning and thunder right about now, she guessed. He wasn't pleased with her answer.

"You're not a witness, Dana. You are the worst thing that could possibly exist." His eyes pinned her. "Potential gone awry."

He still thought in terms of himself, of what he had wanted her to do, not what she wanted. He'd made that very clear from the moment she and Megan began attending school. They were to become lawyers, like him. Successful, like him. But never quite as successful. That, too, had gone unsaid, but it was just as important. For no one was allowed to challenge his position as supreme leader.

She stood her ground, refusing to shout, refusing to apologize. Both, she had a feeling, would have given him satisfaction. "No, Father, I was a daughter. A person, not a thing."

He sat looking at her without saying a word. Dana decided she was being dismissed and turned to leave a second time, only to be stopped again.

"Your room is still there."

Was he asking her to stay? She couldn't bring herself to believe that.

"Barring an earthquake—" she turned to face him "—I imagine it would be." Dana tried to read his reaction, but more astute people than she had failed at that. "Was that an invitation?"

Too much had happened between them for Morrow to welcome her back with open arms. He wasn't going to act like some pathetic, sentimental old fool. It was enough that he'd kept tabs on her all these years.

"That's a statement." Even as he said it, he waved it away with his hand. "Do with it what you will."

Dana stared at him, trying to understand. Was he extending a peacemaking gesture, however feeble? It didn't seem possible. It certainly wasn't like him.

And yet…

She studied his face as she spoke. "If I make use of it without your specific invitation, that's breaking and entering, isn't it?" she asked wryly.

She'd always been infuriatingly obstinate, he thought, from the moment she took her first breath during an earthquake that had shaken the foundations of the hospital. It had served as an auspicious announcement of her birth. "Not if the police aren't notified."

Dana watched his eyes as he spoke. There wasn't a flicker of emotion there. He had an ulterior motive. He had to. All her old emotions came flooding back to her, rebellion, anger, hurt. It had taken, what? All of five minutes in his presence? The man was truly in a class by himself.

He wasn't going to get away with it. Ill or not, he was going to be responsible for his actions, for his words. And if, for some strange reason, he'd changed his spots and meant to be kind, in whatever minor fashion, he had to own up to that, too.

"Why would you do that, Father? Why would you allow me to remain?"

He glared at her for questioning him. It was a look that would have frozen the blood in a man's veins. But Dana had gained an immunity over the years. And her own blood ran too hot.

"Your mother would have wanted me to," Morrow finally said.

Oh, no, he wasn't going to hide behind her mother. "You never did anything Mother wanted you to when she was alive. Why start now?"

If she was going to question his actions, then she could damn well take herself out of here. "You want to go, go, you want to stay, stay. It makes no difference to me." He turned the chair so his back was to her.

As if by magic, the anger was siphoned out of her. Maybe it was the sight of his shoulders, once so broad, so arrogant, now the slightest bit bowed. She didn't know. She had no idea why she wanted to throw her arms around him, to comfort him and be comforted. It was a stupid, weak feeling, given the man it was directed toward. But it was there just the same.

"I want Mollie to meet you."

She saw his back stiffen. She knew that Megan making her Mollie's guardian instead of him had angered her father. She would even have said wounded, except that his skin was far too thick for that. The fact that he had thrown Megan out of the house and disowned her when she married George didn't seem to enter into it for him. He saw life only from his point of view.

When he said nothing, she added, "I thought she should know her grandfather."

The chair was turned sharply. He'd been practicing, she thought. Paul Morrow wouldn't allow something like a wheelchair to interfere with the way he conducted himself.

"Why?" he demanded. "Megan didn't think she should."

Something snapped within her when she heard him utter her sister's name so contemptuously. If not for him, Megan and George would still have been in the area. And alive.

Anger gathered, hot and pulsating. "You don't know anything about Megan!"

His tone matched hers. "I know she married beneath her! I know she threw her life away!"

Shouting wasn't going to accomplish anything. Neither were the tears that gathered, a result of the tension she felt. She battled to restrain both. "George was a good man."

Morrow's eyes narrowed beneath brows that were still dark. "He was a *common* man. He didn't have a college education."

She knew it was futile to try to convince him that education was not the measure of a man. Megan had tried in her gentle way and failed. Of the two of them, it had been Megan who had been the favored one. Because Megan had listened, had tried so very hard to please. But he'd never softened to her, either.

"Don't you understand?" Dana demanded. "George made her *happy.*"

The dark look dissolved into a sneer. "There are more important things than being happy." There were responsibility and honor. He'd worked too hard to arrive where he was to watch it threatened by some simple, grinning idiot who could only work with his hands and not his mind. That wasn't part of the image. The carefully crafted image that had cost him so much to maintain.

Her eyes held his, and she didn't flinch. "I don't think so."

"So where is he? The scum you ran off with. The one who made *you* so happy?" He knew exactly where the worthless bastard was, in Texas, bedding some exotic dancer he'd picked up two weeks before Dana had left him. It was all there, every last sordid detail, in the report the detective his firm retained had given him. A coda to the ongoing eight-year assignment of keeping tabs on her.

She didn't want to tell him, but if she wasn't prepared to be honest, then returning was meaningless. She gave him the briefest answer she could. "Steven and I went our separate ways."

Morrow snorted, obviously pleased at being proven right. "About time you came to your senses."

She hated that tone, that smugness. "I didn't come back to talk about Steven."

He leaned forward in his chair, the tough attorney intent on making the witness break down on the stand. "Why *did* you come back?"

She kept it simple. She'd learned a long time ago that the less she said, the less could be used against her. "Sheila Pollack told me that you weren't well."

"Sheila Pollack can mind her own damn business and go to hell. I'm doing fine," he insisted with haughty malice. It would have made her explode in the old days. "So, if you came back to see if you were going to get your inheritance, you're in for a disappointment."

He'd pushed her over the edge. "Damn it, is it always about money with you?"

"No, it's always about money with *everyone*." He saw the world for what it was. He always had. That was his gift. From the time he'd run away at the age of fourteen from an abusive father and a mother who was too frightened of her own shadow, too drunk to care what was happening to her son, he'd learned what truly mattered in this world. Money and power. If you had those, no one would touch you. If you didn't, you were plowed under. "There are the haves and the have-nots. The have-nots want what the haves have, and they'll do anything to get it." A mirthless smile twisted his lips. "Like that character you were shacked up with."

Even though when her father said *black* she had an uncontrollable urge to say *white*, it wasn't in her to come to Steven's defense. "Shacked up? Thousand-dollar suits, and that's the best word you can come up with?"

"Low words for low life."

She'd been wrong—she wasn't impervious to his words. At least, not all of them. "Are you talking about Steven—or me?"

He was tired of this. He was tired of a great many things these days. "As I said, the room's there. Do with it as you will. I've got to get to the office."

He moved his chair to his desk and pressed a button on a

console. Within moments, a tall, fair-haired man wearing a chauffeur's uniform appeared in the doorway.

Someone new, she thought. Her father went through employees the way women went through panty hose. They were serviceable only for a short time before a defect crept up.

"Bring the car around, Dickinson, and then come for me," he ordered the man.

"Very good, sir." The chauffeur retreated quickly.

Maybe she should do the same, Dana thought.

"So, are you back?" Morrow demanded sharply.

Startled, Dana looked up. His eyes held hers, dark, demanding. She made a decision and hoped she wouldn't regret it.

"I'm back."

"Are you sure you know what you're doing?" Slade studied Dana's face. He didn't need any of the skills he'd honed as an investigative reporter to tell him that his wife's friend was not at ease with her decision to move into her father's house, however temporarily.

Dana paced the length of the patio. Inside, Pilar was playing a game with Mollie. Dana was grateful for the diversion. It gave her time to calm down. All the way home, she had felt like a person on a high-wire trying to work her way to the other side without falling.

Had she done something tremendously stupid by coming here? By trying to find a way to bridge the gap between her father and herself one last time? She couldn't settle on an answer.

"No, I'm not." Dana dragged a hand through her hair restlessly. "I don't know if I know what I'm doing." She turned to face Slade, voicing her thoughts, using him as a sounding board. "All I know is that this is where it all started going bad. This is the beginning. Maybe, if I retrace my steps, I can set things on the right course and go from there." She shrugged, wondering if that sounded naive. "I just know that, right now, my life feels like a hopeless mess, and I need to sort things out. I have to start somewhere. This seemed as likely a place as any.''

Slade took the hand that feathered restlessly through her hair. "We're here for you if you need us.''

She smiled her thanks. "That means a lot. Really.'' Why couldn't she meet someone like this? Someone who said he cared and meant it? She felt happy for her friend's fortune but wistful at the same time. "Tell Sheila she's got a great guy.''

He laughed, sinking down on a chaise longue. Having wrapped up a seven-part series, he'd elected to take a few days off and was determined to enjoy his family in something other than snatches. "Every chance I get. I think she's even starting to believe it.''

Sheila walked out to join them. The office closed at noon on Wednesdays. If she got out by two, she felt like a kid being sprung early from school. "Believe what?'' She bent over and greeted Slade with a kiss.

He hooked his arm around her waist and pulled her onto his lap. "What a great guy I am.''

Making herself comfortable, Sheila laced her arms around his neck. "Ha, I just took pity on you because you're Rebecca's father and you looked like you needed a home.''

This was what she wanted, Dana thought, watching them. What Sheila had. If she hadn't witnessed this with her own eyes, she would have sworn that happy marriages, happy unions, didn't exist except in the minds of filmmakers and novelists.

No, that wasn't true, she corrected herself. There had been Megan and George. They had been happy together. It was only her father's disapproval that had cast a shadow on their happiness.

Her father. It always came back to him. Her father was the root of all the discord, all the turmoil that haunted her and tainted everything.

Could peace be made with someone like that? It was something she intended to find out.

And then there would be only nine hundred ninety-nine problems to face, instead of a thousand.

"So, how are you doing today, Mollie girl?" Rafe asked as he walked into the examining room.

Dana swung toward the door at the sound of his voice. She'd intended to take Mollie to meet her grandfather, but Mollie had been particularly wan this morning. So much so that she'd called up for an appointment. The only opening had been at four, and she'd jumped at it.

"I think she's getting worse, not better," Dana told him.

And her aunt was getting edgier, he thought. He wouldn't have pegged Sheila and this woman as friends. As far as he could see, they were complete opposites in temperament. Sheila was laid-back, calm. Dana reminded him of a fire-cracker about to go off.

He looked at Mollie. "Have you been taking your medicine?"

Mollie nodded solemnly, then smiled at him. "It tastes like pink gum."

"It does?" He pretended to be surprised at the comparison. "Gee, maybe I'll give it a try sometime." He scooped her up and set her on the examining table, then took out a fresh tongue depressor. "Okay, you know the drill. Open wide for me." He placed the depressor lightly against her tongue. "Oh, wow."

Dana's heart lunged. "What? What do you see?" She was beside him, attempting to peer down Mollie's throat, but it was impossible with him in the way. "Is it her tonsils? Are they enlarged?"

"You've got dinosaurs in there," he told Mollie, then spared a smile for Dana.

Dana could have hit him for the scare he'd given her. She didn't need added stress.

Mollie looked at him, her eyes huge. "I do?"

"Yup, but it's okay." He tossed out the tongue depressor

and proceeded to examine her ears and nose. "They're the friendly kind. They're going to make sure you get better."

"Will they protect me from mean people?"

He glanced toward Dana, wondering if that was a childish question or if there was something behind it. "You bet. Is someone being mean to you, Mollie?" he asked casually, checking the sides of her throat for enlarged glands.

"No." Mollie fidgeted on the table, picking at the paper covering. "But Aunt Dana said she's going to take me to meet Grandpa, and he's mean."

So she'd never actually met the man. Things fell into place. He figured what Mollie was experiencing was a case of nerves.

"Remember what we talked about," he reminded her. "You're supposed to give him a chance first."

She smiled at him brightly, clearly enamored. "Okay."

Stepping toward the doorway, Rafe called out, "Sara, I'd like you to take a throat culture." Mollie immediately clamped both hands around her throat, clutching it as if she'd swallowed a giant chicken bone. Very gently, Rafe removed her hands one at a time. "She's just going to tickle your throat with a long magic wand, Mollie. It'll be over before you know it." As Sara entered, Rafe looked at Dana. "Can I see you outside for a second?"

Mollie was frightened at the prospect of being left alone. "Aunt Dana?"

"We'll be right by the door," Rafe assured her. "Sara has pointy elbows and she needs a lot of room when she moves around. If we stay, we'll just get in her way."

To Dana's surprise, Mollie settled down. The little girl didn't ordinarily trust people so quickly. She supposed Sheila was right about the doctor. He was good.

She looked at him anxiously as soon as they stepped out of the room. "What did you want to see me about?" Dana asked, her voice low. "Is it about Mollie?"

"Yes. I think you should lighten up."

Dana stared. This wasn't what she'd expected him to say. "Excuse me?"

He turned his back to the doorway so his voice wouldn't carry. "You're scaring her. Kids have got fantastic radar, and she knows you're worried, so she's worried. Stop worrying. She'll be fine in a week, and this'll be all in the past. Kids get sick. It's a fact of life. You don't want a junior hypochondriac on your hands, do you?"

His tone was calm and soothing and irritated the hell out of her. Sheila had told her that he wasn't married. Well, he might treat children all day, but he had no idea what it felt like to be solely responsible for one. "Of course not, but—"

"Then do as I say and take it light. You'll both feel a lot better."

She caught his arm before he had a chance to walk into the room, surprising him. "Is that your considered medical opinion?"

Was she deliberately trying to get on his nerves? "Yes, it is. And if you don't agree with it, you're completely free to get a second opinion." With that, he entered the room.

Annoyed, she followed him as Sara walked out of the room with the culture. Dana wondered if Sheila would take offense if she asked her for the name of a different pediatrician. This one rankled her, and he had too high an opinion of himself. She didn't need two men like that in her life at the same time. Dealing with her father was going to be rough enough.

She heard Mollie giggling.

Mollie definitely responded to him, though, she thought, walking into the examining room. She hadn't heard her laugh like that in a long time. Not since Christmas, when she'd gone to Megan's for a visit. Steven had conveniently picked an argument with her before they were to leave, and she had gone alone. Megan and George had gone out of their way to make it up to her. They'd all had a wonderful time.

That had been just before the accident, she remembered with a pang that threatened to reopen the wound that had only now begun to heal.

Forcing the sadness back, Dana concentrated on the sound of Mollie's laugh.

"Okay, you're free to go." Mollie leaned her head against his shoulder as he picked her up off the table. Smiling, Rafe placed Mollie on the floor. "I'll see you, okay?"

Mollie nodded with enthusiasm.

Rafe turned to Dana. "Just keep up with her medicine. I'll have someone from the office call you if the culture comes back positive. In the meantime—" Rafe opened Mollie's folder and extracted several forms "—I'd like you to fill these out and bring them back the next time you come." He handed them to her.

Dana flipped through them. Even if her degree was in law, it didn't affect how she felt about paperwork. She hated it. "What's this?"

"Health history forms," he said needlessly, then flashed a grin at Mollie, who appeared to be hanging on his every word. "I like knowing all about my patients."

The same forms she'd passed on filling out the first time she was here, Dana thought. But she folded them and slipped them into her purse.

"All right," she promised. "The next time."

With luck, that wouldn't be for a while. Her funds were all but depleted by now. Most of them had been eaten up by Mollie's hospital bills. Megan and George hadn't had insurance. And there was no way she would ask her father for so much as a dime, not even as a loan.

That meant she had to find a job, and soon.

Chapter 5

"Dr. Rafe is nice, isn't he, Aunt Dana?"

Dana changed lanes, easing over to the left in order to make a turn at the light.

"He's okay."

She supposed maybe she was being a little too hard on the pediatrician, taking feelings out on the man that really had nothing to do with him.

Glancing at Mollie, she smiled. "Sounds like someone's got a crush."

Mollie squirmed beneath the seat belt that restrained her, trying to turn toward her aunt. Her face was puckered the way it always was when she was trying to understand something. She was forever asking questions. It was her endless questions that had made Steven label her an annoying pest. And *that* had made Dana finally see the kind of man he really was.

"What's a crush?"

She looked so small, Dana thought, so fragile beneath that seat belt. Mollie was a little past the mandatory weight requirement for car seats. The current pale cast to her skin only contributed to that impression of fragility. She usually looked so pink, so rosy. Dana wished the medicine would do its thing already.

"A crush is when you like someone a whole bunch, sweetie."

Dana had no doubt that Dr. Rafe had a great many groupies of all sizes, shapes and ages. His looks put him in the same category as Steven. He was the kind of man who made women's heads turn, their hearts skip a couple of beats and their minds indulge in fleeting fantasies. It was a category she had little use for. Men that good-looking traded on their appearances. And the trade was never an equal one.

Mollie cocked her head. "Oh." A small smile fluttered over her lips. "I guess that means I've got a crush on you, huh?"

Dana laughed. She'd forgotten how literal an age five could be. "No, honey, the person you like has to be someone of the opposite sex."

This was even harder for Mollie to figure out. She blinked. "What's sex?"

Dana slammed on her brakes as a blue van cut directly in front of her, then sailed through the light that was already turning red. She let out a slow, measured breath, glad she had swallowed the name she was about to christen the other driver with before Mollie could hear it.

"A whole lot of trouble, sometimes," Dana finally answered. Was it her, or had traffic gotten heavier since she'd last lived in the area? Settling back, she tried again. "Okay, how about this? Girls can only have crushes on boys, and boys can only have crushes on girls." She peered at Mollie's face to see if that explanation generated any problems. "Better?"

Mollie's head bobbed up and down. "Uh-huh." Hesitantly, she asked, "Aunt Dana, did you have a crush on Steven?"

Dana couldn't think of Steven without a mixed collection of memories playing tag with one another as they raced through her head. Some good, some bad. Maybe that summed up most relationships except that, in the end, in her case, there had been a lot more bad than good.

"Yeah, I had a crush on Steven." And it had been wonderful to be in love, to feel loved. If only that hadn't turned out to be an illusion, no, a lie. She kept her eyes on the road, determined not to allow the bitterness to creep in. "But I'm all over that now."

"I'm glad."

The smile was weak, but definitely there. Mollie's lower lip protruded a little as she stole a glance at her aunt and told her what she had been afraid to say before. Afraid because, if she said it, then maybe her aunt wouldn't love her anymore or let her stay with her. And then there would be nobody to hold her when she was afraid.

"I didn't like him." Mollie wiggled in her seat, tired and impatient to get to the end of the ride. She wanted to lie down. She was so very tired. Her eyes began to drift shut. "But it's okay if you have a crush on Dr. Rafe."

Dana choked back a laugh. She would probably have to take a number, like at a bakery. But, for simplicity's sake, when Mollie looked at her quizzically, she said, "I think Dr. Rafe might have something to say about that."

Sighing deeply, Mollie settled into her seat. She was beginning to fall asleep. "Why?" she murmured.

Glad to leave the flow of traffic behind her, Dana made a right turn into Sheila's development. "Because men like to think they decide these kinds of things for themselves."

Mollie's eyes were little more than blue slits as she shifted them toward Dana. "But they don't?"

Mollie was too young to be told that men didn't like making decisions about anything, least of all commitment. Dana had learned firsthand that urges dictated their actions and any thinking that was done was generated from below their belts. Or cerebrally, like her father. But never from the heart.

No, she couldn't say that to a five-year-old, even though

her illusions would disappear soon enough. For now, they had to be preserved for as long as possible.

"We help, honey, we help." Before turning the corner onto a street that fed into the block where Sheila and Slade lived, Dana eased her foot onto the brake and brushed a kiss over her niece's head.

Rafe Saldana might think she needed to lighten up, but she swore that Mollie felt warm to her, despite her pale color. She was going to take her temperature as soon as they reached the house. Maybe she was being unnecessarily worried, but aside from her father, Mollie was all the family she had. And *she* was all the family Mollie had. Mollie's welfare was entirely in her hands.

"Looks like Sheila is going to have to put up with us a little longer. You're going to bed as soon as we get home, young lady." Any plans to move into her father's house would have to be put on hold. And she certainly had no problem with that.

"Okay," Mollie agreed.

The fact that she didn't protest going to bed so early *really* worried Dana. She pushed down on the accelerator, anxious to get Mollie to Sheila's.

She saw the long black limousine from a distance. It was parked directly in front of Sheila and Slade's house. Dana felt something twist inside her even as annoyance gelled. Without seeing the license plate, she knew the limousine belonged to her father.

"Oh, God, what's he doing here?" This was all she needed, a confrontation with her father in front of Sheila and Slade.

The sharp note in her aunt's voice roused Mollie. She peered out the window, looking around. "Who, Aunt Dana? Who's here?"

For a moment Dana felt like turning the car around and going back. But there was nowhere to go, and Mollie was sick.

She was in no mood for this. He had no right to hound her. "Your grandfather. That's his car up ahead."

Mollie stared out the window, searching for someone matching the description of her grandfather she had conjured up for herself.

"Is he a giant?" The question was a hushed whisper.

"He likes to think so."

A giant among men, that was the sort of legacy he had always tried to carve out for himself. And no success he attained was ever great enough.

Dana realized that Mollie was shrinking in her seat as if she was trying to vanish into it. "Mollie, what's the matter?"

When she was really little, Mollie used to shut her eyes and think no one could see her. She wished she could do that now. "I'm afraid, Aunt Dana. I don't want to meet him."

Dana couldn't have faulted her niece for feeling that way, if she'd ever met the man before, but she hadn't. Dana pulled the car over. She had to find out why Mollie was so afraid before she allowed her to meet her grandfather.

"Mollie, did someone say something to you about your grandfather?"

Mollie shivered, huddling into herself. "No. I heard Mommy and Daddy talking once. They thought I was sleeping. Mommy was crying, and Daddy was mad. He said Grandpa was an o—" Frustrated, she tried to remember the word.

Bastard started with *b,* Dana thought. Besides, George had never used profanity, even the mildest kind. What started with *o?* Mollie had asked if he was a giant.

"Ogre?" Dana guessed.

"Yeah." Mollie nodded hard. "Like the one in my book that eats kids."

Well, that explained that. She leaned over and slipped her arm around her niece. Dana hadn't thought she could laugh about anything connected to her father, but Mollie had proven her wrong.

"Oh, honey, he's not an ogre, he's just an old man in a wheelchair. He won't eat you, and he can't hurt you."

Mollie bit her lower lip hesitantly. *Just like Meggie,* Dana thought. "Promise?"

"Oh, yes, I promise." *He's a bastard, capable of a lot of things,* she added silently. *But he'd never physically hurt you.* "Okay?"

Mollie gave her a brave smile. "Okay."

Dana saw the trust in Mollie's eyes. It was at once humbling and a huge responsibility. One she swore she would never neglect. Not the way her father had neglected her.

And what about the baby? a small voice whispered in her head. *The one you don't want. Are you going to shirk your responsibility to it?*

Annoyed, guilty, Dana shut the voice away. With a sigh, she took the car out of Park and drove the remaining few yards to Sheila's driveway. Taking her time, she got out of the car and then rounded the hood to open Mollie's door.

"C'mon, honey, let's go inside." Because Mollie looked so unsteady on her feet, Dana scooped her up in her arms. "You *do* seem a little warm," she commented, as if Mollie had asked her for confirmation.

Dana's first inclination was to ignore the limousine parked at the sidewalk like a loitering, silent shark, but that wouldn't get rid it. So, holding Mollie to her, she approached the vehicle.

As she did, the chauffeur stepped out. The windows were rolled up in the back, darkening her view of the sunset. She wondered if her father was behind them, watching.

"Dickinson, isn't it?" she asked the chauffeur.

The man politely touched the brim of his hat. "Yes, miss, it is. Tom Dickinson."

She nodded toward the limousine. "Is my father inside, Tom?"

Dickinson looked surprised at the question, as if she should know better than to think Paul Morrow would be content to wait for anyone. "No, he's at home, miss. He sent me to bring you and his granddaughter to the house."

Dana shifted Mollie to her other side, instinctively protective. "A command performance?"

The chauffeur looked as if he wasn't sure whether he should or could safely comment. He didn't. "Mr. Morrow said that you should bring your things with you."

So, the invitation had turned into something with a little more teeth to it. She wasn't surprised. For as long as she could remember, her father had liked being in control of every situation. This was no different.

"How did he know I was here?" Dana was sure she hadn't mentioned it. Every syllable uttered during her visit with him this morning was still fresh in her mind. She had deliberately *not* told her father where she was staying, to give herself time if she needed it.

Dickinson was as devoid of curiosity as humanly possible. Morrow paid well, and that was all the information he needed. "I don't know that, miss. I was just instructed to wait until you were ready."

Nothing had changed. Her father thought that because he snapped his fingers, she would obey. She'd returned to mend fences, not to place her hand beneath his boot.

Dana raised her chin. "Tell him I have my own car, and I'll drive over when I'm ready." She paused, then added, "In the morning." No use fanning the flames too high. She didn't want another argument. She just wanted the respect he would accord one of his judicial adversaries.

"Trouble, Dana?"

She turned to see that Slade was standing in the doorway of the house.

She smiled. The cavalry. A cavalry on loan, but a cavalry nonetheless, just as she remembered Sheila saying once. Mollie murmured something unintelligible against her shoulder, and Dana feathered a hand gently along her head, soothing her.

"No, but thanks for the backup. My father sent his chauffeur to pick me up."

Slade stepped off the porch to join her. "Yes, I know. We told him you weren't here. Two hours ago."

"Well, Tom doesn't have to wait any longer." Dana saw a look of uncertainty cross the chauffeur's face. He was probably nervous about being the bearer of bad news. She didn't blame him. Her father's moods were probably worse than ever. "Please tell my father that I can't come tonight. With any luck—" she kissed the side of Mollie's head "—Mollie and I will be there in the morning."

Dickinson looked at her doubtfully. Those weren't his instructions. "Mr. Morrow was very specific about your coming tonight."

Dana laughed shortly. "I'm sure he was." She paused, choosing her words carefully. It wasn't the chauffeur's fault that her father was the way he was. And she didn't want to say anything that would generate a further tear in the already weak fabric between her and her father. Reconciliations weren't built on angry feelings. "Tell my father that I appreciate his thoughtfulness, but Mollie isn't feeling well, and I'd like her to be fresh when she meets her grandfather for the first time."

With that, she turned and walked into the house. Slade followed, closing the door behind them.

He took Mollie from her. Dana dropped her purse on the hall table and led the way upstairs to the room she and Mollie were sharing.

"What was that all about?" Slade asked.

She went into the bedroom and drew back the covers. "I'm not sure. I think my father is having me followed."

"Followed?" He laid Mollie on the bed. He knew Dana's history, but still, that didn't sound like the way a father would treat his daughter. Maybe his paternal feelings were coloring his perception, he thought.

Dana nodded, taking Mollie's running shoes off. "I never told him I was staying here." She dropped the shoes on the floor, trying to control her temper. She didn't like the idea of being followed. Of having to look over her shoulder.

"Maybe he just took an educated guess," Slade suggested for the sake of argument.

That was highly unlikely. Dana thought of her father sitting in his chair, playing God with those around him. Arranging their lives to suit his purposes. Why had she thought he'd mellowed? Not everything mellowed with age. Cheese just turned sharper.

"My father never guesses. He likes knowing."

With a dinner plate carefully held in each hand, Kate Mulligan moved cautiously into the tiny dining room that was little more than an alcove. A fastidious person, she would normally have set the table long before now. But after three broken dinner engagements in a row, she'd learned to play it by ear. It didn't matter. Rafe was worth it.

Placing one plate on either side of the two tapering candles she had lit only minutes ago, Kate smiled at Rafe. He looked so pensive. And tired, she thought. She longed to hold him, to help him find peace. She would have given anything if he could find it with her.

"I was beginning to think we were never going to get a chance to get together," she told him.

He watched her hands flutter, smoothing napkins, straightening silverware that was already straight. The candlelight brought out red highlights in her auburn hair. She was wearing it down to please him. Rafe felt a stirring of affection. But nothing more.

He shrugged noncommittally, knowing she wasn't trying to pin him down with the comment. Kate wasn't like that. "It's been pretty rough lately. Every time I turn around, someone else is coming down with the flu."

She nodded, understanding. They were backlogged at the lab. "Well, you can relax now." She glanced at the small, dark rectangle at his belt. Hardly bigger than a tie clip. She hated it. "Why don't you turn your pager off?"

He took the bottle of wine he'd brought and uncorked it. After filling her glass, he poured some into his own. But, though he'd selected it, he found himself uninterested in sampling the wine. He felt restless, as if there was a storm coming. As if there was something he'd left undone.

Probably a combination of the weather and fatigue.

He smiled tolerantly at her suggestion. "You know I can't do that, Kate."

At times, she thought, he was too damn dedicated. "But you could get someone to take your calls for you once in a while. Trade-off," she pressed. "Like every other sane doctor does."

What other doctors did didn't interest him, unless it directly affected his patients. He sat and waited for her to join him. "When my patients' parents call with a problem, they want to talk to me, not to some doctor they don't know."

Kate frowned as she moved the salad bowl toward him. "You need to have a life, Rafe."

Her comment made him smile. "Being a doctor *is* my life, remember?"

That wasn't what she'd meant, but she knew better than to argue with him about it. Kate knew about Debra, and how being a doctor was what had kept him going after she died. "If you're not careful, you're going to burn out."

In order to burn out, there had to be something left within him to burn, and there wasn't. Not the way it would have mattered to Kate, he thought.

He looked at the meal she had prepared. Eggplant parmesan. She'd called his mother for the recipe. He knew, because his brother had kidded him about it. It made him feel guilty.

"You didn't have to go to all this trouble. Take-out would have been fine."

She took a sip of wine, hoping it would quell her nerves. "But then I couldn't impress you with what a good cook I am."

His eyes rose to meet hers. "You don't have to impress me, Kate."

Kate pressed her lips together. She should have downed the entire glass for courage. She was running pitifully low right now. "Oh, yes, I do. I have to do something to nudge you along to the next level."

He pretended to be interested in his meal. "I don't nudge very well, Kate."

"Sorry." She flushed. They had an agreement, she knew that. It was just that sometimes she wanted to go beyond the confines of the agreement. She wanted him to look at her with love in his eyes. Love like she felt. "You'd think a research biologist would learn to be patient."

He set down his fork. This was his fault, not hers. Rafe reached for her hand and covered it. "No, I'm the one who's sorry, Kate. Sorry if I'm being testy. Like I said, I'm tired."

Relieved that he wasn't leaving, she placed her hand on top of his, confirming the friendship, placing everything else on hold a little longer. Again.

"You can sleep here if you'd like," she offered. "After dinner. You can stretch out on the couch or my bed. I promise I won't jump your bones unless you want me to."

He heard so many things in her voice, and for her sake he wished he could return them in kind. But it just wasn't in him. "Kate..."

She raised her hand, knowing what was coming. "Hey, no promises asked, no commitment required. I know the rules." Her smile was patient, resigned. "You were very clear, and I accepted the terms."

He shook his head. This wasn't fair, not to her, and maybe in the long run not even to him. "Kate, you need to get a nice guy."

"I did get a nice guy," she insisted. The smile curled into her brown eyes. "I just need to have him want to get me." Leaning over the tiny table, she kissed his mouth, her lips warm, willing.

As she deepened the kiss, his pager beeped. A moan of defeat escaped her as she reached to turn it off. Rafe placed his hand over hers, then drew his head back. "It's my service."

She knew that. She damn well knew that. With a small sigh, Kate dragged her hand through her hair, backing away, surrendering. She knew what was coming. One by one, she removed the dishes from the table. He was going to leave. No one called a doctor at this hour just to ask a question.

Rafe frowned as he hung up the telephone. "It wasn't my service."

Kate stopped midway between the kitchen and the dining room. She looked at him hopefully. "Does that mean you're staying?"

Preoccupied, he looked up. It took a second for her question to register, though he failed to pick up on the hope in her voice. "No, the call was from the hospital. One of my patients came into the emergency room."

She crossed to him, taking his hands in hers. As if that could make him stay. "Good, then they'll be well taken care of."

Very gently, he extracted his hands from hers. "The patient's aunt requested that I be called in. I've got to go."

"An aunt now?" Kate sighed. Next it would be neighbors and total strangers. With a shake of her head, she went to the kitchen. "You know, you can't keep running off every time someone calls." She reached for the cellophane wrap, then looked at him as he entered behind her. "Someday, Rafe, you're going to have to stop running."

"You're right," he agreed vaguely. Quickly, he brushed his lips against hers. "Thanks for the meal. Sorry I couldn't stay to finish it."

She was right. Someday he would have to stop running. Maybe. But someday, Rafe thought as he closed the door behind him, wasn't now.

"Not coming?" Morrow demanded, his face turning pale then red. "What do you mean she's not coming?"

Dickinson was twice his employer's size. There was no

earthly reason he should feel the inclination to cringe. And yet, held by the glacier gleam in Morrow's eye, he did.

"She said that your granddaughter wasn't feeling well, and that she wanted her to be fresh when she met you for the first time."

"That's a lie. Don't you know a lie when someone tells you one?" he demanded. "When I send you to bring someone, I damn well expect you to bring them to me. Do I make myself clear?"

"Yes, sir. She said to thank you for your thoughtfulness." That gave him pause. "She did?"

"Yes, sir." Dickinson worked the brim of his hat through his hands, turning it as he waited to be dismissed. Hoped to be dismissed. From the room, not his position.

"But she still didn't come."

Dickinson's throat felt dry. "No, sir."

Uttering a well-turned oath, Morrow sent the man from the room. He waited until the door was closed and he was alone before he slumped in his wheelchair. Anger exhausted him.

Kate's penthouse apartment was located across from the hospital. The easy access was what had brought Rafe and Kate together. Seeing how exhausted he was after rounds one day, she had offered him a place to crash when he needed it. Eventually, purely through her perseverance, they had drifted from friends into a comfortable relationship that included the physical and was pleasant, but devoid of passion. At least on Rafe's part.

But he liked her company. He enjoyed talking to Kate. They shared a great many interests, and while he bore affection for her, he wasn't in love with her, and she knew it. He knew she knew it, too. He'd been very careful not to lead her on, and she had been just as careful in making him understand that she was willing to settle for whatever was available. She made no demands on him.

Rafe slipped through a yellow light, then drove into the hospital compound. Kate was a good woman, and he supposed that if he ever was to marry again, it would be to her. A comfortable relationship where he was in sync with the person he was married to was the best he figured he could hope for.

But that, too, wasn't today.

After leaving his car in the doctors' parking lot, Rafe hurried through the automatic emergency room doors. A quick scan to his left took in the crowded waiting area. It looked as though it was going to be a busy night.

Rafe bypassed the registration desk and looked for the head nurse. She was walking out of the patients' area. He made his way to her before she could call the next patient.

"Hi, Nancy, I got a call that one of my patients was here."

The nurse, a tall, sleek woman with skin like lightly brewed coffee, flashed a smile at him. Though it was worn around the edges, there was still a tiny dash of flirtation in it.

"She's in the back, Dr. Saldana. We've got her on oxygen. Looks like the croup to me. Come on." Nancy pushed open the door she had just walked through. "I'll take you to her."

He knew exactly what he would see when he pulled back the curtain. Even so, the sight of the small figure on the gurney wrenched at his heart. He was never, never going to become immune to the sight of a suffering child.

Mollie had an oxygen mask covering half her face. Her eyes were huge with fear, the sheen of perspiration on her brow.

"I suppose you still think I should lighten up." Dana couldn't help the bitterness in her voice when she saw the doctor walk in.

"Yes, I do," he answered without looking at her. "You're still scaring the hell out of her." With Nancy at his elbow, Rafe picked up the chart, quickly making an assessment of the information. He added several tests to be done in addition to the ones already listed. Nancy left to set things in motion. "She's going to be fine."

Dana placed a hand over the chart, forcing him to look at

her. "You said that this afternoon." She waved a hand at Mollie. "Is this your definition of fine?"

"No, this is my definition of the croup." He moved the chart from Dana's hand so that he could return it to its place at the foot of the bed. "I think it's best for her if she remain here overnight."

He heard Mollie whimper beneath the mask.

Dana glared at Rafe before she hurried over to Mollie.

Chapter 6

With soft, soothing strokes, Dana brushed the damp hair from Mollie's forehead. The ends were dark with perspiration.

"It's okay, baby, it's okay. If you have to stay overnight, I'll be right here with you." She threaded her fingers through Mollie's. The small hand felt so cold, so damp, as it grasped hers. Dana squeezed it, wishing she could transfer some of her strength to Mollie. She hated seeing her frightened. "I won't leave you, I promise." She looked at Rafe, her eyes daring him to tell her she couldn't remain with Mollie.

He nodded. "We can have a cot brought in for you."

Dana sincerely doubted she would get any sleep. "I don't need a cot. All I need is a chair."

Amusement highlighted his features. "We have chairs."

"Good." A tired, relieved smile rose to her lips as Dana looked at Mollie. "See, baby? It's all settled. We'll be room-mates."

Debating, Dana raised her eyes toward Rafe. She didn't like leaving herself open to pity but she had to be up-front with him. She didn't believe in playing games. That was for people like Steven. Very gently, she began to draw her hand from Mollie's. The girl hung on tightly, as if her very life depended on it.

"Mollie, I have to talk to Dr. Rafe for a second." With reluctance, Mollie let go of her hand. It had to be awful, Dana thought, to be so young and so afraid. She kissed the damp forehead. "I'll be right back."

Like two blue homing devices, Mollie's eyes followed as Dana moved to the other side of the curtain.

Rafe waited until she said the first word. He couldn't even begin to guess what this was going to be about.

Dana lowered her voice. This was hard enough to say to him. There was no need for anyone else to overhear.

"Is this going to be for just one night? Her hospital stay," she clarified, when he looked at her.

"That depends on Mollie, but I think there's a good chance she'll be able to go home sometime tomorrow." There was no telling with children. Her fever was low grade, and she'd stopped choking. All things considered, it looked promising, but he knew it was safer to remain guarded, just in case.

He studied the woman before him. Did she plan to contest his decision if he wanted Mollie to remain an extra night to be on the safe side? Rafe couldn't tell. She wasn't an easy woman to read—just an exasperating one, but that could be because she seemed so wound up.

"Good." Dana weighed her next words, not quite sure how to proceed. Being in financial difficulties was not something she was accustomed to. It felt awkward, uncomfortable. She hated it, hated admitting to anyone she was in this position, however temporarily—and she intended for it to be very temporary. As soon as she could, she was going to find a position at a law firm, even if she had to trade on her father's name to do it. But right now, she needed to get this straightened out.

"I left my last job rather suddenly." It wasn't easy to withstand the scrutiny she saw in his eyes, but she refused to look away. "Consequently, we don't have any health insurance at the moment. But I can make arrangements to pay—"

He waved the remainder of her explanation away. This was obviously very awkward for her, and he had no desire to watch her discomfort. There was nothing here that couldn't be worked out. The hospital budgeted a certain amount to be written off each year as charity. As a last resort, Mollie's bill could be referred to that department, though he had a feeling Dana wouldn't particularly appreciate hearing herself referred to as a recipient of charity.

"Why don't we worry about that later?" he suggested tactfully.

Later had a habit of catching up to you when you least wanted it to. "I'm only saying this because your bookkeeper is worried about payment *now*. I thought if you told her it was going to be made—maybe not as quickly as she'd like, but it *will* be made—she might feel better about it." Dana looked at him pointedly. "I always pay my debts, Dr. Saldana, no matter how big they might be at the outset."

"It never crossed my mind to doubt that." His eyes held hers. Pride was important to everyone, especially to stubborn, headstrong women. He allowed her hers. "I'll talk to her."

It was past eleven by the time everything had been arranged and Mollie was settled in her room. Pulling a few strings, Rafe had managed to get her one where the other two beds were empty. A minor miracle, after the way things had been the other day.

Rafe knew he should go home like, as Kate had pointed out earlier that evening, any sane doctor would have done hours ago. Even so, he found himself returning to Mollie's room to look in on the little girl one last time.

And maybe, though he didn't really know why, to look in on her aunt, as well.

If it hadn't been for the time he spent with his parents and his brother, Gabe, Rafe would have said his entire world was enclosed within the relatively small circle formed by his office and the hospital. Diagnosing and caring for children was what took up most of his time and his energy. In return, it gave him a sense of satisfaction and worth the way nothing else could. He found he needed very little else to define him as a person.

Almost all the lights were off in Mollie's room. The one above her bed was on the dimmest setting. Soft shadows hovered beyond the bed. Everything seemed peaceful, in contrast to the way things had been a short while ago.

Good, Rafe thought.

He saw Dana sitting beside Mollie's bed, her body tense, like a bow about to release an arrow. What sort of an arrow would she release if she was freed of the tension that outlined her body?

It might be interesting to speculate about, if he had the time for things like that.

He entered quietly and kept his voice low. "How's she doing?"

Startled, Dana swung her head around to look at him. She'd been holding Mollie's hand for the past hour or so. Somewhere along the line, Mollie had fallen asleep, but Dana didn't want to risk waking her by moving. She'd lost most of the feeling in her arm, and her fingers were almost numb.

She let out a shaken breath, waiting for her heart to stop pounding.

"Sorry," he whispered.

She nodded, accepting the apology. It was so quiet, she wondered why she hadn't heard him approach. Gingerly, she drew her hand slowly from Mollie's, then got up. Indicating that he should retreat to the doorway, she joined him there.

"She calmed down a little," Dana told him in answer to his question. It had taken a while, though. She could only guess what kind of terrors Mollie was trying to deal with, being in a hospital again. "I think placing her in the oxygen tent was a good idea. We pretended that we were camping out and that she was in this magic see-through pup tent. After that, it became a game to her."

He smiled. "I've got to remember that the next time I need to put one of my patients in an oxygen tent." He wouldn't have pegged Dana as someone with an imagination. But then, he'd only seen her when she was coming on like gangbusters.

Dana dragged a hand through her hair, trying to smooth it. She had to look like hell. God knew she felt like it. She knew it didn't matter to him, but it did to her. She hated being at her worst.

"And how are you doing?" He couldn't help it. The doctor in him had taken over. It was something Gabe kidded him about. He approached everything as if it was a triage situation.

The question surprised her. After all, if she was being honest, she'd hadn't exactly been the model of politeness to him.

Massaging the stiff muscles of her neck, Dana answered, "I've been better." Then she shrugged as a small smile emerged. "But then, I've been worse, too, so I guess you could say I'm breaking even." She looked over her shoulder to check if Mollie was still asleep. The gentle rise and fall of the small chest reassured her. "Maybe I'm even on the plus side of the ledger."

Dana paused. Apologies never came easily to her, but she did owe him one. And she'd always hated owing anything.

The only way to do it was to do it. She pushed the words out, trying not to sound as uncomfortable as she felt.

"Listen, if I sounded as if I was going to bite your head off earlier, I'm sorry. I had no right being angry with you. It's just that Mollie means a great deal to me, and I worry about her."

It wasn't exactly news. A smile twitched his lips. He understood where she was coming from. Maybe he'd been a little hard on her. "I can't fault you for that, but you do know that you can't insulate her in bubble wrap, don't you?"

Yes, she knew that, but it didn't stop her from trying. "Maybe not, but a little padding until she's older won't hurt." Her smile was sincere. A peace offering. "Thanks for coming so quickly."

"It's my job." He thought of what Kate had said. Poor

Kate, she really had to find someone else. He wasn't any good for her. "If I didn't want to be on call, I wouldn't be. Anyway, I was in the area." He knew he should be going. He had to be at the hospital again within a matter of hours, making rounds before going to the office.

But he lingered a little longer in the darkened hallway talking to a woman he'd thought he disliked. They'd both made mistakes. "Listen, are you going to be all right here? Can I get you anything?"

A nurse had already been by to ask her that. At the time, she'd said no, far too concerned with Mollie to think of anything else. But Mollie was asleep. And getting better.

Her mouth curved. Maybe he wasn't so bad, after all. "A fairy godmother would be nice, but I'd settle for some—" She wanted coffee, but knew that wasn't wise, not in her condition. "Hot chocolate," Dana amended with reluctance. Encouraged by his offer, she risked imposing. "If you could stay with her for a couple of minutes and point me toward the vending machines, I'd really appreciate it. I never got a chance to eat dinner tonight—Mollie's attack came on very suddenly." She'd never felt so helpless, watching Mollie gasping for air, terror in her eyes, and not being able to do anything about it. "I'm afraid that if my stomach rumbles any louder, it's going to wake her up."

She looked way too exhausted to be wandering around the halls. "I've a better idea. You stay here, and I'll go get the hot chocolate."

Dana began to protest, but the words never surfaced. With a nod of thanks, she accepted his offer. "I'd give you an argument if I had more energy."

He grinned. "I know."

Rafe was back in ten minutes, carrying several containers on a tray he'd borrowed from the nurses' station. He set everything on the shelf beside the sink.

She'd almost fallen asleep waiting for him. Rousing herself, Dana crossed to where Rafe was standing and peered around his arm. Unless she was seeing things, he'd brought three containers. She'd only asked for one.

"What's this?" She looked at the containers without taking one. "Did the hot chocolate become fruitful and multiply on the way back from the vending machine?"

So she did have a sense of humor. That, too, surprised him.

"I decided that if you were going to camp out here with Mollie, you needed to be running on something other than empty. But the cafeteria's closed for the night. All I could come up with is chicken soup." He pressed a container into her hand. "It's not bad, really."

She looked at the container dubiously. Food that emerged from vending machines was notoriously long on salt, short on taste. "Are you trying to convince me—or yourself?"

"You. I've had this before. Lots of times." Taking a second cup of soup from the tray, he raised it to his lips and sampled, then nodded his approval. He saw the question in her eyes. "I didn't have a chance to eat, either."

And that was her fault, she thought. She'd called him away from the table.

"Sorry," she murmured. She smiled at the cup in her hands. "The eternal magic cure-all, chicken soup." She took a sip and was surprised to find it was pretty decent. And hot.

"Careful," he urged as she winced. "You don't want to burn your tongue."

"Too late." Eyes tearing, Dana sucked air in, trying to relieve the burning sensation dancing along her tongue.

"Sorry." He flashed her an apologetic look. "I should have warned you."

Dana let out a breath slowly. The tears retreated. "That's okay." She could feel bumps forming on the edge of her tongue. It would be days before she was rid of them. "I can still talk."

He laughed softly. The sound washed over her, uniquely comforting. For a split second, she had the oddest sensation of being warm and contented. She figured that was probably due to the soup.

"Somehow, I thought you might be able to."

She took no offense, because he meant none. Dana indicated the cup in her hand and the one still on the tray. "What do I owe you for this?"

He could certainly afford to spring for hot chocolate and soup. Especially since the latter was his idea. "Consider it atonement."

Her eyes narrowed as she tried to make sense of that. "Excuse me?"

She was going to make him spell it out, wasn't she? Well, if she could apologize, he supposed he could, too. "Maybe my bedside manner was a little abrupt when you brought Mollie in," he allowed, then added, "Sheila tells me I need to work on it sometimes."

The admission, personal in nature, took them out of the realm of strangers. "You *were* a little sharp," she agreed. "I figured it was because of me."

"It was." She looked at him, ready to square off again. It didn't take much with her, did it? he thought. "You and a lot of other things." His eyes met hers. He tried to decide if they were a royal blue, or if that was because of the dim lighting. "That's still no excuse for being tactless, though."

She agreed with him, but it was enough to hear it. She wasn't her father, to keep a man twisting in the wind for her pleasure, yanking a little on his rope whenever it threatened to go slack until such time as she saw fit to let him go.

Dana changed the subject. "Mollie's crazy about you." Deep-seated affection crept into her voice. "I think she's planning on a wedding."

He laughed. He thought he'd detected the makings of a crush earlier this afternoon.

"I guess it'll be a long engagement." And then he smiled at Dana. She was, after all, in some way responsible for the way the little girl behaved. "She's a great girl."

"No argument." The soup was cool enough to drink. It was gone in a few gulps.

He waited until she put the container down. "What happened to her parents?"

It was on the tip of her tongue to change the subject, but that wouldn't change what had happened. Besides, as he'd pointed out, he needed the information for his files. And for any intelligent work-up on Mollie.

So she recited the words that, when she had first heard them, had ripped open her heart.

"They were killed in a car accident a little more than six months ago. Her mother was my sister. Megan. Megan died on the way to the hospital. Her husband, George, died instantly. Mollie was in the car, too." With all her heart, she wished she could have changed at least that much of the tragedy, that Mollie could at least have been somewhere else when it happened, not right there, to see it, to feel the crash that killed her parents.

Dana didn't realize that she shivered. "Mollie still has nightmares, but not as often as before." Progress was made by inches, not giant leaps. "That's why she was so afraid of staying here."

He looked at the chair. It couldn't be comfortable, not for the whole night. "Is that why you stayed?"

She nodded. "Mollie's had enough upheaval in her life. She needs to know there's something she can count on."

"And that would be you." It wasn't a question, it was a softly voiced statement.

"That would be me." She didn't know why, but she couldn't turn her eyes away from his. A very strange sensation rippled through her. No, rippled was the wrong word. Drifted was more like it. Drifted like a lazy, slow-moving river making its way to the sea with an eternity to get there. Mentally, she shook herself free of the feeling.

"How about her grandfather?"

Dana stiffened. She'd almost forgotten about him. Her father wouldn't take kindly to knowing he could so easily be put out of someone's mind, especially his daughter's. "That's something that has to be worked out."

Her tone told him that this was a private area, one where trespassers weren't welcome, and he was a trespasser.

If he was going to be of any use to anyone, Rafe thought, he had to get going.

"Well, I wish you luck." He crushed the empty soup container in his hand. "I'd better be going. If you need anything, ask one of the nurses. You'll find they're a friendly bunch." He moved closer for one last look at Mollie. "I think everything's going to be all right. Some of her color's coming back."

Her panic had settled to something manageable. She knew he was right. "Thanks for the soup."

He tossed his container into a wastepaper basket near the door. "Don't mention it."

But she had, she thought as he left. She always made it a point to mention a kindness. Accustomed to doing without them, acts of kindness always surprised her when they happened.

Just as, she mused, settling into the chair, Rafe Saldana had surprised her.

Rafe struggled to keep the grin from his lips the next afternoon.

"I never saw a little girl get well so fast before." He looked properly amazed for Mollie's benefit.

In a complete reversal from the previous evening, Mollie looked as if she was ready and able to convert the hospital bed into a trampoline and bounce right out of the room.

"That's 'cause you and Aunt Dana took good care of me," Mollie told him gleefully. Her eyes shining with happiness, she seemed light-years away from the terrified little girl who had been brought in the night before.

Concerned, Dana drew Rafe to one side. "Is this normal?" she asked doubtfully, keeping her voice low. "To be so sick one day and so full of energy the next?"

He could see why she was skeptical. It was a drastic change.

"It is when you're five. I've known kids to be sick in the morning, great in the afternoon, feverish again by five and then perfectly fine by bedtime." Rafe smiled. It never failed, that deep feeling of satisfaction that came over him whenever one of his patients pulled through. Never mind how often it happened, it was still a high. "They're exceedingly resilient at this age." He winked at Mollie, and she giggled, ready to bounce higher to impress him. With a practiced arm, he caught her and settled her down. "I don't want to be forced to put stitches in that pretty little head of yours." He glanced toward Dana. "They don't spend a lot of time lingering over things."

Unlike adults, Dana thought. She said, "Except their shoes and socks, when you want them to get ready to go somewhere." A smile lifted the corners of Dana's mouth as she exchanged looks with Mollie. The struggle over getting dressed was one they went through every day. Mollie preferred the freedom of bare feet to the confinement of shoes and socks.

Dana had a nice smile, he thought. Too bad she didn't use it more often. "I wouldn't know about that aspect of it."

Mollie looked at him, surprised. "Don't you have any kids of your own?"

"No," he told her solemnly. "I don't."

Pity filled her eyes. At five, she had a tremendous capacity for sympathy. "I could stay with you sometimes. Aunt Dana could come, too."

Sympathetic or not, Mollie was getting far too carried away here, Dana thought. She was about to change the subject when Rafe said, "That sounds like an intriguing offer, but I'm hardly ever home. We wouldn't see very much of each other."

He really was nice, Dana thought. Not everyone had the patience to listen to children. It was an admirable quality. Her thoughts drifted to Steven and the way he'd acted toward Mollie. Too bad that quality was in such short supply.

Mollie saw no problem with Rafe's revelation. "Then you'll just have to come home more."

He laughed and gave Mollie a hug. "I know someone who would agree with you."

He had someone, Dana thought suddenly, then wondered why that should surprise her. Men like Dr. Rafe Saldana were born with someone in their lives. Not having anyone would have been the surprise, not the reverse.

Rafe paused to write something on Mollie's chart. Setting it down, he looked at Mollie, then smiled. "You're free to go, Mollie."

Dana looked at her watch. It was approaching one. They'd been here a little more than twelve hours. "Then you *are* discharging her?"

"Looks that way." He lifted Mollie and set her on the floor. "C'mon, off with you. Someone else can make use of this bed."

Mollie's spirits soared at the prospect of leaving the hospital. "Are you going to make him all well, like you did me?"

"It's a her, and she's someone else's patient." Actually, the child was assigned to the bed by the window. He'd overheard the admitting doctor discussing the little girl with the head nurse. Another case of the flu. Mollie was leaving the room just in time.

Mollie looked at Rafe with pure worship in her eyes. "But you'll help, right?"

There was no point in contradicting her. Instead, he smiled at the confident little face. "Absolutely. Now, I don't want you to overdo it for a couple of days. And come by and see me at the end of the week." He looked at Dana. "If Alice gives you any flak, tell her I told you to come."

Mollie, eager to please, nodded vigorously. "Right, no flak."

Rafe exchanged glances with Dana. When he grinned at her, suppressing a laugh, it felt as if his smile went straight to her core.

* * *

"How long did you say you'd known Dr. Saldana?"

Sheila sat on the bed, watching Dana toss the few possessions she'd come with into a suitcase. Sheila still felt incredibly guilty for not being home last night when Mollie had gotten so ill. She and Slade had gone to see a play at the Performing Arts Center. Slade had gotten the tickets five months in advance to secure good seats. While the Sharks had confronted the Jets on stage, Dana had been confronted with a gasping, choking child. The thought squeezed her heart.

"Since we interned together. Four, no, five years ago. Why?" She peered at Dana's face. Her friend's expression gave nothing away. Her father's daughter, Sheila thought. "What's up?"

"Nothing." Dana folded another one of Mollie's shirts, then tucked it into the suitcase. She'd called and spoken to Esther when she arrived at Sheila's a little while ago. It was a great deal easier talking to the housekeeper than to her father. Dana asked her to relay the message that they would be arriving early that evening. "I was just wondering how long he's been practicing."

"Long enough to be good." Sheila couldn't help wondering if that was all that was on Dana's mind. There wasn't a woman alive who hadn't expressed interest in Rafe on some level. "Actually, he was good right from the start. He's got a natural knack for it, for understanding children." Sheila thought of it as a gift. Not all pediatricians had it. "It's the parents he occasionally has trouble with." She smiled. "He can get a little terse with them, but that's only because he cares so much."

Dana closed the suitcase, snapped the locks. Done. "He said you thought he needed to improve his bedside manner."

That didn't sound like something Rafe would casually volunteer. He usually remained pretty close-mouthed. "Seems he did a lot of talking with you."

"Not that much," Dana countered. She set the suitcase on the floor. The box of photographs was already in the car, along with Mollie's toys. It seemed like so little to represent the sum of two lives. "Besides, it was quiet. There wasn't much going on, so he looked in on Mollie around midnight," she explained when Sheila raised one eyebrow. "We talked a little over chicken soup."

"Chicken soup?" Sheila repeated. She couldn't picture Rafe sharing chicken soup with someone at midnight.

"He brought me some from a vending machine." Why was Sheila looking at her like that? They had only exchanged a handful of sentences. "I mentioned that I'd skipped dinner."

"Chicken soup and conversation." Sheila laughed. Maybe she would make it her business to run into Rafe and have a few words with him. This was beginning to sound interesting. "In some countries, you would be betrothed by now."

Dana rolled her eyes. "Something tells me you need more than an occasional evening out with your husband. You, Dr. Pollack, need a genuine vacation."

"As a matter of fact, we're going on one." In all the excitement over Mollie, she'd forgotten. "Just Slade and me. He thinks it's about time we had that honeymoon we keep postponing. He says he wants to go before he's too old to remember why he's there."

Dana had seen the looks, the touches exchanged between them. Easy, without thought, just part of their everyday lives. It gladdened her heart even as it filled it with envy. "I don't think Slade will ever be too old."

Sheila grinned. "That's exactly what I said." She thought of his reaction to that, and her skin warmed, just as it had then. "While we're gone, you're welcome to stay on. Pilar will be here, taking care of Rebecca, but you can have the run of the place."

Dana couldn't allow herself to be swayed. Otherwise, she would never leave. "Tempting, but I've put this off long enough. The longer I wait, the more ominous her grandfather becomes for Mollie."

Sheila nodded. Dana was making sense, but she still wished her friend didn't have to go. "Okay, but if you change your mind, or if you need a place to retreat for any reason, my house is yours.''

Dana smiled. Just like the old days. ''Thanks. I'll keep that in mind.''

Chapter 7

The fact that her grandfather was in a wheelchair made no difference whatsoever to Mollie. Or to Dana. Standing or sitting, Paul Morrow had always been, and continued to be, a formidable man.

It was his manner that induced and inflicted fear.

Dana and Mollie had arrived a few minutes earlier. Dickinson, who she assumed lived somewhere on the premises, opened the door to them, instead of Esther, as she'd expected. He assured Dana that their things would be immediately attended to.

There had been nothing left but to get on with Mollie's introduction to her grandfather.

He was in the den, reviewing some obscure point of law to see how he could use it to skewer his opposition. He laid the tome on the desk as soon as they entered the room.

For once, Dana noted with a sense of satisfaction, he didn't pretend to be so taken with what he was reading that he didn't hear her come in. If she hadn't known better, she would have said he'd been waiting for this. It went beyond the power of imagination to think he was actually looking forward to it.

"So, we finally meet."

Hands folded before him, Morrow looked down a nose that was a little too short to be termed hawklike, assessing his granddaughter the way he might have a client who had entered his office for the first time. Having had little time for his own children, he had no idea of the kind of care or conversation children required, only that it was annoyingly different from what he was accustomed to.

Dana placed a soothing hand on Mollie's shoulder. She could see agitation flickering across the small face. Ushering her only as far as she was willing to go, Dana softly said, "Mollie, this is your grandfather, Paul Morrow."

"No need to tell her," Morrow snapped. He hated stupidity. To him, it was the worst of all possible sins. The child wasn't slow—why did Dana have to explain who he was? "She knows who I am, don't you, Mollie?" Working the controls on the armrest, he moved his chair forward and reached out to her. Afraid, Mollie shifted so that she was partially hidden behind Dana. His blue eyes glinted. "What's the matter with her?"

"Offhand, I'd say you're frightening her." Taking her hand, Dana coaxed Mollie forward. "It's okay, Mollie, there's nothing to be afraid of." *He's just a grumpy, disgruntled old man, nothing more.*

As if he read her thoughts—she'd believed he could when she was Mollie's age—her father demanded, "What did you tell her about me?"

The silent accusation annoyed her, since she'd done the exact opposite of what he implied in an attempt to calm Mollie. And he was ruining her carefully laid groundwork by behaving the way he always did. Demanding, insensitive and overbearing. Nothing had changed.

"That you didn't eat children for breakfast," Dana answered coldly. She draped one hand around Mollie's thin shoulders, silently trying to reassure her. But the scowl across her grandfather's face did little to assuage Mollie's fears.

"What?"

This wasn't going to work, Dana thought. At least, not right away. It was going to take time, the one thing she wasn't sure she had. But there was no one to ask about that. God wasn't answering his phone today.

Dana squared off with her father, shifting so she was between him and the little girl. "She has this impression that you're an ogre because you made Megan cry."

He took umbrage. "I never made Megan cry."

There was no feeling in her smile. It was as cold as those she had seen grace his face. "You underestimate yourself, Father. At one time or other, I'm willing to speculate that you made everyone cry."

Incensed, Morrow bristled at the image she was fabricating before the child. It was a blatant lie. And he could easily prove it. "I never made you cry."

Dana raised her chin, pride forbidding her from making the admission. She wouldn't give him the satisfaction of knowing that he had twisted her young soul. A great many tears had been shed in secret before she knew better than to let him get to her.

"No, you never made me cry."

His eyes shifted once more to Mollie, to take measure. She looked well enough. "Esther said she was sick."

He was old and ill and probably afraid of contracting something. "Don't worry, she's better." As Dana spoke, she stroked Mollie's hair. Though silent, she knew Mollie was absorbing everything, every word, every nuance, just like Megan used to do before her. "She won't contaminate you."

True or not, the fear made him sound weak, and he refused to acknowledge even a hint of weakness. "That wasn't what I asked."

She knew him, and that annoyed the hell out of him, Dana thought. For a moment it almost made her feel smug. "No, but that was *why* you asked."

He damned her for her impertinence, for knowing. "I want her checked out by my doctor."

Amusement curved her mouth further. "You have a pediatrician?"

Was she laughing at him? There was a time when he wouldn't even have stopped to wonder. He would simply have had her removed. But that time was gone. Other things had moved forward to prey on his mind. He hadn't become more patient, just realized that there was a need to act as if he had in order to win. "I have the best," he countered.

The last thing Mollie needed was to be subjected to more doctors. After last night, Dana was satisfied that what Sheila said about Rafe Saldana was true. He was at the top of his profession. There was no need for a second opinion.

"So do we. Dr. Rafe Saldana." She exchanged looks with Mollie. The little girl nodded vigorously, the first sign of animation since she'd entered the house. "He signed her out of Harris Memorial and said she was fine. I believe him." Dana took Mollie's hand, ready to lead her out of the room. "I'd like to get her settled in, if you don't mind."

Though tiring, he was surprised at their withdrawal. He gestured toward Mollie. "We haven't had a chance to talk yet." They'd barely said hello.

Dana was firm, though her voice was amiable for Mollie's sake. "I thought maybe the two of you could take this in slow doses." To convince him, she knew she needed something more than her own judgment, since he'd never thought much of it before. "Dr. Saldana said not to tire her out too much."

Morrow accepted that. With a stipulation. "I still want her examined by my doctor."

There was no negotiating on this point. "Sorry, Father, I'd like to keep the poking and prodding to a minimum." She saw his face cloud. There was a time when she would have taken that as a sign to run, but that time had passed. She had nothing to lose now, and perhaps, she thought, even respect to gain. At the very least, she could protect Mollie. "Mollie is afraid of doctors. After what she's been through, I'd say she has good reason to be.''

She turned and saw the housekeeper in the doorway. "My old room?"

Esther smiled. "Yes, miss. I had Dickinson put your things there." Looking at Mollie, Esther felt as if something was squeezing her heart. The little girl was the image of Megan at that age. "Have you ever met Logan?" she asked Mollie.

Mollie shook her head solemnly, trying not to seem as eager to leave the room as she felt. Her mother had always said not to be rude. She didn't want to do anything to get her grandfather mad at her. "No."

Esther's smile was mysterious. "Well, he's waiting to meet you."

Mollie raised her eyes to Dana, hoping for an explanation.

She'd saved it, Dana thought, a bittersweet sensation wafting through her. Esther had saved the toy all these years. Why?

"Logan was my old teddy bear," she told Mollie.

"Oh." Mollie brightened immediately. "Okay." She took the hand Esther extended to her. Before leaving the room, Mollie looked over her shoulder at her grandfather. "Good night," she said politely, her expression once again subdued.

The subdued look disappeared the moment she turned toward Esther and hurried off.

This, Dana thought as she followed behind them, had the makings of a lovely friendship. Esther had been the haven she'd sought again and again during her stormy younger years.

"You kept my teddy bear?" she had to ask. She'd thought it had been thrown out years ago, when she had outgrown it. Now she realized childhood things were not really outgrown, merely put to one side.

Esther's reply was matter-of-fact and practical, giving not even the remotest hint of the sentimentality that governed her. "I thought you might like it for your own children someday."

Though Dana gave no indication, the words hit far too close to home.

Morrow watched them leave. His own granddaughter and she lit up like a damn Christmas tree because a housekeeper waved a bribe in front of her like some damn carrot before a rabbit. A bribe that wasn't even hers to wave.

She was *his* granddaughter, damn it. He'd allowed her to come here. He'd allowed Dana to come here, and she didn't even have the decency to behave as if she was grateful.

Neither of them did. He knew what kind of situation his daughter found herself in, knew how low her funds were almost to the penny. And yet she behaved as if she was doing him a favor by being here.

He was the one doing the favors, damn it, not her. Not—

Morrow pressed his lips together in frustrated anger as he felt his hand begin to tremble. Glaring at the offending limb, he willed it to stop. But the palsy continued as he cursed it.

Hating what was happening to him, to the body he had always taken for granted, he placed his other hand over the one that was moving independent of his wishes. He pressed down hard, hard enough to cause tears to spring to his eyes, trying to make it stop.

It refused.

Dana couldn't sleep. Though she felt exhausted beyond words, for some reason sleep refused to come.

It had taken her the better part of the evening to get Mollie settled. Time had crawled by before she finally fell asleep. Dana had been sure that all she would have to do was lay her head on the pillow and she would be asleep within seconds.

The seconds came and went, and she was still awake.

She'd lain there with her eyes shut, waiting to be overtaken by sleep. Instead, she'd remained wide awake as the minutes, then the hours, ticked away.

Maybe it was her surroundings keeping her awake. There

was no denying they were a factor. It was hard for her to believe she was here after all this time. Back in a place she had sworn never to return to as she fled, watching the house disappear in her rearview mirror.

She'd meant it at the time.

But at the time her father had been healthy, at the top of his game. And Megan had been alive, pandering to his every whim. When she'd left home, her sister hadn't begun to develop a backbone.

That hadn't happened until George entered her life.

Dana didn't want to think about that. She really didn't want to think about anything.

Restless, she sat up and threw off the covers. Moonlight seeped through the window, a campfire lantern whose batteries were waning. It made everything look eerie, distant.

It had felt that way even when she was a child, she thought. This had never been her sanctuary. It was another room in her father's house when he was here. And even when he was gone, away in another state, defending another affluent or influential client, his presence was still felt. Felt so strongly it left a pall over the house that no amount of sunshine could lift.

Damn, what had she been thinking of, coming here? And with Mollie, too. She must have been crazy.

At two in the morning, returning felt like a colossal mistake.

Why had she been optimistic enough to think she could somehow accomplish something that had eluded her for so many years? Did she really think she had a chance of being able to coexist with her father in something other than a battlefield? She'd come to the table without any bargaining chips, without the cards stacked in her favor. How could she hope to win?

But she had come to play, and she did have one thing in her favor. He couldn't intimidate her anymore. She was an adult now. A bar-certified lawyer, just like he was.

Well, not just like he was.

No one would pay her the kind of money he could demand to defend them, but then, she wasn't ruthlessly bent on annihilating the opposition, either. And her record wasn't perfect, like his.

Dana smiled. What kind of a lawyer did that make her?

A pregnant one.

The thought reared from nowhere, attacking her unannounced as it had a dozen or so times since Sheila had dropped the devastating bombshell on her in her office.

Pregnant.

With Steven's baby.

Dana scrubbed her hands over her face. She couldn't get used to the idea. Still prayed Sheila was mistaken, although in her heart Dana knew that wasn't possible. Pregnancy was the mainstay of Sheila's profession. She should know a pregnant woman when she examined one.

Sighing deeply, Dana wrestled with her conscience. That, too, was a by-product of the hour. It was incredible, the thoughts that crawled out of the woodwork at one in the morning. Like guilt. Guilt that in the light of day would have seemed laughable.

Guilt because she hadn't told Steven he had fathered a child.

As if he really wanted to know that.

But what if he did? Bastard or not, he deserved to know. Deserved the right to hang up on her, she thought cynically.

The idea of talking to him left her cold. Given a choice, she never wanted to see him or hear from him again. She didn't have that luxury. It had to be done. Sooner or later, he had to be told.

Damn, why was life filled with so many have-tos? Why couldn't she drift through it, being taken care of by someone? Someone kind, caring. Someone like Rafe Saldana, who loved children and was dedicated to making them feel better.

Startled by the path her mind had veered onto, she abandoned the entire line of thought.

No use in wallowing in self-pity. That accomplished nothing except for wasting time. She was who she was. She was the one who took care, not the one taken care of. That was the way things were.

Muttering, she dragged the telephone from the nightstand and dialed the number that had so recently been hers. It was late, but she didn't care. She wanted to get this over with.

Her heart felt like a heavy stone in her chest as she listened to the phone ring.

Two, three, four.

And then there was a noise. Sharp needles jabbed at her nerves until she realized it was his machine that had picked up, not him.

Where the hell was he at this hour?

With that bimbo, that was where. The one he'd been sneaking around with while telling her he loved her. While verbally abusing Mollie.

"Hi, this is Steven. I can't come to the phone right now—"

Dana let the receiver drop into the cradle. He'd changed the message, she thought, irritated. *I* can't come to the phone instead of *we*.

Well, what had she expected, to have him build a shrine to her memory? If he'd been into shrine building, he wouldn't have gone tomcatting around while she was living with him. And he would have been kind to Mollie instead of treating her as if she was some subhuman irritant.

Dana glared at the telephone, cursing her stupidity. There was no reason to tell him he was going to become a father, other than the moral rightness of it. He didn't want children. He'd made that perfectly clear by the way he treated Mollie. She would have given anything if, just once, he had behaved the way Rafe Saldana did.

Her thoughts shifted to Rafe as she lay down again. She had no idea what the man would be like as a husband, but as a father, there was no question in her mind. He would be wonderful. You could tell.

And maybe, just maybe, that meant he wouldn't be so bad as a husband, either. A man who was good with kids had potential. And Rafe Saldana definitely had potential, she thought, beginning to drift off. Potential for a lot of things…

Daylight crept in, slipping between her lashes, prying apart her lids. She had half a second or so of peace before morning slammed into her with the force of a sledgehammer applied to her midsection.

She jackknifed up, stunned, confused and utterly nauseated.

Taking in her surroundings with unfocused eyes, she was unnerved. She was in her old room, amid the highly polished dark wood furniture and oppressive drapes. In the living tomb with vaulted ceilings.

If she hadn't felt so sick, that reality might have preyed even more heavily on her mind.

Her feet hit the floor, and she had just enough time to make it into the bathroom before her stomach rose up to meet her throat, determined to purge itself. She had absolutely no say in the matter.

Mercifully, this morning's episode was briefer than usual. Maybe her body was finally getting accustomed to the invader that had entered it, she thought, rising from her knees.

There had to be a better way.

Bending over the sink, Dana rinsed her mouth and splashed water on her face. She looked at her reflection, her eyes bleary from lack of sleep. Trust Steven to find a way to make her feel sick to her stomach even when he wasn't around.

It took her a while before she could summon the strength to get dressed, and even longer to find enough to face her father over breakfast.

She was grateful for the diversion of having to fetch Mollie.

Her father was at the table when she came down, Mollie's hand in hers. Dana had known he would be. Just as she'd known the look in his eyes would be critical as he observed them. It was a given.

He nodded a curt greeting as his daughter and granddaughter walked into the wide dining room. The table, too formal for a family to converge around, was intended for entertaining his peers and his clients. He favored it, foregoing the one in the kitchen. Kitchens were for working in, not for dining in, he staunchly maintained. He'd forbidden his daughters from eating there as children. Common people ate in the kitchen, he'd told them. People with no education, no future, huddled about an uneven table that wobbled each time they sat down or rose from it. Or tried to eat.

Dana and Mollie sat at the far end of the dining table, accentuating the distance between them. Annoyed, he waved his granddaughter closer.

"Sit here," he ordered Mollie, indicating the chair to his left. "Where I can see you better." Instead of obeying, Mollie looked hesitantly at Dana. He could feel his temper fraying. Why couldn't she just do as he asked? "You don't have to get your aunt's approval for everything I say. This is my house, girl."

"Mollie," Dana corrected tersely. They moved closer and reseated themselves. "Her name is Mollie."

His eyes narrowed. He didn't like being corrected. "I called *you* 'girl.'"

That was just the point. "And I hated it."

She wasn't making any sense. "Why?" he demanded.

His habit of calling her that, especially while lecturing, had irritated her for years. "Because I figured it meant you couldn't remember my name. You called Megan 'girl,' too."

Mollie looked from her grandfather to her aunt. "Did that make you girl one?"

It took a second for the words to register. When they did, Dana experienced an uncontrollable urge to laugh. And then, because tension was so close to the surface, so close to exploding, she did. It was a hell of a lot better than screaming.

"No, honey. Too as in also, not as in the number." Her eyes slid toward her father. "Your grandfather didn't give out numbers." Everyone was the same to him. Beings beneath him.

"So, Mollie—" Morrow emphasized her name pointedly, momentarily raising his eyes to Dana "—do you go to school yet?"

"I went to preschool for a while."

He knew she'd dropped out of class after the accident, unable to attend. And then Dana had come for her and moved the girl out of state. Dana had been called, not him. That had been per instructions—his late daughter's instructions. Megan hadn't trusted him with her child. That, more than anything, rankled him. As if he, and not they, had not lived up to the faith placed in him.

"Well," he informed Mollie as he poured a dollop of syrup on his French toast, "you have to go again now. To kindergarten this time."

"It's summer, Father." Had he forgotten? Of course he had. The seasons were all one and the same to him, just as she and Megan had been. "School's out in the summer. I'll have her registered by fall."

"In your old school?" The private school's rates were prohibitive to the average person. It was one of the reasons he'd chosen it. He liked being associated with things other men could not afford to even think about. It had been a long, hard climb to this pinnacle, and he meant to savor everything, however small. "Just how do you intend to pay for that?"

Did he think she was going to ask him for money? "She's going to public school."

"Public school?" He spat the words out as if they left a horrid taste in his mouth. "Are you out of your mind? My granddaughter is—"

"—going to public school," Dana said firmly.

"If it's a matter of money, I could—"

"No," Dana contradicted quietly, "you couldn't, and you won't." She said the next sentence slowly, so that each syllable would sink in. "Mollie is my responsibility."

"Responsibility is next to impossible without money to back it up."

No, Father, responsibility is a feeling, a pledge, not a check. "I have money."

He knew better. The insurance policy was almost gone, eaten up by Mollie's medical bills, as was her bank account. "Not enough."

That tore it. Dana dropped her knife on her plate with a clang. Mollie's eyes darted toward her. She hadn't meant to scare Mollie, but she was angry.

"Oh, I forgot, you would know that. Just as you knew where I was staying. And probably how many vitamins I take in the morning. Just what don't you know?" She leaned over the table. "Tell you what, why don't you tell me exactly what your detective failed to report to you, and I'll see if I can fill in the gaps!"

He threw down his napkin. A corner fell into his coffee cup, absorbing the drops that were left. "I don't know what you're talking about."

"Yes, you do. You had me investigated, tailed and God only knows what else." She drew herself up. "How dare you? How dare you invade my life like that?"

"How dare I?" he echoed. Fury entered his eyes at the challenge to his authority. No one talked to him like that. Ever. "How else was I supposed to know about you?"

It wasn't like him to miss the obvious. Except when it came to her. "There's such a thing as the telephone, Father. In eight years, you could have found time to pick it up just once. Besides, explain this to me. Why would you want to know?"

How could she even ask that? "Because you're mine."

Like a possession. Her anger rose to meet his. "Only if I want to be."

She was wrong, he thought. "Blood isn't a matter of choice, Dana. It just *is*." He looked at Mollie, who shrank from his glare. "Remember that."

"Yes, sir," she mumbled, afraid to look away.

He pushed his chair back from the table. "I have to get to the office."

Dana looked at his plate. He'd hardly touched anything. "You haven't finished your breakfast."

He missed the veiled concern and heard only the accusation. "I've lost my appetite."

She rose, as if to restrain him. "You're not well. You can't afford to skip meals."

He wouldn't be dictated to by someone he'd brought into the world. "Don't tell me what I can and can't do."

She wasn't about to back away, though she wanted to. "Somebody should."

He fixed her with a cold look. "Well, it won't be you." With that, he directed the motorized wheelchair out of the room.

"Does he hate you, Aunt Dana?" Mollie was whispering, even though he was gone.

Dana took a deep breath before answering, trying to calm her nerves. No one could irritate her the way he could.

"No, sugar, I think it's himself he hates." She gave her a heartening smile. "C'mon, don't let him spoil your appetite. Esther makes the best French toast around." She urged some on the girl.

Chapter 8

"I see you have a new address."

Rafe looked up from the patient folder he was reading as he walked into the examination room. He placed Mollie's folder on the small counter against the wall. Mollie had regained her color. No loss of energy here, he thought, pleased.

"Did you move?" He directed the question to the little girl.

She nodded. Though she would have liked to stay with Slade and Sheila, she didn't say anything to Aunt Dana. She didn't want to make her feel sad. "We're at my grandfather's house now."

The statement, so seriously uttered, made him smile. He had an image of Shirley Temple, playing Heidi, saying the very same thing.

"So you did finally meet him." His hands on either side of her waist, Rafe gently lifted her and placed her on the end of the examining table. "Up you go. Say, have you been working out?"

She giggled, covering her mouth. There was pure adoration in her eyes. "No."

"Well, you certainly feel like it to me." He reached for his otoscope. "So, you're living with your grandfather, huh? Is he as scary as you thought?"

She tilted her head, patiently enduring the exam even though she wanted to wiggle. "Kinda."

"Eyes clear," he pronounced for Dana's benefit. "Ditto ears." He took a tongue depressor from the breast pocket of his lab coat. "But you're giving him a chance, right?"

Mollie eyed the wooden stick with resignation. She didn't like this part. "Uh-huh."

"Say ah." He waited until she did as he asked. "Must be a pretty nice guy to let you come live with him. Throat normal." He jettisoned the depressor into the basket in the corner, making the shot. Mollie clapped. Playing along, Rafe modestly bowed his head in thanks.

"It's a large house."

Dana had no idea why she felt compelled to say that. Maybe she didn't want him thinking she'd moved back with her father because she had no options, or that she was someone who had to have other people take care of her. Not that it mattered what he thought, just that he did seem to be a pretty decent guy, and there was no point in him getting the wrong idea about her.

She'd spent part of the past hour sitting in the waiting room, listening to one testimonial after another about the fine young doctor. Sheila hadn't been kidding when she said Rafe Saldana's patients' parents sang his praises. Dana could almost hear the accompanying music as first one, then another mother volunteered stories of how good Rafe was with his young patients, how he could always be reached day or night, not like some doctors they'd had. And how he was never too busy to explain things to them. Never too busy to care.

Thirty-five minutes of that and she'd half expected to see him coming into the examining room wearing wings and a halo.

The image seemed slightly incongruent with the look in his eyes when he glanced in her direction. He had green eyes. Beautiful, soulful, light green eyes that seemed incredibly sensual when he looked directly at her. She wondered if he realized how sensual. If he did, he hadn't capitalized on it, at least not according to Sheila or his groupies.

"Any complaints?" Rafe retired his stethoscope. Her lungs were pure music. When Mollie shook her head, he raised his eyes to Dana for confirmation.

"She's been fine," Dana said. "Full of energy, as if she'd never been sick."

Nice not to see her brow furrowed with worry for a change, he thought.

"I told you, kids are wonderfully resilient." Rummaging in the coat's deep pockets, he found what he was looking for. Rafe took out a lollipop and looked at Dana before offering it to Mollie. "Is it all right?"

His thoughtfulness impressed her. She wouldn't have thought he would bother asking but just hand the treat out. Feeling oddly touched, she nodded.

He presented the cherry-flavored treat to Mollie. "This is for you, kiddo, for being such a good patient."

"Thank you." The wrapper was off before she said *you*.

Because the atmosphere was relaxed, Dana found herself thinking of Rafe as someone other than a stranger whose services she required. "Do you realize you have a fan club out there?"

He arched an eyebrow, then took the information in stride. "My nurses are required to sing my praises or I don't give them their paychecks on Friday." He made a few notes on Mollie's chart.

"No, I meant the women in the waiting room. This one women in particular—she had twins with her…"

Rafe reviewed his appointments. "That would be Nicole Lincoln. I've been taking care of Ethan and Erika since they were two months old." He'd seen them through a harrowing bout of pneumonia before their first birthday, he recalled.

"Her husband's with the Justice Department. I mess up, I'm history." He winked at Mollie.

In the line of fire, Dana found the wink extremely sexy, though she knew he hadn't meant it to be. If she wasn't careful, she was going to start to sound like those women she'd been talking to.

She found his modesty an incredible change of pace after Steven, and especially her father. "She thinks you're the best thing since rain on a dry crop."

That was a new one, he mused. "She's also friends with Sheila." It was Sheila who had delivered Nicole's twins. And Sheila who had recommended him to Nicole when she sought a second opinion about a minor problem with Ethan. After the first visit, Nicole had wound up bringing both twins to him. "That makes her prejudiced."

That wasn't an obvious connection. "*I'm* friends with Sheila, and I was prepared to dislike you."

Adding a line to the file, he raised his eyes to hers. "I think you're prepared to dislike everyone." Finished, Rafe flipped the file closed. "Why is that?"

He'd delved further than she wanted him to. But because she was feeling less defensive around him, she answered, "It's safer that way."

He could see her argument. He saw something else, too. "Also colder."

Colder. The word hit her with the jarring force of a two-by-four. That was, she realized, what she'd often accused her father of being. Colder than snow. That the term was being applied to her was something she didn't care for. She cared even less for the fact that it was true. At least, looking in from the outside.

Seeing he'd struck a nerve, Rafe directed his attention to his patient. "You, young lady, are in perfect health." Laying his finger on the tip of her nose, he pressed it lightly, as if to impress his next words upon her mind. "See that you stay that way."

Mollie shifted the lollipop to one side in her mouth in order to answer. It pouched out her cheek, making her look like a chipmunk storing nuts.

"Yes, Dr. Rafe."

He set her on the floor. And then, because he didn't want to leave the air between them cluttered with awkward discomfort, he asked Dana, "So, eaten any good chicken soup lately?"

"No, not since the hospital." She smiled, remembering how kind he'd been, then roused herself. Though she appreciated the care he gave Mollie, she didn't want him thinking she was becoming a card-carrying member of his fan club. "Right now, I'm more interested in finding some decent Tex-Mex food."

The declaration interested him. "Haven't you been to La Reina Simpatica yet?"

She was unfamiliar with the name. But then, so much had changed since she'd lived here. There were shopping malls where she had left fields ripe with corn and strawberries.

"No."

He laughed softly. Dana found the sound almost hypnotically engaging. "You don't know what you're missing. It's in Newport Beach on Pacific Coast Highway, just before you hit Laguna Beach. The food's out of this world, if you like that sort of thing."

That was the whole point, wasn't it? "I do," she maintained. Then, because he sounded so sure of his assessment, she sniffed. "But I doubt it can compare with this little hole in the wall I know in Dallas." Squeezed between what had once been a storefront church, now vacated, and a discount shoe store that was perpetually going out of business, it wasn't even remotely familiar with the term *ambience,* something that was written into the leases of the restaurants here. She paused, thinking. "I don't think it even had a name. Just a rude owner who knew the value of an excellently prepared meal." Once she'd found it, the restaurant had quickly become one of her favorite places. She'd frequented it so often, the owner had upscaled his attitude toward her to only slightly patronizing.

Steven's comment on that, she recalled, had been to ask her if she'd been sleeping with the old man.

Rafe grinned, as if tolerant of her naïveté. "Oh, I'm sure La Reina could not only compare to but surpass your little hole in the wall."

She should have let it go at that, but she couldn't. Dana had no idea what possessed her, but she heard herself asking, "You wouldn't like to make a bet on that, would you?"

His laugh, rich and deep, made her think of a streetwise con artist about to separate her from her money. "You're on. Five bucks too rich for your blood?"

She almost jeered. "No, but it shows me that you're made of the same stuff you brought me in the hospital." When he looked uncertain, she pursed her lips and said, "Chicken."

He couldn't put his finger on why her cockiness amused him. Or why the way she pursed her lips aroused him. He dismissed both. "Okay. Loser pays for the dinner."

Dana inclined her head. "Sounds fair."

Fair, the key word. He held up a finger. "One hitch. This all hinges on you." His eyes held hers. "How will I know if you're telling the truth?"

The smile on her face remained, but it grew serious around the edges. With eyes like his, she caught herself thinking, he could see right into her soul if it was necessary. But it wouldn't be.

"Because I don't lie."

No, he thought, she didn't. No matter what. Here, too, he had no idea why he believed her. He just did.

"All right. So how does tomorrow night sound? Six-thirty all right with you?"

Dana hesitated. Maybe she had gotten carried away, here.

Almost finished with her lollipop, Mollie tugged on Dana's sleeve. When Dana looked down, she asked, "Are you going out on a date with Dr. Rafe?"

For a moment, caught up in the exchange, she had forgotten Mollie was in the room. How had that happened? Dana wondered. Mollie was the only reason she was here.

Self-conscious and trying hard not to show it, Dana cleared her throat. "Not a date, honey, dinner."

Mollie didn't see the difference. "But dinner can be a date."

Was that a flush she felt creeping up her neck? God, she hoped not. "Yes, but—"

"Yes!" Mollie shouted, making a fist and bringing her elbow to her waist with a triumphant jerk, the way she'd seen people do on television. Aunt Dana was going on a date with Dr. Rafe. Maybe she would get to like him a lot, more than that mean old Steven. Everything was going to be perfect.

Embarrassed, Dana was at a loss. Rafe looked too amused for her to apologize, so in the end she said nothing.

He opened the door for them. "I'll pick you up at the new address?" Dana nodded, feeling the slightest bit numb. "Don't forget to bring your wallet," he told her. Was that mischief in his eyes? "You'll be paying for the evening."

As she walked toward the reception desk with Mollie, Dana had the uneasy feeling he might be right—and in more ways than one.

Over the next twenty-seven hours, Dana carried on half a dozen arguments with herself. Depending on her state of mind, the final verdict regarding her going out to dinner with Rafe was sometimes yes and sometimes no.

She was leaning toward no, but yes kept cropping up like a cork that couldn't be sunk.

A woman carrying another man's child had no business going out with someone. The thought, the protest, echoed in her brain more than once, louder each time.

But as she had taken great pains to point out in front of both Mollie and Rafe, this wasn't a date. It was a meal. People had meals with one another all the time, and it didn't mean anything. Right?

Dana flounced on her bed, frustrated and not sure why. If

going out to La Reina Simpatica didn't mean anything, why was she having this damn debate with herself?

Because it had been so long since she had gone out with anyone except Steven that the prospect of doing it with anyone else felt unsettlingly new to her.

It was just because her escape from Steven had left her stressed and on edge, she silently pointed out.

Dana pulled her knees to her chest, warding off the shiver that threatened to ripple through her body. Escape. The word hummed in her brain. That was what it had been, an escape, pure and simple. An escape from a life that was swallowing her up.

A life she didn't want.

There was absolutely no doubt in her mind about that. She didn't want to spend her life emotionally tied to a man who didn't care. She'd spent her youth that way, and that was more than enough.

But she'd come back to her youth, hadn't she? The thought mocked her.

It wasn't the same.

She'd returned because her father was ill, and because there were things that needed to be fixed, loose ends that needed to be tied. Fences that needed to be mended. And then she had to close the gates.

For good.

That still didn't help her decide whether she should go through with this tonight.

Disgusted with herself, with this Ping-Pong game taking place in her brain, Dana decided it was best not to think at all.

Or would it be best not to *go* at all?

No, that would be the coward's way out, and she refused to be a coward. Besides, she was making too much of this. This wasn't a date. If it had been, he wouldn't have asked her in front of Mollie, wouldn't have worded it the way he had. This was nothing more than two people settling a bet.

She buried her head against her knees.

Excitement in her eyes, Mollie skipped into the room. Not waiting for an invitation, she scrambled onto the bed, wiggling into position beside her aunt. She deliberately mimicked her aunt's pose, scooting her knees up and wrapping her arms around them. It didn't seem all that comfortable to Mollie, but she desperately wanted to be just like Aunt Dana.

"Whatcha gonna wear tonight?" she wanted to know. "Something pretty?"

She didn't own anything pretty, Dana thought. She hadn't packed very much when she'd left Steven. Only her photographs and some of Mollie's things. Her own clothes had been a very low priority. She had just wanted to leave before she weakened and lost her resolve. Sheila had lent her a few things, but she didn't feel right about keeping them.

Dana feathered her fingers through Mollie's baby-fine hair. "I don't have much to choose from, sweetie."

"Don't these closets have things in them?" Rather than wait to be told, Mollie climbed off the bed and went to see for herself.

Dana hadn't bothered opening the walk-in closet behind the mirrored, sliding glass doors. There was no point, since she expected it to be empty. She'd used the bureau to house her things.

But when Mollie struggled and pushed one long sliding door to the side, Dana saw the closet was full.

There were clothes hanging there.

Her clothes.

Stunned, she got off the bed and crossed to the closet, a child in a fairy tale. Or, more to the point, a woman who didn't know whether she was dreaming or not.

It wasn't a dream. Or a hallucination. The clothes were there. They were real. Amazed, excited, confused, Dana slid one dress after another along the pole.

He hadn't thrown them out.

She was sure he'd had them all destroyed when she left home against his wishes. Or, at the very least, had given them away to charity.

Why had he kept them? Had he expected her to return someday? He would have known better than that.

But she had, hadn't she? she thought. She *had* returned home.

Her hands flew over the familiar items, nudging forth memories as she looked at a favorite dress or blouse. Dana pressed her lips together, rivers of happiness and sadness running together, pouring through her veins. She blew out a shaky breath as she tucked away an oversize sweatshirt the boy she'd had a crush on her junior year in high school had given her. What was his name? Jim? No, Joe. Joe Taylor.

She smiled, sentimentality tugging at her. Well, at least this solved the problem of having nothing to wear.

Mollie entertained herself by moving in and out between the long line of dresses against the back wall. "You've got lots of pretty things to pick from, Aunt Dana." She turned to look at her, awed. "Whose clothes are they?"

"Mine," Dana answered quietly, looking at a burgundy suit.

This was the suit she'd worn on her sixteenth birthday. She'd sat on the window seat, looking out. Waiting for her father to come home to take her out to celebrate, just the two of them. The way he'd promised. She slid her fingers along the sleeve. He'd called two days later to wish her a belated happy birthday. He'd been in Washington, D.C., at the time. Detained. She no longer remembered who he'd been defending. Only that she'd sworn that day never to be stupid enough to believe anything he said to her again.

Never to let him hurt her again.

Mollie burrowed into another line of clothes, reveling in the new playground she had discovered for herself.

"Are they *all* yours?"

"Yes, they're all mine. Or they *were* all mine," Dana amended. "Before I left home. I guess your grandfather kept them."

Mollie popped her head from between a mauve sundress

and a white sheath to look at her. "That was nice of him, huh?"

Nice was stretching it. But it was definitely *some*thing. She wasn't sure what. "Yes, it was," she murmured.

"How about this one?" Eager to help, to make her as pretty as possible to Dr. Rafe, Mollie held out a light blue chiffon skirt. She'd unearthed the dress Dana had worn to her senior prom. "It's very soft. Dr. Rafe'll like it."

Oh, God, she had a junior matchmaker on her hands. "I think it's a bit too formal," Dana told her tactfully.

Nodding, Mollie let the fabric go. The skirt retreated amid the rest of the garments. "Okay. You can wear that the next time."

Dana opened her mouth to correct Mollie, then shut it. It might be too daunting for Mollie to hear that there wasn't going to be a next time. This was a one-time thing. And she had accepted not because of her craving for Tex-Mex food but, she admitted to herself, because of her underlying craving to talk to a decent man for the space of an evening. It would be a nice change.

Her head filled with testimonials to Rafe Saldana's "wonderfulness," as one preschooler had said, she'd gotten carried away by the moment.

And, she supposed, by her need to be able to spend an hour or so with a man she knew she wouldn't have to fight off. Or fight with. Rafe didn't look like a pushover, and she knew he spoke his mind, but he seemed like a fair man, and that was all she required, the company of a decent, fair man. A man she didn't have to watch her back with. Or any other part of her anatomy, either.

On their first date, Steven had barely been able to keep his hands off her in the restaurant. At the time she'd found it thrilling. But she was a hundred years older now, and maybe six months wiser.

It counted for something.

She heard the front door open and then close rather loudly, then the sound of an angry voice raised in a tirade. Her father's words reverberated up the stairs. He had a voice that could carry to the back row of an opera house. He was proud of that, even boasted of it.

Glancing at her watch, she saw it was only a little past five. It was too early for her father to be home. When he wasn't in court, his usual pattern was to remain late at the office and to have dinner out. Rarely did he come home before eight, and usually sometime after ten.

But that was before, she reminded herself. Now the shell was wearing out and, she supposed, taking what passed as his soul with it.

Dana crossed to the door. She heard Mollie behind her. Turning, she motioned her back.

"Stay here, Mollie. See if you can find me something to wear," she added, hoping to keep her busy. Hoping, too, that she wouldn't regret it.

Mollie retreated willingly. "Can I play dress up?"

"Be my guest." Looking over her shoulder, Dana grinned. "Knock your socks off."

Dana went to the landing and peered at the foyer below. Her father was no longer in view, and she didn't hear his voice. Wondering what was going on, she hurried down the long, curved stairway, only to encounter Esther at the bottom.

Dana looked around, but they were alone. "Where's my father?"

Esther nodded toward the rear of the house. When he had first become confined to a wheelchair, Paul Morrow had had a master bedroom added on the ground floor and a connecting door put in the den. The two rooms, as spacious as some houses, comprised his lair. He hadn't been upstairs in over a year.

"I think he's gone into his den." When Dana stepped past her, Esther added, "He doesn't want to see anyone, Miss Dana."

No, she didn't imagine he would. But that didn't change her mind. "I didn't come back to hide in the shadows when he was home."

As she turned, Esther placed a hand on her arm. "I think it might be better if you let him have some time to himself. He doesn't like people seeing him when he's…indisposed."

Dana ignored the delicate euphemism. "I know what he has, Esther. I know the whole story. Sheila Pollack wrote to me in great detail. A lot of time's been wasted. Some of it my fault, a lot of it his. I don't want to waste what's left."

Concern for her rose in the housekeeper's brown eyes. "What are you going to say to him?"

Dana straightened, bracing herself. "I'll start with hello."

Chapter 9

Dana knocked on the door to the den. There was no answer. Knowing she was going to be met with extreme displeasure, she went in anyway.

There was an open decanter on his desk. The sun was filtering through it, casting an amber shadow on the opposite wall. Scotch. Her father favored brandy for socializing and Scotch for darker moments. She saw his hand shake ever so slightly as he raised the bottle and poured.

"Get out, Dickinson," he roared, never raising his eyes from the glass he was trying to fill. Why did something so simple require so much damn effort?

She nearly backed away. His tone unearthed memories she'd taken great pains to bury. But if those memories were to be eradicated, they had to be faced, not buried. She knew that. And that could only be accomplished one way.

Sheer grit made her hold her position. "I came in to see what's wrong."

The decanter slipped from his fingers and made it the last

two inches to the desk with a thud. A trickle of Scotch splashed over the thick cut-glass rim.

The look of surprise melted into one of malevolence, and his eyes narrowed. "Why? So you could bask in my mortality?"

How could he sit there and accuse her of something so heartless, so vindictively cruel? Didn't he know that no matter what had happened between them, she could never be capable of something that heinous?

The simple answer was no, he didn't know.

She stared at him in wonder that bordered on fascination.

"You really think I would do that, don't you? Be just like you." She watched as his eyes grew dangerous, but she didn't flinch. "You have no idea who your daughter is, Father. Who Megan was." Even as she said it, even though she'd been there during all his absences, it seemed incredible that he'd lived with them all those years and had still remained a stranger. "You haven't got a clue."

"I don't need clues." He gripped the armrests, his fingers channeling his fury. "I *know.*"

Dana shook her head, more sad than angry. "You don't know anything."

She refused to allow him to cow her. Instead, she forced herself to move closer, until she was standing in front of him. Close enough to smell the alcohol. Close enough to smell the fear the alcohol was meant to veil. Something was very wrong.

"Why did you come home so early?" She searched his face for an answer, knowing he wouldn't volunteer one. "I can remember you staying out so late, Megan and I were convinced you never came home at all. That you were just a figment of our imaginations."

He threw back the contents of the glass the way he'd seen his father do countless times when he was a boy, then waited for the numbness to come. It didn't. He needed more. An ocean more, and then maybe the pain would go away. Or not matter.

"None of your damn business." He reached for the decanter.

Dana claimed it. "You're wrong." With an easy movement, she poured two fingers into his glass, though he had downed more than that. "It *is* my damn business." She set the intricate cut-glass bottle down. "You would have learned that, Counselor, if you had come home early once in a while when it counted. What goes on in a family is every member's business."

Her eyes met his. She searched in vain for his soul, for some small indication that she was getting through to him. A self-mocking smile curved her mouth.

"But I suppose that's really stretching it, isn't it? We were never a family. Just four people trying to survive with each other." Even that didn't ring quite true. "Or maybe three people trying to survive with you would be more accurate," she amended. The smile on her face wasn't bitter. It was the shadow of things that could have been. And hadn't.

He hated her in that moment. Hated her for what she was saying. Hated her for being young and healthy. And for having the years before her that he wouldn't. Hated her for being right.

"Get out."

Funny, once his look would have sent her running. Now it made her dig in. Did that mean she'd grown up, or that he had lost his touch?

"I didn't come home to get out, Father. I came home to take down this damn wall between us, one brick at a time if I have to." Right now, that felt like a completely impossible goal. "But maybe I flattered myself too much. I don't seem to have the tools."

She focused on why she had returned, why she had come here instead of half a dozen other places that would have done just as well. She'd returned because she realized his time was no longer endless. And she was the last of his family. She'd returned not just for herself, or for him, she'd returned for

Mollie and, in a way, for Meggie and for her mother. There had to be peace in the family.

Did he understand what she was attempting to do? She doubted it.

"You know what happens when there are walls, Father? People on either side of them don't get to see a thing that's going on on the other side. They miss a lot." She wasn't getting through. Stymied, resigned, she crossed to the door. "Good night." Dana turned the doorknob.

"I stuttered."

Not even daring to breathe, Dana slowly turned to look at him. Had her imagination conjured up his response? "What?" she whispered.

Damn it, was she going to make him say it again? "I stuttered." He spat the words, a cobra spitting venom. "Oh, it wasn't in court, it was during the briefing." For some, that might have mitigated the occurrence. Not for him. "But I stuttered."

Dana stepped away from the door, knowing what he was saying. Knowing that even the act of sharing the event was a significant step.

"So? Everyone stutters sometimes." Because it was her nature, because that much concern had survived despite everything, she tried to bury the incident for him. "The excitement of the moment, your thoughts racing faster than you tongue, even—"

Didn't she get it? This was his reputation they were talking about. "I'm not everyone. I don't stumble, and I don't stutter."

She looked at him pointedly. "Except that you did." He couldn't dwell on this. There would be other setbacks, and if he dwelled on them, they would eventually undo him. "Accept it and move on."

"Don't preach at me."

He was like a wounded animal, Dana thought, snapping at the hand that was extended only to aid him. "I wasn't aware I was preaching. I thought I was comforting."

His anger prevented him from seeing the difference. The look in his eyes was meant to make her back away. "I don't want your comfort or your pity."

She struggled to keep from lashing out at him. He made her so angry that she wanted to pummel him with both fists.

Now there was a pretty headline, she thought, restraining herself. *Renowned wheelchair-bound lawyer pummeled to death by irate estranged daughter.* The tabloid reporters would be lined up six deep for that one. A miserable coda to what had been, after all was said and done, a brilliant career.

"You don't have my pity because you stuttered or you faltered, Father. That's only human. You had my pity a long time ago because you're alone. You always were. And you know the worst part of it?" She studied his face, waiting for a spark of understanding or recognition. There was none. "It was of your own choosing."

Fury colored the sunken cheeks. "You don't know what you're talking about."

She sighed. What was the use? He only heard what he wanted to hear. She was just so much noise in the background.

"Have it your way."

Dana left the room and closed the door behind her, wishing she could do the same to this chapter of her life. Wishing she could walk away as she had the first time.

But she couldn't. Her stubborn determination forbade her.

Even when she heard the resounding crash of glass meeting wood, she kept on walking. It wasn't the first time.

Rafe arrived at her door an hour later. She'd almost called his service to cancel, then decided she needed to get out to clear her head. It was simpler just going along with the arrangements she'd made.

The first thing Rafe thought when he saw her at the door was that she cleaned up nicely. It was the first time he'd seen her in something other than jeans and a T-shirt, and he had to admit the difference was striking, even if the jeans were flattering to her curves.

Jeans didn't tell him that she had gorgeous legs. And denim did not create the same effect that formfitting fabric could. The lemon sheath definitely made her look like a sunny California girl.

The second thing that struck him was that she seemed in a hurry to leave. He found himself trailing after her to his car.

Rafe closed the passenger door for her, then rounded the rear of the car and got in himself. "I had no idea that Paul S. Morrow was your father."

It had suddenly come to him as he was going up the long, winding driveway to the house. He'd seen this shot in the Sunday *Times Magazine* section two or three years ago. Intrigued by the kind of person who would want to live in a house large enough to merit its own zip code, he'd read the article. And come away with mixed feelings about the man revealed in the pages of the article.

"Yes, Paul S. Morrow is my father." She blew out a breath. If she didn't watch her step, she was going to be as rude as her father. She slanted a glance at him.

"What does the *s* stand for?"

"Shark." And then she shook her head. "Sorry if that sounded snippy. There was a time when I thought everyone knew my father was Paul S. Morrow, that I had it stamped on my forehead, kind of like the mark of Cain."

She sounded, he thought, threading his way to MacArthur Boulevard, defensive. And hurt. "That bad?"

She was usually good about keeping her feelings in check, but this thing with her father was wearing on her. "I didn't say it was bad."

He kept his eyes on the road. "You didn't have to." A casual observer would have picked up on it.

She brushed it off. "A lot of people don't like lawyers." She left it to him to infer that she'd endured childish teasing rather than so much more.

"So why did you become one?" Feeling the way she did, he would have thought she would have picked any other career but that one.

He caught her off guard. "How did you know—Sheila?" she guessed.

"No, the form you filled out in the office. You put down lawyer under occupation."

She'd forgotten that. She had to be careful about the conclusions she jumped to. There was no reason to think he asked Sheila about her. Why would he? They were only having dinner to settle a bet. Living with Steven had left its mark, she realized. It had made her look for hidden meanings in simple statements, hidden agendas where there weren't any.

"Are you a practicing lawyer?" he asked, when she made no response to his earlier question.

She thought of the letter of resignation she'd posted from Sheila's house the day after she arrived. She'd enjoyed working for Greene and Jefferson. The firm was small enough to fit into her father's coat pocket, but it had a heart. Something she hadn't thought law firms were allowed to have.

"I practice," she acknowledged. "But at the moment I'm temporarily between positions." Temporarily between lifestyles, too, she added silently. Currently residing in limbo.

The logical solution occurred to him. "Will you be joining your father's firm?"

"As a doormat, maybe." The comment had just come out. It shouldn't have. Dana sighed. She didn't know what was wrong with her lately. She felt so edgy, so completely at odds with herself. With her world. It was as if she was revisiting the years of her teenage rebellion. "Sorry. My father and I had words before I left."

He glanced at her before looking back at the road. Her jaw was rigid enough to pass for stone. "I take it they weren't very good words."

Dana laughed shortly. "With my father, they never are."

Rafe rolled the comment over in his mind. "I felt that way

about my father." Coming to a red light, he eased his foot onto the brake, stealing a look at her. "Fifteen years ago."

"You're lucky. Your father grew up." She looked for a way to direct the conversation away from her. She was always uncomfortable discussing herself, her life as Paul Morrow's daughter. "So what made you want to become a doctor?" She went with the obvious. "Your father's example?"

The light changed. Rafe sped up. Sunset was still more than an hour away, but he was in a hurry to get to the restaurant. Tonight, he was hungry. "He's a cop. So's my younger brother. Me, I liked fixing things."

She thought of George, who had been nothing short of a magician with his hands. "Why didn't you become a mechanic?"

Rafe grinned. She liked the easy way his face softened.

"Living things," he clarified. "I was ten years old when this baby sparrow fell out of his nest, right at my feet. Ugly little thing. I kind of related to it—" He caught her dubious look out of the corner of his eye. "I was a hell of a homely kid. My hands and feet were way too big for the rest of me. Anyway, I took the sparrow's unexpected appearance in my life as an omen. So I brought the bird home, tried to keep it warm, nurtured it. I was consumed with getting this tiny, helpless thing well. By the time it was, I was hooked on the process."

It was hard to imagine those large hands handling something so small. "What happened to the bird?"

Something that bordered on sentimentality tugged at the corners of his mouth.

"I set it free. My dad said it wasn't right to keep something like that as a pet. It was meant to be free." The grin widened. "It bit me just as I let it go. It was either giving me a peck goodbye or letting me know I was taking too long in releasing it. It wasn't easy for me to let go until he did that."

The road opened up, and so did he, pressing on the accelerator. There was no traffic in either direction. With houses visible on the hillside to their left and the ocean quietly flow-ing on their right, a sense of peace settled around him. Only Dana beside him sent ripples through it with her restless presence.

"How about you?" he prodded again. "Why did you become a lawyer?"

She remembered the moment of her decision as if it had happened only a few hours ago. Remembered, too, the way she'd felt when she made it. Not unlike Scarlett O'Hara when she'd taken her oath never to go hungry again.

"To spite my father," she said simply. "To show him I could do it. He didn't think much of my abilities."

Rafe realized that there had never been anything but supportive words for him and for Gabe for as long as he could remember. He tried to envision how it would have felt if it had been otherwise. "Why's that?"

"Because I didn't agree with him. And he was always right." Dana crossed her ankles, shifted in her seat. "I'd really rather not talk about my father, if you don't mind."

"No problem," he said obligingly. It had only been idle curiosity that had prompted him to ask. A teasing smile appeared. "Did you remember to bring your wallet?"

The expression on his face lightened her mood. She grasped the opportunity. "You really are convinced that this meal is to die for, aren't you?"

"No," he corrected. "To live for. If it weren't for the fact that being a pediatrician keeps me so busy, I'd be over at La Reina all the time. Tex-Mex is my Achilles' heel." He laughed, picturing the result. "I'd be a blimp in no time." He shrugged. There were worse things, he supposed. "But a happy one."

"Despite the snow job, I'll reserve judgment until I sample this fabulous cuisine for myself."

He nodded. He'd expected nothing less. It was what made her interesting. "You struck me as a stubborn woman the first time I saw you."

At least he had worded it politely, she thought. She'd heard the observation put in far less pleasant terms. "What gave me away?"

"Maybe it was the way you wouldn't let Alice plow you under." He thought of the older woman. Alice had been with him from the day he had opened his practice. "She's very protective of my time."

What else was she protective of? Dana wondered. Was there something going on between them?

She stopped abruptly. The direction of her thoughts annoyed her. Just because Steven liked keeping reserve entertainment around didn't mean every man was like that.

No, just the good-looking ones, she thought.

"What would she say if she knew you were frivolously using some of that time to take me to a restaurant?"

His answer wasn't the one Dana had anticipated. "She'd say it was a good thing. She's of the opinion that I don't get out enough."

It had to be a line, and not a very good one at that. Somehow, she couldn't see him as a cloistered monk. "Do you?"

He shrugged. After Debra died, he'd felt no desire to see other women. What was the point? He was never going to get married again. Most women didn't want a relationship that led nowhere. That Kate accepted those terms made her unique. But it didn't change how he felt.

"Enough to suit me. I love my work. There isn't anything I'd rather be than a pediatrician."

She believed him. And, in a way, envied him. "You're lucky. I never felt that kind of satisfaction."

Her voice was oddly empty. He looked at her. "With anything?"

How had the conversation veered from small talk into areas she'd had no intention of touching again? This was supposed to be a careless evening out, not a baring of souls.

Dana was spared the awkwardness of making an inane comment as she changed the subject, because when she opened her mouth, the sound of squealing tires and metal

crashing against something large, solid and immovable interrupted her.

Dana jumped. "Oh, my God, what was that?" Eyes wide,
she scanned the road.

Her breath caught in her throat, almost choking her. Less
that a hundred yards ahead was a car, or what was left of it.
From where they were, it gave the appearance of being a
mangled toy that had been foiled in the act of attempting to
climb a tree. Battered and crumpled, its hood was at a forty-
five-degree angle to the ground. The crash had caused the
antitheft alarm to go off, its pealing adding a surreal quality
to the scene.

The driver was slumped against the steering wheel, but the
other occupants had been thrown clear. Even at a distance,
she could see that there was blood everywhere.

And smoke was beginning to curl from beneath the car.

Rafe jammed on his brakes. The car careened to the right,
fishtailing before it finally stopped. Alert, his adrenaline running on high, Rafe was out of the vehicle even as it rocked
in response to the emergency brake he had jerked into position.

Of like mind and separated by less than a heartbeat, Dana
was right behind him, running toward the smoldering wreck.
Her ears throbbed from the piercing noise made by the alarm.

He sensed rather than heard her. "Get back!" he shouted
over his shoulder. It wasn't safe to be in the vicinity of the
vehicle.

She had no intention of listening. "You're going to need
help!" she insisted, raising her voice to be heard above the
din. And because he had shouted at her. She didn't take that
tone well, even if it was meant in her best interests.

Rafe would have argued with her, but there wasn't time to
pause or push her aside. Resigned, he nodded. "Let's get the
driver out."

He was wedged behind the steering wheel. Rafe tried to
move the steering column, but it wasn't going anywhere. For

a split second a chill passed over Rafe when he thought he wouldn't be able to rescue the man.

Dana had tried to pull the man out as Rafe pulled on the wheel, but there was no budging either one of them. "You're going to need a crowbar," Dana said.

It was worth a try. He didn't want to leave her, but he had no choice. Swallowing an oath about her damn heroics, Rafe sprinted to his car and got the crowbar out of his trunk. He was back in less time than it took to think the matter through.

Moving as quickly as possible, he worked the bar between the spokes of the steering wheel. He felt his muscles fairly screaming in protest as he managed to work the steering wheel back just a fraction. It was up to Dana to pull the man free.

There was no way she could manage it, Rafe thought in frustration, but there was nothing else he could do. He couldn't be in two places at once.

"Pull, Dana, pull," he coached. Every fiber in his body tensed as he tried to move the wheel a little more.

Sucking in air, working on panic and adrenaline, Dana wrapped her arms around the driver's rib cage as best she could. Braced, she tugged with all her might. Her face was streaked with blood and turning a bright shade of red beneath the grime when she managed to pull the man to the side. It was all that was needed.

Rafe took it from there. He released the wheel, then dragged the man upright and slung him over his shoulder fireman style. With one hand hooked beneath Dana's arm, he hurried the three of them away from the vehicle. A moment later, the flames came, quickly eating their way up the car.

Breathless, her lungs feeling as if they were going to explode, Dana struggled to steady herself. She looked around, trying to take in the scene.

She zeroed in on the other people. There were two of them, one male and one female, both teenagers like the driver. Both conscious and crying for help.

"I've got my medical bag in the trunk." He set the unconscious teen on the ground as gently as he could. "Why don't you stay here and catch your breath?"

She didn't need to be pampered. It was the others who needed his attention. "My breath is fine. What do you want me to do to help?"

He wasted no more time. "C'mon, then." Hurrying, Rafe led the way back to his car.

Along with his medical bag, he took out the fire extinguisher his father had talked him into carrying out of his trunk. God bless the old man, Rafe thought.

"Here." He handed it to her quickly. "See if you can put out the fire before some breeze spreads it any farther. We can't take a chance on having the hillsides catch."

They were well into fire season in Southern California. Whole acres of land had already been destroyed by fires.

"Leave it to me," she promised.

He had no other choice. He had injured people to help.

Chapter 10

If he had thought, for one moment, that Dana would get in his way with her efforts to help, Rafe quickly realized how wrong he'd been.

She was right there alongside of him, eager to do what she could to help.

It amazed him that instead of being squeamish, as most people were when exposed to the bloodied, mangled bodies involved in an accident, Dana seemed to be oblivious to the horror, focusing only on the fact that these were people who needed help and needed it in a hurry.

When he saw her toss away the empty canister, the flames mercifully extinguished, he breathed a sigh of relief. At least there wouldn't be an out-of-control fire storm to contend with.

"Dana, call the paramedics," he called out to her. "Use my cell phone in the car."

She merely nodded, doing as she was told. It took only a minute to make the connection, another two to give all the pertinent information.

"They're coming," she announced, hurrying to his side.

He was trying to immobilize the driver's broken arm. "See anything we can use for a splint?" Rafe asked her.

Dana looked around, but there was nothing. "No. Why don't you tape it to his side until the paramedics arrive?"

It was what he was about to do, but he was surprised at the suggestion coming from her. "Good thinking." He wanted to ask her where she had learned that, but there was no time.

They worked well together, quickly, competently, two halves of a team with an identical goal. With luck, the paramedics would be on the scene shortly. But they both knew that there were too many seconds within "shortly" that could prove fatal.

Not wanting to move any of the victims more than was absolutely necessary, Rafe and Dana found themselves spread out. Rafe remained with the two teenage boys while Dana tended to the girl.

"What's your name?" Dana asked.

Her voice was as calm as if she was carrying on a conversation with someone she'd encountered in the checkout line at the supermarket. While she spoke, she was ripping the edge of the girl's T-shirt in order to make a bandage for her head wound.

"Carol." Her face a mask of twisted pain, the girl watched her every move. "Am I going to die?"

Dana pressed the material against the gash in an attempt to stem the bleeding. It was far from sanitary, but it was the best she could do under the circumstances.

"No, you're not going to die," she said firmly. "No one's going to die tonight."

Dana prayed for the ambulance to come.

Was this the way it had been for Meggie? The doctor said she died on the way to the hospital. Had she lain in the car, crying, begging for help, calling for her husband, for her child? Calling without anyone hearing?

It froze her heart to think about it.

Carol clawed at her hand, desperate to hold on to something, to someone.

"It hurts so bad," Carol gasped, sobbing. "I'm afraid." Huge brown eyes, filled with shock and fear, begged Dana for something, anything, to make the pain and fear go away.

Dana held Carol's hand tightly, saying what she knew the girl wanted to hear. Saying what she would have said to Megan if she'd had the chance.

"I know. But it's going to be fine. *You're* going to be fine. Don't you give in, you hear me?" Dana raised her voice, determined to keep the teenager awake. "It can't conquer you if you don't give in."

Carol's lashes were beginning to flutter as consciousness fought injury for possession of her. "What can't?" she asked hoarsely.

Dana had to keep her talking, had to keep her awake. She said whatever came into her head. This wasn't some teenager who was a stranger to her, it was Megan. And it was for Megan she fought. "Fear, pain, you name it. All you have to do is hang on long enough."

All the color, all the strength, seemed to be draining from the young girl. It wasn't the onset of evening dusting everything around it. Carol was retreating. Fading.

"But I just want to go to sleep." She was silently begging Dana to let her go.

Dana clamped her hand on the thin shoulder. She knew she couldn't shake Carol, but she did what she could to rouse her attention.

"No, don't close your eyes," Dana ordered, struggling against the onslaught of panic. She couldn't call Rafe over to help her. He had his hands full with the other two. Who knew, maybe he was up against the same thing. Where was that damn ambulance? Why hadn't they gotten here yet? "Pain is on your side, Carol. It's trying to keep you awake. Do you hear me, Carol?"

"Yes, I...I hear you," Carol murmured distantly. The next

moment, she began to shiver. Her whole body was enveloped in one huge tremor she couldn't control.

Out of the corner of her eye, Dana saw Rafe approaching them. "Rafe, do you have anything in the car I can put around her? A blanket? A sweater? Something?"

Squatting beside Dana, he looked at Carol and shook his head. "Nothing, why?" And then he saw the reason before she said another word. "She's going into shock." Quickly he stripped off his jacket.

Between the two of them, they managed to wrap it around the girl without moving her.

"Keep her as warm as you can," he instructed, though he knew it was unnecessary to tell. Rafe couldn't help being in awe, not only of her cool competence, but also of the compassion he saw in her face. The lady was special.

Dana tucked a corner of the jacket closer to the girl. "Okay, now stay awake," she ordered. But Carol's eyes were drifting shut again. Dana caught the girl's face in her hands. "Do you hear me? Stay awake, Meggie. They'll be here soon. I swear they will."

Her words were swallowed by the distant wail of a siren. Dana had never heard anything so wonderful, so sweet in her life. She could have cried.

"Hear that? They're already here. Don't let go, don't let go," she coached, wrapping her hands tightly around Carol's again. "Hang on just a little while longer, honey. Please."

The two ambulances arrived within a heartbeat of each other. Two gurneys were unloaded from one vehicle, one from the other. Drawing Dana to her feet, Rafe moved out of the paramedics' way. Questions and answers mingled with cries of pain.

In short, concise sentences, Rafe told the first set of paramedics what he could about the accident and the condition of the two boys, then moved on to help Dana explain what they knew of Carol's injuries.

"Anything else, Doctor?" the first driver asked him.

Rafe shook his head. "No, that's it." He watched the second gurney being lifted into the ambulance. "Where are you taking them?"

The driver checked his sheet. "Dispatch said South Community's backed up tonight. We thought maybe we'd take them to—"

"Are you independent drivers?" Rafe cut in. When the driver nodded, Rafe said, "Then take them to Harris Memorial."

The distance to the other available hospital, St. Anne's, or to Harris Memorial was almost identical. Rafe wanted to be able to keep tabs on the teenagers.

"I'm a doctor there." He reached into his back pocket for his wallet, opened it and took out two business cards, then handed one to each of the drivers. "We'll follow you in my car." It occurred to him that he was taking a lot for granted. He looked at Dana. "That is—"

That he was checking to see if she was willing to go along surprised her. It had never crossed her mind not to. They'd come this far with the victims. How could she not know if they pulled through?

"Of course we'll follow. We can't walk away now. Hey, don't forget your jacket," she said to Rafe as he began to walk away from the ambulance.

Retrieving the jacket as the second paramedic team eased Carol's gurney into their vehicle, Dana sighed, watching the rear doors being slammed shut, then turned and offered the jacket to Rafe. They had to be all right. They just had to be.

The jacket was far too bloody to put on. Fingers hooked in the collar, he slung it over his shoulder. He took her arm with his other hand. As he escorted her to his car, it felt as if a hundred years had passed since they'd gotten out of it, instead of half an hour.

Rafe opened the door for her. Dana slid in. She looked tired, he thought. After shutting the door, he walked around to his side and got in. He looked at her for a long moment before he started the car, wondering what was going on in her head, what she was thinking.

"You're sure you don't mind?"

What did it take to convince him? She would have asked to follow if he hadn't volunteered.

"We're not exactly dressed to waltz into a restaurant anymore." She glanced down. There was grease from the wreck mixed with dirt and blood across the front of her dress. "I don't think they welcome blood in the dining room unless it's coming from a rare steak."

He laughed under his breath as he followed the ambulances. He had the second one in his sights. "You're one unusual lady, Dana Morrow."

She wasn't sure just how he meant that. *Unusual* might have been synonymous with *freak* to him. It had been to some. "That's me, a square peg in a round hole."

"Not the same thing," he countered. But all the same, it was a telling remark, Rafe thought. "I'm going to call ahead to the emergency room to let them know what to be prepared for."

How could anyone be prepared for that? Dana thought, as he pressed a button on his cell phone. The musical tones she heard in response told her the number was being dialed automatically. "This happen to you often?"

"What? Oh. No, I'm not calling the emergency room directly. I'm calling the hospital switchboard." And then he was talking to a woman there, asking to be put through to the emergency room.

Dana slumped in her seat, trying to gain control of the emotions that had been rubbed raw by what she'd just lived through.

Oh, God, Meggie, I wish someone had been there for you. If not me, then someone. Someone who could have saved you.

"Who's Meggie?"

The question, coming on the heels of her thoughts, made her jump. "What?"

He tucked the telephone into his pocket with his left hand. "You called that girl Meggie. The boy who wasn't driving told me her name was Carol."

He glanced at Dana, waiting. There was dirt smeared across the front of her dress, most of her makeup was gone, and her hair was a mess. And he'd never seen any woman look more compelling.

"Meggie was my sister." She shrugged, staring straight ahead. "I guess I got a little confused in the heat of the moment."

He understood now, at least part of it. Her need to help, the fierce way she'd talked to the teenager, trying to keep her awake. She was reliving the past.

"Were you there? When the accident happened?" he clarified.

Her lips felt very dry, as did her throat. "No." Her face was immobile, her voice devoid of emotion as she added, "But I wish I had been."

He told her something his mother had said to him after Debra died. Something very basic that needed saying. "We can't control everything, no matter how much we want to."

She blew out a long breath. It didn't help. Her nerves still felt as brittle as matchsticks. "No, we can't."

He strove to lighten the air. They both needed it. There had been enough heaviness for one evening. "All right, I'll bite. Where did you learn all that?"

She blinked. It took her a moment to focus on his question. "What?"

Rafe switched on the headlights. Twilight seemed to have tiptoed in earlier than usual. "You came through like a complete trouper, and you really seemed to know what you were doing when I gave you instructions. You're not like any lawyer I know."

"I'm not like any *anything* you know," she corrected him with a glib smile. It was the cocky tone she used with her father, but she softened it enough so there was no mistaking there was no attitude behind it.

She wasn't trying to prove anything to Rafe. And right now, she was beginning to feel pretty good about herself. About the lives they had saved. Together. There was no question in her mind that if they hadn't been there just after the accident occurred, the driver would have burned to death, and the others might have bled to death before another car came along.

Dana savored the whiff of euphoria that passed over her. Taking a deep breath, she rotated her shoulders, stretching muscles that felt taut. When she turned her head in his direction, she saw that Rafe was watching her with a bemused expression on his face. He was still waiting for her answer.

"Eyes on the road, Doctor," she teased. "Or the paramedics are going to have to double back for us."

Maybe it was the moment, or the fact that they had aided in cheating death, at least for a little while. Whatever it was, she felt comfortable enough with him to share a piece of herself.

"My mother was a nurse practitioner who thought it was important that her daughters be up on first aid." That was before she'd descended into a far-reaching, black depression that ate away at her soul far more rapidly than the alcohol she used to anesthetize herself ate away at her liver. "And for a while, when I was studying for the bar, I drove an ambulance to support myself."

Rafe tried to picture that. A would-be lawyer who drove an ambulance. It boggled the mind. "Hell of a combination."

She could guess what he was thinking. "Hey, at least I drove the ambulance instead of chasing it." And then she grinned as she shook her head. "Besides, I'm not that kind of a lawyer."

The road began to snake its way to Newport Boulevard. He had to remain alert so he wouldn't miss the turnoff. "What kind of lawyer *are* you? Besides good, I mean."

She wasn't accustomed to compliments and considered them suspect or, at the very least without substance. "How would you know whether or not I'm good?"

Was that distrust he heard in her voice? Why? It didn't make sense.

"I think you'd be good at anything you put your mind to.

It's that stubbornness factor coming in again.'' He made the turn and wove his way onto the boulevard. He waited until traffic was clear enough for him to cross three lanes. "I don't think you'd allow yourself to be average. That wouldn't satisfy you.'' He eased the car into the left turn lane. "I heard you talking to that girl about not giving in. It didn't sound like something you picked up by reading a book.''

"I *am* good,'' Dana confirmed. There was no ego, no false modesty. There was just fact. "A good criminal lawyer.''

The choice surprised him. "Like your father?''

"No, not like my father.'' She'd made that a goal, not to be anything like him. "He only goes after the high-profile cases, the ones with big headlines and big money. I figure poor people can be innocent, too.''

"A public defender?'' He could picture that. It seemed more in keeping with the woman who was beginning to emerge.

"Something like that.'' She didn't particularly feel like going into details. She'd talked more than enough about herself for one night. "We're here,'' she pointed out to forestall any other questions.

He took the hint. "So we are.''

Driving onto the hospital grounds, he made a choice. Rather than go all the way to the doctors' lot, he decided to park in the emergency room lot. When he got out, Dana was right beside him.

The emergency room teams he'd asked Nancy to assemble were working on the victims when he and Dana entered the ER. Rafe saw the flash of a blue uniform in the background beyond the electronic doors. That would be the police. He'd asked Nancy to notify them, as well. This had the makings of a very long evening.

He wondered if he should call a cab to take Dana home. His next thought was that he was being presumptuous. She wouldn't take kindly to his making any decisions on her behalf. She would call a cab if she wanted to leave. She'd proven she wasn't a hothouse flower.

In the Family Way

Nancy's dark eyes shifted from the doctor to the woman beside him. They both looked worn. Seeing them together triggered recognition. The woman had been here before, with her niece. She'd asked for Dr. Saldana.

"You're back?" she asked Dana in mild surprise.

"Can't seem to get enough of this place," Dana quipped. "But this time I'm here strictly as an observer."

Nancy raised a quizzical brow toward Rafe.

"Don't let her fool you—she's an emergency room groupie." He grinned at the head nurse.

Nancy had a feeling she wasn't going to get the straight story for a while, if ever. But this was definitely food for the hospital gossip mill.

"Whatever." She moved so her body blocked Rafe's access to the examining rooms. "We can take care of things, Doctor. You both look like hell." She waved them away. "Why don't you talk to the policeman, get cleaned up and go back to what you were doing?"

Dana, he noticed, wasn't about to remain behind. Or be dismissed. Certain kinds of stubbornness, he decided, could be appealing.

"Can't," Rafe replied. "The restaurant has a very strict no-blood code."

Dr. Weinstein, the orthopedic specialist Rafe had told Nancy to call, came by, nodding to Rafe in recognition. "I'll take it from here, Nurse," he informed her.

As Dana watched, he disappeared behind the swinging glass doors where the rest of the team was assembled, leaving her outside to wonder over the fate of the three victims.

"I could have Harry get you a couple of burgers and fries from the cafeteria," Nancy volunteered, nodding toward the tall, distinguished-looking man at the reception desk. "They're about to close, but the short-order cook has a thing for Harry."

Now that she thought of it, she could stand to eat something, Dana realized. Hunger pangs were working their way through the knots that had formed in her stomach. "She'll open the grill for him?" Dana asked.

"It's a he," Nancy corrected her, a smile playing over her lips. "And yes, he will. He's trying to win Harry over."

Rafe exchanged looks with Dana. She nodded. Rafe took the nurse's hands in his. "Nancy, you're an angel. Right now, burgers and fries sound like heaven."

"Good. I'll tell Harry to get charming." She placed her arm around Dana's shoulders. "While you're waiting for him to get back, why don't you come with me and get cleaned up?" Taking charge, she led Dana off.

Dana looked over her shoulder at Rafe, but he merely shrugged his shoulders in an exaggerated motion, then went to talk to the policeman.

"This isn't exactly the way I planned for this evening to go."

It had taken Harry longer than anticipated to return with their impromptu take-out dinner. In the interim, they'd given statements to the police and been told that, so far, all three victims were in stable condition.

When Harry returned with their dinner, Rafe had taken it and Dana to the beach across from the hospital. There was a private little stretch where he thought they could be alone and eat in peace. They'd had enough excitement for one night.

Sitting on the fence that ran along the perimeter, Dana finished the last of her hamburger. She couldn't remember when she'd had anything better.

"Can't say I was bored," she told him in response to his comment. She gestured toward the sky. "And the floor show's lovely." Every single star ever created had come out tonight, blanketing the sky with myriad tiny, winking lights.

Sitting beside her, Rafe looked up. "Yes, it is, isn't it?" He smiled to himself.

She watched a dimple wink in and out of his cheek. "What?"

She would probably think it was silly, but right now, image

didn't seem so important to him. "When I was a boy, I used to think angels had cut holes in the sky so they could look down on us. I thought the stars were heavenly lights shining from their eyes." He shrugged, a self-deprecating smile on his lips. "I was six. What did I know?"

She was charmed by the concept. "I've got to remember to tell Mollie that. Maybe we can start some sort of legend."

Dana knew Mollie would take to the concept immediately. She was convinced her parents were angels, watching over her. There were times, when she was bone weary, that Dana felt like embracing the idea herself. It made her feel less alone.

Rafe balled up his burger wrapper in his hand, then eyed hers. "Finished?"

She nodded, regretting that there wasn't more. "You sure this is hospital food?"

He took the wrapper from her and threw it into the paper bag. He offered her the last of his soda. She'd finished hers halfway through the meal. "I only work for the best. Care to go for a walk?"

Dana drained the soda, then surrendered the container. He threw the lot into the cylindrical waste basket. "Here?"

Rafe gestured. The moonlight was skimming along the water, leaving wavy yellow ribbons to mark its path. "We seem to have the beach to ourselves."

Going with impulse, Dana took off her shoes and slipped them into her oversize purse before rising from the fence. "All right."

Rafe took off his shoes and socks. He tucked the latter into the former, then picked them up with his left hand. He took her hand in his right.

It was the first time, she realized, that they'd touched all evening. The first time they'd touched at all. Oh, he'd slipped his hand along her back or her elbow, but that was to guide her or usher her along. This was different.

Right from the start.

A tingling sensation worked its way through her with the

speed of a minor electrical jolt. Not enough to shock her, just enough to make her aware that it was there. She wasn't sure if she wanted it to be.

He felt her stiffen, then force herself to relax. "What's the matter?"

"Nothing." The lie made her mouth feel dry. Words stuck to the roof of her mouth like peanut butter. "Must be the hamburger repeating itself."

That wasn't it, he thought, but he pretended to believe her. "That wouldn't have happened if we'd gotten to La Reina."

She laughed, grateful to shift attention from herself. "Yeah, yeah, I'll believe it when I taste it."

"All right, are you free tomorrow?"

"Yes," she answered before she thought. Before she could stop herself.

"Care to try again?" he proposed. "This time, I hope, without any daring rescues?"

She tried to make light of the invitation. They would merely be completing what they'd set out to do, to see which was the best restaurant. That he'd asked her out twice in two days didn't mean a thing. "You really are determined to be parted from your money, aren't you?"

His smile was slow, even sexy. "No, determined to prove I'm right."

"All right, tomorrow night," she agreed. Dana stared straight ahead, watching the moonlight shimmer and trying very hard not to think about anything. Least of all how good his hand felt around hers.

The tide was coming in closer than he'd anticipated. It lapped at the sand inches from their feet. Looking over his shoulder, he saw that behind them the tide had erased their footprints in some places. In others, it seemed to have deepened them.

The silence was not uncomfortable. But it did feel oddly pregnant, as if there were things waiting to be said, though he had no idea what.

"You were pretty terrific tonight."

Pleasure, warm and comforting, crept through her like ivy working its way up a trellis. Still, she tried to dismiss his words. She hadn't done anything out of the ordinary, just what she had been trained to do. If she'd gone about it a little more zealously, it was only because she'd been thinking of Megan.

She shrugged off his compliment, paring it down to size. "I'm at my best during an emergency. Doesn't leave much time to think, just act."

Rafe stopped walking and turned toward her. "There's something to be said for that." As he spoke, his eyes skimmed over her lips. Just as his hands skimmed along her arms to her shoulders.

Dana's heart took the elevator up and stopped at the top floor, settling in her throat. She knew what he was going to do. Knew just as surely as she knew that the sun was going to rise tomorrow.

Knew, too, that there was no place for this in her life. No place for a complication of this nature no matter how she packaged it and tried to make it acceptable.

But no matter how she argued, she couldn't force herself to do the logical thing. She couldn't turn her head away. With the wind playing with the ends of her hair, the breeze caressing her body with transparent fingers, she stood perfectly still, waiting for his lips to find hers.

And staunchly told herself that no matter what, it wasn't going to mean anything beyond a single pleasurable moment.

A moment she found herself desperately wanting.

Chapter 11

His lips touched hers slowly, gently. Smooth as silk, sweet as honey, the kiss enveloped Dana until, one by one, all her senses were drawn in. Captured. Willing prisoners in a cell with no bars.

Wonder, vast and endless, filled him. Pushed him forward. Urged him to seek more. Rafe deepened the kiss until he lost his way. And didn't care.

She could feel her heart fluttering like an agitated falcon trying vainly to navigate against a strong wind. Instincts ingrained since the moment of her conception rose up, refusing to allow her to be passively taken anywhere, even into pleasure. If her head was going to go spinning, her pulse racing, well, then, so were Rafe's.

Rising on her toes, Dana encircled his neck with her arms, bringing her body closer to his.

Bringing her soul into her kiss. And losing it.

If his socks hadn't already been off, she would have metaphorically knocked them off right then. What had begun as an impulse had turned into something he couldn't define, couldn't put a name to. In that single moment, Rafe felt freer than he had in a very long time. Free to feel, to react. Free to soar above the clouds that surrounded him.

He felt his body heating and knew he had to stop while pleasure was hot but not yet sizzling. It took effort to listen to reason while his body begged for things that lay beyond reason.

His pulse wouldn't slow down even though he drew his lips away.

Dana took a deep breath, her lips pressed tightly together. Absorbing the taste of him. Without realizing it, she ran the tip of her tongue along the outline of her mouth. She looked at him, fighting her way out of the haze around her brain.

"Why did you do that?"

He was asking himself the same thing. This wasn't something he'd ever done before with any of his patients' parents. But he didn't think she would appreciate hearing that. It sounded too much like a protest. And this, whatever this was, wasn't something to protest.

Rafe took the wisp of hair that insisted on dancing about her brow to a tune only the wind heard and tucked it behind her ear. He saw the quickening in her eyes, felt it mirrored in his body.

"I didn't think kisses needed to be explained."

"Some do." This one did. Then maybe she would understand the diametrically opposed feelings that were dueling so madly within her.

He shrugged, looking away. He wasn't sure if he should run like hell or not. All he knew was that he wanted to kiss her again.

Maybe that was why he should run like hell.

"French fries mixed with starlight raise my sugar level. I lost my head." Turning, he looked at her. "Why did you kiss back?"

Served her right for asking. A smile, more nervous around the edges than she would have liked, played over her lips. "I guess echoing the Twinkie defense would be out of order here.''

His laughter was in his eyes, not on his lips. ''Completely.''

''Then it's the hamburger.'' She nodded, then elaborated on the ridiculous answer. ''Hamburger and sea breezes.''

''Hamburger and sea breezes,'' he echoed, amusement framing his mouth.

It was just as good as French fries and starlight. Or Twinkies. Damn, why wouldn't her heart settle down? ''Does it every time.''

He liked her sense of humor. And he liked the taste of her mouth. Liked it very, very much.

''I'll have to remember that.'' Did that sound as if he meant to kiss her again? He didn't want to frighten her away, and there was something in her eyes that told him she could be frightened. ''Strictly for research purposes, of course. The AMA would be interested in hearing about this.''

Dana turned to face the hospital. From here, it looked like such a small building, perched far above them. A small, pristine white building, stretching itself to reach the sky.

She'd stayed too long. She should have gone home before he kissed her and messed with her head. Too late.

Dana nodded toward the hospital. ''Maybe we'd better get back.''

''Maybe,'' he agreed. It was getting late, and he had an early day tomorrow. Besides, if he stayed here in the moonlight with her any longer, he was going to kiss her again.

And he had a feeling that it might not be good for either one of them if he did. At least, not now.

Dana let herself into the house quietly. In the distance, she heard Rafe's car pulling away. She'd shaken his hand in the car, refused his offer to walk her to her door and gotten out as quickly as possible. A deer bolting into the forest before the hunter could get off a second shot.

Maybe that was cowardly, but in the long run, she knew it was better this way.

A feeling of déjà vu filled her as she eased the door shut.

How many times had she come sneaking in like this when she was a teenager? Even younger, she thought, than the girl who'd held her hand so tightly tonight. Her father had labeled her a bad seed and once even said he was glad her mother hadn't lived to see what she had become. She'd cursed him for having the audacity to make any reference to her mother when he was the one responsible for her death. He was the one who had driven her into her depression.

She'd thought he was going to kill her. But he never raised a hand. He didn't have to. His tongue had been his weapon of choice, doing more damage than a hundred beatings. Shredding self-esteem. Except that he hadn't managed to shred hers. Not completely.

Maybe that was what goaded him now.

Dana drew her hand from the door, satisfied that her entrance had been silent.

"You haven't changed at all, have you? Still coming in at all hours of the night."

Dana jumped, barely managing to stifle a scream as her pulse pumped hard. Swinging around, she saw her father in the living room doorway. His eyes seemed to burn holes into her flesh. Slowly, he moved forward, an eerie figure, half man, half machine, emerging from the shadows.

"What the hell happened to you?" He gestured at her dress. Despite Nancy's help, she still looked disheveled, as if she'd played hide-and-seek with a dirty barbecue grill and raw meat. "Were you in an accident?"

She couldn't tell if that was concern or accusation in his voice. Probably the latter. He didn't waste his time with petty things like concern.

"No." Dana's response was terse. "But I was at one."

His eyes narrowed, sharp blue scalpels making incisions in her statement. "What is that supposed to mean?"

Why did he always think she was trying to put something

over on him? "It means that there was an accident on the road ahead of us, and we stopped to help." She began to walk toward the stairs.

He blocked her path with the wheelchair. "Who's *we?*"

Had he displayed the slightest bit of interest in her life, as if she was an actual person rather than an extension of himself, at any time during the years she lived here, she wouldn't have found his question so offensive. But she knew from experience that her father's only concern when it came to her was how her actions reflected on him.

Nothing, apparently, had changed for him, either.

Stubbornly, she refused to answer his question directly. "The man I went out with."

His mouth twisted in a smirk. "Didn't take you long, did it?"

A scathing retort hovered on the tip of her tongue, aching for release. Struggling, she held it back. Telling him what she thought of him wasn't going to help anything. Or change him. It was what he expected. So she didn't give it to him.

Instead, she shook her head. "I'm not underage anymore, Father. That means I'm not accountable to you."

He moved his chair again, refusing to let her pass. "What about Mollie?"

She glared at him, her eyes just as deadly, as challenging, as his. "What *about* Mollie?"

He leaned forward, wishing for the thousandth time that he wasn't imprisoned in this fancy piece of polished technology. That he could stand when he spoke. "Aren't you accountable to her? What kind of an example do you think your lifestyle is setting?"

Suddenly, Dana felt bone weary. "I don't have a lifestyle, Father." She resented the implications in his tone. "I'm just settling in."

Who did she think she was fooling? She'd lived the wild life once, thumbing her nose at him, at his reputation. And given half a chance, she would still do it. "That'll be your excuse when you're fifty."

"It's not an excuse, it's a fact." She wanted to run to her room, to slam the door in his face, even if he couldn't follow her. But because he couldn't follow her, because he was bound to this chair by a disease that threatened to take away what he held most dear, his dignity, she forced herself to calm down. To be civil. "Tomorrow—today," she corrected, glancing at her watch, "I'm taking Mollie with me to check out a summer program so she can be prepared to enter kindergarten in the fall. Once that's settled, I'll take the next step."

His eyes held hers. She couldn't tell whether he believed her or not. "Which is?"

"A step above the one I've taken." She pressed her lips together, sighing.

What was it about him that always made her ready to go ten rounds? One of them had to make the first move. The first ten moves, if necessary. And it looked as if that was going to fall to her. No moves were going to be made if she continued sparring like this.

"I'll be looking for work."

Her father sneered, his laugh disparaging. "I'll believe that when I see it."

"Fine, have it your way. Now, if you'll excuse me, I have to get to bed." Determined to get away before she said something vitriolic, she deliberately moved past him. "I'm very tired."

He swung his chair around, facing her back. "Living in the fast lane will do that."

Stiffening, Dana turned, suppressed fury in her eyes. "Are you accusing me of something?"

With his family, he'd always believed it was a matter of guilty until proven otherwise. "I don't have to. The evidence is all there."

She wanted to scream at him, to demand to know why he had opened his house to her only to revert to the behavior that had driven her away in the first place. What was he trying to prove, to gain? Was this all some twisted game?

"Then I suggest you get yourself another pair of glasses, Counselor, because your eyes are deceiving you. There *is* no evidence." Too tired and too angry to think clearly, Dana hurried up the stairs, knowing that if she remained, she wouldn't be able to keep her temper in check.

Detouring to Mollie's bedroom, she was gratified to see that their raised voices hadn't woken her. Dana retreated to her room. Wanting to slam her door, she eased it shut instead. Barely harnessed anger shook her body. Why did he do that to her? Why did he deliberately bait her that way?

And what the hell had made her think that if she returned, things would be different between them? If anything, they were worse.

Dana collapsed on her bed, too exhausted to undress.

Paul Morrow stared after his daughter as she fled up the stairs. Fled his accusations. Fled the truth. It wouldn't be long, he thought, before he had enough evidence against Dana to take Mollie from her. Anyone could see she was unfit to raise the child.

And if they couldn't, he meant to make them see.

Feeling suddenly exhausted, he turned the wheelchair and went to his room. With any luck, tonight he would sleep.

It had gone well.

Despite everything that had happened the night before between her father and her to color Dana's mood, the interview with the preschool staff and administrator had gone exceptionally well. For once, everything had gone beautifully from start to finish.

Mollie had chattered in the car, asking Dana all sorts of questions about her "date with Dr. Rafe." Dana gave her only the highlights, mentioning the burgers and fries and the walk on the beach. Mollie seemed enthralled, absorbing every detail like a miniature matchmaker in training.

Consequently, when they arrived at the preschool, Mollie

was relaxed, forgetting to be afraid. Defenses down, her bright, sunny nature came through loud and clear. The teachers loved her, and she ate it up. By the time they left, Mollie had made one new "best" friend, with the prospect of half a dozen more. Best of all, she was eager to return.

This was what Mollie needed, Dana thought, children her age to socialize with. She made a mental note to call Nicole Lincoln to thank the woman for the referral. Nicole's twins were enrolled in the school and attended three half days a week, just to get them in the swim of things. Twins, Nicole had pointed out, tended to depend too much on one another, creating their own world and shutting everyone else out.

Not unlike she and Meggie had been, Dana thought, as Mollie went on about the preschool. Oh, they hadn't been twins, but they'd behaved that way, being each other's buffer when it came to their father. Trying to make one another feel better.

And then Megan had changed. Always the gentler, quieter one, she began to do anything to please their father, feeding his ego with her compliance.

Dana became unacceptable and lacking. Megan was the good one, while Dana was the wild one.

Dana pressed her lips together. She was allowing last night's encounter with her father to get to her. Why couldn't she dwell on the good things? Like Mollie's enthusiasm about preschool? Like saving a life? Like Rafe's kiss?

Startled, she reined in her thoughts. The first two events were valid reasons for satisfaction. The last didn't belong in the same category. Dwelling on it was borrowing trouble, and God knew she had enough of that as it was.

"Aunt Dana, we're here. Aren't you going to stop the car?"

Mollie's voice penetrated Dana's thoughts. She was almost at the end of the driveway. How had that happened? "Yes, baby, I'm going to stop the car. Thanks for watching out for me."

Her response made Mollie puff up her chest. A moment later she practically skipped out of the car.

Esther opened the door for them, looking at Mollie. "So, how did it go?"

Mollie beamed at her. "They like me," she announced proudly.

Esther laughed, hugging the little girl quickly before she could restrain herself. Warm hugs were against type for her. "Why wouldn't they like you? You're the most likable little girl in the whole world."

Pleased by the compliment, Mollie cocked her head. "Better than Aunt Dana was?"

The housekeeper shook her head as she looked at Dana. The older Dana had become, the more difficult she'd been to deal with. "Your aunt Dana was a handful."

Mollie's eyes grew huge, darting toward Dana and then back again. "She fit in your hand?"

Esther's laughter mingled with Dana's at the literal interpretation. "No, but there was many a time I wanted to fit my hand to her bottom."

The admission surprised Dana. "I never knew that, Esther."

Esther drew herself up to her full five-foot stature. "I was very good at hiding my feelings."

Dana caught her tongue between her teeth. "Especially when your face turned purple."

Esther remained undaunted. Living here had made her ready for almost anything. "I was busy counting to a hundred and holding my breath."

Dana looked at her dubiously, wondering if the woman was putting her on. "And that helped?"

Esther nodded. "Made me too light-headed to think about wanting to throttle you. By the way, you had a phone call."

She thought of Rafe immediately, then silently called herself an idiot. "From who?"

Esther had seen the sudden light in Dana's eyes and interpreted it correctly. She hadn't been around the Morrow girls all those years without gaining some insight. She hadn't been available last night to admit Miss Dana's escort, but she'd watched them leave from a second-story window. Whoever he was, he was a handsome one, she thought. "Not a man. From Dr. Pollack."

Dana made no comment about Esther's glib comment. Instead, she focused on the information. "Sheila? Sheila called here?" She hadn't heard from her in a few days. Why had she called in the middle of the day? "Did she say what it was about?"

"No, only that you should call her back when you had the chance."

Dana started for the stairs. "Esther, do you think you can see about getting a certain young lady some cookies?"

Dana loved seeing the way Mollie's face lit up over such little things. She looked so like Megan then. Would she see the same sort of light in her own child's face? she wondered suddenly. Or would she see Steven each time she looked into the small face?

Would she be able to stand it if that was the case?

The answer was yes. Dana realized that, with no conscious debate, she had made her peace with what was happening to her. This was her child's heart beating beneath her heart. *Her* child.

And she loved it.

It helped, knowing that.

"There might be one or two cookies lying around," Esther said. She laced her fingers through Mollie's. "Want to help me find them?"

Mollie nodded and tried to contain her eagerness. Grown-ups didn't like it if you were too bouncy all the time. "Yes, please."

Esther smiled as she looked at Dana. She thought the younger woman looked a little preoccupied. But her color seemed to be improving. That was something. "Stunning manners on this child. Easy to see she was Miss Megan's."

Dana pretended to take offense. "*I* didn't have manners?"

Esther sniffed as she ushered Mollie toward the kitchen. "None that I recall."

The claim brought a smile to Dana's lips. Except for a few more gray hairs, Esther was still the same. Pretending not to care, to be aloof and distant. But it was an act. She knew Esther cared. The woman had been there for her and would have been there even more had Dana allowed it.

She went to her room to make her call.

She spent several minutes on hold before she was finally put through to Sheila. "You know, you really have to put on some more up-to-date music for people to listen to while they wait for you to get to them."

Sheila laughed as she recognized Dana's voice. "I like oldies, and they're staying on."

Dana shifted on the bed, trying to get comfortable. Her back was aching. Was that normal this early on? "To each his own. Anyway, Esther said you called while I was out."

"Right." Sheila edged into her reason for calling slowly. "I just wanted to call and check how you were feeling."

Dana thought of the confrontation last night, deliberately letting it overshadow what had come before. It was easier than exploring it. "As well as can be expected, under the circumstances."

"Circumstances?"

Dana sighed. She leaned forward on the bed, pressing a hand to the small of her back. Maybe soaking in the tub would help. It certainly couldn't hurt.

"My father is not exactly making this reconciliation easy." Maybe the blame wasn't totally his. "And I guess he still rubs me the wrong way." She paused, then added, "A lot."

"Oh, I see." That wasn't what Sheila was after. She plowed ahead. "I ran into Rafe this morning at the hospital."

It was stupid to feel her stomach tighten, Dana upbraided herself. Too stupid for words. "And?"

Sheila thought of Rafe's expression. She hadn't seen him look like that in a long time. "He seemed rather buoyant."

It didn't mean anything. She didn't want it to mean anything. Right? "You saw him floating? Was he going out to sea?"

Sheila knew that tone. Dana was slipping behind her protective shield. "Stop being flippant. He told me the two of you went out last night." When Dana made no comment, she said, "Simon added a little color to the event."

"Simon?"

"One of the attending physicians in the ER. He said Rafe and you came in with some victims of a car wreck." The rumor mill had picked up the tidbit that Rafe had come in with a young woman and run with it. Someone had made a point of mentioning it to Kate at the lab. The reaction, Sheila had heard, was not good. "Interesting way to conduct a first date."

"It wasn't a date," Dana protested quickly. "It was a bet."

Her friend was definitely in denial, Sheila thought. "You're going to have to clarify that one for me."

Dana moved restlessly from the bed, and the telephone clattered to the floor. She stooped to pick it up. "Sorry about that. Rafe wanted to prove that some restaurant he likes serves better food than the one I used to go to in Dallas." She heard Sheila's soft laugh in her ear.

"A rose by any other name—"

"Still has thorns," Dana cut in. Her mounting frustration about her situation, about everything, stripped the situation of any humor. "You know I can't date anyone right now."

"You're pregnant, Dana. You don't have the bubonic plague." Maybe Dana and Rafe would be good for one another. God knew they'd both been through a lot.

Dana refused to capitulate. "In either case, I'm not exactly in a position to socialize widely."

Sheila decided to let the matter drop. Maybe she was jumping to conclusions. Maybe they *had* gone out to eat just to settle a bet. Being so happy with Slade made her want to pair everyone off so they could find the same sort of joy she had. "About the baby, Dana."

Dana tensed. "Yes?"

There was no easy way to broach this, but she was Dana's doctor as well as her friend. If Dana was planning to sweep her dilemma from her life, it had to be done soon. "What are you going to do about it?"

"Do about it?" She repeated the words as if she was barely aware of what they meant. "I'm going to have it."

Sheila exhaled the breath she'd been holding. She should have known Dana wouldn't choose an abortion. Dana had always loved children. But people did change, and their priorities changed with them. "And then?"

Since she'd learned she was pregnant, the baby hadn't been out of her mind. It had lingered, hiding behind every thought she had, every response she made. It wasn't just physically a part of her. It was *part* of her, emotionally. Part of every breath she took. She knew that. Inconvenient or not, there was no denying this child. Dana placed her hand over her taut, flat belly, wondering how it would feel to have it swollen out of all proportion. "And then I'm going to love it the way every baby has a right to be loved."

Sheila hesitated, then forced herself to ask, "Even though it's Steven's?"

"Hey, the baby can't help that." Still unborn, and she was already taking its side. That had to be a good sign, right? "Just like I couldn't help being Paul Morrow's daughter."

Sheila rose to the last hurdle. "When are you planning to tell Steven that he's a father?"

"I've already tried. I can't reach him. Whenever I call, all I get is his damn answering machine. It's not the kind of brief message that belongs on a tape. If and when I get *him* rather than his annoying recording, then I'll tell him."

That brought up other problems. Problems Dana was going to have to face. Better now than down the line. "And if he wants custody?"

Dana's laugh was harsh. Steven's inability to tolerate not being the center of attention, his attempt to seize that spot from a child, was why she'd left.

"That, dear Dr. Pollack, will be the day you should sink

all your available money into winter clothing, because it will mean that hell has frozen over.''

Sheila laughed, and a few minutes later she rang off.

Dana hung up and stared at the telephone, her thoughts waffling from one emotional extreme to another.

Her next call was to Rafe's office. Speaking quickly before she could change her mind, she left a message with the nurse. She asked Alice to extend her regrets to the doctor, but she wasn't going to be able to go to the restaurant with him after all.

Dana stared at the phone after she'd hung up. She'd done the right thing. She knew that. So why did doing the right thing have to feel so bad?

Chapter 12

Rafe let himself into the one-bedroom apartment he'd sublet several years ago from a friend. At the time, he'd leased it because it suited his budget.

His practice was thriving now, but he saw no reason to move. Nothing else had changed for him. He hadn't acquired any expensive hobbies that threatened to crowd the apartment with possessions, and he harbored no desire for extra space. For him, the apartment was a place to sleep and shower and, once in a while, to eat. If he wanted a good meal, there were restaurants around.

Or, better yet, there was always his parents' home. His mother loved to cook for him, and he found her meals infinitely preferable to restaurant food. The company was better, as well. Aside from a little teenage rebellion, he'd always gotten along well with both parents. That feeling extended to his brother, too. Once he and Gabe had both gotten past the age of ten, their fierce competitive streak had mellowed into something that was manageable and only reared its head occasionally when they played a little one-on-one basketball.

He knew that, day or night, the door of his parents' home was always open to him. It was a comforting thing to fall back on, but tonight, he wanted to be alone.

That being the case, he supposed that things had worked out for the best, with Dana canceling at the last minute.

Rafe stretched out on the sofa, a can of soda in his hand. Briefly, he flirted with the idea of calling for take-out, then decided to make do with whatever he found in the refrigerator.

He reached for the remote and clicked on the television set. He ignored it the minute it came on, needing only the soft blur of colors, the indistinguishable buzz of noise in the background, as company. He popped the top of the can, then brought the drink to his mouth and drank deeply, trying to quench an even deeper thirst.

It made no difference to him, Rafe thought. If Dana Morrow had decided she didn't want to go out with him, he wasn't about to push the matter. It just wasn't meant to be, that was all.

He wasn't aware of the sigh that escaped him. A lot of things weren't meant to be.

On the other hand, some things were. Sometimes, things just came together and turned out well.

The way they had with Timmie.

Toasting himself with the half-empty can, Rafe smiled. Timmie was even now undergoing treatment to purge his blood of the toxins that had come perilously close to killing him.

Who would have thought that what amounted to a few bites of contaminated ground beef could nearly destroy a boy as vibrant, as energetic, as Timmie? The boy had been afraid to confess to his mother that, curious, he had sampled the raw meat. He'd almost taken the secret with him to his grave.

And he would have, Rafe thought, if he hadn't badgered him, making the boy go over everything he'd done, everything he'd touched, in the days before he'd gotten sick. In forcing Timmie to recite the events over and over again, Rafe had almost reduced them both to tears, but he'd gotten his answer.

And now Timmie was getting his life back.

Rafe drained the rest of the soda, then placed the empty can on the coffee table, still feeling thirsty. A man couldn't feel down when he'd managed to cheat death of such a young trophy. And he did feel good, very good.

So why was there this small, nagging feeling echoing in the back of his mind, humming of dissatisfaction? The message from Dana, tendered secondhand through Alice, had taken the edge off his victory. It shouldn't have, he knew, and yet it had.

Women.

He blew out a breath and then got off the sofa. He needed another drink. Something stronger than soda.

Dana stared at the man who had been her father's partner for the past fifteen years. Jefferson Wallace had called her earlier today and mysteriously requested a meeting. A fussy, precise man who could never be accused of being larger than life the way her father was, Wallace had been very specific in selecting both the time and locale for their meeting. He wanted to see her at one o'clock in her living room. A time when he knew her father was going to be safely in court.

Dana had had absolutely no idea why Wallace wanted to see her, even after Esther had shown him in and she had taken her seat across from him.

Once he'd told her what was on his mind, Dana felt she was being set up for some sort of macabre joke. It couldn't be anything else. She waited in vain for the punch line that didn't come.

Finally she asked, "You're kidding, right?"

A mouth created for frowning pursed as eyes the color and shape of ebony marbles scrutinized her every move. With narrow, thin shoulders that hunched forward and hands that were too large for the rest of him, he was like a small, ugly statue that was so off-putting it bordered on fascinating.

"Dana, I don't have time to waste with ill-conceived pranks or poorly constructed jokes. I am very serious about this. Will you come to work for the firm?" Wallace repeated.

If her father had wanted her to join the firm, she thought, he would have said so.

Or would he?

Was this some kind of test? And if it was, which way was she to answer in order to pass? It wasn't easy, being Paul Morrow's daughter. At the very least, it bred a strain of paranoia that was hard to shake.

Cautiously, she entered the waters. "This is my father's firm. I don't really think he'd like having me there."

The marbles never shifted. They continued to bore straight into her. "It's a firm your father began," Wallace replied, correcting her. "But I'm a senior partner, and we would very much like to have a Morrow on our staff."

"You *have* a Morrow on the staff. My father."

Wallace watched her reaction to his next words. "We've been thinking of asking him to step down. Retire. For reasons of health," he added expansively.

He wasn't concerned with her father's health, Dana thought. He was concerned with the fact that her father might do something to embarrass the firm.

"And you think having me at the firm will somehow soften the blow of his knowing he'd been eased out?" She laughed harshly. She would have thought that someone at the firm would have done his homework. Paul Morrow wasn't the kind to bust his buttons with pride at his offspring's accomplishments. Especially not if it came to that offspring supplanting him. "Boy, do you have the wrong number." Her laugh faded. Wallace continued looking at her, his eyes unfathomable. She felt something twist in her stomach. Revulsion? Or fading morning sickness?

Dana leaned forward in her chair. If she hadn't thought it would give Wallace heart failure, she would have caught his hand between hers to underscore her entreaty.

"You can't do this to him." Neither she nor the family

physician she had called the other day for a prognosis knew how long her father had—six months or six years—but one thing she did know for certain. "If you force him to retire, it will kill him. He'll have nothing to live for." Her voice became impassioned. "Being a lawyer is his *life*, Mr. Wallace. His *whole* life. It's who and what he is."

Wallace appeared uncomfortable but unmoved. "He has you, his granddaughter and more money than Monaco." Every reason in the world to retire, in his book.

Dana shook her head. "Unimportant. All unimportant. He *needs* to be Paul S. Morrow, criminal lawyer. Take that away from him and you're guilty of putting a gun to his head."

Her eyes could be just as cold as her father's. It was a look she had practiced and perfected in the mirror when she was very young. It never worked on her father, but it did on others. She aimed the look at Wallace, nearly succeeding in making him squirm.

"Do you want that on your conscience?"

"No, of course not." He tried again, a little less pompously. "But there is a danger of his becoming an embarrassment."

She didn't have to summon a practiced expression. The look in her eyes cut him dead. "To whom?"

Wallace faltered a little. And as he faltered, he thought that Dana Morrow might indeed be the perfect heir apparent to her father. "To himself."

"Then he'll be the one who knows when to leave." She knew her father well enough for that. If he felt he was a liability, if he felt that others were laughing at him, he would leave immediately. She rose and looked down at Wallace. "It *is* his firm, Mr. Wallace." Clamping a lid on her anger at the other man's presumption, she thought the situation over. Wallace's concern did have some validity. Her father *was* slipping. Something had to be done to pick up the slack. *That* she could do.

"If it will be of any help," she said, measuring her words. She'd never thought about working for her father, never wanted to work for him, but it wasn't a matter now of her values or her desires. Her father, completely unknown to him, needed her. Needed her to be his buffer. Maybe somewhere along the line, if she joined, she could even manage to have the "S" in his name stand for something other than shark. "I'll come to work for the firm. I'll do what needs to be done to smooth over any rough edges you feel are showing. I can help prepare the briefs, that sort of thing." She could hear the explosion when her father was told. "I need the work, anyway."

Because he knew in his gut that he had no choice, the compromise appeased Wallace. For the time being.

His stomach settling, he allowed himself to sample one of the pastries that Esther had put out. The amaretto-laced tart coaxed a ghost of a smile from him. "Don't know why he didn't bring you in before. You could argue the ears off a brass monkey."

That wasn't always a compliment, but she took it as her due. "If I have to."

Wallace carefully wiped his mouth with his handkerchief. "Your sister was a great deal quieter."

Until her falling out with her father over George, Megan had clerked for the firm, hoping to someday become at least a junior partner. It was a carrot her father had dangled before her but never actually offered.

"That was my fault." Her fond tone was for the memory, not the man. "I never let her get a word in edgewise."

It occurred to Wallace that condolences might still be in order. It was something he'd never been any good at. "I'm sorry about...well, about..."

She nodded, putting him out of his misery. His words meant nothing to her, nor did the social code he adhered to, which necessitated offering them. "Thanks. So, do we have a deal?"

Relieved, even entertaining a dollop of hope, Wallace extended his hand to her, sealing the bargain. "Deal."

* * *

As everyone else slept that night, sleeplessness once again haunted Paul Morrow, as it had more and more each year. He sat in his den and reviewed the surveillance tapes Dickinson had brought to him. The tapes from cameras no one else knew existed.

They were hidden strategically in several rooms in the house. Originally intended as part of a security system, of late they enabled Morrow to feel as if he was still in control of things by allowing him to eavesdrop on what was going on.

The tape from the living room camera had him leaning forward in his wheelchair. His eyes narrowed as he watched and listened to his partner, a man he trusted as much as he trusted anyone, plot to push him out of the firm he had established.

The spineless bastard was going behind his back, trying to ally himself with Dana.

If asked, his guess would have been that his daughter would have jumped at the chance to be a party to that. It amazed him to learn otherwise.

He heard his daughter, a woman he hardly knew and liked less, come to his defense. Reading people was second nature to him, a craft he'd honed over the years to help him win his cases and survive. As he watched, a side of Dana emerged he'd never been privy to. A side she'd kept hidden as they went head-to-head over everything. There was passion in her face, feeling in her voice, as she came to his defense.

Why?

Why would she come to his aid? Why would she care if his career ended? She'd never tried to reap any rewards from it. She'd made it plain that she hated the limelight, hated the notoriety of being Paul Morrow's daughter.

The question lingered in his mind. Morrow stared at the monitor long after the tape had ended, no longer seeing the screen.

Why?

* * *

Sweat poured into Rafe's eyes, stinging them. He blinked it away. Every fiber of his being was intent on making this shot.

It was a simple game of basketball. Two teams comprised of a potpourri of medical personnel, doctors, nurses, orderlies, whoever didn't mind getting sweaty and fancied himself or herself as the next Michael Jordan—or at least capable of dribbling a basketball. At stake were a couple of rounds of drinks at McGinty's, a local hangout. Losers footed the tab. The fate of the world was not riding on this shot.

Just his pride.

Which was why it would have cost him dearly had he missed. And he almost did. Because as he was lining it up, as he was about to release the ball, out of the corner of his eye, he saw Dana. Dana, with her hand holding Mollie's, came into his line of vision. Looking his way.

If it hadn't been a free shot, if he'd been in motion on the court, someone would have knocked the ball out of his hands.

"Hey, Saldana, you going to take the shot or pose for a statue?" Moore, the new plastic surgeon, hooted impatiently.

Gaining his concentration, Rafe made his shot. The basketball sailed toward the hoop and made it through cleanly. As his teammates and somewhere around half the people scattered in the bleachers in the local high school gym cheered, Rafe watched Dana usher Mollie into a seat, then sit next to her.

What were they doing here? And why should the sight of a woman he had put out of his mind make him lose his concentration?

Annoyed with himself for his lack of a satisfactory answer, he ran to the other end of the court with his team.

Mollie's eyes were glued to him from the moment she'd spotted her beloved doctor. "Dr. Rafe looks all sweaty, Aunt Dana."

Yes, he did, didn't he? She could see it from here. Sweat gleamed on his body, making it almost glow. Dana shifted restlessly in her seat.

"He's playing basketball. It's sweaty work." She found it difficult to look at anyone else.

"How come Dr. Rafe's not wearing any pants?"

Dana bit back a laugh. "He's wearing shorts, honey. It makes it easier for him to play." Dana watched Rafe's muscular legs tense and pump as he ran from one end of the court to the other. You wouldn't think a man that tall could move so fast. "Man's got a pretty nice pair of legs on him," Dana murmured to herself.

She had to admit he was in possession of a magnificent form. Dressed, there was only a hint of the body beneath. Wearing only shorts and a T-shirt and gleaming with sweat, he looked as if someone had carved him out of golden rock.

The man appeared to be solid muscle, she realized in awed fascination.

Glancing around at the female spectators, she saw she wasn't alone in her assessment.

Dana bit her bottom lip. She still didn't know what she was doing here—other than having thoughts she shouldn't about her niece's pediatrician's body.

Dana looked around, but Sheila was nowhere to be seen. Leave it to Sheila to all but strong-arm her into coming to watch her play basketball and then not have the decency to show up.

Signaling for a time-out, Rafe dropped into the stands and grabbed the water bottle he had stashed under his seat. He took a long pull and let the warm liquid trickle down his throat before turning to look at Dana. She was sitting several rows behind him. He raised a quizzical eyebrow in her direction.

She felt awkward as she lifted her shoulders in a shrug. The next thing she knew, Mollie was working her way down to where he was sitting. Muttering under her breath, Dana had no choice but to follow.

Well, this was a dumb idea, she thought. There was no question that she should have her head examined for going along with it.

"Come to the game," Sheila had said. "I need someone to cheer me on, and you need to get out. It'll be perfect. Bring Mollie."

That she needed to get out was right on the money. But she didn't need to be here, looking at Rafe when he was all sweaty and sexy as hell, suddenly reliving a kiss that had had no business happening.

Why hadn't she thought to ask Sheila if Rafe was going to be there? Because that would have made it sound as if she wanted him to be there, that was why. So she hadn't, and now look.

Irritation born of embarrassment flooded her. Damned if you do, damned if you don't.

Mollie was a one-woman fan club. She'd made herself comfortable on the bench beside Rafe. "You play good."

He took another pull of the water bottle, then laughed as he tousled her hair. "Just what I like, an unbiased opinion. How're you doing, kiddo?"

"Very well, thank you," she answered primly, her eyes sparkling like dew on tender green buds.

"Still got your manners, I see." He raised his eyes to Dana's face as she joined them. She looked flushed. And pretty. "And your aunt. What brings you here?" he asked Dana.

She told him the truth and thought it sounded like an excuse. "Sheila asked me to come and cheer her on. She said Slade couldn't make it."

Frustrated, Dana looked around, willing Sheila to materialize and save her from this awkward moment. Being face to face with Rafe served to remind her she hadn't even had the courage to break their date last week in person. It galled her that she'd behaved badly, impulsively urged on by a fear she'd momentarily been unable to manage.

It galled her more that he probably knew it, too.

"Neither could she," Rafe told her. Confused, Dana looked at him. "Sheila had an emergency delivery." His attention shifted to Mollie. "Since *you're* here, want to act as *my* cheering section?"

"Yes!" Mollie shouted. She clapped her hands to demonstrate.

"That's all the encouragement I need," he pronounced. He left the almost empty water bottle under his seat and got back into the game.

By the time the game was officially over, both sides were ready to drop. Rafe's team won by one basket, the winning shot made by an anesthesiologist who barely came up to Rafe's shoulder.

Detaching himself from his high-fiving teammates, Rafe came over to join Mollie and Dana. Mollie was standing on the bleacher, applauding wildly.

"We're going to McGinty's to celebrate." Rafe raised his voice above the din of crowing winners and grousing losers. "Want to join us?"

"I don't think so. Mollie's too young to hoist a few," Dana pointed out. She was grateful she'd brought Mollie. Otherwise she would have been tempted to say yes, and that probably wouldn't have been a good thing.

Victory and the sight of her cheering for him had made Rafe forget they were going to a bar. A sheepish grin curved his lips.

"Sorry, what was I thinking? How about Chocolate Heaven?" He presented his case to Mollie. "They make the best ice cream sodas."

Mollie looked as if she was ready to take off with him like a shot. Only ingrained training had her looking at Dana. "Aunt Dana?"

She'd never heard her name said so hopefully. Dana couldn't find it in her heart to say no. She supposed that, with Mollie between them, she was safe from making any foolish mistakes. Like kissing Rafe again.

Unable to quite shake the feeling that she had stepped into quicksand, Dana nodded. "All right."

He couldn't explain the electrifying zip that went through

him at her words. He didn't even try. He began to move away, then stepped back.

"I've got to change." His eyes pinned her down. "Be here when I get back?"

"Yes."

It wasn't good enough. Dana had said yes before, then changed her mind. Rafe directed his appeal to Mollie. "Keep her here, okay?"

Mollie grinned broadly as she laced her fingers through her aunt's. "Okay."

"I'm counting on you." Leaning forward, he slid his finger down the pert nose. "She's slippery." With that, he hurried off.

Mollie's brow was puckered as she turned to her aunt. "What did he mean, Aunt Dana?"

Dana shrugged broadly. "I don't know," she lied. "He must have gotten hit on the head with the basketball before we got here." Leaning over, she whispered confidentially, "It makes him say silly things."

Mollie accepted the explanation. After all, Aunt Dana knew everything.

Rafe hurried through his shower and into his clothing. He had a feeling that, if he didn't, Dana was likely to take a powder, pint-size bodyguard or not.

"Hey." Kim Lee stopped toweling his hair dry to look bewilderedly at his friend. Rafe was dressed and stuffing his sweaty clothing into his gym bag while the rest of them were still dripping from the shower. "They timing us or something?"

Rafe didn't bother zipping the bag closed. Grabbing the handles, he was off. "No, only me." He tossed the words over his shoulder as he left the locker room.

Watching him go, Kim grinned. It had to be a woman. No man moved that fast if he didn't have someone to go to. He wondered if it was the blonde in the stands he'd seen Rafe talking to. All he could think was that it was about time.

* * *

Half of Rafe didn't expect to find Dana and Mollie there when he got to the gym, but there they were in the bleachers, right where he'd left them. Rafe exhaled slowly. He couldn't remember ever getting ready so fast, even when he was in medical school. Not even the morning he'd overslept after pulling a thirty-six-hour shift.

Seeing him coming their way, Mollie ran to greet him. "Aunt Dana thinks you have nice legs."

If there had been a hole in the gym floor to crawl into, she would have done it. Mortified, Dana made a mental note to give Mollie a lesson about the need to keep secrets.

"Oh, she does, does she?" Rafe grinned, looking at Dana, who was slowly coming toward them. "Tell Aunt Dana thank you."

"She's right here." Grabbing his hand, Mollie tugged on it, pulling him toward her aunt. "You can do it yourself."

Instead of following, he dropped to one knee beside Mollie. "I'm afraid I'll spook her, like I did the other night."

If it qualified as a whisper, it was of the stage variety. Dana met his eyes, her embarrassment dropping away. "What I said to Mollie was that your legs didn't look as bad in shorts as some of the other players' did. And for the record, you didn't spook me."

He rose to his feet, his eyes on hers. "Then why did you cancel?"

She shrugged vaguely. "Something came up."

"Something?" he repeated, waiting for her to be a little more specific.

He had a long wait ahead of him, then, she thought. "Yes, something." She took a breath. "Now, just exactly where is this Heavenly Chocolate?"

"Chocolate Heaven," he corrected.

Dana waved away the correction. "Whatever. Is it far?"

He paused, thinking. "About a mile. C'mon, I'll take you there." Reaching for Mollie's hand, he was ready to leave the gym.

Dana held out. She wanted a clean getaway available if she needed it. "You lead the way. We'll follow in my car."

Turning, he regarded her for a moment. "Can you be trusted?"

She supposed she had that coming. "Yes, I can be trusted." Biting back a comment, she raised her hand as if she was in court. "I promise."

Rafe looked at Mollie solemnly. "You're a witness, Mollie. She promised. You know what happens to people who break their promises, don't you?"

Mollie hung on his every word. "No, what?"

"They can never eat chocolate again." He deliberately made his voice sound stern.

After wavering for a second, Mollie giggled, deciding that he was teasing. "We'll follow you," she promised. "Aunt Dana loves chocolate."

This was promising. "Then she's going to love their amaretto sundae." He took Mollie's hand again. "So, did you like the game?"

Mollie thrust her other hand into her aunt's. She liked the way it felt, walking between them. Almost like when she used to walk with Mommy and Daddy. "Uh-huh. It was cool."

"Cool, huh?" he repeated. "Who taught you that word?"

"My new best friend, Becky. She goes to my preschool. Aunt Dana signed me up. I get to go three times a week. My teacher's name is…"

Mollie was off and running. And much to Dana's eternal relief, she kept up a steady stream of chatter all the way to the parking lot.

Chapter 13

Chocolate Heaven was a small shop devoted to the axiom that all good things involved chocolate in some way. The owner, who could be found on the premises at any given time, knew how to reel people in from the streets if they were passing by on foot rather than by car. Even the latter were immune only if the windows were firmly rolled up. Otherwise, the aroma of chocolate, decadent and tempting, floated out, beckoning to one and all like the crooked finger of a mischievous enchantress. Very few could resist the call.

Dana didn't even try.

Her senses were aroused and her mouth watering long before she and Mollie crossed the threshold. She took a deep breath, drawing in the scent.

"They know how to get you, don't they?" Rafe asked her, amusement in his eyes.

She laughed, looking around the shop. Several booths and small, white-topped circular tables surrounded by chairs, the kind found in old-fashioned soda shops, were scattered throughout the room. To one side was a long soda fountain, complete with stools. The back of the room was devoted to chocolate. Chocolate bars, gold-foil-covered chocolate coins, chocolate in boxes, chocolate figures and any combination of food covered with chocolate the mind could conjure up.

Wow, was all she could think. "I think I gained three pounds just by breathing."

Mollie scrunched up her face, trying to understand. "How can you do that?"

"When you're older, you'll find out," Dana assured her. She found herself wishing she could burn off excess calories as easily as Mollie could.

Rafe selected a booth, then looked at Dana for approval. She smiled, letting Mollie slip in first, then sitting beside her.

And that put her right across from Rafe, she realized. Right across from eyes the color of leaves budding in the spring. Dana decided that close scrutiny of the menu Rafe had picked up on their way in was in order.

Mollie frowned at the menu in front of her. She knew how to recognize all her letters and a few words, but this had curly stuff written all over it. She couldn't pick out a single thing she knew.

Frustrated, she looked at Rafe. "What's it say?"

He began reading the different selections to Mollie, along with their flowery descriptions. He did it with such feeling that by the time he was finished, Dana had no idea what to order.

Mollie was in the same boat. "I don't know what to get," she confessed. Her appeal for aid, Dana noted, was to Rafe, not to her.

"How about the banana split?" Rafe suggested. "At least then you can pretend it's healthy." When he winked at her, Mollie giggled.

It amazed Dana that Rafe seemed content to let Mollie chatter endlessly as they sat, waiting for their orders to be brought. He even responded in the few places where she paused for air. He wasn't just allowing Mollie to talk, Dana realized, he was listening to her.

She had to admit that the man was a rarity.

Rafe's grin widened as he looked at the expression on Dana's face. "What?"

Faced with a direct question, Dana roused herself. "Excuse me?"

She probably wasn't aware she was staring at him, he thought. "You have this look on your face like you're trying to figure me out."

Caught, she had no choice. She raised a shoulder, then let it drop. "I am."

"Not much to figure," he said simply. "I'm a doctor, I like kids. Especially bright ones." He winked at Mollie, then raised his eyes to Dana's. "If there's anything else you want to know, ask."

She did have questions, she realized. Questions about him, about his life. But answers would only lead to an intimacy she didn't want right now. An intimacy she wouldn't know what to do with.

Dana toyed with her silverware. "I don't believe in prying."

That would put her in a class by herself, he thought. "It's only prying if the other person doesn't want to answer." But even though he paused, she made no effort to ask anything. "You might be interested in knowing that the three people you helped save on our auspicious non-date have been discharged and gone home."

"You helped save people, Aunt Dana?" Mollie asked, her voice bubbling with curiosity.

Dana didn't think it was a good idea to discuss a car accident in front of Mollie. Her eyes met Rafe's, and she subtly shook her head, hoping he understood her meaning.

He did, but he couldn't ignore Mollie's question. "Your aunt's a brave lady. At least," he added significantly, "where some things are concerned."

Dana bit back a retort. Any discussion of the subject was tabled as the waiter returned with their order. Mollie's looked almost larger than she was. She beamed in anticipation.

"Looks like our fall from grace has arrived." Rafe raised a spoon to something described as "fudge decadence à la mode."

"No, it hasn't," Mollie corrected, confused. "This is ice cream."

Rafe laughed. He enjoyed the gusto with which she dug in. There was an innocence to children that faded and then disappeared completely when they got older. An innocence that gave him hope for future generations.

"For you it's ice cream," he pointed out. "For me, it's three hours at the gym."

Dana had begun to believe that, except for rare aberrations, Rafe was always at his office or the hospital. "You work out?"

He noted her incredulous tone. "Obviously not enough, if you have to ask."

She took a sip of her drink, something that combined vanilla ice cream, chocolate syrup, whipped cream and Kahlúa, mint and amaretto flavorings, and let it seduce her taste buds before continuing.

"No, I just meant I thought maybe it was natural. The muscles and everything." She was putting this very badly. The amusement in his eyes wasn't making it any easier for her, either.

"No, just a natural by-product of working out." He thought back to the photographs in his mother's album. The ones he couldn't convince her to throw away. "My natural look is early Pillsbury doughboy." Mollie's delighted laugh urged him to elaborate. "No, seriously, my mother can cook like nobody else in this world. The only thing she likes more than cooking is watching Gabe and me eating." Only a rapid growth spurt in his late teens and a good metabolism had prevented him from being wider than he was tall. "I started exercising in self-defense. It was either that," he confided to Mollie, "or look for a job as Humpty Dumpty's stand-in."

Now that Dana didn't believe. She let her eyes roam over his upper torso. It could have been chiseled out of rock. The blue jersey he wore accented biceps and pectorals that were usually only found in the pages of a physical fitness magazine.

She shook her head. "I can't picture you heavy."

And she was really trying. He could see it in her eyes. "Remind me to show you a few pictures sometime."

Sometime. That meant he intended to see them, her, again. Or was it a throwaway line? She didn't know. More than that, she didn't know whether or not she wanted it to be.

Common sense was weighing in on one side, but other factors were beginning to gather on the other. A side that could definitely complicate things for her.

Dana lowered her eyes and concentrated on the tall glass in front of her.

Throwing herself into eating her dessert with abandonment, Mollie still found time to eye the one before Rafe. "Boy, that looks good, too."

He could read what was on her mind as if it was printed on her forehead in big block letters. "Want a taste?"

Mollie practically glowed. "Yes, please."

Enthusiastic, but still polite. He got a tremendous kick out of Mollie. He and Gabe had never been remotely this polite when they were kids. Scooping up two layers of brownie decked out in three kinds of chocolate sauce, he offered the prize to Mollie. She leaned forward and cleaned the spoon with one bite.

"Good?"

Her mouth full, she could only respond with a pleased noise. "Uh-huh." Mollie swallowed, her eyes gleaming. Then she pushed her plate toward him. "Would you like some of mine?"

She seemed so eager to share, he couldn't refuse. "Sure."

Mimicking him, Mollie fed Rafe some of her banana split. A little ice cream was lost to the table, but Rafe pretended not to notice.

Her father would have ordered her from the table, Dana thought. And Steven would have hit the ceiling because of the mess. She felt herself smiling as she watched. Rafe Saldana was going to make a hell of a father to some lucky kid someday.

"Now you, Aunt Dana. You feed Dr. Rafe, too."

The wide grin on Rafe's face made Dana's stomach flip over. She found herself looking at her glass instead of at him. "No, I don't think he wants any of this."

"Sure I do."

"Sure he does," Mollie echoed.

She might have known he would do this. It was either give Rafe a taste or subject herself to an onslaught of Mollie logic.

Something warm and unnamed washed over her as she dipped her spoon into the tall glass and then held it out to Rafe. Her breath hovered in her lungs, not going in, not going out.

Waiting.

Rafe saw the slight tremor of her hand. Did he make her nervous? And why was that so appealing to him?

Holding her hand steady with his, his eyes on hers, Rafe guided the spoon slowly to his mouth. He closed his lips over it, then slid the spoon out even more slowly. The arousal he experienced was nothing new. But the intensity was.

Her breath finally materialized, evacuating her lungs rapidly. But not nearly as rapidly as her pulse was pounding. Dana dropped the long spoon into the glass, her fingers feeling oddly boneless.

"If you want any more, you can have it." She pushed the tall glass toward him.

He shook his head, smiling. "No, that's all right, you finish it." His eyes lingered on her face, caressing it. "Want any of mine?"

"No!" She reddened as she realized that she'd declined a little more loudly and forcefully than she'd intended. The amused, knowing smile on his face only served to irritate her, although she couldn't have said exactly why.

He nodded, lifting his spoon to his mouth. "Well, let me know if you do."

For a second her eyes were drawn to his mouth, It was a strong mouth, a firm mouth. A…

Rallying, annoyed with herself, with the way she felt herself slipping, Dana squared her shoulders. "Believe me, you'll be the first to know."

Was it his imagination, or had he just been privy to a battle cry?

The evening and the company charmed her far more than she'd thought possible. And she wasn't the only one who felt the effects of spending some time with Dr. Rafe Saldana, first-rate physician and star of the basketball court as well as chocolate advocate par excellence. It was clear that Mollie was completely enamored with him.

If she'd had any lingering doubts of that, they were dispelled once she and Rafe had pulled up in her driveway. He had insisted on seeing them home, even if that meant he had to follow them in his car. Apparently chivalry was not dead.

As soon as the two cars stopped, Mollie scrambled out of theirs and ran to his, waiting impatiently for him to get out.

Hands tucked behind her back, rocking on the balls of her feet, Mollie looked at him adoringly. "Dr. Rafe?"

She sounded so serious, he suppressed the smile the mere sight of her evoked. "Yes, Mollie?"

"Will you marry me?"

The proposal caught him completely off guard. She was so earnest, so sincere, he knew it would crush her if he laughed. Banking down his initial reaction, Rafe crouched beside Mollie, taking her small hands in his. He kissed them one at a time.

"Mollie, I am very, very honored that you want to marry me."

Mollie's expression was the picture of eagerness. "Then you will?"

Regret was evident in every fiber of his countenance. How did he manage to do that? Dana wondered. Was it kindness or practice that he drew on?

"I can't, kiddo. Not right now. You're too young."

With the deadly accurate logic of the young, Mollie pointed out, "But I'll get older."

He inclined his head, conceding the point. "So will I."

Stymied, Mollie shook her head. "I don't care about that. I love you."

She touched his heart. Lightly, he feathered his hand through her hair. "And I love you, Mollie. Tell you what, I'll wait for you, and if you still want to marry me in, oh, say thirteen years—"

Her eyes widened as her voice filled with despair. That seemed like an eternity. "Thirteen years?" she wailed.

He nodded. "Thirteen years. You'll be eighteen then and can do whatever you want. If you still want to marry me, I'm all yours."

"Oh." The clouds lifted from her face. Hope existed, waiting for her at the end of eternity. "Okay."

Mollie was adorable. Rafe had a sudden image of Dana at that age and decided she'd probably been more in the spice category than sugar.

"So, it's decided," he said. "If you still want to get married in thirteen years, I'm your man."

"It's a deal!" Mollie stuck out her hand like a grown-up.

Rafe shook it solemnly before rising. He made eye contact with Dana and saw that the look in her eyes had softened considerably.

"That was very nice of you," she whispered.

As she spoke, her breath touched his cheek. Warming him. Reminding him. Funny how some things lingered in your mind, he mused. Just enough to haunt you.

He smiled at her. "Just covering my bets. I figure by the time she's eighteen, I might be ready to settle down, and they'll be lining up six deep for her." The look in his eyes was soft as they slid over her. "The way they probably did for you."

Thirteen years, huh? She wondered if he was putting her on notice that he wasn't available. As if that were necessary.

"No lines." She kept her voice low. "My father wouldn't have stood for it. When he was here."

And from her tone, that hadn't happened very often. "And when he wasn't?"

"Hasn't Sheila filled you in yet?" She was surprised, but maybe he just hadn't been curious enough about her to ask. "I was the original wild child."

Wild. That was the word for her. Not in the way she conducted herself, but there was a certain look that came into her eyes, a certain way she lifted her chin. A vitality that she exuded, even when she was being subdued.

He should be going, he thought. For lots of reasons. He lingered for one that remained unacknowledged. "I'd like to do this again sometime."

Nervousness danced through her. "Have ice cream, go out with the two of us or stand in my driveway and talk?"

His laugh was quiet. She couldn't be accused of making this easy. "All of the above." He paused, almost at ease with his discomfort. It kept him on his toes. "This is very awkward for me. I'm not really up on my dating skills—not that this is exactly a date." To him, a date was dinner, dancing, moonlight, the whole nine yards. But this was close.

Because he seemed momentarily uncomfortable, she wasn't. "Whatever this is, you're doing very nicely."

"Good." He looked into her eyes. "Does that mean I can call you sometime?"

"Yes." She was leaving herself open to disappointment, she upbraided herself. But somehow, the word no just didn't want to materialize on her tongue.

"Good," Rafe repeated. "I'll see you." He smiled at Mollie, then bent and kissed her cheek. "Stay healthy." Rafe surprised Dana by kissing her cheek, as well. "You, too."

Not if he kept making her heart flutter as if it was going to take off, she thought, watching him drive away.

Dana waved in unison with Mollie only because Mollie urged her to.

"I really am going to marry him, Aunt Dana," Mollie declared, taking Dana's hand. "He's the nicest man I ever met—except for Daddy. But I think he's as nice as Daddy." She paused, her small face suddenly troubled. "Is that wrong?"

Dana pushed her jumbled thoughts to the side. "No, baby, there's nothing wrong in liking someone else." *Maybe you should listen to yourself sometime. You've got feelings for the man you won't let come out and you're running for the hills.* "Let's go inside."

All she wanted when she walked into the house was some time to herself to sort out feelings that were ricocheting through her with the energy of handballs in play. But all personal desires had to be put on hold until Mollie went to sleep.

Chattering ceaselessly about Dr. Rafe and her wedding plans thirteen years in the future, Mollie gave every indication of being able to go on all night. But eventually the little girl wore herself out and fell asleep.

Relieved to finally have some time to herself, Dana slipped out of Mollie's room. Dickinson was waiting for her in the hall. Dana started, her hand flying to her chest. She looked at him accusingly.

"Sorry, didn't mean to frighten you," he murmured.

She drew in a long breath, then let it out, getting herself under control. "How long have you been standing there, Tom?"

The thin lips curved. "She was planning her wedding. I didn't want to interrupt."

Dana smiled, her annoyance vanishing. "Thanks."

And then Dickinson was all polite business again. "Your father would like to see you."

Now what? Dana turned toward the stairs, resigned. "All right."

Paul Morrow's eyes met hers when she entered the den. She had the impression he'd been staring at the door the entire time, willing her to come. Waiting. "Took you long enough."

"Mollie was too excited to sleep." That was enough of an

explanation. "Tom said you wanted to see me. What's this about?" She had a feeling she knew. Somehow, her father must have found out about Wallace hiring her. He was undoubtedly going to forbid her from setting foot in the office.

Prepared for the clash, she was surprised to hear her father ask, "How is Mollie adjusting?"

Dana watched his face warily. Where was this leading? "Fine. She seems to be a lot more resilient than I thought she'd be."

His shrug was careless, vague. "They say children are."

"But you wouldn't have any firsthand knowledge about things like that, would you?" The look in his eyes was sharp, alert. "Sorry. I can't remember you ever asking after anyone's well-being before."

Though he stared at her intently, what he was seeing was the girl she'd once been. Even at Mollie's age, she'd stood before him defiantly. He remembered being torn between annoyance and a certain amount of pride at the backbone she'd displayed, even then. "Maybe I've learned a few things."

Dana studied his expression. There was more here than what she was hearing. "Such as?" she asked slowly.

"Such as perhaps I might have conducted some business the wrong way. Such as perhaps I've placed my trust in the wrong people." His eyes narrowed. "And distrusted the wrong ones."

The calm before the storm. Dana braced herself for the onslaught of temper she knew was to come. "What wrong people?"

For the second time in the space of five minutes, her father surprised her. "The former? People I work with. The latter? You."

Her head felt as if it had been punted straight into a thick fog. "You're going to have to get more specific than that, Counselor."

"I know that," he snapped, then struggled with his temper, something he'd never bothered trying to contain before. Not here, in his own home, where pretenses weren't necessary.

Where he could throw off the harnesses of frustration and image and act upon their effects. "You think this is easy?"

She refused to be intimidated. Instead, she met his look and matched it. "If I knew what you were doing, I could answer that."

He blew out a breath. Words, they were only words. He'd used endless words before. He was a master. Why was this so difficult for him?

Because these words mattered, really mattered.

Every one of them stung as they left his tongue. "I'm trying to apologize."

She stared at him, the fog worsening. "About what and to whom?"

"Don't play dumb, gir—Dana," he corrected himself, gritting his teeth.

He couldn't be doing what she thought he was doing. Could he?

"In this case, I don't have to play, I am." A ghost of a smile flirted with her lips. "And thanks for remembering my name."

He looked at her in annoyed surprise. "Of course I remember your name. I gave it to you."

Dana stared at him. "You gave— I didn't know that."

She'd assumed her mother had named her, just as she'd named Megan. Megan was named after their maternal grandmother. Dana had never asked who she was named after. That way she could make up stories in her head when she was very young. Stories that made her feel special. As special as she desperately wanted to be.

For a second her father savored the minor triumph. "There are a great many things you don't know. A great many." His eyes grew distant, looking into the past. His past. "Dana was my sister's name."

Dana sank on the love seat facing him. "You have a sister?"

Her question jerked him to the present. "Had. She died when she was little more than Mollie's age."

Sadness. Was that sadness she heard in his voice? Her father? Dana studied him more closely. "How…"

"Parental neglect." It had been more than that. It had been parental abuse, but he had no desire to go into that. His agitation grew. "I wasn't there." He looked at her sharply, helpless frustration in his eyes. Just as there had been in his soul when it had happened. "What does it matter? Dead is dead."

It mattered, she thought. Mattered a great deal. Dana realized that this was the closest she'd ever felt to her father. "If you named me after her, you must have loved her."

He was about to deny it, to clamp the lid on his personal feelings, but that would have been like denying his sister's existence, and he couldn't bring himself to do it.

"Yes, I did. Mollie reminds me a little of her." And then suddenly, because this had cost him too much, his expression changed completely. Darkened so quickly it startled her. "I know that Wallace came here, offering you a job. Trying to get you to side with him."

"And just how do you know that?"

He waved her question away. "That's unimportant."

But Dana stood her ground. "Not to me."

His energy was limited, and he wasn't about to spend it on trivial details. "Will you just listen?" he demanded. "I also know what you said to him. Verbatim. Why?" His eyes pinned her. If she lied to him, he would know.

She tried to recall her exact words to Wallace. Just what was it her father was after? "Why did I say that to him?" she asked, guessing.

"Yes." He spat the word out.

She didn't understand why he was so angry with her. Did he resent her being on his side? Was that it? "Because it was true."

He both hated and admired the fact that she read him so well. "Why should you care?"

She looked at him for a long moment, trying to fathom what he was thinking, what he was after. It was impossible.

"If you have to ask, then the answer won't mean anything to you."

He nodded slowly, as if to himself. He had his answer, his confirmation. Hearing it seemed suddenly superfluous. "I do the hiring and firing at the firm."

Dana rose. "That's what I thought. I accepted Wallace's offer because—" When he caught her by the hand, she could only stare uncomprehendingly at him.

"I know why you accepted. And I appreciate it."

"You do?" She almost stuttered.

As if realizing he'd taken her hand to keep her from leaving, he dropped it. "Stop interrupting. You're making me tired." He drew a deep breath. "Perhaps, for once, Wallace had a good idea." The man's name left a bad taste in his mouth. He and Wallace were going to have it out when the time was ripe. Right now, he was gearing up for Senator Johnson's trial. "At least, half a good idea. I want you to come work for the firm."

Dana felt as if she was hallucinating. "You do?"

"Didn't I just say that?" he snapped, growing exhausted.

That was more like it. "Yes." Dana smiled. "You did."

He nodded, terminating the meeting. "All right then, I expect to see you there in the morning. Don't mess up. Being my daughter doesn't entitle you to any privileges."

She couldn't stop smiling. "I already know that."

"Good. Now get out."

Her smile, bemused and still somewhat confused, didn't fade this time, not even as she left the room.

Chapter 14

The telephone beside her bed was ringing when Dana walked into her room. She picked it up automatically. Only when she'd lifted the receiver from the cradle did it occur to her that the call was most likely for her father.

But it wasn't. The familiar masculine voice on the other end of the line was asking to speak to her.

"Rafe?"

The pleased laugh, unintentionally seductive and sexy, curled through her belly. "I'm flattered that you recognized my voice."

It was so distinctive, there was no way she could mistake his voice for anyone else's. Why was he calling her? "Is something wrong?"

Why would something have to be wrong for him to call her? Couldn't she conceive of him calling just to hear her voice? Or wanting to prolong what had been a very nice evening, dropped in his lap like an unexpected gift?

"No, it's just sometime."

"Sometime?" she repeated when he didn't say anything further. "Sometime what?"

She'd forgotten. It wasn't in her to act coy, he thought. "I asked if I could call you sometime, and you said yes. I decided that this was as good a sometime as any."

No one could ever have accused her of being the nervous type. Yet with Rafe that was exactly what she became. A woman whose nervousness kept surfacing, full blown, with the thought of each encounter. She felt like someone stuck in a dream, doomed to repeat it until someone woke her up.

"But I just saw you," she pointed out.

"Which is what makes this a good time," he countered. The soft chuckle made her feel itchy. Itchy in places that couldn't be scratched. "You know, we never did get to go to La Reina Simpatica."

"No," she agreed slowly, "we didn't." She wrapped both hands around the receiver, waiting. Calling herself an idiot for acting so adolescent. So confused. She was hoping he'd spell it out and ask her for a date. Yet if he did…

She looked at her still-flat belly. If he did, where could this go? Nowhere.

"I'm free Friday night. Would that be all right with you?" The soft-spoken question seduced her senses and secured the answer before she realized she'd formed it.

"Friday would be fine with me."

He gave her the particulars. She heard herself murmuring, agreeing. And her fate was sealed.

Dana hung up feeling better than she knew she should. But no self-inflicted lecture to the contrary could wipe the smile from her face.

T.G.I.F.

Dana turned the letters and the phrase they stood for over in her mind as she let herself into the house. Thank God It's Friday. It was a good phrase. She acknowledged it down to the very bottom of her being. She didn't think she could have borne it if it was only Thursday.

On an absolute scale, working for her father was turning out to be far more difficult than rescuing the victims of that car accident had been.

She dropped her purse on the hall table, missed and left it where it fell on the floor, too tired to pick it up. She stepped out of her shoes while rotating her stiff neck. Her mind was on the last encounter she and her father had had. Last battle was more like it. He wanted his answers almost as quickly as he thought of the questions, and he expected her to produce them, not excuses. She was in a position to have to anticipate his tartly worded requests, none of which was ever easy.

Dana dropped onto the sofa, every bone in her body aching. Just the way her head was. Paul S. Morrow was a demanding son of a bitch, she thought with a silent nod. He kept her on her toes constantly, dancing to his tune, in what had all the makings of a never-ending nightmare.

But she had to admit that there was a fair amount of satisfaction in continuing the dance, in—so far—not faltering. In showing him she could survive whatever he dished out. For the first time in her life, she was meeting her father on his home turf. And she was keeping up.

It felt good.

She would have sung if she wasn't too damn exhausted to carry a tune. This past week had seemed endless. She would no sooner drop her head on her pillow at night than it was time to get up again and begin the cycle all over. Work and Mollie, Mollie and work. She felt as if she was juggling, and so far, the balls were staying in the air.

With luck, they would continue that way. With more luck, she would get better at it.

One could only hope.

Hope.

She smiled. She liked the sound of that word. It was nice to feel it was in her life again.

She heard the doorbell ring. Odd. Her father was still at the office. Why would someone be calling for him here? She hoped Esther would get rid of whoever it was. She didn't feel like having to put her shoes on again to greet someone.

Out of the corner of her eye, she saw Mollie come flying into the room. The next second, she was being tackled enthusiastically.

"You're home!" Mollie exclaimed.

"Looks like it, pumpkin. Been a good girl?"

"Uh-huh. Irene invited me for a sleep over tonight. Can I go? Can I? Can I?" The words tumbled out faster than the speed of light.

Irene, Irene. Which one was she again? Oh, yes, the one with the heart-shaped face and straight, jet black hair. "Well, I don't know. Did Irene's mother say it's okay?"

"Yes, and she gave me this." From the pocket of her pink and yellow overalls, Mollie pulled out a crumpled envelope.

Dana scanned the contents quickly. It was an invitation to a birthday party sleep over. "Looks in order. But we're going to have to give Irene something. You can't go to a birthday party without a present." And where was she going to get one on such short notice?

"I've *got* a present for her," Mollie told her importantly. "Esther got it for me."

She might have known. God bless Esther—the woman was a saint.

"Then you can go." Mollie's energy was infectious, but only up to a point. "Give me a minute to catch my breath and I'll take you."

"Have you been running?" Mollie peered at her closely.

"It feels that way, baby. It sure feels that way." As she was mustering her strength to rise to her feet and face the prospect of putting her shoes on, Esther entered.

"There's a Dr. Saldana at the door, Miss Dana," she announced politely. It was the voice she used around company.

Mollie looked pleased enough to burst. "Here?" she squealed.

Dana shut her eyes. "Oh, no, I forgot."

The next moment, Rafe was in the room behind Esther, catching Mollie as she hurled herself at him. "Forgot what?"

Dana was on her feet instantly, struggling for the balance she almost lost as she shoved her feet into her shoes. At the last minute, she braced herself on the edge of the sofa. How could shoes that fit so perfectly in the morning pinch so damn much now?

Dana swung to face him. "Our—our bet. I'm not dressed."

Still holding Mollie, who had wrapped her legs partially around him like an agile little monkey, Rafe scrutinized Dana. She was wearing a teal suit with a pencil-slim skirt and a hot pink blouse. The hot pink reminded him of a strawberry sundae and conjured up the words *good enough to eat* in his mind like a reflex.

"Those look like clothes to me," he noted mildly, his tone betraying neither what he was thinking nor what he was fantasizing about.

Dana looked at the single-breasted suit she'd unbuttoned long ago. This wasn't what she would have chosen to wear on a date. Unless it was a date with an accountant. "Well, yes, but—"

"La Reina doesn't have a dress code, and neither do I. Clothes are clothes." He set Mollie down.

"Are you taking Aunt Dana out?" Mollie wanted to know.

With the crush she had on him, Mollie might feel left out, Dana thought. Why not take her along? There was safety in numbers.

"I'm trying to, Mollie," he admitted. "Give me a hand?"

She gave him two and placed both on Dana's posterior, then shoved as hard as she could. "Go," Mollie ordered.

"You heard her." Rafe laughed, hooking his arm through Dana's. "C'mon, Miss Morrow, you're not talking your way out of this one. I've actually got another doctor covering my calls for the rest of the night. Don't tell me I've done all this juggling for nothing."

Esther slipped out, then rematerialized, silently holding

Dana's purse aloft. There seemed to be no fighting city hall tonight.

Dana sighed, giving up. "See that Mollie gets to her slumber party," she told Esther as she took the purse from her.

Esther nodded. "Already done, miss."

"No, it's not," Mollie protested. "I'm still here."

"A slumber party, huh?" Rafe asked. "Why don't we drop Mollie off on the way? That way you get to see her off yourself and check things out. You'll feel better."

"Yes," she agreed. "I will."

He was thoughtful without being prodded. That said a lot about a man. There seemed to be no antidote for the warm, pleased feeling tucking itself around her. Nor was she looking for one. For now.

Dana discovered that Mollie was already ready. Her overnight case had been packed within half an hour of her return from preschool. The present, a large picture puzzle, was wrapped in paper decorated with teddy bears leapfrogging over birthday cakes. Rafe carried both to his car while Mollie danced beside him, telling him all about Irene and what they planned to do tonight.

Watching, Dana thought Rafe looked incredibly domesticated. The scene suited him. She wished with all her heart that someone like Rafe had been the father of her child. Then she would have someone to share this with. Someone to love her child along with her.

"Don't get left behind," Esther told her. She waved Dana on her way. "When shall I tell Mr. Morrow you'll be back?"

"Before Christmas," Dana called, then closed the door firmly behind her.

Rafe looked amused when she approached the car. He placed Mollie in the back, then helped her with her seat belt. "I had no idea you took that long to eat a meal."

"Old habit." Dana checked the security of Mollie's seat belt before getting into the front seat. "I don't like being held accountable for my time." The metal tab of the seat belt clicked as it slid into the slot, punctuating her statement. And terminating it.

Rafe turned the key, and the car rumbled to life. "Esther's probably only asking because she knows your father might worry if he doesn't know when to expect you."

When had he gotten Esther's name? She didn't remember introducing them or mentioning it. He must have asked her, she surmised. As for why Esther had asked, she knew the answer to that. And she also knew why her father would want to be informed. Because knowing her whereabouts, her time-table, kept him in control, and he always had to be in control. Obsessively so. Now more than ever, to prove that he was still the man he once was.

"My father doesn't worry," she told Rafe simply. "He just likes being in charge."

"I take it working for your father isn't turning out."

"Oh, it's turning out," she informed him. "But it doesn't put blinders on me, either."

He sincerely doubted, as he glanced at the address on the invitation Dana handed him, that anything could blind Dana to what she perceived as the truth.

"So?"

His gaze, penetrating, unwavering and amused, made her want to wiggle her toes. And, just maybe, other parts of her body, as well.

"So?" she repeated innocently. She hid the smile she felt forming behind her glass of cider. The soft murmur of voices in the restaurant faded into soothing background noise as she looked into his eyes. For a nonalcoholic drink, the cider certainly packed a punch. Or was it his eyes that did that?

"What's the verdict, Counselor?" Rafe prodded. "About the food?"

The term, the one she used with her father, caught her by surprise. It took her a moment to collect herself.

"All things considered..." Dana paused long enough to keep him dangling, then smiled. "I guess I'll be picking up the tab for dinner. You win. This is better—although it is pretty close." She looked at her empty plate. It had been so good that even when she was full, she had continued eating.

The waitress arrived with the check. When she placed it on the table, Dana reached for it, but Rafe covered the small tray with his hand. She looked at him in surprise. "What are you doing?"

He raised a brow. "Taking the check."

That wasn't their agreement. "I thought I was supposed to pay."

He'd never meant to collect. That wasn't the way he'd been raised, current mores notwithstanding. "I only said that to appeal to your sense of competition." He glanced at the total to calculate the tip. "I thought it was the best way to get you to come."

She didn't know whether to be flattered or uneasy that he seemed to have her number. "How would you know if I had a sense of competition?"

Rafe rolled his eyes. "Oh, please. I've never met a more competitive woman in my life." He took out his wallet. "You live for it. It's in your body language."

She stiffened. "I wasn't aware that my body had a language."

His smile unfurled slowly as his eyes slid over her. Dana felt as if her suit just vanished, leaving her in a teddy that would all too soon be snug.

"Trust me, it does." Instead of his charge card, Rafe took out several bills and placed them on the tray to cover the bill, along with a healthy tip.

Dana looked at the tray. "Money. How quaint. I didn't think people used money anymore." Good with numbers, Dana knew exactly what their dinner had cost. The size of the tip wasn't lost on her. Thoughtful *and* generous. The man was almost too good to be true. Where was the flaw? There was always a flaw.

"Old-fashioned, I guess. I only keep plastic for emergencies." He pocketed his wallet as the waitress came to claim the tray. He smiled his thanks at her, then turned toward Dana. "So, what would you like to do next? Go dancing?"

Her feet miraculously no longer hurt, but she didn't think that being in his arms, even in a crowd, would be the wisest move for her to make at the moment. She was seeing too much in his favor to remain on the safe side of her feelings right now.

"Truthfully?"

"Always."

She almost believed he meant that. But in her experience, people didn't always want the truth. Not when a lie could do better.

Dana sighed. "I'd like to walk off this meal. I feel like I've gained a ton. I think seeing you is definitely bad for my waistline." It was intended as a joke, but the words stuck in her throat. It wasn't seeing Rafe that was going to erase her waist.

Rafe leaned back as if studying her. He didn't need to. Her trim figure had become etched in his mind, though it had happened unintentionally. "Your waistline looks fine from where I'm sitting."

She laughed, dismissing the compliment. Right now, she wanted him to be nasty, to say one wrong thing, even half wrong, so she could pick a fight and go home. So she could squelch this desire to linger with him. "That's because from where you're sitting, you can't see it."

He laid his napkin on the table. "Then by all means, let's go for a walk, so I can make a better assessment of the subject under discussion."

Rafe rose and managed to pull back her chair for her before she could do it herself. Once again she thought he moved fast for a man his size. Almost too fast to suit her.

When Dana got to her feet, he slipped his hand around her waist to guide her out.

"Feels fine to me," he commented, as if he was taking her measure. "Maybe even on the thin side."

Color flooded her cheeks. That would change, she thought.

And soon. But as quickly as the thought surfaced, she banked it down. It had no place here, tonight, with him.

She had no place here tonight with him, she insisted silently. What had she been thinking, accepting his invitation?

She'd been thinking it would be nice, just for the space of an evening, to enjoy the company of a man she was beginning to think a great deal of—just as a friend, she insisted to herself.

"Are you warm?" he asked inside the entrance.

"What?"

"Your face, it's flushed." He pushed open the door, and a rush of night air swirled in.

"Yes, it's warm in here," she agreed, taking the handy excuse he'd unwittingly tendered. Standing outside, she took a deep breath, hoping that the color and the warmth that had generated it would leave her.

It was a beautiful night. Soft, serene, with the sky above them like freshly spun velvet. "Would you care to go for a walk on the boardwalk?"

Dana didn't answer. Not out loud. Instead, she laced her fingers through his, unwilling to let words spoil the mood.

There was something almost magical about the boardwalk in Laguna Beach in the early evening. She'd always believed that. During her teens, she'd come here a lot. Sometimes with friends, sometimes hitching a ride, knowing the act was stupid but taking comfort in the fact that it would have turned her father's hair gray if he'd known.

She'd done a lot of stupid things in her time. Maybe this was stupid, too, but she couldn't help herself. Didn't want to. She needed the paradoxically exciting serenity she felt being here with Rafe.

Dana smiled. She felt very close to being at peace for one of the few times in her life. The ocean softly sighed on her right, while on the left small arts-and-crafts shops and homes were interspersed with trees as old as the California coastline. The soft late spring breeze that accompanied them on their stroll completed the scene, making it almost too perfect.

Could something be too perfect?

Yes, she thought, when it wasn't real. Perfect was never real.

"So, you didn't tell me. How does it feel, working for your father?" Rafe asked.

The question, following on the heels of a comfortable, mutual silence, roused her. But she didn't have to think to answer.

"Scary. Exhilarating. One minute I think he's waiting for me to fall flat on my face, the next I almost feel he's hoping to see me succeed." Even as she said it, it seemed hard to believe. "I think being sick has mellowed him. I never thought anything would."

He knew better than she did about that. "Mortality has a way of kicking you right in the gut, making you see what a fool you've been about taking things for granted."

There was something in his voice that caught her attention. When she looked at him, his face was turned from hers. He was looking up. At someone he saw in his mind's eye?

"You sound as if you have firsthand experience."

He looked at her, a little embarrassed at drifting away. "I do. My wife died a few years ago."

"Your wife? I didn't know you were married." Somehow, she'd assumed he hadn't been. The information created a crack in the intimacy that had been building. And maybe that was for the best, she thought. If there were things in the way, obstacles, she couldn't, wouldn't be drawn to him.

He nodded, concentrating on fighting back the pain. Like an adversary relentlessly searching for a weak spot, it always found him if he let his guard down.

"Two years. It should have been longer. But Debra wanted to wait until I was through with medical school." His smile was distant, wistful, shrouded with memories. And suddenly Dana ached to have someone feel that way about her. "Thought she'd distract me otherwise."

Her response was automatic. She squeezed his hand, wanting to hug him, to tell him that, in a way, she understood.

That though their paths were different, that the events they'd gone through were different, she'd lost love, too, at the hand of someone she'd mistakenly loved.

"I'm very sorry, Rafe."

He heard the feeling in her voice, and it warmed him. "Yeah, me, too. She was a wonderful person. Supportive, always thinking of others, always willing to put other people ahead of herself." He glanced at Dana. "You know, she wasn't a thing like you."

He was smiling, and his eyes were kind, but his words... His words weren't. Dana stopped walking. "Excuse me? I'm a little confused here. Was that just an insult?"

It had come out wrong. "No, I didn't mean it that way. You're independent, Debra wasn't—" He tried again. "What I'm trying to say is that the two of you are very different from one another. Your personalities are like night and day. And yet...and yet I find myself very attracted to you."

"Attracted?" she whispered.

There was a noise in her ears, a thumping sound. Her heart? The air going in and out of her lungs? Or her pulse, which was suddenly competing in the hundred-meter dash?

"Completely." Unable to hold himself in check any longer, Rafe wove his fingers into her hair, tilting her head slightly as he brought his mouth close to hers. "I haven't felt anything for another woman since Debra died. But I feel something for you. I think I did the first moment I noticed you."

The noise stopped only long enough for her to hear him, then started again. Louder. Oh, God, was he going to kiss her?

Oh, please, let him kiss her.

"I guess I made it difficult not to notice me."

"Very."

He brought his mouth to hers. This time there was no hesitancy on her part. No list of reasons she shouldn't. Only one reason she should.

Because she desperately wanted to.

Her mouth met his with the urgency of a woman who needed to feel like one. With contact, with just the promise of contact, her blood heated instantly.

Stretching to the maximum, Dana wound her arms around his neck, letting herself go. Free-falling into the kiss, into the haven he had to offer, her body pressed close against his.

Rafe felt around the wall until his fingers came in contact with the light switch. He flipped it into the up position, and his apartment became instantly visible.

He couldn't help wondering if she was comparing it to what she was accustomed to. It probably didn't hold a candle to anything she'd ever seen. Still, he couldn't bring himself to feel embarrassed by it. This was home, such as it was, and it suited his purposes.

But none of those purposes had ever included bringing a woman like her here.

She liked it, Dana thought. There was the feel of home to it. Oh, not like hers, but then, hers had never felt like home, only a neatly cleaned display case.

Dana surveyed the room. There was just enough clutter to make it look pleasantly lived in. Her father couldn't abide clutter. As a child, she was never allowed to spread her things on the floor even for a little while. Everything always had to be put neatly away. After a while, she ceased bothering to take anything out. It was easier that way.

His apartment made her feel safe. Which was absurd, because she wasn't. Not here, alone with him, the one person she realized she could so easily let herself make a mistake with.

Dana glanced toward the door he closed behind him. "Rafe, maybe I should go."

Her bravery was gone. She was someone else now. Someone who attracted him even more. "Are you afraid of me?"

"No, of course not." She shot the words back too quickly. It was herself she was afraid of. Her weakness. Her needs. "It's just that—"

He didn't wait for her to finish. His mouth skimmed over

her lower lip, barely tasting it. Barely branding her. "Just that...what?"

Her head was spinning. "I forget," she breathed as his lips slowly worked their way down her throat. Her eyes began to flutter shut even as her body tingled with razor-edged anticipation.

With the feel of his hands along her skin.

From out of nowhere, a frenzy took hold of her. A frenzy, powerful and overwhelming, that urged her to take what he offered, to lose herself in the solace of his mouth, his touch, his body, before her mind gained control.

Before she could stop herself.

Because she didn't want to. More than anything, she wanted this, wanted to feel again, to glory in a man's desire again. *This* man's desire. She began to tug urgently at his shirt, pulling it from his waistband, fumbling at his buttons, even as he responded in kind. They undressed each other in a flurry of garments, questing hands and warm, promising kisses that raced faster than their fingers did.

Rafe wasn't sure how it happened or who took the first step. All he knew was that suddenly he was playing with fire.

And if he got singed, if he got burned to a crisp, it was one hell of a way to go.

He'd had that feeling, even if he hadn't acknowledged it, the first time she'd walked into his life, breathing fire, demanding the best for Mollie.

He'd brought her here to be alone with her. In his heart, he hadn't really known he was going to make love with her until it began happening. And then there was no question but that, somehow, it was meant to happen.

The time-honored tradition of lovemaking became something new to him that night. New because, even at the height of what he'd had with Debra, he'd never encountered such passion, such need, before. Debra had been pliable in his arms, loving and giving, but she'd never been quicksilver, first one thing and then another. Never fire and passion. Never raw need and sex.

As soon as it began, Rafe felt his desire ignited and brought to new highs, new levels. It took all he could do to harness it, to keep from taking her then and there. Somehow he maintained a shred of control. Control so he could show her what he felt before it consumed him.

He was putting her needs above his own. The thought startled her. Dana could feel him holding himself back while his hands evoked symphonies from her body. Finding secret places to make her vibrate with feeling, with sensations that rocked her and left her exhausted, yet wanting more, he stroked, caressed and conquered.

He took her breath away, not with his technique, not with his magnificent body, hard, primed, but with the gentleness that was at the heart of him. He seemed determined to bring her to the heights ahead of him, to keep her on that edge, drawing her back and taking her there again, until he was finally ready to meet her there himself.

This was something new, something entirely different. Entirely wondrous. She didn't want it to end, didn't want the coldness of thought and logic to find her here, hiding in the shelter of his arms, of his body as it cleaved to hers.

But more than that, she wanted him. Wanted him to feel this echoing crescendo of climaxes he'd created within her. With her last ounce of strength, she arched against him, tempting him. Opening for him.

There was nothing left in him with which to resist. Holding back was no longer possible. Murmuring her name like a prayer, he entered her. And burned all the bridges that ever existed behind him.

Chapter 15

Horror and guilt, sharpened, hurtful, pushed through the layers of euphoria, peeling them apart from within like so much ugliness, swelling, emerging and destroying a thing of beauty.

And then there was only a glaring awareness of what had happened. What she had allowed to happen.

How could she have done such a thing?

It was bad enough making love with one man while carrying another man's child, but how could she have put herself at risk like this again, baring her emotions, her soul, to a man? All but handing herself over to him, to do with what he would, after she had sworn never again to give any man that kind of power over her.

Dana didn't know what had come over her. Never, even in her so-called wild period, had she gone to bed with a man after knowing him such a short time. No matter what her father thought, she had values.

That was just the trouble. Somehow Rafe seemed to fit in with her values.

And that scared her most of all. Because it felt right,

seemed right. But it couldn't *be* right. Dana knew all about being lulled into a false sense of security. Believing herself to be at a wonderful place in her life, only to have it blow apart on her. Just like her mother before her.

Just like her relationship with Steven.

Wow.

All Rafe could think of was *Wow,* with a capital *W.* Whatever had just happened here, sex, lovemaking, passion, whatever name it chose to go under, he'd never experienced anything like it before. He felt as if every fiber of his being was carrying on its own celebration of the Fourth of July.

Rafe wasn't sure he could even move. But when he felt Dana stirring beside him, he knew he had to. Wanted to. Turning, he moved to put his arm around her, to hold her close and soak in this feeling that was blanketing him.

But Dana was already sitting up.

The sheets were too tangled to be of any use, and her clothes were out of reach, so Dana gathered Rafe's jacket around her to cover herself as best she could. Shame, embarrassment and anger all tugged relentlessly at her, fighting for the larger share.

How could she have let this happen?

Dana felt tears gathering in her eyes, and she cursed herself for this inopportune overflow of emotions. It had to be the pregnancy playing havoc with her hormones. She never cried, yet right now, she felt like she was comprised completely of tears.

He saw them immediately, the tears shimmering in her eyes. Bewildered, confused, Rafe sat up beside her.

"What's the matter? Did I hurt you?" He brushed one tear away as it emerged on her cheek. It felt as if it burned his fingertip. He felt instantly guilty. "Oh, God, Dana, I'm sorry. I meant to be gentle, to go slower, but you were so incredible, so passionate, all I could do was just hold on." Talking about it gave him a rush, the depth of which still rocked him. "Anyone ever tell you how extraordinary you are?"

She struggled hard not to shake, not to let any more tears free.

"All the time," she retorted hoarsely. "Men take out full-page ads in the *Times* telling the world how extraordinary I am in bed."

He heard pain beneath the words and didn't understand why, even though he was trying. "I'm sorry, that was insensitive. You're going to have to wait until my brain catches up to my body."

She was on her feet instantly, agilely executing a maneuver that kept her modesty intact. *A little late for that, don't you think?* a small voice asked inside her brain.

"I can't wait." Quickly, she swept her clothes into her arms and propelled herself toward his bathroom. "I've got to go."

"Go?" He jumped off the bed, naked and unembarrassed by it. "Dana, don't go. Not yet. Dana, what's wrong?"

He found himself talking to his bathroom door as she closed it in his face. He heard the lock click. Stunned, stumped, he hurried into his pants, wanting to be ready for anything.

"Dana, if it's something I did, something I said, I'm sorry. Dana, please, don't run off this way. Talk to me." He was at the door, talking through it. Trying to reach her. "Just tell me what I did and give me a chance to apologize."

Dana pushed her hands through the sleeves of her blouse. With shaking fingers she did up the buttons and managed to mismatch them by one. She didn't have time to redo them. She had to get away from here. Away before she made even more of a fool of herself.

"You made love with me," she accused.

He waited and heard nothing more. "Yes, and...?"

She looked in the mirror. Tears made her look like someone suffering through a bad bout of the flu. Hurriedly, she threw water on her face, trying to make herself presentable. "That's it."

"That's it?" He stared at the door as if, somehow, his

expression, his thoughts, could penetrate the wood. "Dana, I can't apologize for that, for being made to feel for the first time in so long." Frustration, needing an ally, roused anger. "Besides, you weren't just a passive recipient here. You made love back." He thought of the way she'd thrown herself into their lovemaking. "Hell, you started it."

The door swung open. She glared at him, breathing fire.

"*I* started it? I'm not the one who nibbled on your lower lip. I'm not the one who kissed your throat, making it impossible for you to breathe."

A sense of satisfaction rose, ready to quell the argument before it went any further. It felt good, hearing that she'd reacted to him the way he had to her.

"You did later," he reminded her.

"Later doesn't count." Pushing past him, she located her shoes and scooped them up.

He was right on her heels, growing more confused.

"What the hell is that supposed to mean?" He passed his hand over his head, a tension headache sprouting just above his eyes. "And what are we fighting about? I lost the thread."

She spun on her heel, furious with him, but even more furious with herself. "We're fighting about lovemaking, we're fighting about trust, we're fighting about—oh, damn it all to hell, you're just confusing me." With a strangled cry, she grabbed her purse and ran for the door.

"Dana, at least let me drive you home," he called after her.

"No!"

She was gone before he had a chance to put on his shoes. Cursing, he went after her barefoot. The magnitude of the curses grew as he hurried after her. The entrance to his garden apartment was paved with rough stones that bruised the soles of his feet as he ran. The pain made him angrier.

He caught up to her quickly enough. "Damn it, woman, you are not going out at this time of night to try to hail a cab."

"I can do whatever I want!" she retorted, moving away

from him. He was already trying to control her. She'd been right to run when she did.

"The hell you can." He grabbed her arm and pulled her roughly toward the carport and his car.

Angry, afraid, she tried to pull away from him. She might as well have been playing tug-of-war with a grizzly. Her chances of winning were about the same.

Desperate, not sure what he was capable of, Dana tried to brazen him out. "Let go of me or I'll scream."

Working hard at controlling what was going on inside him, Rafe unlocked the car. He yanked open the door on her side.

"I wouldn't advise that." With his hand on her head, Rafe pushed Dana into her seat, policeman-style.

His temper was begging for release, but he knew he would say something that he wouldn't be able to take back, and there was just the slimmest chance that, someday, he might want to. Although right now, he figured they would be ice-skating in hell before that happened.

He kept his silence, knowing he wasn't ready to trust himself yet. Dana stared straight ahead, not uttering a word, cocooning herself in silence.

Though she hated herself for it, for the weakness it symbolized, one rebellious tear overflowed and slid down her left cheek.

Rafe saw it as he turned toward her at the intersection.

Instantly, guilt ate a hole through him.

"Oh, damn it, Dana. I can't stand to see a woman cry." His mother had cried once in helpless frustration because of the way he and Gabe were behaving. It had almost broken his heart. Seeing her that way had generated a turnaround in him. From that day forward, he'd made sure he and Gabe never gave her any more trouble.

It hurt almost as much, seeing Dana cry.

Unable to stop, unwilling to talk, Dana turned her head away.

"I didn't mean that you had to—oh, hell, have it your

way.'' For a second, he swore roundly, then shut his mouth. He left the rest unsaid. But he thought it.

They arrived at her house in what seemed like record time. Still, Rafe had managed to calm down enough to attempt to reason with her again, to find out what it was that had caused her to do such an about-face.

He never had the chance. Dana bolted from the car the instant it came to a stop.

Frustrated all over again, Rafe thought of running after her, of demanding to know what the hell was going on. He decided against it. Her old man would probably have him up on some kind of trespassing charges before he got within two feet of her.

And besides, they could both stand a little time apart to cool off.

It sounded reasonable. Only trouble was, he wasn't feeling very reasonable. He was feeling cheated and abandoned and a great many other things he didn't even know how to begin to describe.

Resigned, Rafe drove away.

Dana let herself into the house as quietly as she could, praying her father was asleep. Or at least out of the way.

For once, her luck held.

She raced up the stairs as silently as she could, her heart pounding with each step she took. She thought her throat was going to burst before she reached her room. Once she did, she threw herself facedown on her bed.

The comforter muffled her sobs.

Like red dye that can never be completely eradicated once it has come in contact with something, Dana remained on Rafe's mind all his waking hours. Sleeping, it was even worse. She slipped into his dreams, and suddenly he was making love with her all over again, experiencing an entire kaleidoscope of feelings, just as he had the first time.

Then he would wake up, more exhausted than when he'd first lain down. And still wanting her.

Angry and confused by the way she'd invaded his mind, he thought of calling her, but to say what? He'd tried to apologize, and that had led to nothing.

And nothing was what he had.

This was absurd, to let a woman, a woman he hardly knew, get to him this way. Especially when there was a good woman waiting for him.

As if to talk himself out of the madness buzzing in his brain, Rafe sought out the one person he thought could neutralize what he was going through. The woman he *should* be having these feelings about.

It was late, and Kate was about to go to bed when she heard the doorbell. Wondering who could be calling at this hour, she made her way to the door and cautiously looked through the peephole.

She had to be wrong.

Kate opened the door and looked at Rafe in stunned but immensely pleased surprise. "Rafe, what are you doing here?"

"Looking for my sanity. Can I come in?"

She realized she was blocking the way. "Of course." She stepped back, letting him enter. "I don't think I understand. What do you mean, you're here looking for your sanity?"

Rafe shook his head. "Never mind, poor joke."

He looked beleaguered, but he was here, and that was all that mattered. Kate thought of quickly changing into her clothes, then decided not to. Maybe he wanted to find her like this, ready for bed. Maybe bed was where he needed her.

She laced her fingers through his and drew him to the bedroom. "You look tense, Rafe. I told you that your hours were too long. Looks like they finally caught up to you."

It wasn't his hours that had caught up to him, Rafe thought. It felt more like his heart had finally found him in.

But he wasn't here to think of Dana. He'd come here looking for Kate, for what he could have with Kate if he only let himself.

"Here, let me help you work out the knots." Kate made him sit on the edge of the bed. She knelt behind him and began kneading his shoulders. "I used to do this for my father at the end of the day. He'd come home tense, frustrated. I'd start kneading his shoulders, and pretty soon he was himself again." As she worked, Kate leaned forward and pressed a kiss to Rafe's neck.

He closed his eyes, wishing he could feel something. Knowing that he was capable of feeling, really feeling, not just reacting like a normal male. But there was nothing, nothing like what he'd experienced with Dana.

Damn Dana, anyway.

He felt sorry for Kate and wished with all his heart that it was different between them. That it was her scent that lingered in his head, instead of Dana's. That it was her voice he heard echoing in his brain, instead of Dana's. "Did you do that for your father, too?"

"No, that's special," she whispered, her voice husky. "Just for you."

Dropping her hands and all pretense of massaging the tension away, Kate moved in front of him. She slipped her robe from her shoulders. Wearing only a thin cotton nightgown, she slid onto his lap, linking her hands around his neck.

The kiss was deep, ardent and soulful. She moaned, pressing herself closer to him, wanting him. Trying her best to make him want her. His heart didn't have to be in it. She could wait for that. As long as she had a part of him, it would be enough for now.

Rafe tried, really tried, to feel something, to let Kate's kiss captivate him the way Dana's had. It would be so simple with Kate. He knew where he stood with her, knew what she wanted of him. He didn't have a clue when it came to Dana. In all honesty, he didn't even know what it was he felt for Dana, only that with her, he *was* capable of feeling.

Unlike with Kate.

Very slowly, he took her hands from his neck. When she

looked at him, dazed, bewildered, he felt like the cruelest man alive. "Kate, I just can't do this. It's wrong. I'm sorry."

Kate sighed, dragging her hand through her hair. The air seemed to shudder from her. Embarrassed, she rose and picked up her robe, then slipped it on. She knew in her heart what he was saying to her, even if she didn't want to hear it.

"So am I, Rafe. So am I." She tied the sash tight, as if that could somehow protect her. "Why did you come here tonight?"

He wouldn't insult her by lying. "I was hoping that I could feel something."

For a moment, temper rose in her eyes. "The way you can with her? The woman who came into the ER with you? You're running some kind of comparison test? What am I, the control case?" she guessed. "Litmus paper?"

"No, you're a wonderful woman, with wonderful qualities." He wanted to hold her, to make her feel better, but he knew it would only accomplish the opposite if he did. "A man would have to be crazy not to want you."

She tried to muster a smile and almost succeeded. "So why don't you?"

He released her hands and rubbed the back of his neck. "Maybe I am crazy. I honestly thought everything that could feel that way about a woman was dead inside me." Gone, along with Debra.

Rafe looked at Kate, trying to make her understand. He hadn't come with the intention of using her, only of seeking her aid. "I thought that if anyone could bring those feelings to life, you could."

Bitterness twisted her lips even as she accepted the inevitable. "But I can't, and she did. To the victor, the spoils." Her expression softened a little as she looked at him. It would be so much easier if she could be angry at him, but she couldn't. It wasn't his fault. It just wasn't meant to be. "So what's her name, this victor?"

They were still friends. There was solace in that. "Dana

Morrow.'' His expression was rueful. ''And I don't know about the victor, Kate. She's a hell of a complicated woman.''

Kate took in the information philosophically. ''Maybe that was my problem right from the start. I was too damn simple.'' She looked into his eyes, hoping, she supposed, for a spark of something to work with. She knew before she looked that it wouldn't be there. ''My message was there in big block letters.'' Kate sighed and sat beside him on the bed, a bed she knew they would never share again. ''So now what?''

He shrugged, at a loss. ''I wish I knew.''

''I have a suggestion.'' When he looked at her, waiting, she told him pleasantly, ''Get out of my house.'' Then she smiled. ''And thanks.''

He rose to his feet when she did. ''I don't understand.''

Kate led the way to her front door. ''It's very simple. Another man would have tried to use me, to use the situation, before he went on his way. Gotten what he could. But you didn't. It's pretty obvious the way I feel about you.'' Fondness entered her eyes as she lightly touched his cheek. ''Even you couldn't miss it.''

He took her hand and lightly pressed his lips to her knuckles, sincerely thankful for her understanding. ''I care too much about you to do that to you.''

He still didn't see it, did he? Still didn't see what attracted her to him. It wasn't his killer looks, it was his soul.

''It's not me, it's you, Rafe. You're too damn decent.'' She could have been good for him, Kate thought. Really good. Someone else might not be. ''It's going to get you stomped on.''

Kate had the wrong idea about Dana. ''No, it's not like that. Dana's not interested in stomping. Or even in having a fling.''

Opening the door, she could only shake her head. What a waste. ''If she's passing up a fling with you, she's an idiot. Sure you want an idiot?''

He wasn't sure what he wanted, only that he wasn't going to string Kate along when there was no hope. There might

have been. If Dana hadn't entered his life, he wouldn't have
known he was capable of feeling. He would have thought that
what he had with Kate was as good as it could be for him.
Affection based on mutual respect. But now he knew differently, and it wasn't fair to Kate to give her only half of what
she deserved.

"Goodbye, Kate." Lightly, he kissed her lips.

Kate bit back her tears. "Goodbye."

When she closed the door on Rafe, she knew it was for the
last time.

The others around her rose, clearing out of the conference
room as quickly as possible. They gave the impression of
being well-trained rats off to do the piper's bidding. She supposed it was a pretty accurate description.

Dana took her time gathering her files. Friday morning
meetings were always long and grueling, and she wasn't feeling that well.

She hadn't felt well since she'd left Rafe's apartment.

"You seem preoccupied these last few days."

She hadn't realized her father had drawn closer to her.
Showed how bad off she was, she thought. "Just trying to do
a good job, Father." It took an effort to sound aloof, professional, when she felt as if she was falling apart at the seams.

He placed a skeletal hand over the wine-colored leather-
bound pad. Looking at it jarred her back into her surroundings
and completely out of her mental wanderings.

Having caught her attention, he withdrew his hand. "I
know when one of my people is thinking about work. And
when they're lying to me."

Dana tried to bluff her way through. "You missed your
calling, Father. There's a great deal of money to be made in
clairvoyance if you have the right manager." She picked up
the pad and began to leave the room.

Things were better between them than they had ever been,
but that was a long way from perfect.

He was right behind her. "Don't let this, whatever this is,

get in the way of your performance here." He brought the chair around so he blocked her way. "I won't think twice about firing you."

Her office, little more than a glorified cubicle though that made no difference to her, was next to the entrance of the conference room. All she wanted was to reach it.

"I never doubted it for a moment." Taking a chance, she circumvented his chair. "If you'll excuse me, I have some work to do on the Johnson case, as you might recall."

She slipped into her office and sank into her chair. What was the matter with her? Why was she allowing what had happened between her and Rafe to color everything? It had been a week, a whole week since she had run from him, from the trap she'd very nearly walked into. Wasn't that enough time for everything inside her to have settled down?

Apparently not.

She opened a drawer and slipped her pad into it. Contrary to settling down and obligingly shrinking away, her feelings had grown, threatening to become almost unmanageable.

Nothing was unmanageable, she thought, slamming the drawer shut.

Except maybe her waistline.

Today she'd had to struggle with the button on her skirt. Maybe it was her imagination or simple water retention, but it had brought everything home to her that much more vividly.

Hadn't she learned her lesson? Didn't she know that there was no such thing as everlasting love, not for her? Rafe was wonderful now, but Steven had been wonderful once, too. And now look.

Steven.

Dana blew out an impatient breath. She knew what she had to do. She had tried to get in contact with Steven six times. Five more times than she'd thought she would have. Each time she'd gotten his machine. This time—the last time—she was going to leave a message. And if it got erased or was never heard, well, that wasn't her fault. She'd done everything

humanly possible to let Steven know he was going to become
a father.

As if he wanted to know that.

No one would want to know that, she thought. Not Steven
and certainly not her father. Now there was a fun hurdle waiting for her. She didn't look forward to telling her father she
was pregnant.

Dana decided to put that off as long as she could, because
there was no doubt in her mind as to the outcome. Her father
would throw her out, along with Mollie. She wanted to earn
a little more money before that happened. She needed to be
able to afford a decent apartment when the time came.

She'd originally thought she would eventually have to tell
Rafe, as well. But now that wouldn't be necessary. She didn't
need the baby to force them apart. They were apart already.

So why the hell couldn't she stop thinking about him?
About the way he'd looked when passion had claimed her
and they'd made love with such abandon? Every image felt
as if it was burned into her brain.

And she didn't like it.

She also didn't like what she had to do now. Dana pulled
the telephone over, then tapped out the familiar number on
the keyboard.

The phone on the other end rang three times. She braced
herself for the message she was about to leave after his recording ended, but instead of a recording, she heard his
voice—his nonrecorded voice.

Dana swung her chair around to the window, closed her
eyes and tried to pull her thoughts together. *You can get
through this.* She took a deep breath and plunged in. "Steven,
this is Dana."

There was silence, then the voice on the other end mocked
her. "Well, Dana, I wondered when you'd come to your
senses and call."

He rankled her right from the start. "I came to my senses
the day I walked out on you." The hell with preambles and

niceties. Steven didn't deserve them. "I'm calling to tell you I'm pregnant."

She found the curse he uttered offensive, but she said nothing. The sooner she got off the phone, the better.

"Oh, no, you're not pinning that on me. No way are you suckering me into taking this fall."

A part of her had expected him to deny responsibility, but hearing the words uttered with such rancor hurt more than she'd thought it would. "I'm not trying to pin anything on you, but this baby *is* yours. I was faithful to you."

"I can get three guys to swear you hopped into bed with them." A sliver of panic made his voice gain momentum. "More, if I have to. All of them will testify that you slept around. Are you prepared for that?"

How could she ever have been stupid enough to think she loved him? "I'm not even prepared for *this,* though I thought I was." Anger came to her rescue. The slime ball. The pathetic slime ball! "Listen to me, you poor excuse for a human being. I don't want anything from you. I just thought you'd want to know that you were going to be a father."

"Well, I don't. And I'm not. That bastard you're carrying isn't mine, do you hear me?" He was shouting. "It's not mine!"

Her voice was calm, as steely as his was loud. "I hear you, Steven. Loud and clear."

"Good, and don't bother coming back for anything. I threw all your things out, and the brat's, too."

She'd taken most of Mollie's things with her. As for hers, those things belonged to a person she no longer was. She wouldn't have wanted them even if they were still available, but he'd had no right to throw them out.

Without saying a word, Dana let the receiver drop in the cradle. She would have thrown it and the telephone across the room if it wouldn't have gotten her attention she didn't want.

Boy, could she ever pick them.

Trying to tell herself it didn't hurt, that it certainly didn't matter, Dana turned her chair to face her desk. It was then she realized her door was ajar.

And that her father was sitting in the hall.

Dana swallowed a groan. Things were just getting better and better, weren't they?

Chapter 16

Their eyes locked.

There was no way for Dana to pretend her father wasn't there. That he hadn't heard. Unable to dodge the situation, she plowed straight into the heart of it.

Striding over to the door, Dana pushed it open all the way. Her voice was even, deceptively calm, as she asked, "Is this how you operate, Father? Eavesdropping on your employees?"

He directed his chair into her room and turned to face her before answering. His eyes were steely and unfathomable. "Sometimes that's the only way I get to learn things."

Dana closed the door, wishing she'd been this careful to begin with. She crossed her arms and leaned one hip against her desk, bracing herself for the explosion to come. "Conversation would be another."

Dana knew that expression. He was studying her, and she hadn't a clue what he was thinking.

"Up until very recently," he pointed out, "we haven't had

conversations. What we've had were encounters where you would do as much damage as you could, then flee the scene.''

Oh, no, she wasn't about to shoulder the burden of the missteps their relationship had taken. "I wasn't the only one.''

"No," he admitted, "you weren't.''

The admission stunned her. Her father had always portrayed himself as above reproach. Normally he would have lashed out at her, cutting her to ribbons with his tongue. Or trying to. What was going on? And why was he continuing to look at her like that? As if he was sorting things out in his mind, weighing them. Why didn't he say what he had to say and get it over with? Was it that he'd perfected his game since she'd been away, toying with offenders before summarily drawing and quartering them?

When he finally spoke, it was almost a relief. "So, you're pregnant." There wasn't a trace of emotion in his voice.

The calm before the storm.

Dana raised her chin. "Yes, I am." He continued to look at her. Was he waiting for her to apologize? "I suppose you're going to fire me now."

"Why?" The question was so mildly put that, for a moment, she thought she'd imagined it. "There's nothing in your contract with the firm that forbids you to be pregnant."

When she'd returned, he'd raked her over the coals for coming in late. Now he was shrugging off her pregnancy. What the hell was he up to? Dana pinned him with a look, wishing she could see past his facade. "I don't understand."

"How much more simply do you want me to put it?"

Was she hallucinating?

No, this was real, all right, but it was hardly her father's usual m.o. Dana met his eyes, still waiting for the torrent of vilifying words, the anger, the name calling. None of it was happening.

"What I don't understand, Father, is this display of kindness, this show of—for lack of a better word—support on your part."

Was that a shadow of a smile on his face?

Her father turned his chair and looked out the window. The offices of Paul S. Morrow and Associates occupied the entire top floor of the twelve-story building. From here, when it was clear, like today, he felt he could almost look into the heart of the ocean. The wide, bottomless, endless ocean.

That was the way he'd pictured life once, when he'd begun to make a name for himself. He'd felt there was nothing he couldn't accomplish, nothing he couldn't conquer, if he tried hard enough. But he'd been wrong. He couldn't conquer this. Couldn't conquer what was ahead of him. He could only come to terms with it. And it wasn't easy.

"Perhaps," he said slowly, "when a man comes face to face with his own mortality, it has an effect on everything around him, making it appear different than it once did."

Dana moved so she was directly in front of him. Maybe she was crazy, flying in the face of this reprieve, but the memory of her mother wouldn't allow her to let the comment slip quietly by.

"And what kind of effect did Mother's mortality have on you?" There had been no remorse, no hint of acknowledgment of the guilt he bore for that wasted life. If it hadn't been for the showy funeral, Dana would have said he hadn't even noticed her mother had died. Not his wife, but her mother. Jane Morrow had long since stopped being his wife except in name.

Morrow squared shoulders that appeared to be growing ever thinner. "It made me live faster, play harder, expect even more from you and your sister than I already did." His eyes grew distant. Memories intruded on his thoughts, clouding them. "It made me expect more of myself than I already did. I took higher-risk cases, hell-bent on winning at all costs." His mouth curved as his eyes shifted to his daughter. "Justice be hanged, it's the winning that counts, Dana. The thrill of besting the other side. Your mother's death intensified my need to hold on to life." He saw the look entering her eyes and anticipated her. "But your sister's death showed me that no matter what, I couldn't hang on to what was mine."

"If you felt that way, why didn't you come to Megan's funeral?"

"I couldn't. I couldn't face her death. The wounds hadn't healed after your mother's death."

Wounds. Then he *had* felt something, *had* loved them.

"You could have talked to me. We could have been there for each other."

"I didn't know that. I thought you'd only be too pleased to see I had a vulnerable side. Besides, I'd spent all those years building up walls where no one could touch me, hurt me. I didn't know how to dismantle that." He shrugged, helpless to follow any other path than the one he was on. "I'm an old dog, and I don't know any new tricks, so I'll keep doing this one until the circus is finally over for me."

Circus. That was what she'd called their life, *his* life, once. And in truth, at the height of it all, it had seemed that way to her. But not now. Now he and it were respectable and sought-after. There was a great deal of prestige associated with the firm. She supposed he had a right to that. He'd worked hard, sacrificing his family to earn it.

Because the firm's image was tied so closely to his pride, his identity, Dana recanted the irreverent term. "Hardly a circus, Father."

Other memories rose, whispering to him, reminding him of the boy he had been. The boy, at bottom, he would always be. "No, you were right. It is." It was to himself, not to her, that he said, "No matter what I do, I can't leave the con behind."

Dana stared at him, bewildered. Was his mind wandering? Had the disease tainted that, too? "Con?"

Hearing her repeat the word splashed icy water on his thoughts. Regaining himself, he waved his hand, dismissing what he'd said. That belonged to his youth. She needn't know he'd lived by his wits, doing things he wasn't proud of just to put something into his belly.

"Never mind." Before her eyes, he pulled himself together, becoming the man she was accustomed to seeing. Haughty, proud, unyielding. "I'm glad you told that bastard where to get off. You don't need him."

They were in complete agreement on that one. Whatever love she'd felt for Steven was deader than she'd once deemed her father's compassion to be.

"No, I don't." And then a sadness crept in. "But we all need someone."

He looked at his daughter pointedly. "And you have someone."

"You?" she asked uncertainly, unable to believe he was willing to go this far to extend an olive branch to her.

He'd already said more than he should have. She was bright enough to understand. Briskly, he became all business. "I need the notes on the senator's mistress on my desk by three." And then a little of his gruffness receded. "If you're feeling up to it."

"I'm feeling up to it," she answered slowly. It was difficult for her to accept this change in his behavior. She kept waiting to wake up. Or have the trap spring.

But it wasn't a dream, and there was no sign of a trap. Maybe he was on the level.

A bemused smile curved her mouth. "Careful, Father. You act too nice, someone is liable to think you're an impostor."

He laughed shortly. "No chance of that." He opened the door and wheeled himself out. "Remember, no later than three."

"Three," she echoed, closing the door. Dana shook her head in bewilderment. Just when she thought the surprises were over...

"So they still have an annual county fair in Bedford," Dana murmured.

Finishing her toast, she put the A section of the local newspaper on the dining room table. The coming fair, promising to be the best ever—as usual—was the weekly paper's lead story.

It was nice to know there were a few things that hadn't changed. Dana smiled. Some of her favorite memories were centered around going to the fair with Megan. At first, when they were very young, Esther had been in charge of taking them. Although there was one year—one very special year, Dana recalled—when their mother had taken them. That was just before she finally succumbed to her depression. It was as if she'd tried to give her daughters one last memory to treasure.

Later, when they were older, they'd gone to the annual affair with friends. She'd lost her heart and her virginity at the fair late one night behind the fortune-telling tent after everyone else had left the grounds.

This time, her smile was wistful. She'd been so terribly in love. It had lasted all of two months. Two very intense months. It was her first taste of how disappointing love could be.

Still, the fair usually represented the four best days of the year, she remembered. It might be fun to see what it was like now.

Finished with breakfast, Mollie scooted off her chair and rounded the table to Dana's side. Her grandfather had already left for the office. Otherwise, she would never have dared to leave her place without asking.

Mollie peered around Dana's arm at the newspaper. There was a photograph from last year's fair on the front page. "What's a county fair?"

Dana moved her chair back and drew Mollie onto her lap. "A place where we're going to have lots of fun. Are you game for it?"

Excitement colored her cheeks to a faint pink. "Sure. Let's go!"

"Hey, not so fast." Dana laughed, tightening her arms around the wiggling child. "We can't go yet. You have to go to preschool, and I have to go to work," she pointed out.

"Besides, it doesn't start until tomorrow. We'd be standing all alone on the fairgrounds."

"No, we wouldn't," Mollie insisted. "We'd have each other."

Touched, Dana laid her cheek against Mollie's silky hair. "Oh, baby, where would I be without you?"

"Alone?" Mollie guessed. Dana laughed in response. "Aunt Dana?"

"Yes?" Dana continued hugging her, grateful for the precious gift she'd had bestowed on her. Mollie was all that was pure and good in this world. As long as she had Mollie, everything would work itself out.

"You're squishing me."

Dana laughed, releasing her. "Sorry about that. Just getting a little carried away. So, you ready to go to school?"

Mollie was on her feet instantly. "Ready."

The furrows on John Saldana's forehead deepened as he looked at his older son. He'd gotten Rafe to come under the pretext of needing help to load his van with some of the acoustical equipment for the fair tomorrow. Three separate groups from the police department were going to be performing on one of the stages and that required a network of speakers, amplifiers and microphones. It was an excuse to get the son he hardly ever saw over to the house.

His wife worried about Rafe, saying he worked too hard. That he needed to get out more. Most of all, that he needed to get on with his personal life. John was in agreement, but he figured there was no need to verbalize it.

He waited until he had his breath back. Loading the speakers was bad enough. The drums were a bear.

"I'm not taking no for an answer, Rafe. You're coming to the fair, and that's that." John paused, then hit his son with his best shot. "Your mother wants you to. And she could use the company, not to mention the help. You know what she's like. She's so damn generous, she starts giving all those baked goods away."

There was a time when he'd loved the fair. Now it was just another one of the things he didn't have time for. It seemed almost trivial to him. But Rafe knew better than to say that to his father. Especially since his parents were so involved in it.

Rafe blew out a breath, pausing over the kettledrum until his father was ready to begin again. Maybe it was just his mood, he thought. He'd been out of sorts since that night with Dana.

"What about your help?" Rafe pointed out. "You're going to be there."

The look John gave his firstborn said he'd expected better than that from him. He hoisted the kettledrum onto the truck.

"Hey, the Bedford police department is keeping me plenty busy." He climbed on behind the drum and secured it to the side of the van. "Don't forget, the department's one of the major sponsors of this little shindig. All us boys in blue are supposed to be there." He eased himself off the van, deliberately ignoring the hand Rafe offered him. "And that includes your brother, so don't be looking to him to take your place." He went into the garage, Rafe on his heels, to get the last kettledrum. Together he and Rafe moved the instrument to the driveway. "When's the last time we did anything together as a family?"

Rafe angled the drum so the bulk of the weight was with him as they lifted it into the van. "Last month. Mom made Sunday dinner."

Thank God that was the last of them. "Besides eat," John said shortly. Then his expression softened. Rafe was a good kid. It killed him to see his son cutting himself off from the best part of life. A wife, a family. It was all out there waiting for Rafe, but he had to break free of the past and a woman who could no longer be anything more than a memory for him.

John placed his arm around his son's shoulders as best he could, given that Rafe had four inches on him. "C'mon, getting away from the hospital will do you good, and it'll make your mother happy. You can invite Kate.'' There had been no fire there the one time he'd seen the two of them together, but with the right background, who knew?

"Kate and I aren't seeing each other anymore, Dad."

John looked at him in surprise. Wait until he told Carol. "Since when?"

"A week ago." Rafe didn't embellish. There was no point in telling his father he had met a woman who had unfrozen his heart, only to slash his pride.

John nodded, taking the news in stride the way he did everything that came his way. Looking for the bright side. "Then going to the fair will give you a chance to look over what's available." He grinned at his son, momentarily chasing away the years that marked him. "Like I said, I'm not taking no for an answer."

Rafe sighed. His father was like a junkyard dog when he latched on to something. "Then I won't bother giving it."

John laughed, rubbing his hands together in victory. He'd had a bet riding on the outcome, and Carol was going to have to pay up. "I told your mother I'd win you over."

All right, so he was enjoying himself, Rafe thought. Even if he'd had to unload, carry and then arrange enough folding chairs to seat half of Bedford. Sometimes doing something physical was enjoyable. He needed the diversion of working up a sweat.

He'd arrived at the fairgrounds before seven and immediately been put to work. His mother had claimed him before his father had a chance to. Both belonged to committees that were responsible for putting on the fair.

Carol and John Saldana believed in being a part of whatever was happening in their neighborhood, in their schools, in their community. Good neighborhoods, his father insisted, began with being good neighbors. With his father on the police force and his mother teaching elementary school, they were always in the thick of things. And naturally he and Gabe had always been dragged along in their wake.

They'd had a hell of a good upbringing, he thought.

Rafe glanced toward where his brother was helping harness a horse to a wagon for the hayride. He supposed there were worse ways to spend a Saturday than surrounded by family and friends. The trickle of fairgoers that had begun early this morning was turning into a steady stream of people. A lot of his patients and their families were here. After a while, it was almost a challenge to spot a face he didn't know, at least in passing.

And then there was one he did know but hadn't expected to see. He almost let the pie he was putting out drop on the table.

"Rafe, be careful," Carol admonished. A fondness that was never far away when it came to her sons entered her voice. "I certainly hope you don't hold newborns that way."

"No," he quipped, setting the pie tray down, "I dangle them upside down by their ankles."

From the moment they arrived, Mollie looked as if she'd fallen headfirst into Wonderland. Pulling Dana one way, then another, Mollie couldn't make up her mind where to go. And then her eyes widened with pleasure.

"There's Dr. Rafe!" she exclaimed excitedly, pointing. "Let's go say hi!" Without waiting for Dana's answer, Mollie took off across the grounds.

The last thing Dana wanted was to say hi to Rafe. "No, Mollie, wait." But Mollie was off and running. "Oh, God."

Dana had no choice but to go after her. There were so many people milling around, she was afraid that if she looked away for as much as a second, Mollie would be completely swallowed up.

Like a missile, Mollie hurled herself right into Rafe, throwing her arms around him as he caught her. "Hi, Dr. Rafe! Are you here, too?"

He laughed at the rhetorical question and the enthusiasm with which she'd uttered it. "Looks that way, kiddo." He set her down. "I was just helping my mother set up."

"Your mother?" There was wonder on the small face. "You have a mother?"

As if on cue, his mother came up to join them. No doubt drawn, he thought, by the sight of Mollie. His mother had a weakness for anyone under four feet. It was from her that he'd inherited his love of children. "Yes, Mollie, even doctors have mothers."

Carol smiled at the little girl. "Hello, Mollie." Very formally, she extended her hand. Mollie shook it solemnly. "I'm very pleased to meet you." And then Carol fell back on what she deemed to be her biggest asset, her culinary talents. She pushed forward one of the pieces of pie she'd just sliced. "Would you like some custard pie? I seem to have too many pieces here. I wouldn't want to see them go to waste."

As she stared at the pie, Mollie's mouth watered. She looked over her shoulder, confident her aunt was there. Dana was just coming up behind her. "Can I, Aunt Dana? Can I have a piece of pie?"

Dana couldn't have cared less about a piece of pie. She'd sailed after Mollie, terrified of losing her. She dropped down on one knee, grabbing the little girl by the arms. "Don't you ever, ever do that to me again, Mollie. You know better than to run off in a crowd."

Seeing Dana's worried expression, Mollie's face clouded. "I'm sorry. But I wasn't running off. I was running *to*."

Dana sighed, releasing her. She rose, painfully aware that she was much too close to Rafe. "You sound like a lawyer already." She couldn't stay angry, not with Mollie, even if her nerves did feel as if they were walking the plank because she'd been forced to all but run into Rafe. "Just don't do it again."

One arm around her shoulders, Dana pressed Mollie to her. Her heart began to settle down. Ready to face the next challenge. Rafe.

"And yes, you can have a piece of pie." She looked at Rafe's mother. "I'm sorry, we haven't been introduced."

Dana offered her hand, deliberately avoiding looking in Rafe's direction. "I'm Dana Morrow, Mollie's aunt."

Twenty-five years of teaching had taught Carol Saldana how to read people quickly, and silent looks even faster. There was tension vibrating alongside the polite nods her son and this woman exchanged. Dana Morrow might have been a stranger to her, but definitely not to her son.

Carol smiled warmly, placing her hand in Dana's. "Nice to meet you, Dana. Would you like something to eat?" Not waiting for an answer, Carol began slicing another piece of pie.

Mollie had made herself comfortable at Rafe's feet, sitting cross-legged and savoring her pie. He couldn't have moved if he'd wanted to. "Ma, you keep giving it away, you're not going to raise any money."

Carol nodded. "Good point." She handed the paper plate to Dana. "All right, Rafe, pay for the lady." She placed the knife on the table and put her hand out. "And while you're at it, you can pay for Mollie, too."

He sighed and dug several bills out of his pocket, shaking his head as he gave them to his mother. "That'll teach me to open my mouth around you."

"Yes, it will." Carol smiled, pleased with herself and with the situation she saw. "I won't be needing you any longer, Rafe. You're officially free. Why don't you show Dana and Mollie around?"

Could his mother have been any more obvious? He doubted it. "I was going to see if Dad—"

Carol killed the half-baked excuse. "Dad has the whole police force to work with, not to mention your brother. You were mine for the morning, and I'm setting you free." He'd learned a long time ago there was no arguing with that tone. "Now take advantage of it before I think of something else I need you to do."

Mollie looked at him. "Can you show us around, Dr. Rafe?" she asked prettily. "This is my very first fair ever."

There was no way he could refuse that face. "I guess I can

do that." He indicated the last row of folding chairs he'd arranged. "Why don't we sit down over here until you finish that?"

"Okay." Eager to please, Mollie nodded so hard, she almost let what was left of her pie slide off her plate. Rafe righted it, preventing a collision between dessert and grass.

He stepped out of the way to let Dana pass first. Sitting with Mollie between them, Rafe couldn't have felt more awkward than if he'd just been asked to dance *Swan Lake* as the female lead. They still hadn't exchanged so much as one word.

He was determined to be civilized about it, even though he didn't feel very civilized. "So, how have you been, Dana?"

The sound of his voice, a voice that echoed in her brain at the most inopportune times, had her struggling to maintain her composure. "Busy. My father really has me hopping."

Mollie looked at her puzzled, loaded fork in midair. "I didn't see you hop, Aunt Dana."

Trust Mollie to ease the tension. Dana leaned over and kissed her head. "Just an expression, sweetie. Dr. Rafe knows what I mean."

His eyes met hers over the curly head. "In this instance, yes." And then he looked at Mollie's plate. It was empty. "You're finished already?"

She grinned, nodding. "I was hungry."

He took the plate from her and threw it in one of the trash cans he'd put out. "Don't they feed you where you live?"

"Sure," Mollie answered, "but not pie like this."

Rafe laughed. He loved the honesty that existed in children. He glanced at Dana. The honesty that fell by the wayside once children became adults.

"My mother will be very happy to hear your endorsement." He offered Mollie his hand. "Want to go on the Ferris wheel?"

"Yes!" And then she paused before asking, "What's a Ferris wheel?"

"Come on, I'll show you." He was already leading the way.

Mollie hesitated for only a fraction of a second. "Can Aunt Dana come along?"

"Only if she wants to." He looked over his shoulder at her. Dana had finished her pie, as well. "I wouldn't want her doing anything she doesn't want to do."

She took the direct hit and recovered immediately. "Don't worry," she assured him, keeping pace. She dumped the plate as she passed the trash can without breaking stride. "She won't."

Rafe stopped, and before she could draw her head back, lightly passed his thumb over the corner of her mouth. Her heart lunged against her chest.

"You had some custard right there." Still looking at her, he licked the custard off his thumb and then hurried off with Mollie.

So much for congratulating herself that the situation was under control, Dana thought.

Why did he have to be so damn charming? They'd gone from the Ferris wheel—which they had ridden twice—to the pony ride—three rides—to the carousel, which was so packed, they only rode once. During all that time, Rafe was completely attentive to Mollie.

He was making it so difficult for her to remain detached. For the past two hours, traipsing from one ride to another, answering Mollie's endless questions and chasing her through the fun house, Rafe had displayed the kind of infinite patience Dana thought was only allotted to mothers, and only to a limited few, at that.

Dana wasn't accustomed to a man showing such warm affection for a child. It certainly wasn't anything she'd grown up with.

With all her heart, she wished she'd never left home. Then maybe, somehow, fate would have led their paths to cross before now.

Dana laughed at herself. She had too much of her father in her to believe that. Besides, there was no use wishing for things that weren't. She was having enough trouble coping with things that were. Like her pregnancy.

With Mollie flagging just a little, Rafe brought her to the rows of folding chairs that were still by and large empty, and would remain so until that evening, when the entertainers began their acts.

"This is fun, Aunt Dana," Mollie announced, as if it was news. "I'm glad we came."

"So am I," Dana agreed. At least for Mollie's sake. Tired, she eased herself into a chair beside her niece.

"Hey, who is this little doll?"

Dana turned to see a man coming up behind them. As she looked closer, it occurred to her that he looked like an older, shorter version of Rafe.

Mollie looked at John Saldana solemnly. "I don't talk to strangers, sir."

Impressed, John nodded. "That's a very good habit, but it's all right to talk to me. I'm a policeman."

The solemn expression vanished, chased away by her smile. "Okay. I'm Mollie Aliprantis." Twisting in her chair, she did the honors. "This is my aunt Dana, and this is my doctor."

John had trouble keeping his expression properly sober. When it came to kids, he was used to Carol exaggerating, but she was right this time. This one was adorable. "Do you always bring your doctor along?"

Mollie shook her head. "No, we met him here."

Rafe laughed as he leaned over to whisper to Mollie, "He's just pulling your leg, honey. This is my father."

Mollie looked down at her leg, which seemed to be right where she expected it to be, unpulled. "A mother *and* a father?"

"And a brother, too," John told her. He beckoned his other son over. Gabe looked reluctant to leave the company of the blonde he was talking to, but he did. It was the uniform that

In the Family Way

attracted them, John thought. That and the killer Saldana smile. "Gabe, come on over here. There's someone I'd like you to meet."

Joining them, Gabe paused to give Dana a quick but very thorough once-over. He definitely liked what he saw. He also noted the proprietary look in his brother's eye.

Well, well, well, that should certainly make their mother happy.

Mollie was staring at Gabe, clearly smitten all over again. He was as good-looking as Rafe, with a certain boyishness to him that Rafe had clearly outgrown. "I *like* your family, Dr. Rafe."

Rafe saw his mother, busy selling her homemade pies, pausing to look their way. He could see her antennae going up. *Don't get your hopes up, Mom.* "They like you, too, Mollie."

John and Gabe were flanking Mollie. Nothing he liked better than a well-mannered kid, John thought. "Ever ride in a police car?" he asked.

"No," she breathed, a hopeful expression wreathing her face.

Gabe laid claim to her before his father could, picking Mollie up. "Well, then, let me give you the grand tour." He glanced at Dana, then looked at his older brother. *Nice taste, bro.* "Why don't you two get some punch or something? This might take a while."

Mollie was eating this up, Rafe thought, but he pretended not to notice. "Okay with you, Mollie?"

She looked at Gabe. "Are you going to be there with me?"

"Stuck to you like glue," he promised.

Her face would have been in danger of cracking if she grinned any harder. "Okay."

Dana shook her head as she watched the two policemen disappear with her niece. "She has the makings of an A-one flirt."

"A flirtatious lawyer." Rafe made the association from her

earlier comment. He looked at Dana. "Must run in the family."

Dana opened her mouth to retort, then let it go. "I guess I had that coming to me." She pressed her lips together. Apologizing didn't come any easier to her than it did to her father, but she owed it to Rafe, if for no other reason than for the way he'd treated Mollie today. "I'm sorry about what happened."

His hand at the small of her back, he guided her past a cluster of people. "Which part are you sorry for?"

She looked at him. Did he have to ask? "What do you think?"

He took out two dollars and paid the woman at the concession stand for two glasses of punch. He handed one to Dana. "I'm not sure what to think."

If he could be honest, so could she. Dana took a sip before turning toward him. "Rafe, I'm coming from a very rocky place in my life. Trust isn't something I can just give, even if I want to."

"And do you? Want to?" he prodded when she didn't answer.

She was probably going to regret this. "Yes."

He smiled. "Good enough. We'll take it from there. Slow." He glanced toward the police car that had been driven onto the grounds for the day. He could see his father talking Mollie's ears off. "But right now, I think we should rescue Mollie from my father."

"I have a hunch it might be the other way around." She fell into step beside him as he walked toward the police car. And when he took her hand, she left it there, content, for the space of the afternoon, to pretend that everything was all right.

Chapter 17

Chapter 17

The evening air was soft and filled with music as it swirled gently around them. On the stage a group was doing justice to the songs that had made them popular more than a quarter of a century ago. The audience, who spanned ages from pre-schoolers to people in their eighties, swayed and clapped in time, keeping the beat alive.

When he looked behind him, Rafe saw his parents sitting several rows back. They were holding hands instead of clapping. His father was whispering something into his mother's ear. She laughed and swatted at him in that playful way she had when he made her feel like a young girl again.

That was what he wanted, Rafe thought, turning. To have a life like that. To have a love like that in his life. Again.

He glanced at Dana's profile. She seemed completely absorbed in the music, in the moment. Moonlight was as kind to her as sunlight, caressing her skin, accentuating a sensuality that needed little help to stir him.

He felt a pull so strong, so overwhelming, that he thought

it would wrench out his very gut. When he sucked in his breath to steady himself, she looked at him quizzically.

He thought fast. "I think we're losing someone." Grinning, he indicated Mollie, whose head kept nodding as she fought valiantly to remain awake.

Dana felt guilty. She should have taken Mollie home hours ago. It was just that today had been so perfect, she didn't want to see it end. After Mollie had satisfied her desire to ride every ride, they'd run into some of Rafe's patients and their parents making a day of it. Dana recognized several of the women immediately and lost no time telling Nicole Lincoln how happy Mollie was at the preschool.

One of the others, Nicole's older sister, Marlene, had suggested they all take a breather for lunch and Dana had found herself assimilated into a circle comprised of young parents and their children. A group that welcomed her. A group, Marlene confided, that Sheila had once dubbed her baby-of-the-month club, since their due dates had all been a month apart. Nicole added that Sheila had rounded out the club with the birth of Rebecca. As she listened, Dana's secret weighed heavily on her conscience and on her heart.

Mollie had had a ball with the other children, and Dana had felt as if she belonged. With Rafe sitting on the grass beside her, it had had the feel of an impromptu picnic. The years and the sorrow that had brought her had temporarily disappeared.

After lunch, the group had broken up, but not before promises of getting together soon were exchanged. The contented glow that get-together and all the rest of the day had generated was still with her. Maybe it was selfish, Dana thought, but she'd wanted to hang on to it just a little longer.

To remain here with Rafe a little longer.

Yes, it was selfish. Dana put her arm around Mollie, gathering the little girl against her. "It's way past her bedtime."

Pavlov's dog reacting to the dinner bell couldn't have responded faster than Mollie. Her eyes popped open, a protest coming from her rosebud mouth. "Not yet, Aunt Dana. Please, I don't want to go to bed yet."

If there had only been herself to consider, Dana would have remained until the last person left the fairgrounds. But with Mollie added in, the equation changed. Mollie needed her rest. Even Cinderella knew she had to withdraw before midnight struck.

Careful not to jar her, Dana began buttoning the sweater she'd coaxed Mollie into putting on once the sun had gone down. Actually, Rafe had had more to do with getting her into it than she had. All he'd had to do was back up Dana's request, and suddenly Mollie was pushing her arms through the sleeves with zest. Dana smiled. Mollie was crazy about Rafe, there was no doubt about it.

As for her, well, there were a lot of doubts about that. And a lot of rampaging feelings, as well. All she knew right now was that she would have given anything if this night could have gone on forever.

"Oh, I think you've had enough for one day, sugar plum." She glanced at her watch, angling it into the light so she could read the face. It was after ten o'clock. "We've been here almost eleven hours." She took the whimper to be a protest. Poor baby, she thought. "And we can always come back tomorrow."

"Tomorrow," Mollie murmured. The battle with her eyelids was almost completely lost. They were barely fluttering open, each time they sank down.

Rising, Rafe picked Mollie up in his arms. "Up you go, kiddo." With Mollie's head tucked against his shoulder, he looked at Dana. "I'll walk you to your car."

She didn't want him going to any extra trouble. He'd already done so much for Mollie. Dana reached for her niece, ready to take her from him. "I'm parked way over to the side. It's a long walk."

Mollie was staying right where she was. Her last act before surrendering to sleep had been to wrap her small arms around his neck. He laughed softly, holding her to him.

"I don't mind. I'm young, I can handle it. Just lead the way." He nodded toward the exit, then looked at Dana, a smile in his eyes. "Better yet, walk alongside me."

She did as he asked, happy at the way things were turning out. But she felt obligated to warn him.

"You'll be sorry." She wasn't kidding about how far away she was parked. When they'd arrived, the lots were already jammed. She'd had to look for a parking space way out on the perimeter.

It was a great night for a stroll, he thought. Funny, until Dana had come into his life, he'd stopped doing things like that, stopped taking walks, stopped enjoying the simple things around him. Without intending to, she'd awakened him to things he'd let slip by since he'd lost his wife.

It felt good to be alive. To be here with her and Mollie.

"I'm sorry for a lot of things, Dana, and I'll probably do things in the future I'll regret. But carrying a little girl to her car won't be among them."

Dana couldn't help herself. The question came out before she could think to stop it. "What *are* you sorry about?"

Amusement crossed his face. She'd once accused him of prying when he'd asked her personal questions. "Now who's prying?"

Dana bit her lower lip, looking away. She was letting the borders between them blur again, but that was because the day had been so magical. But the day was over. "Sorry."

He'd only meant to tease her, not make her back away. "No, I'm the one who's sorry." He flashed a grin at her. "See, I told you I'd be sorry in the future." He took a breath before he began. "You want to know what I'm sorry about?" He looked at her, their eyes momentarily holding. "I'm sorry I didn't call you the day after I dropped you off at your house."

He'd shifted the emphasis onto himself when she'd been the one who'd run away. She was beginning to believe that was in his nature. To be kind, to spare others' feelings.

"Why?" she asked. She'd wanted him to call, hoped he

would call even as she prayed that he wouldn't. A few times she'd thought of calling him, but then she'd talked herself out of it. There was no point in seeing him. It couldn't lead anywhere.

They'd passed the first lot and were walking through the second one. The lights were fewer out here, spaced farther apart. He was glad he'd insisted on coming with her. For the most part, Bedford was a safe city, but even paradise had its serpent.

"Because," he told her truthfully, "maybe we could have cleared things up sooner."

Nothing concrete had been said. Just feelings piled onto a day that had gone well from the start. "I wasn't aware that we *had* cleared things up."

He stopped walking because he wanted to see her face, all of it, when he asked her, "You had a good time today, didn't you?"

She had. She couldn't remember laughing so much in years. Or feeling so good. "Yes."

Then they were moving forward, which meant things were all right again. Words would come later. For now, it was enough that they were enjoying each other's company again. "Then things are clearing up."

But they weren't, she thought. It wasn't that simple. She was still afraid of being hurt, still afraid of risking her feelings, although she was beginning to feel as if the choice was being taken away from her, slipping through her fingers a little more each time she was around him.

And there was still the secret she was keeping from him. One that would put a whole different slant on their relationship, if not terminate it altogether.

With a pang so strong it startled her, Dana realized that she didn't want to terminate their relationship. Not yet.

She decided it was safest to drop the subject and move on. "What else do you regret?"

He liked the way her hair brushed against his arm as they

walked. Softly, silkily, just the way she'd felt in his arms that night.

"That the evening is over." Mollie began to slip to the side. Gently, he shifted her into place. "I'd like to take you home, Dana," he said quietly, "but I promised to help with the cleanup."

Home. Hers? Or did he mean his? Was he saying that he wanted to make love with her again? She felt her breasts tingling at the very thought of it.

Or was he talking about sex? It would have been easier on her if it was the latter, because then she could dismiss him as being like all the rest.

But she was beginning to think that he wasn't like all the rest. Not at all.

You've been wrong before, she told herself. Look at Steven. He wrote you poetry and swore with tears in his eyes that he loved you.

"I brought my own car," Dana pointed out. "That would make it difficult for you to take me anywhere."

"I'd still like to." His voice was low. If she concentrated, she could almost feel it skimming along her bare skin. Along her face, her arms, her legs. She struggled to shut out its effects. "I'd like to take you places, Dana. Places you've never been."

She'd always been good at game playing, doing it to survive in a world she didn't like. But she didn't want to play games with Rafe. She felt she owed him the truth.

"You already did." Dana looked at him. "What happened between us was very special to me. No one's ever treated me like that before, as if I what I felt mattered more than…" She was saying too much, giving too much of herself away. And allowing him to have too much power into the bargain. That wasn't supposed to happen. Dana shrugged, playing down the emotion behind her words. "Well, no one's ever done that, that's all."

He promised himself never to ask. The past wasn't supposed to have any effect on whatever was happening between them. But maybe it did. Maybe the last man in her life really had scarred her. Scarred her so she couldn't give herself completely.

He needed to know. "You said you were coming from a rocky place in your life—"

"I am. I was." Dana stopped, searching for the right words. Shadows bathed her face as she walked beside Rafe, hiding her expression from him. She tiptoed around the subject carefully, not wanting to say too much, afraid of driving him away too soon. "I was involved with someone. Someone I thought I would be with for the rest of my life."

Someone she'd loved, he thought, maybe even the way he'd loved Debra. It gave them common ground. "What happened?" he prodded gently.

She took a breath. When she spoke again, her voice was devoid of all feeling. She'd learned from the master, she thought.

"He didn't turn out to be the person I thought he was. We began as soul mates and wound up as cell mates." To buy herself some time, Dana smoothed Mollie's hair, though there was no need to. "The last straw came when he was cruel to Mollie. I took her in after my sister and her husband were killed. Steven resented the attention I was giving her."

The name sprang at him. Steven. The man who had made love with her, who had hurt her, was named Steven. He'd never liked that name.

"He gave me an ultimatum. It was either Mollie or him." She shivered. Whether from the breeze or the memory, she didn't know. "I picked Mollie." Her smile was enigmatic. "It wasn't really a contest."

The bitter taste in his mouth surprised him. How could she have stayed with someone like that? "Sounds like a real winner."

She gave Steven his due, knowing he would never have returned the favor, given a chance. She had no doubt that he had run her down in front of all his friends. "Oh, he had his good points." She shrugged, feeling suddenly very cold.

"Unfortunately, they weren't the lasting kind." Without meaning to, she stepped up her pace. "I'd really rather not talk about him."

Rafe noted her increased speed but didn't mention it. "Sorry, wasn't my business to ask. I was just curious about the kind of man you allowed into your life."

She balked at what she took to be criticism. "It's not a matter of allowing or not allowing, it's…"

"Closing the barn door after the horse is gone?" he suggested helpfully.

She thought of the pony ride he'd taken Mollie on. And the hayride they'd all gone on. Remembering nudged some of her bad humor to the side. "You're letting the fair get to you."

"Yeah, that and other things." He didn't want to leave her thinking he had pumped her. "Since we're exchanging personal information, for the record, I loved my wife very much. Her dying much too soon, cheating me of growing old with her, is one of the things I regret the most." He glanced at her. "I really didn't think I was ever going to feel anything for anyone again."

He left the sentence dangling. Dana looked at him. "But?"

"But," he repeated, nodding, as if the one word said it all. Because she clearly didn't understand, he explained, as much as he was able. "That's what I need to explore. That disturbing little word, *but*." And to explore it, he needed to be with her. "Listen, there's this policemen's ball coming up—"

She knew where this was going and needed a minute to gather her thoughts. To make sense of her ricocheting feelings. Dana played for time. "You're not a policeman."

He wished she wouldn't keep interrupting. He still wasn't any good at this sort of thing. "No, but my father and brother are, and they're trying to stick me with all these tickets."

A smile played along her lips as she asked innocently, "Are you trying to sell me some?"

"No," he said in exasperation, "I'm trying to *use* some.

Two, to be exact." And then he saw the grin. She was putting him on. "Come with me?"

Senator Johnson's trial date was coming up soon. Her father was insisting that everyone devote all their time to it, in and out of the office.

But she needed this, too. "When?"

"Next Friday."

Where had she parked, in the next state? he wondered. They were coming to the end of the last parking lot, and she still wasn't giving any indication that they'd reached her car.

Dana thought, trying to put things in order. Friday. A week from Friday the senator's murder trial was scheduled to begin. More than any of her father's cases in the last few years, this one promised to be a real media event. But it was still two weeks away. Her father couldn't expect her to work every evening.

Dana reconsidered. Well, actually, he could, but she wasn't going to. At least, not next Friday.

"Friday will be fine."

"Great." As he said it, he almost felt like a kid again, getting a date to the prom. An odd reaction for a man his age, he thought, savoring it nonetheless.

Dana stopped beside a dusty-looking white sedan. "We're here."

He didn't bother hiding his relief. Even forty-five pounds of spun sugar and heaven began to feel heavy after a while. "I was beginning to think you'd decided to walk home."

"I warned you." Dana unlocked the door.

"Yeah, you did. I'm not very big on listening to warnings." Rafe carefully slipped Mollie into the back seat.

She felt her heart flutter the tiniest bit and told herself she was an idiot. "That gives us something in common."

Mollie, her eyes shut tight, murmured, "No bed," then curled up in the back seat. Rafe chuckled as he straightened, carefully drawing his large frame out of the car. "She's your niece, all right. Stubborn to the end."

Dana began to check the seat belt, then stopped herself.

Rafe was perfectly capable of buckling Mollie up. She had to start trusting someone sometime. With a snap, she shut the rear passenger door.

And turned straight into Rafe, their bodies brushing against each other. Stiffening ever so slightly, Dana pretended not to notice, but the unguarded look in her eyes gave her away.

She felt something, just as he did, Rafe thought. The question still remained—what?

When she began to open the door on her side, he placed his hand on hers. "I said we'd go slow."

She raised her eyes to his face, her breath catching in her dry throat. "Yes?"

"What I want to know is, is asking to kiss you good-night going too fast?"

She felt the smile coming from the soles of her feet. "I believe Goldilocks said it best, 'No, it's just right.'"

He couldn't think of anything he wanted more than to kiss her. "Always been one of my favorite fairy tales."

Touching her face with the tips of his fingers, trailing them slowly along her jawline to the point of her chin, he allowed himself a moment to savor the feel of her skin before finally pressing his lips to hers.

It felt as if everything within her had been holding its breath, waiting for this moment to happen. When it did, every fiber of her body came alive, leaning into the kiss, into the sensation it created within her.

As it deepened, as it took her away from everything she knew to everything that was wondrous and good, Dana could feel her head spinning again. In the distance, a hundred crickets serenaded them as the night spread its cloak around them.

She could feel her body yearning again, yearning for him. Yearning to feel again the way only he had made her feel. Wanted, precious. Beautiful.

He wanted her. Sweet heaven, but he wanted her. Right here, in this field of neglected weeds, with the lights of the fair shining dimly in the distance, he wanted to make love with her.

Rafe felt as if he was no longer the man he'd been only a little more than a month ago. He wasn't quite sane anymore.

What he was was alive.

Exercising whatever control she had left, Dana placed her hands against Rafe's chest and drew her head back. It took her a second to focus, to struggle out of the swirling haze surrounding her. "I'd better get Mollie home."

Dana was only grateful that she managed not to gasp the words.

Rafe nodded. For a moment he'd forgotten about Mollie. Forgotten about everything except this crying need within him. Denied and locked away for so long, it was ravenous.

He stepped back and held the door open for her. "I'll see you Friday." He closed the door as she buckled her seat belt.

"Friday," she echoed.

He watched her pull out and remained standing there until he could no longer make out her car. Then he walked to the fairgrounds to join cleanup detail. Whistling.

The days between Sunday and Friday were filled with work and second thoughts for Rafe. A great many second thoughts, despite the ragging he'd gotten from his father and Gabe on Sunday when he turned up to help set up again. He'd withstood it all good-naturedly and even suffered his mother's questions, though there were only a tactful few. But underneath, he still wasn't sure what it was he felt when he was around Dana. Whether it was purely physical attraction taken to the extreme, or if there was more to it than that.

There was no denying that their lovemaking had been incredible. Maybe what was bothering him was that he couldn't get a handle on things. On her. Feisty, independent, yet there was obviously something going on under the surface, an inner hurt he saw in her eyes at unguarded moments. He could relate to that.

More than that, he could relate to her. That scared him even as it reeled him in. He wasn't sure if he was ready for that kind of connection to someone again. Could he handle it?

Logically, he knew he should be able to. But emotionally, it was a different story. One that refused to allow him to sneak a peek at the last page.

A call from the hospital had him leaving the fairgrounds just after setup. And just before he figured she would arrive. When he tried to call her later, Esther told him she wasn't in.

They played phone tag. He called her house several times that week, only to be given the same message. The few times Dana returned his call, she got his answering machine at home or his service at the office, never him.

By Friday night, he was wondering if this had been such a good idea. Maybe there was a message in their inability to make contact. Maybe he should let things slide for a while.

He was still saying maybe when he arrived at her door to pick her up.

And to have his breath taken away.

She was wearing a silver gown, one that came demurely to her throat and then wantonly used up all its available material before it reached her back. The shimmering material, slashed all the way to the middle of her thigh, clung to her with every move. It was the kind of gown that could bring a grown man to his knees.

It nearly did him. Especially when he placed his hand on the small of her back and realized that he was touching skin rather than fabric.

"Aren't you afraid of catching cold?" he asked.

But she merely smiled in return. "I think the look in your eyes will keep me warm enough."

"I don't know about you, but I'm going to stay plenty warm tonight trying to keep every available man from running off with you."

"That's the nicest thing you've ever said to me."

"I get better with practice," he promised, opening the car door for her.

"Mind if I cut in?" Gabe asked his brother even as he took possession of Dana.

He danced away with her before Rafe had a chance to say anything. Most likely no, Gabe thought. It would be just like Rafe to be selfish with Dana. Gabe tucked her hand against his chest, smiling at her. He felt pretty confident that most eyes were on them, the way they'd been on Rafe when he had danced with her.

"You look terrific." The look in his eyes, as sensual as Rafe's, reinforced his words. "Has he told you that yet?"

Dana smiled, remembering. "He might have mentioned something along those lines."

Whatever Rafe had said, Gabe knew it wasn't enough. "He was never any good with words. I'm the one with the gift of gab." Gabe inclined his head. "So, on behalf of the Saldana men, let me tell you that you're the most gorgeous woman here." He grinned. "Although my mother gets honorable mention."

"Thank you." Dana's amusement shone in her eyes. She decided that she liked Rafe's brother a lot. And it was easier, being friendly, even being flirtatious, when it didn't count. "Tell me, does that list include your own date?"

"Rosemary?" He grinned broadly. Rosemary DeAngelo was his lady of the month. He liked her the way he liked all the women he went out with. But there was nothing serious in the offing. Just two people enjoying each other's company. Rafe was the serious one, not him. He intended to enjoy himself until he died. "Rosemary's okay. She doesn't make my eyes shine the way you make Rafe's shine, though."

Dana turned her head, trying to find Rafe in the crowd. He hadn't looked very happy when Gabe cut in. "He doesn't look like his eyes are shining to me."

Not conceited. He liked that in a woman. He gave Rafe more points on his choice. "You should have seen him before." For a fleeting second, he was serious. "Whatever you're doing, thanks."

Wait a second. The waters were getting a bit too deep for her. She didn't want Rafe's family misunderstanding things. "But I'm not—"

Gabe didn't need or want explanations, whatever was going on was between his brother and the lady. He might like annoying Rafe from time to time, but he did have a sense of honor about some things. "Hey, it's none of my business, really."

Rafe was suddenly between them, elbowing his brother out of the way. "You've had her long enough."

Hands spread in surrender, Gabe stepped back. "He always did like to hog things," he told Dana. "Have him tell you about the time he took my bike."

"It was *my* bike," Rafe reminded him as he danced away with Dana. He smiled at her. "Thanks for putting up with him."

There was nothing to put up with. "I like him," she said honestly. "I like your whole family. And your friends," she added, thinking of the other day at the fair. "They say you can tell a lot about a man by the kind of friends he has."

"Oh?"

She nodded. "Yours are all so easy to talk to, so down-to-earth."

He glanced to his right, where Gabe stood with some of other men on the force. Most of the faces were familiar to him. "That's because they all want to crowd around you."

"Another compliment?" she marveled. "Two in one evening?"

He drew back a little to look at her. "Hey, I'm as capable of giving one as the next guy."

She laughed, leaning her cheek against his chest again. "Not according to your brother."

"My brother is too busy drooling over you to think straight." He could feel her breath along his chest, even through his jacket and his shirt. Having his hand against her bare back only made him ache for her. "How did you get into that dress?"

"Why?" She raised her head to look at him. Did he suspect? Afraid, she glanced down to see if she was suddenly showing. "Is it too tight?"

"What was it you said the other night? It's just right?" He grinned at her. "Well, it is. But it does make me wonder, though."

"About?"

"About what you have on underneath." He had his suspicions.

Unable to resist, Dana raised herself on her toes and whispered against his ear, "Skin."

He felt the ripple of desire possess him. His body quickened, reminding him how much he wanted her. Ever since he'd taken her in his arms to dance, all he'd been able to think of was making love with her.

His thoughts were on a collision course with the promise he'd made to her. The promise that said he would go slow.

He meant to keep it, he really did. But it wasn't easy. Especially not when she pressed herself against him like this. And not when she smelled this good, like sin served on a golden platter, all warm and tempting.

He tried to focus on taking a cold shower. It didn't help. "That's what I thought."

She smiled as she felt his heart beating hard against her cheek.

Chapter 18

"Looks like the party's breaking up, Cinderella," Rafe murmured against her hair.

The strains of the last dance, a slow one, were fading. Rafe had noted that the crowd had been steadily thinning for the last half hour or so. There was just so much dancing people could take, he mused. He saw his brother getting ready to leave with a redhead he didn't recognize. Nothing new there. Gabe seemed determined to avail himself of the companionship of every female on the planet between the ages of twenty and forty-seven.

Not him. He only needed one. A very particular one. And he was beginning to think that just maybe lightning had managed to strike him twice.

"Hmm?" Dana looked at him. He'd said something, but she hadn't heard. She'd been too busy enjoying the comforting sensation of his heart beating beneath her cheek.

"I think things are winding up." He pointed to several couples who were milling around the exit. Gabe made eye contact before leaving and gave Rafe the high sign. He waved his brother away. Placing his hand lightly on Dana's shoulder, he began guiding her toward the door. "Time to go." They sidestepped several people still gathered around the bar, swapping stories. But even they appeared to be winding down. "Do you want to go home?"

"Yes." Dana turned her head to look at him. She'd made up her mind. "Yours."

If a rush of excitement met her words, he managed to keep it under wraps. "Are you sure?" he asked carefully.

Her eyes held his, and then she smiled. "I'm sure." And she was. Sure that she wanted this last time with him. And when it was over, when the delicious sensation of his love-making and the feelings it brought to life had settled and faded, she would tell him. Tell him what wouldn't be a secret for very much longer. Oh, she might be able to continue for another month or maybe two. She knew of women who didn't show right up to the date of their delivery, but that was rare. He would have to be told before that.

Before their feelings were permanently entangled.

A smile, self-deprecating and small, played across her lips. It might be too late for that.

But come what may, she had to tell him. It was the only decent thing to do. If he turned from her, well, then he would be like all the others, wouldn't he? Putting his feelings before hers. There would be nothing surprising if that was the way he reacted.

And if he didn't…

If he didn't, then he would be one of those rare men who glowed in the dark and made the demons go away. A man who would love her and make her feel safe. Either way, she would know what she had.

Or didn't have.

On the way out, Rafe guided her toward his parents. He'd slipped his hand to the back of her neck, leaving it there.

"Please don't do that," she whispered.

Her voice might be low, but there was no disguising the emotion in it. "Do what?"

"Lead me around like that, like I'm a puppet. It—it re-minds me of someone." Steven used to do that. Keep his hand at the back of her neck, moving her around as if she was a mindless rag doll who couldn't walk on her own. It was all part and parcel of the power trip Steven had been on.

Rafe dropped his hand. "Sorry."

She felt bad immediately. "I know it's silly, but—"

"Hey, I said I was sorry, and I am. I don't want to do anything to remind you of someone who hurt you. Anything else?" She shook her head. "Okay. Mind if I just stop to say goodbye to my folks?"

"Only if you don't let me say goodbye, too. And, Rafe?"

"Yeah?"

"It's okay to put your arm around me. I like that."

He grinned as he slipped his arm around her shoulders. "As long as I know."

The road seemed almost serene this time of night. Traffic was minimal, and it felt as if they were masters of all they saw. Ordinarily, that would have been a very secure feeling.

But tonight Dana wasn't feeling secure. She was feeling damn nervous.

It was strange to feel like this, to have all these pins and needles dancing along her body. She knew exactly what lay ahead, at least for the next hour or so. They would make fabulous love and then hold each other as the feeling mel-lowed. And for just a tiny space of time, she would feel safe.

Until she told him.

Suddenly she didn't want to tell him, didn't want to face what might happen in the wake of her admission. Didn't want to see him turning from her.

But she had no choice.

It was the telling that made her feel like this. That, and the fear that he might think she had been deceiving him all along for her own purposes. Or, worse, for her own amusement.

Well, wasn't she? Wasn't she leading him on in a way, pretending to be free when, in the purest sense of the word, she wasn't? She wasn't free to do what she wanted with whom she wanted. She had an obligation. An obligation to the child she was carrying.

Leaning over, she turned the radio on. She needed something to fill the spaces in her mind, to chase away her thoughts.

Since she'd turned on the radio, Rafe turned it to a station that played the blues. It seemed to match the mood. When he was a kid, he'd thought the blues were depressing. But as he grew older, as he listened not so much to the words but to the music, he'd become a fan.

"You're awfully pensive," he said. "Are you having second thoughts?"

Dana shook her head, trying to sound upbeat. Maybe she was worrying for no reason. "No, I'm still working on my first ones."

"Which are?" He wanted to know every thought in her head, every feeling in her heart. He knew all about personal space and people's need for privacy, but right now he wanted to know everything there was to know about the woman beside him. He smiled. Maybe there was a little of the cop in him, after all.

She couldn't think of anything to tell him, and she wasn't about to tell him what she was really thinking. Not yet.

Dana shook her head. "Never mind."

Maybe she thought he was presuming too much. "None of my business?" he guessed.

She didn't want him to feel she was pushing him away. That wasn't it at all. She was afraid of pushing him away. As afraid of that as she was of admitting what it was she was beginning to feel for him. "I didn't say that."

He shifted slightly, turning his face in her direction, while one eye remained on the road.

"I know, but maybe that's what you thought." He wanted her to understand, at least a little. "Dana, I know I said I'd go slow—"

He saw her eyes widen slightly. "Maybe you'd better."

There was apprehension in her expression. Was she changing her mind? "Then you don't want to come to my place?"

"No, I really meant slow, as in slow down." Dana pointed to the speedometer. "You're doing sixty." Rafe glanced at the dash and immediately eased up on the accelerator. "I figured that maybe not all of Bedford's police force is gathered at the Colony Hotel tonight."

"Damn."

Mentally, he upbraided himself for being so careless. He was usually a very conscientious driver. But being around Dana seemed to rob him of the edge he ordinarily had. Like heady perfume, she clouded his mind.

"Now, what was it you were trying to say?" she coaxed as they continued at an acceptable speed.

Maybe what he had to say was best left unsaid for now. Maybe saying it would only make her back away. Or damage what was between them. If you held on to something too tightly, it broke. He knew that, and he didn't want this to break. He wanted to nurture it until it was strong enough to withstand being handled.

"I don't know." He lifted a shoulder carelessly and let it drop the same way. "Must have lost my train of thought."

He was lying, Dana thought. She was about to prod him, then decided against it. Maybe she wouldn't want to hear what he had to say. Because she knew that if he had questions, real questions, she would have to answer them truthfully. She couldn't bring herself to lie to him. There was more involved than keeping to her own code of ethics. She couldn't lie to him, because to lie would cost her the one thing she could always bargain with. Trust. If she lied to him, he wouldn't trust her, not completely, and possibly not ever. And she might want him to...someday.

Wasn't not telling the same as lying?

God, her head was beginning to hurt. Turning the music up louder, she refused to let herself think about it any more.

Light flooded the room, illuminating the clutter. It looked like a family of bears had run riot here. Dana couldn't help grinning. Her grin widened as Rafe hurriedly began to make a vain attempt at cleaning the place up.

"I guess you weren't expecting to bring me here."

He stuffed newspapers that defied folding into a magazine rack. The rack fell over, spilling its contents. Rafe sighed, frustrated. "It does look pretty awful, doesn't it?"

She turned to face him. "Not as far as hurricanes go. But I didn't come here to critique your housekeeping."

He shoved the overflowing laundry basket behind the recliner. There was no way he could hope to make a decent dent in all this. He gave up trying. "Why *did* you come?"

She moistened her lips, nervousness beginning to rise again. "Because I like your company."

Behind him, the basket, top-heavy, toppled. He didn't care. He crossed to her, took her in his arms and held her against him.

God, but she felt good, smelled good. She made his senses churn. Doing nothing more than standing here, he could feel the excitement all through his body. His breath didn't seem to want to last as long as it should. Damn, but she had him almost panting. Any minute now, he was going to sit up and beg.

"Are you really wearing nothing underneath that?"

The question, softly whispered, made her pulse accelerate. Dana raised her eyes to his. "Why don't you find out for yourself?"

He wanted to. Damn, but he wanted to tear the gown from her beautiful body and make love with her right here in the middle of this chaos he called a living room. But then he would be just like the man in her past. The man who treated her like an object. Someone who had seemed one thing to her at the outset, becoming another all too soon. Rafe didn't want her to feel that way about him. Her wanted her to...

To what?

To care for him. The rest, if there was going to be a rest, would come later. Right now, caring was enough.

Gathering her close to him, he made her another promise. One she didn't hear. A silent promise. To take what she offered so generously and savor it the way it should be savored. Slowly, with reverence. Even if it killed him.

Very lightly, with his hands barely touching her shoulders, he grazed her mouth with his, kissing her once, twice, and then again, each time more deeply than the last, until he finally lost himself completely in the kiss.

He discovered that he liked being lost. Liked feeling as if he'd lost his way, as long as it was with her.

Like a man who suddenly had to rely on his other senses in order to see, Rafe skimmed his palms along her body. Touching her, memorizing every curve, every dip, every tantalizing swell. He passed his hands along her body slowly, knowing he was exciting her. And, in knowing, he excited himself. The rush was incredible.

She could feel the frenzy beginning, beating its wings wildly within her. Was it humanly possible to want someone so much and still live? She wasn't sure. All she knew was that she felt as if she was bursting inside. She wanted to feel him, to touch him the way only lovers touched. And to have him desire her.

Even as he molded her to him, Dana began to unbutton his shirt, eager to feel his skin against hers. When one of the buttons held fast, she tugged, almost ripping it off.

He stopped her hands with his, leaning in to nibble on her lower lip. "Hey, slow down, we have all night."

"All night?" She was going to have to get back to Mollie. And if she came in with the morning, it might initiate an argument with her father. She didn't want to risk that. "But I can't—" Rafe kissed her throat, making the words that were forming melt away. Her hands tightened on his shoulders, not to stop him, but to steady herself as she began to lose feeling in her knees. "I've got to—"

"Call home," he urged as one kiss rained down in the wake of the last. "Tell them you'll be there in the morning." And then he drew his head back to look at her. Her pupils were large, her eyes dazed. She'd never been more beautiful to him. "Stay the night with me, Dana."

Oh, God, she wanted to. With all her heart, she wanted to.

"I can't." Her voice became progressively less forceful. "Mollie. My father—"

"Stay for me." The words were whispered along her skin, seductive, sensual. Erasing the last of her protests.

Dana wound her arms around him tightly. The imprint of his hard body heated hers. She was already losing. "God, but you drive a hard bargain."

"I mean to win."

He took full advantage of having her like this, gently making love to her with his hands until she thought she was going to vibrate out of her skin.

He was searching for a zipper at the base of her spine. Dana felt her loins quickening. "How do you take this thing off?"

"First you unbutton it here." Her eyes on his face, she unfastened the three buttons at the back of her neck. The two sides floated down, coming to rest on the tempting swell of her breasts. "And then you tug."

"Like this?" Carefully, as if afraid of hurting her, he drew the material away from her. As it dropped to her waist, he cupped her breasts with his hands, his thumbs gently rubbing against her nipples. Dana moaned, pressing against his palms reveling in the sensations he was arousing within her. She could feel herself growing damp. Could feel her emptiness crying out for him to fill her.

"Exactly like that," she murmured.

His breath catching in his lungs, Rafe tugged at the gown easing it over the swell of her hips. The effort was minimal. In a heartbeat the gown sank to the floor.

Venus rising from a silver seashell, he thought. Without word, Rafe picked her up in his arms and carried her to his bedroom.

Even as a rush came over her, she couldn't help noticing

the state of the bed. In direct contrast to everything else in the apartment, it was neat. She began to laugh.

"What?" Whatever it was, even at his expense, he wanted to share the joke with her. Wanted to share everything with her. Always.

"You made your bed."

The grin was lopsided and sheepish. "That's ingrained. My mother always nagged me about it. Now I make my bed first thing after I get up, usually when I'm still three-quarters asleep."

Gently, he placed her on the blue and beige comforter, then lay down next to her.

"Does nagging work?" She peeled his shirt from him and threw it on the floor.

"Only about making the bed." Though it took an effort to remain still, to keep his hands off her, Rafe let her unbuckle his belt. Anticipation drummed through him as she undressed him, lightly skimming her cool fingers along his upper thighs, knowingly driving him crazy.

Unable to take it anymore, he flipped her onto her back after his slacks and underwear were discarded. For the next part of eternity, he fascinated himself and pleasured her by exploring her body like a man who had never made love to a woman before. He feasted on her with his eyes, with his hands, with his lips and tongue, until there was nothing left of her but a throbbing mass of needs and desires.

When he made her come the first time, she had to bite on her lower lip to keep from crying out, the explosion within her was so violent. So wondrous.

She squirmed against him, feeling his breath hot on her thighs, on that most sensitive part of her. As she began to protest that it was too one-sided, he began again, teasing her, slowly working his way in with his tongue. She grabbed the comforter beneath her and would have torn tufts of it out if he'd had the strength as another explosion rocked her.

Summoning her last bit of strength, she rolled onto him, reversing their positions. Using the same techniques he'd employed on her, she teased, explored and aroused. Growing bolder and more wanton, testing her newfound power, she took her turn at making him want, at making him twist with mounting desire.

She branded him with lips that were by turns cool, passionate, then fiery. With eyes that flashed with delight, she teased him just the way he had teased her, pulling back just before he reached his climax.

Had there been other men who'd felt like this with her? Other men she'd done this with? As quickly as the questions came, they died. He didn't want to know about the men who had come before him.

The only thing he wanted was to make her forget them tonight and all the nights afterward.

His body glistening with sweat, primed, aching, he linked his fingers through hers, pinning her with his weight. Then, holding her a willing prisoner, he kissed her over and over again. Lightly, then passionately, then lightly again, alternating until she was writhing so hard beneath him that he was afraid she would make him come before he entered her.

Unable to hold back any longer, Rafe parted her legs with his knee. His eyes holding hers, he slowly sheathed himself within her.

Dana felt the pulsating need, the hardness she had created, and felt desperately empowered, desperately excited.

Then they gave themselves up to the rhythm that seized them, moving ever faster toward what they both wanted, both needed. And when it happened, when the climax enveloped them both, they clung to it as if it was the very salvation that neither had ever dreamed they would find.

Rafe slowly rolled to the side, gathering her to him. Breathing in deeply of her scent mingled with the sweat of their lovemaking. Wanting her all over again.

He wanted to keep her with him all night, to make love with her over and over again for as long as was humanly possible. Or until he expired. He didn't care which. All he cared about was having her here.

He rubbed his cheek against her hair. He hadn't thought it was possible to feel this content. "Stay with me, Dana."

The euphoria was already leaving, taking her giddy peace with it. In its wake came the burden of what she had to tell him.

What she didn't want to tell him.

Maybe if she said it now, while his eyes were mellow with lovemaking and his body was still warm from hers, he would find it in his heart not to blame her. Not to hate her. "Rafe, I—"

The rhythmic beep emanating from his pager chased away what courage she had, silencing the words she was about to say.

Relief shivered through her at the reprieve. She pulled the comforter around her, then dragged her hand through her hair, trying to make herself presentable. "Shouldn't you answer that?"

It was too late to wish that he had thought to ask someone to take his calls all night. He'd thought a few hours would be enough, never thinking she would come home with him after the dance. "Yes." He sighed, zeroing in on the pager, still clipped to the pocket of his trousers. "I should."

It was his service. Checking in, he listened to the particulars, then nodded. "Tell them I'm on my way and to meet me in the emergency room. And not to panic."

Hanging up, he turned to look at her. She had already gotten her gown and was slipping into it. "I'm sorry about this."

"Don't be. It's nice to know you care. About kids," she added quickly, in case he thought she was taking something for granted. If he cared about her, he would tell her. Until then, she would assume that what was going on between them was a very torrid affair.

It was probably better if she just went with that assumption.

"Whoever called your service at this hour is probably going out of their mind with worry—the way I was. It's nice to know there's a knight in shining stethoscope we can turn to."

"That's me," he muttered. "Sir Pediatrician." He reached into his closet for a pair of jeans. "No chance of my talking you into staying here until I get back, is there?" Rafe knew what her answer would be before she shook her head. "I didn't think so."

"There's no telling how long you'll be gone, and I should be getting back." She slipped her shoes on. "Can you drop me off on your way there? Or should I call a cab?"

He pulled a jersey on and shoved his feet into a worn pair of running shoes "No cab." He took her arm, heading for the front door. "One look at that gown and the cab driver will drive straight to Acapulco with you. I'll take you home." Longing and a sense of something missed suddenly hit him with the force of a well-delivered punch to the gut. Turning her around, he kissed her passionately. When she stared at him, speechless, he smiled. "One for the road."

Dana swallowed, waiting for her voice to return. He certainly knew how to rock her world. "Kiss me like that again and I won't let you go on the road."

He laughed, taking her hand again. "Promises, promises."

That was all she had to give, she thought, tugging on his hand to make him stop as she grabbed her clutch purse from where she'd dropped it earlier. Promises. Promises he might not want once he knew everything.

Chapter 19

She was setting herself up for a fall.

Dana frowned at her reflection in the mirror as she opened a drawer. There was no getting away from it. She had to face the fact that a reckoning was coming. It was just a matter of time.

Time, the one thing she needed. The one thing she didn't have.

Dana shoved the drawer closed with her hip. They had been seeing each other whenever they could for the past two weeks, filling in the wide gaps in between with short, impulsive phone calls. She'd never believed she could feel so happy, so alive.

As long as she banked down any thoughts of the inevitable.

Dana tossed the underwear she'd just chosen into the cloth overnight bag that lay open on her bed. A pair of white shorts followed.

Funny how feelings refused to be packed away so neatly. No matter how hard she tried to deny it, to keep the lines clearly drawn between enjoying herself and falling in love, she'd gone and done it. No two ways about it, Dana thought, she was an idiot. Reason and logic, joined with the past, hadn't been enough to stop her. Hadn't been enough to prevent it from happening. Like a headstrong child, she'd plunged headfirst into something she'd sworn she would never do.

She'd fallen in love with Rafe.

Dana sighed, adding a pink and white striped pullover to the bag. Emotions weren't subject to sanctions and controls. You couldn't fall in love with someone just because you gave yourself permission to do it. And you couldn't *not* fall in love with someone just because you knew it was wrong. Just because you were so afraid of being hurt again.

Dana pulled a turquoise bathing suit out of her dresser. It was halfway to the bag before she changed her mind. No sense tempting fate. She still wasn't showing, but she didn't want to risk drawing Rafe's attention to her body any more than necessary. That was why all the tops were loose, all the shorts baggy. Her precautions might seem silly since he would certainly see her naked when they made love, but that was different. Because when she was naked, he wasn't really looking at her, he was in the grip of passion, the same as she was, and passion always blurred things.

Like common sense.

She had to tell him. After this weekend, she would have to tell him. She could almost feel the burden weighing her down. The longer she waited, the worse it would seem. She knew that, and yet something within her kept stopping her from telling him. Something within her kept crying out, "More, just a little more."

Her mouth curved. Just like Oliver Twist, she thought, who'd asked for more.

Dana sank down on the bed beside the overnight bag. The problem with more was that it was endless.

Just like her craving for Rafe.

She knew there was no satiating her where Rafe was concerned. It wasn't a matter of once or twice and then she was satisfied and on her way. Until the day she died, she would go on wanting Rafe, wanting to make love with him. Wanting to lie in his arms when the lights were low and breathing returned to normal, feeling safe. Pretending that what there was between them was love. It wasn't such a stretch.

After all, part of it was already true. She loved him.

Dana drew the overnight bag to her. Well, that was it, she decided, closing the flap. She wasn't going to need very much for this weekend.

Rafe had told her to pack only a toothbrush and a favorite lure, if she had one. Dana smiled at the memory of that conversation. She'd thought he was talking about a sexy nightgown. Turned out Rafe was talking about a real lure, the kind used for fishing. She'd been surprised to discover that he loved to fish. She'd never been near a pole in her life. When he heard that, the agenda for the weekend was set—fishing lessons and lovemaking, not necessarily, he made it clear, in that order.

Dana couldn't wait. She didn't particularly want to go fishing, but for him, she was willing to put up with it, hooks, worms and all. Who knew, it might even be fun. Everything, it seemed to her, was fun as long as it was with him.

Early Saturday morning, they were going to drive up to the cabin his parents owned on Lake Elsinore. It would be just the two of them—and the fishing lures. He'd wanted to do something special with her, because he knew this was the last weekend before the trial got under way, now that jury selection was over. From here on in, her hours would be even more limited than they had been. And he understood that, she marveled. There was no indication that he resented having to share her with her work, and certainly no hint that he didn't like sharing her with Mollie. He was in a class by himself.

Maybe, just maybe…

The doorbell rang. Rafe. She grabbed her bag and flew down the stairs, anticipation fluttering through her.

One last weekend, she thought, her feet hitting the stairs.

Forty-eight hours more, that was all she wanted. And then she would tell him.

Rafe looked at her, trying very hard not to laugh. How could anyone with such a graceful body have such an awkward form while fishing? She looked like a mannequin someone had hastily posed before hurrying away.

That was all right, he mused. She had other virtues. If he concentrated, he could still feel her lips racing along his face, her hands eagerly divesting him of his clothing the moment they'd walked into the cabin.

She was like a tigress, a wild creature just barely tamed. He almost hadn't been able to keep up with her. The thought made him grin. The grin grew as he watched in silence while Dana tried to cast again and failed miserably. The line had skimmed the stream and floated back to her like a misshapen boomerang.

At least it was better than her first two casts, which had gotten tangled in the branches above them. Given enough time and patience, he figured he could make a fisherman out of her yet.

And he meant to give her all the time in the world.

"What are you grinning about?" she demanded, reeling her line in, determined to attempt another cast. Eventually it would have to go where it was supposed to, wouldn't it?

"Nothing," he answered innocently, but his eyes continued smiling as Dana got her line caught in the branches again. God, but it was peaceful here. He loved his work, but it was nice to leave everything behind once in a while. As long as he had someone to share it with.

Rafe glanced toward her. "I know I should have told you to bring Mollie, but I wanted to be alone with you."

Maybe it would work better if she ventured a little farther into the stream, the way he did. Standing on the bank and casting wasn't working. She yanked her line from the lowest branch.

"Just you, me and several hundred fish." Or so he had

said. She had yet to see any evidence of that. "Very romantic."

Rafe laughed softly. "You have to keep your voice low, or they'll hear you."

The pole slipped in her hands as she tried her umpteenth cast. The lure caught the edge of her cutoffs, barely missing her thigh. She gritted her teeth in frustration, working the lure out of the frayed edges. "I'm not ashamed of what I'm saying."

He could only shake his head. Maybe this wasn't such a good idea after all. Fishing relaxed him, but it was obviously doing just the opposite with her. "It's not that. The noise might scare them away."

"I knew that." She blew out a breath. There was a trick to this, she knew it. Why couldn't she get it? "What I don't know is how to cast this stupid thing into the water."

Rafe reeled in his line. He'd offered to help her when they started, but she'd insisted on doing it herself. Maybe she would let him help her now.

"Want my help?"

She looked at him, exasperated. Pride shuffled away, head bowed. "Yes."

As he began wading toward her, she decided to meet him halfway. The cool water would be a welcome relief on her legs. But as she began to gingerly pick her way over the rocks, she lost her footing. Her feet flew out from under her, and she came down hard, hitting her tailbone on a rock.

For a second Dana felt light-headed and disoriented, and then the pain descended in full force to claim her. An involuntary groan escaped her lips.

Rafe dropped his rod and ran the last few feet to her. Worried, he fell to his knees beside her. "Are you all right?"

She couldn't speak. All her faculties were focused on trying to deal with the pain that was firing in all directions through her abdomen. Without realizing it, she clutched at his hand, holding on so tightly her fingers were turning white. The pain wouldn't leave.

"I'm okay," she whispered raggedly. "Just let me catch my breath."

She was definitely *not* okay. She was rocking like someone trying to find a place for themselves amid a fiery pit of pain. He turned her face toward the sun for a better view. Her eyes looked dazed.

"I think that's enough fishing for—Dana, you're bleeding."

She couldn't assimilate what he was saying. Something about bleeding? He was staring at the water beneath her. Confused, she looked down.

The water around her shorts was turning a dirty, dull shade of pink. Or was that red? She couldn't think. The pain wouldn't let her. It refused to subside.

And then, suddenly, she realized what it was. Blood. Her blood.

Her nails dug into his hand. "Oh, my God, the baby." Her breath left her as panic leaped into the center of the circle of pain. "I'm losing the baby." Her eyes widened as she stared at the water again. "Rafe, I'm going to lose the baby."

It was his turn to feel confused. What was she talking about?

"Baby?" He stared at her. She wasn't pregnant. Was she? "What baby?"

Hysteria threatened to break through, to sweep her away. This couldn't be happening, not after she'd come to terms with having this baby. Not after she'd braced herself to sacrifice everything to bring this child into the world.

"*My* baby!" Dana cried.

The first time he'd made love to her was over a month ago. It was possible, just possible, that—

Oh, God.

"Why didn't you tell—damn, never mind." This was no time for recriminations or demands. Words could come later. There would be time enough then to sort everything out. He had to concentrate on the emergency he had on his hands.

His thoughts, so jumbled a moment ago, threw themselves

into a structured whole. There was nothing in the house that would be of any help in this situation. She needed a hell of a lot more than peroxide and Band-Aids, or even what he had available in his medical bag. "I've got to get you to the hospital, baby."

Baby, her baby. Dana clawed at him. He had to help, had to save her child. "Rafe, I can't lose this baby. I just can't."

Fear tied a tourniquet around his heart as it fought for control of the rest of him. He couldn't let her see what he was going through. It would only make it worse for her. Damn it, he was trained for this.

No, he was trained for other people's emergencies, not his own. It was always different when it was yours. What if she…

No!

He wasn't going to go there, wasn't going to think that. Nothing was going to happen to her, *nothing*. He wouldn't allow it.

His voice was calm as he said, "You're not going to lose the baby. Just hang on, everything's going to be all right. Do you hear me, Dana?"

Weakly, she nodded, clutching at his words. Holding him to them.

She swallowed a groan as he picked her up, biting hard on her lower lip and not even feeling it. Every step he took vibrated through her, intensifying the pain.

Rafe moved as quickly as he dared. His heart was pounding by the time he reached the car. As gently as he could manage, he eased her into the back seat. "Lie down, Dana."

There was horror on her face, "You've got blood on your shirt."

He looked down. Her blood was smeared across the bottom of his shirt. He had to stop the bleeding, or at least slow it down. He stripped off his shirt, wadded it up, then pressed it between her legs. He wedged his medical bag under her hips, elevating them as best he could.

He guided her hand to the shirt. "Now hold that there. Press as hard as you can," he ordered. "It's the best I can do to stop the bleeding.'' Because she looked so helpless, he stopped to kiss her. It was a rough kiss, an urgent kiss, meant to make him feel better as well as her. ''I won't let anything happen to you, I swear.''

He prayed in his heart that nothing would make him break his promise.

''Hang on,'' he ordered, jamming the key into the ignition.

He knew he was in a race against time. As long as she didn't lose too much blood, there was hope.

Memories of Debra, of the insane ride to the hospital as he tried to outrace death that last time, haunted him. He hadn't made it then, although what he'd expected the hospital staff to do he didn't know. She'd died before he could reach it.

That wasn't going to happen again. Sweet God, that wasn't going to happen again.

Rafe drove from the cabin and its idyllic setting like a madman. There was no hospital between here and Harris Memorial. Familiar with all the back roads, all the shortcuts, he took them at speeds that would have horrified him if he was paying attention to the speedometer. But he wasn't. All he could think was that he had to get Dana to the hospital. To people who could help her. Nothing else mattered except saving Dana.

Sheila felt drained. Perspiration plastered her scrubs to her body, and she could feel a fresh line of sweat trickling down her back. It had been touch and go there for a few minutes. She didn't want to dwell on how it might have gone had Rafe arrived any later.

This, she reminded herself, was one of the good moments. One of those magical saves she had been trained for. It felt a little surreal when it involved a friend.

Two friends, she amended, coming out of the room. Rafe was in the hallway, standing like a steadfast tin soldier, his back pressed against the wall. No doubt for support. He looked terrible, she thought, her heart going out to him. He looked like a man who thought he was on a deathwatch.

He had called her on his car phone, snapping out details, and she'd never heard him sound like that before. As if he was holding himself together through sheer grit. She'd gone racing to the hospital and met them in the emergency room. The rest was a blur of hands, transfusions and efforts that were superhuman and ingrained.

It had worked. Mother and unborn child were both going to be fine.

Rafe came to attention as soon as he saw Sheila. He refused to try to read her expression. Sheila was always determined to be upbeat about everything, no matter what. He wanted to hear the words.

"How is she?"

Sheila wasted no time before reassuring him. "She's going to be fine, Rafe. You got her here just in time. A little longer and…well, no need to go there." She paused. "I'd like her to stay overnight, just to rest, but there's no need to worry. She'll be able to go home in the morning."

An almost overwhelming relief, bordering on euphoria, washed over him, leaving him weak. She was all right. Dana was going to be all right. "And the baby?"

Sheila nodded, looking at him closely. Trying to read his expression. "The baby's safe. Like I said, you got her here just in time." Sheila paused, not knowing exactly how to proceed. How much did he know? "She told you about the baby?"

"No, not exactly." In the absolute sense, she hadn't told him at all. She'd just blurted it out in her panic. He wasn't even sure if Dana knew what she'd said to him. She'd clearly been in shock.

Being a friend meant placing curiosity by the wayside sometimes. The problem was, she was friends with both of them. The only side she wanted to take was the side that saw them happy.

Sheila nodded toward the door behind her. "You can go in to see her now if you'd like."

His mouth hardened a little as he looked toward the room. "Yeah."

When she placed her hand on his arm, Rafe didn't even seem to notice. "Are you all right, Rafe?"

A baby. Why hadn't she told him? Why did he have to find out this way? He shook off his thoughts when he realized that Sheila had asked him a question. "Shouldn't I be?"

There was a defensiveness in his voice. And something else she couldn't quite make out. Tactfully, she backed away. She knew he wouldn't take kindly to being the target of advice right now.

"No, of course not. I'll see you later."

Rafe barely acknowledged her words. He eased open the door to Dana's room and let himself in quietly, in case she'd fallen asleep. He wanted to see her, to assure himself that she was all right, before he released the other feelings that were beating their fists inside him.

Her eyes darted toward the door the moment he entered. Her fear of losing the baby had been set to rest, but another, equally strong fear had taken its place. She held her breath, watching him walk toward her. She expected anger to crease his face, but it didn't. Instead, there was an expression there she couldn't read.

The fear wouldn't go away.

Still weak, she held her hand out to him. "Rafe, I'm so sorry." The words sounded hopelessly insignificant to her ears.

"It's okay, baby, it's okay." Rafe took her hand, wrapping his around it. Color was beginning to slip into her face. She looked exhausted. He knew he should let her rest, but he had to know, had to understand. "Why didn't you tell me you were pregnant?"

They'd given her something to make her relax. She struggled against its effects. She couldn't think, couldn't find the words to make this sound right. Her brain felt like so much wet cotton.

She shrugged helplessly. "Not enough courage."

What did courage have to do with it? Did she think he would reject her? Didn't she know him well enough to realize he wouldn't do that? "Dana, as the baby's father, I had a right to know."

As the baby's father. He thought it was his.

Dana closed her eyes, fighting tears. He'd given her a way out, handed it to her on a silver tray. It was so easy. So easy. She could...

No, she couldn't. Not ever. Not even to keep him.

The next words that came out of her mouth were the hardest she'd ever had to say. "Rafe, it's not your baby."

"Not my—" What did she mean, it wasn't his? "Then who—" An icy hand passed over his heart. "Steven?" He dropped her hand as he spoke.

She pressed her lips together, feeling the tears gathering in her soul, the sickening taste of fear filling her mouth. But he had to be told.

"Yes."

Numb, he could only stare at her. "How long have you known?"

She felt as if every word she uttered was pushing him away from her. "Since the morning before I met you."

He couldn't believe it. Couldn't make himself believe it. She'd known all along. Making love with him, she'd known. "And you didn't say anything?"

His voice was low, emotionless. Steely. Fear slid down her back like an icicle. Not even facing her father had made her feel like this.

Confused, dazed and backed into a corner, she felt herself irrationally lashing out. "What could I say? 'Hello, I'm Dana Morrow, cure my niece and, oh, yes, by the way, I'm pregnant by a man who hates children'?"

She could have found a way to tell him, he thought. There must have been an opening, some point when she felt they were getting serious, when she could have told him. He deserved that from her.

"Does he know?"

She nodded. "He knows," she said bitterly. "And denies it's his. Says he can get a whole clubhouse full of his friends to swear I was the town slut." Dana looked at him. He had to believe her. "I wasn't. I don't sleep around. I never did. And it matters to me that you believe that. You matter." She reached out to him, but he didn't take her hand.

Temper heated the blood in his veins. He raised his voice. "If I mattered so much, why didn't you tell me?"

She wasn't going to cry. She wasn't going to give him the satisfaction of knowing he was hurting her. Didn't he realize the hell she'd been going through? Was still going through? "Don't yell at me," she snapped.

That only added fuel to the fire. "What do you expect me to do, stand up and cheer? Applaud? Just how long did you think you could keep this from me?" he demanded.

"I don't know." As suddenly as her anger had filled her, it drained away. She told him the truth, even though she knew he wouldn't believe her. And it was her fault. "I was playing for time. Days. Minutes. Every minute you didn't know was a minute longer I had with you."

Frustration tore holes in her. She didn't know how to make him understand. She could argue eloquently before a jury, but where her own case was concerned, she couldn't summon the words with which to plead. She could only pray.

"At first there was no reason to tell you. And then there was every reason *not* to tell you." She threw her last card onto the pile. "I was afraid, all right?"

But he shook his head at her, at the words. "I don't know if it's all right. I don't know anything at all anymore."

He was backing away from her. Leaving. And she couldn't blame him. Not rationally. But emotionally, she felt like hurling things at him for disappointing her this way. For deserting her.

Dana drew herself together, trying to ignore the emptiness that was growing within her. "I'm sorry if I can't live up to some pristine image that you have. I can't be like Debra."

She'd struck a direct hit. "Leave Debra out of this."

It was as if he'd stuck a knife into her heart and then twisted it. She'd been wrong about him all along, about his gentleness, his kindness. Terribly wrong. Wrong again. What a surprise.

"Not even good enough to talk about her, is that it?" She spat the words out. "Fine, I won't. Now you get out of my room, Dr. Saldana."

For a second he hesitated. No matter what she'd done, he didn't want to leave her this way. "Dana, I—"

But she wasn't going to listen, didn't want to look at him anymore. "Just get out. Now!"

She maintained her cold fury just long enough for the door to close behind him. And then she dissolved into tears and cried her heart out.

What was left of it.

Chapter 20

"Dr. Saldana, would you be willing to squeeze in Allison Adray this afternoon?" Knocking as she opened the door, Alice peered into the doctor's office. "Her mother just called. She thinks Allison's coming down with something."

Irritated at being interrupted, Rafe glared in the nurse's direction. Was it too much to ask for five minutes of peace?

"Her mother always thinks she's coming down with something. The woman is trying to make hypochondria a family affair. If we're booked, Alice, tell her so," he snapped.

The look on Alice's face brought him up sharply. He could see exactly what she thought of the mood he was in. The mood he had resided in for the past two and a half weeks.

Silently, Alice turned on her heel and walked away. "As you wish, Doctor."

He sighed, trying to control his temper. Of late, he felt as if he was teetering on the edge of losing it all the time. Everything annoyed him. Misplaced tongue depressors, interruptions, the color yellow. Everything and anything. He had to get hold of himself.

"No, scratch that," he called after Alice. "Tell her to get down here as soon as she can. I'll see what's wrong with Allison this time—besides her mother."

"Fine, I'll tell her."

He wasn't forgiven, Rafe thought as he shut the door. But that was her problem. He had other things to deal with than an overly sensitive nurse who doubled as a receptionist.

When the door opened again almost immediately, Rafe threw down his pen in exasperation. Since when had his office been declared an intersection?

"What is it now? All I asked for was a few minutes of peace to write up some notes."

Instead of Alice or one of the other nurses, it was Gabe who walked into the room. He looked a little surprised at the greeting. "Wow, your bedside manner has really gone to hell, hasn't it?"

Rafe gave up on the report. Maybe he could get to it later. "Sorry, just a little on edge lately." He pushed himself back from the desk and looked at his younger brother. Gabe was in uniform, so he was still on duty. "What are you doing here?"

Gabe made himself comfortable in the chair across from Rafe's desk. He noted the tension in his brother's face. Something was up.

"I was in the neighborhood, and I thought I'd let you take me to lunch, seeing as how you're the successful brother." His lopsided grin appeared. "Unless, of course, you're seeing your lady."

His lady. No, she wasn't his lady, Rafe thought. She wasn't his anything, not anymore. Nearly three weeks had gone by since he'd seen her. Three weeks down and a lifetime to go. He figured it would take that long to get his life on an even keel again. Right now, it was completely upended, and he had all he could do to make it from one end of the day to the other.

Rafe turned his attention to the file on his desk. "No, I'm not seeing her."

Though they didn't see each other much anymore, he and Rafe were close enough for Gabe to pick up the nuances that might have escaped others. He'd only seen his brother like this once before.

"You say that with a lot of conviction." He lowered his face until he could get a better look at Rafe's. "Trouble in paradise?"

It was useless to try to concentrate. Not with Gabe yammering at him, getting in his face. And not with his head so messed up.

"No, we just weren't right together." Rafe's voice was cool, detached. "You know how it is." Why did he have to explain himself to Gabe, of all people? "Hell, you go from one woman to another like a bee goes from flower to flower, pollinating them."

Gabe continued studying Rafe as he spoke. "Yeah, I guess I do. But that's me, not you." His eyes met his brother's. "You don't pollinate, Rafe. You're a one-flower bee." Rafe was hurting, Gabe thought. And too bullheaded to admit it. Like all the Saldana men, he supposed. "And you don't attach yourself to that flower unless you're damn sure. Okay, tell me. What gives?"

Talking about his feelings had never come easily to Rafe. It was no different now. "Nothing."

Gabe rose and went to the door. But instead of leaving, he closed it, then returned to face Rafe. "Behind this smiling exterior is a damn good cop, bro. I'm not leaving until I get the goods." Pulling the extra chair around until it was positioned directly beside Rafe's, Gabe straddled it. "Now, are you going to tell me, or are we going to sit here all day, staring at each other?"

Rafe hated being put on the spot, but he knew Gabe wouldn't back off. He hung on like a damn terrier when he wanted to, just like their father. "You want to know? All right, I'll tell you. She's pregnant."

The information took a minute to sink in. And then Gabe

was reaching for Rafe's hand, slapping him on the back. "Hey, congra—"

Rafe pushed his brother's hand away, rising. "It's not mine." He began pacing the room, impatience bubbling in his veins.

Thrown, Gabe could only stare at him. "Not yours? Then whose..."

Angry, without a target to take it out on, Rafe shoved his hands into his pockets. "The last guy she was with."

Gabe was trying to make sense of the fragments coming his way. "She sleeps around." Even as he said it, it didn't feel right. The woman he'd seen with his brother, the woman he'd danced with, didn't seem to be that type.

Rafe wheeled around, defending a woman he'd blocked out of his life. "No!"

Though his brother banked it down quickly enough, Gabe didn't miss the emotion on his face. No matter what he said to the contrary, Rafe had feelings, strong feelings, for Dana. Gabe was willing to bet his badge on it.

Gabe continued studying Rafe's face, his movements. "She break up with this guy before she met you?"

The shrug was halfhearted and dismissive. "Yeah."

Then why was Rafe so mad? Unless...

"And is she going back to him?" Gabe guessed.

"No, and that's not the point." Rafe glared at Gabe, tired of being grilled.

He was good at untangling things, Gabe thought, but he was going to need a little help here. "What *is* the point?" he asked seriously. "It can't be that you don't want kids, because I've seen you with them. Hell, you're better with kids than most people."

Because they were brothers, and because he knew Gabe cared, Rafe struggled to hang on to his temper. To keep from telling Gabe to take his questions and get the hell out. "The point is she kept it from me. She wouldn't tell me, wouldn't be honest with me. If she hadn't fallen..."

Gabe jumped on the information. "She fell?"

"Stop interrupting, damn it!" Rafe dragged his hand through his hair, trying to collect himself. Everything inside him felt raw. "That weekend we went up to the cabin, she slipped on a rock. She came down hard and started bleeding. That's when she told me." Even talking about it upset him. Made him relive it all. "I drove her to the hospital." He began pacing again. "I don't even remember driving. All I could think of was saving her, saving the baby." His mouth twisted in a mocking smile. "I had this crazy notion the baby was mine."

Gabe watched him steadily. "But she told you it wasn't."

"What does it matter what she told me? It's over."

If that was the case, Rafe wouldn't have looked like something the dog dragged in. "Is it?"

Rafe was in no mood for rhetorical questions. "I just said—"

"Yeah, words. I know you, Rafe. Once you're in, you're in. You're not the type to back away. I think you're using this whole thing as an excuse. A smoke screen to hide what's really going on." He knew his brother better than he knew anyone, probably including himself. Gabe rose to face him. "I think you're afraid."

That was absolutely ridiculous. "Of what?" Rafe demanded.

"Of being hurt again. Of what you went through when Debra died." Gabe put his hand on Rafe's shoulder, only to have it shrugged off. Gabe took no offense. If the tables had been turned, he would probably have taken a swing at Rafe. "Think about it."

Gabe crossed to the door. He'd said as much as he could. He couldn't make Rafe see what he refused to see. That part was up to Rafe.

"I'll see you around, bro. Think about it," he repeated closing the door behind him.

"Dana, I need you."

Startled, Dana looked up slowly from the briefcase she wa

packing. Without realizing it, she tightened her fingers on the notes she'd prepared for her father's cross-examination of one of the prosecution's key witnesses.

She had to be dreaming.

All her life, she'd secretly waited for those words. But there had to be some mistake. Her father had always made a point of not needing anyone. He liked comparing himself to a venerable oak. He stood alone.

She let the notes drop into the open briefcase. "Excuse me?"

Impatient, her father pushed his chair into her room. "Something wrong with your hearing? I said I need you." She was still looking at him blankly, as if she'd lost the ability to understand her native tongue. "At the trial today, I need you to sit at the table."

The table was full. There was her father, then David Headley, the second chair, and Alex McGuire, who rounded out the defense team.

"But David and Alex—"

His impatience grew. He didn't stand protests well. "Alex was in a waterskiing accident yesterday." He dismissed the incident as being beneath his interest. "Trying to impress someone. The fool knew better than to take chances." Morrow hated the unexpected when a case was being tried. "I expect my people to remain sane during a case."

She thought of his partner. Surely Wallace would have something to say about him choosing her, even if her father's name was the first on the door. He didn't like using "untried talent," as he called it. The trial was beginning to turn in their favor, with new evidence that cast doubt on the senator's guilt, but it wasn't like her father to venture out on uncertain ground.

"What about Mr. Wallace?"

Morrow's eyes seemed to glitter. "Wallace has taken an early retirement." There was nothing but contempt in his voice for the man he deemed to be a traitor in his ranks. "The very thing he wanted for me. I thought it only fair to return his thoughtfulness." Elbows on the armrests, he brought his fingertips together, watching her face. "That leaves you."

He'd forgotten about the others, all of whom had seniority on her. "And—"

He was through bandying this about. "I know who else I have working for me. I also know their abilities." His eyes narrowed. "I watched you try a case once. You were good. Not spectacular, and you could stand work, but you were good."

"When? When did you see me?" He had never been in any courtroom she'd pleaded in. Dana would have sworn to it.

Morrow didn't brook questioning, either. "My house, girl. I ask the questions. You're who I want. Will you be up to it?"

She swallowed, suddenly feeling breathless and confused at the same time. "Yes, of course, it's just that you've taken me by surprise."

The admission pleased him. He laughed to himself. "That's what I do best. I take people by surprise." Feeling expansive, he shared something with her. "Ever since I was a skinny, snot-nosed kid, I've taken people by surprise." He looked away. "I probably took my father by surprise. He expected me to die in a gutter somewhere."

Dana felt like someone on the bomb squad, reaching to touch a wire, hoping not to set off an explosion but to prevent one. And to learn from it. Dana kept her eyes on his face, watching for a warning. She inched a little further into uncharted territory. "You never told me anything about my grandfather."

He knew that. He'd never told anyone about the family he was ashamed of, the background he'd buried so successfully. Not even his wife. She'd been given very little information, and what there was of it had been false. "That's because I've always operated on a need-to-know basis. You didn't need to know."

"And now?" she asked. Did he think she needed to know now? "I'd like to know now," she added.

He looked at her for a long moment, as if a debate was being waged in his mind. And then, finally, he spoke. "There's not much to tell. He was an abusive drunk. That's what made him the perfect match for my mother." There was no nostalgia in his voice, no wistfulness. Just disgust. "Between the two of them, they must have drunk half of Oklahoma dry."

"Oklahoma?" she repeated, confused. "Why Oklahoma?"

He spoke curtly. "Because that's where I'm from."

That wasn't what her mother had told her. "I thought—"

He knew exactly what she thought, because he'd invented it, down to the last detail. And covered his tracks well. "The official story is San Francisco. Wealthy background, breeding, trust fund, best schools." He rattled it off, knowing it by heart. The heart people claimed he didn't have. "The only part of it that's true is the best schools. And you know why?"

Dana slowly moved her head from side to side, her eyes riveted to her father.

"Because I did anything I had to to get into them. I was on the street by the time I was fourteen." There was no humor in his laugh. "If I hadn't been, my father would eventually have killed me." Even as he said it, the beatings returned to him. A belt buckle, newly sharpened, catching his flesh, tearing it as it came down. "It was just a matter of time. I didn't intend to wait for it. So I left, survived, made something of myself. You get famous by being the best, so I became the best, courting the limelight as if it was half debutante, half whore. But you can't court it if you come from roots you're ashamed of. So I cut my roots and didn't look back. After a while, I began to believe in the image I created. I *became* that man.

"There," he said dismissively, "you have it. The real story." It was a moment before he looked at her. She looked appropriately surprised. Good. If there had been pity in her expression, she would have paid dearly for it. "If I left compassion out, it's because I never really came across it until it was almost too late.'' He'd said this much, he thought, he might as well say the rest of it. ''Your mother was compassionate at first, but it was wasted on me, because I had my eye on a goal, and nothing was going to get in my way. Not even her love.''

Dana didn't understand. After years of keeping her out, why the sudden change? ''Why are you telling me all this?''

He didn't like explaining himself, but he supposed, in this instance, because he was the one who had initiated it, he could cut her some slack. ''I thought maybe you should know. And there's no one to tell you but me. Who knows how much longer I'll be around?''

She hated this talk of dying. Science was progressing all the time. There had to be something that could be done for her father. ''Don't say that.''

He was careful not to show any emotion. Emotion clouded your brain, made you clumsy. And it made you lose.

''Never be afraid of the truth. If you have it, you can use it as a weapon.'' Time was growing short, and he had yet to talk to his people about Day Thirteen of the trial. ''Ready? The car is waiting.''

She nodded. He turned the chair and began to leave the room. ''Father?''

He waited for her to join him. ''Yes?''

''Thanks for telling me.''

He didn't want her thanks, he wanted her loyalty. ''I did it for me, not for you.''

It had a grain of truth in it, but there was more to it than that. She smiled at him and then walked behind, pushing the chair. ''I know, but thanks just the same.''

The second day into that week's proceedings, her father surprised her again. Handing her the notes she'd prepared for the second chair, he had her take over the cross-examination. Stunned, Dana had less than five minutes to pull herself together. She used her edginess to her advantage, wielding i like a well-honed saber. Thrusting, parrying and leaving wounds the prosecution had to deal with.

She was, to his satisfaction, her father's daughter. As he'd known she would be, given the right direction.

When Dana had no more questions for the witness, the judge called a recess. Dana felt as if her knees were about to give out, but it was a good feeling. Her father trusted her. Maybe she was finally on the right track to getting her life in order.

The courtroom rustled as people left their seats. Dana looked in her father's direction, catching his eye. He nodded, saying nothing. She knew better than to expect praise. He'd given her the praise by trusting her.

Relieved, exhausted, Dana sat at the table and began gathering her things. She had two hours before she had to sit here again. Two hours in which to go somewhere and unwind.

Her father and David Headley, the second chair, left while she was still packing her briefcase. She'd turned down their invitation for lunch. She was much too tense to eat.

Thinking she was alone, she was startled when she sensed someone in the room directly behind her. She turned, expecting to see anyone but who she saw.

"Rafe?"

He crossed to her and pushed open the wooden gate that separated the spectators from the players. The greeting he'd rehearsed in his head a dozen times while watching her today seemed trivial and unnecessary.

"My father called me and said he saw you on the news last night. That you were sitting at the defense table. I thought I'd see for myself." The smile was small but genuine. "Pretty impressive." He didn't add that he'd felt proud of her when she'd held up her end against a top assistant D.A.

"Thank you," she responded stiffly, snapping the locks on her briefcase, then picking it up. "If you'll excuse me, I have to be somewhere."

To her exasperation, he fell into step beside her. "Mind if I come along?"

"Yes, I do mind." Dana stopped and swung around to face him. She wanted no misunderstandings. "The somewhere I have to be is anywhere that you're not."

He took the direct hit and tried not to wince. "I guess I had that coming."

Did he think that made them even? That now he could come waltzing into her life and she would welcome him with open arms?

"No, you have a lot more coming than that, but as a criminal lawyer, I know that justifiable homicide isn't always easy to prove."

He saw the fury in her eyes. And the hurt. He'd done that to her, he thought. The last thing in the world he'd wanted to do.

"Dana, I'm sorry."

Oh, no, it wasn't going to go like that. "That's it?" she demanded. How dare he? How *dare* he? "You yank my heart out, walk away from me when I need you most, and you're *sorry?*"

He nodded, unable to put it any better than that. "Yes, I'm sorry. Very sorry."

She wasn't going to be taken in by this. She wasn't. "Fine. Apology accepted. Most men wouldn't be able to deal with the idea of the woman they were currently involved with carrying some other man's child. I understand." She was trying very hard not to let her voice break under the stress of hiding her emotions. Knowing that was a clear and present danger, she began to push past him. "Now get out of—"

She had to hear him out. He caught her hands in his to keep her from walking out. "I'm not most men, I don't get currently involved, and it's not your baby I have a problem with. It's you."

She wasn't buying it. She didn't care how sincere his eyes looked. It was a trick, all a trick. "Nicely put." Her expression was hard, unyielding. She'd learned well from her father. "You're good at twisting knives once you inflict a wound."

"I have a problem," he continued, as if she hadn't jus

done everything except tell him to go to hell, raising his voice as she walked away, "because I love you."

Dana stopped walking. But she was afraid to turn around. Afraid to hope.

So he came to her. He would have crawled to her if it would have helped.

"Because when I was driving like a madman to the hospital with you bleeding in the back seat, I was completely scared out of my mind that I'd lose you. That you'd die and leave me." Slowly, he circled her, stopping when he faced her. He had to make her understand. "That it was happening all over again, the way it had with Debra. I went to hell and managed to come back the last time. I didn't think I could do it again."

"So you wanted to leave before anything else happened to make you face that kind of ordeal again. All right, I understand. You want—"

"What I want," he interrupted, his hand on her shoulder to keep her from leaving, "is you. The hell of not having you, knowing I could, is worse than anything I could have imagined. I don't even know myself anymore. My patients are backing away from me, my nurses are on the verge of a mutiny, and Sheila…Sheila is threatening to cut off very important portions of my anatomy if I don't straighten up and fly right. I figure that flight has only one destination in its flight plan." He took her hands in his. "Marry me, Dana. Marry me and make me sane again. You'll gain the undying thanks of an awful lot of people."

He was proposing to her. Actually proposing. "It's not every day a girl gets to be a savior."

"No, it's not. Be mine. And I swear, no one will ever love you the way I do."

She smiled. "I already know that."

She'd misunderstood him. He wanted everything to be perfectly clear. "In and out of bed."

"Oh." And then the smile faded, along with the temporary dream. She was an optimist, but not foolishly so. "And the baby? Will you be able to face the baby, knowing it's not yours?''

She was wrong there. "But it is," he insisted. "The way I see it, if I hadn't gotten you to the hospital in time, that baby would have died. That means I gave it a second chance. I gave it life. That baby is mine as much as it is yours."

Dana could only look at him in complete disbelief. She was surprised she could find her tongue. "You would have made a very good lawyer."

"I'll leave that up to you. One lawyer per couple is plenty." He searched her face, trying to find an answer in her expression. "So, will you? Will you marry me?"

There was so much happiness inside her, she thought she was going to burst. "What do you think?"

"I think," he murmured, feathering his fingers along her face—God, how had he managed to stay away so long? "If I don't kiss you soon, I'm going to die."

"Can't have that happening." Her eyes were teasing. "Who would take your place at the wedding?"

"I don't intend for you to find that out. Ever."

Dana brought his mouth to hers and kissed him. She saw it as an act of mercy. For both of them.

Epilogue

Dana fell back against Rafe's hands, drained, as another hellish contraction receded. Even her eyelashes were heavy with perspiration. It felt as if she'd been at this for hours.

She looked at Sheila, then blinked to see her clearly. Everything looked out of focus in the delivery room.

"Damn, why didn't you tell me it was going to be this hard?"

Sheila shifted on the stool, her back aching. This wasn't going as quickly as she'd hoped, for Dana's sake, it would. Her friend's labor had been going on for seven hours.

She lifted her head to allow the nurse to dry her forehead before the sweat went into her eyes.

"Trust me, you'll forget all about this the first time you hold little what's-it in your arms." She saw the look on Dana's face. Another contraction was coming. Sheila pulled her stool closer. "Just a little more, Dana, push a little more."

Dana wanted to run from the pain, to hide somewhere, anywhere, but it kept finding her, exhausting her. She felt

Rafe gently pushing against her back, moving her into an upright position.

"I don't have a little more," Dana groaned.

Still supporting her, Rafe brought his face in close to hers. "Sure you do. You're the stubbornest woman I know. The stubbornest human being I know," he corrected himself.

He hated seeing her suffering, but there was no way around it. He tried to give her something to hang on to besides the sides of the gurney. He was betting on her feistiness to get her through this.

"Mollie's been waiting outside for hours to find out whether she has a little brother or a sister. How much longer do you intend to keep her waiting?"

They'd made it official. Too impatient to wait, Rafe had married Dana before Senator Johnson's trial was over. Instead of a honeymoon, they'd immediately gone to court to begin adoption proceedings to make Mollie theirs. And then Dana had gone on to be on the winning team of the trial of the decade as the jury brought in a verdict of not guilty. All in all, it had been a hell of a month.

But it was nothing compared to this moment, being here with Dana, waiting for his child to be born. *His* child and no one else's. The bastard whose seed had gone to create this miracle that was happening right before him had signed away all rights, all claims to the baby, in exchange for a set sum of money. This baby was theirs.

"That's right," Dana said, panting, only half feigning anger, "make me feel guilty."

His laugh had tension laced through it. "Hey, what's a husband for if he can't take care of the little things?"

Dana managed to turn her head to look at him. "You wanna have this baby?"

He could always count on her spirit to pull her through. "I'll have the next one."

He would have to, because she sure as hell wasn't going to. She wasn't all that sure she was going to survive this if it went on much longer. "I'll hold you to that," she gasped,

Sheila spared Rafe a glance. It wouldn't be long now, she thought. She could see the baby's head. "She will, you know. You're going to be sorry you made that rash offer in front of witnesses." Sheila peered at Dana. One or two more good pushes were all it was going to take. "I'm just sitting here with my hands out. Give me something to catch, Dana. Push."

Dana gritted her teeth. "Easy for you to say."

And then, as another contraction came, threatening to rip her in half, Dana summoned what was left of her dwindling supply of strength. Concentrating, straining, she pushed with every fiber of her being until there wasn't a breath left in her.

"Good girl, good girl," Sheila coached. "A head, I have a head," she announced excitedly. Her hands flew as she cleared the baby's mouth and nasal passages. "Now give me some shoulders, Dana."

Dana scrunched the sides of her gown in her hands, desperate to hang on to something. "I'll give you more than that if you don't stop sounding like a third-string auctioneer trying to up the ante." She'd never hurt like this before, and she felt too exhausted to try anymore. She'd been pushing for so long. "Can't you just pull it out?"

Sheila empathized. "Not yet."

Rafe could feel Dana flagging. He'd never been on this side of things before, and he struggled to contain his agitation.

"C'mon, baby, you can do this. You came back and reclaimed your life through sheer grit. You made your father into a human being and me into a true believer. This should be a piece of cake for you."

The hell it was, she thought, too drained even to be irritated. "If it was a piece of cake I was trying to pass, I'd be done— *Ow*." Her eyes flew open as a king-size contraction seized her, showing absolutely no mercy. Only stubborn determination kept her from screaming.

Sheila held her breath. "Good one?"

"There is no such thing as a good contraction." The words were individually strained through clenched teeth. Another one was coming on the heels of the last, not even giving her enough time to draw breath. Her hand darted out, clutching at Rafe wildly. He caught it in his. "Oh, Rafe, hold my hand, hold my hand."

"I am holding your hand." And it felt as if she was breaking the bones of his fingers. He saw the expression on Sheila's face, saw the movement in the overhead mirror. His baby was being born. "Oh, honey, here he comes."

"She," Sheila corrected, easing the rest of the tiny body out. She grinned as she cut the cord. "You have a she."

"We have a she," Rafe repeated in awestruck wonder. He had a daughter. Another daughter. There were tears in his eyes as he pressed a kiss to Dana's damp temple, his heart brimming with love. "I always liked being surrounded by females."

Dana offered up a silent prayer. It was over. She slumped against Rafe's waiting arms.

With quick, competent movements, the attending nurse cleaned the baby and wrapped her in a blanket. Sheila took the minutes-old infant and brought her to her parents.

"Dr. and Mrs. Saldana, may I present your daughter to you?" Very gently, Sheila placed the tiny bit of humanity into Dana's arms. This, she thought, was her very favorite part.

Dana pressed her lips together. She wasn't going to cry like some foolish twit. Tears were for sorrow, not for joy. She felt them forming just the same. Comfortable in this new world she found herself in, their daughter was already falling asleep.

Dana looked at Rafe. "Oh, God, Rafe, she's so tiny."

With all the wonder of a first-time father, he touched the tiny clasped hand resting on top of the blanket. It felt so smooth, so doll-like. "They do start out that way," he murmured.

He'd been in this position countless times, looking at tiny newborns, but it had never filled his heart the way it did now

Sheila smiled. "Well, you're all ready for the recovery room."

Dana certainly felt ready for it. But there was a roomful of people waiting down the hall. She knew what they had to be feeling. She'd waited in a claustrophobia-inspiring room all night for Mollie to be born.

Dana looked at Sheila. "Can we make one side trip?"

Sheila had expected nothing less from Dana. "All right, but then I want you to rest." She grinned at her friend, affection in her eyes. "It'll be the last time you get to until this little princess goes off to college."

Dana shifted, looking at her husband. "Rafe?"

"On my way."

As soon as Rafe walked into the waiting area, all but one of the occupants rose. Mollie was the first to reach him. She stifled the urge to jump into his arms.

"Is it here yet?" she asked eagerly. She peered behind her new daddy, hoping to see a bassinet with a baby in it. "Is it here?"

He grinned at her. He was still getting used to the idea of having one daughter, and now he had two. It was a good number.

"You have a sister, Mollie. Want to see her?" Mollie's head bobbed up and down as she took his hand and held it. He looked at the others. His parents and Gabe had insisted on being notified the moment Dana went into labor. "You might as well come, too. She's in the hall."

"You left my daughter in the hall?" Paul Morrow demanded, moving forward as the others stepped to the side to allow him to pass.

Rafe had gotten accustomed to the man's crusty manner. According to Dana, her father had softened up considerably. He would hate to have known the man before his so-called transformation.

"She's en route to the recovery room," Rafe answered, "but she wanted to see you all." A smile played over his lips as his family crowded around him. "Can't see why."

Mollie moved into the hall first, followed closely by her grandfather. That Paul Morrow had insisted on being here at all had been a surprise to both Dana and Rafe. Who said a leopard couldn't change at least a few of its spots?

Family, Dana thought as they gathered around her, was definitely God's greatest invention. Her life had never felt this full.

Mollie hovered beside Dana's gurney on tiptoe. Her attention was riveted to the baby. "She's so little," Mollie whispered.

"So were you," Dana told her. Mollie looked at her in disbelief. Dana smiled. "I'm going to need a lot of help with her. Think you're up to it?"

"Yes, Aunt Da—I mean Mommy." Mollie liked fitting her mouth around the word. It felt good being able to call someone mommy again. Just as good as calling Dr. Rafe daddy. She looked at the baby, wanting to touch her but afraid of disturbing her new sister. "What's her name?"

"We wanted to call her Megan." Dana looked at her father. "Megan Jane."

Paul Morrow nodded, his mouth a tight, neutral line. But there was emotion in his eyes. "It's a good name. She'll be special right from the start."

Standing beside her, Rafe took Dana's hand and kissed it, looking at his newborn daughter. "We already knew that."

*See next page for an excerpt
from Marie Ferrarella's next book,
FIONA AND THE SEXY STRANGER,
available in July 1998 only from
Silhouette Yours Truly.*

1

"**P**ainless Parties," Fiona Reilly announced into the receiver. "Catering to suit your every whim. How may I help you?"

For a moment there was only silence on the other end.

Fiona frowned, unwilling to hang up and make herself the target for more of her sister Bridgette's nagging. "Hello?"

Bridgette looked up, mildly interested. "If it's an obscene caller, don't hang up," she instructed. "You need the practice."

Fiona waved an annoyed hand at her sister. Why did Bridgette always pick the worst times to play matchmaker? "Hello?" she repeated. "Is anyone there?"

"Are you the woman who called me about my misdirected résumé?" the voice on the other end asked.

He didn't have to say who he was. Even if he hadn't mentioned the résumé, Fiona would have recognized the drawl instantly. Though she'd made the call over three weeks ago, the voice had remained in her memory, and the fantasy she'd built around it now sprang vividly forth.

"Henry?"

Out of the corner of her eye, she saw that Bridgette had stopped packing the cream puffs and had come instantly alert, her face alive with questions. Fiona deliberately turned her back on her sister.

Fiona's guess as to his identity was rewarded with a deep chuckle that undulated along her nerve endings, unsettling her in all sorts of delicious ways she meant to mentally record and savor later, when she wasn't under Bridgette's intense scrutiny.

"How did you know?" he asked, his voice curling around each syllable.

"I recognized your voice from your answering machine. Besides, it's not every day I get a résumé lodged in between an order for a hundred guinea hens and a request for lobster bisque."

This time the pause on the other end was shorter. "Excuse me?"

"I run a catering business," she explained. She vaguely wondered if the drawl meant he was also slow in the uptake. She'd mentioned the name of her company before she'd said her name.

A short laugh warmed her ear. "Oh, that's the kind of parties you meant."

Fiona struggled not to sink into the sound. "Yes, why? What did you think I meant?"

He laughed again, this time more heartily. "Never mind, doesn't matter. Listen, the reason I'm calling is to tell you that they hired me a couple of weeks ago."

It didn't occur to her to ask why he'd felt he had to call her with this information. She was genuinely happy that she'd managed, in a small way, to help. "Congratulations."

"I figure if it hadn't been for you taking pity on a misdialing stranger, I'd still be sitting here in my living room, wondering if Collins Walker was ever going to call me for an interview. I'd just like to express my gratitude."

"All right." Fiona paused, waiting for him to say something else, perhaps launch into a lengthier thank-you. She would have been willing to sit and listen to him read the phone book just to hear the sound of his voice a little longer.

"Where would you like to go?" he asked.

Had she missed a step? Fiona turned again. A very curious Bridgette was almost in her face, her lips forming the word *who* over and over again, as if she were a determined owl. "Excuse me?" Fiona said into the phone.

"I'd like to say thanks over dinner," he clarified. "As you probably guessed if you looked at my résumé, I'm new around these parts. Where's the best place to eat?"

"My kitchen." The reply came automatically. Fiona was confident about very little when it came to herself, but she had no doubts about her ability to produce minor miracles in the kitchen.

When the laugh came again, she realized what she had said. "No, wait, I didn't mean that the way it sounded."

"How *did* you mean it?" he drawled, wondering what had produced the change in her voice. She sounded almost nervous.

"I mean, I never go out to eat. I'm too busy."

"Couldn't you make a little time?" he coaxed. A debt was a debt, and besides, she had him curious.

She could feel her palms going damp around the receiver. Damn it, he wasn't even in the room. Why was she having this absolutely ridiculous reaction? "I'm sure you can, but that still doesn't change the fact that I'm very, very busy. This is June, and I've got six weddings to do in the next three weeks. I really don't have any time to spare." Her voice was picking up speed, making the contrast with his drawl even more pronounced.

"I really would like to express my gratitude somehow," he insisted.

Even insisting took on new ramifications when done in a voice that was richer than molasses pouring from a pitcher in midsummer. She struggled not to allow herself to drown in the sound. "You already did. You said thank-you," she pointed out.

Bridgette was circling her like a shark looking for a way into the diver's protective steel cage. Each time Fiona turned, Bridgette moved with her, gesturing madly. Fiona felt as if she were being besieged from without *and* within.

There was only one thing she could do.

She would have to say yes.

THE ATTRACTION WAS ALL TOO REAL

"This position you mentioned," Claire said. "Is it in your bank?"

"No."

She eyed Garrett suspiciously. "Another hotel?"

He shook his head slowly. "The position I have in mind is a bit out of the ordinary."

"How so?"

Garrett moved a step closer, and Claire felt as if he were engulfing her. Her reaction was silly, since he was standing a good three feet away, but she couldn't push it aside. For the second time that evening, the penetrating strength of Garrett's gaze seemed to soften, and Claire found herself immobilized by the peculiar sensations racing up and down her spine.

"I'm a very wealthy man," he said finally, coming even closer, "with an ailing grandmother and a house on the Hill. You're a single young woman who needs to keep a roof over her head while she searches for her brother. If you pose as my fiancée, I will provide you with a place to live and hire a private investigator to locate Donald."

"You can't be serious?" The words tumbled out of Claire's mouth.

"Think about it." His voice dropped to a seductive whisper. "All you have to do is play the part of an attentive finacée and I'll take care of all your problems."

Right now, Claire's biggest problem was Garrett Monroe. He was standing so close, she could feel his breath in her hair. Her heart was racing and her head was spinning. Did the man think she was made of wood? How could he possibly think that she could *pretend* to love him without eventually falling in love for real?

A GENTLEMAN'S BARGAIN

Patricia Waddell

ZEBRA BOOKS
KENSINGTON PUBLISHING CORP.

http://www.kensingtonbooks.com

Chapter One

San Francisco, 1887

Claire Aldrich counted the splattering of coins on the white bedspread. Whatever she was going to do, she had to do it quickly. The rent was due in three days and the boardinghouse owner had made it abundantly clear that she wasn't a woman of patience when it came to delinquent tenants. If Claire didn't have the rent come Friday morning, Mrs. Kruger would show her the front door. Then where would she be? Out in the streets and no closer to finding her brother than she'd been three weeks ago when she'd arrived in San Francisco.

"Where are you, Donald?" Claire mumbled to herself as she walked to the window that overlooked California Street.

She'd spent almost as many hours at the window, contemplating the future, as she had walking the streets of the unfamiliar city looking for her brother. The

address on Donald's last letter had turned out to be
a clapboard cottage on Filbert Street. The family had
admitted to knowing her brother but not his present
whereabouts. He'd been hired to paint the two-story
house that could only be reached by climbing a rock
staircase. Where the young man had gone after he'd
applied the last coat of white paint the owner couldn't
be sure.

Realizing that her brother's letters hadn't been
entirely truthful, Claire had gone to the police. The
uniformed officer sitting behind a scarred wooden desk
had been very sympathetic, but he hadn't been very
helpful. Since her brother wasn't a current resident of
the jail, nor wanted by the authorities for any offense,
the officer had suggested she try asking the Benevolence
Society for help. Again, she'd found a sympathetic ear
and a recommendation for a boarding house that
catered to single young women, but no news of her
brother. After renting a room, Claire had done the only
thing she could think of doing. She'd started walking
up and down the streets, making inquires of shopkeepers and peering into the windows of drinking establish-
ments, hoping to catch a glimpse of her brother.

She'd met several industrious-looking men, who
worked on the ships anchored across from the Presidio
at Black Point. Donald had worked on the riverboats in
Cincinnati, and she had hoped that he might be making
his way in a similar fashion. Unfortunately, none of the
men had recognized her brother's name or his description. Not that Donald was all that memorable. Her
brother was six feet tall with brown hair and brown eyes.
Although Claire loved his smile and the brittle quality
of his laughter, she had to admit that Donald wasn't
the kind of man who left a lasting impression on the
people he met. The only unusual thing about her
brother was his thirst for adventure. He'd been born

with ants in his pants, or so their mother had claimed. Donald liked seeing new things and exploring new places. He'd left home on a riverboat the day he'd turned sixteen. Claire had waved good-bye to him after wrangling a promise that he would write.

The letters had been few and far between since Donald had left their small family. Their mother had died and Claire, never able to grasp the art of fine needlework, had closed her mother's shop and accepted a position as a companion to an elderly lady. Mrs. Shurman had been more friend than employer and Claire had enjoyed the time she'd spent in the Cincinnati mansion, reading and writing letters for the frail matron. Mrs. Shurman had been in her eighties and when her heart gave out, Claire was alone once again. The bonus she'd been assigned in Mrs. Shurman's will had provided the train ticket to San Francisco and enough money for a new dress and two meals a day.

But the money was running out and Claire was afraid that she'd followed her brother to California only to discover that he'd gone off chasing another sunset.

"Staring out the window won't find Donald," Claire told herself. She turned and reached for her hat. "And it certainly won't pay the rent."

Pinning the small hat, with two bright yellow feathers, on top of her honey brown curls, Claire gave the mirror over the spindle-legged vanity a quick glance. She was too consumed with thoughts of finding her brother to notice her amber eyes or the classic features that frequently turned a gentleman's head. Her petite figure didn't require a corset and she rarely wore one. Nevertheless, fashion dictated that a lady wasn't properly dressed until she'd donned layer after layer of clothing. First there was the drawers and bodice, then the corset, then the petticoat and more petticoats. And, of course, the hated bustle. Not to mention the buttons down the back of dresses that often required a second pair of hands to fasten. To Claire's way of thinking, it was a wonder any woman ever changed out of her nightgown.

Making her way from the third floor of the house, Claire stopped in the parlor and informed Mrs. Kruger that she hoped to be back in time for dinner, but if not, the landlady shouldn't worry. Mrs. Kruger was a stout, hard-built woman with gray hair, a prim mouth, and squinty brown eyes that rarely showed a flicker of approval for anyone or anything.

"Miss Haydon is going to do a poetry reading after dinner. I do hope that you will attend," Mrs. Kruger said in a flat voice after giving Claire a tense, despairing look that said she didn't approve of a young lady galli-vanting about town without an escort.

"I'll do my best to be back by then," Claire told her as she draped a cream-colored shawl over her right arm and headed for the front door. "If I'm not, please give my regrets to Rebecca."

Rebecca Haydon was a button-eyed young girl with reddish hair and an abundance of freckles on her round cheeks. She worked in a millinery shop not far from the boarding house, and although Claire liked her well enough, she couldn't imagine Rebecca reciting poetry with any enthusiasm while Mrs. Kruger judged her every word.

Putting aside the landlady's apparent disapproval, Claire stepped off the lattice-trimmed porch with its pots full of red posies and into the late morning sun. Like most homes on the street, the boarding house had been constructed in the Queen Anne style with an elaborate display of gingerbread trim, bay windows, and peaked gables. Glancing to her left, Claire looked toward Nob Hill, dominated by the Stanford mansion. She hadn't made any inquires on the Hill, thinking it unlikely that Donald would have gained the association of the city's elite. It was more than likely that he'd gotten himself into a card game and lost the money he'd earned from painting the house on Filbert Street. Which meant that he could be anywhere in the city, doing almost anything, or that he'd decided to try his luck elsewhere.

Claire frowned as she decided against using one of the cable cars that trudged up and down the lofty San Francisco hills and began walking. Her feet were free and necessity dictated that she either find her brother or a job before the day was over.

Garrett Monroe walked into his friend's office, grunted a welcome, and poured himself a stiff drink.

Christopher Landauer waited until Garrett had made himself comfortable in one of the two leather chairs that fronted the lacquered desk before he spoke. "I heard you were back. How was jolly ole England?"

"Wet and cold," Garrett complained before downing a good portion of the blended whiskey.

The two men had been friends for nearly twenty years, and although Christopher knew Garrett better than anyone, he was the first to admit that he rarely understood the handsome banker. Underneath his friend's good looks was a tough, hardheaded businessman who went after what he wanted. Garrett possessed as many physical assets as he did financial ones. Tall with raven black hair and piercing silver eyes, the banker drew female attention like a horse drew flies. But in spite of the best efforts of the ladies of San Francisco, no woman had won Garrett Monroe's heart. All they received for their valiant efforts was the banker's charming smile.

"How's Grams doing? I heard that Dr. Baldwin had to pay her a visit the other day."

Grams was the affectionate diminutive used to address Garrett's seventy-eight-year-old grandmother. Christopher was one of the privileged few who could call her *Grams* and get away with it. Theodora Monroe had been an honored matron of San Francisco society for the last thirty years, but she'd come West with a double-barrel shotgun across her lap, along with the backbone to use it. No one gave Grams any trouble, and if they did, they quickly found out that she may have lost her youth but she hadn't lost her gumption.

"Dr. Baldwin said her age is catching up with her," Garrett told his friend. "I don't believe it. Grams has the heart of an ox."

Christopher gave him a pensive look. "She is getting up in years."

"She isn't that old," Garrett argued.

Garrett adored the old woman, who had raised him after cholera had taken his parents. His grandmother was the only woman who had ever come close to touching his heart. When it came to women, Garrett had the appetite of a starving coyote and the hide of a grizzly bear. He was the first to admit that he wasn't a marrying kind of man, but his indifference seemed to challenge rather than discourage, which meant that he didn't have to put much effort into finding a willing bed partner. The ladies practically stumbled over their dainty feet in their rush to gain his attention. If he availed himself of their charms, then graciously forgot their names, there was no malice in his actions. He never got involved with virgins and he never promised his women more than the physical pleasure he could give them, which according to his reputation was more than enough to keep a sated smile on their faces while he gathered up his clothing and made use of the nearest exit.

"If Grams is getting her second wind, what's got you looking like a preacher who just discovered that the world is fresh out of sinners?"

Garrett let out a frustrated sigh. "I shouldn't have

gone to England," he admitted. "If I had been here, Grams wouldn't have spent the last six months flitting around the city like a seventy-year-old butterfly. Now, I'm back and . . ."

"You're her grandson, not her guardian," Christopher reminded him. "I know you love the old woman, but . . ."

"But nothing," Garrett countered, clearly frustrated about the situation.

He began pacing the hotel office. Garrett had loaned Christopher the money to open the hotel and the investment had proved to be a profitable one. So profitable that the two men were now partners in several hotels that stretched from the stylish streets of New York City to the windy shores of Chicago to the exotic avenues of New Orleans. They shared other investments, as well as an appreciation for good whiskey, beautiful women, and fast horses.

It was his lavish way of life that had his grandmother worried sick, Garrett admitted to himself as he turned and retraced his steps across the plush red and gold carpet. The woodwork and doors were painted a deep majestic red in bold contrast to the black lacquered furnishings and brass fixtures. An elaborate red lacquered overmantel dominated the fireplace, its shelves artfully displaying several Chinese vases as well as the delicate jade carvings Christopher had collected over the years. A large twelfth-century samurai sword hung on the wall behind his friend's desk. Garrett studied the sword for a moment, wondering if having his arm severed by the shiny blade would be as painful as the thought of losing his grandmother. The cantankerous old woman was the only family he had and even though they argued over almost everything, he truly loved her. The emotion came easy for him where Grams was concerned, but Garrett couldn't imagine himself feeling it for anyone else.

Marriage was a velvet cage and he was determined to stay free of it. The thought of sharing his bed with a woman came easily enough to mind, but sharing more than that wasn't something he could imagine easily. A wife expected to know what her husband was thinking whenever he was thinking it. She expected him to open the door to his heart and mind and let her waltz in and out as she pleased. The concept seemed as ridiculous to Garrett as leaving the vault of his bank unlocked and open to the public.

"Grams wants me blissfully married with a devoted wife and a baby perched on my knee before she departs this world for the next," Garrett announced out loud. "She's done nothing but lecture me since I returned from England. She's convinced that if I don't marry soon, she won't be alive to attend the wedding."

"She's been lecturing you for years," Christopher retorted. "When did you start listening?"

"When Dr. Baldwin told me that her next heart attack will probably be her last one."

The expression on his friend's face wasn't one that Christopher had seen before. Garrett was known for his self-control. He rarely lost his temper. One glaring look from his silver eyes was all it normally took to convince people that he wasn't a man who backed down easily.

"You really are worried about her, aren't you?"

Garrett's mouth thinned into a hard line as he nodded. "She's always been so full of life. It's strange seeing her propped up in bed like a china doll."

Christopher knew the anguish in his friend's voice was real. What he didn't know was what to do about it. "I gather you're going to postpone your trip to Seattle."

"I can't leave Grams again. I've only been back a few days. I'll wire Jared and let him know to go ahead with the negotiations. He can handle the deal. It isn't complicated."

"The deal might not be complicated, but Phillip Paige is. He's part barracuda."

Garrett laughed. "Jared's not as soft as he looks and Paige needs the money. He'll put up a fight, but I'll get what I want in the long run."

Jared Clarke was the Boston attorney Garrett had hired as the bank's legal advisor. Garrett hadn't accumulated his substantial fortune by sitting behind a rolltop desk waiting for depositors to plunk their money in his safe. His reputation for becoming actively involved in his investments had persuaded the young lawyer to come to San Francisco to try his luck in the banking industry. Jared was in Seattle at this very moment negotiating a deal that would add a lumber mill to the banker's list of financial assets.

"So what are you going to do?" Christopher asked. "Sit on the Hill and hold Grams' withering hand? Somehow I can't imagine you sipping herbal tea and reading poetry until she drifts off to sleep."

Garrett's eyes narrowed as he thought about the frail woman who had been both mother and father to him over the years. His reckless youth had turned Grams' hair a silvery gray and his adult restlessness had added more wrinkles to her delicate features. The last few years had increased their differing viewpoints to volcanic proportions as they argued more and more about his lack of interest in finding a suitable woman to marry.

"You can't keep traveling around the world to avoid your responsibilities, dear boy. Sooner or later you're going to have to marry and have children. If you don't, there won't be a Monroe to inherit what you've spent a lifetime building. Then what will you do? Grow old all alone and regret the majority of your days while you're waiting for the last one to arrive. Stop dallyin' about like a shy girl at a barn dance and get on

with it. I'm not going to live forever, no matter how much I'd prefer otherwise, and I won't be content until I know you have a family to keep you company after I'm gone."

Grams' words came racing back as Garrett tried to think of what he could do to ease her mind. Dr. Baldwin's prognosis of her declining health had brought some guilt to bear on his shoulders and he didn't like thinking that his Gypsy attitudes might subtract precious days from his grandmother's life. Maybe he should marry?

He didn't realize he'd spoken the words aloud until Christopher leaned back in his chair and started to grin. "Married? You! Don't make me laugh. You'd never be satisfied with just one woman. Monogamy goes against your natural grain. Besides, who would you marry, Belinda Belton? The girl's too proper to have a backbone. A woman like that would bore you to death."

"Belinda Belton isn't the only young lady in San Francisco," Garrett pointed out, grimacing inwardly at the thought of marrying the mousy girl just because she was his social equivalent.

Henry Belton was the president of the city's second largest bank and his ambitious wife, Ada, was constantly shoving her daughter under Garrett's nose. Everyone who was anyone in the city knew Ada Belton was determined to snag Garrett for her mundane daughter. Although her father wasn't as obvious, it was common knowledge that Henry Belton wanted to merge his bank with Garrett's and reap the rewards the younger man had gathered.

Garrett couldn't conjure up the image of Belinda Belton moaning with passion on their wedding night. If anything, his mind's eye saw just the opposite. She'd walk dutifully to the bed, slide beneath the covers with her white nightgown still covering her skinny body and lie there dormant, her eyes closed, while he mounted her. The consummation of their marriage would be more sacrifice than pleasure.

Garrett helped himself to another whiskey and stared out the window. He was too absorbed in thought to see the newest cable car move sluggishly up Nob Hill or to hear the clack of the bell as it made a stop in front of the hotel. Christopher was right. He wouldn't be a contented husband and he sincerely doubted that he could be faithful to one woman for more than a few months. He liked variety too much to curtail his sexual appetite. He kept a small but comfortable house on Bartlett Street, where he'd just installed his latest mistress. He'd met Evelyn Holmes in London and had brought her back to San Francisco with him. Petite with wide blue eyes, pouty pink lips, and a talent for making a man feel like a man, the English beauty was already beginning to bore him.

Garrett let Christopher ramble on about a recent altercation in the hotel lobby that had ended up with one of the hotel guests getting his jaw broken, but his mind wasn't on the comical fistfight. If finding himself a wife would make Grams happy, then maybe he ought to give the matter some serious consideration. After all, he did owe the old lady. She'd raised him, educated him, and even though she tested his patience, he loved her as much as she loved him. Perhaps marriage to the right woman wouldn't be that bad. The problem being, of course, that Garrett couldn't think of any woman as the *right* woman. Women in general tempted and intrigued him, but he couldn't imagine sharing more than his bed with a member of the opposite sex. He liked his independence.

Garrett's mind raced as Christopher continued his storytelling, jumping from the fisticuffs in the hotel lobby to the social gossip that kept tongues wagging on Nob Hill.

Maybe a fiancée would satisfy Grams?

Yes. That would do it. If Grams thought he'd finally found the *right* woman, then maybe she'd stop worrying about him and start worrying about her health.

But the imaginative solution brought about another problem.

What lady in her right mind would agree to an engagement for the mere sake of prolonging Theodora Monroe's life? None that Garrett could name. He wasn't vain, but he knew enough about socially acceptable young ladies and their greedy mothers to know that he wouldn't find a fictitious fiancée among the elite of San Francisco. He was the most eligible bachelor in town and one of the wealthiest men in the state. Few women would draw in their claws once they'd hooked him.

"What are you frowning about now?" Christopher asked.

"I need a woman," Garrett grumbled.

Christopher Landauer's smile was pure devilry as he poured himself a drink. "From what I hear, the one you brought back from London should be able to take care of whatever needs arise. Andy told me she's very pretty."

Andy was the hotel clerk who handled discreet errands and messages for Christopher. He was tall and thin with deep-set brown eyes and pale skin that turned ruddy in the summer. On occasion Garrett availed himself of the young man's services. He had employed Andy to drive the carriage that had delivered Evelyn Holmes to the cottage on Bartlett Street.

"Evelyn isn't the kind of woman I need," Garrett said as he turned away from the window. "She's pretty enough, but she'll never be able to fool Grams. The old woman's heart may be failing, but her eyes are as sharp as ever."

"What are you talking about?"

"Fooling Grams into thinking that I've met my match," Garrett said impatiently. "If she thinks I've fallen head over heels in love, she'll stop badgering me about my future happiness and start doing what Dr. Baldwin says she should do—rest."

Christopher placed the top on the crystal decanter with calm precision then looked at his friend as if Garrett had lost his mind. "And how do you plan on finding the right woman? Are you going to place an ad in *The Chronicle* and hope that a gifted actress appears on your doorstep?"

"It would be easier if the lady wasn't known in San Francisco," Garrett mumbled more to himself than to his doubtful friend. His silver eyes took on a mischievous sheen as he put down his whiskey glass. "In the last year I've spent time in London, New York, St. Louis, and New Orleans. Pick a city."

Christopher's skepticism turned into amusement as he realized Garrett was serious. "I've always been partial to New Orleans, but I can't see Grams accepting an ebony-eyed Creole enchantress as her future grand-daughter-in-law."

"You're right. New Orleans is too exotic. What about St. Louis?"

"What about it?" Christopher mused as he leaned back in his chair and propped his feet on the top of his desk. "You don't really think you can get away with conjuring up a fiancée, do you? Actress or no actress, someone is sure to find out the girl is a fraud. Grams will have an old-fashioned conniption fit before she keels over for good, and you'll have a scandal on your hands."

"There won't be a scandal," Garrett told him. "Not if I find the right woman."

* * *

Claire sucked in a deep, unladylike breath as she silently cursed her aching feet and the afternoon heat. She was exhausted from soliciting a position in the business district that fronted San Francisco Bay. Her skills were limited but she could read and write and she wasn't too proud to do an honest day's work. The proprietors had been gracious but hesitant to hire a young lady who was new to the city. Chinese help was cheaper and less likely to cause trouble, they'd told her. Her only offer had come from the owner of a men's haberdashery. He could use a clerk to watch the front counter, or so he'd said, and was willing to pay her on a weekly basis. Claire had declined the offer, sensing that the balding man in wire-rimmed spectacles had had more in mind than her ability to dust shelves and address delivery slips for his well-to-do customers.

Exhausted from trekking all over the city, Claire looked for someplace to sit down and feel sorry for herself. She gazed longingly across the street at a stately hotel, painted a pristine white. The hotel literally turned the corner in an assertive manner with its lobby entrance facing California Street and a secondary entrance facing Taylor Street. The building's triangular shape did nothing to distract the eye from its elegant architecture. The apex of the triangle was a rounded corner tower with large bay windows. The turret roof was delicately ridged with cast-iron finials. Four stories high with plaster medallions decorating the thick window panels that artfully separated the second and third floors, the hotel looked like an oasis for the wealthy. Thick green ferns grew in fat-bellied ceramic pots near the front door, currently being held open by a uniformed attendant. Claire got a brief view of the lobby. It looked cool and inviting and she wished she had the courage to stroll inside so she could sit down on one of the red velvet settees. Settling for a bench near the entrance, Claire made herself as comfortable as the weathered wood would allow.

She was debating whether or not to return to the boarding house when she realized that hotels needed maids. Although the idea of changing bed linens and fetching towels for strangers didn't appeal to her, Claire knew she couldn't afford to be choosy about how she made the money she needed, as long as she earned her wages honestly.

Guided by necessity, she crossed the street and approached the hotel. Once she was inside, she hesitated. How did one go about asking for a job in a hotel? Thinking the desk clerk might offer her some guidance, she dried her sweaty hands by pretending to smooth the wrinkles from her skirt as she approached the oak counter. A young man with chestnut hair, a lean face, and an even leaner body, wearing a white shirt and dark brown jacket, greeted her with a cordial smile.

"May I help you?" he said, sounding even younger than he looked.

Claire returned his smile with one of her own, not realizing that the expression changed her already pretty face into one that stole the young man's breath for a moment. "Is the hotel manager available?" she asked, deciding the manager probably did the hiring and firing. The owner would be too busy counting his fortune. The hotel was even grander on the inside than it was on the outside and Claire realized the cost of a room for one night was probably more than she'd paid Mrs. Kruger in the three weeks she'd been living at the boarding house. "If so, I would like to speak with him."

"I hope everything is to your satisfaction," the clerk said, looking a little worried. "We pride ourselves on making our guests comfortable."

"I'm sure you do," Claire replied. "But I'm not a guest."

The young man's brown eyes narrowed just a bit. It wasn't unusual for the male guests of the hotel to arrange discreet liaisons during their stay, but this girl didn't look like anyone's mistress. He studied her for a moment, noting that her features were delicate without being frail and that although her dress wasn't as expensive as the ones he was accustomed to seeing, it was well made and fashionable.

"Is there something I can do for you?" he asked.

Realizing that she was going to have to get past the desk clerk before she could see the manager, Claire took a more direct approach. "I'm looking for a job."

It was easy to see that the young man didn't believe her. His eyes went from skeptical to suspicious in a blink of brown lashes. "What kind of job?"

Grateful that the lobby was void of guests for the moment, Claire glanced over her shoulder to make sure the man stationed at the door was still at his post. She moved closer to the counter, reminding herself that she couldn't let her pride stand in the way of doing what had to be done. "I thought to inquire about a position as a maid."

The clerk went back to looking skeptical. "You want to work as a hotel maid?"

Claire let out a small sigh. "It isn't exactly a question of wanting," she replied quietly. "It's more a matter of having a roof over my head and food on the table."

Working in a hotel had taught Andy to be a quick but accurate judge of character and something about the young lady standing in front of him caused his instincts to come alive.

"What's your name?"

"Claire Aldrich."

"Please have a seat, Miss Aldrich," Andy said, motioning toward one of the three settees positioned strate-gically about the elegant lobby. "I'll see if Mr. Landauer has time to speak with you."

Smiling her thanks, Claire sat down and waited while the young man disappeared up the wide carpeted stair-case that led to the hotel's upper floors. Thinking to calm her quivering nerves and take her mind off the interview ahead, she studied her surroundings. The lobby was a wide room with a parquet floor done in a singular design of golden oak. The front windows were dressed in a bluish gray velvet, pulled back and secured with thick gold braids. In addition to the three settees, there were several balloon-backed chairs and small oval tables. A brass gaslight chandelier hung from the vaulted ceiling. Crystal prisms dripped off the chandelier's brass stems like tiny jewels and large white globes diffused the light and directed it toward the ceiling rather than the floor. Large ceramic pots brimming with tropical ferns filled in the corners of the rectangular room.

While Claire gazed at the hotel's elegance in silent awe, one of its owners was pacing the office on the second floor.

"The idea isn't ludicrous," Garrett argued. "All I need is a beautiful woman who's more interested in money than marriage. I'll hire her to pose as my fiancée."

"That's the problem," Christopher insisted. "Find-ing a woman who's more interested in money than mar-riage makes whoever you find the *wrong* kind of woman. Grams isn't going to accept a gold digger and she's seen enough of them to know one on sight. Besides, proper young ladies aren't for hire. They're for marrying. The very thing you're trying to avoid."

Garrett was opening his mouth to protest when a knock on the door interrupted him.

"Come in," Christopher Landauer called out.

Andy opened the door and poked his head inside. "Excuse me, Mr. Landauer, but there's a young lady in the lobby looking for a job."

"Let Crawford talk to her. That's what I pay him for," Christopher said, somewhat surprised that Andy would interrupt him for such a thing.

He watched as the clerk scratched his head, then frowned. "I don't think . . . I mean, I don't feel like that would be the right thing to do in this instance. There's something about her that . . ."

"What something?" Garrett prompted impatiently. He did own half the hotel, after all.

"I'm not sure," Andy said, stepping inside and closing the door behind him. "For one thing, she's too pretty to be a maid."

Christopher shared the same admiration for the opposite sex as his friend. But unlike Garrett, he wasn't always discreet in expressing that admiration. "How pretty?"

Andy smiled, then blushed. He was trying to think of the right words to describe Claire Aldrich when Christopher instructed him to bring the girl upstairs.

"I'll talk to her. It's better than wasting my time trying to convince my partner that he's lost his mind."

Knowing better than to interfere in what was none of his business, Andy exited the room with a quick nod.

"I haven't lost my mind." Garrett glared at his best friend. "The more I think about it, the more the idea appeals to me. I can keep Grams from worrying herself to death and discourage Belinda Belton at the same time. Once my engagement is announced, I'll be as good as married. I'll be off the market, so to speak."

Another knock kept Christopher from continuing their argument. The two men waited as Andy opened the door and motioned a woman inside. Garrett felt his frustration over his grandmother's health take on a different form as the job-seeking young lady walked into the hotel office. Petite, but definitely full grown, she had honey brown hair and wide amber eyes that reminded Garrett of a curious kitten. Her features were classically delicate and there was a determined tilt to her chin. Her pink, bow-shaped mouth practically begged to be kissed, but Garrett was willing to bet a sizable fortune that she'd never been touched by a man. Everything about her shouted innocence.

Chapter Two

Claire took one look at the dark-haired man and felt something inside her pop open like a bottle of French champagne exploding when the cork was removed. The feeling was so distinct that for a moment she was tempted to gather up the skirts of her chocolate-colored dress and run out of the hotel. His silvery eyes continued to appraise her as Claire stepped into the room, assuming that one of two well-dressed men was the manager of the hotel.

"Andy's right," the second man said, stepping forward. "You're much too pretty to be a maid."

The compliment gained Claire's attention. "Are you the hotel manager?"

"I'm Christopher Landauer. I own this hotel. Actually, I own half of it. May I introduce my partner, Garrett Monroe."

The dark-haired man nodded his head in silent acknowledgement, then smiled. Claire felt her stomach quiver then knot. When she looked into his face, she felt the same strange sensation she'd experienced when she'd walked into the room. It was more intense this time, and much more intriguing, as if the man possessed some deep dark secret and she was destined to be the woman to discover it.

Realizing that she was staring, Claire forced her reverie aside and remembered her manners. "Mr. Monroe," she said.

Garrett frowned slightly as he studied her more carefully. It was a pity that she was a virgin. The thought of watching those jeweled eyes burn with passion sent a rush of heat through his body. The stubborn tilt of her chin said she wouldn't surrender to temptation easily, but once conquered she would be a willing participant, demanding as much from her partner as he did from her.

Realizing his mind was wandering, Garrett stepped forward. "And you are, Miss . . . ?"

"Claire Aldrich."

"Please, sit down, Miss Aldrich." He indicated one of the chairs that faced the desk. "Andy, have some lemonade brought up for our guest."

The desk clerk nodded, then closed the door with a soft click. Claire almost sighed out loud at the thought of a cold drink. She was thirsty from the long walk up the hill. Taking a moment to smooth the full skirt she was wearing, she tried not to look at either of the hotel owners. Although Mr. Landauer was handsome enough in his own right with tawny brown hair and warm brown eyes, there was no comparing him to the tall man whose smile made her heart flutter and her knees go weak.

She knew who Garrett Monroe was. Because she was concerned that Donald might have gotten himself into some sort of trouble, Claire read every word in the city papers, searching for some scrap of news about her brother. She'd seen Garrett Monroe's name in print more than once in the last three weeks. He lived on Nob Hill with his grandmother. He owned one of the city's most successful banks, which he used to finance hotels and other investments. He'd just returned from England, or so she'd read.

He was also considered the city's most eligible bachelor.

Seeing him in the flesh convinced Claire that the newspapers weren't speculating on Garrett Monroe's popularity with the ladies. He was devastatingly handsome. The dark gray suit he was wearing was impeccably tailored and his highly polished boots were made of expensive leather. His raven hair absorbed the sunlight streaming through the bay windows. It looked like India ink and Claire knew it would feel soft against her fingers. His eyes were an eerie blend of silver and gray and somehow she knew instinctively that they got darker when he was angry. Garrett Monroe wouldn't be a gracious enemy. He looked as powerful as he was handsome, and she imagined that he wielded his wealth and influence like an ancient sword, severing the political and financial heads of anyone who didn't bow to his wishes.

"Are you new to the city, Miss Aldrich?"

Mr. Landauer's question forced Claire's whimsical thoughts back to the present. "Yes. I arrived by train three weeks ago. I expected to find my brother waiting for me at the station."

"But he wasn't there," Christopher supplied the sad ending to Claire's once-hopeful westward adventure. "And now you're seeking employment in my hotel."

Claire nodded. Mr. Landauer was looking at her with more than a glint in his eye, but she didn't feel offended as she had been earlier in the haberdashery when the balding shop owner had stared at her. The gentlemen in the room might be predatory in their nature, but they were gentlemen, and she knew she wasn't in any immediate danger. As for the future, she'd have to be very careful. She was innocent, but she wasn't naïve. A woman's reputation was like her virginity, once lost, it couldn't be regained.

A soft knock preceded the desk clerk. He was carrying an oval tray with a pitcher of lemonade and several glasses. He sat the tray on the edge of the desk then turned to leave, but not before he gave Claire a mischievous wink. She was pondering the reason behind the unexpected gesture when Garrett stepped forward and poured her a glass of lemonade. She found herself studying his hands as he went about the task. His skin was bronzed, his fingers lean, and his nails clean and well manicured. Claire wondered if he had inherited his dark coloring from the original dons who had once owned the Presidio of Yerba Buena.

One thought led to another and Claire quickly found herself thinking fanciful thoughts about the romantic days of Spanish guitars and bullfights. When Garrett handed her the glass, their hands touched. Claire wasn't wearing gloves and she almost flinched from the contact. Stopping herself at the last moment, she thanked him for the drink and forced herself to sip it slowly. She might not come from money like Garrett Monroe, but she had impeccable manners. Mrs. Shurman had seen to that, along with Claire's education. She could play piano and her literary repertoire included Shakespeare and Byron.

"Why don't you tell us about your brother," Christopher Landauer suggested, returning to his seat behind the desk. "A young lady shouldn't be alone in a city like San Francisco. Do you have other family?"

"No," she admitted. "Donald is my only living relative."

"Where are you from?"

The question came from Garrett Monroe and Claire turned toward the sound of his deep, rich voice. It matched everything else about him. Strong and authoritative.

"I was born in Cincinnati," she told him. "My father died when I was very young. My mother owned a millinery shop, but I sold the store after she died."

"So you could come to San Francisco and live with your brother," Garrett added.

An idea was forming in his head and for the first time he was willing to agree with Christopher. He must be losing his mind. Either that or Claire Aldrich was a miracle. She'd only been in the city for a few short weeks. She had no relatives, excluding a brother who hadn't taken the time or inclination to meet her at the train station, and she was apparently in need of money. She was also more than passably pretty. Her movements and mannerisms were graceful and her words had an educated flair. Her innocence was apparent in the amber depths of her eyes and there was no risk of Grams mistaking her for anything but a well-mannered, well-bred young lady.

Once again Claire nodded in lieu of words. Something about Garrett Monroe stole her ability to think and communicate at the same time. It was very disconcerting. She wasn't unaccustomed to male attention, but she'd never encountered a man who affected her the way Garrett Monroe was affecting her. Her normally calm composure felt completely muddled by the man's presence and she couldn't stop thinking about what it would feel like to have his strong hand holding hers while they danced to the vibrant melody of a Viennese waltz.

"I'm afraid I don't need any more maids for the hotel," Christopher said, searching for a polite way to send Claire away from the hotel without ruining his chances of escorting her to dinner. "However, if your circumstances dictate that you have a job to support yourself, then I'd be glad to make some inquires for you. Do you have any particular skills I should know about?"

Claire tried to mask her disappointment. "Not anything I can boast of," she replied. "I can read and write, of course. I'm afraid that I didn't inherit my mother's talent with needle and thread, which is why I sold her shop. However, I've been told that I have an amicable personality. Or at least Mrs. Shurman thought so."

"Mrs. Shurman," Garrett interrupted. "Would that be Mrs. Elizabeth Shurman of Cincinnati?"

"Yes." Claire smiled in spite of her nervousness. "I was a companion to Mrs. Shurman before she died. I worked for her for almost five years. She was a kindhearted woman. Her death will always be one of my greatest sorrows."

If Claire had been a companion to Mrs. Shurman, who was known for her stringent attitudes, then she wouldn't have a problem getting along with Grams.

"I know the grandson," Garrett said, willing his eyes away from Claire and back to Christopher. "Henry Shurman doesn't have the finesse of his father, but he's done well for himself in the coach business. He owns a factory that supplies most of Pullman's cars."

He changed the subject, once again pinning Claire to the chair with the force of his pewter eyes. "What duties did you perform for Mrs. Shurman, other than offering her companionship?"

"I handled her correspondence and managed the household staff. Mrs. Shurman's heart was very weak and she spent most of her time in bed. Her grandson was rarely at home. His business demanded most of his time."

Garrett didn't mention that Henry Shurman's business included a lust for ladies and gambling. The young man was known for his addiction to poker and his family's fortune staked him in some of the most notorious games ever held on the riverboats that connected Cincinnati to the thriving cities along the Mississippi River. He wondered if young Shurman had ever directed his attention to Claire, then decided against it. Henry preferred his women experienced and voluptuous.

"I assume that you've been unable to locate your brother," Garrett added casually.

"I tried the address on his letter, but he wasn't living there any longer," Claire admitted. What she didn't say was that Donald had never actually lived in the clapboard cottage on Filbert Street. Mr. Landauer and Mr. Monroe seemed like pleasant, well-meaning men, but she didn't know them well enough to tell them her life story.

"Have you talked to the authorities?"

"Yes," she said, then added, "my brother wasn't arrested for any crime, Mr. Monroe. I'm sure he's somewhere in the city. All I have to do is keep looking."

"San Francisco isn't getting any smaller, Miss Aldrich," he pointed out. "And it has its faults. It certainly isn't the place for a young woman to be on the streets without the benefit of a chaperone."

"I can take care of myself," she said, controlling her temper. She rarely lost it, but when she did, it was formidable. "If there are no openings at the hotel, I'll thank you for your time and be on my way."

Claire set her unfinished glass of lemonade on the desk and started to leave. She might need a job, but she didn't need one badly enough to grovel. At least not yet.

Garrett saw the indignation on her face and realized she was about to walk out the door. "There's no reason to be insulted, Miss Aldrich. If your brother is still in the city, he can be found. If not, you need to know where he's gone. Either way, questions are necessary. What's his occupation?"

Claire forced herself to relax. Mr. Monroe was right in spite of his blunt approach. A young lady of good character didn't comb the city in search of a wayward brother. But she didn't have the money to hire a private investigator.

"I'm sorry," she mumbled. "I've been so worried about Donald and I don't know anyone else in the city." She settled back in the chair. "When he was younger, Donald worked on the riverboats that carried the mail from Cincinnati to New Orleans. After he left, he did a lot of things. In one of his letters, he told me that he was working as a train conductor. In another, addressed from Chicago, he was still working for the railroad but he'd been promoted. He didn't go into any details, but I got the impression he was doing very well. The letter after that came from Denver. He was trying his hand at mining, but he didn't like it so he moved on to Texas." Claire paused and licked her lips. "Donald has an adventurous spirit."

Garrett's insistent gray eyes studied her a moment longer. He could see the apprehension on her face in spite of her best efforts to hide it. Claire Aldrich was young and alone and that made her vulnerable. She was also extremely beautiful and very proud. Garrett could understand pride since he had a sizeable amount of it himself. What he couldn't understand was a man deserting his family. Whoever Donald Aldrich was, he deserved a good thrashing.

There was a very strong possibility that Claire's brother had left the city. San Francisco was full of wandering men; men who arrived by train and left by sea, or arrived by sea and then disappeared into the interior of the country. The city was a gateway to all sorts of people, rich and poor alike.

If Claire's brother had wanderlust in his blood, he could be anywhere. If he wasn't particular about the way he earned a living, he could also be dead. The city's docks weren't known for their hospitality. The opium trade was still running strong, although the Chinese businessmen who supplied the drug were careful to keep their business discreet.

Garrett gave his decision another moment's thought before he spoke. "I believe I know of a position that may alleviate your financial stress, Miss Aldrich. If you're interested, we can discuss it over dinner. The Landauer Hotel serves a delicious roast duck."

Claire wasn't sure what to say. She looked at Christopher Landauer. He appeared to be angry over something. He was glaring at his partner as if the handsome banker had just foreclosed on the luxurious hotel. Before she could think of an appropriate response to the unexpected invitation, Garrett walked to the door and called for Andy. The desk clerk appeared a moment later.

"Andy, please escort Miss Aldrich home." He turned to look at her. "Where are you staying?"

"I've rented a room in a boarding house," she said, coming to her feet. "It isn't all that far. I can manage."

"Nonsense," Garrett said. "The hotel keeps several carriages. Andy can see you home." ·

Realizing that the banker was used to taking charge of other peoples' lives and not wanting him to think her spineless, Claire started to protest while she tried to think of a way to decline his dinner invitation. She didn't like the idea of being in this particular man's debt. "Really, Mr. Monroe, it isn't necessary. As for dinner, I'm sorry but I promised to attend a poetry reading this evening. Perhaps we can discuss the position you mentioned tomorrow."

"I'll have Andy pick you up at eight o'clock," he said, ignoring her politely voiced refusal.

Their eyes collided for a brief moment and in that short second Claire wasn't sure what she felt, all she knew was that she'd never felt anything quite like it before. An odd combination of surprise and curiosity raced through her blood. Garrett was looking at her mouth and for the first time in her life, Claire found herself wanting to feel a man's kiss instead of just imagining it. She averted her gaze and looked at Christopher Landauer.

"It was a pleasure making your acquaintance, Miss Aldrich," Mr. Landauer said, coming to his feet.

Claire got the impression that the man was wishing her luck at the same time he was bidding her good-bye. Refusing to meet Garrett Monroe's steely gaze and fully intending to tell Andy that he was not to return to the boarding house and call for her later that evening, Claire thanked Mr. Landauer for his time and followed the hotel clerk from the room. She was halfway down the stairs when she realized that she had insulted Mr. Monroe by not telling him good-bye. *Serves him right,* Claire thought. *The man's far too arrogant for his own good. And I am not going to have dinner with him. I'll find a job without his assistance.*

While Claire was arguing with herself about whether or not she could afford to turn down Garrett Monroe's offer of dinner and a possible job, the man was arguing with his partner.

"You can't be thinking what I think you're thinking," Christopher Landauer remarked as Garrett moved to the window and watched Andy help Claire Aldrich into the carriage.

"I'm thinking that Donald Aldrich needs to be horse-whipped," he said harshly. "You know this city as well as I do, Christopher. Men like that come and go every day. I doubt that she's going to find him singing in a church choir."

"That doesn't mean you have to adopt her," Christopher argued. "Or worse. The girl just walked in off the street. You don't know anything about her. And you can't be sure that her brother won't show up eventually."

"Let me worry about the brother," Garrett said confidentially. Once the carriage had pulled away from the front of the hotel, he turned to face Christopher. There was a lethal quality about his voice when he spoke. "From this moment on, Miss Aldrich is my concern, not yours."

The other man gave him a knowing smile. "Am I being told to mind my own business?"

Garrett reached for his hat. "You're being told to keep your charm on a short leash. I don't intend for Miss Aldrich to end up living in one of our hotel suites, installed there for your personal gratification."

"Are your intentions any better?"

"Whatever my intentions, they're definitely more honorable than yours." Garrett laughed. "I don't seduce virgins."

"No. You only hire them to pose as your fiancée. Be careful, Garrett. Something tells me that the lovely Miss Aldrich could end up being very, very expensive."

"I can afford it," Garrett retorted as he headed for the door.

Claire's curiosity was hard to control during the carriage ride that took her down the hill much faster than her feet had taken her to the top. She clenched her jaw to keep from asking Andy all sorts of questions. The most important one being if she could trust Mr. Monroe. Was there a job or did the man have other intentions? Normally she wouldn't question a gentleman of his status, but the peculiar sensations she'd felt at the hotel hadn't completely subsided and Claire couldn't ignore them.

No matter how many times she told herself that she had too much on her mind to think about Garrett Monroe, the man slipped into her thoughts like a snake into a bird's nest.

Admittedly, she'd never seen a more striking man, but she wasn't interested in men. She had come to San Francisco to find her brother and to hopefully begin a new segment of her life that would one day include a husband and children.

But not now. She had turned twenty-one a few months ago, but Claire didn't attend the school of thought that assumed an unmarried woman past that age was doomed to spinsterhood. She wanted to experience more of life before she resigned herself to the confines of marriage. And what better place to do it than San Francisco. The city was known for its sophistication.

Thinking one or two discreetly posed questions might gain her some insight about Garret Monroe and his motives for helping her, Claire asked Andy how long he had been working for the hotel.

"Mr. Landauer hired me when I was twelve," Andy answered with no hesitation. "My pa shipped out on a freighter and didn't come back. Ma couldn't earn enough to feed us all, so I went to work."

"Then you have brothers and sisters?"

Andy laughed. "I've got two younger brothers and one sister. Katie's a handful."

"That's what Donald used to say about me." She laughed. "He's my only brother and I haven't seen him in almost seven years."

"Is that what brought you to San Francisco?"

"Yes. He's here. Somewhere. All I have to do is find him."

"It's a big city," Andy told her, then smiled. "But don't you worry. If anyone knows San Francisco, it's Mr. Monroe. If your brother's in town, Monroe can find him."

Claire wasn't so sure. Garrett Monroe had nothing in common with her brother, and even less in common with her.

The sun was sinking into the water of San Francisco Bay as Andy brought the carriage to a stop. Claire sat quietly for a few moments, enjoying the bold color of the California sunset.

"I'll be back at eight o'clock," Andy said as he helped her down from the carriage. "Mr. Monroe's a stickler for punctuality."

Recalling the hard glint of Garrett's eyes, Claire reminded herself that he wasn't the kind of man she could underestimate. Still, she shouldn't have dinner with him. It wasn't entirely proper, even if she desperately wanted the job he had referred to. "I'm afraid that I've made other plans for the evening. Please convey my apologies to Mr. Monroe. I'll be unable to join him for dinner."

Andy frowned. "I'm not sure I'd do that if I were you, Miss Aldrich. Garrett Monroe carries a lot of weight in this town. He can help you find the kind of job that won't have people looking down their noses at you."

Claire chewed on her bottom lip. Andy didn't live on Nob Hill, he worked there. Like her, he hadn't been born into a wealthy family. Realizing that she and the hotel clerk shared a common ground, Claire lowered her defenses. "I do need a job. I don't have enough money to pay next week's rent and my brother seems to have vanished off the face of the earth."

"Mr. Monroe can help you find him," Andy told her. "He knows everyone in town, including some people that might surprise you. Like I said, if your brother's in the city, Garrett's got ways of finding him."

Claire wasn't as confident as the hotel clerk, but she kept her doubts to herself. Deciding that she could survive Garrett Monroe's arrogant ways long enough to find out about the job she needed and perhaps gather some help in locating her brother, Claire reviewed her decision to eat at the boarding house. "Very well, Andy. You may return for me later this evening. I'll dine with Mr. Monroe."

He smiled in approval and climbed into the front seat of the open carriage. "By the way, my name's Wilkes. Andrew Wilkes. I think we're going to be good friends."

"I hope so, Mr. Wilkes," Claire replied with a smile. "Thank you for seeing me home."

He winked at her again and Claire bit back a laugh. She watched as Andy negotiated a full turn in the busy street and headed back to the hotel. Several seconds passed before Claire's smile turned into a frown. The only dress she had that was suitable for dining at the hotel would need a good ironing to take out the wrinkles and Mrs. Kruger kept the irons in the kitchen. She turned and went inside, hoping she could avoid the landlady long enough to heat the iron and sneak it upstairs.

An hour later, Claire was stripped down to her underwear. The shear cotton felt cool and comfortable against her skin as she moved about the room, gathering her brush and the tortoise shell comb Donald had sent her for Christmas last year. The drapes were drawn and she'd just finished pressing the blue dress she planned on wearing that evening.

Still confused over her reaction to Garrett Monroe, Claire forced herself to sit down instead of pacing the room as was her habit when she was worried. Of course, she didn't have anything to be worried about. The term was an overstatement. She was anxious, that's all.

The last five years of her life had been spent in the luxury of Mrs. Shurman's home and although she'd had Wednesday afternoons and Sundays off, she had rarely ventured beyond the confines of the estate gardens or the busy stores in the shopping district near the Ohio River. Her only experience with gentlemen had been to avoid the ones Henry Shurman had invited to his grandmother's Cincinnati home, being told by Mrs. Shurman that it wasn't proper for a servant to mix with the guests. Claire hadn't been offended by the older woman's bluntness. She'd sensed the protection in Elizabeth Shurman's words and had kept to herself whenever Henry and his friends occupied the house.

The only adventurous thing she'd ever done in her entire life was learning to ride a bicycle. Mrs. Shurman had been appalled when Claire had come home looking like she'd run into a train. It had taken several Sunday afternoons, riding along the trails in Eden Park, before Claire had mastered the fine art of keeping the two-wheeled contraption upright and moving forward at the same time. Cycling was fast becoming the passion among the middle and working class. While the rich still had their private carriages to get them about town, the bicycle offered the same freedom of movement to the less financially fortunate. Claire had thoroughly enjoyed her speedy romps in the park, although she'd found her female clothing quite cumbersome. It was extremely difficult to peddle while wearing a bustle and petticoats. She'd been thrilled to read that the popularity of the bicycle was beginning to have an affect on ladies' fashion and some predicted that the bustle would soon disappear completely.

Other than cycling, Claire had spent her time reading about all the exotic places the world had to offer. She was sure that Garrett Monroe had been to some of those glamorous cities. After all, he was rich and one had only to look at him to know that he was sophisticated. But it was more than that and Claire knew it. There was a sensual mystique about Garrett Monroe that went beyond his expensive clothes. It radiated from him like heat from the sun.

Claire felt her body reacting to her thoughts and frowned. She'd never had such notions before, at least not in broad daylight and certainly not about a specific man. It was shocking to realize that the short time she'd spent with Garrett in the company of other people could affect her so dramatically. Of course, she knew he hadn't felt the same way. He was a man of the world, which meant he'd been with beautiful women under much more intimate circumstances.

Feeling her face color at the thought of what Garrett had done with those women was enough to bring Claire out of the chair and into a frenzy of activity. Once again, she debated with herself about accepting the dinner invitation. What would they talk about? The only place she'd traveled to was San Francisco and she hadn't had the money to explore the cities she'd passed through on her way to the coast.

Claire supposed Garrett Monroe would think her boring and bland, but then she wasn't trying to win his heart so what did it matter. What mattered was finding her brother and getting on with her life. She wasn't interested in gaining more than a temporary position that would tide her over until Donald was found. She certainly wasn't interested in conquering Garrett Monroe's heart. She doubted that the man had one. After all he was a banker and everyone knew how cold-blooded they could be.

Chapter Three

Garrett stood in front of the mirror, his fingers automatically knotting the black silk tie. Since encountering Claire Aldrich at the hotel, his mind had been preoccupied with how he was going to breach the subject of her becoming his fraudulent fiancée. It was apparent that she was inexperienced, but very beautiful, a combination that could endanger her if she remained in the city without family supervision for too long. Her brother might be adventurous, but living under his roof would at least offer her some protection. Without it, Claire was more vulnerable than she realized.

The attraction Garrett had felt when Claire walked into Christopher's office was another complication. What he needed to fool his grandmother into thinking that he'd one day marry and take up the settled, routine life of a family man was an employee who would conduct herself according to his wishes and collect her pay without any hoopla. As much as Claire may need the money,

Garrett wasn't so sure he could write the check with total indifference.

She was a pretty little thing and her uncultured innocence appealed to his masculine senses like spring flowers to a bumblebee. His plans to convince Grams that his intentions to marry were sincere meant that he'd need to bring Claire to the house on Nob Hill. With his grandmother and ten servants in residence, no one would question the propriety of the arrangement. He intended to introduce her as his fiancée and to inform people that she'd recently lost her mother. The years she had worked for Mrs. Shurman didn't have to be mentioned. Claire's experience as a companion to the belated Cincinnati matron meant that she could assume the same position, although much more informally, with his grandmother. It also meant that Garrett would be forced to treat her like a fiancée.

The mirror reflected Garrett's frown. He wasn't the kind of man who could hold hands and brush chaste kisses over a beautiful woman's cheek without wanting more. He hadn't controlled his sexual appetite since he'd turned fifteen and taken his first woman. She'd been the young widow of one of his father's clients and more than willing to help him through the rite of passage from randy adolescence to experienced manhood. Since then his money and good looks had kept his bed comfortably filled with females, none of whom he'd ever introduced to his grandmother.

First things first, Garrett told himself as he slipped his arms into a black evening jacket. Before he introduced Claire Aldrich as his future bride-to-be, he had to convince her to play the part. That might take some doing. The short flare of temper he'd witnessed at the hotel said the young lady may not be as easy to control as he needed her to be. However, he did have the advantage of knowing that her funds were limited. A young lady with her social graces wouldn't be looking for a job as a hotel maid unless she was near the point of desperation.

Garrett smiled as he stepped out of his room and headed for the parlor where his grandmother was resting. If there was one thing a banker understood it was financial desperation and Garrett wasn't shy about using it to his advantage. Not if it meant putting a smile on his grandmother's beloved face.

"It's about time," the woman on the chaise longue said as Garrett strolled into the family parlor.

Theodora Monroe tilted her face at just the right angle for her grandson to place a kiss on her pale cheek. "You're going out," she said, not bothering to hide her disappointment. "Don't tell me that you have a business meeting tonight, because I won't believe it. You've done nothing but hide away in that stuffy bank office since you came back from England."

Theodora "Grams" Monroe was an elegant woman with silvery hair and sparkling blue eyes that gave her grandson hope she'd regain her strength. Reclining as she was with an ivory and green blanket covering her from the waist down, all he could see of her silk dress was the expensively embroidered black bodice and lace neck. But Garrett didn't have to see her standing up to know that she barely reached his breastbone. Grams was a bright-witted, small woman with an extraordinary sense of neatness and order. She liked everything in its place and a place for everything, which was why the house on Nob Hill was run like a military institution. Surprisingly, the servants who staffed the house had been with the family for years. Grams might be a hard taskmaster, but she was a fair one, and the servants idolized her. They weren't the only ones. Garrett loved her to distraction and whenever he was in her company his steely eyes took on a warm glow.

He sat down and smiled his best smile. "That stuffy

bank office pays for this comfortable little nest you call a home. And you know damn good and well that most of my business is conducted in the evening. It's the nature of the beast I've taken up as a career."

"Don't lecture me," Grams said indignantly. "And don't patronize me, either."

"I wouldn't dream of doing either," Garrett said, chuckling. "After all a woman of your severe age is due respect."

He laughed when Grams reached out and swatted his shoulder.

"Pour me a sherry," she instructed him. "And don't frown while you're doing it."

Garrett not only frowned, he refused to pour the drink. "I don't think Dr. Baldwin would approve."

"As if I care what that pompous bag of wind approves or disapproves of," Grams said, tossing aside the crocheted comforter and slowly swinging her feet off the lounge. "If I listened to him, I'd be dead and buried by now. And I don't intend on being either one until I've seen you properly married."

Garrett sighed, then reached out and caught his grandmother by the wrist. "I'll pour the sherry. You stay put."

He swung her legs up and over, returning her to her original reclining position before he walked to the liquor cabinet across the room and poured a miniscule helping of sherry into a glass. Pouring himself a more substantial brandy, Garrett didn't see the playful smile that brightened his grandmother's face.

"So, where are you going?" she asked, once he'd returned to sit beside her.

"To dinner," he replied matter-of-factly.

"With whom?"

"None of your business," he replied, reaching out and tapping her upturned nose.

Grams smiled warmly at him. "I'll know as soon as the paper is delivered tomorrow morning. You can't escort a lady to dinner without everyone in the city hearing about it."

"And what makes you think I'm having dinner with a lady?"

"My female instincts are as old as my heart, but they're in no danger of giving out," she said with a smile. "I'm the one woman you can't fool and you know it."

Garrett didn't bothering arguing. In the thirty-five years since his birth, he'd never bested his grandmother at verbal warfare. She was an experienced general when it came to finding out what she wanted to know. He didn't like lying to her, and in fact, he couldn't think of a single time when he'd blatantly done so. But he couldn't make mention of Claire Aldrich until the time was right.

"I'm having dinner at the Landauer."

Garrett could tell she didn't believe him.

"I thought you housed your mistress on Bartlett Street," she said candidly. "Are you keeping her at the hotel now?"

Garrett was surprised he could blush at his age, but he could. He took a sip of his brandy to avoid a direct answer, but the gleam in his grandmother's eye made him smile. "A man doesn't discuss his mistress. It isn't considered proper conversation."

Grams wasn't dissuaded. "What's proper and what's practical aren't necessarily one and the same, dear boy, and you know it. What I can't understand is why you insist on keeping a mistress when you can't seem to remember their names a day after they've vacated that adorable little cottage you bought a few years ago. And I have no idea how you got that way. Heaven knows your father didn't flit from woman to woman like a hummingbird. I'll admit he had his wild days, but after he met your mother, he changed. I wonder if you're ever going to settle down."

Garrett hesitated, then smiled. "And what if I did? You'd have nothing to lecture me about and you'd die of boredom."

"There's nothing boring about having a house full of children," she chided him. "And that's what you need. Half a dozen little hellions running around would settle you down in no time."

"Perish the thought." Garrett grimaced.

He finished his brandy and set aside the glass, before turning a fierce gaze on his grandmother. "Don't wait up for me. Dr. Baldwin said you need lots of rest."

"Stop frowning at me." She shooed him off with a wave of her elegant hand. "I'll be tucked in as tight as a bug in a rug before the waiter serves your dessert. Now go."

Garrett searched her face, lined with age, but still compassionate. Theodora Monroe ruled San Francisco society without being a member of the Temperance League or the church choir. She ruled by example, making sure her life was as spotless as a newly washed apron, and demanding the same level of morality from the people around her. If she announced her dislike for something or someone, they were immediately shunned by the people on the Hill. On the other hand, if she recommended a charity, its coffers were filled, and if she mentioned that she liked a particular painting or the prose of a new author, the artist's work was an immediate success.

She was revered and respected by everyone who knew her. Hating the thought of what his life would be like without his grandmother's sharp wit and cutting chastisements, Garrett leaned down and placed a kiss on her forehead. "If you're a good girl, I might have a surprise for you this weekend."

"I'm too old for surprises," she teased him. "They're not good for my heart."

He laughed. "Behave yourself and go to bed early. I'll see you at breakfast."

Claire wasn't surprised when Andy brought the carriage to a stop in front of the boarding house at precisely seven-thirty. She'd had to do some fancy footwork to keep Mrs. Kruger from barring the door when she'd told the landlady that she'd accepted a dinner invitation with one of the city's gentlemen. Of course, she hadn't mentioned Garrett Monroe's name. If Mrs. Kruger assumed that Andrew Wilkes was her escort for the evening, then so be it.

Fortunately, the hotel clerk had changed his clothes. He knocked on the front door, looking every inch like an acceptable young man. His brown hair had been washed and brushed and his clothing, a dark suit and a crisp white shirt, met the landlady's sharp scrutiny as he stepped into the parlor.

Not wanting to linger, Claire had her shawl draped around her shoulders and the black beaded reticule she'd inherited from her mother, dangling from her right wrist.

"You look lovely," Andy said as she came down the steps that led into the foyer of the boarding house.

"Thank you," Claire replied before making the formal introduction that Mrs. Kruger insisted upon before letting any of her girls venture into the night. Knowing that there was nothing threatening about Andy's outward appearance, Claire tried to relax.

It was impossible. The closer the time came for her to confront Garrett Monroe again, the tighter the knot in her stomach got. She'd almost backed down again, but a quick recounting of her funds changed her mind.

She needed a job and if the banker could find her a position as a lady's companion or temporary governess, then she'd be glad to accept it.

"Be sure she's back by a decent hour, young man," Mrs. Kruger instructed, following them outside. She gave the carriage a thorough going-over with her eyes before insisting that Claire keep her shawl close at hand. The fog had rolled in off the bay and the gaslights were straining to illuminate the misty streets.

Claire entered the carriage with Andy's helping hand, thankful that he'd raised the canvas top, shielding her from the landlady's sharp eyes. The smile on her face, painted there since she'd descended the staircase, quickly turned into a frown. Andy noticed, but gratefully didn't comment on her sudden change in attitude as he snapped the reins and sent the carriage on its way.

Seeing the hotel at night was even more impressive than seeing it in the daylight. Rows of streetlamps positioned every twenty feet or so flooded the lobby entrance. The upper windows were ablaze with light and the sound of an orchestra drifted through the open doors and out into the street. The fog wasn't as prominent at the top of the hill, and Claire gazed at the fashionable ladies and gentlemen entering the hotel. The night air had a briskness about it and most of the ladies were wearing fur wraps that accentuated their husbands' wealth and their own keen fashion sense. Claire gazed down at the blue skirt of her taffeta gown and realized that she had a long way to go before she caught up with the cream of San Francisco society.

Too nervous to see the admiring glances sent her way, Claire stepped down from the carriage, unaware that Garrett was watching from the second floor window of the hotel's office. His astute eye immediately noticed Claire's change in hair style. Her petite face was framed by wispy ringlets while the rest of her silky hair was held back by a thick velvet ribbon tied at the nape of her neck. A paisley shawl was draped over her shoulders, hiding most of her from view, but Garrett smiled as he saw the ruffles on her petticoats and the small but unavoidable fashionable bustle on her dress.

God, how he hated bustles.

Reminding himself that what he had in mind for Claire didn't include stripping her clothes away so he could memorize her body with his eyes, Garrett collected his determination and went into the private dining room adjacent to the office. He'd instructed the hotel manager, Mr. Crawford, to have the room prepared for the evening ahead. Garrett had used it for business meetings in the past and he knew Christopher often employed the room when he wanted to be alone with a particular lady, usually a guest of the hotel who was bored because her husband was playing poker or enjoying the sinful delights of the waterfront district.

The small dining room was reached by opening a set of pocket doors in the rear of Christopher's office. The panels were made of California redwood with elaborate carvings that added to the elegance of the room they revealed when opened. The room was carpeted in shades of green and gold. The fabric matched the velvet drapes covering the rectangular windows that overlooked a small courtyard in the back of the hotel. A set of French doors opened onto a balcony. The table was large enough to seat six, but small enough to allow genteel conversation if one was wooing a lady. Draped with an ivory lace tablecloth, the cherrywood table displayed a massive silver and gold centerpiece commissioned from a fashionable city jeweler. The built-in china cabinet housed a set of china with the hotel's insignia, as well as cutlery. A large gilded mirror, hung opposite the doorway, reflected the tasteful décor of the room at the same time that it gave the illusion of space, making one think that the dining area was much larger than its actual measurements. The quaint intimacy of the room gave its guests the impression that they were dining in a private home, not a hotel.

Mr. Crawford had arranged for one of the hotel's most trusted maids to serve the meal and Garrett knew that his first private meeting with Claire Aldrich would remain a secret. Libby had been hired before the hotel had opened some six years before and she had risen in the servant ranks because of her loyalty. Whatever she saw or heard she kept to herself, a trait that the young Andy shared. Their discretion was the source of their job security and Garrett was confident that neither one of them would breach it willingly.

He smiled as the robust maid came into the room, carrying the first tray of the evening. Libby was in her midforties with graying hair. She was wearing the hotel's customary uniform, a dark navy dress and white apron.

"Good evening, Mr. Monroe," she said, sitting the tray down on the low, claw-footed table that occupied the space between two high-backed brocaded emerald green chairs. "When shall I start serving?"

"Give me half an hour with the lady, before you interrupt," he answered.

Libby nodded, then left the room. A discreet knock on the door that led into the main corridor of the second floor brought Garrett around. He assumed a relaxed stance as Andy opened the door and escorted Claire Aldrich inside.

"Good evening," he said, taking a step forward as his guest's eyes went wide. The room always impressed people, and Garrett found himself wondering just how much of life young Miss Claire had experienced so far. Not enough by the look of her, he decided. Her eyes swept the room, taking in the expensive furnishings and the fact that they would be eating dinner alone.

Claire managed to find her tongue. "Good evening."

The Shurman home had been elegant, but Elizabeth Shurman had, like most women her age, been obsessed with knickknacks and clutter. Claire had searched for years for an inch of shelf space that wasn't occupied. In many ways the house had resembled the lady, since Claire couldn't think of a time when Mrs. Shurman's own person hadn't been cluttered with pearl necklaces and heavy jeweled brooches.

This room was different. The furnishings were undoubtedly expensive, but they had been placed with careful thought to the human eye. The table was in exact proportion to the size of the room, which Claire realized wasn't all as large as it seemed. The candelabra looked like it belonged in a London palace along with the crowned jewels. The draperies and carpet matched perfectly. The man standing a few feet in front of her seemed completely at home in the lush décor that surrounded him. Claire felt like a fish out of water.

As Andy closed the door behind him, Garrett reached for the blue and gold paisley shawl that covered Claire's shoulders. She flinched at the slight touch of his hands, then relaxed when she realized her reflex had been insulting. It was perfectly acceptable for a gentleman to help a lady remove her wrap.

"I wondered if you'd come," Garrett said, hiding his smile as he draped the shawl over the back of a walnut armchair. "I'm glad you did."

Claire licked her lips, unaware that the gilt-framed mirror revealed her every move to the man standing behind her. "I'm anxious to discuss the position you mentioned earlier today."

"There's plenty of time for that," Garrett told her, walking to the tray that Libby had brought in earlier. The sight of Claire's pink tongue darting out to moisten her lips had him thirsty for more than liquor. He calmed the unexpected rush of desire by telling himself that Evelyn was waiting for him at the cottage. Whatever sexual satisfaction his body required could wait until after dinner.

A vintage French champagne was among the bottles on the silver tray. Garrett poured two glasses and handed one to Claire. "Sip it slowly," he said. "And relax. I'm a banker, not a cannibal."

"Some people might say they were one and the same," Claire retorted. She'd assumed that they would be having dinner in the hotel's main dining room. She'd never expected the quiet elegance of a private suite.

Garrett's laughter surprised her. "I assure you I don't eat young ladies for dinner."

Claire didn't look convinced as she raised the glass to her mouth and tasted the champagne. It had a lighter, sweeter taste than the wines Mrs. Shurman had served with dinner.

Garrett knew that Claire was nervous. What he didn't know was why it excited him to have her at his mercy. Normally he detested young inexperienced women who giggled and hid behind their eyelashes. But Claire Aldrich was different. Something about her enticed him in a way he'd never been enticed before. He looked at her and liked what he saw. Her dress was a deep royal blue with an ivory lace skirt panel trimmed in black velvet. The lace pattern was repeated on the bodice that covered her upper chest and throat. The sleeves were long, which meant she wasn't wearing the gloves that most women favored for evening wear. The dress hadn't been fashioned in New York or Paris, but it suited her slender form, as did the soft ringlets that framed her face.

It was a lovely face, Garrett decided. Much lovelier than he remembered and he realized that Claire was one of the few women who didn't cover their natural complexions with powder. Her skin was soft and creamy with just a hint of color in her cheeks. Her mouth looked more kissable than ever and her eyes glowed in the soft candlelight. Garret smiled without realizing it.

Claire smiled back.

"Would you like to see the view?" he asked.

Claire nodded, once again stricken with an inability to speak. She remained silent as Garrett took the glass from her hand and set it aside. He motioned her toward the French doors at the opposite side of the room and she was thankful that he didn't touch her. There was something strangely intimidating about him, but it wasn't a fearful intimidation and Claire's female senses, inexperienced as they were, warned her that she mustn't give him the impression that she was interested in more than a job.

Garrett unlatched the French doors and pushed them open, revealing a long narrow balcony. Claire stepped outside, instantly awed by what she saw. The balcony overlooked a small courtyard, but it wasn't the silhouette of the well-trimmed trees and marble benches that caught her attention. From the balcony it looked as if the whole of San Francisco had been laid at her feet. Thousands of gaslights gleamed like golden stars, outlining the streets that crisscrossed the city like strings on a tennis racket. Parlor windows gleamed like tiny diamonds up and down the hills that bordered the bay. The night air cooled her skin and Claire leaned her head back to get a better look at the moon. It was full and bright and rimmed by silvery clouds that made the night seem almost magical.

"It's beautiful," she said in a whispery voice.

"Very beautiful," Garrett replied, looking at Claire. The moonlight added a new dimension to her features and he fought the urge to pull her into his arms and kiss her.

He'd meant the evening to be a job interview. Making

a mental note not to forget that important fact a second time, Garrett forced himself to look out over the city.

"Tell me more about your brother," he said.

Claire found herself smiling again. Maybe Andy was right. Maybe Mr. Monroe was just the man she needed to help her find Donald. He surely had contacts in the city, people who could ferret out things that it would take her months to discover.

"What do you want to know?"

"Does he drink? Gamble?"

"He's a man," Claire laughed. "What do you think?"

Garrett found himself smiling at her candor. "What about friends? Did he mention any in his letters?"

"None that I can recall," Claire replied. She treasured each and every letter Donald had ever written and she'd read each one dozens of time. Her brother had written her about the places he'd gone, not the people he'd met.

Garrett got the impression that Claire didn't know a great deal about her sibling. Trying to be tactful, he asked a few more questions. None of Claire's answers were very helpful. When she finally mentioned that she hadn't seen her brother in almost seven years, Garrett felt certain that the elusive Donald Aldrich wasn't the sort of man to be responsible for his sister even if his whereabouts were discovered.

"Donald favors our father. He has brown hair and brown eyes. He's not as tall as you. But he always looked big to me."

"Most men would," Garrett said simply. "You're a tiny little thing."

"I'm not that tiny," Claire said, thinking he meant childlike.

His eyes slid over her and he found himself once again forgetting the reason he'd invited her to dinner. He was struck by the subtle quality of her innocence

and the contradicting flair of defiance in her catlike
eyes. The combination was more intriguing as his gaze
moved slowly downward, taking in the soft curves of her
body. Chastising himself for his inability to keep his
mind on the business at hand, Garrett stepped back. "I
promised you a sampling of the chef's roast duck. Shall
we eat?"

Claire nodded and went inside. For a moment she
thought that Garrett was going to kiss her. His eyes had
turned a soft, smoky gray and in that brief second she'd
felt something. Something intangible, but very real.
Something that warned her to proceed very carefully
where this man was concerned or she could end up
with more than a lost brother. If she wasn't careful,
Claire knew she could lose her heart to the San Francisco banker.

By the time Libby served the main course, roasted
duck glazed with a sweet orange sauce, Claire was beginning to feel slightly more comfortable in her surroundings. Garrett made conversation easy and she found
herself telling him about her life in Cincinnati and how
she'd shocked Mrs. Shurman by buying a bicycle.

"You'll see them in the parks around the city," Garrett told her. "But our hills keep them from being very
useful for more than Sunday afternoon entertainment."

"I'm used to hills," Claire replied. "Cincinnati isn't
exactly flat. It has seven hills, just like Rome."

"Can you name them?" Garrett teased.

The champagne was having its desired effect and
Claire was relaxing enough to talk to him. Everything
he'd learned so far confirmed his first impression. She
was the perfect candidate for a fraudulent fiancée.

Claire laughed. "Mount Adams, Mount Auburn,
Mount Washington, Mount Carmel, Mount Airy, Mount
Healthy, and Mount . . ."

"Mount something or other." Garrett smiled, as Claire sipped on her second glass of champagne.

"I'll think of it," she mused, squinting her eyes as she concentrated. The name was on the tip of her tongue. It must be the champagne, she decided. Or maybe it was the company? "Mount . . ."

"You can tell me tomorrow," Garrett said, smiling. "Would you like some dessert?"

"No, thank you," Claire told him. "Will I be seeing you tomorrow?"

"That depends on if you say yes or no to my job offer."

"*Your* job offer?"

Garrett nodded as he pushed back his chair and stood up. As much as he'd like to keep refilling Claire's champagne glass, he didn't want her tipsy when he presented his job proposal. He rang the service bell, summoning Libby. When the maid appeared, he requested coffee.

Claire held her breath as Garrett pulled her chair back so she could leave the table. Although he didn't touch her, his proximity was unmistakable. She could smell the subtle scent of his cologne and feel the faint brush of his breath over her temple. His nearness prompted a deep, almost painful sensation in Claire's chest, as if her lungs had forgotten how to breathe. When Garrett stepped back, the feeling didn't go away for several more seconds, and she wondered if the champagne had heightened her senses or dulled her wits. Either way, Claire knew she had to put some distance between herself and the San Francisco banker. The balcony doors were still open, so she went outside, thinking the night air might have a soothing effect on her befuddled nerves.

Claire was so shaken from the unexplainable feelings swirling around inside her that she clutched the wrought-iron railing like a lifeline. Garrett had been a perfect gentleman all evening, but beneath the pleasant dinner conversation she'd sensed a storm brewing. Having him announce that the job she so desperately needed was actually a position working for him added a dose of apprehension to the excitement she'd felt since walking into the private suite.

While Claire took some air to dispel the effects of the champagne, Garrett poured two cups of coffee, adding cream and sugar to Claire's before joining her outside. Seeing her standing in the moonlight accelerated the sexual tension he'd been feeling all evening until he had to question what he was about to do. It was going to take all his talent to convince Grams that he was seriously in love with the young lady he presented as his fiancée. Accepting that meant he also had to accept the sexual frustration he knew he was going to suffer having Claire within reach. It had been a long time since he'd had to abstain from having a woman if he wanted her, and Garrett couldn't deny that he wanted Claire Aldrich.

He took a moment to weigh the consequences of what he was about to do before he stepped through the French doors and joined Claire on the balcony. She accepted the china cup with a softly spoken thank you, then turned back around to look out over the city.

"The position you mentioned," she finally said. "Is it in your bank?"

"No."

She eyed him suspiciously for a moment. "Another hotel?"

Garrett shook his head slowly.

Claire hesitated. The only thing left was a position in Garrett's home. Suddenly the thought of being a maid became distasteful. The idea of touching linens still warm from the heat of his body made her heart skip several beats.

"The position I have in mind is a bit out of the ordinary," Garrett said, trying his best to conduct the conversation the same way he would any other business meeting.

"How so?" she prompted.

Garrett moved a step closer and Claire felt as if he were engulfing her. Her reaction was silly, since he was standing a good three feet away, but she couldn't push it aside. His eyes narrowed as he watched her take a sip of coffee and she wondered what he was thinking. For the second time that evening, the penetrating strength of his gaze seemed to soften and Claire found herself immobilized by the peculiar sensations racing up and down her spine like tiny bolts of lightning.

Garrett took a drink of black coffee to clear his head of the tempting thoughts that seemed synonymous with Claire Aldrich. When he spoke it was in the same deep, authoritative voice he used at the bank. "Like you, Miss Aldrich, my family is limited to only one relative. In my case, the relative is my grandmother."

Claire's curiosity peaked. A dozen questions formed on the tip of her tongue, but she didn't dare ask them yet. Garrett was standing tall and the tone of his voice was all business.

"Grams is a formidable old woman with a heart of gold."

"Grams?"

"That's what I've always called her," he explained. "I'm not a boy any longer, but old habits are hard to break."

"I think it's sweet," she commented, as her mind conjured up the image of a little dark-haired boy crawling into his grandmother's lap. Somehow the fantasy made Garrett seem less intimidating.

"She'll be seventy-nine on her next birthday and her

mortality is catching up with her. Her heart isn't strong and her doctor has advised lots of rest."

"I see," Claire replied, thinking she did. She'd told both Garrett and Mr. Landauer that she'd been a companion to Mrs. Shurman in Cincinnati and now Garrett wanted to hire her to perform a similar function for his ailing grandmother. Part of Claire was relieved that he didn't need a maid, but on the other hand . . . She wasn't entirely sure how to describe the mingled emotions that included both anticipation and apprehension. Being a companion meant that she'd be living under the same roof as Garrett's grandmother, and Claire had read enough about the esteemed family and its legendary matron to know that Garrett lived in the same house as Theodora Monroe.

"Then the position you mentioned involves caring for your grandmother?"

"To some degree," Garrett said. "Actually, it's a little more complicated than fetching tea and writing letters."

"I'm not a nurse," Claire said, once again thinking that she understood the direction he was taking her. "But I did take care of Mrs. Shurman on a daily basis. Toward the end, she was almost an invalid and she seemed to prefer my company to that of anyone else."

"Grams isn't an invalid," he said, smiling as he recalled the way his grandmother had teased him about the cottage on Bartlett Street. He searched for the words, then decided if the arrangement he planned had any chance of succeeding, it demanded a certain degree of honesty between himself and the lady he wished to hire.

"Perhaps I should stop and clarify a few things," he began again. "First of all, I admire you for deciding to stay in San Francisco to find your brother. Most young women, when faced with your circumstances, would return to the place they called home."

"When I find Donald, I'll find my home," Claire said, surprised by Garrett's expression of admiration. "Family is home."

"Yes," he agreed. "Which is why I'm willing to do almost anything to make what remains of my grandmother's life as pleasant as possible."

Claire wasn't sure how to respond so she didn't say anything. She sipped her coffee and waited for Garrett to finish his explanation.

"Like most women," he continued, "my grandmother is convinced that my complete happiness won't be obtained until I marry and have a family."

Claire smiled. "My mother was the same way. She always complained that Donald needed to come back to Cincinnati and settle down."

"What about you, Miss Aldrich? Most young women would agree with their mothers. Did you leave someone behind in Cincinnati?"

Claire shook her head. "I have no desire to marry, Mr. Monroe. At least not yet."

He smiled. "Then we have something in common. I'm not inclined to marry, either. In fact, I'm almost certain that I never will."

The conversation was taking a personal turn and Claire wasn't sure how to reply.

"As I said, I have no desire to marry, but my grandmother is determined to see me happily married before she departs this world for the next, which brings me back to the job I mentioned this afternoon. It seems I can do you a favor, Miss Aldrich, and you in turn can do one for me."

Claire was getting confused and this time she couldn't blame it on the champagne. Garrett was talking in riddles.

"You need funds to remain in the city and look for your brother. And I need a fiancée who can convince my grandmother that she's willing to take responsibility for my future happiness."

Claire's coffee cup stopped midway to her mouth. She looked at Garrett for a moment, unsure if he was adding another riddle to the conversation or explaining the first one.

When he laughed, it confused her even more. "Let me put it another way," he said. "I'm a very wealthy man with an ailing grandmother and a large house on the Hill. You're a single young woman who needs to keep a roof over her head while she searches for her brother. If you pose as my fiancée, I will provide you a place to live and hire a private investigator to locate Donald. In the interim, I'll provide you with a new wardrobe and all the other amenities that go along with being the future Mrs. Monroe."

"You can't be serious?" The words tumbled out of Claire's mouth.

"Ahhh, but I am."

She eyed him warily for several seconds and Garrett thought he might have misjudged her. When she kept staring at him, he realized that he hadn't insulted her as much as he'd shocked her. "I realize my offer isn't exactly what you had in mind, but I'm sure if you think about it, you'll see it's a practical solution to both our problems."

"Practical!" Claire got her voice back. "But we're strangers. I only met you this afternoon and . . ."

"The position isn't based on our arrangement becoming a permanent one," Garrett reassured her. "I'm offering to hire you, nothing more. In payment for your acting abilities, I'll provide food, clothing, and shelter, as well as the means to locate your brother. And, of course, you'll be paid a salary. We can discuss the details later."

Claire handed him her coffee cup and walked back into the dining room. She was reaching for her shawl when Garrett stopped her by saying her name. She turned around to look at him, unsure if she should run out the door or take the time to slap him.

"I don't know what you're up to, Mr. Monroe, but I don't want any part of it."

"You're overreacting, Miss Aldrich. My offer is strictly business."

Claire replied with a dry laugh. "Business! What kind of businessman sets out to deceive his own grandmother? I think it's a terrible thing and . . . I think you're terrible and I never want to see you again."

She was reaching for the doorknob when Garrett stopped her again. This time, his hand appeared over her shoulder, holding the door shut while she fumbled with the knob. The fringe on her shawl got in the way and she cursed under her breath.

"That's a habit you'll have to break," Garrett said, amused by her temper. "What will people say if I announce my engagement to a young woman with the manners of a . . ."

"Don't call me names," Claire said, swirling around so fast she bumped into him. She backed up until the cool wood of the door was pressed against her back. "You're . . ."

"Rich," he said matter-of-factly. "Rich enough to hire a team of investigators. Rich enough to buy you anything you want. Rich enough to help you or . . ."

"Don't you dare threaten me," Claire said furiously.

Garrett looked down at her. His eyes were as cold as a winter storm. "You don't stand a chance of finding your brother without someone's help, Miss Aldrich, and you know it. San Francisco is a very big city. Besides, who's to say that your brother is still here. What if he's shipped out on a freighter bound for Hong Kong? What will you do then? Work in a dress shop and sleep in a rented room until you're forced to accept some dull young man's attention and get married?"

Claire closed her eyes, knowing that if she let go of her temper, she'd end up being hauled off to jail for murdering the banker. She took a deep breath, hoping that when she opened her eyes Garrett wouldn't still be standing as close as skin.

"Think about it," he said softly. His eyes slid over her and he had to fight the urge to kiss her. She was lovely when she was angry. Her eyes, before she'd closed them, had sparked with amber fire. He wanted to kiss her until she was purring like a kitten or clawing like a wildcat. Either way, he'd enjoy it.

"Think about it." His voice dropped to a seductive whisper. "All you have to do is play the part of an attentive fiancée and I'll take care of all your problems."

Right now, Claire's biggest problem was Garrett Monroe. He was standing so close she could feel his breath on her hair. Her heart was racing and her head was spinning. Did the man think she was made of wood? How could he possibly think that she could *pretend* to love him without eventually falling in love for real?

Because, he doesn't know that I'm attracted to him already, Claire told herself. *He wants to make his grandmother happy. Not me. He wants to hire me the same way he'd hire a maid to sweep the floors of his grand house on the Hill. The problem is, he's right. It's going to take more than money to find Donald, especially if he's left the city. And if I don't find Donald . . .*

Claire refused to finish the thought. She had to find her brother. If she didn't, she was all alone in the world and she didn't want to be alone.

Garrett watched Claire's face and knew that she was arguing with herself. He also knew the moment she'd

reached her decision. Her body relaxed and her eyelashes fluttered ever so slightly before she raised them
and looked up at his face.

"I'll think about it," she said in a faint whisper.

The urge to kiss her was almost uncontrollable as he
removed his hand from the door and stepped back.
"I'll have Andy bring the carriage around," he said,
but instead of motioning her away from the door he
walked to the service bell and pulled the cord again.
"I'm sure your landlady wanted you home at a proper
hour."

Claire straightened her shawl around her shoulders
in preparation for leaving. "If I decide to accept your
offer, should I send a message to the bank?"

"No," he told her. "I'll have Andy call for you tomorrow afternoon. Shall we say two o'clock. We can discuss
the details more thoroughly then."

He sounded as if she'd already made up her mind.
Claire had every intention of penning a curt refusal,
but she didn't want Garrett to know that. At least, not
now. She needed to go back to her room so she could
think.

The service entrance opened and Andy walked into
the room.

Claire managed a smile, then wondered if the young
man knew about Garrett's outrageous proposal. Sensing
that he didn't, she tried to act as if dinner had been an
ordinary event.

"Andy, bring the carriage around to the Taylor Street
entrance."

"Yes, sir," the young man replied before disappearing.

A few moments later Claire found herself being
escorted out of the hotel. As before, instead of entering
through the main lobby, Garrett led her down a second-

ary staircase and into a smaller lobby that fronted Taylor Street. Andy was waiting outside.

"Mount Lookout," Claire said unexpectedly.

"What?"

"The seventh hill," she told Garrett. "It's Mount Lookout."

Garrett smiled. "Good night, Miss Aldrich."

"Good night," she said, then went still as he reached out and took her hand. His mouth was warm on the skin above her knuckles and Claire couldn't help but wonder what it would be like to have his lips pressed against her own.

"Until tomorrow," Garrett said.

As the carriage moved away from the hotel, Claire was left with the image of the pewter gray eyes boring into her soul and the knowledge that all the money in the world couldn't save her if she made the mistake of falling in love with Garrett Monroe.

Chapter Four

The next morning arrived to find Claire frowning at herself in the mirror. She hadn't slept well and it showed. Her eyes lacked their usual brightness and her body felt bruised from endless hours of tossing and turning. She'd gotten ready for bed, determined to send Garrett a blunt note declining his outrageous offer, but as the night wore on, Claire couldn't think of a plausible alternative to her dilemma. The possibility of employment in a dress shop or similar business was still a possibility, but time wasn't on her side. She needed to pay her rent or vacate the room, and she didn't have anywhere to go.

As Claire drew a brush through her tangled hair, she couldn't help remembering the touch of Garrett's hand. His fingertips had felt strong and slightly rough. She'd been surprised because she'd expected them to be weak and soft like a bank clerk's. Then again he wasn't a clerk. He was a banker, a man of power and consequence. The kind of man who could call in favors and pay investigators to comb the streets of San Francisco until they found her brother.

The more Claire thought about Garrett's offer the more she realized she had little choice but to accept it. The thought of returning to Cincinnati never entered her mind. She had no one there but a few friends who had turned into old acquaintances. There was only her brother and her hope that he'd be content to share a home with her while she found her own direction. One that she hoped would eventually lead her to a man who could love her and give her children.

There were no grand dreams in Claire's head as she pinned up her hair and began her morning toiletry. She'd lived in a mansion for five years, but she had no desire for one of her own. She'd be content with a normal house and a normal man, as long as he held her close at night and shared his heart with her.

She wanted the intimacy of a family and the contentment of knowing that once she gave herself to a man, he would be content with her, as well.

The morning passed with the speed of a tortoise inching its way uphill. By the time the clock in the foyer chimed two, Claire was so anxious to get the meeting with Garrett over with she practically slid down the banister to answer the door when Andy knocked. Dressed in a light blue skirt with brown velvet trim around the hem and a white cotton blouse, Claire tugged on her jacket as she descended the staircase. The jacket was fitted at the waist with brown velvet lapels and cuffs. Andy gave her an approving smile when she opened the front door of the boarding house and stepped onto the porch.

"I'm to take you to Willows Park," Andy told her as he helped her into the carriage. "Mr. Monroe will meet us there."

Claire had heard about the fashionable park at the

corner of Mission and Eighteenth streets. She noticed
a small basket sitting next to Andy's feet. Its contents
were covered with a checkered towel and she wondered
if Garrett meant for them to share a quiet lunch while
they discussed the job he had offered her last night.

Claire was too busy rehearsing what she'd say to the
banker to notice the city's buildings and the people
milling up and down the sidewalks. It was a beautiful
day and there was a hint of rain in the breeze blowing
in from the Pacific. When they reached the park, Claire's
eyes went pleasantly wide. The park was everything its
name implied. Tall, wispy willow trees graced the
entrance, their limp green branches bowed toward the
ground. More trees dotted the well-manicured landscape, offering cool little arbors where people sat
appeasing their appetites while children darted among
the flowering shrubs and rosebushes.

Claire smiled as a young man maneuvered his way
along a gravel path on a high wheel bicycle. Several
children stopped playing and applauded his skill. The
front wheel of the bicycle was almost four times larger
than the rear wheel, but the young man controlled the
awkward-looking contraption with ease.

Andy turned the carriage toward the north end of
the park and a grove of thickly boughed trees. Claire
strained her eyes to catch a glimpse of Garrett, but the
banker was nowhere to be seen. When the carriage
rolled to a stop, she looked at her driver. The young
man smiled.

"He'll be along any minute," he said, pulling a small
round watch out of his vest pocket and giving it a quick
glance. "Mr. Monroe rides here every Thursday."

Claire was about to ask if he rode a horse or a bicycle
when she realized the question was ridiculous. Garrett
Monroe was far too dignified to ride a bicycle. No doubt
he'd come galloping up on a black charger like a medi-

eval knight threatening to lay siege to an ancient castle.
The thought gave her pause as she realized Garrett
might not be a warrior, but he had the same kind of
power. His name was well respected in the city. His
wealth, added to the strength of his reputation, made
him a very powerful man.

While Claire admired the fragrant blooms of a mean-
dering vine, Andy unloaded the basket and a small blanket that had been tucked away underneath the carriage
seat. He spread the blanket on the ground under the
shady limbs of the trees, sat the basket in the middle,
and climbed back into the carriage.

"I won't be far way," he told Claire when she gave
him a questioning look. "I don't want to crowd you and
Mr. Monroe."

Claire tried not to show her apprehension as the
carriage rolled away, leaving her alone.

She wasn't alone for long. The sound of a horse,
blowing and snorting, caught her ear and she turned
around to find Garrett riding her way. Instead of a
thick-muscled black war horse, he sat astride a sleek
Appaloosa stallion. The well-bred animal pranced and
danced its way through an artful array of azalea bushes,
but Claire quickly lost her interest in the animal. Her
eyes were glued to its rider. Garrett's dark hair gleamed
in the afternoon sunlight and his face, bronzed by the
California sun, was the most handsome Claire had ever
seen.

The sensations she'd battled all night came rushing
back, along with several new ones. Garrett was looking
at her as if he'd just found a misplaced treasure.

"Good afternoon, Miss Aldrich," he said, bringing
the energetic stallion to a halt with a firm grip on the
reins. "I'm glad you decided to join me. Have you
eaten?"

The last thing Claire wanted to think about was food,

but she didn't want the handsome banker to know that
her stomach was doing somersaults, so she smiled and
walked to the blanket Andy had spread over the grass.
Kneeling down, she uncovered the basket and found a
neatly prepared lunch for two. There were slender slices
of roasted chicken served between wedges of bread that
was still warm from the oven. The hotel had prepared
the food and Claire smiled at the plump grapes and
apple slices wrapped in a white napkin. There was
cheese and a bottle of red wine.

While she spread the small but impressive banquet
on the towel, Garrett watched her. Claire had the poise
of a young woman who had been raised with a house
full of servants. Her movements were calm and graceful.
His grandmother's keen eye wouldn't be able to tell
that Claire Aldrich wasn't what she professed to be. That
suited Garrett just fine. What didn't suit him was the
uncomfortable feeling he got every time he looked at
the young woman from Cincinnati. It was an unnerving
combination of desire and something he wasn't able to
name as yet.

He supposed a bit of it was his innate male instincts.
It was natural for him to feel protective of a young
woman alone in a strange city. The panic he'd felt when
he returned to San Francisco and found his grandmother ill couldn't compare to the fear a young woman
must feel when she realizes that she's all alone in the
world. At least Garrett had his business, a home, and
friends. Claire had nothing but a brother who hadn't
bothered to meet her at the train station.

Anger threaded through Garrett as he tied his mount
to the branch of a nearby tree and left the animal to
munch on the rich spring grass. When he found Donald
Aldrich, and he would find him, Garrett intended to
give the man the trashing of his life.

Claire did her best to concentrate on the lunch she

was preparing, but she couldn't keep her eyes from darting toward Garrett as he moved toward her. Dressed in a dark riding jacket, tan trousers, and black boots that stopped just below his knees, he was an impressive sight. He was a big man, but he had no extra weight to slow him down. His legs were long and lean. His upper body was wide at the shoulders and he moved with the ease of a cat strolling along a tree branch. She'd never been so aware of a man's physical presence before and it alarmed her. As Garrett sat down on the blanket, Claire reminded herself that he only wanted her to *pretend* that she cared for him. Telling herself that a hundred times a day might keep her from letting the pretense turn into a reality, but she wasn't entirely sure she could undo the damage Garrett had already done to her nervous system. All he had to do was look at her and her bones seemed to melt.

"Since you came to the park, I assume that you've decided to accept my offer of employment," Garrett said as he reached for one of the sandwiches.

Claire took a deep breath and forced herself to meet his piercing gray gaze. "I have to find my brother, Mr. Monroe, and as much as it stings my pride, I also have to admit that there doesn't seem to be any other way."

Garrett admired honesty and he knew that Claire wasn't happy about her current circumstances. He also had to admit that he'd never had to pay for a woman's attention. Reminding himself that this was a business relationship, he poured the wine, and offered her a glass. "I'm a businessman, Claire. And this will be a . . . What's wrong?"

"I didn't give you permission to address me by my Christian name."

Garrett laughed. "People who are engaged to be married tend to call each other by their given names, Miss Monroe. Mine is Garrett. Say it."

"We're not engaged, Mr. Monroe." Claire took a sip of wine to fortify her wits. When she raised the glass she found Garrett staring at her and it wasn't a friendly look.

"I'm hiring you to play the role of my fiancée, Miss Aldrich, and I don't pay for a job unless it's done well. Now, say my name."

The authority of his voice frightened Claire just a little. She was about to stand up and call a halt to their meeting when she remembered the two coins tucked away in the dresser drawer at the boarding house. She didn't have enough money to pay for another week's rent. Feeling defeated by circumstances and the steely power of Garrett's stormy eyes, she sighed.

"Garrett."

"That's better." He smiled. "Now say it again, but with a little more enthusiasm this time. We are supposed to be *fond* of each other, remember."

"Garrett."

The name rolled off her tongue in a sultry whisper that turned Garrett's short burst of anger into a flood of desire. He smiled again and this time the expression reached his eyes.

"That's better. Now, let's talk about your duties. I don't want this drama to unfold improperly. My grandmother is ill, but she has the instincts of an alley cat. One misspoken word and she'll know something is wrong."

The comment didn't reassure Claire's nervous stomach. She took another sip of wine.

"You need to eat something," Garrett told her. He handed her one of the sandwiches and watched until she bit into it. "We met on the train from St. Louis," he began. "You're a distant cousin of Elizabeth Shurman and we were introduced by a mutual friend."

"But that's a lie."

Garrett frowned. "I appreciate your dislike of false-hoods, but they're necessary. Now, eat and listen."

"Are you going to order me around all the time?" she asked, returning his frown with one of her own. "I'm not sure I like it."

Garrett ignored her. "We met on the train from St. Louis and fell in love."

Claire chewed on her bottom lip for a moment, then nodded. She wasn't in any position to argue about the terms of her new job. She needed the money too desperately to let her conscience beat her to death over the way she was going to earn it. Garrett was a gentleman, and as such, he wouldn't make demands that weren't proper and acceptable.

"When I introduce you to my grandmother, she's going to ask about your family. You can tell her the truth, as long as it doesn't compromise the impression I want to give her. Understand?"

"My parents are dead and my brother is . . ." Claire hesitated.

"Your brother is employed by the railroad," Garrett supplied. "His job takes him away from home a great deal and you're not sure when he's returning to the city. Of course, you've written him about our engagement."

"You make it sound so simple."

"It is simple," he told her. "All you have to do is be charming and act besotted."

"Besotted?"

Garrett made a frustrated sound. "You have to appear to be madly in love with me, Miss Aldrich. Anything short of that and my grandmother will know that I've got something up my sleeve. The whole point of this exercise is to brighten her spirits. That isn't going to happen if you keep frowning at me."

Claire softened her expression. "I'm not an actress, Mr. Monroe."

"Garrett," he corrected her. "And I don't want an actress. I want an amiable young lady with acceptable social graces and a pretty face. You have both."

She dropped her eyes for a moment, hoping that the flush of heat she felt at his words wasn't showing on her face. His next remark said she hadn't succeeded in hiding her feelings.

"Don't be coy," Garrett said, sounding irritated. "You have a lovely face and I doubt that I'm the first man to tell you so." He hesitated, wondering how many suitors Claire had left behind in Cincinnati. Realizing that his mind was straying, Garrett reached for some grapes and continued what was becoming a very difficult conversation. He'd never had to come out and literally ask a woman to pretend she was attracted to him. "Let's get back to the business at hand, shall we? For starters, it only makes sense that I would find you attractive. Following that is the obvious conclusion that the same thing applies to you."

Only, I don't have to pretend, Claire thought. *I am attracted to you. Far too much for me to be comfortable about the corner I'm about to paint myself into.*

Deciding she'd be better off to at least act like she was pretending, Claire raised her head and met Garrett's gaze. "I'm not totally ignorant of what happens when two people fall in love, Mr. Monroe. And I'm not a child in a classroom. Please stop sounding like a teacher."

The question of her experience was on the tip of Garrett's tongue, but he squelched the urge to ask it. He'd bet the gold nameplate setting on his desk at the bank that Claire Aldrich had never been kissed. At least not the way she should be kissed. Long and deep and passionately. Kissed until she moaned and went limp in a man's arms. Kissed until her pretty pink mouth was swollen and her hazel eyes blurred with desire.

"Excuse my tone," he said, softening his voice until it resembled the tone he'd used the previous night when he'd had her pressed up against the hotel door. "I'm a businessman, but this isn't my usual business. In fact, this whole situation is just as awkward for me as it is for you."

Claire knew what he was talking about, although most young ladies weren't supposed to understand the real facts of life. Hiring a woman to pretend affection for him was new. The stories in the newspaper came rushing to mind as Claire realized any woman in the city would be more than willing to be seen with Garrett Monroe. She supposed it bruised his male ego to have to instruct a young lady in the female arts, but then she hadn't been the one to plot against his grandmother's tender feelings. A touch of anger replaced her embarrassment and she tilted her chin slightly higher.

"It would seem to me that your performance is just as important as mine," Claire said candidly. "Tell me, Mr. Monroe, can you *pretend* affection for one woman when you no doubt have a dozen young ladies flirting with you at any given opportunity. I'm sure you'll be bored by week's end."

Garrett's smile was smug and very masculine. "I see my reputation precedes me."

"I may be a stranger to the city, but I can read," she told him. "Your name isn't new to the social page of the newspapers."

"Unfortunately not," he admitted. His smile returned as he noticed her fidgeting with her napkin. He popped a plump grape into his mouth, letting his eyes roam over her as he chewed it. After a short pause that was poignant with possibilities, he finished his reply. "Don't worry about me becoming bored, Claire. In fact, I think you and I will get along very well."

The arrogance in his tone pricked Claire's temper.

"And just how do you expect us to get along, Mr. Monroe? Will I be given a daily script from which to read, or shall I consult with you as to the frequency of my smiles? I certainly wouldn't want to appear overly affective or unduly complacent."

He laughed out loud. At that moment, he wanted to cover Claire's sassy mouth with his own and kiss her senseless. "I suspect we'll have to work out some sort of secret signals," he suggested, clearly amused by her indignation. In fact, he was delighted to find out that she had a sense of humor. "My name is Garrett," he repeated. "I insist you use it from this moment on."

Claire was about to send another fiery retort his way when Garrett surprised her by standing up and holding out his hand.

"I think you're right. We need to get better acquainted. Shall we take a walk? The park isn't crowded this time of day, and I intend to introduce you to my grandmother this weekend. If she hears a bit of gossip between now and then, no harm will be done."

He'd taken off his riding gloves and laid them next to the picnic blanket. Claire looked at his bronzed hand like Eve must have looked at the forbidden apple before plucking it off the tree.

"I'm afraid holding my hand is also a requirement of your employment," Garrett said teasingly. "Come along, I don't bite."

Claire wasn't so sure. In fact, the longer she was with Garrett Monroe, the less confident she became about what she was getting into. Engaged couples did walk hand in hand. They also talked to each other in soft whispers and exchanged affectionate smiles. It boiled down to the simple fact that people in love liked being close to one another.

That realization was the cause of Claire's hesitation. She already liked being close to Garrett. The sound of his voice, when he wasn't being dictatorial, was pleasing and his smile had the strangest effect on her. It made her heart pound and goose bumps sprout on her skin.

When Garrett's strong hand closed around hers, Claire felt her knees go weak for a scant second. Reminding herself that she was looking for her brother, not a suitor, she allowed Garrett to help her up from the blanket. He led her toward a small pond not far from the trees and she smiled when she realized that the tiny reservoir was crowded with fat goldfish swimming around in circles. Nothing was said for several minutes and she became conscious of the tension between them. They were strangers who had agreed to play at being in love.

She looked up and searched his face. His eyes masked his feelings and she suspected that he'd learned the art of keeping his thoughts secret because of his profession. Bankers were known for their standoffish attitudes. Of course, there was nothing standoffish in the way Garrett was looking at her. His eyes roamed over her face, then lower, taking in her entire body. Claire felt herself warming under his predatory stare and she pulled her hand away.

It was time to say what she had to say before she lost her nerve completely.

Garrett saw the subtle change in her expression. "What is it?"

She glanced down at the fishpond. "I can't promise you that I can fool your grandmother," she said honestly. "I've never met the lady, but if she's as nimble of mind as you say she is, then I fear your plan will have a disastrous ending. I don't want to cause anyone harm."

"I don't think you could harm anyone if you tried," Garrett replied candidly. "You have a gentle nature and a soft heart."

His remark brought Claire's head up and around. "You only met me yesterday."

"I'm a banker," he replied, smiling. "But I don't always depend on numbers to make my decisions. I've been known to give loans on nothing more than a gut feeling. I'll trust my instincts where you're concerned."

There was more Claire had to say and she dreaded the words. She'd swallowed her pride when she'd accepted Garrett's offer, and it was still caught in her throat. "You said that you intended to introduce me to your grandmother this weekend."

Garrett gave her a slight nod. He could sense that the words she was struggling to find weren't easy ones. His protective instincts came into play again and he reached for her arm, turning her to face him. "Our arrangement isn't a conventional one, Claire. It's going to demand honesty between us, even though we will be deceiving others. If we can't talk to each other in private, how are we going to carry off a successful charade in public?"

"You mentioned a salary," she said in a shaky voice. "I'm afraid I require an advance. My rent is due and . . ."

His fingertips, placed over her lips, stopped Claire from further humiliation. The gesture was soft and it carried no threat, but it was a little scary to realize how the slightest touch of Garrett's hand could affect her.

"We can talk about your salary over dinner," he said, realizing he was looking forward to it already. He also realized that Claire's financial situation was worse than he'd first suspected. Another reason for him to beat Donald Aldrich into the ground when they finally came face-to-face. "As for your rent, it won't be necessary. I've arranged for you to have a suite of rooms at the hotel. Andy will take you there after you've packed your belongings."

Claire wanted to argue, but Garrett's finger was still

resting against her mouth. The soft pressure made her think of a kiss.

"I've also arranged for a dressmaker to call on you tomorrow morning. You'll need a complete wardrobe, including numerous gowns for evening and a fur wrap. The nights can get quite chilly here. I'm afraid our engagement is going to spawn a flock of invitations. Everyone will expect to see you at all the right social functions."

His hand dropped away and Claire felt a strange sense of disappointment when his touch vanished. Drawing herself up to her full height of five feet four inches, she frowned. "Is all that really necessary?"

"I'm afraid so," he remarked. "You aren't that shy are you? Most young ladies would be thrilled at the prospect of being the belle of the ball."

"I'm not most ladies," Claire said, wondering just how she explained who and what she was to a stranger. Of course, they wouldn't be strangers for long. She was going to move into Garrett's mansion on top of the Hill. It was part of the plan and she knew she couldn't talk him out of it. But she still had her pride. She'd agreed to play the role of Garrett's fiancée. She hadn't agreed to be a kept woman. "You can deduct the clothing from whatever you were going to pay me."

Garrett knew she was battling her pride. He had no desire to dampen her spirits, so he said nothing. Claire was the key to his scheme and he had to keep her moderately content in order for things to go smoothly. "We can work out the details of your compensation later. For now, I have an appointment and you have some packing to do."

They strolled back to the blanket. Claire didn't protest his hand this time. In fact she liked the warm, secure feeling it gave her. Until today, she'd been all alone in the city. Now she had one of its most prominent citizens escorting her around the park and she wouldn't have to fall asleep wondering how she was going to pay Mrs. Kruger the rent.

While Claire repacked the basket, Garrett mounted his horse and rode to where Andy was waiting with the carriage. The two men exchanged some words and Garrett rode back to where she was standing. "I'll see you at dinner," he said, tipping his hat. "If you need anything ask for Andy or Libby Marlow, she's the maid who served our dinner last night. Do you remember her?"

"Yes."

"Good," he replied. "Now, stop frowning. I'll take care of everything."

The words were a balm to Claire's worried mind. For the last three weeks she'd been struggling with the unknown. Where was Donald? Was he in some sort of trouble? What if she couldn't find a job? What if Mrs. Kruger tossed her out on her ear? The what ifs had kept her from sleeping and she'd paced her rented room until her feet hurt. She blinked back a tear, unable to control the relief that suddenly overtook her. She liked being independent but knowing that her temporary burdens had been shifted to the banker's shoulders was a small miracle.

Garrett saw the gleam of moisture in her eyes and dismounted. He didn't think about his actions. He simply did what came naturally and pulled her into the circle of his arms. "Don't cry," he said in a soothing whisper. "And don't worry. I'll find your brother."

Garrett's words shocked him as much as they reassured Claire. He wasn't the type of man who reacted to a woman's tears, but the soft shudder of Claire's body touched him in more ways than one.

* * *

Claire acted just as unconsciously as she put her hand, palm down, on his chest and tried not to let three weeks' worth of tears dampen the front of his jacket. She should protest the improper familiarity of being held in Garrett's arms, but she couldn't. At the moment, it felt wonderful. She could smell the soap he'd used to bathe with that morning. His arms felt strong and secure around her and she wanted to sink into that strength until all her doubts disappeared.

Garrett was too much of a man, and not enough of a gentleman, to ignore the way Claire fit so perfectly against him. Her hair, a thick mass of honey brown curls, teased his chin and he could feel the feminine contours of her body in spite of all the clothes she was wearing. His hands ached to tighten around her narrow waist and bring her even closer, but this wasn't the time or the place. She needed reassurance, not seduction.

Several moments passed and Claire realized that they were in the middle of a park. Anyone could see them. She pulled away, taking a step backward as Garrett's arms relaxed and gradually released her. Pulling a linen hankie out of her pocket, she dabbed at her eyes, more embarrassed now than she'd been the previous night when he'd cornered her between his hard male body and the hotel door. The man had the power to make her forget everything she'd ever been taught about being a lady.

Garrett smiled at the blush that covered Claire's cheeks. He couldn't resist the urge to touch her again. His hand reached out and he tilted her chin, forcing her to meet his gaze. "I'll see you this evening."

Claire gave him a weak smile. Her emotions were getting out of control and she wished he'd remember his appointment and leave so she could get back her composure. It was impossible as long as he was touching her.

"Andy will wait while you pack your things," Garrett told her. "Take a nap when you get to the hotel. I don't want you falling asleep while I recite my accomplishments in life. Grams will expect you to know something about me."

Being reminded that she was being hired to play a role brought reality crashing down on Claire's head. How could she forget something so important in the space of a few minutes?

"I'm sure I won't be bored, sir. After all, your name is legendary in this city."

"You mean my money is legendary," Garrett replied stiffly.

His hand dropped away. Once he was in the saddle again and looking devilishly handsome atop the spirited stallion, he smiled down at her. "Until this evening, Miss Aldrich."

He tapped his riding crop against the horse's flank and galloped away, leaving Claire to wonder if she hadn't just jumped out of the proverbial frying pan and into the fire.

Chapter Five

The present arrived shortly after Claire closed the door of her hotel room and let out a sigh of relief. She'd just removed her hat and placed it on the vanity table when Libby tapped on the door. Claire opened it, hoping to find the hotel maid armed with a tray of tea. Instead of tea, Libby was carrying a small box wrapped in gold foil and tied with a black velvet ribbon.

"Mr. Monroe had this delivered," Libby said, stepping into the room. "He said to tell you that he'll meet you in the lobby at eight."

Claire accepted the box, then watched as Libby began milling about the luxuriously decorated suite, rearranging the flowers in a vase and adjusting the curtains so just the right amount of light drifted through the Irish lace panels covering the windows. The suite was spacious and decorated in shades of royal blue and ivory. Large pocket doors opened, revealing a bedroom that was fit for a queen. The bed was covered with a white canopy.

A comfortable silk damask chair, upholstered in deep purple, sat beside a marble-topped Italianate table. Claire had only gotten a peek at the bathroom, but what she had seen was enough to make her hope for a long steamy bath in the claw-footed ceramic tub.

She sat down on the blue-and-white-striped settee and stared at the elegantly wrapped box. If Garrett was meeting her in the lobby, she could assume that they would be dining in the main restaurant of the hotel. That meant the curtain was going up on her performance. Claire wondered if he was testing her at the same time she wondered just how much Libby knew about her relationship with the banker.

The maid had gone into the bedroom and Claire could hear her unpacking the small trunk Andy had deposited at the foot of the bed. Putting Garrett's present on the table in front of the settee, Claire walked into the bedroom.

"That isn't necessary," she said as the hotel maid undid the straps on her canvas valise and began unpacking.

"Of course, it's necessary," Libby replied, smiling. "I got my orders directly from Mr. Monroe. I'm supposed to take very special care of you."

Claire was about to ask how many times Libby had been turned into a lady's maid, but she caught herself before the question tumbled out. If Garrett was testing her, then she had to act in front of Libby the same way she'd act in front of the other people she'd soon be meeting.

Instead of protesting, Claire thanked Libby for her efforts and returned to the parlor. She reached for the present, hesitated, and then folded her hands in her lap. Whatever Garrett had put into the box could wait for a moment of privacy before being revealed.

Once Libby had put Claire's dresses in the walk-in

closet, and placed her clean undergarments in the narrow top drawers of the large chest, the maid joined Claire in the parlor. She was carrying the gown Claire had worn the night before over her arms. "I'll have this pressed for you," Libby said.

The maid didn't comment on the limited state of Claire's wardrobe. The blue gown was the only dress Claire owned that was suitable for a formal dinner and she suddenly regretted that Garrett would have to see it again tonight. *What more can he expect,* she thought to herself. *I wouldn't have asked for an advance on my salary if I could afford a new dress.*

"Would you like some refreshments before you rest, Miss Aldrich?"

"Yes, thank you," Claire replied, realizing that Garrett had given Libby very detailed instructions, including the one about taking a nap. "Some tea would be nice."

Libby gave her a quick nod before quitting the room.

Once Claire was alone, her eyes moved back to the present. She reached for the box again, consumed by curiosity. Why would Garrett send her a present? Her hands were shaking as she touched the velvet ribbon binding the box together. She lifted the lid of the tissue-lined box and withdrew the gift. It was a cameo. Claire had never seen such a finely crafted work of art. The classic female face was in profile and the pinkish shell inlay looked as delicate as a baby's breath. She held the small brooch in the palm of her hand. Her heart was pounding fiercely, as if Garrett had personally pinned the jewelry to the lapel of her suit. Tears burned her eyes and Claire tried to remember the last time anyone had given her such a lovely present.

Donald had sent her the tortoise shell comb, along with several linen handkerchiefs trimmed with lace, but he was her brother. This present was from a man, a man she was supposed to convince the world she loved.

Unsure of how she should be reacting, Claire sat staring at the cameo brooch. It wasn't proper for a young lady to accept such an expensive gift, but then nothing about her relationship with Garrett Monroe could be considered proper. She supposed he was accustomed to bestowing expensive baubles and bangles on the finer sex, and she should be angry, but she wasn't. The gift touched her heart the same way Garrett seemed to be touching it.

The implications of her feelings toward the banker began to take hold of Claire and she frowned. She would be out of her mind to let herself feel anything for the man, but she couldn't squelch the sensations that had taken hold from the first moment they'd met. In less than forty-eight hours Garrett Monroe had become embedded in her mind and heart.

Claire was about to take a mental step back from her emotions and analyze her situation when Libby tapped on the door again. Quickly placing the brooch back in its box, Claire smoothed her hair away from her face and opened the door.

"I've brought you hot tea and some ginger cookies," Libby said, sauntering into the room. "While you eat, I'll run your bath."

Claire opened her mouth to respond, but the maid didn't give her a chance.

"Your dress will be pressed and ready by six. I'll bring it up when I come to do your hair."

"Thank you," Claire said, resigning herself to a day or two of pampering. She poured a cup of tea as she eyed the present and silently reminded herself not to fall into the trap the banker was setting for his grandmother and the rest of San Francisco society.

* * *

Garrett regarded his grandmother with a raised brow. He had joined her in the back parlor for a few minutes of conversation and to make sure that she had taken the tonic Dr. Baldwin had prescribed for her on a daily basis. "What gossip are you referring to?"

Theodora Monroe waved her grandson's matter-of-fact tone aside. "You know very well what gossip. Ada Belton is giving a charity ball for the new orphanage and she's hinting that your engagement to her daughter will be announced."

Garrett smiled. He removed his jacket and tossed it over the back of a nearby chair. Grams had a way of getting right to the point. It was one of the things he liked about her. He was about to reply that the Bay would go dry before he married Belinda Belton, but Grams wasn't in the mood to wait for his response.

"I swear if you've asked that spineless girl to marry you, I'll disown you here and now. As much as I want to see you settle down, I won't accept Belinda Belton into this family. Do you hear me?"

Garrett dropped onto the end of the sofa where his grandmother was sitting. The marmalade tomcat that had appeared at the back door several years ago and been instantly adopted into the family crawled off his grandmother's lap and onto Garrett's. He stroked the well-fed feline from head to tail as he met his grandmother's questioning gaze. The cat stretched lazily under his hand, then jumped down and took up its customary place in the windowsill.

"I have no intentions of marrying Belinda Belton. And I have no idea what initiated the gossip."

"I do," Grams grumbled. "Ada Belton's tongue is loose on both ends. She knows I'm encouraging you to marry and she thinks . . ."

"I don't care what Ada Belton thinks," Garrett interrupted her. "And neither should you. Dr. Baldwin wants you to rest, not worry."

"I'll stop worrying when you're married to a decent woman who loves you more than she loves your money," Grams replied bluntly.

Garrett took a deep breath, letting it out as he stood up. His grandmother had a higher opinion of the female gender than he did. "I'm having dinner at the hotel. Don't wait up for me."

Garrett could feel his grandmother's eyes on his back as he walked out of the room. He was halfway up the staircase that led to his bedroom before he allowed himself to smile. Saturday was the perfect day to introduce Claire to his grandmother. The Beltons' party was Saturday night and he intended to walk into the Nob Hill residence with his fiancée on his arm. Whatever Ada Belton had up her sleeve would be worthless after that and he could concentrate on his business again while Claire's presence calmed his grandmother's worried brow.

After he bathed and changed clothes, Garrett went into the library for a brandy. It was his private domain, his retreat within the well-furnished house, and one of his favorite rooms. The walls were lined with leather-bound books. It was a room for inspiration and instruction and Garrett found himself staring out the window, thinking about the night ahead.

He'd spent most of the afternoon making arrangements for Claire's public introduction. A prominent dressmaker would arrive at the hotel tomorrow morning. He'd given the discreet lady specific orders as to what he expected, along with the promise of a sizeable bonus if a gown was ready for Saturday night's party. After that, he'd paid a visit to the jeweler. He'd selected an engagement ring. Large but elegant, the star-cut emerald had caught his eye almost immediately. He'd been on his way out of the shop when he saw the cameo. The brooch reminded him of Claire's delicate features and he'd bought it, then given instructions for it to be delivered to the hotel as soon as possible. The shopkeeper's withered face had drawn into a smile when Garrett added a diamond and ruby necklace to his purchases.

The mantel clock struck seven as Garrett finished his brandy. He was used to escorting beautiful women to dinner, but tonight was different. Tonight was the beginning of the deception. He wanted the other guests in the hotel, many of whom knew him on sight, to notice that *this* lady was different. He wanted them to whisper that he was talking to her differently, looking at her differently. By the time he escorted Claire out of the dining room and invited her to take a walk in the hotel garden, Garrett wanted everyone to realize that he wasn't entertaining his current mistress.

He had no doubt that Claire would play her role to perfection. It was his own performance that was in doubt. As he gathered his hat from the foyer table and reached for his gloves, Garrett wondered if he could pretend to be in love. Never having experienced the mysterious emotion he had nothing to go on. He'd seen his share of besotted young men, but he wasn't fresh out of short pants, and he had no intentions of making a fool of himself. He knew how to conduct himself around a lady, but being engaged demanded a certain change in his demeanor.

Garrett could cope with the young widows and sophisticated women he'd taken as mistresses over the years. He knew what they expected from him and what he gleaned in return. He understood the unwritten laws of the bedroom, but he knew next to nothing about how a man treated a woman who held a place in his heart rather than in his bed.

As he climbed into the carriage that would take the

twisting gravel lane down the hill and into the city, Garrett supposed that he'd do well enough if he treated Claire like any other lady, with the exception of the acceptable familiarity that was allowed between engaged couples in public.

The carriage was halfway to the hotel before Garrett thought about Evelyn Holmes, the young Englishwoman he'd moved into the cottage on Bartlett Street. He hadn't visited her since her first day in the city, the evening after he'd encountered Claire in the hotel office. The last two days had been consumed with thoughts of Miss Aldrich, not the succulent blonde who had amused him since leaving London. He made a mental note to call on Evelyn later, after he'd bid Claire good night. Although none of his peers would expect him to deny himself the pleasure of a mistress, before or after his alleged marriage, Garrett wanted Evelyn to hear the news from him. If she responded as he expected her to respond, he'd offer her return passage to England, or better yet, he would introduce her to Christopher. His friend was between liaisons at the moment and knowing Christopher's appetites, Evelyn would suit him well.

That thought aside, Garrett's mind turned to a more immediate problem—Donald Aldrich. His first inclination was to make sure that Claire didn't find her brother. It was apparent that the man felt no responsibility or commitment to his sister. If he did, Claire wouldn't have been left alone after the death of their mother. Garrett had a gnawing feeling in his gut that when he did confront Donald Aldrich, there was going to be trouble. He decided to put Mr. Wilson on the case. Hiram had worked for him in the past, privately gathering useful bits of information about potential investors or grumbling stockholders. The middle-aged man was dependable and extremely discreet.

By the time the carriage stopped in front of the hotel, Garrett had dismissed any lingering doubts about the scheme he had hatched to keep his grandmother happy. Her reaction to the gossip churned up by Ada Belton confirmed his suspicions. Grams wasn't going to be content until her grandson appeared to be happily resigned to a wife and family.

Several people were milling around the hotel lobby as Garrett entered through the main entrance. Andy was standing behind the counter wearing a brown, double-breasted jacket. He gave Garrett a quick nod, excused himself from the front desk, and went upstairs to inform Claire that her dinner companion had arrived. Garrett took off his gloves and hat, handing them to a bellboy, who then placed them in the coatroom adjacent to the lobby.

"Thought I'd see you tonight," Christopher Landauer said, strolling across the lobby to shake Garrett's hand. "I understand Miss Aldrich has been installed in one of the upstairs suites."

"Only temporarily," Garrett told him.

Christopher led him to the side, away from the people who were gathering in the lobby for a small party to be held in one of the private dining rooms that overlooked the courtyard. "I can't believe she agreed to your outrageous proposal. The girl must be more desperate than I thought." Garrett gave him a scathing look, but Christopher wasn't deterred. "Is this to be her formal coming-out dinner? Should I order up a bottle of our best champagne?"

"You can stop smiling like you've just found a lost gold mine," Garrett replied curtly. "And yes, Miss Aldrich has agreed to my offer of employment. An offer I trust will remain confidential."

Christopher held his hands up, palms out. "I won't breathe a word. Promise."

"See that you don't," Garrett warned him, then smiled. "Actually, a few well-spoken words should get the gossip wheels turning in time for Ada Belton to realize she's put her foot in her mouth again."

His friend laughed. "Heard that particular piece of news, did you. I for one accepted an invitation to the gala event just to see Mrs. Belton's reaction when you walk in with the lovely Miss Aldrich on your arm."

"She is lovely, isn't she," Garrett mused, as if he'd just realized Claire's beauty.

His friend looked past Garrett, toward the carpeted staircase. "From here, I'd say she's the loveliest lady in San Francisco."

Garrett turned around. Claire was standing on the small landing, halfway between the first and second floors of the hotel. Her hand was resting on the mahogany banister as she scanned the lobby and caught his gaze. Although he'd seen her earlier in the day, she looked even more beautiful than he remembered. Her hair was done up in a thick cluster of curls, accenting her slender neck and the classic rise of her cheekbones. He smiled when he saw the cameo. She'd pinned it to a strip of black velvet ribbon and was wearing it around her neck.

"If you'll excuse me," Garrett said, leaving Christopher to stare, along with several other men in the lobby.

The air became charged with tension as Garrett approached the bottom of the staircase. Claire couldn't keep herself from staring at him as he stopped next to the wide banister at the end of the staircase and looked up at her. She took a deep breath and began walking slowly toward him, totally unaware of everyone else. Garrett held her gaze like a magnet.

Garrett made no attempt to look anywhere but at Claire. He boldly surveyed her body as she came closer. He studied the shape of her waist, letting his eyes move ever so slowly upward over the swell of her breasts, not stopping until he was staring at her tempting mouth.

"Good evening," he said in a deep voice.

"Good evening." Claire's voice shook. She couldn't help it. Just looking at Garrett made her nervous. Unconsciously, she raised her hand and touched the cameo. It felt warm under her fingers and she smiled. "Thank you for the present. It's lovely."

"Not as lovely as the woman wearing it," Garrett said as he held out his hand.

Claire hesitated for a moment, then accepted it, letting him wrap his lean fingers around her trembling ones. He tugged her gently forward and she stepped down onto the lobby's tiled floor. He was still staring at her and the impact of his quicksilver eyes made her feel naked.

"I hope you're hungry," Garrett said, placing her hand on his bent arm as he escorted her into the formal dining room. He caressed her face with his eyes. "I'm famished."

The words were innocent but his tone was laced with sensuality and Claire had to look down at the floor to keep from blushing. She nodded, put a smile on her face, and met his gaze again. His eyes were still burning with unreadable emotions and Claire's heart started pounding so loudly she feared he could hear it.

As they stepped through the wide doorway into the hotel's main dining room, several heads turned in their direction. Claire forced herself to act as if being with Garrett was an everyday event. She smiled cordially as they passed through the maze of linen-covered tables. Garrett acknowledged several greetings, but he didn't stop long enough to introduce her to the well-dressed men and their equally fashionable companions. A waiter, dressed in stark black trousers and vest with a white starched shirt, appeared out of nowhere. He pulled back the chair at a corner table and waited for Claire to be seated.

Garrett ordered champagne and told the waiter that the chef already knew what he wanted served for dinner.

"I'm nervous," Claire whispered, once the waiter had left them alone. The table was far enough away from the other guests for her voice not to be heard but she didn't want to take the chance. "Everyone's staring at me."

"That's because you're worth staring at," Garrett told her, amused by her confession. "Relax and enjoy your meal. They're only curious."

So was Claire. Questions started buzzing around in her head. If Garrett loved his grandmother enough to go to the trouble of hiring a fiancée, he couldn't be as coldhearted as she'd first thought. Coldhearted men didn't weave compassionate schemes.

Garrett gave the room a quick glance. "The bearded gentleman who spoke to me on the way in is Alexander Stockton. Railroads and gold mines," Garrett said, as if everyone owned at least one of each. "The lady with him is his second wife. The first Mrs. Stockton died after giving her husband four sons."

Claire absorbed the names of the people as Garrett listed them and their various assets. "Are they guests at the hotel?" she asked.

"Some of them," Garrett replied. "Others are here because the Landauer has one of the best chefs in the city."

She was about to comment on the quality of the champagne, when Garrett changed the direction of their conversation.

"I attended school in England," he told her. "Cambridge."

She was duly impressed and her expression told him so. Garrett smiled, then casually began telling her about his family. His father had been a banker in St. Louis, and having an adventurous spirit, he'd decided to move West. His insight into the possibilities that California and its neighboring states would soon offer helped to make him a large fortune in a very short period of time.

"How old were you when your father died?" Claire asked.

"Twelve. I was an only child, as was my father. That's why Grams is so important to me. When cholera killed my parents, it almost killed her, too."

"Your grandmother is the only family you have."

Garrett nodded as he reached for his champagne glass. "That's why making her happy is so important to me. I owe her more than I can ever repay."

"But you're willing to deceive her," Claire reminded him.

"I'm willing to do all that I can do to make her happy," he replied dryly. His smile disappeared for a moment. "Let this be the last time we discuss this particular issue, Miss Aldrich. You've accepted the position as my fiancée. It's done. Our appearance together tonight is only the opening act."

Claire accepted the reprimand, but she didn't like it. Reminding herself that the reason she was having dinner with Garrett Monroe was because she wanted to find her brother, Claire sipped her champagne and smiled. "How will you go about looking for Donald?"

"I have a talented investigator at my disposal," he replied, knowing that her financial situation was the key to her cooperation. It pricked his temper to think that if Claire wasn't in dire straits, she'd probably stand up and walk out of the room. "If your brother's alive, Hiram will find him."

Claire went pale and her glass wobbled precariously for a moment. Garrett took it out of her hand and set it on the table, regretting his choice of words. "I'm sorry," he said. "It was a figure of speech, nothing more."

Claire closed her eyes for a moment. The thought of Donald being in trouble had plagued her since she'd arrived in the city. The thought of him being dead made her blood run cold. "He's the only family I have," she said shakily. "If anything's happened to him . . ."

"I'm sure your brother is alive and well," Garrett said, placing his hand on top of hers. "Hiram will find him, don't worry."

"You must think me a coward," Claire said, wishing she could withdraw her hand but knowing the people still giving them curious glances would notice. She put on her best smile and looked across the table at Garrett. "And you must think Donald a terrible man. I assure you, he isn't. He's generous and fun-loving and I know he's going to feel terrible about my being in the city without his knowledge. My letter didn't reach him. If it had, he would have been at the train station."

Garrett didn't want to discuss Claire's brother. Time and Hiram Wilson's investigation would tell him everything he needed to know. The waiter brought their food and they began to eat. He was telling Claire an amusing anecdote about one of his investors when Christopher walked into the dining room and headed for their table.

"Miss Aldrich," Christopher said, giving her an admiring look before he acknowledged Garrett. "I hope your stay at the Landauer is satisfactory. If it isn't, be sure to tell me. I know the owner personally."

Claire laughed softly. "Thank you, Mr. Landauer."

"Call me Christopher," he said with his customary charm. "After all, Garrett is my best friend, and as far as Grams is concerned, I'm an official member of the family."

"He's the proverbial black sheep," Garrett told her.

"But Grams invites him to Sunday dinner regardless of his unsavory reputation."

Claire smiled as the two men exchanged polite insults.

"I look forward to seeing you at the Belton ball," Christopher said, before telling Garrett that some men had to work for a living and excusing himself.

"The Belton ball?"

"It's Saturday night," Garrett told her. "Henry Belton is another banker. The two of us maintain a gentlemanly game of competition for the city's money. His wife is giving a charity ball. The timing is perfect. I'll introduce you as my fiancée."

Claire's stomach knotted momentarily. She had thought Garrett would give her some time to get to know him better before he pushed her into the lion's den. "But I'm only meeting your grandmother Saturday afternoon. Isn't the party a little too soon to announce our engagement."

Garrett smiled again. Claire wished the expression didn't make him look so roguishly handsome.

"If I don't announce it, Grams will," he told her. "I've never invited a lady to my home before. The moment you walk through the door, my grandmother is going to know there's a reason to my madness."

"Of course," Claire said softly. "We're supposed to be in love."

"That's right," Garrett reminded her. "So, finish your dessert. It's a lovely night. We can take a walk around the courtyard before I'm forced to call an end to the evening."

It wasn't that late, but Claire didn't question his remark. Whatever Garrett did with his time was none of her business. She was nothing more than a paid employee and he was her boss. What he did, and who he did it with, were of no concern to her. All that mattered was finding Donald and keeping her heart safe.

As Claire dipped a spoon into the small silver bowl filled with peach cobbler, fresh cream, and chopped nuts, she had a premonition that finding her brother was going to be the easier of the two tasks.

The courtyard was cool and filled with shadows. Overhead the moon hung like a bright silver platter in the sky and the sound of laughter drifted out of the hotel. There was a party and Claire wondered what the people were celebrating.

Garrett walked beside her, his expression blank, his hands tucked casually behind his back. Claire cast him a leery look, her mind racing with all the facts he'd recited while they'd eaten. She'd never remember them all, but she liked observing people and she was sure that if she kept her eyes and ears open, she'd learn even more from Garrett's grandmother than she'd learned from the handsome banker.

Garrett stopped suddenly and looked at her. Claire found herself gazing into his smoky eyes and wondering what thoughts filled his head. Was he worried that she'd make a mess of things or was he having second thoughts about the charade they had set into motion? His features had a worried look as he motioned for her to sit down.

Claire made herself comfortable while Garrett looked over his shoulder toward the hotel. "Christopher Landauer and I have been friends most of our lives," he said. "While you're at the hotel, I want you to act like a guest."

Claire didn't like the tone of his voice and she didn't care for the implication of his words. "How else would I act?" she answered. "I am a guest."

Garrett let out a frustrated sigh. He wanted to warn Claire about Christopher's insatiable appetite for women, but he didn't want to scare her off the deal they'd made. Thinking through his words, he met her searching gaze. "Christopher is attracted to you and I don't want that attraction to get in the way of our arrangement."

"If you're implying that I have encouraged your friend, then . . ."

"Don't get your temper up," Garrett said. "Christopher isn't always the gentleman he appears to be. My words were meant to be a caution. Nothing more."

"Your words are insulting," Claire said as she stood up. "And I'm beginning to question your behavior, as well. After all, you're hiring me to join you in a fictitious charade to fool your grandmother into thinking that you have honest feelings for a lady. That doesn't speak too highly of you, Mr. Monroe."

His pride felt the sting of Claire's well-aimed words. After a tense moment he forced himself to relax. His new fiancée was right and they both knew it. "I'm sorry if I offended you. Just keep in mind that Christopher's reputation is even more unsavory than mine and keep your distance when I'm not around."

The apology lacked the enthusiasm Claire wanted, but then Garrett didn't have to apologize at all. He was in control of the situation and if her actions didn't please him he could retaliate by ending their arrangement and finding another woman. Claire couldn't afford that at the moment.

"It's time you went in," Garrett said, turning toward the hotel. "I'll see you again Saturday afternoon. We usually have lunch out on the patio, weather permitting."

Claire walked back to the hotel beside him. He didn't touch her until they reached the door of her room.

"Good night," he said, reaching for her hand.

Once again the heat of his mouth pressed to the skin just above her knuckles had an intoxicating affect on her body. The caress only lasted a brief moment, but it was enough to make Claire realize she was in for another sleepless night. She watched as Garrett moved down the hall, away from her. When he disappeared from sight, she slumped against the door of her room and released a deep sigh. How was she going to stop herself from falling in love with the man when she could already feel herself plunging off the cliff into a romantic abyss that offered no promise of his love in return?

"Think about your brother," Claire chided herself as she unlocked the door and entered her room. The silent battle continued as she undressed and got into bed. It didn't take her long to realize that she'd be the loser if she forfeited her heart too easily to her new employer. Garrett had told her in plain, precise words that he had no inclination to marry.

Snuggling under the covers, Claire closed her eyes and told herself the same thing. She was young and she had plenty of time to fall in love with the right man. In spite of her good intentions and reasonable thoughts, the night brought more dreams of the San Francisco banker, but this time Garrett was waltzing her around a brightly lit ballroom and Claire was dressed like a bride.

Chapter Six

By the time Saturday rolled around, Claire was pacing the floor of her hotel suite like a caged lioness. She was wearing a golden brown faille dress with a full chemisette front of gold taffeta. The puffy sleeves narrowed as they approached her wrists, which was the current style. A large leghorn hat accented with dark gold ribbon was lying on the bed, waiting to be placed on Claire's head the moment Libby tapped on the door and informed her that Mr. Monroe was waiting in the lobby.

They were to lunch with Theodora Monroe, the grandam of San Francisco society, and Garrett's beloved grandmother.

Claire passed by the mirror and stopped to look at the dress one more time. The autumn colors suited her own natural coloring. She'd been amazed at how quickly the alterations had been done. Mrs. Carlton, the dressmaker, had arrived the previous morning with the enthusiasm of an invading army and Claire had been measured, pinched into a corset, and measured again. She'd argued that the six evening gowns, twelve day dresses, and the other assorted items Garrett had ordered were excessive, but Mrs. Carlton had only smiled and insisted that each and every garment was essential. The robust lady had added a "poor dear" to her remarks, offering her regrets that Claire's luggage had been stolen from the train and left her with so little to wear. Claire hadn't corrected her misconception, knowing that Garrett had fabricated the likely excuse to explain the need for her services.

Shortly after Mrs. Carlton had filled the suite with her fabric samples and chatter, the clerk from the millinery shop had arrived. The leghorn hat was only one of the six fashionable hats and bonnets that had been selected, with the dressmaker's help, to complete Claire's wardrobe. Then came shoes, silk undergarments that made Claire blush, and three parasols to keep the California sun from ruining her fair complexion.

As Claire looked at the fashionable dress delivered early that morning, her smile turned into a frown. She'd realized that Garrett was rich, but she was beginning to see that her definition was limited by her experience with the upper class. Filthy rich was more like it.

Libby's firm tap on the door brought Claire out of her miseries. At least the waiting was over. As usual, Libby came sauntering into the room with a smile on her face. She frowned when she saw the breakfast tray she'd left earlier that morning. Claire had been too nervous to eat more than a small slice of dry toast.

"Mr. Monroe is downstairs," the maid told Claire. "I'll pack up your things and have them delivered to the house."

"I won't be returning to the hotel?" Claire asked, then realized she shouldn't have seemed surprised by the bit of news. Garrett made the rules. She was being paid to follow them.

Libby shook her head. "Mr. Monroe told Andy to have everything sent up to the Hill right away. Do you need help with your hat?"

"No, thank you," Claire said as she picked up the expensive piece of headwear and set it on top of her head. She secured it in place with a pearl-tipped hat pin while a flock of butterflies gathered in her stomach. Turning to the maid, she smiled. "Thank you for all your help, Libby. I've enjoyed getting to know you."

The maid seemed genuinely flattered. "Oh, you're welcome, Miss Aldrich. Everyone in the hotel is abuzz with the talk. I wish you and Mr. Monroe a long and happy future."

Claire gave her a warm smile. "Thank you."

With nothing left to be said, Claire gave her appearance one last scrutinizing glance before she left the suite. The noon hour was fast approaching and the corridor was void of guests. She nodded to another maid, whose arms were loaded with bed linens, and Claire realized that a strange twist of fate had prevented her from being occupied with the same task. If she hadn't entered the hotel a few days ago and asked for a job, she would never have met Garrett Monroe. Now, she was on her way to the top of Nob Hill to have lunch with Theodora Monroe and to take up residence for weeks, or maybe months.

As Claire reached the lobby, she realized that praying for a timely end to her role as Garrett's fiancée meant praying for his grandmother's quick demise. The thought sent a wave of guilt through her and she hastily corrected her petition to the Almighty. She'd gotten herself into this mess, with a little help from her wayward brother, and now she'd have to make the most of it until . . . Claire was searching for an answer when she saw Garrett. Her mind went blank the moment they made eye contact.

Garrett stared at the elegantly dressed young woman who had just stepped away from the staircase. For several long seconds, he absorbed the way the clothing accentuated Claire's natural beauty. The golden shades of the dress and hat made her hair glow and her hazel eyes seem larger than life. The skirt lay smoothly over her hips and stomach. The bodice hugged her exquisite figure, making Garrett's mouth water to taste the pale skin and womanly nipples it concealed. He closed his eyes for a moment and imagined removing the dress slowly. Very slowly. So he could kiss and caress each inch of skin he bared. He imagined holding her breasts in his hands and circling their rosy tips with his tongue until they hardened into tiny pearls. He imagined making love to her, moving over her, in and out of her, until they both relented to a release so sweet it was painful.

Every muscle in his body was taut with control as he stepped forward to meet Claire and he knew every man in the lobby could read his thoughts as easily as they'd read the headlines of the morning paper.

"You look lovely," he said, his voice thick with emotion.

Claire's heart was beating so hard she could barely reply. Her eyes scanned his face and she could feel the butterflies in her stomach being tossed around as it did a flip-flop that nearly made her gasp. Garret held out his hand and she accepted it, feeling the warmth of his touch travel up her arm and penetrate her own body. The sensation made her feel self-conscious and she looked away for a moment.

"Grams is waiting," Garrett said lightly. "Although she thinks that she's only waiting for me. Tomorrow is her birthday. You're going to be her surprise present."

"Is that good?" Claire asked, mindless to the envious stares Garrett was getting from the other men in the lobby, including Christopher Landauer. "I mean, if she has a weak heart?"

"She's going to be thrilled," Garrett told her. What he didn't say was that he was feeling something akin to the same emotion as he placed Claire's hand on his arm and escorted her out of the hotel lobby.

Claire had never ventured to the top of Nob Hill and she sat in the carriage, awed by the grandeur of the homes. When the carriage turned into a circular cobblestone drive, Claire gasped with surprise. Garrett's home was a miniature palace. The front entrance was approached by a flight of steps that terminated in a covered porch of gingerbread trim and elaborate Romanesque columns. Three stories high with rounded towers on each end, the house was painted a light beige with white trim. The residence was a beautiful but complex structure of bay windows, gables, and several tall white-brick chimneys.

"It's lovely," Claire said, turning to look at Garrett for the first time since the carriage had pulled away from the hotel. He'd seemed equally content with silence while she'd studied her new surroundings. "It must be the grandest house in all the city."

"Not quite," he told her. "But my grandmother likes it and it's comfortable. Your room overlooks the rear garden."

Mentioning that Claire would soon be sleeping under his roof brought back the desire Garrett had thought he'd had under control once they were in the carriage. He'd intentionally avoided conversation, knowing that the sound of Claire's voice would only agitate his aroused condition.

Claire was having a similar reaction to the statement. Sitting in a carriage with Garrett was bad enough. How was she going to keep her composure when she was actually living in his house, seeing him all hours of the day and night? No woman was that good of an actress and Claire knew that no matter how many times she reminded herself she was being paid to play a role, her feelings were going to get in the way. They already were.

Garrett helped her down from the carriage. "Don't be nervous," he told her. "My grandmother is a wonderful woman."

Claire was more worried about her performance than his grandmother's personality. Garrett led her through an elaborately carved oak door into a tile-paved vestibule. The foyer area was lighted by beveled glass that diffused the morning sunshine. A butler appeared to take Garrett's hat and gloves, telling them that his grandmother was waiting in the parlor. Claire took a deep breath, hindered by the sudden tightness of her corset as they moved through a large doorway trimmed in antique oak and into the parlor. The silver-haired lady sitting on the velvet settee looked up in surprise. She was dressed in a deep purple day dress with black lace around the collar and cuffs. Her hand was pale and delicate as she raised it to her chest and for a moment Claire feared that she had been right. The lady was shocked by her unexpected appearance.

The older woman's blue-gray eyes lingered on Claire for what seemed like an eternity before her face lightened with a smile. "What do we have here?" Theodora Monroe asked of her grandson.

"Grams, may I present Miss Claire Aldrich," Garrett said as calmly as if he were introducing a business associate. "Claire," he said, reaching out to take her trembling hand, "This is my grandmother."

"I'm very pleased to meet you," Claire said, dipping into a small curtsey. "Garrett has told me so much about you."

Theodora's welcoming smile faded into a frown as she looked from Claire to her grandson. "Has he? Well, the young scamp has told me nothing of you, Miss Aldrich, but I'm sure he's going to remedy that oversight immediately. Aren't you, Garrett?"

"As soon as Claire is comfortable," Garrett replied lightheartedly, leading Claire toward a brocaded chair fronting an art-glass window. "Would you like some tea while we wait for lunch to be served?"

Claire shook her head slightly. She was too nervous to hold a cup and saucer.

"Stop dallying and tell me about this lovely young lady," his grandmother interrupted. "I don't believe I recognize the name."

"I'm not from San Francisco," Claire said as Garrett walked across the room to sit down beside his grandmother. When he kissed the elderly lady on the tip of her upturned nose, Claire began to relax. Garrett was right. His grandmother wasn't the stiff ogre she'd envisioned. Theodora Monroe was as stately and elegant as the home in which she resided, but her smile was pure sunshine. "My family is from Cincinnati."

Grams folded her jeweled hands in her lap. "Cincinnati. I haven't been there in decades. Do the riverboat whistles still wake up the city like roosters waking up a weary farmer?"

"Every morning," Claire replied as a prim-looking maid dressed in a black skirt and white apron came into the room carrying a silver tea service.

While Garrett poured tea, his grandmother divided her attention between Claire and her grandson. Finally, her gaze settled back on Claire. "Forgive me, Miss Aldrich. If my wits seem scattered, it's because my grandson has never brought a young lady home before. I confess, I'm a bit unsure what to make of it."

Just as unsure of what to say, Claire smiled and waited

for Garrett to take the stage. He did so with the same confidence he'd boasted since walking into the parlor.

"Miss Aldrich is here because I wanted her to meet you," he began. "We were introduced on the train from St. Louis. She has a brother in the city whom she planned on visiting. He's away on business and I've had the pleasure of entertaining Claire until he returns. Unfortunately, an unexpected situation is going to keep him out of the city for quite some time, so I've invited Claire to be our houseguest. I thought you might enjoy her company."

Grams gave him a skeptical look as she raised a teacup to her mouth. When she put it down, there was a sparkle in her eyes that hadn't been there before. Claire knew the first few minutes of their charade were the most important ones, but she couldn't tell how Garrett's grandmother was reacting to the performance. Theodora Monroe was either amused by her grandson's attempt at trying to please her or blessedly happy that he'd been struck by Cupid's arrow. Unable to decide, Claire's eyes returned to Garrett. He seemed perfectly at ease with the situation. She envied him his composure. Hers was definitely on the shaky side.

"I've also invited Miss Aldrich to attend the Beltons' party with me this evening," Garrett added. "I think she'll be the most beautiful woman in attendance, don't you agree?"

"Without a doubt," his grandmother said, then turned to Claire. "Well, I'm surprised. Pleasantly surprised, of course. You can't imagine how long I've waited for a young lady to capture my grandson's attention. Now, Claire, you must tell me how you managed it. Did you bash him over the head with something? No, I think not," Grams continued. "It was your eyes, of course. They're lovely."

Claire blushed to the roots of her hair.

Garrett laughed. "Mind your manners," he teased his grandmother. "I don't want you scaring her off when I only just got her inside the door."

Before Grams could respond, the butler announced that lunch was served. Standing up, Garrett offered his grandmother his arm. She took it, coming to her feet with a grace that made Claire wonder about her frail heart. Theodora Monroe moved with the elegance of a queen at court.

Presenting his other arm to Claire, Garrett gave her a reassuring smile. "Come along," he said gently. "You can get to know Grams over lunch. I'll do my best to keep her from pestering you with questions."

Grams swatted his arm. "You'll eat your lunch and leave the business of my acquaintance with Miss Aldrich up to me," she said, scolding him. "As for questions, you're the one who'd better have some answers. How long have you been hiding her from me?"

"Not long," Garrett replied, giving the older woman a wink.

The friendly banter between the banker and his grandmother continued as they walked down the tiled hallway toward the east end of the house. Claire took in the elegant décor while Grams chastised her grandson for keeping secrets. By the time they reached a small portico, furnished with a table and four chairs, Claire felt the butterflies in her stomach disappear. Whatever role Garrett was playing with her didn't extend to his grandmother. Anyone could see that he loved the old woman. His eyes and voice softened when he was talking to her and Claire felt something tug at her heart as she watched the camaraderie between the two people. She prayed that Garrett found her brother soon and then that he found a way to dissolve their fraudulent engagement before Claire found herself as attached to Grams

Monroe as she was becoming to the lady's handsome grandson.

Lunch was a delightful meal of fresh vegetables, cold sliced ham, and animated conversation. Grams asked Claire about her family, reaching over to pat her hand when Claire admitted that it was limited to one brother. The conversation centered around the differences and similarities between Cincinnati and San Francisco. Once the maid had cleared away the dishes, Claire was surprised to discover that her stomach was accepting the food she'd eaten without protest. Grams had made her feel welcome and it showed in the smile Claire offered the older woman when Garrett led her away from the table, insisting that his grandmother take a nap.

"Wait for me in the garden," Garrett told her. "Once I've got Grams tucked in, I'll be right back."

"Tucked in," Grams scoffed. "He makes me sound helpless."

"He makes you sound treasured," Claire replied sincerely. "I'm so glad you don't mind me being a houseguest. I think you and I are going to become friends."

Garrett gave Claire a smile that said "well done" as he escorted his grandmother into the house. Grateful for a few minutes of privacy, Claire stepped off the portico and into the garden. Narrow, cobblestone paths crisscrossed their way through dark green grass and she stopped to inhale the heavy perfume of the rosebushes along the way to a small fountain in the center of the private courtyard. A tall, adobe wall separated the residence from its neighbors and she relished the private feeling of the place. As she sat down on a marble bench, Claire thought she'd found a small peace of heaven.

"She's very beautiful," Grams said to Garrett as he escorted her up the stairs.

"Yes, she is."

His grandmother stopped on the landing, forcing him to stop as well.

"Am I reading too much into this meeting and the invitation for Miss Aldrich to be our houseguest?"

"That depends on what you're reading into it," Garrett replied, giving her a friendly nudge that started her up the stairs again. "She's lovely, charming, and very much a lady."

"Are you falling in love?" Grams asked bluntly.

Garrett took a moment to prepare his answer. It was crucial that his grandmother believe his reply. He looked down at her and smiled. "I've never met anyone like her. She's shy and I find that I like that about her. She makes me laugh and I like that, too."

His grandmother searched his face and Garrett said a silent prayer that she believed him. He wasn't lying. Claire was shy and her shyness was part of her appeal. And she did have the ability to make him laugh. When she got her temper up, her eyes sparkled with anger, and it made him smile to think of the passion that was just waiting to be ignited. Of course, his interest in her was fueled by physical desire. He didn't want love messing up his well-ordered life. It was an inconvenience he was determined to do without.

Once he had his grandmother lying on her bed with a crocheted coverlet draped over her legs, Garrett sat down beside her. He reached into his jacket pocket and took out the small box holding the emerald engagement ring he'd purchased the previous day. He opened it and showed it to Grams. "Do you think she'll like it?"

"Oh, my," his grandmother said, staring at the ring in disbelief. "You are in love, aren't you?"

Garrett laughed. "You always told me if I found the right girl, I'd know it."

"Well, it's easy to tell that she's enamored of you. The girl's eyes sparkle every time she looks your way."

His grandmother hesitated, as if weighing the pros and cons of having her dream come true. "I like her," she finished. "I'll trust my instincts and keep my fingers crossed that she says yes."

Garrett gave her a quick kiss on the cheek before he stood up. "I'm a little nervous," he said, hoping it sounded natural. "I've never asked a woman to marry me before." He straightened his tie and returned the ring to his pocket. "Wish me luck."

"And happiness," Grams added as he turned to leave the room. His footsteps were still echoing in the hall when she tossed back the coverlet and got up from the bed. Walking to the window that overlooked the garden, she pulled back the curtain and saw Claire sitting on the bench. When Garrett appeared, Grams crossed the fingers on both hands and said a fervent prayer.

"Your grandmother is charming," Claire said as Garrett joined her. "I hope entertaining me didn't overtire her."

"It didn't," he said, sitting down beside her.

The bench wasn't that large and Claire felt his presence the way she had in the carriage. The man had a predatory magnetism. She knew she was in danger, but she couldn't move, especially when Garrett reached out and took her hand.

"If I know my grandmother," he said, smiling wickedly, "she's watching from the upstairs window. No, don't look up. You're supposed to be enthralled by my presence, remember."

Claire licked her lips. She was getting nervous again. Garrett was an expert at seduction. His voice was as smooth as freshly whipped cream and his hand felt warm and strong as he rubbed his fingertips over her knuckles. "I'm going to present you with an engagement ring," he continued as calmly as if he was instructing a bank clerk to lock up for the night. "You're going to smile, then shake your head yes."

"Okay," Claire whispered.

"Then, I'm going to kiss you."

Claire's eyes went wide. "Is that really necessary?"

Garrett laughed softly. "Trust me, it's perfectly acceptable behavior under the circumstances and my grandmother knows me well enough to know that I wouldn't pass up the opportunity. Surely, you've been kissed before."

"Not exactly," Claire mumbled, looking at her hand. Garrett was still holding it. She could feel her pulse quickening as his thumb glided slowly back and forth across her wrist. When he reached out with his free hand and tilted her chin up so she had to look at him, she stiffened.

"Either you've been kissed or you haven't, Miss Aldrich. Which is it?"

"Donald kissed me good-bye when he left home," she stumbled over the words. Garrett's eyes were as dark as sin and just as tempting. She could feel her body melting under his fiery gaze and she licked her lips again, as her mouth went dry.

The unconscious gesture sent a knife of desire through Garrett's body. He wanted to kiss her right then and there. He wanted to kiss her until she was clinging to his shoulders and begging him to never stop. The urge was so strong he cursed its power over him. This was all an act. He was playing a role to keep his grandmother happy and that role didn't include being trapped in the clutches of a beautiful, cat-eyed virgin.

As Garrett withdrew the jewelry box from his jacket pocket a second time, he knew having Claire within reach on a daily basis was going to test his self-control. He was used to having a woman whenever the need arose and right now it was rising with embarrassing speed.

Claire watched as the lid of the small box was lifted. When Garrett took out the ring and slid it on her left hand, tears came to her eyes. She couldn't help it. The ring was the most beautiful thing she'd ever seen. The emerald gemstone was breathtaking and the tiny diamonds on either side twinkled like newborn stars.

The tears surprised Garrett. He stared at Claire. His grandmother had mentioned that she seemed enamored of him. He didn't want her falling in love. Love would only complicate what could end up being a very pleasing relationship. Needing to remind them both of their circumstances, Garrett's voice had a harsh tone when he spoke. "You're a better actress than you think, Miss Aldrich. Tears are a nice touch. Although, I doubt if my grandmother can see them."

Claire tried to pull her hand away, but Garrett wouldn't allow it. "I'm going to kiss you now," he said.

Claire stiffened. She couldn't help it. She'd never been kissed before and Garrett looked almost angry. She felt her eyes closing, but he told her to open them.

"I'm not going to hurt you," he said impatiently. "Relax. A kiss isn't the end of the world. Lick your lips again but don't close them as tight as a bank vault."

Her eyes widened again as he leaned closer. She felt unsteady, as if the bench had taken on wings and was suddenly flying.

"Lick your lips." His voice was husky and butter smooth and Claire complied, unable to do anything else.

He brought his head down and her eyes drifted closed. She couldn't have opened them again for all the money in Garrett's bank. He moved his mouth over her, softly devouring it, coaxing her to relax and return the kiss.

Claire forgot the ring on her finger and the elderly woman watching from the upstairs window. She forgot everything but the unique pleasure of Garrett's mouth as it moved on hers. His breath was warm and he tasted like the spiced apples he'd eaten at lunch. Her hand moved to the front of his jacket, but it didn't push him away. The delicious sensations he was creating consumed her will; she was his to possess and there was nothing she could do to stop it.

Garrett had meant to kiss Claire with affection, but he couldn't resist the urge to taste her more deeply when she made a tiny female sound in the back of her throat and parted her lips to his teasing tongue. His hand was trembling as he brought it up and cupped it around the nape of her neck to hold her still. His tongue dipped into her mouth once, then twice. She tasted sweet and innocent and the knowledge that he was the first man to kiss her fed his pride. Kissing her turned into a test of endurance. How many times had he imagined kissing her over the last few days? At least a hundred, he was sure. His tongue brushed the sweet interior of her mouth and she stiffened for a moment, as if he'd touched her in a much more intimate way. He thought of that, too. Of stripping her naked and caressing every inch of her pale skin until she was moaning with need. Desire hammered through his body and Garrett had just enough self-control to break the kiss. His eyes roamed over her face, her swollen lips, her partially closed eyes. God, she was beautiful. Beautiful and young and too damn innocent for him to think he could seduce her without having a mountain of consequences come tumbling down around his head, but at that moment Garrett wasn't thinking about the ramifications of his actions. All he could think about was kissing her one more time. The sooner the better.

The second kiss was a long, deep matching of mouths.

Garrett pulled her close, hating the clothing that separated their bodies while he drowned in the sweetness of Claire's untutored mouth. His tongue dipped and teased while she trembled in his arms. The passion the kiss ignited was more surprising to Garrett than it was to Claire. He was an experienced man and she was an innocent lady, but the soft moan he pulled from the back of her throat had his senses riling and his body on fire. The only thing that kept Garrett from losing complete control of the situation was the surety that his grandmother was watching his every move.

Claire felt the world return to normal as Garrett pulled away from her. Her hands were trembling, but not with fear. She'd never imagined a kiss being so wonderful. She'd lain awake a good part of the night, thinking of the very thing that had just happened. But the reality of it was much more shocking. She never knew that men used their tongues to kiss. She'd never imagined that being kissed could make her body tremble and her blood feel like it was boiling in her veins.

Reluctantly, Garrett let his hand slide away from Claire's neck. With a sound that was a soft growl, he stood up. His body protested what he'd started and couldn't finish.

"It's time for me to introduce you to Mrs. Smalley, our housekeeper. She can show you to your room and help you unpack. I have some work waiting for me in the library."

Claire came to her feet. Her knees wobbled for a brief second and she prayed that Garrett didn't notice her faulty composure. Suddenly, Claire felt more vulnerable than ever. The banker was her employer, nothing more. Besides, he'd probably kissed dozens of women. Hundreds. The thought turned her green with envy and she hated the emotion. She was being foolish and silly, but the realization didn't diminish the jealousy she felt when she thought about Garrett's mouth being pressed against another woman's lips.

"The Beltons are expecting us by eight," Garrett continued, unaware of the battle Claire was fighting with her emotions. "Mrs. Smalley can fill in as your maid until Christopher finds a replacement for Libby."

"You're moving Libby to the house?" Claire was surprised.

"She told me that she likes you and since you've already made her acquaintance, I thought it might make the transition more comfortable."

"It will," Claire admitted. "Thank you."

They walked inside together, but this time Garrett didn't touch her. He didn't trust himself not to kiss her again. His body was used to having what it wanted and it wanted Claire.

While his new fiancée was recovering from the splendid shock of her first kiss and Garrett was trying to regain his self-control, Grams tucked herself back into bed and drifted off to sleep with a smile on her face.

Chapter Seven

Garrett was still brooding over his unexpected reaction to a simple kiss when he came downstairs later that evening. Dressed in black evening wear and a crisp shirt with gold studs, he walked into the parlor to say good night to his grandmother.

"Where do you think you're going?" he asked as he surveyed her gown and formal jewelry.

"To the Beltons' ball, of course," Grams told him. "I've been cooped up in this house for weeks. A few hours out won't kill me." Garrett scowled, but Grams kept smiling. "Do sit down. And stop frowning. I'll have Henry bring me home early."

Garrett didn't sit down and he didn't stop frowning. He poured himself a short brandy and told his grandmother in no-uncertain terms that she was to spend the evening resting.

"I've rested until I'm bored," she retorted. "Besides, Dr. Baldwin will be there. If I feel ill, you can fetch him to my side. Now, stop worrying and tell me about my future granddaughter-in-law. Does her brother know you're planning to marry?''

"No," Garrett said. "He had already left the city by the time Claire arrived. She's going to write him, of course. I have no reason to assume that he will oppose the marriage."

"He'd be crazy if he did," Grams replied smugly. "You're the best catch in the city."

Garrett smiled as he reminded himself that he was supposed to be in love. "As long as Claire agrees with you, I'm a happy man."

He was about to reiterate that his grandmother should forego the excitement and stress of a large party when Claire appeared in the doorway. Her gown was the exact color of the emerald ring he'd slipped on her finger earlier in the day. The full satin skirt had a scalloped hem, held in place with black rosettes. A black lace panel trimmed in black ostrich feathers gave the gown a unique elegance. The bodice was fitted and cut low enough to be fashionable without being overly revealing. Her hair was pinned up in a stylish cluster of curls. Once again the cameo was pinned to a black velvet ribbon, circling her pale throat. Small jet earrings dangled from her ears. The effect was enough to keep Garrett staring as Claire moved into the room.

"You look absolutely lovely, my dear." Grams supplied the words Garrett was thinking. "Come sit by me. I'm in need of an ally. My grandson is determined to banish me to my room and I refuse to go."

Claire gave Garrett an awkward smile. He was still looking at her and she became self-conscious of the gown the dressmaker had delivered a few hours ago. It was much lower cut than the gowns she was used to wearing and she could feel the heat of his gaze on her upper body. Her mind raced back to the moment in the garden when he'd kissed her and Claire prayed that she wouldn't blush. She was supposed to be a sophisticated young lady.

"Are you sure the party won't be too much for you?" Claire asked Grams, covering her thoughts with a cool façade.

"I'm sure," the older lady replied. "And I have every intention of being present when Garrett announces your engagement."

Garrett gave his grandmother a cursory frown. "Two hours and not a minute longer. I'll have Henry wait with the carriage."

Grams laughed. "That was easier than I thought it would be." She reached out and patted Claire's hand. "In case you don't know, my grandson can be quite stubborn."

"So I've noticed," Claire said, remembering the way Garrett had talked her into taking on the role of his fiancée. "What he doesn't know is that I've got a stubborn streak of my own."

Grams looked at Garrett. "I think you've met your match, young man. And not a moment too soon," she added before turning back to Claire. "I'm thrilled about the engagement, my dear. Absolutely thrilled."

Garrett wished he could say the same thing as he listened to Grams begin a conversation with Claire. He should be happy that his grandmother was preparing her for the deluge of people she'd be meeting in a short while, but he couldn't seem to free his thoughts. Claire had a grip on his mind and Garrett didn't like it. He glanced at the graceful curves of her body and the soft swell of her breasts, sheathed in emerald satin and black lace. He couldn't shake the memory of how she'd felt in his arms, the scent of her, the taste of her lovely pink mouth. She was as innocent as a rosebud and she was making his body ache all the way to his bones. He recalled Christopher's warning that Claire could be expensive and Garrett finally realized that his friend hadn't been talking about money. Trapped between unrequited desire and the knowledge that he couldn't seduce a virgin, Garrett began to admit the cost of his folly. Like it or not, he'd have to bear the sexual discomfort and make the best of a bad situation.

Concealing the nervousness that lay beneath her calm exterior, Claire listened while Grams Monroe told her what to expect from the cream of San Francisco society. She'd been to enough social functions to know that her manners and demeanor would pass a stringent test. She wasn't worried about being accepted as a social equal. It was knowing that she was going to be the center of attention that had Claire's stomach knotted like a fisherman's net.

The knots tightened into a painful lump a short time later when Garrett helped Claire down from the carriage. The Beltons' home lacked the elegance of the one she'd just left, but what it lacked in style, it made up for in size.

"Breathe, before you faint," Garrett whispered as he stepped alongside her. Grams was still in the carriage and he didn't want her to overhear the exchange of words.

The teasing quality of his tone belied the concerned look on his face and Claire managed a smile. "Now I know what Daniel must have felt like before he walked into the lion's den," she whispered back. "I feel numb."

Unwittingly, Claire moved closer to Garrett. His presence was a strange form of security. Once she stepped inside the Beltons' mansion, she was going to drown in a sea of strangers. The shyness she'd thought she'd mastered as a child came rushing back and for a moment Claire considered fleeing like a convicted criminal. What in God's name had made her think she could do something like this? It wasn't like her to be devious or deceptive in her actions. If she allowed Garrett to introduce her as his fiancée, she'd be an out-and-out liar.

"This isn't the time for second thoughts," he said in a low, gruff tone. "Grams saw me give you the engagement ring. There's no going back now."

Claire blanched at having her mind read so expertly. She was about to tell Garrett as much when he turned around to help his grandmother exit the carriage. Claire sucked in a deep breath, knowing Garrett was right. She was in too deep to undo the damage now.

A few moments later, a stiffly dressed butler opened the front door and they stepped inside. Claire looked around the large foyer. What she could see of the house said more attention had been given to expense than tasteful décor.

A robust woman in a dark maroon dress and several ropes of pearls came rushing their way. Fat curled around the woman's neck like white sausages and her hands were heavy with jewels. *Our hostess,* Claire decided. As the introductions were made, she felt the woman's dislike as strongly as she felt the subtle touch of Garrett's hand at her elbow. It was apparent that Mrs. Belton wasn't happy with an uninvited guest. The awkwardness of the situation stretched like a taut bow for seconds and Claire feared that the overweight matron might actually ask her to leave. Fortunately, the arrival of Mr. Belton kept that from happening.

"Good to see you, Theodora," the older banker said, giving Grams an affectionate peck on the cheek. "Dr. Baldwin told me to expect you. I'm glad to see you looking so well."

Henry Belton was such a contrast to his wife that Claire almost laughed. His voice was soft and his body was long and lanky. His dark hair had a sprinkling of gray at the temples and his eyes looked weary, as if he'd grown tired of life a long time ago.

"And who is this?" he asked, turning to Claire.

"Henry, may I introduce Miss Claire Aldrich," Garrett said, sounding very proud.

"Miss Aldrich," Mr. Belton said, smiling as he made a quick appraisal of the situation. It was obvious that he was accustomed to his wife's rudeness and an expert at rescuing the victims of her snobbery. "Welcome to our home. I hope you enjoy the party."

"I intend to make sure she does," Garrett said with a rakish smile. "If you'll excuse us, I need to speak with Christopher."

The sound of stringed instruments drifted through the open doors of the house as he led Claire toward the music. She felt anxiety snaking through her body as they entered the ballroom.

"You're holding your breath again," Garrett whispered as he escorted her around the edge of the overpopulated room. "Smile."

"Do hush," Claire rebuked him. "This is hard enough without you snapping at my heels."

Garrett chuckled softly before draping his arm around her waist and swishing her off onto the dance floor. "Relax, sweetheart," he said as he guided her to the music. "You're supposed to love me, remember."

At the moment, Claire couldn't remember her own name. Being in Garrett's arms again, innocently this time, was too reminiscent of the way he'd touched her in the garden. She followed his graceful movements instinctively, the way she'd followed his lead in the garden when he'd molded his mouth to hers and taught her just how intimate two people could touch each other with only their lips doing the touching.

A fire leaped in Garrett's blood as he swirled Claire around the room. His arms tightened around her narrow waist until she was too close for polite dancing, but he didn't care. The feel of her suited him for the moment and he justified it by telling himself that a man in love would naturally hold the woman he loved a bit too closely.

Claire glanced around her, noting that several of the guests had stopped dancing to watch them. Her nervousness returned and she pressed lightly against Garrett's palm to let him know that they were drawing attention. His hold didn't relax. She looked up at him and their eyes met. The world around them melted away. There was the vague sound of music and the heat of Garrett's hand. There was the shiver of sensation traveling up and down Claire's spine and the searching quality of Garrett's silvery gaze as he looked down at her. His eyes lingered on her mouth and Claire relived their kisses all over again. She could feel his eyes the same way she could feel the heat of his hand at the small of her back, burning her through layers of fabric. She suddenly felt weak and her insides quivered with an odd yearning.

Garrett watched Claire as he flexed his fingers around the curve of her back, massaging her ever so slightly. She responded to his touch like a cat being stroked and he stifled a groan. What was she thinking? Moments ago she'd been nervous and stiff and now . . . now she was relaxing in his arms and looking like . . . a woman caught in the throes of love. He smiled. Of course, she was being paid to look that way. Garrett wasn't sure he liked her playing the role so convincingly. He allowed his gaze to linger on her mouth, then let it slide slowly down to her breasts, hidden by expensive satin. He suppressed the primitive urge to drag her out of the room and into the moonlight, to strip her naked, to touch her until the desire throbbing in his body was a thing of the past.

The music ended. Garrett hesitated a moment before releasing Claire. The room filled with the hum of conversation as he led her toward a serving table filled with silver trays of tasty food and glasses of champagne punch. Christopher Landauer materialized out of the crowd. He flashed Claire a smile before introducing the young lady at his side.

"Belinda, I'd like you to meet Miss Aldrich. Claire, this is Belinda Belton, the daughter of our host and hostess."

Claire was glad to see that Belinda Belton favored her father instead of her mother. She was slender and immaculately dressed. She had a pretty little face under curly brown hair, fashioned in an elegant coiffure.

"Miss Aldrich." Belinda acknowledged her with a slight smile before shifting her attention to Garrett. "I saw your grandmother. I'm pleased that she's feeling better."

Polite conversation was exchanged, but Claire got the distinct impression it was what wasn't being said that mattered most. Christopher was smiling too smugly and Belinda seemed uncomfortable. They were joined by another couple. More introductions were made and before too long, Claire felt the momentary security she'd experienced while dancing with Garrett fade away. The names she'd read in the paper began to have faces; lawyers, railroad tycoons, city officials and their wives. Although everyone she met was well mannered and polite in their speech, she knew she was being measured for approval. The gentlemen weren't as obvious in their scrutiny as the women. She was surveyed from head to toe by several pair of jealous eyes and Claire knew that half the women in the room had set their caps for Garrett.

He didn't leave her side for a moment. She was certain that he wanted to make sure she didn't say or do the wrong thing and upset his well-planned scheme. When Christopher invited her to dance, Garrett allowed it, but he didn't looked pleased.

"Since you're here, I assume all went well with Grams," Christopher said once they were on the dance floor.

"As well as can be expected," Claire said, feeling awkward that Garrett's partner was aware of her role. She wasn't entirely sure she liked the man. He was handsome enough, but there was something about him, something that pricked at Claire's sense of well-being.

She reminded herself that Christopher was Garrett's best friend, and as such would know him better than most. If she was smart, she'd use that to her advantage. The more she knew about Garrett, the safer she'd be from the feelings he ignited with little more than a glance.

"Grams is all that matters, at least to Garrett," Christopher replied, then gave her a wicked smile. "My friend stepped on our hostess's toes this evening when he showed up with a lovely lady on his arm. Ada Belton had other plans," he added, still smiling.

Claire gave him a puzzled look.

"Belinda," he said matter-of-factly, "Ada Belton has been planning their marriage for the last two years. A merger of banks and bedrooms, you might say."

Claire wasn't sure what to say. She didn't know anyone in the room, including the man she was pretending to be in love with. The only place she'd ever called home was thousands of miles away. Suddenly, she realized that she'd always been an outsider. She could count her close friends on one hand and have fingers left over— her mother, Donald, and Elizabeth Shurman. Donald was the only one left alive and she didn't have the vaguest idea where her brother was. She was a stranger to the city and the people. The realization of just how alone she really was hit Claire like a runaway train. She stumbled ever so slightly but Christopher was too much of a gentleman to remark on it. The music ended and she stepped back, searching the room for an exit.

She needed a moment to herself. A moment to calm the fear that was washing over her like a tidal wave. What if she couldn't find Donald? What if . . . The possibilities swarmed around in her head as Claire turned to find Garrett behind her. He was joined by a man in his later years, balding with square rimless spectacles and a well-trimmed beard.

"Claire, this is Dr. Baldwin," Garrett said. "Chester, this is Miss Claire Aldrich." Garrett reached out and wrapped his arm around her waist, pulling her gently to his side. "Claire is our houseguest and she's also given me the great pleasure of agreeing to be my wife."

The people standing nearby overheard Garrett's announcement and went into silent shock. Christopher grinned from ear to ear and Belinda Belton seemed to let out a small sigh of relief. Dr. Baldwin's smile was contagious as he leaned over Claire's hand.

"May I be the first to congratulate you, Miss Aldrich. Garrett's one of the finest men I know. She's lovely," he finished, looking at Garrett. "I'm sure your grandmother's health improved instantly. Happiness can be a miraculous tonic."

"She's pleased," Garrett said modestly. "But not as much as I am," he added, looking at Claire with perfectly feigned affection. "Grams is in the parlor. Why don't you check on her for me while I escort my fiancée outside for some fresh air. It's unusually warm tonight."

The news of their engagement rippled through the room like a wave cresting on a beach. Claire could feel people staring at her in amazement as Garrett led her toward a pair of French doors. She was too busy trying to look calmly in love to notice that Garrett was smiling with smug satisfaction.

"The worst part is over," he announced as a servant appeared out of nowhere to open the door. "We'll spend a few minutes outside while the gossips attend to business."

The garden beyond the ballroom was a carpet of neatly trimmed shrubs and dark grass. The light from the house gave the stone patio a yellowish appearance until it faded just beyond the walkway and the garden began a maze of shadows and vague floral images that eventually became unrecognizable. Garrett released her arm and Claire walked to the railing, staring at nothing in particular as she tried to focus her thoughts. Her employer seemed pleased with himself. Too pleased.

"Mr. Landauer told me that Mrs. Belton had hopes of a marriage between Belinda and yourself," Claire said.

Garrett laughed. The sound was rich and deep and totally male. Claire felt it rack across her nerve endings. Her composure wasn't going to last much longer. She had to suffer people gawking at her, the touch of Garrett's hands when they danced, and now she had to wonder if she'd inadvertently caused Belinda Belton's heart to be broken. It was too much.

"Mrs. Belton's hopes and my reality are two different things," he told Claire. "I told you, I have no intentions of marrying anyone. Especially Belinda Belton. She's a shy church mouse. I scare her to death."

"Being shy doesn't make you weak," Claire said in self-defense.

Garrett gave her a crooked smile. "Your temper is showing, Miss Aldrich."

Claire stiffened. "I agreed to play a part for other people," she said in a low voice. "But I have no intention of continuing the role when we're alone, Mr. Monroe."

A servant carrying a tray of crystal glasses filled with punch walked onto the patio. Garrett took two glasses from the tray, offering one to Claire. He didn't speak until the servant had returned to the ballroom. Smiling coldly, he stepped closer. "My name is Garrett."

Claire didn't need to be reminded. She sipped the punch, ignoring his arrogance.

Garrett didn't like being ignored. Anger sluiced through him as he looked at Claire dressed in satin and moonlight. Jealousy had visited him when she'd danced with Christopher. He wasn't used to the green emotion. It bothered him in more ways than he was willing to admit. "My name is Garrett," he repeated in a low husky whisper. "I'm the man who put a roof over your lovely head and an engagement ring on your finger. I'm the man who's going to find your brother and return you to the bosom of your family. I'm the man who doesn't intend to have his grandmother upset over anything. You will be whatever I want you to be, Claire, whenever I want you to be it."

Claire's courage wavered for a moment. She was seeing the real Garrett Monroe, a man who was used to getting what he wanted, a powerful man who could be an influential friend or a fearful enemy. Well, she wasn't going to be intimidated. Her pride had suffered all it was going to suffer for the time being.

"In other words, you think I'm at your mercy," she said tartly. "Well, think again. I won't be coerced into soothing your ego, *Mr. Monroe*. If you don't like my temper, then I suggest you stop fueling it with rude remarks."

Garrett set aside his glass, then took Claire's out of her hand. She felt as if she were reliving the evening at the hotel when they'd had dinner the first time. His presence was even more overwhelming now that they'd shared a kiss and Claire felt her body trembling with anticipation. Something was happening to her and she didn't understand why her heart kept responding when her mind told her to be afraid. The absurd idea occurred to her that she couldn't keep herself from falling in love with Garrett Monroe because she had already fallen— hook, line, and sinker to coin her brother's favorite phrase.

Unaware of what Claire was feeling and unable to define why he was pushing the point, Garrett pulled her into his arms and tilted her chin up with his hand. Her eyes were sparkling with defiance and something he'd never seen there before, but he didn't want to take the time to evaluate it. He wanted to kiss her again.

The pressure of his arms became a hot fire that engulfed Claire the moment Garrett touched her. He drew her up close, so close she could see the silver flecks in his eyes. "The door to the ballroom is open and people can see us," he said in a soft whisper that brushed over her skin like a warm breeze. "I'm going to kiss you, again. Relax and enjoy it."

"It isn't proper," Claire said, using the only argument she could think of at the moment. She wanted him to kiss her. She wanted it so badly her hands were shaking as she pressed them lightly against his dark jacket in a frugal attempt to keep him at bay.

"It's expected," he told her. "And I'm paying for the privilege, remember."

His blunt words pricked Claire's temper at the same time they sliced a hole in her heart. She tried to pull away, but Garrett wouldn't let her. He smiled, an arrogant smile that said he was in control whether she liked it or not. His mouth hovered over hers, and she could feel the warmth of his breath for a brief moment before it was replaced with the fiery taste of his mouth.

Claire tried to suppress the wild surge of pleasure that rushed through her at the feel of Garrett's mouth, but she failed. The kiss was mild by his standards, but it made Claire's insides start to bubble and her knees go weak. Garrett went on kissing her, robbing her of her senses while he fought the temptation to turn the kiss into something more—something Claire couldn't deny.

He'd lied when he told Claire that the kiss was expected. It wasn't proper and Garrett knew it as well as she did, but he hadn't been able to resist the opportunity. It was more than that, but he wasn't in the mood to dissect his motives. Claire fit his arms like she'd been made for them and he liked the tiny, female sounds he forced from her throat.

The sound of the orchestra came to a halt and Garrett's sanity returned. He released Claire and stepped back, satisfied that he'd proven his point. She was being paid to do what he told her to do.

Once her mouth was freed, Claire brought her hand up and wiped the kiss away. Her heart was racing with a strange combination of joy and anger. Garrett thought he owned her, at least temporarily. He was arrogant and rude, but even that didn't stop her from wishing he felt something for her. Feeling used and furious at herself for being such a fool, Claire stepped back. "Don't kiss me again. Regardless of our arrangement, I'm not a woman who sells her favors, Mr. Monroe, and I refuse to be treated like one."

A slap would have served the same purpose. Garrett flinched inwardly at her sharp words. He was tempted to show Claire just how much of a man's touch a woman could suffer and still moan with pleasure, but his pride and the time and place kept him from pulling her back into his arms. He had to admit he deserved the insult, but he was only willing to admit it to himself. Damn it to hell! The woman was getting under his skin and he didn't like an itch he couldn't scratch.

"Men use whores for quick pleasure and no complications," he said curtly. His words were shocking but then he'd promised her honesty. "You are my employee, nothing more and nothing less. I'll kiss you whenever the situation calls for it, and if you wipe my touch off again, you won't like the consequences."

The threat hung between them like a cloud of smoke and Claire's anger heightened until she thought her head would explode from containing her temper. "Don't threaten me."

Garrett's smile was as cold as the ice keeping the champagne bottles chilled. "I don't make threats, Claire, I keep promises. And I expect you to keep yours in return."

"There you are," Christopher said, strolling onto the patio. "Mrs. Belton is puffing like a locomotive and everyone else is still recovering from the shocking news that the city's most eligible bachelor is officially off the market. But I have to admit, Grams looks better than I've seen her looking in years."

"That's the whole point of this charade," Garrett said none too politely as he offered Claire his arm. "Shall we rejoin the party, Miss Aldrich?"

An insane feeling came over her and Claire bit her tongue to keep from saying that all the money in the world couldn't persuade her to continue her role. Garrett had driven his point home with expert precision when he'd said that he was the man who could find her brother. Without Donald, she had nobody.

Claire laced her arm through Garrett's. When they

stepped through the doorway and entered the ballroom, she looked up at him like a woman lost to love. Unfortunately for Claire it wasn't an act. Her heart was breaking as Garrett swept her onto the dance floor while his grandmother watched from across the room.

Chapter Eight

Claire stood perfectly still while Libby slipped several petticoats over her head. She was having lunch with Garrett. He'd left instructions for Henry to drive her to the bank to meet him. The Beltons' ball had passed into history three weeks ago and since that time Claire had been forced to endure at least a dozen social events. Invitations were arriving daily for even more parties, afternoon teas, and Sunday dinners. Everyone in the city wanted to meet the lovely young woman who had turned Garrett Monroe into an attentive fiancé who smiled like a man truly trapped by the arms of love.

While Libby fluttered about the room like a butterfly in a rose garden, Claire tried not to think of another day consumed by shy looks, polite smiles, and the pretense of being in love with a man who was pretending to be in love with her. The strain was beginning to take its toll and Claire feel restless and tired. The worse part was playing a role for Grams. During the last few weeks, she had come to genuinely like the older lady. Theodora Monroe was full of life, despite her failing heart. She was witty and candid and Claire felt herself growing more fond of Garrett's grandmother with each passing day.

The longer she was in the Nob Hill mansion the more Claire had to confront her feelings for the man who had brought her there. Garrett was the epitome of a gentleman whenever they were together. There had been no more kisses, but the tension between them hadn't eased. It was growing in equal proportion to Claire's uneasiness and she knew the reason why. When Garrett wasn't reminding her of the reason for her presence, he was charming and fun to be with. She enjoyed listening to him discuss politics and arguing with his grandmother over the increasing interest in women's rights. He was intelligent, well educated, and still the most handsome man she'd ever had the pleasure of encountering. Although she had convinced herself that what she felt wasn't love, but merely a girlish infatuation, the feelings persisted. The more she learned about the handsome banker, the more he filled her thoughts and dreams. She felt like a keg of dynamite, ready to explode at a moment's notice.

When they waltzed, Claire couldn't ignore the feverish sensations that overtook her body and the sense of security that came with having him close to her. After days of arguing with herself, she'd reached the conclusion that there was little she could do but brave the circumstances and pray that Hiram Wilson found news of her brother soon.

Garrett had asked her for the few letters Donald had written over the years, thinking the private investigator might find them useful. Claire had surrendered them into his keeping as easily as she'd surrendered her heart.

"I think the pink silk would be perfect." Libby interrupted Claire's private thoughts as she laid the dress out on the bed. "It's a lovely day. The dress has a matching parasol that will keep you from getting too much sun."

Claire looked at the garment Libby had selected. It was lovely, like the dozens of other dresses and gowns Garrett has purchased for her. On the outside, she had everything a young woman could want. The house was magnificent, her clothing drew the attention of the most fashionable ladies in town, and her fiancé was every woman's dream come true. On the inside, Claire was miserable. The smile she kept plastered on her face was a mask that vanished the moment she was alone in a room with the door shut to keep anyone from seeing just how miserable she looked when she wasn't pretending to be the woman who had the world at her feet. She felt like a liar and a cheat. Grams was a wonderful woman and she could finally understand Garrett's reason for the fraudulent engagement, but understanding didn't make her part in his scheme any more pliable.

The bitter taste of knowing she'd exposed her heart to a man who liked women too much to love only one added to Claire's misery. As she sat down so Libby could arrange her hair, Claire looked in the mirror and silently told herself that she'd get over whatever emotions Garrett sparked. Time and distance would cure her ills. Once Donald was found, she could use the excuse that she needed to oversee her brother's home to end her stay at the mansion. Then, she'd gradually wean Grams of her companionship, and eventually, when Dr. Baldwin was sure that the ailing woman wouldn't suffer another heart attack brought on by bad news, she and Garrett could stage an argument that would end their relationship without ruining their reputations.

Thinking back to the previous night, Claire could have accomplished the task with little effort. They'd attended a small party at the home of one of Garrett's

investors. Grams had stayed home since the meeting
was mostly business and she wasn't overly fond of the
investor's wife. Claire had found the woman as distasteful as Grams had predicted, but she'd managed
to survive the boring dinner conversation and Mrs.
Fletcher's constant chatter about herself and her family. Grams had explained that William Fletcher had
married into money and his wife wasn't about to let
anyone forget it.

After dinner, Garrett and Christopher Landauer,
whose dinner companion was Belinda Belton, had
adjourned to the library for brandy and cigars. The
ladies had retired to the front parlor, where Marian
Fletcher dominated the conversation until Claire
excused herself to use the powder room. She'd stolen
a few moments for herself by slipping outside into the
garden. The night had been warm and the windows to
the library open and she couldn't help but be drawn
by the sound of Garrett's voice. He and Christopher
were alone, or so it seemed by their conversation, and
she was shocked when Garrett's partner mentioned the
fact that the banker had been neglecting his mistress
by keeping himself busy with his new fiancée. Claire
knew she shouldn't be surprised to discover that Garrett
maintained a woman for his private pleasure; she knew
such things weren't a rarity. But it was his words that
turned the balance of the evening into a painful experience that didn't end until she closed the door of her
bedroom and collapsed in a fit of angry tears.

"If you're so concerned about Evelyn, by all means,
attend her yourself," Garrett had said with no audible
hint of remorse. "My interest in the English lady has
waned since returning home and I'm too busy to worry
about her bruised feelings."

"You're a coldhearted devil," Christopher had told

him. "But then, that's part of your charm. Women like you because you're a challenge."

"I'm a *rich* challenge," Garrett had pointed out.

"I don't think Miss Aldrich is impressed by your money." Christopher's reply came to Claire's defense in a limited way. "In fact, I'm not sure the lady is impressed with you in general. She's a very good actress when she has an audience, but I've seen a frown or two slip over her beautiful face when she thinks no one is watching."

Garrett wasn't pleased and he'd said as much. He'd also warned Christopher to keep his *watching* to a minimum. "Claire is my business, not yours."

"What about her brother?"

"Wilson is working on it. Whoever Donald Aldrich is, he's good at not leaving a trail. The more Wilson can't find out the more I'm inclined to believe that Claire's brother is up to no good. An honest man doesn't need to hide."

"If that's the case, what happens to the sister?" Christopher had asked.

"I'll take care of Claire."

"You mean marry her for real."

"Good God, no," Garrett had blurted out. "She's tempting, but not that tempting."

"Then you plan to install her in the cottage after Evelyn returns to England or finds herself another lover?"

"Maybe," Garrett had replied. "She'd make an interesting mistress."

The response had cut Claire to the quick. She'd stood outside the window, shaking with anger and fighting back tears. Just when she'd begun to think that Garrett might have some redeeming qualities, she'd discovered that he planned to seduce her. *Mistress.* The word conjured up images of painted women in low-cut red dresses and things that made Claire blush to the soles of her feet. How dare the man think she could ever be his mistress! It was more insulting than anything he'd said to her so far.

His remarks about her brother's integrity had cut just as deeply. No matter what Garrett thought, Claire knew her brother. Donald wasn't a bad man, and he wasn't one to shirk his responsibilities. Once he discovered she was in San Francisco, he'd come running.

Garrett's unguarded remarks had given Claire a new resolve. She was going to find her brother, with or without Garrett's help, and then she was going to begin a new life. A life that didn't require her to play-act. The only drawback to her plan was Grams. She truly liked Garrett's grandmother and she refused to do anything that might put the older woman's health at risk.

As Libby put the finishing touches on her coiffure, Claire decided she'd worry about one thing at a time. For the time-being, she had no choice but to continue as she'd begun.

Once the dress was buttoned and she'd slipped on a pair of white cotton gloves, she reached for the parasol trimmed with white lace and pink flowers.

"Mrs. Monroe asked if you'd stop in the back parlor before you left for the city," Libby told her as she gave Claire's appearance a nod of approval. "She needs some thread and thought you might have time to stop by one of the shops for her. If not, I'll fetch it later."

"I'll make the time," Claire announced. Although she didn't need anything for herself, she liked the idea of doing some shopping. It would give her some time alone.

She went downstairs in search of Grams, knowing she'd find her in the back parlor. The comfortable room was one of the lady's favorite places and she could often be found there, sewing or reading.

"Do come in," Grams said as Claire appeared in the doorway. "And don't you look lovely, my dear. Garrett will be hard-pressed to return to his office after spending time with such a beautifully dressed young lady."

"Libby said you needed some things from town," Claire said. She didn't want to think about Garrett pretending to enjoy her company when all he wanted was her body. "What shop do you frequent?"

"Miller's Yard Goods on Market Street," Grams told her. "It's a few doors down from the bank. Garrett will show you. Here's a sample of the thread." She handed Claire a strand of dark blue thread. "After you get back, we need to discuss the wedding. Plans need to be made and a dress will take months. Madame Napier is the best couturiere in the city, but she's a stickler for detail."

Claire didn't want to think about a wedding dress. It added insult to injury. "We have plenty of time," she said. "We haven't set a date for the wedding."

"You need to," Grams said unceremoniously. Then smiled. "Don't be so modest, my dear. Your marriage to Garrett will be the social event of the year. Everyone will expect to be invited. Have you heard from your brother?"

"Not yet," Claire said, thankful that she could at least be truthful about Donald. "He'll want to be there, of course."

"Of course," Grams agreed. "He can give you away. Christopher will be Garrett's best man. I can't imagine him asking anyone else. The Episcopal Church is large enough to hold a thousand or more guests." She smiled at Claire's gasping mouth. "Oh my, I never thought to inquire about your faith. Is the Episcopal Church a problem?"

"I'm Methodist," Claire replied automatically. The thought of a wedding dress and a thousand guests had her reeling. The situation was getting more complicated by the day.

"Close enough." Grams laughed. "Now, hurry along. You don't want to keep Garrett waiting. And tell my grandson that I want a date set before you finish your lunch. I'm not one to dally about and wait until the last minute for things. I hope you don't mind me saying that I'm glad you don't have a maiden aunt in the city to take my place. I rather like the idea of planning the wedding. It gives me something to look forward to."

Claire smiled as she leaned down to place an affectionate kiss on the older woman's cheek. "If it makes you happy, then Garrett and I are happy."

Grams gave her a pensive look, before she smiled again. "I don't know what my grandson did to deserve you, but I'm glad he did it. I couldn't have picked a more perfect wife for him if I'd interviewed every woman in the state of California. In the short time that you've been here, I've come to think of you as family, Claire, and I'm sure that you and Garrett will have a wonderful life together."

"I'm sure we will," she lied, hating the words. "Now, be sure and take a nap. You know how grumpy Garrett gets when he thinks you aren't getting enough rest."

"He's a pain in the backside more times than not," Grams retorted.

"He loves you," Claire replied. That much she could say without doubt or hesitation and know that it was true. Garrett adored his grandmother. He could love. The banker wasn't as coldhearted as Christopher Landauer believed. But Garrett didn't love her. Claire had to admit that heart-wrenching fact and get on with her plans to find Donald. She didn't belong in the mansion on Nob Hill. Sooner or later she'd have to leave and make a life for herself, one that didn't include Garrett Monroe.

Claire stepped down from the carriage a short time
later. She had seen the exterior of the bank on several
occasions, but having no money, she'd never had a need
to pass through its door. When she did, she felt as if
she'd discovered another facet of Garrett's personality.
A clerk showed her to his office. He was sitting behind
a large desk, going through ledgers. He looked like a
banker. His suit was dark and impeccably cut. The room
carried the faint odor of cigars and male cologne. She'd
entered a male domain and Claire felt it as surely as
she felt the heat of Garrett's silver eyes as he stood to
greet her. He ruled supreme here and she suddenly
realized that the decisions he made affected more than
just one young lady from Cincinnati. He could make
or break people with a cast of the financial cards.

"You're right on time," Garrett said. His expression
didn't reveal that he'd been thinking about her for the
last hour. He'd counted the passing of the minutes
instead of concentrating on the figures on his desk. It
wasn't like him to let his personal life interfere with
business. He justified his obsession by reminding himself that Claire was business. He'd hired her to perform
a specific task and up to now, she was doing it very well.
There were times when Garrett could almost convince
himself that she really did love him.

But not today. There was no hint of adoration in
Claire's hazel eyes as she looked at him. On the contrary,
she looked angry. Angry enough to bash him over the
head with the brass paperweight sitting on the corner
of his desk. He resumed his seat and unlocked the right
drawer of his mahogany desk. Withdrawing his personal
ledger, he made an entry.

"I'll have one thousand dollars deposited in an
account under your name by day's end," he said. "An
equal amount will be deposited at the first of each
month for as long as our engagement is active."

Claire's mouth dropped open. She'd never imagined her *salary* being that excessive. "It's too much," she said, doing her best to steady her breathing. "I can't accept it."

"You most certainly can," Garrett replied in an autocratic voice. "And you will. I insist."

"You can't always have what you want," Claire said, remembering this was the man who wanted to turn her into a ruined woman. "The money you've spent on my wardrobe and jewelry is more than I can ever repay."

"Your clothing was part of our arrangement, Claire. And I must say, it's money well spent. You look very pretty today."

The compliment sounded sincere, but Claire couldn't let herself believe it. Like her, Garrett was becoming accustomed to the roles they were playing. He was being polite, nothing more.

"Shall we have lunch at the hotel?"

He came to his feet and Claire looked up at him. Where was the anger that had consumed her ever since she'd heard him speaking with Christopher Landauer in the Fletchers' library? How could she hate the man one moment and love him the next? She wasn't some silly schoolgirl. She was a woman full grown with a mind of her own and a missing brother who was going to beat Garrett to a bloody pulp if he found out the banker wanted to turn her into a mistress instead of a wife.

"Before we have lunch, I want to talk to you about my brother. Has Mr. Wilson turned up anything?"

Garrett shook his head. "Nothing more than you already know. Donald painted a house, collected his pay, and disappeared like a puff of smoke. But don't worry yourself over it. San Francisco is a big city and these things take time. Hiram will find him. Eventually."

"Eventually isn't soon enough," Claire told him. "Your grandmother wants us to set a date for the wedding. I can't keep this up much longer, Garrett." She had gotten used to calling him by his first name. "I've grown very fond of Grams. I don't want to hurt her."

"Then don't," he said, coming around the corner of the desk to perch on the edge of it. His legs brushed against her dress. "Let me do the worrying. It may take months to find your brother." He held up his hand to silence her when Claire started to reply. "I know you don't like hearing that, but it's true. Until your brother is found, you'll remain a guest in my home and continue playing the part of my fiancée. As for the wedding date, one year is the customary period of time between an engagement and a wedding. That should satisfy Grams."

It seemed like forever, and Claire didn't like the idea of continuing her charade that far into the future. In fact, she was sure she couldn't continue it. She'd only known Garrett for a month and she was already hopelessly in love with him. If she didn't find her brother soon, Claire knew her heart would be beyond repair.

"Now, let's have lunch. I'm famished."

Claire stood up. She watched as Garrett locked his desk, thinking of all the times he'd held her in his arms while they danced at parties. She could recall with vivid clarity every instant of the two times he'd kissed her. The memory was so real she woke up at night, thinking he'd stolen into her room to wake her with a kiss. She trembled whenever he touched her and she pretended that it was natural because people were watching them. But it was natural. Her feelings for him had become a part of her. Loving him seemed as easy as breathing and she couldn't do anything about it but pretend to Garrett she had no feelings whatsoever where he was concerned. Either way, she was forced to play a part. The only certainty in the whole sordid mess was knowing that she'd never allow herself to become Garrett's mistress. She had too much pride to ever let that happen.

* * *

It was midweek and the hotel dining room was filled with businessmen. Claire recognized a good portion of them now and she smiled as they spoke to her. As always, Garrett was at her side. She was reaching for her napkin when a blond woman walked into the room. The attractively beautiful lady was escorted by Christopher Landauer and he smiled as he guided her toward the table where Claire and Garrett were sitting. She couldn't be sure, but Claire thought Garrett's eyes flashed with anger for a brief moment before he came to his feet.

"Christopher," he said in a neutral voice.

"Garrett," his friend replied. "Of course, you know Miss Holmes. I believe you and her father conducted some business while you were in England."

"Miss Holmes." Garrett acknowledged the beautiful woman with his usual charming smile. He motioned toward Claire. "May I introduce my fiancée, Miss Claire Aldrich."

"Christopher told me all about you," Miss Holmes replied. Her accent was definitely British. "No one expected Garrett to marry," she added. "May I offer my congratulations."

Claire was smiling until Christopher addressed the woman by her first name. *Evelyn. So that's what a mistress looks like,* Claire thought. The woman was beautiful. Claire felt her heart sink to her feet.

"We didn't mean to intrude," Christopher said. "Enjoy your lunch."

Claire watched as the couple moved away to a corner table. They were still in sight and her stomach churned at the thought of eating while Garrett's mistress was in the room. Her appetite vanished and she looked over to find Garrett's face an unreadable mask. She wasn't sure if he was upset over Christopher taking him up on his offer to entertain Evelyn Holmes, or if he was jealous because another man was with the woman who normally warmed his bed. Claire didn't want to think that while she was lying awake at night, mooning over the banker, Garrett was sneaking out of the house to satisfy his carnal appetites. More importantly, she didn't like to think that Garrett had kissed the beautiful Evelyn Holmes the same way he'd kissed her.

But then men did more than kiss their mistresses. They . . . Claire blocked out the image of Garrett's naked body entwined with the beautiful blonde.

"She's lovely," Claire said as Garrett's eyes drifted toward the table where his mistress was sitting with his best friend.

"In her own way," Garrett replied as he turned his attention back to Claire. "Would you like me to order?"

"Yes, please," Claire retorted, surprised that he could act so casually about the matter. Then she realized he was a good actor. After all, he'd convinced the whole of San Francisco that he was in love with her.

Garrett talked about the upcoming Fourth of July picnic while Claire concentrated on chewing her food and swallowing it without becoming sick. The more she thought about the mess she'd gotten herself into the more her stomach rebelled. Halfway through the meal, she put down her fork.

"What's wrong?" Garrett asked, sounding concerned.

"Nothing," Claire lied. "I'm just not very hungry."

"Would you like to leave?"

"No." She shook her head. "Finish your lunch. I'm content to sip my tea."

It wouldn't do to let him think that seeing Christopher and Evelyn Holmes had upset her. The only way she could account for knowing the woman's identity would be to confess that she'd eavesdropped on a private conservation. Feelings of rage and betrayal snaked through Claire as the sound of Evelyn's laugher drifted across the dining room. Christopher was smiling, clearly amused about something, and Claire wondered if Garrett's mistress knew the truth about her lover's engagement.

"How about a walk?" Garrett said, coming to his feet as he tossed his napkin onto the table. "It's a nice day and you should show off that dress. It suits you."

Forcing a well-rehearsed smile to her face, Claire reached for her parasol. Once they were outside, she opened it, shading her face from the noonday sun and Garrett's probing eyes.

"Tell me what's wrong," he said, once the sidewalk had cleared of other pedestrians and he'd told Henry to follow with the carriage.

"Nothing's wrong now that wasn't wrong ten minutes ago," Claire retorted a little too hastily to convince him. "I'm worried about my brother."

Garrett didn't believe her, but he didn't push the point. There was no way that Claire could know that Evelyn had been his mistress for several months. The relationship was in the past tense. Garrett hadn't visited her since Claire had moved into the house he shared with his grandmother. The lovely blonde didn't interest him. Garrett wasn't sure she ever had. He was simply used to having a woman at his beck and call. He thought about Christopher mounting Evelyn, but the image didn't spark any reaction. No jealousy. Nothing.

He looked at Claire. A similar image flashed in his mind, but this time it wasn't Christopher and the sophisticated blonde. It was him and Claire. Naked. Their bodies were damp with sweat and she was moaning as he rode her until she convulsed in his arms, caught up in the sensual storm of her first climax. The illusion had an immediate effect on Garrett and he cursed under his breath.

Claire looked at him. "Grams asked me to do some shopping for her. Do you mind if I excuse myself to buy some embroidery thread."

"Not at all," Garrett replied, thinking of the bottle of imported Scotch he kept in his desk drawer. He could use a drink.

He motioned for the carriage and helped Claire inside. Once he was seated next to her he turned the conversation back to the Fourth of July picnic being held at Russ Gardens. The gardens were a pleasant blend of wide spreading trees, flowering shrubs, and cool little arbors where people celebrating the Fourth of July would gather with picnic baskets while children ran about the grassy knolls, tossing balls and spinning brightly colored hoops. The city resort had become a playground for its wealthy residents and the day's celebrations would end with a fireworks display that rivaled any in the world.

"Christopher has invited Belinda Belton again."

"What about Miss Holmes?" Claire dared to asked. "He seems very attracted to her."

If the question caused Garrett any discomfort, he didn't show it. "The Fourth of July celebration is the city's biggest summer affair and Mrs. Belton has hosted the party for the last several years. It wouldn't be to Christopher's advantage to bring Miss Holmes. I think my friend has visions of owning his own bank someday and Belinda's father is a banker."

Claire frowned. She liked Belinda, in spite of her mother. "He shouldn't escort her to parties if he doesn't have any feelings for her," she said. "I'd hate to see Belinda, or any woman, in a loveless marriage."

"Marriage for money is as old as time," Garrett said candidly. "Belinda isn't the sort to defy her family. She's expected to marry well and Christopher isn't a pauper.

He's a shrewd businessman who's made a small fortune in the import business."

"I thought he owned hotels."

"He has other interests along with the hotels. His father was a missionary in China. Christopher was born in Peking. He speaks their language and understands their customs."

"That explains the exquisite jade carvings in his office," Claire remarked. "But it's hard to picture him as a minister's son."

Garrett laughed. "I doubt that Christopher has been inside a church since his father's death, although he's given generous donations to every parish in the city. And yes, he collects Chinese art, among other things," Garrett told her, thinking of the string of young Chinese girls his friend had entertained himself with over the years.

Garrett had taken a Chinese mistress years earlier and the woman had proven to be very skilled in the sexual arts. He still visited her on occasion, when he wanted to experience the exotic pleasures she'd taught him to enjoy.

The carriage stopped in front of the bank and Garrett looked at Claire. What would she think if he told her that he wanted to feel her mouth traveling over his body, licking and tasting until he was fighting desire like a demon? Would she straddle his hips and take him inside her, wanting the pleasure as badly as he did? Would she cry out in her passion, demanding as much from his body as he demanded from hers? He couldn't image Belinda Belton casting her inhibitions to the wind and submitting to Christopher's Oriental appetites, but the image of Claire, her hair unbound, her body flushed with desire, her eyes glowing with need, stayed with Garrett as he stepped down from the carriage and entered the bank.

He found Hiram Wilson waiting to see him.

"Any news?" Garrett asked as he closed the door to his private office.

"Perhaps," the investigator replied.

Hiram Wilson was a short, thin man with a distinct pride in his profession. Well dressed in a dark brown suit, his eyes gleamed with enthusiasm about the assignment in front of him. Hiram liked solving puzzles and Donald Aldrich had become an intriguing one.

"Tell me," Garrett said as he took off his jacket and rolled up his sleeves. He had a lot of work to do before the day ended. Now that he had a *fiancée* waiting at home, he did his best to join Grams and Claire for dinner.

"I've been able to locate a gentleman, an old railroad worker, who apparently knows our elusive Mr. Aldrich. I contacted him by telegram and he's agreed to see me. I've arranged to leave on the afternoon train for Tucson. I should be back by the end of the week."

Garrett nodded, keeping his opinion to himself. "I'll expect a full report."

"Yes, sir." Hiram turned on the heels of his well-polished shoes and left Garrett to brood about what the timid-looking investigator may or may not discover while the rest of the country was celebrating the Fourth of July.

Chapter Nine

Claire dressed for the Fourth of July picnic with a heavy heart and a sense of dread. Libby had laid out an apple green silk dress with white lace around the cuffs and collar. There was a matching parasol to shade her face and delicate white leather slippers to cover her feet, but Claire was more concerned with Garrett's mood than her wardrobe. He'd come home from the bank the day they'd had lunch with a sour look on his face. Immediately after dinner, he'd retired to his library for the evening, claiming that he had work to do.

Knowing that banking wasn't as easy as simply having money to lend, Claire wanted to believe that Garrett was preoccupied with matters of business, but she couldn't help but wonder if the change in his mood had anything to do with Evelyn Holmes and Christopher Landauer. She'd come to know Garrett well enough over the last few weeks to realize that he was a possessive man by nature. Although he'd acted with indifference at having his best friend escort his mistress to lunch, and he'd all but offered Evelyn to Christopher on a silver platter that evening in the Fletchers' library, Claire was sure it had to sting Garrett's pride to think of his best friend and his mistress sharing an intimate relationship.

All Claire had to do was imagine Garrett kissing the beautiful blond woman and her pride was replaced by jealousy. She hated the thought of Garrett kissing anyone except her.

At the sound of footsteps coming down the hall, Clair felt her nerves tighten. A light tap on the door from Libby brought a forced smile to her face. The pretending was beginning to take its toll and Claire wasn't sure how much longer she could keep up the façade of being the happiest woman alive. She dared not think too far ahead for fear that she'd lose her nerve completely. If Grams noticed a change in her personality, the older woman would start asking questions Claire wasn't prepared to answer, not until she found her brother.

An hour passed before Claire walked down the steps and into the parlor. Grams was waiting along with Garrett. Claire's forced smile took on a genuine quality as she stepped into the room and heard the two people arguing. When Garrett and his grandmother exchanged opposing viewpoints, the conversation was always a lively one.

"I didn't reach the ripe old age of seventy-eight by always doing what I was told," Grams said. "I'm going to the picnic and I'm going to have a good time."

"It's too hot for you to be there all day," Garrett pointed out. "Rest today and attend the dance this evening."

Grams made a sound and wrinkled up her nose. "I'll come back before the heat is unbearable and take the blasted nap you always insist on, but I'm not going to miss all the excitement. Now, say hello to Claire, and stop fuming like a medieval dragon. We'll be late."

Garrett let out an exasperated sigh as he turned his attention toward the doorway. Claire met his gaze, fully expecting his face to show the same rigid expression he'd been wearing for days. When he flashed her a warm smile, she wasn't sure how to react.

"You look lovely," he said, walking across the room to take her hands. He pulled her toward him and placed a chaste kiss on her cheek. The fleeting touch of his mouth was enough to make Claire's body churn with excitement. "Grams is being stubborn again."

"So, I heard," Claire replied. She looked past Garrett to where his grandmother was placing a thin lace shawl around her shoulders. Feeling suddenly impish and not knowing why, Claire said, "Stubbornness must be a family trait."

Grams laughed while her grandson frowned.

"Feeling feisty, are we?" Garrett said in a low whisper meant only for Claire's ears. His smile of greeting turned into one of pure devilry as he laced her arm through his and turned toward the door. "That's going to cost you a kiss, Miss Aldrich. A real kiss."

Claire was so surprised by the unexpected remark all she could do was stare as Garrett went in search of his jacket and hat. By the time Grams joined her, Claire was back to looking perfectly happy. She prided herself on her acting abilities as they got into the carriage and began their way toward Russ Gardens. Garrett cast several promising glances in her direction and by the time she stepped down from the carriage, Claire was back to feeling as though her stomach were tied in knots.

Russ Gardens was an elaborate park with large trees and colorful, fragrant flowers. Claire was amazed at the number of people already gathered around the tables and booths that offered everything from lemonade to

Italian sausages rolled in crisp bakery dough. Streamers of red, white, and blue ribbon decorated everything. Musicians were seated in a large gazebo in the center of the park and music drifted on the crisp breeze blowing inland from the bay. Women dressed in their summer finery mixed with gentlemen and children of all ages.

"Let's claim a place for our picnic before there isn't a tree left in the park," Garrett said, reaching for the large basket Mrs. Smalley had packed. Since it was the nation's anniversary, Garrett had given everyone in the household the day off. "I want to get Grams out of the sun."

"Stop hovering," his grandmother retorted. "I want to mingle before I'm forced to take root under some tree for the balance of the day. Find a place for our basket, then enjoy yourself."

With that, she gave her grandson a quick smile and started walking toward a group of elderly women standing beside a table that was offering fresh watermelon for a penny a slice.

"I wasn't hovering," Garrett said, looking toward Claire.

"Yes, you were," she chided him. "Don't worry, I'll keep an eye on her."

"Good," he said. "Then I can keep both eyes on you."

Claire pretended to be busy with her gloves and parasol. The tone of Garrett's voice had taken on the seductive quality he only used when they were alone.

Garrett smiled. He knew she was doing her best to ignore him, but he didn't intend to be ignored. He'd woken up that morning determined to enjoy the day, and the night ahead of them. He hadn't danced with Claire for over a week and he missed having her in his arms. "Let's try over there," he said, pointing toward a large tree with long, sprawling branches and a canopy of rich green leaves. A wrought-iron bench decorated with blue and red streamers sat underneath the tree. "We can stake out our share of shade and then take a walk around the park."

Claire walked alongside him as a cheer broke out. She looked toward a group of older men playing horseshoes. One of the men, as thick as he was tall, with a bald head that gleamed in the late morning sun, was wagering that he could win the second game as easily as he'd won the first. His opponent, several inches taller and a good deal slimmer, reached into his pocket and pulled out some money, apparently willing to take the bet.

"Ben Corwin takes his horseshoes very seriously," Garrett told her.

"You know him?" Claire asked. The plump little man with thick suspenders holding up his pants didn't look like someone who had ever made the banker's acquaintance.

"I loaned him the money to start his own business," he said. "Ben's one of the best cabinetmakers in the city. He's one of those rare people who can turn wood into a work of art."

Claire smiled in spite of her apprehension over Garrett's promised kiss. "Did he work on your house?"

"For over a year," Garrett replied as they reached the shade of the tree and he sat the basket on the bench. "Ben's a good man."

"Which means he makes his bank payments on time," Claire teased.

Garrett laughed. "Be careful, Miss Aldrich, or you'll find yourself owing me more than one kiss."

Claire did her best not to blush. "I don't owe you any kisses. You only think I do."

"We'll see about that," Garrett said, reaching into his pocket and pulling out a coin. He tossed it to a young boy standing a few feet away, promising the child another one if the blanket and basket were still there when they got back. "Let's walk awhile."

With a firm grip on her arm, Garrett led her away from the tree and back into the sunlight. Claire opened her parasol and allowed herself to be guided through the park. They walked, stopping to talk to people along the way. The park's population was growing as more families flocked into the gardens to enjoy the variety of games and foods being offered to celebrate the summer holiday. When they reached the pond, Claire pulled away from Garrett long enough to help a small, pink-cheeked little girl unravel a kite string.

When she returned to his side, he gave her a pensive look.

"What's wrong?" she asked.

"Nothing," he said, much too quickly for her to believe him. "Would you like something to drink?"

When she said no, he maneuvered her away from the pond and toward a cluster of small trees. Their leisurely stroll ended under an arbor heavy with dark leaves and plump grapes that wouldn't be ripe enough to eat for several more weeks. The tangled vines created a natural wall between them and the other people milling about the park. Claire knew the moment she looked up at Garrett that he was going to collect on his promise to kiss her.

Claire tried to pretend that Garrett's closeness wasn't having a powerful effect on her, but she couldn't. She reminded herself that he wanted to make her his mistress. The insult alone should be enough to make her hate him. It wasn't. All she could think about was how wonderful it was going to feel when he finally lowered his head and put his mouth over hers.

The day was growing warmer and the park was alive with the sound of voices. The sun was playing hide-and-seek through the thick grapevines, casting small shadows on the ground as it tried to penetrate the natural shelter of the arbor. Birds chirped and insects buzzed, but all Claire could hear was the thumping of her heart as Garrett stepped closer. His hand slowly snaked around her neck, forcing her head to tilt back so he could have better access to her waiting mouth.

"Tell me you want me to kiss you," he said in a low husky voice.

Claire kept silent although she was screaming inside for Garrett to stop talking and get on with kissing her until her mind went blank and all her reasons for doubting him and the future melted away. Her lashes lowered in perfect timing with the descent of Garrett's head. His mouth brushed lightly over her slightly parted lips, but it didn't stay. Instead she felt the light touch of his teeth on her earlobe and the soft rush of his breath.

"Say the words, Claire. Say them so I can hear the need in your voice. Let me know you want what I want."

A hundred reasons not to say the words raced through Claire's head, but they were pushed aside by the singular fact that she wanted Garrett's kiss. She wanted it desperately.

"Please, kiss me," she whispered.

The words were barely spoken because Garrett ended them with a kiss that scorched Claire's body all the way to her soul. His arms were around her and she felt a rush of pure joy as he tightened his hold, pressing their bodies close together. His mouth was hard and hot and hungry, and she loved it. He kissed her more passionately than he'd ever kissed her before. His lean fingers threaded through her hair, holding her captive, while his mouth taught and teased and made her body shudder from head to toe.

Totally defenseless against what Garrett made her feel, Claire let the sensations flow through her, surrendering to the kiss and all it offered. What he did to her was unlike anything she'd ever experienced before. Reality drifted away, leaving nothing but the feel of Garrett's arms and the taste of his mouth. The moistness of his tongue, probing gently then withdrawing, sent shivers up and down her spine.

Garrett tried to restrain his desire, vaguely remembering that they were in a public place, but it was the most difficult thing he'd ever done. His hands soothed over Claire's back, pressing her closer, wanting to feel the softness of her body. He wanted her to know that she was safe in his arms, and wanted. Very much wanted. The guilt of seducing a virgin vanished as his mouth moved from her lips to the tender flesh of her neck. His tongue dampened the skin before his teeth nipped just enough to make her tremble in his arms.

She moaned softly as he returned to her mouth, taking the sound before it could be heard by anyone else. His mouth covered hers fully, his tongue moist and hot on hers as it dipped once then twice.

Claire didn't want the kiss to end. Her hands slid up the front of his jacket, feeling the hard muscles of his torso, as they moved to encircle his neck. The fierce need that had been growing day by day exploded in one wild moment as she forgot all her inhibitions and arched her body into his, telling him in a language both silent and as old as time how much she wanted him.

The laughter of a small boy chasing a wayward ball as it rolled toward the arbor brought them apart. Garrett's hands dropped away while Claire drew in a deep breath. She didn't recall dropping her parasol until Garrett picked it up and handed it to her.

"It's time to find my stubborn grandmother and enjoy our lunch."

They walked out of the arbor as they'd walked in, side by side, close but not touching. Despite the physical distance between them, Claire knew she'd never be able to keep Garrett at arm's length again. Part of her worried that he'd think her submission a few moments before would guarantee her future surrender, and another part wanted to relive the kiss. Torn between loving Garrett and knowing that that love would end with her heart broken and her future forever stained by his memory, Claire assumed her role and greeted Grams with a well-rehearsed smile on her face.

After they'd eaten lunch, Grams was content to sit with Claire while Garrett was enticed into a game of horseshoes by Ben Corwin's challenge that a banker lacked the necessary skill to win such a match.

"Hold my jacket," Garrett said, shedding the summer coat. He handed it to Claire, then swooped down to plant a quick kiss on her cheek. While Claire did her best not to blush, he rolled up his sleeves and walked toward the flat area where small spikes had been driven into the ground.

"He'll win," Grams predicted with a smile.

"Does he ever lose?" Claire asked, trying her best to sound lighthearted.

"Rarely," his grandmother replied. "But then you know Garrett well enough by now to know that he doesn't make promises he can't keep, or accept challenges he isn't confident he can win. His father was the same way. And his grandfather. My Benjamin was a wonderful man. He died so young," she added sadly. "I loved him so much, I wanted to crawl into the casket and be buried with him. The only thing that kept me alive was knowing that I had *his* son to raise. Then Garrett was born, another son, and I felt as if God had somehow given me back my Benjamin."

Claire looked at Grams again, but this time she didn't see Garrett's grandmother, she saw the woman, Theodora Monroe. A woman who had raised a son and a grandson without the benefit of a father for either one. "You're a remarkable woman," Claire said, meaning every word.

Grams shrugged. "I'm no more remarkable than anyone else, my dear. Women don't always have an easy way of things in this world. One day that may change, but until it does, we have to depend on the men we love to take care of us." She reached over to pat Claire's hand. "Garrett is a good man. He has a loyal heart and a quick mind. He'll take very good care of you."

Claire hoped the smile she gave Grams was convincing. At the moment, the only thing certain about her future was its uncertainty. Her brother was missing and she was playing a role that could have disastrous results for both her and Grams, if she didn't find a way out of the bizarre arrangement she'd made with Garrett. The more she thought about the future, the more Claire realized that Grams was right. She had to depend on Donald's willingness to share his home with her once he was found and she had to depend on Garrett's honor as a gentleman to keep the promises he'd made. Either way, it was the men in her life, not herself, who were making the decisions. The truth bruised her pride, but there was little she could do about it for the time-being.

Chapter Ten

Russ Gardens took on a new look for the evening. Grams had elected to stay at home while Claire and Garrett returned to the park for a night of dancing and revelry that would end with Chinese fireworks to celebrate the country's birthday. The scent of wild honeysuckle mixed with garden roses and the smell of the bay as the carriage rolled to a stop. Garrett had driven the sleek single-seat buggy instead of the normal household carriage and Claire's pearl white dress, trimmed with blue velvet tapping, brushed against his legs as the buggy rolled to a smooth stop.

The ride to the Gardens had been a silent one, but that hadn't kept Claire from feeling Garrett's presence every inch of the way. The familiar spark of shocking sensation he always created in her was burning bright by the time he stepped down from the buggy and walked around to help her from her seat. The moonlight glistened all around them and music lifted and swelled from the gazebo in the center of the park. The uniformed band that had played for the picnic guests had been replaced with black-jacketed musicians in stiff paper collars.

Claire looked up at Garrett once her feet were on the soft summer grass. His black lashes lowered to cover quicksilver eyes as he returned her glance.

"Would you like to take a walk in the moonlight before we dance the night away?" he asked.

Claire lost her breath for a moment. The memory of the kiss they'd shared in the grape arbor was as fresh as sunshine in her mind. Mixing caution with boldness, Claire nodded and Garrett extended his arm.

They began a leisurely stroll around the park. The red, white, and blue streamers were still in place, except for the ones the children had taken as souvenirs to remember a day of fun and games. The trees were draped with colorful Chinese lanterns and the crowd that had filled the park earlier had dissolved into a well-dressed mingling of ladies and gentlemen who planned to enjoy themselves in a more civilized fashion now that the children had been put to bed. Most of the booths had been cleared away. There was one near the gazebo, where champagne punch was being served, and another a short distance away for those who preferred cold beer to quench the thirst of a warm summer night.

Large sections of wooden planks, nailed together like rafts, created a dance floor and Garrett stopped so Claire could watch for a moment. She caught sight of Christopher Landauer dancing with Belinda Belton and wondered if the hotel owner would really marry for money without any thought to Belinda's heart or his own. Probably, she realized. Garrett was right. Money had been the motivating force for matrimony for a good many years.

"Ready?" Garrett asked, as his eyes moved to meet hers.

Claire nodded and they began to walk again. The night was warm and there was just enough of a breeze to keep it from being uncomfortable. The couples, promenading around the dance floor, were forgotten as the shadows grew thicker and Garrett led her away from the party. Claire's heart and mind knew she should insist that they backtrack and rejoin the dancers, but she wanted to be alone with Garrett. She wanted to talk to him, really talk. The more she knew him the more she wanted to know him. She was curious about the little things in his life. Did he like peas? Mrs. Smalley never served them. Did he enjoy reading all the books that lined his library walls? She'd only peeked into the room, but what she'd seen had impressed her, and she longed to know what he thought about when he was secluded behind the elaborately carved doors.

"A penny for your thoughts," Garrett said as he stopped near a large wispy willow tree.

Claire shrugged her shoulders lightly. "I'm not sure they're worth the investment."

Garrett didn't say anything for a long moment. His mind was busy with the image of Claire, kneeling on the summer grass next to the pond while she patiently undid a knot on a little girl's kite. Garrett wasn't sure why the image was still lingering in his mind, perhaps because it had seemed like such a natural one. Claire and a child. She'd be a good mother. She was patient and caring and kind of heart. The thought became more upsetting as Garrett realized he'd never thought about children before, except to consider them noisy little hellions and more inconvenient than necessary.

"How are you and Grams getting along?" Garrett asked for lack of anything better to say.

"I like your grandmother," Claire told him as she

reached out to drag her hands though the delicate willow leaves. "She's an extraordinary woman."

"Yes, she is," Garrett agreed.

The evening breeze nipped at the curls arranged around Claire's delicate face and Garrett longed to reach out and touch them. He wanted to feel their silken texture against the palm of his hand. He wanted to kiss her again. And again. And again.

Taking a gentle grip on her hand, Garrett began leading her toward the northern end of the park. Gradually the hum of voices vanished, leaving only the soft melody of the stringed instruments the musicians were playing. Once they were totally alone, shrouded in the dark shadows of tree branches and pale moonlight, he stopped and looked at her again.

They stood and stared at each other for a second and Garrett let the need that had been building in his body all day take over. He reached out and put his hands on her shoulders, pulling her toward him. Slowly, carefully so not to mess up the artful arrangement of curls that Libby had fashioned for the party, Garrett buried his hands in the thick mass of hair at the base of Claire's head, forcing her neck to arch back and her mouth to raise toward his.

The kiss was one of searching intensity when it finally happened. Garrett pressed his mouth against hers and his tongue dipped inside, tasting. The fire in his body terrified him. He'd never wanted a woman the way he wanted Claire. The needing ripped at him, making him furious and disarming him at the same time. God forbid that he actually let some wild-eyed virgin get past his defenses, but Garrett knew the thought was too late.

"You taste like moonlight and sunshine all at the same time," he whispered against her lips. "Kiss me back, Claire. Taste me the same way I'm tasting you."

Claire didn't need to be asked twice. Her mind was

whirling and her body was on fire. There was no point in denying that she wanted the same thing Garrett wanted. Her arms encircled his neck and she let him pull her closer.

Claire tried to think of what she'd say when Garrett stopped kissing her, but the strange quivering in the center of her body wouldn't allow the thought to take hold. Garrett's arms felt warm and strong around her. His mouth felt wonderful and she wondered if the wall he'd erected around his heart could be melted.

When Garrett finally broke the kiss, Claire's eyes fluttered open. Moonlight splashed against the tree leaves and seeped into the shadows before it was gobbled up by the darkness.

"I shouldn't kiss you again," Garrett said as if he was arguing with himself. "But God help me, I can't stop."

Claire stared up at him. Her arms remained around his neck and she could still taste his kiss. "I don't want you to stop," she whispered, her voice shaky from the riot of emotions that had invaded her heart and body.

Her words fueled the fire in Garrett and he pulled her close once again. This time the kiss wasn't gentle. It was hard and rough, as if he were desperate to get his fill of her so he could satisfy himself and walk away once and for all.

One kiss turned into another and another, until Claire was leaning against Garrett's hard body for support. A hot flush raced through her body, ebbing and returning like endless waves of water rippling onto a beach. Garrett's mouth moved from her mouth to rain kisses over her face, her eyebrows, her nose, the curve of her jaw. His hands moved, as well. They traced the outline of her spine through the taffeta of her dress, stopping as they reached the small of her back, then pushing gently, bringing them so close there was nothing between them but clothing. She could hear his heart pounding, or was it hers?

He raised his head and looked down at her. His mouth curved into a satisfied smile and Claire knew in that moment that she'd never be free of the feelings her heart harbored for this man. He kissed her again. It was a slow, gentle glide of his tongue but the passion returned just the same. She couldn't hold on to the rational thought that what they were doing would only make matters worse. She should insist they return to the party, but the words never came.

One hand slid away from his shoulder and down to the front of his jacket. The hard plane of his chest felt warm and she wanted to touch more than the soft satin of his embroidered vest and the black velvet of his jacket lapels. She wanted to touch the man.

A shiver ran through Garret and his face tightened with agony and ecstasy combined as Claire's eyes drifted closed. She liked touching him even in this chaste way and he triumphed in the knowledge that she was as lost in the moment and moonlight as he was. Suddenly Garrett's legs felt weak and he knew that if he didn't sit down, he'd end up falling onto the grass and taking Claire with him. Vaguely remembering a bench not too far way, he took her hand and started leading her further into the shadows.

The bench was there and Garrett sank down on it. He pulled Claire onto his lap and sealed her protest with a hard kiss that gradually softened into one of pure pleasure. He moved her to make both of them more comfortable and to keep her bustle from digging into his thighs. The blissful feelings returned as his mouth moved and tasted.

The heat of desire grew and grew as Claire surrendered to the magic of the moonlight and the temptation of Garrett's arms. When he was kissing her like this she could almost imagine that he cared for her—loved her.

Garrett had to touch more than Claire's mouth. His hands moved to the narrow expanse of her waist, holding her on his lap while he enjoyed the pressure of her bottom pressed against the hard heat of his desire. His hands moved upward, over the narrow cage of her ribs until they stopped just below her breasts. He felt their gentle weight and wondered if her nipples were as pink as her pretty mouth. The tiny row of pearl buttons that held her dress together were no challenge to fingers that longed to touch her creamy skin.

Claire felt the evening air, cool compared to the heat of Garrett's searching hands, and her mind told her mouth to form the words that would stop him. Nothing came out of her mouth but a soft sigh of surprised contentment when the taffeta fell away to reveal her silk chemise.

Garrett's mouth became adventurous as he dropped kisses on her collarbone and the soft curve of her throat. His fingertips traced the delicate lace at the edge of her chemise and he wished she wasn't wearing a corset. He wanted to strip her naked to the waist. He wanted to see the moonlight gleaming on the warm globes of her young breasts. He wanted to pull her hard little nipples into his mouth and suckle like a hungry infant.

His deft hands moved the straps of her chemise off her shoulders, exposing as much of her as he could without removing any more clothing. Her breasts swelled over the hard caging of her corset, beckoning him to kiss the skin that looked like ivory in the moonlight. Garrett's body responded to what he saw. His lips brushed lightly over the milky skin he'd exposed and his fingers eased carefully, cupping her breast before he lowered his head, tugged the silk out of the way with his teeth and kissed the velvet valley between her breasts.

Claire sucked in a short breath. Garrett's mouth was as hot as fire. The sensation of the night air against her skin coupled with the moistness of kisses being planted across her upper chest made her body shiver with a newfound glory. She was a woman wanting a man, and for the first time in weeks, Claire wasn't embarrassed by the feelings of desire. She leaned back, wanting more. Garrett obliged her willingly. His arm supported her as she instinctively arched up to meet the demands of his hungry mouth.

"God, I want to strip you naked and take you right here in the moonlight," he said, his breath hot against her skin. "Your skin tastes like champagne and you smell like roses."

Clouds drifted over the moon and Garrett became a shadow to Claire's eyes. She could feel his body vibrating with male emotions. What were they? Desire, of course, but she couldn't help but wonder if it was more. He was being extremely gentle with her and somehow she sensed that he wasn't a gentle lover with most women. The thought of Garrett doing to other women what he was doing to her had the effect of an arctic wind on Claire's flushed body.

The music stopped and the melodious moment of passion descended into the cold reality of shame and embarrassment as Claire pushed Garrett away and surged to her feet. She kept her back to him as she tried to right her clothing.

Garrett missed the resilient softness of Claire's body pressed against his. He was tempted to jerk her back into his arms and finish what he'd started, but he knew if he tried, she'd end up scratching his eyes out.

Claire was fuming with anger. More at herself than at Garrett. She'd walked into the darkness with him, knowing what he had planned, and she'd surrendered to his charms without a word of protest. She had no one to blame for the humiliation but herself. Once her chemise straps were back in place, she fumbled with the buttons on the back of her dress.

"Let me help," Garrett said, moving up behind her. His hands pushed hers away and he fastened her dress as quickly and as expertly as he'd unbuttoned it moments before.

The surety of his skill with female clothing inflamed Claire even more. She turned to look at him once the task was completed. "I won't be your mistress," she said adamantly. "I won't let you seduce me, no matter how much I like your kisses."

Garrett didn't smile even though he wanted to. He didn't need Claire to tell him that she liked his kisses. The way she'd melted in his arms had already told him that much. It had also told him that when the right moment came along, and it would come along, she'd burn in his arms like heaven's own fire. But for now, her voice was shaky with anger as well as passion, and Garrett knew better than to touch her. If he did, he'd end up pushing her away when what he really wanted was to draw her nearer to the flames of passion. Women with real passion were rare and Claire had real passion. Garrett had felt it in the soft shudders that had racked her body and he'd heard it in the female purr she'd made when he'd kissed her.

"Would being my mistress be such a bad thing, Claire?"

She didn't have to think about her answer. "Yes. Being any man's mistress means that I've lowered my worth as a person and a woman. I'll do what you hired me to do, but that's the only game I'll play," she finished in a clipped voice.

Garrett wanted to pull her into his arms and convince her otherwise, but he knew if he touched her, she'd scratch his eyes out. Her chin had taken on a stubborn angle and her voice was laced with restrained anger. He could also sense her embarrassment. He'd touched her in a way no other man had touched her and Claire didn't like being reminded of it. His voice was soft but confident as he replied to her remark. "I haven't played games since I was a boy, Claire. I liked kissing you and you liked kissing me."

Silence was the only reply he got. Claire busied herself with straightening out the folds of her dancing dress. Her hands were still trembling but the reaction was mild compared to the raging emotions that had taken over her body. She was angry, embarrassed, and in spite of herself, she wanted Garrett's arms around her again. The passion she'd just experienced was still playing havoc with her body.

Garrett's smile was bittersweet as he offered her his arm. "I won't apologize for what happened between us, Claire. I'm more man than gentleman, and you're more woman than lady. One day you'll admit that and when you do, we'll set the world on fire."

His words were as insulting as his intentions. Claire looked at him, loving and hating him at the same time. "The only fire I want to build is one under Mr. Wilson. The sooner he finds my brother, the sooner I can leave your insults and your employment behind."

Her temper amused him and Garrett chuckled lightly. "One thing at a time, Miss Aldrich. For now, we'd better join the party."

In spite of her stiffness, Garrett took Claire's hand and placed it on his arm. The moon had reappeared and he could see the angry line of her mouth. He could also see the soft curves he'd caressed a few minutes earlier. "Appearances are very important," he said in a mocking tone. "Now put a smile on that lovely face. I don't want anyone thinking that we've had a lovers' quarrel."

"The last thing I'll ever be is your lover," Claire told him in no-uncertain terms. "At the moment, I don't even like you."

"You liked me enough a few moments ago," Garrett reminded her. Common sense told him to drop the subject, but his pride wouldn't let him. Claire had been pure sunshine in his arms, warm and vibrant and alive. He'd come too far in his pursuit of her to let her get away now. Time was on his side and he intended to use it to his advantage.

Claire tried to pull away and walk ahead but Garrett wouldn't let her. She measured her words as she looked up at him. He was right, but she couldn't admit it. If she let him think that she'd surrender unconditionally the next time he kissed her, she might as well cut out her heart and give it to him on a silver platter. "You're very good at seduction, Mr. Monroe. But then, you've had a lot of practice." Claire paused long enough for the insinuation to sink in. "I won't be one of your women. I came to San Francisco to find my brother and start a new life, and that's exactly what I'm going to do."

The sound of a woman's light laughter prevented Garrett from remarking on Claire's future intentions. He looked away from her determined face to see Christopher Landauer and Belinda Belton moving toward them. Henry Belton's daughter was gazing up at Garrett's partner as if Christopher had set the silver moon in the sky above her.

Claire used the opportunity to move away from him. They were hidden in the shadow of a large tree and when Claire stepped out into the moonlight she didn't notice a tree root sticking up out of the ground. Her foot caught on the snarled root and she almost tumbled onto her face. Garrett's strong arms kept her from falling, but her ankle twisted to the right and she couldn't bite back the sound of pain.

"Oh, my," Belinda said, leaving Christopher's side and rushing forward. "Are you all right, Claire?"

"She's twisted her ankle," Garrett answered as he scooped Claire up in his arms. The bench wasn't far away and he carried her to it.

"I'm fine," Claire said, although she knew she wasn't. If she hadn't been in such a hurry to walk away from Garrett, she would have been more careful. Her ankle was starting to hurt and she felt embarrassed all over again.

Garrett didn't argue with her. He sat her down on the bench, kneeled in the grass at her feet, and pushed up the hem of her dress.

Claire pushed it back down. "Stop that," she hissed, as Christopher and Belinda joined them.

Garrett's expression said he'd seen a lot more of her than her ankle. His hand found the hem of her dress again and he lifted it up several inches. "Hold out your foot."

"Do you want me to get Dr. Baldwin?" Christopher asked. "He's around here somewhere."

"Yes," Garrett said as his fingers gently probed Claire's exposed foot and ankle. "Tell him I'm taking Claire home and I'd like him to stop by and see her."

"It's only a sprain," Claire protested as Garrett began removing her shoe. He was as good with laces as he was with buttons and her shoe was set aside in no time.

"Wiggle your toes," Garrett said as Christopher excused himself to find the physician.

Belinda stayed behind to offer what comfort she could as Claire moved her toes, then grimaced. "Oh, I'm so sorry," the banker's daughter said, sitting down beside her new friend. "You won't be able to enjoy the dance."

Claire wanted to say that she was almost glad for the

excuse to get away from Garrett, but she held her tongue. Garrett was cupping her foot in his hand and she could feel the heat of his touch all the way up her leg. When she tried to pull her foot away, he tightened his grip, but he didn't cause her any pain. His fingers moved over her ankle one more time, before he looked up at her.

"I'm taking you home," he stated, then tucked her shoe in the pocket of his jacket and came to his feet. Claire came off the bench the same way she had gotten on it. Garrett picked her up in his arms. "Hold on to me," he said as he started walking toward the gazebo.

Not having any choice, Claire put her arms around his neck. She liked the steely strength of his body and the way he was holding her. She liked it so much, she was determined not to show it. Her body went rigid and Garrett stopped walking.

"Relax," he whispered. "I'm not going to ravish you with Belinda Belton standing right behind us."

Claire forced herself to relax. She looked over Garrett's shoulder. Belinda was following them with a concerned look on her face.

Dr. Baldwin and Christopher met up with them by the time Garrett had reached the gravel path where the buggy was waiting.

"My bag is in my buggy," Dr. Baldwin said. "I'll follow you home."

"Thank you," Garrett told him as he deposited Claire on the leather seat. He turned to Christopher and Belinda. "Sorry to cut the evening short."

"Don't apologize," Christopher said. He stepped back and put his arm around Belinda, drawing her close. "We'll come by tomorrow and see how Claire's feeling."

Garrett walked around the buggy and got in. He untied the reins, flicked his wrist, and sent the chestnut gelding pulling the buggy into a brisk trot. Claire waved good-bye to Belinda. Dr. Baldwin was behind them as Garrett guided the buggy out of the park and onto Harrison Street.

"I'll have you home in a few minutes," he said. "Are you in a lot of pain?"

"No," Claire told him. She clenched her jaw against the lie and tried to concentrate on the scenery instead of the handsome man sitting beside her.

The houses they passed were nothing but dark silhouettes against the night sky. Here and there a parlor window glowed and Claire felt her doubts returning tenfold. Garrett had kissed her with desire and what she'd told herself was affection, and she'd been a fool to believe her fanciful dreams and return the kisses.

"I'm more man than gentleman, and you're more woman than lady. One day you'll admit that and when you do, we'll set the world on fire."

Garrett's words came back to haunt her as the buggy began to climb up Nob Hill. He was right and the realization shamed her. She'd returned kiss for kiss and when he'd unfastened her dress, she'd let him. Why? Because his hands were like velvet fire and she'd been mesmerized by his touch.

"Almost there," Garrett said, looking at her.

Moonlight shimmered on her hair and her lips were still swollen from his kisses. He knew Christopher had noticed, but Garrett wasn't concerned about the teasing he'd take from his friend the next time they met. He didn't like the pale quality of Claire's face. She was in pain, although she'd denied it.

Garrett didn't want Claire denying him anything. Not her trust, and certainly not her body. The small taste of Claire he'd had tonight didn't come close to satisfying his appetite.

As Garrett stopped the carriage in front of the Nob Hill mansion, Claire was wrestling with both the pain in her ankle and the humiliation of what she'd allowed to happen at Rush Gardens. She couldn't bring herself to look at Garrett as he stepped down from the buggy and walked around to lift her effortlessly in his arms. Once again she was forced to lace her arms around his neck while he climbed the steps. Belatedly, Claire realized that she couldn't avoid another confrontation with Garrett any more than she could avoid admitting that she'd been an equal partner in the passion they'd shared in the shadows earlier that evening.

"Open the door," Garrett said.

Still not meeting his gaze, Claire reached out and twisted the brass knob. As she gave the door a push, she remembered that Garrett had given the household staff the holiday off. Mrs. Smalley, the housekeeper, had stayed on so that Grams wouldn't be alone, but Claire knew both women were sound asleep.

Dr. Baldwin's buggy came rolling into the drive and Claire let out what she thought was a silent sigh of relief. But it wasn't silent enough. Garrett chuckled lightly as he stepped inside the dim foyer.

"Afraid that I'll have my way with you, Miss Aldrich," he teased as he marched across the tiled floor and up the stairs. "Don't worry. I'll wait until Dr. Baldwin has pronounced you fit as a fiddle before I ravish you again."

"You won't ravish me again. Ever," she bit out the last word. "And keep your voice down. I don't want to wake up your grandmother."

Garrett responded by tightening his hold on her. "You're a sassy woman, Miss Aldrich. Sassy and sweet and too damn independent for your own good. But then, I like my women that way."

"I'm not one of your women," Claire hissed into his ear. Having Garrett compare her to the women he'd taken as lovers in the past fired her temper until the pain in her ankle was forgotten. "Put me down. I can walk the rest of the way."

"Stubborn, too," Garrett teased lightly as he stopped in front of her bedroom door. It wasn't completely closed so he gave it a gentle push with his foot and walked into the room. When he deposited Claire in the center of the large double bed, he was smiling. "Dr. Baldwin is right behind us. Behave yourself."

Claire gritted her jaw until it was aching almost as much as her ankle. She wanted to shout at Garrett, but what she had to say wasn't for anyone else's ears, so she suffered in silence while he turned up the lamp beside her bed. Dr. Baldwin strolled into the room a few seconds later.

"Let's have a look at that ankle," he said, setting his medical bag on the bench at the end of the bed, then shedding his jacket. "It's a good thing Garrett got your shoe off before the swelling started."

At the mention of Claire's black dancing slipper, Garrett reached into his pocket and produced the missing shoe. He put it on the table beside the bed, then moved aside to give Dr. Baldwin more room.

"I need to see your foot," the physician said when Claire hesitated to lift the hem of her gown.

Garrett was standing slightly behind and to the left of the doctor. Claire gave him a quick scowl. She got a devilish smile in return.

"I've already seen your ankle, Claire. And Dr. Baldwin is a physician. This isn't the time to be shy, sweetheart."

Claire wanted to push the endearment back down his throat, but she changed her frown into a brief smile and inched up the hem of her taffeta gown. *"I've already seen your ankle . . . "* The man had seen much more than that. *That's why he's smiling like a little boy with a new toy,* Claire thought. *But I won't be Garrett's new toy. I'll walk out of this house, sprained ankle or no sprained ankle, before*

I'll let him make a mistress out of me and a fool out of my heart.

"This may hurt a little," Dr. Baldwin warned her.

Claire grimaced slightly as the physician examined her swollen ankle. It was tender and the harder he pressed the more it hurt. "Ouch!"

Garrett moved closer to the bed.

Dr. Baldwin waved him back. "It's a sprain, but it is a rather bad one. I need to bind it."

Claire felt like a child, sitting in the middle of the bed while Garrett hovered a few feet away. The man made her nervous and if she hadn't been trying to get away from him in the park she wouldn't have been so clumsy.

"We need to remove your stocking," Dr. Baldwin said matter-of-factly as he opened his bag and reached inside to pull out a roll of white bandage.

Before Claire could reach forward, Garrett was sitting on the edge of bed. He grabbed a pillow and tucked it under her foot, being very careful not to jar her. Claire slapped his hands away when he started to reach under the hem of her dress to remove her stocking.

"I can do it," she said, wishing she could slap his face instead of his hand. The man was impossible. It was bad enough that she'd let him take liberties at the park, but it was even more humiliating to let him get away with them in front of Dr. Baldwin.

Garrett relented but not before his expression said he was remembering how much more of her he'd touched not too long ago.

"I'd like something to drink," she said, hoping Garrett would respond by leaving the room to meet her request. "Mrs. Smalley usually leaves a pitcher of lemonade in the icebox."

"Water would be better," Dr. Baldwin said. "Laudanum and lemonade don't mix very well."

"Is she in that much pain?" Garrett asked, sounding genuinely concerned.

"I want her to rest," the physician replied.

"I don't want any laudanum," Claire said. "I took it once before and it made me sick to my stomach."

"How about a neat whiskey?" Garrett asked of Dr. Baldwin.

"That should do the trick," the physician answered, looking at Claire.

She nodded, wishing Garrett would hurry up and fetch the drink so she could remove her stocking and Dr. Baldwin could get on with binding her ankle. She wasn't about to show her naked limb to the handsome banker. He'd seen more than enough of her for one night and she'd had more than enough of his taunting smiles.

"I'll be right back," Garrett said, giving her a look that said she'd be wise to cooperate with the doctor and do what she was told.

Claire's stocking was lying beside her on the bed and her dress was hitched up several inches when Garrett returned with a small glass of amber liquor. Dr. Baldwin was too busy wrapping her ankle to notice her embarrassment and Claire knew that the smile on Garrett's face was because she was blushing to the roots of her hair. He found a strategic position to stand and watch while she tried her best to pretend he wasn't in the room.

"I want her off her feet for the next three days," Dr. Baldwin said after he tied off the bandage and returned the hem of the dancing dress to a more modest position. "I'll stop by tomorrow to check on her again. Until then, make sure she stays in bed."

"I will," Garrett said. "Thank you."

Dr. Baldwin closed his bag and put on his jacket. "I'll leave some laudanum just in case the whiskey isn't enough. If you mix it with water and a little sugar, she may get by without an upset stomach."

"I'll be fine," Claire insisted. "The pain is better already."

Neither Dr. Baldwin nor Garrett looked like they believed her.

"I can see myself out," the physician said, turning toward the door. "Good night."

Once Dr. Baldwin was gone, Claire went back to being embarrassed. And worried. She didn't want to wake Mrs. Smalley, but she needed to get undressed and there was no way she could manage on her own. With her right foot propped up on a pillow and a bustle under her bottom, she felt lumpy and out of sorts.

"Sip it slowly," Garrett said, handing her the whiskey.

Claire brought the glass to her mouth, wiggled her nose at the scent, and took a sip. The instant the whiskey touched her tongue, she started coughing. "That's awful."

"That's the best Kentucky bourbon money can buy," Garrett said indignantly. "Take another drink. I know your ankle hurts."

Thinking he'd leave once she swallowed the god-awful bourbon, Claire did her best. Her mouth curled into a sour smile as she handed the glass to him. "Thank you."

Garrett laughed, then finished off the whiskey. He put the empty glass on the table. "You can't sleep in all those clothes."

"I can manage," Claire said quickly.

"How? You can't reach the buttons and you can't stand on one foot and wiggle your way out of a corset. Lean forward and I'll undo your buttons."

Claire didn't move.

"This isn't the time for modesty," he said, sitting down on the edge of the bed and pushing the pillow away from her back. "You're injured and regardless of what you may think of me at the moment, I'm not going to take advantage of the situation."

Before Claire could think of another way to unfasten the dress, Garrett's hands were doing just that. His fingers were as skillful as they'd been in the park and in a few seconds her dress was unbuttoned. She clasped her hands to her chest to keep the bodice in place.

"I can do the rest," she said, hating herself because the slightest touch of Garrett's hands and she was back to feeling warm and excited all over again.

Garrett ignored her remark. He stood up and moved to the end of the bed. "You can't sleep with one shoe on and one shoe off," he said simply. Garrett unlaced her left shoe, took it off, and laid it on the floor.

Lightning shot through her body when he reached under the hem of her dress to find the garter holding her one stocking in place. She tried to jerk her leg away. The movement made her bustle dig into her bottom and she almost tipped over on her side. Righting herself and supporting her weight on the hand that wasn't trying to deter Garrett's attempt to pull down her stocking, Claire's temper flared anew. "Stop it," she snapped.

Garrett paid her no mind. His hands moved up the inside of her thigh until they found the lace garter holding her stocking in place. Claire tried to scoot away, but there was no place to go. It took longer for Garrett to remove the stocking than it had taken him to unbutton her dress. The soft glide of his palms over her skin was enough to make Claire grit her teeth.

Once the stocking was discarded, Garrett looked at her. "We can do this the hard way or the easy way."

"Do what?" Claire asked, afraid that she already knew the answer.

"I'll help you stand up long enough to shed your dress and that damnable corset and bustle, or I can hold you down and take them off. You decide."

The gleam in his eye told Claire he'd enjoy stripping away her clothes one garment at a time. She thought about calling out for Mrs. Smalley but the housekeeper's room was downstairs, next to the kitchen. The only person she'd wake up would be Grams and that would create more problems than it would solve.

Talons of desire raked Garrett's body while he waited for Claire to decide to accept his help or fight him tooth and nail. The thought of stripping her naked while she struggled and cursed had a certain appeal, but he didn't want his grandmother charging into the room like a one-woman army to the rescue. He preferred having Claire all to himself.

Torn between embarrassment, anger, and necessity, Claire inched toward the edge of the bed. "I'll need my robe."

The simply spoken surrender was accepted without a word. Garrett walked to the closet, opened the door, and removed the nightgown and robe that hung inside. He carried them back to the bed and then reached for Claire.

"Lean against me," he said, putting his hands around her waist and bringing her gingerly to a standing position.

Holding on to Garrett meant letting go of the dress. When the bodice fell to her waist, Claire reached for it. She wobbled precariously and almost fell flat on her face.

"For God's sake, stop worrying about me seeing what I've already seen and concentrate on standing on one foot," Garrett grumbled. "I'm not going to rape you."

The sharp tone of his voice made Claire flinch. "Stop

being rude,'' she retorted. ''This is embarrassing
enough without you making it worse.''

''Try closing your eyes,'' Garrett suggested with a hint
of humor. He couldn't stay angry with her when she
was wiggling in his arms like a fish out of water. The
more she wiggled, the more she brushed up against
him. It was a delightful kind of torture and he didn't
want it to stop too soon.

''Try closing yours,'' she replied. Being close to Garrett again with her bodice undone and his arms supporting her was too reminiscent of what had happened at
the park. ''If you can hold me up, I can slip the gown
over my head and . . .''

''And nothing,'' he said impatiently.

If Claire thought Garrett was skilled in removing
female clothing before, the speed with which he began
undressing her now was more than proficient; it bordered on an expertise that made her even angrier than
she'd been the night he'd told Christopher that he
planned on making her his mistress. In spite of her
grumbling and protests, Garrett had her stripped down
to her silk drawers and lacy chemise in a matter of
moments. Her bustle was tossed haphazardly into a far
corner of the room, followed by two petticoats and a
corset.

While he undressed her, his eyes roamed and his
hands caressed. When Claire was left standing on one
foot, blushing as red as a summer strawberry, Garrett
lifted her in his arms and put her back on the bed. He
lifted her injured ankle and placed it on the pillow,
then reached for the nightgown.

''Lift your arms.''

Claire jerked the garment out of his hands. ''Turn
around.''

Garrett gave her a disgruntled look, hesitated, then
did as she requested. Once his back was turned, Claire

pulled the gown over her head, mumbling incoherently when it caught on several hairpins. She gave it a jerk, pulling it down, along with her hair.

"Don't peek," she warned Garrett.

Moving as fast as she could, Claire slipped the straps of the chemise off her arms, then slid her arms into the nightgown. It took a good amount of wiggling and squirming to get the chemise unlaced and off so she could get the nightgown on, but she managed it. Then, bracing her weight with one hand she lifted her hips to the left, then to the right. She pulled the gown down over her silk drawers. Once the nightgown passed her knees, she struggled into the blue robe.

"Okay, you can turn around now."

Garrett managed not to smile when he turned around to find Claire tucking the silk and lace chemise under the pillow so he couldn't see the forbidden undergarment. Her modesty pleased him. But seeing her hair free of pins and falling over her shoulders pleased him even more. Her face was colored by embarrassment and her eyes were sparkling with female indignation. She was more beautiful than ever and he wanted her with a savage lust that threatened to steal his breath.

The sight of Garrett standing at the end of the bed, staring at her like an anxious bridegroom, made an odd, fascinating feeling twist through Claire. The contrast of Garrett's formal clothing and her informal attire heightened the tension until Claire thought she'd burst from the effort it took to keep her feelings contained. The longer he stared at her, the more she remembered how it had felt when he'd held her in his arms and kissed the top of her breasts. Just thinking about it made her nipples harden into tiny buds that pushed against the soft cotton of her nightgown.

Garrett's keen eyes noticed the telltale sign. He was delighted to know that Claire couldn't deny what he made her feel. At least not physically. Mentally, he was sure that she'd do everything within her power to resist him. Thinking he could use time and Claire's newly discovered passion to his advantage, Garrett decided to bide his time. *A little temptation can go a long way,* he thought. *All I need is patience and she'll be purring like a kitten in my arms.*

Claire watched as Garrett gathered up her clothing. He folded her dress over the back of a chair, then laid her petticoats, her corset, and the awkward bustle on the bench at the end of the bed. Once her stockings and shoes were returned to the closet, he walked to the bed.

His eyes held her captive for a long moment before he bent down and brushed a kiss over her forehead. "Sleep well, sweetheart. If you need anything, call out. I'll keep my door open so I can hear you."

For some unknown reason Claire didn't mind the endearment this time. She was exhausted and her ankle was hurting. When she looked up at Garrett, the embarrassment she'd felt earlier dissolved under the warmth of his smile. She returned his smile as she leaned back against the pillows, unaware of how alluring she looked to a man whose body was screaming for relief. "I'm sorry that I've been such a nuisance."

"You're too pretty of a nuisance for me to complain," Garrett said. "Are you sure you don't want some laudanum? You won't rest well, if you're in pain."

Claire shook her head. "I'll be fine. Thank you."

Garrett hesitated leaving and Claire suspected it was because he wanted to kiss her again. She didn't dare let him. She was in bed, wearing only her nightclothes and Garrett's charms were too hard to resist. One more kiss and she'd be lost for sure.

"Good night, Garrett."

"Good night," he said reluctantly, then turned to leave.

Claire watched him go. She sighed wearily once Garrett disappeared into the hallway. The night had been an eventful one. She'd saved her virtue, but her heart was still very much at risk.

Chapter Eleven

Over the course of the next few days, Claire became accustomed to Garrett's arms. He insisted that she couldn't spend the entire day in her room, so he carried her down to breakfast, then into the parlor so she could sit with Grams. The older lady had been upset to learn that Claire had injured her ankle, but each time Garrett walked into a room toting Claire like a child, his grandmother's smile took on a satisfied gleam as if she couldn't be more pleased that Claire was an invalid and that her grandson had shortened his business hours to accommodate the young woman's inability to stand on her own two feet.

By the fourth day of her convalescence, Claire bribed Libby into finding her a cane and she was out in the hall and on her way down the stairs when Garrett exited his bedroom.

"What do you think you're doing?" he asked, clearly

disappointed that she wasn't dependent upon him any longer. "You'll fall and break your neck this time."

Claire clutched the pewter handle of the cane with one hand and the banister with the other. Garrett's constant presence over the last few days had begun to annoy her. What had happened on the Fourth of July couldn't happen again.

"I've been practicing in my room," she replied to his remark. "I can manage the steps if I take them one at a time."

"You don't have to manage them at all," Garrett said. "I'll carry you down."

"No." Claire let go of the banister and held out her hand as if she were warning off the devil. "I want to walk down by myself."

Garrett assessed the look on her face for a moment before shrugging his shoulders. "Very well. But I'll go down with you. I don't want you hurt again."

It was on the tip of Claire's tongue to say she wouldn't have been hurt the first time if he hadn't tried to seduce her. Instead, she turned her attention to the task of taking herself from the second floor of the Nob Hill mansion to the first floor. She paused on the landing to adjust her grip on the cane. Garrett was at her side. Claire could feel his gaze, but meeting it was more than she could manage at the moment. Just being beside him triggered memories of how he'd kissed her in the moonlight and the way he'd stripped her down to her underwear after Dr. Baldwin had left. Every time she looked at him, it weakened her resolve to find her brother and depart the banker's house as quickly as she could.

"You don't have to postpone your business because of me," she said as she tackled the last part of the stairway. "I'm sure you have more important things to do than carry me around like a mother cat moving her kittens from one corner of the barn to the other."

Garrett's smile was disarming. "I don't mind," he said, then leaned down to finish his remark in a soft, seductive whisper. "I like kittens. Especially pretty ones with sassy eyes and sharp little claws."

Claire steadied herself against the banister, her frown growing fiercer by the moment. She glanced toward the foyer to make sure they were alone, then said in a firm but polite tone, "I hope this doesn't jolt your ego too much, Mr. Monroe, but I don't particularly care what you like."

Garrett laughed out loud. "Still mad at me for kissing you?"

Claire put on one of the false smiles she'd grown accustomed to wearing since she'd hired on as Garrett's fiancée. "Among other things."

Garrett was about to tell her that he enjoyed stripping her down to her silk drawers almost as much as he'd enjoyed her passion in the park, but Mrs. Smalley's appearance stopped him.

"Breakfast is ready," the housekeeper said, wiping her hands on her apron. "It's on the patio, Mr. Monroe, like you asked."

"Thank you," Garrett replied. Still smiling, he turned back to Claire. "Shall we?"

With as much dignity as the cane allowed, Claire finished off the last two steps and headed for the east garden. Garrett followed her, wondering when he'd lost his taste for sophisticated women. The more he saw of Claire, the more he found himself enthralled by the challenge she represented.

In many ways, he had no idea who Claire Aldrich really was. It was almost impossible to tell when she was acting and when she was being herself. The talented way she blended her own personality with the role he'd hired her to play had him guessing more times than not. The only time he could be sure that Claire was really Claire was when they were alone. When no one was listening, she didn't hesitate to let him know what was on her mind. Her tangy wit amused him. The unique mix of she-cat and house cat was a puzzle Garrett longed to solve. Her eyes sparkled with defiance and her tongue had a sharp edge, but her female ravings weren't strong enough to fool Garrett into believing that she wasn't attracted to him. He knew better and he fully intended to make Claire admit her feelings as soon as she was back on two good feet.

Claire was surprised by Garrett's mood at breakfast. He was being extremely amicable and it worried her. *He's changing his tactics,* she told herself. *Well, it won't work. I won't let him get past my defenses again.* But even as she made herself the promise, Claire was recalling how her pulse raced every time Garrett was near. If only she could find a way around his attitudes about love and marriage. If his behavior toward her the other night had been motivated purely by lust, then why was he being so attentive now?

The man was an enigma in so many ways and Claire didn't have a clue how to go about solving the puzzle he represented.

After breakfast, Garrett joined Claire and his grandmother in the back parlor. He read the morning paper while she and Grams discussed plans for a wedding that would never take place. Occasionally, Claire could feel Garrett's gaze, but she refused to meet it. Let him think what he wanted. She'd promised to convince his grandmother that their engagement was a legitimate one, and if that meant discussing the guest list and the availability of roses for a wedding bouquet, then so be it.

Mrs. Smalley interrupted them to announce that Garrett had a visitor.

"Who?" he asked, setting aside the newspaper.

"Mr. Wilson," the housekeeper told him. "I put him in the library."

Claire's heart flipped over so hard she thought it might bruise a rib. She looked at Garrett, telling him with a silent stare that she wanted to be in on the meeting between him and the private investigator.

"I won't be long," he said, returning her solicitous look with one that said his grandmother would question Claire sitting in on a business meeting. Which meant it was out of the question. "I'll introduce you to Mr. Wilson before he leaves."

Claire didn't like his answer, but Garrett wasn't about to share any information concerning her brother until he'd had time to sort it out for himself.

He found Hiram waiting in the library. Once the door was closed, the investigator didn't waste any time getting around to the business at hand.

"I've found Donald Aldrich."

"Where?" Garrett asked, wishing for once that Hiram hadn't earned his fee in his usual efficient manner. Finding Claire's brother meant a complication Garrett would have rather done without for the time-being.

"He's living in Chinatown."

Chinatown! Claire absorbed the news through the crack in the library door. She'd excused herself from the parlor, telling Grams that she had to take care of a natural need. With the cane to support her weight, Claire gave a quick glance over her shoulder to make sure she was alone, then pressed her ear back to the door.

"What's he doing in Chinatown?" Garrett prompted.

"Working for Chen Loo."

"Doing what?" Garrett's question came after a considerable pause.

"I'm not entirely sure. At least not yet," Hiram Wilson

clarified. "After my interview in Tucson, I returned to the city, having a much better idea of where to look for our elusive Mr. Aldrich. Mr. Mitchell, the retired railroad worker I went to see, was very helpful. He worked with Donald Aldrich during the expansion of the coastal railroad. Miss Aldrich's brother had been employed by the railroad prior to coming to California and Mr. Mitchell said it surprised everyone when the younger man was fired."

Claire shut her eyes. She didn't like the direction the conversation was taking, but she had to listen, like it or not. Donald was her brother; if he was in trouble, he needed her help.

"Why did the railroad fire him?" Garrett asked.

"A small package of opium was found in the passenger's compartment of one of the railroad cars," Hiram explained. "Several workers testified that Mr. Aldrich had been seen in the car shortly before it left the depot. It was also reported that he'd been spending more money than his wages could substantiate prior to the incident."

The word *opium* was enough to make Claire almost drop the cane and collapse against the door. She'd never heard of the drug until she came to San Francisco. It was fairly prominent in the city, at least in the rougher sections of town. She'd heard enough gossip about the Chinese powder to know that it was more dangerous than alcohol. She'd also read in the papers that opium was a legal item of trade in China, although little was grown there. The drug was brought to the Orient from British India and other places in the Middle East. Once it was in China, it was sold to the Chinese people, who had become addicted to the drug. The balance of the cargo was then smuggled into America, most of it through the port of San Francisco.

Claire strained to hear what Garrett was saying.

"If Claire's brother is living in Chinatown, he must be under someone's protection. The Chinese don't give shelter to outsiders on a regular basis."

Garrett's remark was tainted with sarcasm and Claire began to worry even more.

"I have reason to believe that Mr. Aldrich is employed by Chen Loo," the investigator replied.

"Chen Loo is a Chinese viper," Garrett said none too kindly. "The city officials have been trying to have him deported for the last ten years, but every time they find someone willing to testify, the witness ends up disappearing. Never to be found again. If Claire's brother is doing business with Chen Loo, he's lucky to be alive."

Claire gripped the cane so tightly her knuckles turned white. She didn't want to believe what she was hearing. She couldn't believe it. Not Donald. The brother she knew and loved wasn't that kind of man. He wasn't a criminal.

"Here's a complete report of my findings to date," Hiram said.

Claire heard papers being shuffled.

"Should I make contact with Mr. Aldrich directly?" the investigator asked of Garrett.

"No. I want to look this report over more carefully before I decide what's to be done. Until then, continue asking questions, but not in Chinatown. I know someone better suited for that job."

Claire knew Garrett was talking about his best friend. Christopher Landauer spoke Chinese and from what Garrett had told her, he must have friends in the tightly woven Oriental community.

"I'll direct my inquiries to the railroad, then," the investigator said.

"Keep me posted," Garrett told him.

Claire stood up and backed away from the door, being careful not to make any noise. By the time the library door opened and Mr. Wilson took his leave, she was back in the parlor, sitting across from Grams. When Garrett joined them, Claire seemed content with her embroidery.

"I'm sorry I didn't have time to introduce you," Garrett said as he entered the parlor. "Mr. Wilson had another appointment. He offered his apologies."

Claire managed a convincing smile for Grams' sake. "Perhaps you can invite him to dinner. You know I enjoy meeting your friends."

"Once your ankle is healed, I'll extend an invitation," Garrett replied, knowing Claire was impatient for news of her brother. From what Hiram had told him, the news was all bad.

Thinking to postpone a difficult conversation, Garrett leaned down and placed a chaste kiss on her forehead. "I have to go to my office for a few hours. Take it easy with that cane. Dr. Baldwin said it would be another week before you can dance again."

"Will you be home in time for dinner?" Claire turned the probing question into a polite inquiry.

"I'll be back as soon as I can."

After kissing his grandmother good-bye, Garrett went back into the library, opened his private safe, and stuffed the investigator's report inside.

It was midafternoon before Grams retired for her nap. Claire sought her own room. Once the door was closed, she leaned against it for support. Her nerves were brittle enough to break. Since she couldn't pace and worry, she made her way to the bed and sat down.

Opium. Chen Loo. Her brother.

If Donald had been fired from his job with the railroad, it explained why he'd hired himself out to paint the house on Filbert Street. But there wasn't any logical explanation for why he'd been fired. No matter what Mr. Wilson had ferreted out in Tucson, Claire couldn't believe that her brother would be involved in anything illegal. Donald was too straitlaced for that kind of life.

On the other hand, she hadn't seen her brother for over seven years, and people did change.

Her mind bounced back and forth between the good and bad of what she'd heard. Donald was in the city. That meant, she could see him. Once she was eye to eye with her sibling, Claire knew she'd find out the truth. Donald had never lied to her. If he was in trouble, he might not like admitting it, but he'd be truthful with her.

But how could she find him? She already knew that Garrett wasn't planning on telling her what he'd learned in the library that morning. He meant to do some investigating of his own. Claire was sure of it. Her instincts told her she had to find Donald before Garrett confronted him. She was sure that Mr. Wilson had included her brother's whereabouts in the report, and she was just as sure that Garrett had locked the report away.

Feeling caged by circumstances, Claire longed to take a walk in the garden. Since her ankle wasn't up to the task, she stretched out on the bed and stared at the ceiling. If Mr. Wilson's report was accurate, her brother could be in danger. If, and Claire refused to believe it was possible, Donald had taken a wrong turn in his life, then her hopes of a new life in California had taken a wrong turn right along with him. She was back to being alone.

It wasn't a comforting thought. The city that had once held her dreams was suddenly full of painful questions and unanswered riddles. The arrangements she'd made with Garrett were temporary. A matter of weeks or months were raindrops in the sea compared to the years she had in front of her. Claire didn't like thinking about a future without the San Francisco banker, but it was there looming in front of her. With or without Donald, she had to take charge of her life again and make her way in the world.

She needed to talk to her brother, but she was afraid she wasn't going to like the answers Donald gave her. The questions kept Claire from resting and by the time she went down to dinner she was determined to confront Garrett once and for all.

"Where's Christopher?" Garrett asked as Andy pushed a key into one of the pigeon holes behind the hotel counter.

"In Sacramento."

"What in the hell is he doing there?"

Andy cleared his throat, then answered. "He took Miss Holmes to visit the new hotel."

Garrett let out a frustrated sigh. "When's he due back?"

"Tuesday, I think," Andy told him. The clerk wasn't surprised that Garrett seemed more upset over his partner's absence than he did over his missing mistress. Any man with good eyesight could see that Claire Aldrich was worth ten of Evelyn Holmes. "Mr. Landauer said to tell you that if Miss Belton asks, he's in Sacramento on business."

Garrett didn't bother replying to the remark. "When Christopher gets back, tell him I want to see him right away. It's important."

"Yes, sir."

Garrett exited the hotel as quickly as he'd entered. He'd come down the Hill expecting to find Christopher, although he vaguely remembered Claire receiving a note from Belinda Belton apologizing for not being able to visit. Mrs. Belton had taken to her bed with a case of something or other and Belinda was needed at home. Garrett knew Christopher was making use of the opportunity to pursue a more satisfying relationship with Evelyn.

He couldn't blame his friend for indulging himself. Celibacy was for monks and old men. Mentally Garrett tallied the time since Claire had moved into his house. Eight weeks without a woman. In the past fifteen years, Garrett couldn't recall going eight days without a female to satisfy his needs. Ironically, it didn't enter his mind to find a willing woman to break his sexual fast. The only woman he wanted was Claire and even though she wasn't willing now, Garrett was determined to change her mind.

His former resolve not to get involved with a virgin had gone by the wayside. He knew he should be ashamed of himself for even thinking about seducing her, but he wasn't. The thought of a woman like Claire being wasted on a man who couldn't appreciate her vitality and female wonder disgusted him as much as the thought of her being married to a store clerk or farmer. She deserved better. She was beautiful, intelligent, and she needed a man who could appreciate the passion she'd give if properly tutored.

Since he was in town, Garrett decided to go to his office and get some work done. He could use the time to think of what he was going to say to Claire when she asked about Hiram's visit. Garrett didn't want to lie to her, but until he knew more about Donald Aldrich's relationship with the Chinaman Chen Loo, he didn't want Claire knowing her brother's whereabouts.

Garrett had grown up in San Francisco, but Chinatown was a world unto itself. The Chinese community had flourished during the years of gold fever and railroad construction. The Orientals were a reliable workforce that had been exploited, discriminated against, and ill-used for years. While the wealthy moved toward the hills, the Chinese unified and maintained their cultures and traditions. The adversity of being different from their American hosts had strengthened their community rather than weakening it.

For all intents and purposes, Chinatown was a city within a city. You were either a citizen of the new Orient or you were an outsider. Outsiders were allowed to shop in the markets, gamble, patronize brothels and opium dens, but they were never allowed to breach the invisible wall that encircled Chinatown.

Garrett walked into the bank knowing that if Donald Aldrich was involved with Chen Loo he was in trouble up to his neck. The Chinese drug lord ran most of the opium dens in the city and it was rumored that he engaged in white slavery. White women were prized in China and it wasn't uncommon for those with pale hair and light eyes to turn up missing. With ships leaving the port daily, it was easy to smuggle young American virgins out of the country.

The thought that Claire could have stumbled upon her brother and inadvertently been exposed to such a thing was enough to turn Garrett's blood cold. By the time he left for home, Garrett was more determined than ever to keep Claire away from her brother. He'd do anything within his power to keep her safe, and he was a very powerful man.

Chapter Twelve

The clock was chiming seven when Garrett walked into the foyer. As expected, Claire was waiting for him. She was standing on the staircase, her hand resting on the polished mahogany banister.

Garrett stared at her and something inside him flickered like a candle in a draft. He realized it was nice to walk through the door of his home to find Claire waiting, as if she was anxious to see him. For the first time in his life, Garrett had a flashing image of himself as an older man, coming home to a wife and family. It disoriented him for a brief moment and he wondered if he hadn't been caught in the very web he'd woven to satisfy his grandmother.

The image vanished as quickly as it had come and for the moment Garrett had to admit that Claire was more interested in her brother than the man who'd brought her to Nob Hill. Feeling vaguely disappointed,

he put his gloves and hat on the foyer table and walked
to where Claire was standing. "Did you miss me today?"

Claire's hazel eyes went wide for a scant second before
she gave him a disgusted look. "No."

The reply was direct and to the point, but Garrett
could tell she was lying. He took a step upward, then a
second, until he was standing just below her. His hand
reached out and tenderly caressed the one resting on
the banister. When she tried to pull away, he stopped
her. He could see the anger in her eyes, but there was
passion, too. In that instant, he knew that she was playing
dual roles; she was pretending to like him for the sake
of others, and pretending to dislike him for her own
sake.

The realization hit Garrett with the force of a Kansas
tornado. Claire was falling in love with him. He'd seen
the look before, a mixture of desire and hope and
female expectations. If the emotions belonged to any
other woman, he would politely destroy them, but he
couldn't bring himself to say the lethal words to Claire,
and deep inside himself Garrett knew that he was
pleased. If Claire loved him, she wouldn't leave him,
and he didn't want her to leave.

"Grams is dressing for dinner," Claire said, unaware
of Garrett's thoughts but acutely conscious of his hand
holding hers lightly in place. "We can talk without being
interrupted."

"We can talk after dinner," Garrett said. "I need a
drink."

Without further explanation he turned and walked
into his library. His craving for a drink had little to do
with postponing their conversation and everything to
do with the sudden revelation of Claire's feelings for
him. Garrett knew she'd been attracted to him from
the start, but now that he suspected Claire might feel
more than desire, he was forced to evaluate his feelings

for her in return. The very thought that he might actually be falling in love with the young lady from Cincinnati was enough to demand a large dose of Dutch courage.

As he strolled into the library, Garrett felt weakened by the knowledge that he indeed felt more for Claire than a manly desire that was getting harder and harder to control. Absently he lifted the lid off a crystal decanter and poured himself a drink. What had happened to his well-laid plan, his scheme to eventually charm Claire into his bed, and then into the cottage on Bartlett Street where he could enjoy her body with no infringements on his heart?

Claire hesitated in following Garrett, but only for a moment. She'd waited the entire day and she wasn't going to wait another minute.

Being careful not to walk too quickly because the cane felt like a third leg, she followed Garrett into his inner sanctum. Mrs. Smalley had cleaned the room that morning and the fragrance of beeswax lingered in the air. A large vase of fresh flowers decorated a corner table and helped to soften the décor of the masculine retreat. It was the first time Claire had entered the room and she felt Garrett's presence as strongly as she'd felt it on the stairway when he'd touched her hand.

Garrett kept his back to her as he replaced the lid on the liquor decanter and took a sip of whiskey. The sound of Claire settling herself into a chair told him that she planned on staying until he'd told her about his morning visit with Hiram Wilson. He didn't want to lie to Claire, but he didn't want to tell her the truth, either. Knowing how stubborn she could be, Garrett feared that she'd hire a carriage to take her to Chinatown and start knocking on doors until she found the one her brother was living behind.

When Garrett turned around it was to discover that

the library door was closed against unexpected visitors and Claire was looking at him with that same determined stare she'd used the night of the Beltons' charity ball. He'd kissed her then, and he wanted to kiss her now.

"Mr. Wilson believes that your brother may be living in Chinatown," he said as he sat down behind his desk.

Claire didn't show any outward signs that she was disappointed at the way Garrett had turned what Hiram Wilson had said was fact into a possibility. She knew he wasn't happy over the news the investigator had given him that morning. If Donald was nearby, then Claire could begin to sever her relationship and Garrett didn't want to upset his grandmother. Bringing their engagement to a plausible end wasn't going to be easy, especially since everyone assumed they were deeply in love and anxious to marry.

"You say that as if living in Chinatown is a rarity," she replied. If she picked her words carefully, she might be able to learn more about the man called Chen Loo.

"It is, if you're not Chinese," Garrett replied. "Chinatown is a very tight-knit community. Unless you speak the language and have some idea of Oriental customs, most people would find living there awkward. Does your brother speak Chinese?"

"Not that I know of," she told him, then got a thought. "A lot of Chinese worked on the railroad, perhaps Donald learned the language so he could communicate with the workers."

"Perhaps," Garrett mused. "Still, it's unusual for a Caucasian to maintain a residence there."

"What else did Mr. Wilson have to say?" she urged. "Is Donald well?"

"We have no reason to believe otherwise," Garrett replied. "Hiram is still investigating the lead he got from a man who worked with your brother. It may be a few days before we find out anything else. Until then, be patient."

"I want to see my brother," Claire reminded him. "If he's in the city, Mr. Wilson should be able to obtain an address."

"He's working on it," Garrett lied without blinking. His conscience had no problem with the falsehood if it kept Claire out of Chinatown. "As soon as we know where Donald is, I'll take you to him."

"Promise."

"I promise," he said. What he didn't say was that the first time he called on Donald Aldrich, Claire wouldn't be with him.

Claire knew she couldn't push the conversation any further without admitting that she'd been eavesdropping that morning. This was the second time she'd overheard something, the first by accident, of course. In spite of her worries for her brother, Claire found herself thinking about Evelyn Holmes. Had Garrett visited her recently or had he actually turned his mistress over to Christopher Landauer's safekeeping? Were men so callous of heart that they'd share women like they shared unsavory jokes and a bottle of whiskey? Claire didn't like to think so, but she was learning that she knew very little about the male gender. Certainly not enough to form any real conclusions about their actions and reactions.

Forcing her thoughts back to her brother and her need to find a way out of the bizarre arrangements she'd made with Garrett, Claire looked directly at her employer. "The next time Mr. Wilson talks to you about my brother, I want to be present."

Garrett considered the firmly spoken request before replying. "If it's convenient. Hiram doesn't always arrange an appointment with me. If he has information he thinks I should know, he finds me wherever I am. It's the way we've worked together in the past."

"You mean if he comes to your office, I'm to rely on you to tell me what I need to know."

"I'm wounded by your lack of trust, Claire," Garrett said, pretending to be offended. "I thought we were friends."

Being told to be patient when she'd been looking for her brother for months didn't set well with Claire. "I'm not your friend, Mr. Monroe. I'm your employee. Donald is my brother and I want to see him as quickly as possible. He's the only family I have and he's very important to me."

"I know how important your brother is to you, Claire," Garrett said more seriously. He got up from the desk and walked to where she was seated. "You've trusted me this far. Can't you trust me the rest of the way?"

Garrett's words carried a double meaning and they both knew it. He wanted her to trust him so he could seduce her. For days she had imagined that their encounter at the Fourth of July dance had meant as much to Garrett as it did to her. Now, as she sat looking up at him, her eyes fixed on his tall frame encased in a dark suit, all her dreams seemed obtainable. His eyes had softened to a warm, silvery gray and his face was the face she dreamed about every night. He was looking at her as if her trust was important, as if it had held real value to him.

Don't be fooled by looks, Claire told herself. *Garrett doesn't want love. He wants a pliable female to fool his grandmother, then he wants a mistress.*

"I trust you to keep your word," Claire said, using the truth to hide her real feelings. She did trust Garrett. She trusted him to take care of his grandmother and his own desires. Beyond that, she trusted him to break her heart.

Garrett sensed that Claire's answer wasn't an answer at all. There was something in her gaze, something that hadn't been there earlier. He searched her face. Her amber eyes were clear and bright, framed by dark lashes tipped in gold. Her hair was done in loose curls and she was wearing the cameo he'd given her. This time it was pinned to a pale peach blouse, tucked into a dark gray skirt. Garrett realized the only time he'd seen Claire without the cameo was the night of the Fourth of July dance. Her dress hadn't allowed for it then. Her faithful wearing of the gift reaffirmed his suspicions that Claire had come to care for him. Genuinely care.

But how did he feel about her?

He stood there looking at her and felt threatened by the realization that his desire encompassed more than physical lust. He liked being with Claire. He enjoyed her company the way he'd never taken pleasure in a woman's companionship before. He'd come to think of her as a friend, someone who shared his concern for Grams and the little day-to-day things that filled up his life. Had her presence in his home fooled him into thinking that his feelings were love, or had Claire actually wormed her way under his skin and into his heart?

How did a man know he was in love?

The sound of Grams and Mrs. Smalley talking beyond the library's closed doors ended the short silence that had existed since Claire had voiced her trust in him. Garrett looked toward the door. "It's time for dinner. Tell Grams I'll be there momentarily."

Claire came to her feet, using the cane to balance herself. She'd tried walking without it upstairs, but her ankle was still too weak to take her full weight. With some reluctance she left the library, wanting to ask Garrett if she could read the report Hiram Wilson had given him, and knowing that she didn't dare ask.

As usual, dinner was a mixture of well-cooked food and interesting conversation. Grams told Garrett that she'd agreed to sponsor the expansion of a medical clinic that provided care for the less fortunate of the city. Dr. Baldwin had brought the charity to her attention and Garrett agreed that it was worthy of whatever monies his grandmother allotted to its cause. Claire listened as the conversation turned to Christopher Landauer and his anticipated proposal of marriage to Belinda Belton.

"Ada's buzzing like a bee short on summer and long on honey," Grams said. "Lord knows, I'll be glad when Belinda marries, if for no other reason than it will give Ada something else to talk about. Of course, I can't say I'm thrilled at the prospect of Christopher actually marrying the girl."

"I thought you liked Belinda," Garrett remarked as he refilled Claire's wineglass.

"I do," Grams told him. "It's Christopher I have my doubts about. Some men aren't suited to marriage and your friend is one of them."

"Funny," Garrett replied. "I would have said the same thing about myself not too long ago." He looked at Claire. "But then, life is full of surprises."

Claire's heart jumped into her throat. Garrett continued to look at her and Claire felt as if his eyes had taken her captive. His gaze was warm and she suddenly felt as if the whole world had vanished, leaving only her and Garrett. All the hopes and dreams she'd woven over the last two months filled her heart to bursting and Claire knew that she couldn't let go of the small sliver of hope that kept those dreams alive, the hope that Garrett might one day return her affections.

After dessert, Garrett moved away from the table with his usual catlike grace. He seemed unusually tall and intimidating as he helped Claire come to her feet, smiling as he handed her the cane. Once again his eyes seemed to swallow her whole and she felt the implacable masculinity radiating from him.

"I'll be glad when that cane is cast aside and you can dance," he said in a soft whisper. "I miss holding you in my arms."

Claire stared at the smooth buttons on the front of his shirt. It was all she could do to summon the pride that had kept her from walking across the hall and into Garrett's bedroom more nights than she could count. Taking a breath, she looked up into his silver gray eyes.

"I miss dancing, too" she said.

Garrett's smile took on a boyish quality. "Do you?"

Claire steeled herself against the overwhelming urge to kiss his handsome mouth. She was conscious of his long, tanned fingers as they came to rest atop her hand, holding the cane. His midnight black hair gleamed in the light of the chandelier. She knew every line of his aristocratic face but she memorized it once again, loving the dark lashes that framed eyes the color of a summer storm. She remembered the way his mouth had felt warm and moist against her own, and the way his tongue had teased her into returning his kisses. She recalled with crystal clarity the way his hands had felt on her body, strong but gentle, and the memory made her wish all the more than he might want what she wanted— years of love and happiness, a contentment that lasted through the good times and the bad and the sound of children scampering about the house.

He was standing so close Claire could smell his cologne and the faintest hint of the wine he'd drunk with dinner. Her mind reeled with confusion and she was torn between her love for him and the knowledge that her brother was only a few miles away.

Then Garrett stepped back to give her room and Claire felt disappointment wash over her.

"I have some papers that need my attention," he said. "Enjoy the rest of the evening, but go to bed early. Your ankle isn't completely healed yet and the Gromwells have invited us to a party next week. We'll dance again, soon."

He left her with a lazy smile and the unspoken promise of another night, waltzing in his arms. Claire joined Grams in the front parlor. It was their habit to read or sew after dinner, but Claire found her mind wandering toward the library. She knew Garrett was reading the report Hiram Wilson had left with him. By the time Grams retired, Claire was too nervous to sleep.

In spite of her ankle, she decided to take a short walk in the garden. Stepping outside, cane in hand, Claire looked up. A waning moon glowed with soft silver light and stars twinkled with the brightness of a million tiny candles against the black blanket of the night sky. The air was warm as Claire made her way down one of the garden paths to the marble bench where she and Garrett had sat that first day. The day he'd slipped the emerald ring on her hand and kissed her for the first time.

Sitting in the quietness of the garden, Claire rolled things around in her mind. She was vulnerable to Garrett in so many ways. Her body, her heart, her very soul seemed to be his for the taking. And she wanted to give them. She longed to be able to touch a small part of his heart, to make him smile and laugh, to give him children. Another part of her feared that her dreams were just that—dreams—unattainable fantasies that could never come to pass.

And then there was Donald. Had the seven years since she'd last seen her brother brought about circumstances and changes that would make him a stranger to her? Could the high-spirited young man who'd left Cincinnati with a pocketful of hope be a man of criminal means now?

No. Claire refused to believe that her brother was capable of such things. Donald was like their father, strong of mind and true of purpose. Whatever Mr. Wilson had discovered, there was more to the story than he'd told Garrett. Claire was sure of it.

Several hours later, up in her room, Claire was still certain that there was more to her brother's life than the suspicions and assumptions Mr. Wilson had reported to his employer.

Libby had helped Claire undress and change into a soft white cotton gown with tiny flowers embroidered at the collar and cuffs. Her hair was down, and she brushed the long tresses then pushed the thick mane over her shoulder. Without pins to hold it in place, her hair reached her waist, but Claire wasn't thinking about how tempting she looked. She was thinking about the papers in Garrett's library.

It was past midnight. She hadn't heard Garrett come upstairs, but then she'd been so preoccupied with thoughts of her brother, Claire doubted if she could have heard a herd of cattle making their way up the wide, curving staircase.

Slipping a robe over her gown, she looked at the door. The thought of sneaking into Garrett's library and trying to find the investigator's report had been inching into her mind more and more. If she could get Donald's address, she could go to Chinatown and find him.

Reaching for the cane, propped against the vanity table, Claire took a long breath to fortify her courage and headed gingerly toward the door.

Garrett read the investigation report a third time. He closed his eyes for a moment and leaned back in his chair. Hiram had discovered some very disturbing facts. Donald Aldrich had indeed been dismissed from his position with the Union Pacific Railroad. There hadn't been enough evidence to file charges, but there had been enough suspicion to warrant his dismissal. After that, he'd taken on odd jobs. Enough to pay his expenses for several months. Then, almost overnight, he'd turned up in Chinatown with a Chinese girl who kept house for him during the day and probably warmed his bed at night.

The relationship between Claire's brother and Chen Loo was vague, but there was definitely a connection. Claire's brother had been seen talking to several men who were still employed by the railroad and Hiram had ventured a guess that Donald Aldrich was still trying to smuggle opium via the Union Pacific. His years with the railroad, beginning in Chicago and ending in San Francisco, gave him connections in the Midwest where opium dens were becoming the rage. St. Louis and other cities that had once been the gateways for western expansion were taking on a more sophisticated demeanor.

The magical drug had always been in demand. In his more adventurous youth, Garrett had visited several Chinese brothels. Once, he'd even tried opium. The drug had made him feel light-headed and strange, and he'd suffered an excruciating headache for days afterward. The experience had cured his curiosity and he'd avoided both the opium-induced state and the houses that specialized in it ever since.

Opium was big business, which meant that it was smart to transport the drug by the most economical means. The railroad made the route from San Francisco to the interior of the country much shorter than the passage by sea. Chen Loo was a criminal by trade, but his success also proved he was a prudent businessman.

Garrett stood up, stretching his tense muscles as he raised his arms toward the ceiling. He knew he wouldn't be able to sleep. His plans to visit Donald Aldrich and confront Claire's brother face-to-face would have to be postponed until Christopher returned to the city. Garrett didn't know enough about Chinatown to go snooping about on his own. Christopher spoke the language and he had contacts inside the Oriental community that would prove helpful.

Thinking a small snack might ease some of his restlessness, Garrett turned down the lamp on his desk and left the library. Mrs. Smalley usually kept fresh fruit in the kitchen and she knew he was fond of apples and pears. Walking into the foyer, Garrett glanced at the staircase that led upstairs where Claire was sleeping. He hesitated for a moment, wondering if he had the audacity to sneak into the room for a glimpse of her pretty face. Deciding he'd tempted fate enough for one day, Garrett made his way toward the kitchen.

Claire inched her way down the stairs. The house was quiet except for the metallic clicking of the grandfather clock in the foyer. With a bitter pain that she was reduced to the status of a thief, Claire made her way toward the library. The door was slightly ajar and she held her breath as she gave it a gentle push and prayed that Garrett wasn't inside. The door glided open and she released a sigh of relief. The room was empty.

She let out another sigh of relief when she saw several

sheets of paper lying on Garrett's desk. The handwriting was bold, but clear, and she could make out her brother's name at the top of one of the pages. Claire studied the arrangement of the documents, wanting to make sure that she left them as she'd found them, so she didn't raise any suspicions on Garrett's part. Then she picked up the report and moved to the window, using what light the moon offered to read the investigator's words.

Afraid that she might be discovered, Claire hastily read the report, unable to believe what she was seeing. It couldn't be, she kept telling herself. Donald wasn't the kind of man to make his living so notoriously. When she reached the part that gave his address, Claire repeated the street name and number to herself several times. She was more determined than ever to seek out her brother and end her worries. Donald could explain all this, she was certain, and when he had, she'd find a way to ease herself out of the Nob Hill mansion without causing Grams any undue distress.

Claire returned the report to the desk, making sure it appeared never to have left. She made her way to the door. When she was outside, she turned around, holding on to the cane, and returned the door to its former position, not completely closed and resting just an inch or so away from the brass latch.

Garrett found her that way, as if she were reaching for the doorknob.

"I thought you trusted me," he said.

Claire whipped around so quickly she almost lost her grip on the cane and fell. Breasts heaving, she stared at him. His jacket had been shed earlier in the evening and the sleeves of his white shirt were rolled up. She could see the shadow of dark hair that covered his lower arms. It matched the thick carpet of hair on his chest, revealed by the unbuttoned state of his shirt.

Claire was startled by the image he made. Standing in the dim light, Garrett looked rugged and virile, so unlike a banker and very much like a strong man, polished on the surface but strong and hard underneath. The kind of man who made his own path and lived by his own rules. The kind of man a woman found impossible to resist.

Chapter Thirteen

"I assume you're looking for something," Garrett said, stepping closer. He was holding an apple in his right hand and his expression said he wasn't pleased to find her downstairs in the middle of the night.

Claire didn't bother denying the accusation. She'd been caught and now it was time to face the consequences. It might be easier if Garrett didn't look like some ancient god, towering over her with eyes like silver flames. "I thought . . ."

"You thought you could sneak into my library and find out about your brother," he finished for her. "What happened to the trust you proclaimed this evening? Has it vanished so quickly, or did you say what I wanted to hear instead of what you really feel?"

Before Claire could respond, Garrett locked his hand around her elbow and pushed open the library door. He guided her inside, careful not to rush her so she didn't fall. She was tempted to fight him, but Claire knew she couldn't win. Tonight of all nights, she was vastly aware of Garrett's power as a man and her vulnerability as a woman.

The room seemed darker than before and she could feel the night closing in on her. The heat of Garrett's hand seeped into her body as she allowed herself to be led to a chair. He took the cane and motioned for her to sit down.

He stared down at her. Her hair was loose, falling around her shoulders in a mass of honey brown curls. It gave her a wild, untamed look, stirring the desire Garrett had hoped to put to sleep for the night. How would she react if he lifted her out of the chair and carried her to the settee? Would she fight him? Or would she surrender to the fire of passion and the subtle shadows of the moonlight? The hunger inside Garrett grew with the erotic picture of Claire lying under him, her hair in disarray, her body open and wanting as he glided into her.

"I'm sorry," Claire said as she balanced her weight on the chair arms and eased down until she was sitting, looking up at Garrett like a wayward child about to be chastised for misbehaving. "It's just that I sensed you weren't being totally honest with me this evening."

Garrett didn't refute the charge. Instead, he glanced at his desk. The papers seemed to be as he left them. Good. He'd caught Claire before she could read the report.

"I don't deny that I left out some of the more sordid details of Mr. Wilson's summation, but I did it with good reason. I want to make sure your brother is able to provide for you."

"Donald doesn't have your wealth, but he's a hard worker. I'm sure once we've . . . corrected our current arrangement, I'll be content living with my brother,"

Claire defended her sibling. "I can find a job if necessary."

"You deserve more," Garrett said, speaking his mind.

Claire misunderstood him. She thought he was belittling her brother's ability to provide a home for her. "Money isn't everything. It can't buy you the kind of contentment you get from a family, from being with someone who truly cares for you."

Garrett didn't want Claire working in a dress shop or tutoring some merchant's children. He didn't want her living in some clapboard cottage with her brother, cooking meals and cleaning, with an occasional day away from the house to do the shopping. He wanted her living on Nob Hill, where he could see her every day. He wanted to see her smiling again, a genuine smile that reached her lovely eyes. He wanted to hold her at night, close to his body so he could feel her heart beating as she slept.

Suddenly, Garrett wanted so many things, but most of all he wanted Claire. She was so beautiful, sitting there in the chair with her hair hanging over her shoulders, and her tongue nervously wetting her lips. He wanted to kiss that newly dampened mouth, to taste her so deeply, so thoroughly, that she couldn't deny what she felt for him. He wanted to hear her say that she loved him. He wanted her to moan the words in her passion, while she clawed at his back and begged him to satisfy her. He wanted to bury himself inside her warm, willing body until there was nothing but her scent and sound and heat surrounding him. He wanted. God, how he wanted.

"We can talk about your future with your brother some other time," Garrett said, coming away from the desk. "It's late. You should be in bed." He didn't add that she should be in his bed.

Claire tried to avoid his arms, but the chair didn't

give her the freedom of movement she needed to keep from being scooped up and held close to Garrett's chest. As his arms tightened around her, she was forced to hold on to him and she could feel the muscular power of his body as he turned toward the library door. Her nostrils inhaled the tangy scent of his skin and she wanted to put her hands into the thick dark hair at the nape of his neck and feel its texture.

A twitch of fear laced through her as she realized he was going to tuck her into bed. What if he kissed her good night? Could she resist him again? She doubted it and her body was sure of it. She could feel herself warming to his embrace, needing it like a thirsty plant needed life-giving rain.

Garrett didn't hesitate as he climbed the steps. Weeks of wanting had finally come to an end and he knew that this was the night when he wouldn't be able to stop with kisses and a few limited caresses that teased his senses and drove him crazy with desire. Claire belonged to him. He wasn't entirely sure when she'd made the transition from hired employee to a woman he wanted more than his next breath, but she had. The realization was there, pounding in his brain and throbbing in his body, making him harder than he'd ever been in his entire life.

Garrett nudged her bedroom door open and carried her inside. Libby had turned down the bed and starched white sheets gleamed in the moonlight.

Garrett walked across the room and deposited Claire in the center of the feather mattress. She held her breath as he turned to retrace his steps, half afraid that he was going to leave her. When she heard the soft click of the lock, her fears took a new direction.

A frisson that was both frightening and exciting tingled through her body. She couldn't move. Neither could she say a word as Garrett returned to the side of the bed and looked down at her. A disconcerting heat danced in her stomach, like the flames of a bonfire on a windy night, and she knew the yearning she saw in his eyes matched her own.

"I want you to trust me," Garrett said, easing his weight onto the bed. Claire rolled against his hip. "I want you to believe that I want what is best for you, regardless of our unorthodox arrangement."

The impulse to tell him the truth, to expose her heart and thoughts touched Claire briefly, but it disappeared as Garrett reached out and caressed her cheek. Everything vanished, but the scalding touch of his hand. Never had Claire felt so helpless, so vulnerable. And yet at the same time, she felt as if she'd just discovered herself. The need to deny her feelings were gone. No longer could she look at this man and pretend that she didn't want him. She did. She had lain in bed night after night and dreamed of him, longing for his arms, his kisses, his velvet voice whispering in her ear.

Garrett moved his hand from her cheek to the edge of her mouth. His fingertips traced the soft curve of her top lip, then the bottom one. Claire closed her eyes and felt the flame of desire take hold of her, burning her all the way to her soul.

"You're so beautiful," Garrett whispered huskily. "I want you, Claire."

The words, spoken so bluntly, brought her eyes open. Garrett continued to watch her as his hand moved to her hair. His fingers combed through the tangles, bringing her head up so he could press his mouth lightly against her waiting one.

"Let me have you, Claire," he said, his mouth moving against her, his words a deep warm whisper that turned her need into desperation. "Let me give you the moon and stars."

"I don't want the moon," she said weakly. "I want you."

Garrett's smile was arrogant as he brushed her hair away from her neck and placed his mouth against the pulse beating erratically under her smooth white skin. He kissed her gently at first, then more aggressively, sucking on the delicate flesh until she jerked in his arms.

He raised his eyes to her. His dark gaze searched her face as his hands moved to the pearl buttons that held her robe together. They gave way under his deft fingers and Claire held her breath again. He eased the robe off her shoulders, then reached for the blue ribbons laced through the bodice of her gown. They, too, gave way and she could feel the air against her skin.

"I'll go slow, sweetheart," Garrett said as he kissed her cheek, then her jaw, and then her mouth. "I want to feel every inch of your sweet body and I want you to enjoy me touching you. I've dreamed about loving you like this, with those beautiful eyes watching me."

His words made her feel unsettled, but she didn't protest his hands as they inched her nightclothes off her shoulders and down her arms.

Garrett watched her face as he pushed her clothing down to her waist. She sat stiffly as if she expected him to hurt her, but he knew it was the fear of the unknown that kept her from relaxing. He'd meant it when he'd told her that he would go slow. He'd never made love to a virgin before, and he wanted Claire to enjoy it. He wanted to teach her the mysteries of passion, to explore them with her, and eventually yield to its all-consuming power.

He noted the blush of color suffusing her cheeks and his eyes drifted down to where the cotton gown had fallen away to reveal soft white breasts crowned with dusky coral tips. She was as perfectly made as he'd imagined, high and round with sweet little nipples that were begging for his mouth. He wanted her and her body was telling him what she'd already confessed. She wanted him, too.

His hand brushed over the taut fullness of her right breast, and Claire trembled. Then he buried his face in the thick tangle of her honey brown hair and lifted her against him. With one arm around her waist, he used his free hand to push the nightgown and robe down her legs and away. As he felt the silken softness of her body, he thought of the many times he'd ached to touch her and the many times he'd resisted the temptation. Finally, the waiting was over.

Claire had never been naked in front of a man before and when Garrett pulled back to look at her, she reached for the robe he'd pushed to the far side of the bed.

"You're beautiful," he said, taking the robe from her trembling fingers and throwing it aside. It landed on the floor. "Let me look at you."

The words were like a benediction. Reverently spoken, they eased some of her fear. Then he kissed her. Claire went limp as he demanded more and more from the kiss, brushing his tongue into and around her mouth, his hands kneading her scalp, his body hard and male against her nakedness. Soft murmurings came from her throat, but Garrett drank them, the same way he was drinking her breath, her very will to resist him. The last thread of denial Claire had left was swept away by the enticing grandeur of Garrett's kisses. Soon, she was kissing him back with a passion that matched his own.

Shamefully, Claire forgot her morals. She forgot everything but the searching texture of Garrett's hands as they moved up and down her arms, warming her until she was sure the bed would go up in flames. When he moved away to stand up and take off his shirt, Claire thought she'd die from the waiting. She longed to touch his skin, to run her fingers through the thick mat of hair that darkened his chest. His shirt joined her robe on the floor, and he was back in her arms again.

Her shyness almost gone, she reached out to place a hesitant hand on his bare chest. Garrett groaned. "Yes, touch me, sweetheart. God, I've wanted your hands on me for so long I thought I was going to go mad."

While Claire explored his upper body, Garrett studied her. She was close to perfect. Her legs were long and slender, her calves nicely rounded and as smooth as silk. Her breasts were voluptuous. Her waist narrowed before her hips flared out into womanly curves that threatened to steal his sanity. As her hands moved over and around his chest, Garrett slowly eased her onto her back. She stiffened for a moment, but his kiss took her anxiety away and she began to relax in his arms.

His hand drifted over her concave stomach and he vowed to kiss that soft flesh, along with the rest of her. While his mouth pursued her senses, Garrett reached for the buttons on his trousers. He hadn't undressed completely, fearing that Claire's first sight of a naked, aroused man would be too much for her virginal sensibilities to overcome. Instead, Garrett took his time. His mouth moved from her swollen lips to the soft skin of her collarbone. His teeth nipped slightly and she moaned.

"Don't be afraid of me, sweetheart," he said. "Close your eyes and relax. Feel what I'm doing to you. Feel it all the way to your bones."

Claire could already feel it. She was enjoying what Garrett was doing so much she feared that she'd turned into a brazen hussy. When his tongue began to circle one of her nipples, she arched her back, wanting more of the deliciously sinful caress. Garrett obliged her. His mouth was hot and wet and when he closed his lips around the nipple and began suckling, Claire groaned a deep, soft female sound.

Garrett continued stroking her, adoring each curve and valley of her body. He could feel his desire boiling in his veins, scalding him on the inside, and he marveled at the depth of emotion this woman could make him feel. He was quickly learning that there was more to making love to Claire than joining their bodies. Entrusted with the gift of her virginity, Garrett wanted to make her sacrifice something she would treasure, not regret. He fought the burning desire that was testing his control. He wanted the lovely, naked woman lying in his arms to feel as much pleasure as he could give her. He'd always been a generous lover, but tonight he wanted that generosity to go beyond the limits of his past experience.

Claire was too caught up in the throes of newly discovered passion to realize that Garrett was slowly, but surely, stripping away the remainder of his clothes. His shoes made a muffled sound as they hit the carpet, but his wet tongue was drawing tiny circles around her navel and the sensation numbed Claire's ears as well as her ability to do more than lie there on the bed and let Garrett make a feast of her.

Raising his hips, Garrett slid his trousers down and inched them off his legs, until he was as naked as Claire. He pressed a kiss to her quivering body and rested his cheek, slightly rough with a day's growth of beard, against her soft breasts.

Claire cupped her hands around his head and held him close to her heart. She knew she should be ashamed of what she was doing, but it felt too right, too wonderful for her conscience to condemn her. Tomorrow, or the day after, depending upon the strength of her ankle, she would go to Chinatown and find her brother. But tonight, she wanted the dreams that had fueled her heart for the last two months to become a reality. She wanted this special moment. She needed to love Garrett as much with her body as she did with her heart.

Garrett stretched out beside her, letting Claire feel the intimacy of his naked body. He held his breath as hers gushed out in a short gasp of surprise. He kissed her, a slow thorough kiss that stole her fears. His lips played and teased, while his hands caressed her. When he mumbled something low and earthy into her ear, Claire blushed, but her hands didn't stop exploring. She tested the resiliency of his muscles and the warm texture of his naked back. Mouth to mouth, skin to skin, they lay beside each other, learning things about each other they'd only imagined up to now.

Finally, unable to take the sweet torment of Claire's untutored touch a moment longer, Garrett pulled her to him and rolled her over onto her back. He raised his head and stared down at her, their bare legs entwined, his naked chest pressing lightly against her bare breasts.

"Trust me," he said as he inched down her body, kissing and licking his way through the natural valley of her breasts. He kissed the soft, pliable skin of her lower belly as his hand brushed through the curly nest of honey brown curls lying at the junction of her legs.

His hands swept slowly up and down her legs, easing the muscles she'd tensed out of female fear and embarrassment. His touch ignited another fire in Claire and she arched up against him, wanting instinctively what he had to give.

The innate sensual movement made Garrett grit his teeth. He wanted to plunge his body into hers, to join them so intricately, so beautifully that it would bring tears to Claire's eyes, but he was afraid that he might hurt her.

"Easy, sweetheart," he whispered reassuringly. "Let me love you awhile first."

Garrett moved his hands under her, cupping the soft globes of her bottom and lifting her against him. Holding her gently, he pushed his hips against her, letting her feel the hard proof of how much he wanted her. Claire's eyes popped open.

"Don't be frightened," Garrett told her. "We were made to fit together. Spread your legs a little, sweetheart, let me rest against you."

Claire wasn't as confident as Garrett that her body could oblige his, but she shifted her legs, opening them until he was cradled between her pale thighs. Claire looked up at him with a cautious gaze.

Garrett smiled. "Do you know how good you feel?" he asked before he bent his head and licked at her nipples again. "Perfect," he said. "So damn perfect, I'm not sure I can last much longer. But I will, I want you to enjoy this as much as I am."

"I do," she replied in a soft whisper that cooled the hot skin at the base of his throat.

"Not enough. Not yet," he said, knowing that her body would resist him at first.

Garrett allowed her to become accustomed to the new sensation of their naked bodies touching while he kissed her. It was a deep, unrestrained kiss, and when she arched against him again, Garrett let his hand find the sweet, warm center of her being. His fingers combed through the soft nest of curls to find the warm, honeyed core of her womanhood.

Claire flinched at the unexpected caress but she didn't fight it. Garrett's fingers were doing wonderful, shameful things to her, and she didn't want the feeling to end. When he entered her, his finger gliding smoothly into her feminine channel, she couldn't stop her moan of surprise and delight.

Garrett stroked her on the inside, testing her readiness to take him and the natural resistance of her untouched body. He was relieved to find that her virgin barrier was as fragile as the control he was maintaining over his raging desire.

When Claire was making soft pleading sounds, Garrett eased his fingers out of her snug silky center and raised up on his knees. His hands moved from her dainty ankles up her legs, slowing easing them wider apart, then he bent his head and kissed the inside of one thigh.

"Oh, my goodness," Claire said. She'd never imagined a man kissing a woman all over.

Years of practice proved invaluable as Garrett slowly calmed her again. While his teeth nibbled and teased, his fingers found the sensitive nub protected by a nest of tight curls. He touched her then, making her jerk in reaction, then moan out loud as her nails dug into the skin of his shoulders.

When his mouth joined his fingers, Claire almost shot off the bed like the fireworks she'd missed on the Fourth of July. His stroking fingers became bolder and his mouth moved with determination, bringing Claire closer and closer to the mysterious, unknown edge of something wonderful. She pressed up against him, giving herself, offering all that he wanted, unable to hold anything back.

Never in Garrett's wildest dreams had he imagined a woman feeling so wonderful, wanting with such honesty and daring. The incredible joy of giving Claire pleasure welled up inside him and Garrett moved his hand more insistently. His tongue dipped and curled around the bud of Claire's desire until he felt her stiffen, then begin to tremble like a rose petal shaken by a summer breeze.

"Garrett," his name was a question and a plea combined.

"Trust me," Garrett said, lifting his mouth away for a brief moment. "Trust me and let go, sweetheart. I'll keep you safe."

Claire let her body relax and felt the flames of desire burn out of control. She forgot that Garrett was stroking and kissing flesh that no one had touched before. She forgot his grandmother sleeping down the hall and her brother somewhere in the inner city. She was lost to everything but the hot, burning need that raked her body, then found its completion in the glide of Garrett's fingers and the quick, hard pressure of his mouth as he pushed her over the edge into an abyss of swirling, shivering sensations that made the world turn upside down.

"Hold on to me," Garrett said, ending the kiss. "Bite me if the pain's too bad, but don't cry out."

Claire buried her face in the hot curve of his neck and held on. Her body was still vibrating with the wonders of what Garrett had done so far and she couldn't imagine him hurting her. His entry was smooth and firm and she flinched as a prick of pain started then turned into a stretching, throbbing sensation. She could feel Garrett inside her, pushing gently but surely until their bodies seemed to be one.

It's so beautiful, Claire thought. *I love you,* she ached to say. *I love you and I have to believe that you love me. At least for this one special night.*

"God, you feel good," Garrett said in a muffled moan as he rested his forehead against hers. "You're like hot silk and warm honey."

He held himself still, giving Claire time to adjust to the sensation of sharing her body with a man. He kissed her and soothed her with words she didn't understand, but she clung to the words the same way she found herself clinging to the man as Garrett began to move. His hard, hot body stroked her slowly, pulling out, then gently returning until she was arching up to meet the sensual movements and pleasure began to boil inside her once again.

Claire wrapped her legs around him to keep him close. Garrett continued moving. Long, slow sensual strokes that aroused and tormented and promised. They moved and moaned and clung to each other in a sensual dance as old as time. The bed creaked and the night air cooled their feverish skin, and they kept on moving. Each needing something from the other, each wanting, each loving in their own private way.

Slowly, expertly, Garrett made love to her, giving more of himself than he'd ever given any other woman, wanting more in return than he'd ever expected from previous lovers. He knew that having Claire was different, so different that his fears of caring for her vanished as he rode her harder and deeper, moving his body in and out of hers in hard, urgent strokes that tested his endurance. He felt as if his body belonged to Claire, not him. He moved to please her, to torment her, to push her over the edge again.

Claire moved with him, unable to control the need that had instinctively invaded her mind and body. Her pelvis arched and her arms clung to his neck, while she absorbed the buffering, sensual attack. She could feel every male inch of him, lying on top of her, probing inside her, surrounding her as completely as the darkness of the night and the tangled bedcovers that absorbed the sweat of their bodies.

"Don't fight it, sweetheart," Garrett groaned as he felt the sensual tightening of her body and knew she was close to climaxing. "Let go and give yourself to me."

Claire didn't think she could belong to him more than she already did, but she was wrong. Garrett changed his pace, driving deeper inside her as her legs locked around his lean hips. He pumped into her, his body tight with the effort of holding his own release back until she gained hers again. When she buried her face against his damp chest and bit him, Garrett could barely control his reaction. Every muscle in his body flexed and he surged deep, letting go of the world right along with Claire.

Claire's arms stayed around him and her hands eased up and down his spine, needing to touch him as she came back to her senses. Garrett was heavy, but Claire didn't mind his weight. It felt wonderful and she closed her eyes against the tears that threatened to spill down her face.

It took Garrett a little longer to find his composure. God, he'd never felt his body catch on fire the way it had with Claire. He'd been too consumed by desire to think of protecting her and the darkness hid his smile as he thought of her slender form rounding with his child. A few months ago, the thought of creating a new life would have scared him to death, but not now.

Now, he knew what he hadn't known then. He could fall in love.

Garrett eased off Claire and onto his side, bringing her close and kissing the tip of her nose. He wanted to tell her that he cared for her, but he was afraid she'd rebuke his words, thinking them a sad conclusion to his seduction. Instead of words, Garrett gave her soft, tender kisses that slowly turned her face toward his. He looked into her wide, questioning eyes and smiled. He kissed away the tears gliding down her face. "I want to hold you until you fall asleep. Will you let me?"

Moonlight covered their naked bodies. Claire looked at him, loving the intimacy they had shared, her shyness now a thing of the past. Her heartbeat doubled as her gaze moved over him, learning by sight what she already knew by touch. He was a magnificent man. She'd never imagined that a naked man could be beautiful, but Garrett was. His body was a delight and he'd taught her more about her own body than Claire could ever have imagined.

"I like the feel of you next to me," she said in a soft whisper.

She rested her head against his chest. Garrett's arms encircled her and she breathed deeply, taking in the scent of the man lying naked beside her. Her hands roamed over his chest, wanting to touch him again, needing to feel his heartbeat drumming deep and strong inside his body.

Garrett stilled her hand with his, then brought it to his mouth. "Go to sleep, sweetheart."

The words didn't come easy. Garrett knew he could take Claire again and again, sating his desire only to have it return until the sun eased over the horizon and he was too tired to leave her bed. But he couldn't. She'd been a virgin and although her transformation into a woman had been easier than most, she was tender and he didn't want to hurt her.

Claire allowed Garrett to hold her, knowing that leaving him would be the hardest thing she'd ever do. But leave him she would. As much as she loved him, and having no regrets over the passion she'd shared with him, Claire couldn't become his mistress. She wanted more than stolen nights and Garrett's body. She wanted his heart. As naïve as she might be about life, Claire knew that passion was a poor substitute for love.

Chapter Fourteen

"Your grandmother is here, sir."

Garrett looked up from his desk. What was his grandmother doing in the city? "Show her in," he said to the clerk who had worked for him less than a month. He couldn't remember the man's name, Harvey or Harry, or something like that.

The moment Grams walked into his office, Garrett knew that his and Claire's lovemaking hadn't been as quiet as he had hoped. His grandmother was wearing a look that didn't bode well and he knew he was in for a tongue-lashing of the worst degree. Thinking to salvage what he could of a bad situation, Garrett came to his feet. "You shouldn't be out in the heat."

"Don't lecture me about the weather, young man," Grams replied. "I'm old enough to know when I should and shouldn't do something. It's unfortunate that I can't say the same thing for my grandson."

He pulled out a chair and waited until his grand-

mother had made herself comfortable. After a long
pause, Grams looked up at him. "I assume you know
why I'm here."

"I have a fairly good idea," Garrett said, returning
to the leather chair behind his desk.

"Excellent," she retorted. "Then we can dispense
with the formalities and get down to the heart of the
matter. I've instructed Henry to wait for me in the carriage. I plan to stop by the printing office on my way
home and give Mr. Davidson the information for your
wedding invitations. A month from today should give
the few guests that are being invited enough time to
prepare themselves. The wedding will be a small, private
affair followed by a reception at the Landauer Hotel."

He was about to reply that his grandmother was rushing things a bit, then realized that her reply would be
to say the same thing of him. Instead, he asked, "Have
you spoken with Claire?"

"No," Grams told him. "I have no intention of embarrassing the girl by letting her know that I'm aware of
what happened last night." His grandmother's pale eyes
bored a hole through him. "Of all the foolish things
I've seen you do in your life, Garrett, this has got to be
the worst. My God, what were you thinking? You don't
seduce your own fiancée, young man. Claire is a lady,
not a . . ."

"Claire is still very much a lady," Garrett interrupted.
"What happened last night is entirely my fault."

"Of course, it is," his grandmother agreed hastily.
"And I expect you to do the right thing. I won't have
people counting the days between your wedding and
the birth of my first great-grandchild. And I won't have
Claire's reputation tainted by your lack of self-control."

"And you think that a short engagement and a rushed
wedding won't taint her reputation," Garrett remarked.
He'd been thinking about marriage to Claire ever since

he'd left her room before dawn, but he didn't like the idea of it being shoved down his throat. But then, there was the possibility that he'd given her a child. That in itself was enough to demand that they marry as soon as possible.

"I think that everyone will believe what I believe," Grams replied. "You love Claire and you want to marry her."

Garrett didn't dispute his grandmother's opinion. How could he? He did love Claire. And he did want to marry her. The question was did Claire love him? He suspected she did, and her response to him last night had come close to convincing him, but there was still the problem of her brother. Once Claire discovered that he intended to expose any illegal activities Donald Aldrich might be engaged in to the authorities, would she marry him?

"I'll talk to Claire," Garrett told his grandmother. "Don't send out the invitations until I tell you. I wouldn't want a wedding without a bride."

"That's unlikely," Grams said. "I've never seen a woman more in love."

Garrett certainly hoped so.

He escorted his grandmother to the waiting carriage. "I may be late this evening. I've spent more time at home than usual and I have matters that require my attention."

"Don't be too late," his grandmother said. "Claire needs your reassurance now, more than ever."

As the carriage pulled away, Garrett found himself doubting what he'd been certain of last night. Had he seen love in Claire's eyes or had he pursued her because he'd been half crazy with lust and any excuse would do? He was behind his desk again before he called himself a fool. Grams was right. Claire was a lady and a lady didn't give herself easily to a man. In that one mad moment of their mutual climax, Garrett had felt more than he'd ever felt in his entire life. He'd been more aware, more alive, than he'd ever been before. He'd stared into Claire's eyes, eyes that had haunted his dreams and hadn't given him a moment's peace since the day she'd strolled into Christopher's office, and he'd felt the love as surely as he'd felt her passion and her ecstasy. Suddenly, a month seemed like forever.

Claire woke to find her nightgown and robe neatly folded over the end of the bed and her cane propped against the vanity table. She stretched like a cat waking up after a long night's rest on a warm hearth, and realized that Garrett must have retrieved the cane from the library.

Of course, he had, she realized. He wouldn't want anyone in the house to suspect that he'd spent the night in her bed. Claire took a deep breath and inhaled the scent of Garrett on her pillow. Her hand smoothed over the wrinkled linens and she thought of how wonderful it had been to fall asleep in his arms.

The sound of Libby balancing a tray on one hand and tapping on the bedroom door with the other intruded into Claire's memory of the previous night. Hastily, Claire reached for her nightgown and pulled it over her head, then straightening the bedcovers, she leaned against the feather pillows and told the maid to come in.

The next few minutes were spent saying good morning as Libby placed a tray of tea, toast, and fresh fruit on the table beside the bed. When she opened the drapes, sunlight streamed into the room, filling every nook and cranny. Claire realized she'd overslept and apologized.

"Don't worry over it," Libby said as she poured Claire

a cup of tea. "Mr. Monroe left bright and early and his grandmother went into town. She said she had business to attend to. She told me to let you sleep. How's your ankle this morning?"

Claire tucked the blanket up at the corner and wiggled the appendage. "Much better."

"Good," Libby said before taking herself into the bathroom to turn on the tap. The sound of hot water gushing from the spigot was soon heard and Claire smiled, looking forward to a bath.

Suddenly self-conscious of her tangled hair and aching body, Claire finished her tea. She tried to force the thought of leaving Garrett out of her mind, but it kept surfacing, along with the knowledge that one night in his arms wasn't enough. She wanted a lifetime.

Thirsty, but not hungry, Claire sat her empty cup back on the tray and got out of bed. Balancing her weight carefully, she tested her ankle. She hadn't lied to Libby. It felt much better, but Claire reached for the cane anyway. She had a lot to do and straining her ankle again would only slow her down. Since Grams was gone, it would be easy to leave the house. The servants wouldn't ask her for an explanation and the trolley line that went down the hill was only a short distance away. If luck was with her, Claire could go to Chinatown, see her brother, and be back before Garrett returned home.

She was anxious about seeing Garrett again. It would be embarrassing at first, considering what they'd done together, but she was more worried about how to handle his temper once he found out that she'd gone behind his back and visited her brother. Claire reminded herself that she wasn't seeking out a stranger. Donald was her flesh and blood. She had every right to see him.

She stopped in front of the vanity mirror and took a long look at herself. Her hair was a mess of unruly curls and although she couldn't see the rest of her body because of the long cotton gown, she knew it had to show the effects of Garrett's lovemaking as well. He'd taught her that passion could be fierce as well as tender and she blushed at the memory of it.

But the flush of color held no condemnation for her actions. She should be ashamed, she knew; it wasn't proper for a young lady to submit to the baser instincts of life, but Claire didn't feel embarrassed or shamed by what had passed between herself and Garrett. Truthfully, she felt as if she'd taken on a new life, the life of a woman who finally knew what it felt like to be held, and wanted, and perhaps even a little loved. The time she'd spent in Garrett's arms wasn't enough to satisfy her, but it was enough to confirm her love for him.

Holding that thought, she took her bath and with Libby's help put on a blue skirt and matching jacket trimmed in gold braid. A short time later she was insisting that the maid not worry about her.

"I've been cooped up in this house far too long," Claire said, leaning her cane against the foyer table as she slipped on her gloves. "A short walk and a little shopping will be good for me. Don't fret. I'll be back in no time."

Ignoring Libby's worried look, Claire stepped outside the door of the Nob Hill mansion for the first time in five days. The sun was warm on her face and she couldn't help but think of the way Garrett had warmed her the night before. She made her way toward the trolley stop, wondering if he was thinking about her. Not knowing what went on in a man's mind after a night of lovemaking, Claire hoped that Garrett didn't think he'd turned her into a willing bed partner anytime he wanted one. She'd given him her virginity, but her pride was still intact.

The trip to Chinatown soon consumed her thoughts and Claire watched as the trolley moved through the city. She knew the moment she'd reached her destination. The texture of the city changed almost instantaneously. Instead of modest storefronts and quaint cottages with wrought-iron fences, the buildings had tiled roofs painted red and green. Bright banners flowed from the doorways, decorated with bold black lettering that she couldn't decipher. But it was the people that held her attention. The men were short and thin and they wore what appeared to be black silk pajamas and sandals that made a sharp click-clop sound on the wooden sidewalks. The women dressed in a similar fashion and they reminded Claire of fragile china dolls, they appeared so delicately made.

The trolley passed a Buddhist temple. The narrow staircase leading to the Oriental house of worship was lined with Chinese residents who had come to pray and give offerings to their ancestors. The scent of incense was heavy in the air and Claire was intrigued by the building's architecture. Gold painted lions with red eyes guarded the temple and she wondered if the interior of the building was as elaborate as the outside.

When the trolley conductor announced that Waverly Place would be their last stop, Claire stood up. Thankful that she'd brought the cane, she walked to the front of the car and deposited the necessary coins in the box by the conductor's seat before stepping off the car and into the street.

Fortunately the house numbers were written in both English and Chinese and Claire studied the street in both directions before setting out to find her brother. The musical chatter of the Chinatown residents pleased her ears and she strained to understand at least a word of their language, but it seemed impossible.

There were street vendors with large wagons of woven baskets doing business beside wagons filled with exotic fruits. Chickens squawked inside bamboo cages and she laughed and shook her head when a small man, missing a considerable number of his front teeth, waved a half-plucked chicken in front of her and jabbered broken English so fast she couldn't make out what he was saying, although Claire assumed he was trying to sell her the plump hen.

She stopped for a moment to look at a store window. The shop specialized in silk and the window was draped with some of the most beautiful fabric Claire had ever seen. Inside, she could see a slender Chinese woman, wearing black loose-fitting trousers and a high-collared red and gold jacket, talking to a customer. The older Chinese woman seemed to be having a difficult time deciding between a piece of jade silk and one the color of a rare ruby. Claire sympathized with the shopper's dilemma. Both pieces of silk were beautiful and Claire wondered if she dared to take the time to visit the shop after she'd seen her brother.

The thought passed quickly. She had just enough money to pay for a trolley ride back up the hill and another round trip from Nob Hill to Chinatown, if Donald offered her the security of his home. The money Garrett had deposited in an account at his bank would go untouched, no matter how desperately she might need it in the future.

Silently reciting the address she'd discovered the previous night in Garrett's library, Claire continued down the street. She stopped in front of a narrow building with three floors. Both the second and third floors had balconies decorated in brightly colored streamers and brimming with exotic plants. The front door of the house was painted a stark black in contrast to the red walls and red and gold trimmed window frames. Wooden shutters covered the windows, shutting the house off from intruding eyes. Taking a deep breath and praying that her quest for her lost brother would end when the door was answered, Claire knocked on the door and waited.

When the door was finally opened, Claire didn't know what to say. A Chinese girl stood in front of her. Although the young woman was childlike in size, there was a maturity about her face and eyes that told Claire she was much older than she looked. The girl didn't say a word, in English or Chinese. She merely stared at Claire.

"I'm looking for Donald Aldrich," Claire said slowly, hoping the girl would at least recognize her brother's name. "I'm Claire Aldrich, his sister."

A slow smile came to the young woman's face and she stepped back, bowing at the waist and motioning Claire inside. Breathing a sigh of relief that she'd at least found the correct house, Claire entered. The inside of the residence was painted in the same bold colors and the doorways were draped with crystal beads that reflected the sunlight coming through the door like tiny prisms. The light bounced and danced across the floor and Claire smiled.

Her smile changed into one of triumph when her brother pushed aside the long strands of beads and stepped into the hallway.

"How did you get here?"

Donald hadn't changed all that much and Claire recognized him immediately. "By train, and then by trolley," she replied as if they'd been sharing each other's company for the last seven years instead of being separated by thousands of miles of American landscape. "And it was no easy task, I'll admit."

Taken aback by her lively response, her brother stared for a few moments, then laughed. "You haven't changed a bit. You're still as sassy as an alley cat."

Weeks of worry and stress caught up with Claire as she stared at her brother's face. Unable to contain the emotions any longer, she slung herself into Donald's arms and started crying.

"What the hell?" he muttered, then held her close, rocking her back and forth the way he'd done when she was a small girl frightened by a bad dream. "Settle down and tell me what you're doing here."

Claire sniffled, gulped some air, and nodded her head. Donald said something to the young woman who had answered the door.

"You speak Chinese?"

"A few words," Donald admitted. "Come in and sit down."

Once Claire was seated on a faded sofa with red and gold velvet pillows, she wasn't sure what to say to her brother. The young Chinese woman appeared again, carrying a tray with a small round pot and two dainty round bowls that Claire quickly discovered were Chinese teacups.

"This is Mae Ling," Donald said in the way of introduction, then stopped, offering no further information.

The young woman executed another faultless bow, then smiled, saying nothing.

Claire looked at Mae Ling more thoroughly. She was beautiful. Her skin was a soft golden color and her eyes were large and dark. Her hair was arranged in a braid that hung down her back, almost to her knees. After a moment, Claire realized she was looking at her brother's mistress. The thought of her brother and the young Chinese girl sharing a bed the way she'd shared hers with Garrett last night made Claire very self-conscious of the fact that she and Donald were no longer children.

"How did you find me?" her brother asked after Mae Ling had poured Claire some tea and disappeared a second time.

"It's hard to explain," Claire replied. "I've been in San Francisco for over two months."

"Doing what?" Donald asked rather abruptly. "Looking for me?"

"Most of the time," Claire admitted. How did she explain Garrett Monroe and her strange employment circumstances to a brother who looked like he wanted to throttle her for showing up on his doorstep?

Deciding the best way to handle what was certainly going to turn into a loud and difficult discussion, Claire straightened her shoulders and smiled. "I've taken a job," she began. "I'm a companion to a matron on Nob Hill." It wasn't all a lie. She had become a companion to Grams. "I wrote you that I was coming after Mrs. Shurman died. But when I arrived you weren't at the station. I rented a room in a boarding house, but my funds were getting desperately low and I needed a job."

The explanation seemed to satisfy her brother for the time-being. He reached inside a small lacquered chest and brought out a bottle of Irish whiskey. After pouring his cup half full of the amber liquor, he added some tea from the white porcelain pot. "I never got the letter," he admitted after sipping some of the elixir he'd created. "I didn't have any idea that you'd leave Cincinnati. It's your home."

"You can't have a home without family," Claire told him. "After Mama died, I knew you'd never come back. You'd outgrown what adventure the Ohio and Mississippi rivers had to offer. I sold the store. I wrote and told you that much. After Mrs. Shurman died, there was no reason to stay. You were in San Francisco, so that's where I wanted to be, too."

"Why are you walking with a cane?" he asked.

"I sprained my ankle," she said. "It's nothing serious."

A long, tense silence followed as Claire sipped her tea and tried to think of what to say to her brother. Donald seemed strangely upset over seeing her and she began to wonder if perhaps there might be some truth in what Hiram Wilson had reported to Garrett. Well, there was only one way to find out. It was obvious that her brother wasn't going to volunteer any information about his current status.

"Are you still working for the railroad?" Claire queried, trying her best to sound nonchalant about the inquiry.

"No," he replied, then smiled. "I'm working for a man here in Chinatown. This house is part of my salary."

"I see," Claire replied, managing a weak smile. "And Mae Ling, is she your wife?"

"No. And the rest is none of your business. You're my sister, not my mother."

The sharpness of his answer caught Claire off guard. Her cheeks warmed in embarrassment and she looked away. "I'm sorry. You're right. Mae Ling is none of my business."

When she focused on Donald again, he had a brooding look. Several heartbeats passed before he spoke again. "I'm sorry, too, Claire. I wasn't expecting to see you like this. Damn," he said, coming to his feet and pacing the room, "I can't take a sister under my wing right now."

Claire tried not to show her disappointment. She put her cup on the tray and stood up. "I should be getting back, Mrs. Monroe will be worried."

The name brought Donald's head around. "Theodora Monroe."

"Yes, do you know her?"

"Everyone in San Francisco knows who Theodora Monroe is," her brother replied. "And her grandson."

Claire busied herself putting her gloves back on. "Mr. Monroe is a very busy man. I rarely see him." She hated the lie, but she couldn't tell her brother, a brother who hadn't seen her in seven years and who apparently didn't care if he saw her again for another seven, that she'd spent the night making love with Theodora Monroe's grandson.

She walked to where Donald was standing and raised up on her tiptoes to kiss him on the cheek. "If you know who Mrs. Monroe is, then you know where to find me when you have time for a longer visit."

Her brother looked like he was struggling with an inner demon for a brief moment. When he pulled her into his arms and hugged her, Claire felt tears welling up in her eyes again. "I know this is silly," he said, "but don't think I've stopped caring about you. You're my sister for Christ's sake." He held her at arm's length. "There's a lot going on right now. As soon as I've finished some business, I'll come up the Hill and see you. I promise."

"Make it soon," Claire said, wishing with all her heart that Donald's words didn't frighten her so badly.

"As soon as I can," he promised, then walked her to the door. "Can you find your way back to the trolley stop?"

"Yes," she said. "I'll be fine. Don't worry."

The words hung in her throat, but she said them. It seemed like she was forever telling people not to worry about her. She'd be fine. But would she? After months of thinking that once she reached San Francisco she'd have at least a temporary life with her brother, she was back out on the street.

As Claire made her way to the corner where the trolley would stop to pick up passengers, she did her best not to cry. Donald had practically pushed her out the door, he'd been so anxious to get rid of her. Why? The brother she'd known hadn't changed on the outside, but he'd undergone a metamorphosis of some kind. She couldn't believe that he wasn't glad to see her, yet his actions had spoken otherwise.

She didn't want to believe that Hiram Wilson's report

rang with truth, but doubts clouded her mind, joining the ones she already harbored about Garrett's intentions. Her thought of several weeks past, that she'd jumped from the proverbial frying pan into the fire, had come true. Now that she'd found her brother, she was no closer to having the security of a home than she'd been the day she'd stepped off the train. Even worse, she had allowed herself to become intimately involved with a man who wasn't interested in marriage. What had happened to the levelheaded young woman who'd left Cincinnati?

She's fallen in love, Claire told herself. She must be out of her mind, but her heart still pounded with the same strong feelings that had caused her to open her arms to Garrett last night.

Her intense thoughts kept Claire from seeing the carriage stopping a few feet in front of her, but she recognized the voice when a man demanded to know if she'd lost her mind.

"What in the name of God do you think you're doing?" Garrett asked as he came out of the carriage and marched toward her. He had her arm in a viselike grip before Claire could think of a suitable answer. "I ought to paddle your backside," he grumbled under his breath as he all but dragged her toward the carriage. "If I ever catch you in Chinatown again, that's exactly what I'll do. Now, get in the carriage."

"Stop yelling at me," she snapped, then looked up to find Christopher Landauer smiling. "Excuse me," she said, getting into the carriage as quickly as her cane would allow. "The man has no manners," she said as she seated herself across from Garrett's partner. "No manners, at all."

"And you have no common sense," Garrett retorted, climbing in behind her. He sat down beside his friend.

"Do you have any idea what can happen to a woman alone on these streets?"

Christopher reached out the window, tapped the side of the carriage, and the driver pulled away from the sidewalk.

Claire folded her hands in her lap and tried to look as if she strolled in Chinatown on a daily basis. "I find this part of the city fascinating," she replied, offering him a serene smile. "The people are extremely interesting. And the colors. It's like walking through a circus."

Christopher laughed. "That a girl," he said. "Bluff him if you can."

She hadn't expected to see Garrett under these circumstances. At the moment, he didn't look like a man in the market for a mistress. In fact, Claire would almost bet that Garrett would like nothing better than the satisfaction of strangling her on the spot. Grateful for once that Christopher was aware of her unorthodox arrangement with the banker, Claire lifted her chin and met Garrett's fiery gaze.

"What did you expect me to do?" she asked. "I've been looking for my brother for months."

"You read Hiram's report," he said angrily. "You stole into my library, went through my desk, and read the damn report. Admit it. There's no other way you could have found your brother this quickly."

Claire wanted to shout back that if she'd stolen into Garrett's library, he'd done worse by stealing her heart, but she didn't. Instead, she fired another salvo. "You were supposed to help me find my brother, not keep his whereabouts a secret."

"This is getting interesting," Christopher said, leaning back and folding his arms. "Please, go on. If you two keep shouting at each other, I might be able to discern why Garrett pulled me out of a business meeting, tossed me into a carriage, and demanded that I go to

Chinatown with him. So far, the only thing I've been able to figure out, is that you"—he pointed at Claire—"aren't where you're supposed to be."

"She's supposed to be at home," Garrett said.

"It's your home," Claire snapped. "Not mine."

Garrett had to grit his teeth to keep from pulling Claire out of her seat and into his arms. He wanted to kiss her combative attitude away. He wanted to prove to her, as well as to himself, that she belonged to him, not some wayward brother.

"If your brother had proven to be the shining example of manhood you've led me to believe, then why were you walking alone. No man with any sense would let a woman wander about the streets like a lost puppy."

"I wasn't lost," Claire replied stiffly. "I was on my way to the trolley. And stop yelling at me."

"I'm not yelling," Garrett said, raising his voice with each word. "I'm trying to keep you from getting into more trouble than I've got time to get you out of."

"Of all the . . ." Claire stammered, so angry she wanted to bash the handsome banker over the head with her cane. "You're my employer, not my keeper."

"Don't overreact," Christopher cut in. "Even a Chinaman knows a lady when he sees one, Garrett. Claire wasn't in any real danger. At least as long as the sun is up. After dark, things change in this part of the city." He gave Claire a stern look. "I'm forced to agree with Garrett. I wouldn't suggest you call on your brother again without an escort, Miss Aldrich."

"She damn well better not try," Garrett said, sounding convincingly threatening.

Knowing she was outnumbered, Claire sat back and stared out the window. When the carriage stopped in front of the Landauer Hotel, she was relieved. She wasn't up to fooling Grams into thinking that she'd taken a leisurely ride down the hill to do a little shopping.

Garrett stepped out of the carriage, then turned to offer Claire his assistance. She took his hand begrudgingly. "We need to talk," Garrett said, as she stepped onto the sidewalk.

Claire looked at him. There was a fierce glow to his dark eyes and she knew she'd only witnessed the tip of his temper. He said nothing else until she was seated in the hotel's office. Christopher hadn't come upstairs with them. Claire knew he wanted to give her and Garrett the privacy their argument would require.

Claire sat in the chair, admiring the beautiful Chinese carving displayed in a glass case behind Christopher's desk while Garrett poured himself a drink.

Garrett walked to the window, overlooking Taylor Street, staring out at the city while he sipped his drink. Claire suspected he was trying to put a leash on his temper and in a small way she was grateful. On the other hand, she could use a fist-shaking, voice-raising argument. It might clear her mind of the tangled emotions she'd been carrying around for weeks.

When Garrett finally turned around to confront her, Claire knew she was in for more than a small helping of his temper. He looked more furious now than when he'd found her in Chinatown. A chill of apprehension ran up and down Claire's spine as Garrett set his empty glass on the windowsill and walked toward her.

"What did you tell your brother?" he asked in a chillingly calm voice.

Claire blanched at the sound of his voice. She'd never heard him use that particular tone before. The taut lines of his face told Claire that he expected her to repeat every word she'd exchanged with her sibling. Once again, she was seeing the man she'd seen last night in the foyer outside the library. There was nothing about the hardness of Garrett's features that would make anyone think he was a fancy banker who cared only for ledgers and profit sheets. His eyes looked cold and his mouth was drawn into a taut line that said if Claire tried to weasel her way out of anything with less than the truth, he'd make good on his threat and put her over his knee.

"I told him that I'd taken a job as a companion to Mrs. Theodora Monroe," she said defensively. "There was no reason to tell him anything different."

"Does he want you to live with him?"

"No," Claire said, wishing it didn't sting her pride so much to admit the truth. "He has other responsibilities at the moment. He . . ."

Garrett's smile was cynical. "He already has a *house-keeper*," he said. "Or didn't you have time to read all of Hiram's report. The young lady's name is Mae Ling and from what my investigator was able to find out, she's very young and very beautiful."

"Don't mock me," Claire said, shooting up from her chair. "Donald is my brother, not yours, and you have no right to keep me from seeing him."

Before Claire could say another word, Garrett's hand darted out and grabbed her arm. He pulled her against him. "I have every right," he said angrily. "Or have you forgotten what happened last night?"

Garrett didn't give Claire time to say she hadn't forgotten. He buried his hands in her hair, dragging her head back, then he kissed her. A hard, punishing kiss that quickly changed to one of relief, then tenderness.

For Garrett it was a primal reassurance that she was safe and back where she belonged—in his arms. He felt her struggling against his embrace, but the movements of her body only served to intensify what Garrett was feeling. He should release her, but he couldn't. When he'd seen her walking on Waverly Street, alone, anger had sluiced through his veins, followed by an innate need to gather her up and hold her close. The way he was holding her now.

Something called out inside of Claire to fight Garrett, to keep him from thinking that he owned her body as well as her heart, but she couldn't. The sweet pleasure of his kiss robbed her of her anger. Her arms went around his neck and she kissed him back.

Garrett's hands moved to her waist and he lifted her against him. A second later Claire felt herself being put on the desk. She shivered and moaned a throaty protest as he pushed her skirt up and her legs apart. His thigh came to rest between her legs and she could feel the heat of his body through the fabric of his trousers and the thin silk of her drawers. She had vowed not to let him touch her again, to take their one night of passion and be satisfied with the memory. But she couldn't. No matter how much she willed her heart to say no, her body was saying yes.

Garrett went on kissing her as his hands moved from her waist to her breasts. He thumbed her nipples, bringing them to an aching alertness. Claire pressed herself against his open palms. In turn, Garrett kneaded and squeezed and shaped her to fit his hand. The need to touch her, to possess her, stripped away his logic. Damn the woman.

"I have every right," Garrett growled, breaking the kiss and burying his face in the curve of Claire's throat. He kissed her neck. "You belong to me now."

Claire squeezed her eyes shut as he flicked open the buttons of her jacket and reached inside to caress her breasts through the thin fabric of her blouse. His fingers played with her nipples until they hardened and then he kissed her again. Helplessly Claire felt her mind going in one direction while her body followed Garrett's lead. She felt the unsettling return of the sensations that had wreaked havoc on her senses the previous night. The heat, the sound, the smell of Garrett invaded her mind, leaving nothing but the need for the man.

Sanity returned with the sound of Christopher's voice in the hallway. Garrett broke the kiss and stepped back. His chest rose and fell with a deep breath while Claire's hands flew to the front of her jacket to right the damage he'd done.

"Just a minute," Garrett called out when his partner knocked on the door. He didn't apologize as he helped Claire down from the desk. In fact, he looked at her as if she'd started the argument and kissed him, instead of the other way around.

Claire turned her face away from the door, confused over her feelings and angry that Garrett had put her in such an embarrassing situation. Her fingers fumbled with the buttons, and she knew her mouth was swollen from his kisses.

Garrett opened the door, standing between Claire and his friend. "Have Andy bring the carriage around. I want Claire taken home."

Garrett knew his voice was betraying him and that Christopher would know the reason why. His gaze dared his friend to verbalize his thoughts.

"Of course," Christopher replied. "Then I think you and I should have a little chat. I can't help you with your problem in Chinatown, if I don't know what it is."

Claire flinched inwardly at having her brother called a problem, but she didn't argue. She was too exhausted to think straight. She needed some time to sort things out. And some distance. The closer she was to Garrett, the more jumbled her thoughts became.

Garrett escorted her downstairs and into the carriage. Claire barely had the energy to return Andy's smile as the young man greeted her.

"Take Miss Aldrich straight home," Garrett instructed. He didn't have to tell Claire that he expected her to stay there. The steel hard look on his face said it for him.

"We'll talk this evening," he added as he handed her the cane.

Claire didn't answer him. She supposed she should feel some sort of satisfaction because he seemed concerned over her safety. Still, what should she expect. Garrett was a gentleman and even a gentleman showed concern for the woman he'd slept with the previous night. His temper and the way he'd kissed her in the hotel office weren't a confession of love and that's what it was going to take to keep Claire in the Nob Hill mansion.

Chapter Fifteen

Garrett returned to the hotel office. He walked to the whiskey decanters and poured himself another drink. He stared out the window, but all he saw was Claire's face, looking up at him with confusion and passion in her eyes. When he'd seen her walking in Chinatown, his heart had stopped for a cold second. When she'd argued with him in the carriage, he'd wanted to strangle her. A few minutes later, he'd wanted to lay her down on the desk and make love to her.

"Correct me if I'm wrong," Christopher said, breaking the silence, "but I think Miss Aldrich has advanced beyond the status of an employee."

"Mind your own business," Garrett told him. He lifted the glass to his mouth and downed the whiskey. It burned a path to his stomach and Garrett grimaced as he put down the glass and turned to face his friend.

"That's going to be hard to do if you want my help," Christopher replied. "What the hell is going on?"

"Her brother is living in Chinatown," Garrett said.

"That much was easy enough to figure out," his friend replied as he seated himself behind the desk. "What I don't understand is why you don't want Claire to see him. Is the fellow up to no good?"

"He's working for Chen Loo."

Christopher let out a long, low whistle. "That explains a lot of things."

"What do you know about the Chinaman?" Garrett asked, knowing his friend was his best source of information.

"Enough to know he's trouble. Chen Loo is Chinatown. He runs the city like an ancient warlord."

"Have you done business with him before?"

"If you want Chinese goods brought into the city, you have to do business with Chen Loo. No one on the docks is going to argue with a gang of paid assassins. If the Chinese know anything, it's how to kill a man."

Garrett pushed his confrontation with Claire out of his mind and concentrated on her brother. "Do you know anyone close enough to Chen Loo to find out what Donald Aldrich does to earn a house in Chinatown?"

Christopher nodded. "It may take a day or two. What if Claire decides to see her brother again?"

"She won't," Garrett said over his shoulder. He reached for the doorknob. "I'll lock her in the attic if necessary."

The sound of his friend's laughter followed him down the steps.

Knowing he needed some time to cool his temper, and his ardor, Garrett went to the bank. He spent the balance of the day reading correspondences, signing loan contracts, and watching the clock on his office wall slowly tick away the minutes until he could see Claire again.

When Garrett walked through the door of his home

he received a short request from Mrs. Smalley. His grandmother was waiting in the front parlor.

"Where's Claire?" he asked.

"Upstairs resting," the housekeeper told him, then frowned. "She went into town this morning. Libby tried to talk her out of it, but Miss Aldrich insisted that she had cabin fever. I'm afraid she ventured out of the house too soon. When she returned, she said her ankle was paining her and she went right upstairs. I was about to go up and ask if she wanted her dinner on a tray."

"I'll take it up to her after I've seen my grandmother," Garrett informed the housekeeper.

Grams set aside a book of poetry as Garrett walked into the parlor. Her temper had cooled along with his and she greeted him with a welcoming smile. "I assume you know that Claire went into the city this morning."

"I know," Garrett said. "I found her and sent her home."

"I thought as much," Grams said. "She didn't look very happy."

Garrett's bland expression turned into a mild frown. "I scolded her for leaving the house too soon."

Grams laughed. "Scolded. I doubt that, knowing your temper." She gave him a pensive look. "Your display of concern may have been too severe. Especially on the heels of what happened here last night. Claire is a very sensitive young lady."

"She has to learn that I won't tolerate her putting herself at risk," Garrett said, justifying his reaction. "And I don't want her leaving this house again until the cane is put aside completely and Dr. Baldwin assures me that her ankle is healed."

"I can't disagree," Grams told him, "but you can't lock her in her room. She's much too old for that."

"Perhaps," Garrett replied.

His grandmother's laughter was a surprise. "You

remind me more and more of your grandfather," she said. "And in many ways, Claire reminds me of myself. I wasn't always an agreeable young lady, you know."

Garrett smiled for the first time that day. "I can imagine," he teased. "In fact, if my grandfather was alive, I'm sure he'd have an endless repertoire of stories about your wayward youth."

"Perhaps." Grams mimicked his previous statement. "But I'm the only one who knows them now, and I'm not sharing. You'll have to muddle through this one all by yourself."

Garrett wasn't used to muddling through things. He liked a certain order to his life, a certain predictability. He was a banker, a man of numbers. Numbers made sense. Two and two were always four. Unfortunately, he couldn't apply the same logic to the lady upstairs.

Mrs. Smalley tapped on the parlor door, stuck her head inside, and told Garrett that Claire's dinner tray was ready.

"Don't scold her again," Grams cautioned him.

"I'll behave myself," Garrett assured her, knowing he wasn't going to have an easy time keeping the promise. Claire had a way of pricking his temper and there was a lot to be settled before he'd feel comfortable leaving her to her own devices again.

Garrett walked into Claire's room a few minutes later to find her sitting on the edge of the bed, looking at her ankle and frowning as if the expression could cure the inconvenient ailment.

"If you hadn't trekked all over the city this morning, your ankle wouldn't be hurting you now," he said, placing the dinner tray on the vanity table. "I've brought you dinner."

Claire gave him a fierce scowl, saying nothing.

Garrett smiled, walked to the door, and closed it.

"Go ahead, say whatever's on your mind. Everyone is downstairs, they won't hear you unless you scream."

"I don't want to scream," Claire said. "I want to get out of this house. I'm through play-acting."

"Are you?" Garrett mused in a dangerously low voice.

Wishing she could stand up and shout at the top of her lungs, Claire settled for the next best thing. She pushed herself back against the feather pillows, crossed her arms over her chest, and gave the banker a defiant stare. "Yes, I am. I adore your grandmother, but you're going to have to find another way to keep her content."

"It isn't my grandmother's contentment that concerns me at the moment," Garrett said. He lifted the linen towel off the tray. "You need to eat."

"I'm not hungry," Claire lied. She hadn't eaten breakfast and she'd been too upset to eat lunch. The food smelled wonderful and even though she was still upset, she was also hungry. But she wasn't in the mood to be agreeable and she wanted Garrett to leave the tray and vacate her room.

Instead, he carried the tray to the bed and sat down beside her. "Would you like for me to feed you?"

Garrett's eyes searched her pretty face and decided she was much too stubborn for her own good. He picked up the fork and dipped into a fluffy mound of mashed potatoes, then held the fork to Claire's mouth. "Open up, sweetheart. I know you're hungry."

Claire clamped her mouth shut and stared at the end of the bed.

Garrett wasn't going to go away. He was determined to make Claire understand that he wasn't her enemy. He was also equally determined to make her promise to keep her pretty rump on Nob Hill and away from Chinatown. He touched the tip of the fork to her lips. When Claire opened her mouth to insist that she didn't want to be fed like a child or an invalid, Garrett filled her mouth with mashed potatoes.

She wanted to protest, but she couldn't talk with a mouth full of food and Garrett kept feeding her while he calmly lectured her about the danger she'd put herself in that morning. "Chinatown isn't safe, regardless of what Christopher may think. I want your promise that you'll stay here until I've had a chance to speak with your brother personally."

Claire shook her head.

"You know nothing of his current activities," Garrett said. He held up his hand to silence her when she would have argued. "I understand that he is your brother, and that you want to believe the best of him. I'm not agreeing with Hiram's reported suspicions, I'm merely asking that you give me and yourself the time to make sure that your brother is indeed an honest man, capable of providing for himself and a family by legal means."

Claire mumbled something as she chewed on her food.

"You're a stubborn woman, Miss Aldrich," he told her. "But I'm more stubborn. If you think I won't lock this door and keep you here against your will, think again."

Claire swallowed hard, forcing a small piece of roast beef down her throat. "You wouldn't dare."

Garrett gave her the wicked smile she found so fascinating at times. "Oh, but I would. I'll do whatever I have to do to ensure the safety of my future wife."

"Our engagement is a sham," she said, pushing away his hand when he tried to stuff more food into her mouth. "You told me yourself that marriage holds no value in your life."

"Not any longer," Garrett informed her. "As of this morning, our wedding invitations are being engraved.

The tenth of August is the date, according to my grand-mother.''

"Oh, no." Claire groaned as her face reddened with color. "Grams knows what we ... I mean she heard . . .''

Garrett chuckled softly as he used a linen napkin to wipe a small bit of mashed potatoes off Claire's chin. "She knows."

Claire slumped against the pillows and covered her face with her hands. How could she face Grams again, knowing that the older woman had heard her moaning in Garrett's arms. "I'm so ashamed."

Garrett put down the fork and set the tray on the table beside the bed. Placing his hand under Claire's lowered head, he lifted her chin until she was looking at him. "You have nothing to be ashamed of," he said firmly. "If anyone's to blame for what happened last night, I am." His expression softened as he leaned for-ward to press a light, featherlike kiss against her mouth. "Nothing shameful passed between us last night, sweet-heart. I enjoyed you like I've enjoyed no other woman."

Claire's eyes took on a mutinous gleam as she pulled away from him. Enjoyment wasn't love. It was even less than passion. The last flicker of hope inside Claire died a cold and silent death. She'd been a fool to think that Garrett's physical affection had been anything more than lust and she'd been a fool to accept his offer, thinking in the back of her mind that what she felt for him could somehow move from her heart into his. Her voice was filled with conviction when she finally spoke. "I won't marry you."

Garrett was prepared for her argument. He knew he should be wooing Claire with words of love, but they didn't come easy to a man who, up until twenty-four hours ago, would have sworn the heart-shattering emo-tion didn't exist. His fiancée needed a firm hand and he wouldn't hesitate to use one. Claire might rule his heart, but Garrett meant to rule his home.

"What if you're carrying my child?" he asked her. He could see by her shocked expression that she'd been too busy contemplating her brother's situation to think about the consequences of her own actions. If she even knew such things. Her mother had died a long time ago and he doubted that Mrs. Shurman had tutored her on the delicate subject of intimacy. "There are ways to prevent a child from being conceived," he continued as if he were explaining an investment venture. "Unfortunately, I was too enthralled by your charms to incorporate them last night. You could very well be pregnant, Miss Aldrich, and I daresay that even a lady of your high spirits isn't independent enough to think she can raise a child alone. Not that I'd let you," he added firmly. "We will be married."

The words stung Claire far worse than Garrett realized. She turned her face away, refusing to look at him while she thought of a tiny babe suckling at her breasts the way its father had done the previous night. The image brought tears to her eyes and she blinked them away. She loved Garrett and she'd love to have his child, but she didn't want a marriage based on guilt or obligation.

"I've become a very proficient actress," she said, finally meeting his gaze. "Should the necessity arise, I'm sure I can convince almost anyone that I'm a widow with a child to raise."

"Over my dead body," Garrett said. He stared at her, his eyes as hard as the polished pewter cane resting beside the bed. Claire got the distinct impression that he'd be more than willing to put bars on the windows and doors to guarantee she didn't leave the mansion until the day of the wedding.

Garrett poured a glass of wine. Claire accepted it,

wishing she could drink the whole bottle. Her ankle was feeling somewhat better, and her stomach was finally full, but now her head was pounding. She took a sip of the wine and handed the glass back to Garrett.

"If you could send Libby up, I'd like to have my bath and go to sleep. I've very tired."

Claire closed her eyes and tried to concentrate on anything but the sound of Garrett moving about her room. She could hear the gentle clink of silverware and china as he removed the tray from the bedside table. A few moments later, she heard the door being opened, then closed. Thinking she was finally alone, she opened her eyes. Garrett had merely put the tray outside in the hallway. He was standing at the foot of the bed, seemingly content, as if he actually enjoyed looking at her. *Enjoyed.* God, how she hated that word.

Garrett knew he was pushing his luck to think that he could remain in Claire's room too much longer, but he wasn't about to go downstairs to his own dinner until he'd at least had the satisfaction of one kiss. He returned to the bed. Sitting on the edge, he stretched his arm over Claire's lap and balanced his weight on his right hand.

"I want a good night kiss."

Despite the anger and hurt Claire felt toward Garrett, she couldn't keep herself from wanting the kiss, as well. *It will be our last one,* she said to herself. *I'll return to Chinatown tomorrow and force Donald to be truthful with me. If I can't depend on my brother, then I'll depend on myself. I won't marry a man who doesn't love me. I won't.*

Unable to read her mind, Garrett lowered his head and covered her mouth with his own. He wove his fingers into her unbound hair and held her head tightly as his tongue moved over her lips, touching the corner of her mouth and the tiny pout of her bottom lip. When her lips parted to give him entry, Garrett's tongue swept inside her mouth and the kiss became more urgent, more demanding.

Claire returned the kiss with a wild violence that surprised her as much as it pleased Garrett. Her body ached to relive the wonderful magic of the previous night, and her heart hurt to think that she'd never again feel that alive.

Garrett's good intentions to collect a good night kiss and leave Claire to ponder their upcoming wedding disappeared as they mouth-dueled in the delightful, passionate act of pleasing one another. His hands moved from her hair to her shoulders, then downward, exploring and pressing, tracing each ridge of her ribs, then finding her breasts, hidden beneath layers of cotton and silk. Garrett wanted to reach for the hem of her skirt and draw it upward, one delicious inch at a time, but he had just enough sanity left to know that if he touched her that way he wouldn't be able to stop until she was lying naked beneath him.

Slowly, reluctantly, Garrett released her and stood up. "Sleep well, sweetheart. And promise me that you'll stay put until I can escort you to Chinatown myself."

Claire didn't want to lie to him, but she quickly decided one more falsehood couldn't damn her any more than she already was damned. She nodded, letting Garrett assume whatever he pleased.

Thinking he'd won at least one argument, Garrett swooped down, planted a quick hard kiss on her mouth, and left the room.

Claire stared after him, angry at her brother for putting her in a situation where she'd had to accept Garrett's employment in the first place. Men. She was beginning to dislike all of them.

* * *

The next morning, as the servants were stirring about in the kitchen and the sun was creeping over the horizon to shine on San Francisco Bay, Claire was dressed in her old suit. By the time Garrett woke up and walked drowsily into his dressing room to shave, Claire was at the trolley stop. With a small valise sitting beside her, she waited on the bench for the trolley to deposit its load of domestic workers at the top of the hill. She wasn't going to let Donald send her away with nothing but a hug and a poor excuse for his behavior this time. If her brother didn't want to do his duty and put a roof over her head, then she'd find another way to be free of Garrett Monroe.

Claire was too busy berating herself for her own foolishness in believing that Garrett felt any real affection for her to notice the man standing across the street. He was partially hidden by the large stone columns of a residential gate and she had no reason to look his way for more than a moment. Instead, she studied the skirt seam of her brown suit and wondered how long Garrett's enjoyment would have lasted before he turned to another woman.

She wasn't Belinda Belton, and although Claire had formed a friendship of sorts with the young woman, she couldn't imagine herself being a dutiful wife, enjoying the luxury of her husband's wealth and social status, while he dallied about with his mistress. If she couldn't have all of Garrett's heart, she'd have none of it.

The trolley arrived with a tingle of a brass bell and the hum of metal wheels. Several women, dressed in servants' uniforms, got off. Claire smiled briefly as the women passed by, then climbed aboard the trolley, valise in hand, and sat down behind the conductor. Confident of where she'd find her brother this time, Claire looked back over her shoulder. All she could see of the Monroe mansion was its white stone chimneys and the stucco walls surrounding the gardens. Looking forward again, at the metal rails slicing down the hill, Claire thought of her future. She had no idea how to begin a new life, yet she must. Once she was away from Garrett's intoxicating presence and irresistible kisses, perhaps she would be able to think clearly.

She wasn't overly concerned about being pregnant. One of her friends in Cincinnati had been married for almost three years before the birth of her first child and Bonnie had confessed on one occasion that her husband was a lusty man. Claire suspected that Garrett was a lusty man, as well, but they'd only shared one night together.

The man who'd been waiting across the street got on the trolley before it began its journey back down the hill. Dressed in a dark brown suit, he paid Claire no mind as he moved past her to take a seat in the rear of the small train.

The city was just waking up as the trolley moved down the elite hill of San Francisco and into the heart of the city. The sun warmed the air and Claire tried to think pleasant thoughts as the narrow trolley was joined by buggies and carriages on the busy downtown streets. Store clerks were sweeping the sidewalks in preparation for a new day of business and Claire could hear the mournful sound of ship whistles announcing departures at the nearby docks.

The trolley made its way down Waverly Avenue and into Chinatown. Once again she was amazed by the colors and sounds and scents of the Oriental community. The morning sun was chasing the last of the fog from the streets and the soft chatter of shopkeepers and street vendors filled the air.

When the trolley stopped, Claire picked up her valise, filled with what few possessions she could call her own, and stepped onto the street. Thankfully her ankle was being cooperative and she walked toward the small house where her brother lived. The man who'd joined her on the trolley at the top of Nob Hill got off, too. She stepped off the sidewalk to cross a narrow alley when the man came up behind her, clasped a hand over her mouth, and pulled her into the shadows.

Claire fought him, dropping her valise to the ground, but he was tall and twice her weight and no matter how hard she kicked, his hand didn't move. Two Chinese men joined her abductor and Claire was pulled deeper into the alley. Claire continued kicking, moaning as her injured ankle did its best to inflict some damage to the man's shins. Finally her abductor's hand dropped away from her mouth and Claire started to scream for help. The sound was muffled by a cloth pressed against her lower face. A horrible odor attacked her nose and tears flooded her eyes. Claire looked up at a red and gold banner fluttering in the wind just before her world went black.

Chapter Sixteen

"Mr. Monroe!"

Garrett looked up at the frantic calling of his name, closing the ledger that he'd been working on. The bank clerk who had announced his grandmother the previous day came rushing into his office. The man looked like he was ready to jump out of his skin and for a moment Garrett thought the bank was being robbed.

"What is it?" he asked, looking past the frazzled young man and out into the main lobby of the bank. Everyone else seemed calm enough and Garrett relaxed momentarily, thinking the clerk was probably fretting over nothing but a disgruntled customer who didn't want to understand bank policy and had insisted on seeing the head cashier, who was off for the week.

"A message from your grandmother," the clerk said, holding the crumpled piece of paper. "Your driver said it was most urgent."

Garrett snatched the note from the clerk's hand and

broke the seal. He read the short but blunt statement, crushed the paper in his fist, and headed for the door. Looking over his shoulder, he gave the clerk a curt command. "Send someone to the Landauer Hotel. I want Mr. Landauer to meet me at my house. Immediately."

"Yes, sir."

Garrett was outside of the bank in seconds and climbing inside the buggy. "Don't waste any time," he said to Henry. "Get me home as quickly as you can."

A snap of the short driving whip and the horse hitched to the buggy leaped forward. Garrett cursed as he unfolded his fist and read the crumpled message a second time: *Come home at once. Claire missing.*

Garrett knew Claire wasn't missing. The little hellion had taken herself off to Chinatown again, he was sure of it. As Henry expertly weaved his way through the crowded city streets, managing to avoid several small children and a barking dog that nipped at the buggy's wheels, Garrett vowed that this time he would lock Claire in her room. After, he'd beat her black and blue.

By the time Garrett got out of the buggy and rushed up the stone steps leading to the front door, he was shaking with anger. And fear. Hiram Wilson had called on him that morning to report that his discussions with several other railroad officials confirmed his initial suspicions. Donald Aldrich was suspected of helping Chen Loo orchestrate the transportation of opium out of San Francisco, using the Union Pacific Railroad to reach St. Louis and cities to the east.

"Your grandmother is in the parlor," Mrs. Smalley said, meeting Garrett at the front door. "I sent for Dr. Baldwin. She's so worried, I'm afraid she'll have another attack."

Garrett stopped in his tracks, took a long deep breath, and forced a calm, confident smile to his face. As he stepped into the parlor, he appeared to be in no particular hurry.

"What's this about Claire?" he asked, as he sat down beside his grandmother and reached for her hand. It was cold and Garrett hoped he wouldn't lose both the women he loved.

"I thought she was sleeping late," Grams said. "But when Libby went to her room, she was gone. I sent for you right away."

"As you should have," Garrett replied. "But there's no reason to get yourself in a tether. I'll find her and bring her home."

"You argued didn't you?" Grams said. "I was afraid you would. You can be so damn obstinate at times." She gave him a frustrated look. "Well, whatever you did, undo it, and get that girl back in this house."

Garrett didn't answer her. Instead, he poured Grams a small sherry and insisted she drink it. "Now, I want you to relax until Dr. Baldwin gets here. I'll find Claire, and she'll be back before you wake up from your afternoon nap. I promise."

Garrett found Libby in the foyer, wringing her hands and looking responsible for Claire's unpredictable actions. "Stay with my grandmother," Garrett told the maid. "I don't want her left alone."

"Yes, sir," she replied and hurried into the parlor.

Mrs. Smalley appeared from another of the rooms fronting the main entrance. Garrett told her to send someone to the stables. He wanted two horses saddled and ready by the time Christopher arrived. He didn't have time to waste on a cumbersome buggy or trolley schedules.

Marching into the library, he unlocked his desk and withdrew a small wooden case. He flipped the engraved top back to reveal a pistol. He was well versed with firearms and within minutes he had the gun loaded and inside his jacket pocket. After what seemed like a small eternity, Christopher joined him in the library.

"What the hell is going on?" his friend asked, noting the concern on Garrett's face. "Your bank teller showed up looking like he'd just seen the devil himself, and you don't look much better."

"Claire went to Chinatown again," Garrett said. "I need someone who speaks the damnable language. Let's go."

Christopher didn't argue. Within minutes, they were riding down the hill. When Donald Aldrich opened the door of his house, he was greeted by Garrett's fist. The blow was totally unexpected and Claire's brother toppled back against the door, his hand coming up to nurse his bruised jaw.

"Where is she?" Garrett demanded.

"Who the hell are you?" Donald demanded, stumbling to his feet. "And what the hell do you want?"

"Your sister," Garrett said, advancing into the narrow entryway. He twisted his fingers into the front of Donald's shirt and pushed him against the wall. "Claire. Where is she?"

"On the Hill taking care of some old woman," Donald answered, thinking he'd opened his door to a madman. "Now, get out of my house before I . . ."

"Do what?" Garrett challenged him, itching to beat the man's face into a pulp. "Call your friend Chen Loo to avenge you. Don't threaten me," he said in a coarse whisper. "I'd like nothing better than to toss your mangy hide into the Bay."

"Easy, old friend," Christopher said, prying his way between Garrett and Claire's bewildered brother. "Let the man talk."

Garrett needed to release his anger and Donald Aldrich made a perfect target, but he forced himself to rein in his emotions and do what Christopher suggested.

Slowly his hand opened and Claire's brother, free of the banker's deathlike grip, slumped against the wall.

"I haven't seen Claire since yesterday," Donald Aldrich said, then rubbed his jaw and gave Garrett a lethal look. "Not that it's any of your business. She's my sister."

"And she's going to be my wife," Garrett said without preamble.

Donald looked from Garrett to the man standing beside him, then back to the one who'd clipped him with a sound right hook. A trickle of blood was seeping from his split lip. He wiped his mouth with the sleeve of his shirt. "She didn't say anything about getting married."

"That doesn't surprise me," Christopher said with a spark of amusement. "Considering the groom."

"Shut up," Garrett said over his shoulder. "If you haven't seen Claire, then where is she? She left the house before the sun was over the Bay."

"You're that banker, Monroe," Donald said, realizing that he had a lot to learn before he'd have an explanation for being greeted with a fist that packed a helluva wallop.

"Garrett Monroe, at your service," Christopher said. "And I'm Christopher Landauer. A friend of the pugilist, here. We're both concerned about your sister's hasty disappearance."

"Maybe she doesn't like your friend," Donald retorted. "Can't say that I blame her."

Garrett was on the verge of forgetting his common sense and hitting the man again when a young Chinese woman opened the front door of the house and came inside. She was carrying a basket of fruit and Garrett knew she must be Mae Ling, Donald's mistress. One look at her lover's bruised jaw and bloody mouth and she dropped the basket and rushed to his side.

Garrett waited impatiently while the two people

exchanged words in Chinese. Hearing Donald Aldrich speak the language fluently only increased Garrett's convictions that the man made his living smuggling opium for Chen Loo.

"It seems that Claire's brother doesn't know anything more about his sister's disappearance than you do," Christopher said, interpreting what was being said.

Mae Ling pulled a handkerchief from her pocket and wiped at the blood seeping from Donald's cut lip. Another flurry of Chinese followed the affectionate gesture.

"He's concerned," Christopher said, keeping up with the conversation.

"He should have been concerned seven years ago," Garrett said. "Before he walked out on his family."

Donald threw the punch this time, but Garrett was ready for it. He caught the man's fist, twisting his arm behind his back, and pushed him against the wall "You and I are going to have a nice long chat," Garrett gritted out. "I want to know why you sent Claire away in such a hurry yesterday morning."

Donald mumbled a curse, then relaxed, knowing Garrett had the advantage. "Okay, let me go and we'll talk."

A short time later, Garrett and Claire's brother were glaring at each other, while Christopher conversed in Chinese with Mae Ling. Every few seconds, Donald would look at his petite mistress as if to tell her not to say anything too important.

"Are you sure Claire didn't come here this morning?" Garrett asked sharply.

"I'm sure," Donald returned just as curtly. "I think it's time you told me a thing or two, Mr. Monroe. Why would Claire run away from your house?"

"I warned her against seeing you again," Garrett replied honestly. "Unlike your sister, I'm not foolish enough to believe that being her older brother makes you a saint."

Donald flinched at the well-aimed insult, then shrugged his shoulder. "I don't even know how she found me."

"She didn't," Garrett told him. "I did. Or should I say, a well-paid investigator found you."

Letting out a frustrated sigh, Donald sat down on the faded sofa and told Mae Ling to busy herself elsewhere. The young Chinese vanished behind a silk screen that separated the narrow front room of the house from the rest of the residence.

"Claire said she was being paid to be a companion to your grandmother."

"That's how our original relationship began," Garrett admitted. "Since then, it's changed. I have every intention of marrying your stubborn sister once I find her."

Donald smiled, then grimaced as his lip reminded him that Garrett was as talented with his fists as he was with money. "I don't remember Claire being stubborn. She was always a sweet little thing."

"Time changes people," Garrett commented sarcastically. "As well you know, Mr. Aldrich. A few years ago you were a valued employee of the Union Pacific Railroad."

"I still am," Donald replied. "Of course, no one's supposed to know that. Least of all, Chen Loo."

Christopher arched a blond brow and looked at his friend. "I think we've stumbled upon a mystery."

"There's nothing mysterious about it," Donald told them. "And I wouldn't be talking at all if I thought either one of you had anything to do with the Chinaman. Regardless of the banker's obvious opinion of me, Claire is my sister, and I love her."

"Why didn't you meet her at the train station when she arrived in San Francisco?" Garrett asked.

"I didn't know she was coming," her brother replied. "I was moving around, jumping from one odd job to another to make it look like I was desperate for something good to come my way. I never got the letter she sent.''

Garrett began putting the pieces of the puzzle together. ''The railroad wants you to find out how Chen Loo is smuggling opium.''

''That's the long and short of it,'' Donald admitted. He gave Garrett a hard look, then shifted his attention to Christopher. ''I've been working on this project for over a year. The charges to dismiss me from the railroad were part of the plan. I report to the owners, personally. Which means, I'm up to my elbows in lies and secrets,'' he admitted. ''That's why I didn't want Claire hanging around yesterday. Chen Loo doesn't trust his own shadow.''

''What about the girl?'' Garrett asked. ''Is she a link to Chen Loo?''

''No. I've known Mae Ling for a long time. Her father worked on the railroad with me. He's the one who taught me to speak Chinese.''

''If Claire isn't here, then where the hell is she?'' Garrett asked impatiently.

''I don't know,'' Donald told him. ''Does she have any other friends in the city?''

''No,'' Garrett said. ''Not anyone she can depend on.''

He didn't have the time to explain that Claire couldn't call on the people she'd met posing as his fiancée without creating questions he was sure she didn't want to answer. And he wasn't able to confess to Claire's brother that his actions demanded a wedding. Garrett turned to Christopher. ''Find Hiram for me, then send Andy out to start looking for Claire. Have him try the boardinghouse where Claire was staying before she moved to the Hill. Then have someone check the train station. I want her found.''

Christopher was out the door and on his way before Garrett finished giving orders.

"Sounds like you're in love with my sister," Donald remarked. "Glad to know it. I'd like to see her happy."

"She won't be when I find her," Garrett predicted. "Get your coat. This is a big city. I need all the help I can get."

By six o'clock that evening, no amount of help had located Claire. Garrett returned to his house, dreading what he could and couldn't say to his grandmother. Christopher and Donald were with him. All three men had been combing the city since that morning, asking storekeepers if a young lady had inquired about employment and checking on tickets purchased at the city's train depots. Hiram Wilson and a small band of men were still out searching, aided by Andy Wilkes and several of the hotel's other male employees.

Garrett took off his gloves, mentally cataloging all the things that could happen to a young woman alone in a city the size of San Francisco. He'd been silent most of the day, with the exception of the orders he'd given regarding the search. Sensing his concern, increased by his inability to find Claire, his companions followed him inside.

"She couldn't leave the city without funds," Garrett said, as he ushered the two men into the library for a much-needed drink. "She hasn't touched the money I deposited in her account. And I doubt that she had more than trolley fare in her pocket."

Claire's brother sampled the expensive whiskey before he sat in a chair and looked at Garrett. "I think it's time you told me more about your *relationship* with my sister. Like, what in the hell did you do to Claire to make her disappear like gin on Saturday night."

Christopher Landauer laughed. "I think it's time to pay the piper, old friend."

Garrett wasn't amused. The longer Claire was missing, the more worried he got. The thought of her being alone somewhere in the city, with no money and no one to look after her, was ripping his guts apart.

Knowing he didn't have any choice, and convinced that Donald did indeed care about his sister, Garrett confessed the scheme he'd hatched to keep his grandmother content. He omitted making Claire his lover, but the lack of words didn't keep Donald from looking like an avenging angel when he came out of the chair. "You son of a bitch," he growled. "I ought to . . ."

"After we've found Claire," Garrett said, knowing he deserved whatever Donald Aldrich could dish out. "Until then I need your help to keep my grandmother from making herself sick with worry. Can you convince her that Claire is staying at your home. Tell her that you want Claire to spend some time with you before she's handed over to me as my wife. I don't care what you say, just make it convincing."

"I'll try," Donald said begrudgingly. "But so help me God, Monroe, if you don't make my sister happy, I'm going to bury that expensive hide of yours six feet deep."

Garrett smiled. "I'll make her happy. Claire loves me."

"I'm not so sure," Donald replied skeptically. He straightened his tie and dusted off his jacket. "Let's get this over with. It's getting dark and I want to find my sister before I lose my temper and make her a widow before she's been a wife."

"Give Grams my respect," Christopher told Garrett. "I'll be at the hotel if you need me. Until then, try and be patient. No news is good news, or so I've heard."

Garrett wished he could be as optimistic as his friend. Where in the hell had Claire gone? The why he already knew. She was upset because he hadn't trusted her brother and she no doubt thought that he'd proposed marriage out of remorse over taking her virginity. Her refusal last night was proof that he needed to get the words said.

I love you.

He'd said them enough to Grams and they hadn't stuck in his throat, but saying them to Claire was different. He knew Grams loved him in return, she was his grandmother, she was family. Claire . . . God, he hoped he was right. She had to love him. If she didn't, Garrett wasn't sure what he'd do.

For years he'd fooled himself into thinking that he had everything a man could possibly want; money, power, prestige. The void of his parents' death had been filled by Grams, and he'd been content to draw on that love, convinced that it was enough. Garrett lifted the whiskey glass to his mouth and closed his eyes. He had everything, but the woman he wanted. Claire had waltzed into his life with her innocent hazel eyes and her Midwest attitudes and disarmed him as neatly as an army of trained soldiers. Her concern for his grandmother, her devoted looks, that he prayed now weren't pretense but genuine, had broken through his well-constructed shell one day at a time. She'd transformed his elegant life into a yearning to simply come home and see her face across the table, to hear her voice, to watch her as she moved around a room. He'd been bewitched the moment he'd seen her, and he'd fought it tooth and nail, telling himself it was nothing more than a healthy dose of lust. God, he'd been such a fool.

A knock on the library door and Mrs. Smalley's voice interrupted Garrett's bout of self-condemnation. His grandmother was once again waiting in the parlor. He looked at Claire's brother. "She's a grand old lady and I expect a grand performance."

"I'll do my best."

Fortunately, Donald's acting abilities were almost as good as his sister's. He bowed over Theodora's hand and gave her a charming smile. "I'm afraid I'm to blame for your fright, Mrs. Monroe. I wasn't pleased to learn that your grandson had snatched up my sister's heart before I'd had so much as a day of her company. She came to see me yesterday and I suggested that she stay with me for a while, to make sure her feelings for Garrett were strong enough to make the commitment of marriage a real one. She didn't like it, of course," Donald looked at Garrett. "Neither did your grandson. I told Claire I wanted her in my house bright and early this morning. That's where she is now. Pouting and brooding because I'm still not sure if she should marry the first man who asks her."

"Did my grandson give you that bruise, Mr. Aldrich?" Grams asked, looking at Donald's discolored jaw.

Donald smiled. "No, ma'am. I got into a fight in a saloon. I've got a temper and I don't like it when men cheat at cards."

Garrett moved to the mantel and prayed that Grams would believe one more Aldrich performance. He had to keep her calm until he could find Claire. He had to keep himself calm. Claire wasn't entirely lacking in good sense. Surely, she'd taken refugee in a boardinghouse or a small, inexpensive hotel. Garrett told himself that, but he didn't believe it. She'd gone to Chinatown, he was sure of it.

"Why didn't Claire tell me that you wanted her to stay with you?" Grams asked suspiciously. "It's not as if we're strangers. I've become very fond of your sister, and I'm anxious for her and Garrett to marry."

Donald hesitated and Garrett took over.

"You were right," Garrett said, stepping onto the proverbial stage. "Claire and I argued last night. She told me that Donald wanted her to stay with him. I insisted that she not leave the house. One thing led to another, and I'm afraid she felt forced to sneak out this morning to keep the argument from beginning anew."

Grams didn't look totally convinced, but she looked relieved that Claire hadn't been misplaced. Little did she know that her grandson had no idea where to look next. Grams turned to give Donald a brief smile. "Tell Claire that a few days away from Garrett might do her good. My grandson does tend to be overbearing at times, but I'm sure she can forgive the fault. They do love each other, Mr. Aldrich, and in spite of your doubts, my grandson will make Claire a wonderful husband."

"I'm beginning to believe that myself," Donald said. "I'll tell Claire you inquired about her, and don't worry, I won't keep her for long."

"Thank you for coming to see me," Grams told him. "I assume that Claire's asked you to give her away."

"I'd be honored," Donald said, sounding like a proud older brother. "Good night, Mrs. Monroe."

Garrett breathed a sigh of relief once the interview with his grandmother came to an end. He walked to the settee and sat down. "Don't worry. I'll patch things up with Claire and have her home in a day or two." He looked at the doorway where Donald had just made his exit. "Her brother is very protective of her. It took me most of the afternoon to convince him to let me see her."

Grams still didn't look totally convinced. "There's more to your disagreement with Claire than you're telling me, young man, but I won't pry any further. For the time-being," she added. "I do expect to see both Claire and her brother for Sunday dinner. Make sure I'm not disappointed."

"They'll be here," Garrett said, thankful that he'd delayed one catastrophe so he had time to deal with the other. He kissed his grandmother good night. "I'll be at the hotel. Get some sleep."

Taking his leave, Garrett and Donald were about to join Hiram Wilson to search for Claire when Christopher met them on the front steps of the mansion.

"I thought you were going back to the hotel?"

"I was," Christopher replied. "But someone left this note in my carriage."

He handed Garrett a piece of white rice paper.

Unfolding the note, Garrett stared down at it for a moment, then lifted his eyes to his friend. The lettering was Chinese. "What does it say?"

"That Chen Loo has Claire and he wants fifty thousand dollars for her."

Donald cursed and reached for the note. "Damn that Chinaman," he said. He read the message. "He's on to me," Donald said, crushing the note in his clenched fist. "He must have someone watching the house."

"Will he hurt her?" Garrett asked. His blood had turned to ice. He'd never wanted to kill a man before, but he wanted to kill the Chinaman—with his bare hands.

"Not if you pay the money," Christopher replied. "The Chinese believe in honor. You deliver the money. They deliver Claire."

"Where?"

"It doesn't say," Donald said. "The Chinese take their time with this sort of thing. They're experts at mental warfare. We've been instructed to wait at the hotel. We'll get another message."

Garrett marched toward the waiting carriage. "If Chen Loo or his cohorts have so much as touched her, I'll have their heads to decorate my garden wall," he said. He wrenched the door of the carriage open, almost tearing it off its hinges and climbed inside.

Claire's brother and Christopher joined him, neither

one commenting on the banker's words. There was no doubt in their minds that Garrett meant what he'd said. At that moment, Garrett looked more like a gunslinger than a banker. His eyes glowed with a cold hatred that made his friends, old and new, grateful they weren't on the receiving end of his anger.

Chapter Seventeen

It hurt to blink her eyes. Claire leaned against the wall and put her hands to her temples. It felt like a train was thundering through her head at full speed. Her nose and throat were raw and she knew it was from the chloroform that had been used to render her unconscious.

But why?

She looked around the sparsely furnished room. The walls were painted a dull yellow and the baseboards and door trimmings were black. Wherever she was, she was still in Chinatown. Her cane was gone and her ankle was throbbing because she'd kicked the man who had attacked her more than once. She was sitting on a short, thin mattress and there was a small table and a pillow across the room. A gas fixture, suspended from the ceiling, gave off a dull light. No windows. Nothing, except the fierce pounding in her head and the surety that she was in trouble. Big trouble.

Her mind raced despite the pain and she came up with two possible explanations for her kidnapping. One was that Chen Loo or one of his associates had seen her visiting her brother and they thought to use her to get Donald to do something for them. The other possibility was that she'd been followed when she'd left Chinatown the previous day and knowing Garrett Monroe was one of the city's wealthiest men, she'd been taken to hold for ransom.

Either way, Claire knew that Garrett must be frantic trying to find her. She had no way of knowing what time it was. In a room without windows, she had no way of gauging the time of day. Her body told her that she'd been unconscious for several hours. Her legs were cramped and her back ached from lying on the uncomfortable pallet.

Claire was wishing for something to drink when the door opened and a plump Chinese woman came into the room. The door was shut behind her and Claire heard the distinct sound of the lock being set once again. The woman looked to be sixty or perhaps even older. Her face was brown and wrinkled, as were her hands. Her hair, grayed by age, was pulled back into a braid that hung down her back. Her eyes were round and dark and held the same blank expression as her face. She was wearing loose black trousers under a blue and gold embroidered robe that reached just below her knees. Her sandals made a dull sound on the wooden floor as she walked across the room and placed a tray on the table.

"Where am I?" Claire asked, struggling to her feet. Without the cane, she used the wall for support, edging her way toward the woman.

The woman ignored her, not even glancing Claire's way when she spoke. Once a cup of tea had been poured and a bowl of rice set on the table, the woman turned to leave.

Claire reached out and grabbed her by the sleeve. "Who are you? What do you want?"

The woman answered in Chinese. Her tone was sharp as she pushed Claire's hand away and walked to the door. It was opened and she disappeared without looking back.

More frightened than she'd ever been in her entire life, Claire slumped to the floor and stared at the door. Tears came to her eyes, running down her face in a silent stream of despair as she realized that whoever was holding her captive cared nothing about right or wrong. She was a pawn in a game she didn't understand and she couldn't even communicate with her captors.

The aroma of the tea finally reached her nostrils and Claire made her way to the squatty bamboo table. She drank and felt better and then knowing she was going to need all her strength she forced herself to eat the rice. She had to use her fingers, since the Chinese woman had left her no silverware, and the meager meal went slowly. After a second cup of tea, her throat felt better and her headache had subsided a little.

She thought of Garrett, of his handsome face and stubborn nature, of his silver eyes and the arrogant way he'd smiled at her when he'd demanded a good night kiss, and tears welled up in her eyes again. She'd made love with him, but she hadn't told him that he was loved.

Claire regretted it now, wondering if she'd ever see him again, if she'd ever be able to say the words. Even though she knew that Garrett didn't want to hear them, she had an insatiable need to say them. To hear them rolling off her tongue, to free her body and mind and heart of the words.

Thinking of Garrett, of his mulish attitude and his gentle embraces, made Claire's heart clutch in her chest. A sadness she hadn't thought possible enveloped her and she knew in that moment that her plans to start a new life without the banker would be an impossible achievement. No matter how far she traveled or how long she lived, Garrett would always be a part of her.

The door opened again and Claire looked up to find two men. They were slender and dressed entirely in black and she felt a new wave of fear wash over her. One of the men motioned her to her feet and when she finally managed to stand, he snapped out a few Chinese words and pointed toward the door. Claire understood enough to know that she was supposed to go with them. Limping and biting her lower lip against the pain, she slowly made her way toward the door. Once she was outside, the two men changed positions. One led the way down a narrow corridor while the other walked behind her.

A few painful steps later, Claire was forced to stop in front of another black door. It was opened from the inside. The old Chinese woman stepped aside and the man behind Claire gave her a not-so-gentle push to get her inside. When she stumbled, the Chinese woman said something that sounded like a reprimand and the man disappeared, shutting the door with a loud click.

Claire looked around. Once again, the room lacked windows, but it was very different from the one she had woken up in an hour or so ago. The walls were painted a soft green and a mural of a Chinese garden decorated the largest wall, opposite the door. There were candles instead of gaslights and the flickering light gave the small room an intriguing allure, not romantic, but softer and less dangerous than the one in which she'd been confined since her kidnapping.

There was a tall wooden tub in the center of the room. Wisps of steam lifted toward the ceiling. A low bench stood next to the tub and on a low rectangular table to the side there was a thick white towel. The Chinese woman helped Claire to stand. Once she was supporting her own weight, precariously but managing to stand alone, the woman's hands went to the buttons on the front of Claire's jacket. Claire tried to slap them away, but the woman chattered something at her and went right on trying to undress her. A few minutes later, Claire was standing in nothing but her pantaloons and camisole.

The woman slapped her hands together, saying something that made no sense to Claire, and waved at the tub. Claire looked at the inviting water. She inhaled. The air, or was it the water, was scented and she longed to let the steamy bath ease her aches and pains. While the Chinese woman gathered up the clothes that had been tossed to the floor, Claire walked to the tub. Feeling awkward and shy, she stripped off the last of her clothing and got in. Her captors might be considered barbarians by some, but at least they appreciated cleanliness.

The water felt wonderful. Claire stepped up on the bench and eased her body into the tub. She was amazed to discover that the water came up to her shoulders. There was a small bench built into the tub itself and she sat on it, lessening the strain on her ankle. Then the plump Chinese woman opened the door, tossed Claire's clothes into the hall and closed the door again.

Claire wanted to protest, but she sensed that the woman didn't understand English any better than she understood Chinese.

Claire was even more surprised when the Chinese woman stepped up on the bench with a large sponge in her hand. She scooped up some water, wet the sponge, and began washing Claire's back. The natural abrasion of the sponge against her skin felt wonderful and Claire let out a soft moan. A short time later, after being bathed like a child in the scented water, Claire felt the old woman's hands reaching for the pins in her hair. She was treated to a thorough shampooing that left her hair soft and silky and clinging to her shoulders and back as she was helped from the tub and handed the thick towel. Claire wrapped it around her and sat down on the bench, which doubled as a footstool.

The old woman handed her another towel for her hair, mumbled a few short words, and left the room. Claire listened for the sound of the lock and when she didn't hear it, she was tempted to flee the room. But how far would she get, wet and naked and with an ankle that could barely support her weight? The answer became irrelevant when the woman reappeared in less than a minute. She motioned impatiently that Claire was taking too long to dry herself, then moved to the table and laid down what Claire assumed was a change of clothing.

Garrett paced the hotel office with the ferocity of a wild animal. It was almost two in the morning and there was still no word from Chen Loo. Donald had been given a room to rest and although there was several vacancies in the hotel, Garrett couldn't fathom sleeping in one of the elegant suites while Claire was being held in the claws of the Chinaman.

He stopped measuring the room as the door opened and Christopher stepped inside.

"A rather handsome Chinaman just delivered this to the front desk," he said, holding out a small fold of paper. "Chen Loo wants a meeting with me."

Garrett snatched the note from his friend's hand, knowing he wouldn't be able to make sense out of the strange Oriental writing, but needing to see it nevertheless.

"Do you have the money ready?"

Garrett nodded. "Chen Loo will get what he wants," he said harshly. "But not until I have Claire at my side."

"I've instructions to act as the go-between," Christopher told him. "I'll ask Chen Loo to let me see Claire. I'm sure I won't have more than a few minutes with her, if that, but I'll try to let her know that she won't be his prisoner much longer."

"Do you have any idea where he might be keeping her?" Garrett asked.

Christopher helped himself to a cup of the coffee one of the hotel maids had brought up earlier. "She could be anywhere," he said, adding a small helping of sugar to the black brew. "Chen Loo owns half of Chinatown. It would take weeks to search every building."

"Tell me exactly what the note says," Garrett instructed his friend. "I don't want any surprises."

His biggest surprise was discovering just how far in love he'd fallen. The warmth of the day had vanished the moment he'd discovered that Claire was missing and the night had taken on the color of lifeless black when she still wasn't found. The more he thought about her being locked in some strange room in Chinatown with no one to comfort her, no one to hold her close, no one to love her, Garrett's guts knotted so tightly he almost doubled over with the pain.

The anger that had devoured Garrett when Christopher had told him that Chen Loo was Claire's prison master had taken on a new dimension in the long hours since midnight. Instead of burning his insides, it had seeped into his veins, becoming a part of him the same way Claire had become a part of him. Invading his every thought. He'd told his friend that the money was ready, and it was. He'd gone to the bank himself and filled the leather suitcase that was now sitting at the end of

Christopher's desk. But Chen Loo wasn't going to get the blood money he was demanding for Claire, not if Garrett had his way. Hiram had joined him at the bank, along with several armed men to act as bodyguards while Garrett transported the large amount of cash from the bank to the hotel. He'd asked the investigator to make sure wherever they went to redeem Claire, they wouldn't go alone. Once Claire was back in his arms, where she belonged, Garrett intended to make Chen Loo and his Chinese cohorts pay the price of their folly. If necessary, he'd use the fifty thousand in the suitcase to track the fat Chinaman to the ends of the earth.

Claire belonged to him and the Chinese drug lord had signed his death warrant when he'd touched her.

Unaware of his friend's plans, Christopher sipped his coffee and translated the note.

"I'm to go to the Tin How Temple and wait for someone to take me to Chen Loo. Once I've been given instructions, I'll return for you and we'll get on with the actual exchange."

"I want Claire out of there as quickly as possible," Garrett said.

"So do I," Christopher agreed. "Don't worry. I've had dealings with Chen Loo before. He may not be conventional in his approach to business, but he's a man of his word."

Garrett wasn't so sure, but he kept his doubts to himself. "When do you leave?"

Christopher looked at his pocket watch. "Andy is hitching up the buggy. I'm to be at the Temple by four o'clock."

"Why don't you try to get some sleep," Christopher added, putting down his coffee cup. "If I know Chen Loo he will want this business taken care in his usual efficient manner. Probably by dawn."

"That's only a few hours away," Garrett said hopefully.

"Then at least have a quick bath and a shave. As I recall, you've always kept a fresh suit of clothes here at the hotel. I'll have Andy get them for you," Christopher suggested. "If Claire sees you looking like this she might run back into Chen Loo's waiting arms."

Garrett managed a lopsided smile. "I'll make myself presentable. Just make sure Chen Loo hasn't harmed her and get the instructions for the exchange. If I have to wait much longer, I'll take Chinatown apart with my bare hands."

Christopher nodded and left the room. Garrett watched from the window while his friend climbed into the hotel buggy and headed toward the Oriental community where Claire was being held prisoner. Garrett felt the anger washing though his body again as he recalled watching Claire from the same window a few months ago. He looked at her then, thinking only of pleasing his grandmother, but those thoughts had changed, along with his feelings.

He'd found himself looking forward to their quiet evenings in the parlor; he reading the paper while Claire sat on the settee with his grandmother stitching away at lace that would eventually decorate the hem of a pillowcase. He enjoyed the way she bantered with him when no one else was around, insisting that he was stubborn, while she on the other hand wasn't. He had never enjoyed making love to a woman the way he'd enjoyed making love to Claire. His body had craved hers and when he'd finally found satisfaction it had come with a deep contentment he'd never known before, as if something inside had been lacking and he hadn't been aware of it until that night.

He prayed that their lovemaking was fruitful. If Claire was pregnant with his child, she would marry him. She might not love him as much as he loved her, but he wouldn't let her pride stand in the way of giving their child a name. Once she was safe, he'd convince her of that and more. And he'd give her more children, enough to fill the Nob Hill mansion with the teasing of older brothers and the girlish reprimands of little sisters who would grow up too quickly while their brothers protected them the way Garrett vowed he would protect Claire from now on. He closed his eyes and thought of the future, blocking out the horror of the present, until he could see Claire in his mind's eye. She'd be waiting for him on the staircase when he came home. They'd kiss and the children would come running to greet him. He'd lift his youngest son, or daughter, in his arms and spin them around. The evening would be filled with conversation and the nights would be filled with love.

The image slowly vanished and Garrett felt his body tighten with anger. He gripped the windowsill. Where in the name of God was Claire? Was she hurt? Frightened? Of course, she was. Nothing in Claire's life had prepared her for what she was experiencing now. Feeling helpless and utterly useless, Garrett left the office and marched down the hall to the room he used whenever he stayed at the hotel. Andy was waiting inside.

Clean clothes were spread out on the bed. A spare set of boots had been polished and there was a razor and a bar of soap on the vanity table.

"Do you need anything else?" the young clerk asked.

"No, thank you," Garrett said, wanting to ask for a bottle of whiskey but knowing he needed his wits about him. "Give me an hour, then wake up Mr. Aldrich and have him meet me in the office."

"Yes, sir," Andy replied.

The young man moved to leave but Garrett stopped him with some more instructions. "When Hiram Wilson returns, send him to me immediately."

Andy nodded, then quit the room.

Once the door was shut, Garrett took off his jacket and walked into the bathroom. He turned on the spigot and began to fill the tub with hot water. He looked at himself in the mirror over the vanity table. Christopher was right, he looked like hell.

Claire felt odd dressed in the silk trousers and tunic. She had no undergarments on and the slick fabric brushed against her thighs and breasts like a lover's caress. *Like Garrett's mouth when it moved over me, learning every inch of my body.* Would she feel his mouth again, driving her crazy with wanting, making desire burn in her veins until she was consumed by the sensual emotion? Until all she wanted was to join her body with Garrett's, to feel the things only he could make her feel. God, what a fool she'd been to leave him. Claire knew her pride had been her downfall, that and the doubt that she could reach Garrett's heart.

She still had doubts, but she'd regained her determination. Being attacked in the alley, and waking up in a strange house, filled with people she couldn't speak to and the nerve-chilling fear that she might be killed, had taught her just how precious life really was.

And love.

She was blessed to feel so strongly for Garrett. Lots of women went through life never knowing how wonderful love could feel or how intoxicating passion could be. She wondered briefly if Belinda Belton had ever felt her heart skip a beat or her blood run like warm sunshine through her veins when Christopher Landauer kissed her. Somehow, Claire doubted it. Belinda had been raised to know her place and her destination. But Garrett had taught Claire what a woman needed to know. He'd taught her the delights of passion. He'd taught her that her body could offer a man pleasure as well as children.

Claire concentrated on the memory of the one night she'd had in Garrett's arms, as she sat on the stool so the old woman could braid her damp hair. Once the task was complete, she was tapped on the shoulder.

A few Chinese words and a wave of the woman's hand and Claire stood up. Her feet were bare and she could see that her ankle was still swollen. The tiled floor felt cool under her feet as she hobbled toward the door.

The sound of several men, all speaking Chinese, greeted her ears as the door was opened and she stepped outside. The old woman motioned her to turn right and Claire did. Walking gingerly away from the windowless room, Claire studied her prison. There was little to see, except the painted walls and a series of closed doors that shielded rooms filled with secrets.

The two men who had escorted her from the first room were standing in front of a large double door. Unlike the other doors in the house, this one was painted a bright orange-red, the color of a summer sunset. Gold knobs, circled by vines, etched into the wood and painted a matching gold decorated the center of each door panel. When the men opened the doors, Claire was greeted by the light of what seemed like a hundred flickering candles. The light spilled across the tiled floor, illuminating the way toward a large chair where a man was sitting. Perched atop a dais, the chair looked more like a throne. It was high-backed and the arms were covered in velvet. The man's feet were resting on a small stool. The Chinese woman gave Claire a gentle nudge and she stepped through the doorway, sensing that she was about to be introduced to the man who had kidnapped her.

The room was large and sparsely furnished. Oriental statues of life-size proportions lined the walls. Claire looked at them, seeing the faces of Chinese gods and goddesses, arranged as if they were there to pay homage to the drug lord of Chinatown. Two gold lions with gleaming ruby eyes framed the sides of the man's chair and shoulder-high urns, painted with elaborate designs, sat in the corners. Incense burned in a brass bowl and the sweet scent burdened the air, irritating Claire's sensitive nose and throat. There were windows, but they were draped in thick red fabric that denied the room any natural light.

The man waiting for her was just as impressive as the room. Fat around the middle, he was dressed in long black silk trousers that covered his legs. His robe was black silk as well, but high at the collar and adorned with gold braiding and intricate embroidery that attested to the skill of the seamstress. A gold and red dragon decorated one sleeve, while the other was stitched in bright blue and silver and showed a tall-necked bird that Claire didn't recognize.

The man watched her intently as Claire approached his chair. He seemed to study every detail of her face as she stopped a few feet in front of him. She examined him in return. His head was partially shaved and the hair, beginning at the crown, was pulled back into a skinny braid that was draped over his right shoulder. His features were puffy, matching his body, and his eyes were small and slanted and as black as his clothing. His chin turned into fat just before it disappeared into his stiff collar. He reminded Claire of a plump bullfrog. When he spoke his voice was soft, but menacing, and his words were enunciated in perfect English.

"May I introduce myself, Miss Aldrich. I am Chen Loo."

"What do you want of me?" Claire asked, sounding brave while her insides quivered like leaves on an autumn tree.

"For you to be comfortable until it is time for you to leave my protection," Chen Loo replied calmly.

He said something quick and hard in Chinese and one of the men brought Claire a small chair. It was more a stool than a chair, having no back and high, curved arms. The seat was upholstered in dark green fabric. She sat down, thankful to give her throbbing ankle some reprise from the pain that had started anew when she'd walked down the corridor. Tucking her bare feet under the chair, Claire squared her shoulders and looked at the man who smuggled opium in and out of the city of San Francisco.

"I can assure you, Mr. Loo, being kidnapped isn't comfortable."

He smiled, but it was a thin, hard smile that didn't reach the rest of his face. "In China, a woman is taught respect and obedience. She does not insult her host."

"This isn't China," Claire reminded him, reminding herself at the same time that she couldn't let this man know how much he frightened her. "This is San Francisco, and I was snatched off the street like a loaf of bread off a vendor's wagon. Would you care to tell me why?"

He waved her insult away and Claire noticed that his fingernails were long. So long, they curved at the ends, making them look like talons. She shivered inwardly, not allowing her face to show her apprehension.

"The man you are engaged to marry is known for his wealth," Chen Loo said. "And you appear to hold a certain value to him."

Claire breathed a silent sigh of relief. If Chen Loo was holding her for ransom, Garrett had been contacted. "Then you plan to hold me prisoner until Mr. Monroe pays you for my safe return?"

"I am not a violent man, Miss Aldrich, and I am not

inclined to harm you. As long as you do as you're told," he added.

Claire breathed in and the scent of incense assaulted her nose. The pungent odor was a reminder that she was the prisoner of a different culture. It was of little importance that she was still within the municipality of San Francisco. Chinatown was its own city and Chen Loo was its ruler.

Her host turned to one of the men waiting by the door. Claire listened with skeptical ears while the two men engaged in a short conversation. The door opened and the man left the room. Nothing more was said until the door was opened once again and Christopher Landauer walked inside.

He strolled toward her. "Hello, Claire," he said as if he were greeting her at a Nob Hill reception. "I see my brother has already begun your assimilation. Do you find the clothing comfortable?"

"Your brother!" Claire looked from the face of the blond hotel owner to the plump Chinaman sitting a few feet away. There was no resemblance whatsoever. One man was tall and blond with light eyes. The other was stout and dark and completely foreign.

Christopher's laugh had a sarcastic ring. "My half brother," he explained. "My father was a missionary, but like so many pious men, he had his weak points. One of them was Chen Loo's mother."

Claire didn't know what to say. Her mind began to race, sorting through the things Garrett had told her about Christopher Landauer and the feelings she'd had on several occasions when the San Francisco gentleman had danced with her. There had always been something unsettling about him, but Claire had never been able to give it a name. She could now—deceit.

Fear vibrated through her as she lifted her chin and glared at the man who professed to be Garrett's best friend. "Congratulations," she said. "You're much better at acting than I could ever hope to be, Mr. Landauer."

Another laugh. "Fooling people isn't difficult, Claire. All you have to do is let them see what they want to see. A feat you've accomplished very well in the short time you've been *engaged* to Garrett. I believe you even have the talented banker thinking he's in love with you."

"How much money do you expect Garrett to pay you?" she asked, knowing the more she understood, the better prepared she'd be to deal with what happened next. She straightened in the chair, holding on to the hope that Garrett did indeed love her, while she reevaluated her opinion of Christopher Landauer. The man was a chameleon. A tiger who had the ability to change his stripes, friend and confidant, one moment—enemy, the next.

"Garrett's more than willing to part company with fifty thousand dollars," Christopher said matter-of-factly. "And I, of course, am more than willing to accept it."

"Of course," Claire replied. "Then what? You can't let me go. I'll tell Garrett everything and you'll be running from the authorities for the rest of your life."

"I have no intention of running from anyone," Christopher told her. His blue eyes narrowed into sinister slits. "I have other plans for you, Miss Aldrich. Plans that will give me a great deal of pleasure before I put you on a freighter bound for China."

"China!"

"Are you really such an innocent, Miss Aldrich?" he asked, looking at her with a calculated yearning.

"A virgin knows what rape is," Claire said, allowing Christopher to think what he would about her relationship with Garrett. "And kidnapping."

"Ahhh, but I have no intentions of raping you," he

corrected her, then smiled. The expression gave his handsome face a demonic quality and Claire prayed that she could keep up her courage. "Pleasure is an art, Miss Aldrich. An art that the Chinese have perfected over the centuries. By the time you reach Shanghai, you will be well tutored in what will be expected of you. In China, a woman's main function is to please a man, and there are men who will pay well for your fair hair and youthful body."

He turned and began speaking to his half brother. The two men conversed in Chinese and Claire was amazed at how naturally the language flowed from Christopher's mouth. After a lengthy conversation, Chen Loo stood up. Claire watched him walk from the room and tried to imagine him and Christopher Landauer being fathered by the same man.

She did her best not to think of the fate Christopher had threatened her with. Claire couldn't let him frighten her any more than she already was. Garrett knew she'd been taken by Chen Loo and she had to believe that he would do everything he could to get her away from the coldhearted Chinaman.

And the half brother.

"Is your ankle still bothering you?" Christopher asked, taking the chair his half brother had vacated.

"Yes. They took my cane and it's difficult to walk without it."

"A cane can be a very effective weapon," he replied. "I thought it best to have it removed. If the small amount of walking you've had to do since your arrival has been painful, I apologize."

"Apologize," Claire scoffed. "How sincere you sound, Mr. Landauer, especially for a man who plans to steal fifty thousand dollars from his best friend, then sell me off to a Chinese harem."

"I can see why Garrett is so attracted to you, Miss

Aldrich," he remarked. "He's always liked women with spirit. I, on the other hand, prefer my women docile and obedient. Traits you will have to learn if you expect to survive in China. Once there, the man who buys you will own you the same way he owns everything in his house. He can beat you, or kill you, and be entirely within his rights."

"I'd rather die than be a whore," she spit out the terrible word.

"Ahhh, you misunderstand what is expected of you. You will be a concubine, not a whore. There is a difference, Miss Aldrich. And that difference can give you a comfortable home and a comfortable life once you embrace its principles."

"The way you've embraced the principles of dishonesty and deception?" she snapped back. "Garrett will kill you for this. And my brother. You know I've found him. Donald won't sit idly by while I'm smuggled out of the city."

"I know," he said. "That's why I've arranged a nice little meeting just before dawn. Garrett will be there, of course, with a suitcase full of money. And I intend to invite your brother, as well. Once your benefactor sees that you are well and unharmed, he will turn over the money to Chen Loo."

Once your benefactor sees that you are well and unharmed. Christopher was going to let Garrett see her to convince him that she was being returned in exchange for the money, but if she went back to Garrett, she couldn't be sent to China. That meant . . . "You're going to kill them," Claire blurted out her conclusion. "Garrett and my brother."

"Unfortunately, yes." He stood up and stepped off the dais to stand in front of her. "Your brother managed to get too close to Chen Loo. Much closer than we thought anyone could get. My half brother doesn't like his business affairs vulnerable to the scrutiny of outsiders. As for Garrett, he's a stubborn man. If I don't kill him, he'll hound me for the rest of my life. This solution simplifies matters for everyone. Your employer will be dead, along with your brother. You'll have no one to search for you, and as a result, you'll be much more cooperative in assuming your new role in China."

Claire's stomach knotted and the bitter taste of bile mixed with the taste of hatred.

"Now, you will be taken to a room with a bed where you can rest," Christopher said before calling out something in Chinese. "I'll escort you myself."

Claire struggled against his hands as they reached for her. She kicked and screamed and twisted, but Christopher wasn't a small man and she couldn't prevent him from lifting her into his arms. She hated it. She hated him and his touch.

When they walked through the door and into the corridor she saw another Caucasian. The man looked familiar and Claire realized he was the other passenger who'd gotten on the trolley in Nob Hill. His face was pale and potted with scars and she shivered on the inside as she realized he must have been the one who had come up behind her in the alley.

She tried to get free of Christopher's grasp, but he laughed. "I suggest you begin to accept the dire state of your circumstances, Miss Aldrich. I'm not Garrett. I'm not a gentleman. If beating you will quench your insulting behavior, then I will not hesitate to do just that. In fact some women like a taste of discipline before their pleasure. Perhaps we could use the punishment as a test of your potential passion."

"You're disgusting," Claire snapped. "Vile and disgusting."

"And you have a lot to learn," he replied, unaffected by her outburst. "I thought perhaps my friend had already initiated you into the realm of womanhood, but I see that you're as innocent now as you were the day you walked into my hotel.''

"Is that how long you've been planning this?"

"Yes and no," Christopher answered. "Your appeal was apparent at our first meeting, and I have to admit that I was waiting for the right opportunity to offer you my friendship." He grinned mockingly. "Ironically, it was your own actions that spurred the idea of expediting our relationship, Miss Aldrich."

"I don't know what you're talking about."

"I'm referring to your initial visit to Chinatown. It was amusing to watch you defy Garrett. Few women do, you know. After viewing your heated exchange in the carriage, I knew it was only a matter of time before you'd venture out again."

The other man opened the door of a room and Christopher carried Claire inside. She was dumped onto a large bed draped with silk curtains. "I suggest you rest while you can," the blond betrayer said, smiling. "The rendezvous with your fiancé is at dawn. After that you belong to me and I intend to enjoy you before you're put on the freighter. I never sell what I haven't sampled first."

Claire called him every contemptible name she'd ever heard, but Christopher only laughed at her as the door was shut and locked.

The sound of a woman's muffled cries stole Claire's attention away from the door. She looked across the room. Evelyn Holmes was huddled in the corner, crying like a frightened child.

Chapter Eighteen

"Miss Holmes . . ." Claire made her way to the woman crouched in the corner. "Are you hurt?"

Evelyn shook her head. "He slapped me when I called him a bloody bastard, but I've been slapped before. It's being locked in here that's got me ready to go out of my mind. I hate being locked in. My father used to lock me in my room whenever I disobeyed him." Her silvery blond hair hung in disarray about her face and shoulders. She was wearing black trousers and a tunic, similar to Claire's, and her feet were bare, as well. She used the bottom half of the tunic to wipe her face, then looked at Claire. Her blue eyes were swollen from crying and there was a bruise on her left jaw. "He bragged that he'd get you, too," she said in a shaky voice. "I think he's mad."

"How long have you been here?" Claire asked, not sure if she agreed or not. Madness made people do unpredictable, irrational things. Christopher's scheme was premeditated and ruthless. He knew exactly what he was doing. That made him more dangerous than a man who wasn't in control of himself.

"I'm not sure. Two days, I think."

Claire leaned against the wall and looked around the room. Except for the bed, it was void of furniture. A small gaslight fixture, centered in the ceiling, gave off a yellowish light that made the starkness of the room seem even more foreboding. The floor was bare wood, clean but unpolished. Two windows were shuttered on the outside and barred on the inside. Seeing the bars, Claire realized that this wasn't the first time Christopher and his half brother, Chen Loo, had kept prisoners.

Claire continued scrutinizing her prison. She struggled with the fearful sensation stealing the last of her composure. Fear for herself, fear for her brother, but most of all, fear for Garrett. He'd meet with Christopher without suspecting that his best friend was actually his worse enemy. Staggered by her emotions, Claire was thankful that she was sitting down.

She looked toward the bed. The sheets were rumpled and the pillows scattered as if they'd been picked up from the floor and tossed to the mattress without any real thought of tidiness.

"I never sell what I haven't sampled."

Christopher's words sent a shiver of disgust through Claire. A smoldering anger began in the pit of her stomach and she clinched her fists.

"Did you know that Chen Loo is Christopher's half brother?" Claire asked.

Evelyn nodded, then glared at the bed. Her face was blank, but her eyes were burning with hatred. "We were introduced."

Claire wished she had the courage to ask if the introduction had taken place the way she assumed. Was that the reason she'd found the Englishwoman huddled in the corner like a wounded animal? Had Chen Loo raped her? Or had she been forced to endure Christopher's attention after being told that she was to be herded onto a ship and sold into slavery.

Claire closed her eyes and felt the weariness of the last few hours seep into her mind. Tension and a nauseating kind of despair filled her body until she felt tears welling up beneath her closed eyelids. She blinked them away. She couldn't let fear control her. It was what Christopher wanted. To make her feel helpless and intimidated. She'd sensed that when he'd told her about his plans for Garrett and her brother. Evelyn was partially right. Christopher was insane, insanely obsessed with himself.

Claire tried to think of the present instead of the degrading future that Christopher had planned for her and Evelyn Holmes. The uncompromising strength of spirit that had always been a part of her was still there, temporarily buried under the fear. Claire fought to find it. She'd survived on her own for the last five years. She'd worked and worried and hoped for a new life and she wasn't going to give up that dream without a fight.

There was to be a meeting at dawn. She'd be there, of course. Garrett would never relinquish the money until he was sure she was safe. That meant she could warn him.

She looked at Evelyn. The young woman had a defeated glaze to her eyes, as if she'd already given up hope of being rescued. For a moment, Claire tried to dislike her. She'd been Garrett's mistress and then she'd gone to Christopher's bed. But seeing the young woman now, slumped in the corner with tears streaming down her face, Claire could only pity her.

"You have to stop crying and help me," Claire said as Evelyn dropped her forehead to her knees in a display of physical and mental exhaustion. "Christopher is going to kill Garrett and my brother. I'm going to need your help."

"What can I do?" Evelyn asked, turning her head to look at Claire. "I'm locked in, just like you. Christopher told me we're going to be put on a freighter and taken to Shanghai." She swallowed hard. "He said there was a man there who bought women."

"I know," Claire said. "But we aren't on the freighter, yet. We have to think of something. There's got to be a way out of here."

"Where? How? Whenever the old woman brings my food, I can hear men outside the door. Christopher said they'd kill me if I tried to get away. I believe him."

Claire had seen the guards, too. And she didn't have any idea how to get out of the room, but she wasn't going to give up and let Christopher and his half brother kill Garrett and Donald in cold blood. "I have no doubt that Chen Loo and his cutthroats are capable of murder," Claire said. "I'd rather die than spend the rest of my life in a Chinese harem."

Evelyn looked at the bed again. Claire's eyes followed and she saw the ropes for the first time. They were made of knotted silk. Hanging loosely now from the posters at the head of the bed, Claire knew they'd been used to bind Evelyn's hands so she couldn't fight whoever had raped her.

"Help me get us out of this," Claire said adamantly, forcing her eyes away from the bed. "Our only chance may be when they take us to the freighter. I have to know you won't be too frightened to help me if I think there's an opportunity. We'll only get one."

"If we get that," Evelyn said, sitting up straighter. "Okay, I'll help." She looked at the barred windows. "What do you want me to do?"

"I'm not sure. Yet," Claire told her. "But I'll think of something."

Evelyn nodded, then closed her eyes and rested her forehead on her knees once again.

The only sound in the room was the unsteady breathing of the Englishwoman sitting on the floor beside her and her own frantic heartbeat as Claire tried to think of a future without Garrett.

She'd only known the man for a few short months, but he'd taught her so much. About herself. About men. About passion and love and hopes and dreams. Claire knew that no matter what happened, she'd never be able to forget the night they'd shared together. Her body went warm with the memory, then cold as she thought about an auction block in China.

She got to her feet. It was awkward, but she hobbled to the windows and wrapped her hands around the bars like a convict in a jail cell. The metal was cold. She reached through the bars and touched the glass that separated the bars from the wooden shutters outside. The glass was cool to the touch.

It was mid-July. If it was daytime, the sun would have some effect on the glass and metal even if the shutters were closed. The coolness of the bars meant that the sun had been down for several hours. Christopher had told her the meeting was at dawn. But when was dawn? Two hours away? Four hours away?

"He's jealous," Evelyn said unexpectedly.

"Christopher?" Claire turned away from the window. "But why? He and Garrett have been friends most of their lives. They're both wealthy and successful. They're partners. What has Christopher got to be jealous about?"

"You."

Claire shook her head. "You're much more beautiful than I am, Miss Holmes."

"But I'm not a lady," Evelyn confessed. "I like men too much, and money, and fancy clothes. My mother said it would be the ruin of me.'' She wiped her tear-stained face. "She was right.''

Claire wondered if this was the time to do a little confessing of her own. Should she tell Evelyn that she knew the young lady and Garrett were intimately acquainted?

"It's more than jealousy,'' Evelyn continued. "He said things . . .''

"What kind of things?'' Claire urged. She desperately needed to understand why things were happening, even if she couldn't do anything to stop them.

Evelyn shifted uneasily, as if she'd started something she'd rather not finish. "Just things that made me think he was comparing himself to Garrett all the time. He always talked about having his own bank one day. He used Garrett as the yardstick for his own success. He bragged about having Belinda Belton at his beck and call, but underneath the boasting, I think he resisted playing second place to Garrett. I watched Christopher watching you that day in the restaurant. If he could have, I think he would have tried to seduce you away from Garrett. Did he try?''

"No,'' Claire told her. "I never gave him the opportunity.''

"That's because you're in love with Garrett.''

Claire didn't deny it.

She tried not to think about anything for a moment, clearing her mind of the dreadful possibility that she might never see Garrett again, that she'd never be able to tell him how much she loved him. She took a broken breath and then another, letting the air out of her lungs slowly as she pushed the fears from her mind so she could think clearly.

Garrett wasn't a fool. If he'd gotten a ransom request, then he was prepared to meet the men he thought responsible for her kidnapping. Hopefully, he'd be prepared for violence, as well. As for Donald, Claire had no way of knowing where her brother was or if he even knew she was missing, but from what Christopher had told her, she had to assume that Garrett had gone looking for her in Chinatown and encountered her brother. Were they together now, plotting a way to set her free? Or did Garrett still distrust her brother, thinking he was linked to the Chinaman?

"Where the hell is Christopher?" Garrett shouted as Hiram Wilson and Donald joined him in the hotel office. "It's been over an hour since he left to meet with Chen Loo."

Neither man replied because neither man had an answer. Claire's brother helped himself to some coffee while the investigator watched Garrett measure the room in long, impatient strides. Garrett had his anger under control, but the stress on his face showed how much that control was costing him. His jaw was tight and his eyes gleamed with a savage determination.

"What's the plan?" Donald asked as he sat down on the corner of the desk.

"We give Chen Loo the money. He gives us Claire," Garrett answered.

"Sounds simple enough," Donald retorted. "Trouble is, the Chinese aren't simple. The minute you think you know what they're going to do, they do something else."

Garrett wasn't in the mood to discuss Chinese philosophy. "How many men do you think Chen Loo will have with him?"

"At least six. Probably ten," Claire's brother replied. "He'll expect you to be armed."

"We will be," Garrett assured him, then added, "Go downstairs and tell Andy I want the horses saddled and waiting."

Donald nodded, put his cup on the table, and left the room.

"I want twenty men following us," Garrett said to Hiram after the door closed behind Claire's brother. "I want them armed and ready for trouble."

"I anticipated your request," Hiram replied. "Once we know the meeting place, I'll have two dozen men in place. Chen Loo won't get away this time."

Garrett walked to the window. It was just after four in the morning. The city was quiet, the night broken only by the dull glow of gaslights on California Street and the occasional rumble of carriage wheels as some gentleman ventured home after a late evening of cards, followed by the pleasant company of his mistress.

Garrett stared into the darkness, trying not to think of Claire, alone and frightened. It was impossible. The last twenty-four hours had been consumed by those very thoughts. And regrets. Why hadn't he told her that he loved her instead of using the threat of a possible pregnancy to bully her into marriage? His pride seemed unimportant now, as he fought against the blood-chilling fear that he'd never see her again.

"What about the authorities?" Hiram asked, breaking into Garrett's private thoughts.

"You can tell them anything you want once I've got Claire back," Garrett said. "Until then, I don't want any clumsy constables getting in our way."

Being in agreement, the investigator said nothing further about notifying the police.

The door opened and Christopher came into the office. Claire's brother was right behind him, anxious to find out where the exchange was going to take place.

"The meeting is set for dawn," Christopher announced. "We're to meet Chen Loo near the docks."

"Where?" Garrett asked.

"At the end of Washington Street, near The Embarcadero."

The boulevard curved around San Francisco Bay to the northeast perimeter of the city, skirting the edge of Chinatown. Hiram was right. The viper wasn't going to leave his nest. Garrett looked at the clock on the wall, then glanced out the window. "All he wants is the money, right?"

"Fifty thousand dollars in exchange for Claire," Christopher said, reaffirming the terms.

"Did you see her?" Garrett asked anxiously.

Christopher shook his head. "No. He assured me that she's okay."

"Do you believe him?"

"I have no reason to disbelieve him," Christopher replied. "I made it perfectly clear that he has to show us Claire, unharmed and looking as beautiful as ever, before he gets one penny of the money."

"Don't worry about Claire," Donald said. "She's stronger than she looks. She's probably more worried about you than she is about herself.

Garrett didn't comment. Yes, Claire was strong. It took a strong woman to bury her mother and go on with life, supporting herself, taking responsibility for herself. She was steadfast. Unwavering in what she wanted for others and for herself.

Garrett realized it was that serene but constant willfulness of mind and purpose that made Claire such an enigma to him, at least, at first. He was used to women who wanted things; money, fancy clothes, social status. Claire had left everything he'd given her behind when she'd packed and left his Nob Hill home. Everything but the cameo he'd given her the day she'd agreed to pose as his fiancée.

"Very well," Garrett said, looking at the other men

in the room. "Christopher and I will take Chen Loo his ransom."

"Claire's *my* sister," Donald said, making it clear that he wasn't going to be left behind.

"The three of us should be enough," Christopher said, preventing an argument. "Any more and Chen Loo is going to think you don't trust him to keep his word."

I don't, Garrett said to himself. He gave Hiram a quick glance. The two men didn't have to exchange words to convey their thoughts. Chen Loo was going to get more than he'd bargained for.

Garrett hadn't told anyone but the investigator of his plans to overpower Chen Loo and his men once Claire was safe. Initially his reasoning had been to keep Christopher from appearing overconfident when he met with the Chinaman. The reason served the same purpose now. Garrett didn't speak Chinese and he doubted that Chen Loo would speak English when they met, even if he could. Since Christopher was the appointed liaison, the less he knew about Garrett's plans the less he could tell Chen Loo by accidental word or expression. Garrett wanted to make sure that the Chinaman thought he was getting away with his scheme.

Garrett's reason for leaving Donald out of his plan was clear enough.

He didn't know the man well enough to trust him.

Claire's brother seemed certain that the motive behind his sister's kidnapping was his own association with Chen Loo. The Chinaman, being naturally distrusting of outsiders, had had Donald's house watched and Claire followed. When she'd returned to Garrett's home on Nob Hill, he'd made the connection and thought to use it to his advantage. Garrett wasn't so sure. Since he'd learned that Chen Loo had Claire and the frantic search had all but ceased, he'd had time to think.

Something didn't add up.

He'd spent his life balancing ledgers and analyzing debits and credits. The equation wasn't as simple as Donald Aldrich thought. If Chen Loo wanted revenge for Donald's betrayal, then why wasn't he demanding Donald in exchange for Claire? By kidnapping Claire, Chen Loo had involved Garrett, and by involving Garrett he'd taken the risk of having the authorities waiting on the docks along with the ransom money.

The more Garrett thought about it, the more he began to suspect that either Donald was still working for the Chinaman and using Claire to make his employer and himself fifty thousand dollars richer, or there was more to Chen Loo's motive than money and revenge.

He'd have his answer soon enough.

"Excuse me," Hiram said. "I need to make sure the money is transferred to the saddlebags."

Nothing was said for a long time after the investigator left the room. Donald helped himself to another cup of coffee while Christopher poured a drink and lit a cigar. Garrett returned to the window, his back to the room.

A few miles away, Claire was staring at the iron bars of her prison. A hush had fallen over the small room and the two women sat side by side on the floor, saying nothing as the minutes ticked away until someone opened the door and either came into the room or pulled them out of it.

The fear and anxiety that had assaulted Claire a short time before had turned into a dull dread of what would happen next. She knew she was fighting exhaustion. The same exhaustion that had Evelyn staring across the room, her eyes blank, her face an unreadable mask.

The sound of voices brought Claire's senses to life. She came to her feet, ignoring the pain in her ankle. Evelyn tensed by her side.

The door was unlocked, then pushed open, swinging back until it bumped against the wall. Chen Loo stepped inside.

"Ladies," he said, his English words a stark contrast to his appearance, "it's time to go."

"Go where?" Claire asked defiantly.

"Wherever I wish to take you," their captor replied, reiterating his control over them.

The man from the trolley came into the room. He stepped past Claire and reached for Evelyn, jerking the young woman to her feet. When she fought him, he slapped her across the face. "Shut up," he said, although Evelyn hadn't said a word.

Claire raised her hand to repay the cruelty, but Chen Loo caught her arm just above the wrist. "Violence brings violence," he said. "The woman won't be harmed as long as she cooperates."

"You mean as long as she surrenders," Claire said, gritting her teeth. The touch of Chen Loo's hand was revolting. She tried to jerk away, but his grip was too tight. She glared at him. "I wish I knew your language," she told him. "Mine lacks the words to describe how loathsome I find you and your friends."

"One of the things you must learn is respect," Chen Loo retorted. He reached out with his free hand and traced Claire's mouth with the tip of a long fingernail.

She pulled back, but not before she saw the hatred in the Chinaman's eyes. It burned there, deep and dark and deadly, like a smoldering volcano. Claire had never hated a man before, but she hated this man. He was unfeeling, like a wild animal who killed because killing was innate.

She'd seen the same inhuman gleam in Christopher's

eyes when he'd talked about murdering Garrett and her brother. The actions of the two brothers were incomprehensible. Their desires and obsessions were as foreign to Claire as the language they spoke.

Chen Loo's grip lessened and Claire tried to disengage herself from his grasp. The moment she moved, his hand tightened around her wrist until she felt the pressure of his fingers digging into her skin. He was baiting her. Teasing her the way a cat teased a mouse.

"The lessons can be as painful or as rewarding as you choose for them to be, Miss Aldrich" Chen Loo continued, his voice soft and lethal at the same time. "But they will be learned."

Claire, caught in Chen Loo's grasp, was forced to watch as Evelyn was hauled from the room. She knew the Chinaman wanted her to fight him. The brutal gleam in his ebony eyes said he enjoyed her suffering. Knowing that she'd only satisfy him by struggling, Claire allowed herself to be led into the corridor.

There were two carriages waiting outside. It was dark, the silent, lonely darkness that came in the deepest part of the night, just before the hint of dawn softened the sky. Claire looked up and down the alley. It was narrow, just wide enough to accommodate the carriages and the horses. She couldn't see anything else. The man from the trolley put Evelyn in the first carriage, then shut the door. One of Chen Loo's guards stepped forward and opened the door of the second carriage.

The Chinaman pushed her forward. "Get in, Miss Aldrich, and be quiet."

Claire climbed into the carriage. She made her way to the end of the seat, as far away from the Chinaman as possible. Claire sat silently, willing herself not to be afraid, and failing in the attempt. The cold, clammy sweat of fear dampened her body beneath the black silk she'd been given to wear.

The upcoming rendezvous with Garrett was a blessing and a curse. Claire wanted the comfort of his arms. Christopher wanted him dead. Unsure how she was going to warn Garrett and her brother, Claire tried to think of some signal, something the men would know signified danger. Except for screaming at the top of her lungs, none came to mind.

The carriage slowed to a halt and Claire's heart stopped with it. She could hear the water of San Francisco Bay lapping at the wooden dock and the low-spoken conversation of Chen Loo's men as they discussed what they'd come to the docks to achieve. The night air was perfumed with the scent of the bay, rain-dampened streets, and the lingering odor of dead fish. Between the panels of the carriage curtains, Claire could see the silhouette of a steamship. Evelyn was pulled from the first carriage and tossed into a shallow boat. Two of Chen Loo's men started rowing. Whatever hope Claire had had about Evelyn's help disappeared along with Garrett's former mistress.

Claire felt Chen Loo move. She stiffened as the Chinaman reached into his pocket and pulled out a silk scarf. She knew he was going to gag her with it so she couldn't yell out a warning to Garrett and Donald.

Chapter Nineteen

With deadly intent, Garrett mounted the dark bay Andy had saddled for him. Two saddlebags, bulging with money, were strapped behind him. Hiram was nowhere to be seen and Garrett knew that the investigator was with the men at the docks. Christopher was riding to his right, Donald to his left. Neither man spoke as they mounted and joined Garrett.

They rode toward the docks, without conversation. Garrett's eyes swept the alleyways and streets they passed, looking for anything suspicious. The sky was still black and the street lamps glowed against the fading darkness, casting shadows over the storefronts and houses they passed. The city was still sleeping.

Christopher nudged his horse close to Garrett's. "When we get there, don't let your temper get in the way. The sooner we get the money out of your saddlebags and into the Chinaman's hands, the sooner you'll get Claire."

Garrett bristled at the instructions. If he didn't know better, he'd think Christopher couldn't wait to make Chen Loo fifty thousand dollars richer. "Since I don't speak Chinese, calling the Chinaman a greedy son of a bitch won't do me much good. I'll let you do the talking."

Christopher smiled, then nodded.

The cautious cavalcade reached the docks a short time later. Behind them the eastern horizon was beginning to show the first signs of daylight. In spite of his companions and the men he knew Hiram had dispersed among the nearby buildings, Garrett felt very much alone. It was a new sensation, one he hadn't felt before, and he realized that he was alone. Without Claire his life had lost its value. The disparaging view in which he'd held love a few months ago was gone. Love wasn't a complex emotion. It was primitive and basic, like the need for food and water. Once you felt it, it became a part of you. Just as Claire had become a part of him.

Garrett sat on his horse, his eyes scanning the docks where several small fishing boats were moored. Beyond them, larger ships crowded the Bay, anchored in deeper water. Saddle leather creaked as Garrett shifted his weight and felt the heavy metal of his revolver inside his jacket. He was prepared to kill for Claire and the thought held no remorse. If Chen Loo had harmed her, he would do just that. Kill the man and be glad that he'd done it.

They moved along the docks, until they saw the carriages.

"I'll go on ahead," Christopher said. "Don't come any closer until I signal you."

"Make sure Claire hasn't been hurt," Garrett told him.

Garrett's heartbeat quickened as his friend rode forward. He could make out the forms of at least six men.

All Chinese. One was sitting at the reins of the second carriage. The others were lined up like soldiers at review. As Christopher approached them, he said something in Chinese. Garrett didn't understand the words and Donald commented that Christopher was speaking too low for him to make out what was being said.

The door of the second carriage opened and Chen Loo got out. Garrett didn't need a formal introduction to know the man. The Chinaman's clothing was enough.

"That's Chen Loo," Donald said, keeping his voice just above a whisper.

Garrett didn't acknowledge the remark. He was too busy studying the man who had dared to take Claire. He felt a pressure in his chest, like an iron hand squeezing his heart. His hatred for Chen Loo bubbled up from his insides like water gushing from a newly tapped well. It joined the love Garrett felt for Claire, and for a long moment the two conflicting emotions fought for control of Garrett's mind. He took a deep breath, ending the struggle. Claire was more important. Her safety was more important. He'd sit and wait until the right moment before extracting his revenge on the Chinaman.

Claire recognized Christopher's voice. She struggled against the silk rope that had her hands bound behind her back. Her teeth bit into the silken gag that kept her from saying anything to warn Garrett and her brother. When the carriage door opened, she drew back, hating the hands that reached for her.

"You must show yourself, Miss Aldrich," Chen Loo said, wrapping his hand around her elbow and dragging her toward the door. "But I suggest you remember our previous conversations and realize that any disruption on your part will result in nothing but you being forced to watch while your fiancée and your brother are slain."

Claire wanted to free her hands and wrap them

around the Chinaman's fat throat. She wanted to strangle the life out of him, and then she wanted to turn her fury on Christopher Landauer, the deceiving bastard. She'd already seen enough. Evelyn had been pulled from the other carriage and tossed into a small boat. She'd been gagged, as well, her hands and feet bound. Claire had been forced to sit and watch while the young Englishwoman was taken to one of the ships anchored in the Bay.

Once she was outside the carriage, half supported by Chen Loo, half supported by her own wobbling legs, Claire came face-to-face with Christopher Landauer. The man's mouth quirked into a crooked smile.

"Your fiancée is waiting, Miss Aldrich."

Claire said something very unladylike around the gag in her mouth.

Christopher continued smiling.

"Garrett will insist on seeing you before he turns over the money. I recommend that you stand straight and tall and look beautifully defiant while the exchange is being made. After that, it doesn't matter what you do."

Claire looked past Christopher's shoulder. She could make out the shape of two men, mounted on horseback and waiting in the distance. Her eyes were drawn to Garrett and her heart swelled at the mere sight of him. Love rolled through her, pushing the fear away for a brief second, mentally releasing her from the grasp of Chen Loo's hand, and washing away the smirk on Christopher's face. Claire reached for the love, willing it to be enough to see both her and Garrett through the next fatal minutes.

"I'll walk you a short distance from the carriage," Christopher said, replacing Chen Loo's hand with his own. "You'll stand there until the money is exchanged, then you'll walk with me toward my horse. One wrong move," he warned her, "and I'll shoot Garrett myself. Understand?"

He pulled back the flap of his coat and Claire saw a gun tucked into the waistband of his trousers.

She nodded. Her mind raced as she stumbled alongside Christopher, hating the need for his hand, but knowing without it she would fall flat on her face. The boardwalk that ran along the length of the waterfront was cold and damp and slick. The sky was beginning to lighten with the first show of dawn. Small streaks of pink and gold hovered on the horizon, heralding the sunrise. The light profiled Garrett's body. She could see the broad expanse of his shoulders and his dark hair, tousled from a restless night of worry. Claire's feet moved reluctantly, knowing that with each step she took, she brought Garrett and Donald closer to their deaths.

"I've got Claire," Christopher called out, stopping an equal distance between the two men and the waiting carriages. "Ride forward and toss the saddlebags on the ground. Once Chen Loo has them, I can put Claire on my horse and we can get the hell out of here."

Garrett gritted his teeth. Chen Loo had Claire dressed like a Chinese coolie. Her clothes had either been stripped away or taken. Her feet were bare and he knew she must be cold. Other than that, she appeared to be okay. But he couldn't be sure, not until he'd heard her say the words. He nodded to Donald and Claire's brother reached over to unbuckle the saddlebags. Once they were free, he handed them to Garrett.

"Take the gag out of her mouth," Garrett shouted. He was holding the saddlebags up so that Chen Loo could see. The Chinaman hadn't spoken a word or moved an inch since Christopher had taken custody of Claire.

Christopher shook his head. "She's fine, Garrett. Just get the money over here. Chen Loo isn't a patient man."

"Neither am I," Garrett retorted. "Take the gag out of her mouth and let go of her arm. *Now*."

The two friends faced each other. Claire could feel the tension in Christopher's body, the uncertainty. She looked at Garrett, willing her eyes to send him a message, praying he'd understand what she couldn't say. As dawn's faint light inched over the horizon, making the night a thing of the past, she could see Garrett's face more clearly. He had the same dark expression he'd had that night in the hallway, when he'd caught her leaving the library. There was an animalistic alertness about him, a primitive savagery that showed in his eyes.

Claire felt Christopher move. He was reaching inside his coat.

The next second was an explosion of sounds and actions.

Christopher released her arm and shoved Claire to the ground. She landed with a bone-wrenching thud as the sound of gunfire cracked the silence. Garrett called her name and the guttural summons brought her head up. The saddlebags had been dumped on the ground and Garrett was running toward her. She tried to sit up, only to have him reach her and push her back to the ground, covering her body with his own.

"Don't move," Garrett told her.

Claire couldn't argue. The gag was still in her mouth.

Garrett felt warm and solid after the cold uncertainty of the night and Claire didn't move. She lay under him while he raised his pistol and fired. The odor of sulfur assaulted her nostrils and tears came to her eyes. Men were shouting, some in English, some in Chinese.

Claire wanted to see what was happening, but Garrett kept her pinned beneath him. She managed to turn her head toward the carriage. Chen Loo was getting inside, his back to the fight while his men formed a protective circle around him. Claire heard Donald's voice shouting out a curse and a prediction of where Chen Loo would wake up—in hell. A shot rang out and Claire watched as a chunk of wood exploded from the carriage door, a few inches away from the Chinaman's head.

The carriage horses snorted and tried to break free from the harnesses that restricted them. They reared up as one of Chen Loo's men tried to control them and the Chinese man was forced to back away. The carriage rolled forward, then back, as the driver struggled to get the animals under control.

"Hold on to me," Garrett said, as he came to his feet and scooped Claire up in his arms. He ran toward a building, a wooden structure with lead windows and a weather-battered sign. Claire clung to his neck, her head buried against his chest. She felt Garrett's arms give way and she was passed to another man. She didn't recognize him. He was built like a lumberjack, but he handled her like a kitten.

"Don't move, ma'am," he said. "This ain't over yet."

The man pulled the gag out of her mouth, then turned around, pistol drawn, to help Garrett. Claire sucked in a deep breath. She wanted to crawl to where Garrett was kneeling, his body shielded by several large shipping crates, but she knew she would only be in his way. She was the cause of the fight, but it was a man's fight, so she sat where she was, praying the gunfire would cease and that Garrett and her brother would survive uninjured.

"That son of a bitch," she heard Garrett shout out. His raised his gun, aimed, and pulled the trigger.

Claire heard the agonizing sound of a man's harsh scream as the bullet found its mark. She wondered if the man was Christopher Landauer or Chen Loo.

The fighting stopped as abruptly as it had started.

The air was heavy with sulfur smoke and the sounds of frightened horses. Garrett stood up, looked at her, smiled, then moved away from the building. Claire climbed awkwardly to her feet and stumbled after him. The lumberjack stopped her.

"You'd better stay put, ma'am," he said.

Claire didn't obey him this time. When she moved, he stepped aside and she hobbled out into the street. Several men, all Chinese, were lying on the ground. Some were moving and moaning in pain, others were as still as death. Claire looked for Christopher Landauer. Garrett was standing over his body.

"I'm sorry," Claire said. "He was your friend."

Garrett turned around. He walked to where she was standing, her weight balanced on one foot, and pulled her into his arms. "I don't know who he was," he said. "But he wasn't my friend."

She leaned back slightly and looked up at him.

"Are you all right?" His voice sounded hoarse and he looked tired. Bone-weary tired.

"They scared me, but they didn't hurt me," she told him. She was trembling with an aftermath of fear and relief. Her eyes were large and luminous, her hands still bound behind her back. She looked so vulnerable, a young beautiful woman caught by the cruelty of the world.

Garrett cursed out loud. Before he could ask for a knife to free her, one of the men Hiram had hired stepped forward. He handed Garrett a wicked-looking blade, about six inches long and honed to a razor-sharp edge. Garrett gently turned Claire around, and being careful not to cut her, he sliced the silk rope, freeing her hands.

Tears were forming in Claire's eyes as she turned around and looked up at him. She reached for his shoulders to keep from falling and found herself lifted up and held against his chest. She closed her eyes, loving the hard embrace.

"Claire, are you all right?"

Her brother was standing a few feet away. His right hand was cradling his left arm and she could see blood seeping through the dark cotton of his shirt.

"Donald!" She squirmed in Garrett's arms, but he didn't release her.

"I'm fine," Donald told her, grimacing as he moved the injured arm. "That's more than I can say for Chen Loo and his henchmen."

Claire looked toward the carriage. The door was open and she could see Chen Loo's body, slumped lifelessly against the seat. The front of the Chinaman's silk tunic was stained with blood.

"It's over," Garrett told him. "I'll never let anyone hurt you again. Never."

"It wasn't your fault," Claire said, trying to soothe him.

"I should have locked you in your room," Garrett said. "When I think . . ."

"Then don't think," Claire said, cradling his handsome face in her hands. "Kiss me, instead."

Garrett couldn't oblige her fast enough. She groaned softly against his lips. It wasn't a gentle kiss. It was hard and primitive, because the circumstances were primitive, because life and death could be brutal and he needed the primal reassurance that his woman was where she belonged—in his arms.

Claire returned the kiss, needing it as badly as Garrett, knowing now that he did love her. He hadn't validated it with words, but his actions had proven the authenticity of his feelings. He'd come for her, protected her during the gunfight, risking his own life. The words would come later, when they had time to themselves.

Sweeping her up in his arms, Garrett marched toward

the horses. He didn't look at Claire, but over his shoulder as he shouted out more orders. "Hiram, get a message to Dr. Baldwin. Tell him to meet me at the house on Bartlett Street. Then send for the authorities. What you can't tell them, I'll explain later."

"No," Claire said, suddenly remembering Evelyn Holmes. So much had happened in just a short time, her mind was still catching up.

"No, what?" Garrett asked, lifting her into the saddle.

The loose trousers made it easy for Claire to sit the horse. She steadied herself with the saddle horn while Garrett got on behind her. He reached forward to gather the reins and Claire snuggled back against him, feeling completely safe.

"We can't leave," Claire said. She pointed toward the bay. "Evelyn's on that ship."

"Evelyn?"

"Evelyn Holmes," Claire told him. "Your old mistress," she added, no longer afraid of the future. "Christopher kidnapped her, too. He was . . . he was going to steal your money, then sell us to a man in Shanghai."

The stream of curses that followed her revelation burned Claire's ears. She'd never heard such language before, not from Garrett, or her brother, who joined in the chorus.

Claire decided to wait before telling Garrett that Christopher Landauer and Chen Loo had been half brothers.

"Hiram." Garrett's thunderous shout brought a slender man running at top speed. The investigator stepped around the dead body of the man who had gotten on the trolley behind Claire.

She realized she didn't know the man's name, then decided it didn't matter. Whoever he was, he was already paying for his sins. The devil wasn't negligent in collecting his followers.

Garrett pointed toward the ship Claire had indicated. "Get the harbormaster. Make sure that ship doesn't leave San Francisco Bay." His hand moved, sweeping the area. "Then get one of Chen Loo's men to tell you where he was hiding Claire. Search the house. God only knows what you'll find."

The slender man, who surprised Claire by looking more like a bank clerk than a private investigator, assured Garrett that he would take care of everything.

By the time they reached the small house on Bartlett Street the sun was creeping over the rooftops of the city. The cottage was painted a pristine white with dark blue shutters. A small flower garden bordered the narrow porch.

Donald rode by their side, followed by three armed men. Hiram had retrieved the saddlebags and Claire looked at them, draped across her brother's lap.

She leaned her head back, resting it against Garrett's shoulder. "Fifty thousand dollars is a lot of money. I'm flattered that you think I'm worth it."

Claire couldn't see Garrett's smile, but she could feel it. His body relaxed and he chuckled softly. "The saddlebags are filled with old newspapers," he told her, then pulled her back against him when she would have moved away.

"I'll be damned," Donald said, reaching out with his good hand to unbuckle one of the leather pouches.

Her brother tossed back the leather flap and Claire saw newspaper rolled into tight little bundles and tied with string.

"Chen Loo underestimated you," Donald said proudly. "Just as well. The devil doesn't need the money and that's where that fat Chinaman is going. Straight to hell."

"Amen," Garrett mumbled, then leaned down. His

lips pressed against Claire's ear. "You're worth your weight in gold, angel."

Claire smiled, then frowned as Garrett slipped from the saddle and reached for her. She'd been on the verge of asking him why he needed a second house when he'd distracted her by telling her that the saddlebags carried a worthless cargo. As he put his hands around her waist, Claire looked at the house again. This is where Garrett had housed Evelyn Holmes, and the other women who had been his mistresses, but Claire wasn't insulted by his decision to bring her and Donald here. He couldn't take them to Nob Hill without confronting his grandmother.

"Grams?" Claire said, looking at Garrett.

"She's fine," he told her, cradling her in his arms as he made his way onto the front porch. "She thinks you're with Donald."

Claire gave him a questioning look.

"I'll explain everything as soon as Dr. Baldwin's stitched up Donald's arm and examined you. Are you sure you weren't hurt?"

"I'm fine," Claire lied. She was exhausted. All she wanted was a hot bath and ten hours of sleep. After that, she wanted Garrett.

Garrett ignored her. He shifted her weight, dug into his pocket, and brought out a key. Once the door was unlocked, he pushed it open.

Donald followed them inside. He said something about finding a whiskey bottle while Garrett walked through the dim interior of the house. Claire could see a small parlor with a piano. Did Garrett play? There was so much she didn't know about this man, although she'd learned a great deal in the last few days. He was a tender, caring lover. He was strong. Too strong to be intimidated by a man like Chen Loo. Christopher should have known that, but he hadn't. Claire wondered why, then realized that Garrett was a private person, even to his friends.

Christopher had allowed the green curtain of jealousy to cloud his view.

Garrett carried Claire down the hall and into a small bedroom. She looked around. At least the man had had the good sense not to put her in the room he'd shared with his mistress. The bed was narrow with a brass headboard and foot railing and a light blue bedspread with fringe that touched the floor. White lace curtains covered the windows.

Garrett put her down on the bed. Holding her gaze with his own, his hands moved over her body, checking for any injuries she might not have told him about. Claire allowed the tender examination, reveling in the warm feel of his hands against the cool silk that covered her skin. It didn't take Garrett long to realize that she was naked beneath the Chinese clothing.

His face took on a concerned look and Claire smiled. "An old Chinese woman helped me bathe and change clothes," she told him. "I wasn't hurt."

"Thank God," Garrett mumbled, sitting down beside her.

Claire wanted to say so much to him, but seeing the fatigue and stress of the last hours etched on his face, she decided the words could wait.

She raised up on her elbows and kissed him. He groaned like a man in pain and pushed her back against the pillows. His mouth explored hers, his tongue dipping and tasting while his hands continued their investigation, this time to reassure himself that Claire enjoyed his touch. When his hands cupped her breasts, she arched her back and moaned softly, letting him know she liked what he was doing.

Garrett wanted to strip the silk trousers and tunic away and study every inch of her lovely body, but he didn't dare. Donald was waiting in the other room, and Dr. Baldwin would be there soon. The next time he had Claire naked, Garrett intended to keep her that way for a very long time.

Claire felt her body warming as her senses came to life. Garrett's kiss ignited a fire in her heart and she wrapped her arms around his neck. Her mouth was as greedy as his and soon they both knew that the kiss had to end or they'd be making love with her brother in the house.

"Stay put," he said, reluctant to release her. "I'll get Donald settled. Dr. Baldwin will be here soon. He doesn't live too far away."

Claire leaned back against the feather pillows and yawned. "I won't move an inch."

Garrett laughed then left the room. The tension of the last twenty-fours hours was gone, but Claire knew the betrayal he'd suffered would surface soon enough, and when it did, he was going to need her.

Claire's privacy didn't last long. A short time later, Dr. Baldwin knocked on the front door, accompanied by Hiram Wilson. Claire could hear them talking. Evelyn had been rescued from the freighter. Except for some bruises, she was fine, and Hiram had taken her to the hotel. He was on his way to the police station to give the authorities a thorough explanation of the waterfront events that had concluded with the death of Chen Loo, Christopher Landauer, and several other men. Evelyn would be questioned later, along with Claire, but not until Dr. Baldwin had decided that the ladies were up to the ordeal of repeating what had happened to them.

Garrett didn't want Claire questioned at all. "She's been through enough. Tell the police whatever they need to know, but make sure Claire's name isn't mentioned in the papers. Mine either, if you can keep it out.

Grams is going to have a hard enough time accepting Christopher's death without knowing the reason why."

Dr. Baldwin seconded Garrett's motion, then remarked, "Keeping the news of a waterfront gunfight out of the papers isn't going to be easy. You're going to have to tell Theodora something. She's not a fool."

"I'll handle it when the time comes," Garrett said.

Claire could hear the dread in his voice. She cursed her ankle. She wanted to be by Garrett's side, comforting him, aiding him while he wrestled with what had happened, not just to her, but to himself. Men were dead. She and Evelyn had come close to being smuggled out of the city and sold into slavery. Donald had been shot. Claire knew Garrett was carrying the weight of those events on his shoulders.

Claire lay in the bed, feeling content, but helpless. When Dr. Baldwin came into the room, she asked him about Donald's wound.

"Your brother is fine," the physician assured her. "The bullet grazed his arm. He'll have a scar, but no permanent damage." He opened his medical bag for the second time that morning. "Now, let's have a look at you."

Garrett stood near the bed, close enough to watch Dr. Baldwin without getting in his way. He'd shed his jacket and his shirt was unbuttoned halfway down his chest. Claire tried not to notice, but she couldn't help stealing a glance in his direction while Dr. Baldwin examined her ankle. He wrapped it, then told her not to move out of the bed for at least three days.

"I'll be back later to change Donald's bandage," he said to Garrett. "Until then, make sure this lady gets lots of rest."

"I will," Garrett said. He walked Dr. Baldwin to the door.

When he came back into the room, he was carrying

a glass. "I know you don't like whiskey, but you're going to drink this. Then you're going to go to sleep."

"Yes, sir," Claire said. She gave him a mock salute, then reached for the glass. The whiskey tasted awful, but she drank it all. When she was done, she handed the glass back to Garrett. "Send for Mae Ling. She can take care of Donald."

Garrett smiled. "I already did." He shrugged his shoulders. "Someone has to cook and make sure you don't go hobbling around and hurt yourself again. Grams thinks you're staying with your brother. He came back to the city, disliked me on sight, and demanded that you give him an equal portion of your time."

"Grams believed that flimsy story?"

"Enough of it," Garrett told her. "When I realized you were gone . . ."

Claire placed a finger against his mouth. "We can talk later. After we've both had some rest."

He kissed her cheek, then tucked her under the covers. "Sleep well. I have to go to the police station, then I have to convince Grams that I haven't chased you away. She made me promise to have you and Donald at the dinner table, come Sunday."

"We'll be there," Claire said.

Garrett kissed her again. "I've got men guarding the house. Don't worry."

"I'm not worried," Claire told him. "Don't stay away too long."

"I won't," Garrett promised.

Chapter Twenty

Garrett was gone longer than he liked. After returning home to change clothes and reassure Grams that he and Claire weren't arguing and that she'd be there for dinner on Sunday, he went to the police station. Once there, he and Hiram answered a barrage of questions. The police chief sent a deputy to the hotel to interview Evelyn Holmes. Garrett intended to call on her himself and offer her passage back to England. It was the least he could do.

The authorities insisted that they would have to speak with Miss Aldrich as well, and despite Garrett's loud protest, he was forced to give in. The case of Claire's kidnapping couldn't be put to rest until the police had spoken with her and her brother. The railroad would have to be contacted to confirm Donald's part in the events, and they would do their best to keep Claire's name out of the papers. With Chen Loo and Christopher both dead, a trial wouldn't be necessary, but there were a lot of unanswered questions and the case would remain open until a complete explanation could be recorded.

Garrett found three armed men guarding the house on Bartlett Street when he arrived. He spoke to each of them briefly. Mae Ling was inside, taking care of Donald and Claire.

Garrett found Claire's brother in the parlor. He sat sipping a neat whiskey with Mae Ling perched by his side. Donald's good arm was wrapped about the young woman's shoulder. They were talking in hushed whispers and Garrett realized he'd interrupted a private moment.

"How's Claire?" he asked, as Mae Ling stood up to greet him.

"She is sleeping," Mae Ling said.

Garrett wanted to wake her, but he waited. Mae Ling left the room after saying something to Donald in Chinese.

"She's going to start dinner," Claire's brother explained while Garrett helped himself to a drink. "Thanks for letting us stay here. Chinatown isn't my idea of home sweet home after this morning."

"You're welcome to the house for as long as you want it," Garrett replied, knowing he was finished with mistresses. He'd told Grams to send out the wedding invitations. "The police will be here in a few hours. They want to talk to you and Claire."

"Can't blame them," Donald said. "Chen Loo and Christopher Landauer. That's a puzzling combination. How did you know that Christopher was on the sour end of the deal?"

"I didn't," Garrett said, slumping into a chair. He was tired to the bone. He sipped his whiskey before saying anything else. "Something wasn't right, but I couldn't put my finger on it until I saw Claire. She didn't look relieved to see me, or you. She looked scared to death and she was staring at Christopher as if he'd grown horns and a tail. When he wouldn't take the gag out of her mouth, I knew he didn't want her to say anything. Then he reached for the gun."

The two men discussed the events, projecting possible explanations for Christopher's partnership with the Chinaman. When Mae Ling appeared with Claire's dinner tray, Garrett and Donald followed her down the hall.

Claire was awake.

Mae Ling put the tray next to the bed.

"Thank you," Claire said, smiling at the young woman. It was apparent that there was real affection between Mae Ling and Donald, and Claire decided to have a long talk with her brother about the girl's status as a *housekeeper*.

"I hope you do not judge my people by the actions of a few men," Mae Ling said. "Chen Loo had an evil heart. He will not be missed in Chinatown."

"And we won't be missed if we eat in the kitchen," Donald said, taking Mae Ling's hand and leading her from the room. He winked at Garrett. "Make sure my sister cleans her plate."

Claire gave her brother a disgruntled look but it faded into a smile. "He likes you," she told Garrett as he pulled a chair up and sat next to the bed.

"What about his sister?" he teased.

Claire gave him a pensive look, as if she was trying to make up her mind. "No more acting?"

"No more acting," Garrett said.

"His sister thinks you're stubborn, but wonderful. Handsome, but arrogant. Wealthy, but acceptable."

Garrett laughed. It was a genuine laugh. One that came from his heart. "Does that mean you'll marry me?"

"Maybe," Claire teased him. She'd woken up feeling

renewed. She was alive, Garrett and Donald were alive. Evelyn Holmes has been traumatized by her experience, but she was alive and Claire hoped she was strong enough to put her experiences behind her and start a new life.

"Grams is mailing the invitations," Garrett said, suppressing the need to take Claire in his arms until things had been settled between them. "The wedding is the tenth of August. I expect to see you at the church, dressed in white and walking down the aisle."

"Does that mean you like me, too?" She held her breath. She wanted Garrett to do more than like her. If the man didn't hurry up and get the words said, she was going to say them for him. Patience had never been one of her virtues.

"It means I love you." He got up from the chair and sat down on the bed. His weight rolled her against his side as his arms wrapped around her. "I love you so much it almost killed me when I found out that Chen Loo had kidnapped you. I love you so much, it will kill me if you don't agree to be Mrs. Garrett Monroe."

Claire couldn't see him for the tears. She'd dreamed of hearing him say the words, but the reality of it was so much sweeter than she had imagined. He placed short, sweet kisses on her hairline, her eyelids, and finally her mouth. Claire kissed him back, her tongue meeting his in a soft duel of sensual play that made her body tremble and her hands fist in the fabric of his jacket. Garrett shivered in return and made a throaty, male sound as he pushed Claire back against the feather pillows. He jerked down the coverlet, thankful to find a cotton gown instead of Chinese silk. But he was hungry for the woman underneath the cotton. His hands found the laces at the neckline and untied them. A second later, Claire moaned softly and lifted herself against his hands as they covered her breasts.

"I love you, too," Claire breathed out the words as Garrett's mouth lifted away from her lips and moved to nibble at her throat.

Garrett tried to speak, but all that came out was a deep, male purr of satisfaction as his mouth moved to worship more and more of Claire's body.

The sound of someone knocking on the front door brought them apart. Garrett frowned as he watched Claire close her gown and tie the ribbon lacings. He didn't want to share her with questioning police officials. He didn't want to share her with anyone.

"That's Carl Jennings," Garrett said as Donald answered the door. "He's the chief of the city's police department. He insisted on speaking with you and your brother. I tried to talk him out of it, but what happened is too complicated for the police to take just my word and be satisfied."

"I'll talk to him," Claire said, realizing that Garrett was trying to protect her again. She loved him for it, but there were certain things only she could explain.

"Are you sure you're up to it?"

"They have to know," Claire said, reaching for the robe Mae Ling had left with her.

She wasn't sure who the gown and robe had belonged to originally. Mae Ling had walked into the room with the garments draped over her arm and Claire had been too anxious to get out of the silk trousers and tunic to ask questions. Garrett belonged to her now. She didn't like the thought of other women in his life, but they were in the past, she was his present and his future.

Garrett helped her into the robe, then picked her up and walked toward the front of the house. Donald and Mae Ling were in the parlor, along with two men. The older man had a bulbous nose and white whiskers that grew down from his temples and onto his jaws. He was tall, but thick around the middle. He moved briskly for a man of his size and came to his feet the moment Garrett appeared in the doorway. The second man, younger and much thinner, wore spectacles that made his blue eyes seem larger than they actually were. He was wearing a smooth chocolate brown suit and a white starched shirt.

"Claire, this is Carl Jennings, the head of San Francisco's police department. The other gentleman is Stephen Waugh. Mr. Waugh is a detective."

Claire greeted the two men with a shy smile.

"I know this is difficult, considering what you've been through, Miss Aldrich, but it's also necessary. I wouldn't have insisted, otherwise," Mr. Jennings said once Garrett had put her down on the settee. "I need to know exactly what happened." He turned to look at her brother. "And I need to know about your position with the railroad as well, Mr. Aldrich. No one in the police department was notified that the Union Pacific was conducting an investigation of Chen Loo and his opium operations."

"We couldn't take the risk," Donald told him. "Chen Loo had a lot of contacts in the city. Some could be in your department." He held up his hand when the law officer started to protest. "I know you don't like hearing this, but it's the truth. The only way we could be sure that Chen Loo didn't know I was working for Union Pacific was to make sure that no one knew."

"What did you find out?" Jennings asked, silently relenting to the fact that Chen Loo's money might have bribed some of his men.

Claire listened, along with Garrett and Mr. Waugh, while her brother explained what he'd been doing for the last year. He'd been close to proving that Chen Loo was bribing several railroad inspectors to look the other way when opium shipments were mixed with the normal luggage that moved with the train from city to city.

Claire's unexpected appearance had triggered the kidnapping, once Chen Loo discovered that she was engaged to marry Garrett.

Claire disagreed, but she didn't say so until the police chief was done questioning her brother. When Mr. Jennings began to quiz her, Claire squeezed Garrett's hand and told her version of the story.

She maintained the pretense that she'd met Garrett on the train after leaving St. Louis and that they had fallen in love. When she arrived in the city, her brother was missing and Garrett hired Hiram Wilson to make some inquires. Claire couldn't rationalize telling the police the personal details of her relationship with Garrett. It wasn't important now. They were in love and they were going to be married. She told Mr. Jennings that she'd gone to Chinatown to see her brother again, because she was concerned about him. When she got to the part about the nameless man pulling her into the alley and placing a rag soaked in chloroform over her mouth, Garrett shot off the settee and started cursing.

"The man's name was Crane. Walter Crane," the younger policeman told her. "We're still not sure about his connection to Chen Loo."

"That's because he didn't work for Chen Loo," Claire said, gripping Garrett's hand once again. "Mr. Crane worked for Christopher Landauer, Chen Loo's half brother."

Everyone started talking, asking questions, and cursing all at once. Claire waited until Garrett had calmed down enough to hear the rest of her story. Once the room was quiet again, she looked at the police officers.

"Chen Loo didn't kidnap me, Mr. Jennings. Christopher Landauer did. I can't begin to explain everything to you, but I can tell you that Christopher was the one who introduced Chen Loo to me as his half brother.

He also told me that he planned to . . ." Claire stopped
and forced a deep breath into her lungs. "He planned
to smuggle me out of the city and sell me to a man in
China. He had similar plans for Miss Holmes. The room
where we were kept had bars on the windows. I don't
think it was the first time Christopher or Chen Loo had
done such a thing. God have mercy on the women who
weren't saved in time."

She turned to look at Garrett. His eyes were dark with
anger and she could feel the tension in his body when
she reached for his hand. "Christopher was jealous of
Garrett. Insanely jealous. He laughed about stealing the
ransom money, then killing Garrett and my brother.
It's ironic that Donald was investigating Chen Loo, but
he isn't the reason I was kidnapped."

"Half brothers," Carl Jennings mused, shaking his
head. "Who would have thought."

"No one," Garrett said sadly. He looked at Claire.
"All those years and I never knew the man at all."

"He didn't want you to know him," Claire replied.
"He told me fooling people was easy. All you had to do
was be what they expected you to be."

The other people in the room accepted Claire's statement with mild reflection, but Garrett knew they had
a deeper meaning. He'd hired her to do the same
thing—to be what people expected her to be.

After a few more questions, the police officers left.
Apparently Evelyn Holmes had given them a similar
explanation about Christopher's motive. Garrett carried
Claire back to bed and tucked her in.

"I'm sorry," he said, tenderly brushing her hair away
from her face.

"It's all right," she told him. "I shouldn't have gone
back to Chinatown. My stubbornness and pride is more
to blame than you are." She reached up and ran her
fingertips over his mouth. "I love you. No more pre-

tense, no more lies, not for you and not for Grams. I love you both."

Garrett pulled her close and held her. He didn't know what to say because he couldn't find the words to express what he was feeling. Love, anger, and a dozen emotions in between had his throat closed and his eyes damp.

Claire understood and held him. "You can't make sense out of what happened," she told him. "And you can't blame yourself for the jealousy that Christopher let fester into a disease. Evelyn said she thought he was mad, and in a way, I agree with her."

At the mention of the other woman's name, Garrett remembered what Claire had said that morning when she'd pointed at the ship in the harbor.

"You know who Evelyn is?" he asked, pulling away and looking down at her.

"I know who Evelyn *was*," Claire corrected him. "You won't be needing a mistress from now on, Mr. Monroe. You'll have a wife and she plans on keeping you busy at home."

Garrett laughed softly. "I love you."

"It's about time," Claire told him. "Now kiss me good-bye and go see your grandmother. She's going to be lonely without me there to keep her company."

Garrett was glad to kiss her, but reluctant to leave.

By the end of the week, Claire was back in the mansion atop Nob Hill. Her luggage had been retrieved from the Chinatown house, thanks to Hiram Wilson, and she was wearing the cameo Garrett had given her. Grams greeted her with a warm smile and a big hug, then insisted that Garrett join them in the parlor. The news of Christopher's death had hit the newspapers and every tongue in San Francisco was wagging. True to his word, Carl Jennings had kept Claire's and Garrett's names out of the headlines. He'd also muddled enough of the facts when they were released to the newspaper to make Donald Aldrich sound like a hero.

According to the *California Star*, Donald Aldrich, working undercover for the Union Pacific and Central Pacific Railroads, confronted Chen Loo in Chinatown. A fight ensued and the China drug lord was shot. Unfortunately, a prominent San Francisco resident, Christopher Landauer, was also killed. Mr. Landauer's presence had been one of coincidence and the newspaper joined the citizens of San Francisco in mourning his death.

Claire was glad the article spared Belinda Belton the public humiliation she would have suffered if the truth of Christopher's real activities had been revealed. It also spared Grams from discovering the truth. It would take Garrett a lot longer to get over the betrayal of the man he'd thought his best friend, but Claire knew time would eventually heal the wound.

The façade he insisted on maintaining for his grandmother's sake kept him from sharing his real feelings and Claire knew that Christopher's funeral had been the most difficult. Garrett had been forced to sit in the church, originally founded by Christopher's father, and listen to the current minister deliver an eulogy that honored a dishonorable man.

"So much has happened," Grams said, holding Claire's hand as if she thought the young woman might sprout wings and fly away. "Christopher dead. Your brother. My goodness, I never would have suspected that he was an investigator for the railroad. He didn't look the sort at all."

"Looks can be deceiving," Claire said. "I'm sorry about Christopher," she added. "I know you were very fond of him."

"Yes, I was," Grams admitted. "Belinda is going back East to visit relatives. My heart breaks for the poor girl, but I'm sure she'll find a nice young man and marry soon.''

"I hope she does," Claire said with true conviction. "Donald wanted me to apologize for not being able to join us for dinner. The railroad wanted a personal report. He'll be back from Denver in time for the wedding, of course.''

The conversation turned to other things and by the end of the day Claire felt as if she'd returned home after a long and eventful journey. Grams retired for the evening and she sat in the library, reading, while Garrett answered the correspondence that had accumulated over the last week.

Claire put down her book and watched him as he worked, preferring the sight of the man she loved to the fictional hero in the novel. She didn't realize that she'd whispered his name aloud until Garrett looked up from his desk. He smiled at her and she could see the love in his eyes. Suddenly something deep and primal darkened his gaze and he stood up. Claire held her breath as he crossed the room, stopping to close the door on his way to the chaise longue where she was reclining.

The novel was taken out of her hands and placed on the floor. Garrett knelt beside her and his mouth closed over hers. The kiss matched the need in his eyes, fierce and hungry and passionate. Claire matched his need, returning the kiss, returning the love.

Her hand moved from his shoulder to his chest. She could feel the rhythm of his heartbeat. Bold, now that she knew Garrett loved her, she began to unbutton his shirt. He kissed her again, his lips barely touching, his tongue teasing the corner of her mouth.

"I love you," he whispered against her parted lips.

"Show me," Claire challenged him. "It's been so long."

"Too long," Garrett agreed. "Too damn long. I'm starving for you, sweetheart. I'm not sure I can be gentle."

"Just love me," Claire said as she undid another button.

Garrett wanted to do more than make love to Claire. He wanted to consume her, mind, body, and spirit, to lose himself in her and in losing himself to find the peace he hadn't known since their last night together. His breathing grew rough as her hand shyly caressed his exposed chest. Nothing in the world could compare to the feel of her touch, he realized. The heat of her caress went deeper than his skin. He could feel it in his heart.

After a long passionate kiss, Garrett's hand found the buttons on Claire's dress. He undid them, stroking her skin as more and more of her was revealed. His mouth moved to her ear. He whispered words that made the fire burn even hotter.

Still kneeling at her side, Garrett let Claire set the pace. He encouraged her with soft, sensual words and kisses that made her body go limp then rigid with desire. His mouth traced her cheekbones, her nose, the arch of her brows, while his hands explored the satiny texture of her bared breasts and the hard crowns that pouted for his mouth.

He paused to take off his shirt and toss it aside. Claire watched him, her eyes soft with once-imagined dreams that were now a reality. Garrett saw the female triumph in her gaze and it made him smile. She knew he belonged to her and he gloried in the knowledge as much as she did. His breathing increased as he looked down at her lying on the chaise longue, her bodice around her waist, her breasts flushed from the heat of his hands.

"Take down your hair," he breathed the command.

Claire reached for the pearl-studded hairpins. She pulled them out, one by one, slowly letting her hair fall to her shoulders. Garrett watched her with a savage intensity that would have shocked her a few months ago, but Claire wasn't shocked now. She knew that what she felt for this man was love, pure and simple and stronger than anything else on earth. There was no shame in what they shared, no regret, no doubts.

There was only the love between them, the need to hold each other, to be a part of each other, to share their feelings in the magical, elemental joining of their bodies.

Garrett reached for Claire's dress. She smiled as he fumbled with the last of the buttons, cursing their stubbornness. She raised her hips, and the dress was pulled away, followed by petticoats, shoes, and stockings. When she was naked, he looked at her. His eyes lingered for the longest time and she became impatient to touch him again.

"I want to see you dressed in moonlight," he said, walking to the wall switch that controlled the gas-fueled chandelier. The fixture dimmed slowly, until there was nothing but the natural light of a full moon drifting through the windows. "You're beautiful," he whispered reverently. "So damn beautiful, and I almost lost you."

"Almost doesn't matter," Claire told him, raising her arms to let him know she'd have him come back to her. "Don't think about the past. Think about right now, this minute."

Garrett shook his head. "I need to tell you," he said. "I couldn't before. My pride. Not knowing the right words." He hesitated. "That morning at the docks. When I saw your face . . . it made me hate myself for not telling you. You left me because you were angry. It was my fault."

Claire's eyes welled with tears. "It wasn't your fault,"

she said softly, but insistently. "I loved you and I was afraid that you could never love me back. I felt like you'd stolen my heart." She smiled. "You had, and I was foolish enough to think I could get it back if I left."

He kissed her so gently the tears rolled down her face. "I didn't want to give it back. Having you give yourself to me, your body, your heart . . . your love. It humbled me and it scared me, all at the same time." He took a shaky breath. "When I think about what could have happened to you. About Christopher, I . . ."

Claire silenced him with a kiss. "When I think of how much love we have to give each other, of the years ahead of us and the children and the laughter, it makes me glad I ran out of money and walked into the hotel. I'm not a very good actress, Mr. Monroe. I loved you from the start."

"It took me a while longer," he confessed.

He wrapped his arms around her and breathed in the scent of her skin. Perfumed soap and moonlight and woman. His hands closed over her breasts and he moaned a deep, male sound of pleasure into her mouth. Claire fisted her hands in his dark hair, loving the feel of his bare chest against her, loving the sound of his pleasure and the heat of his hands as they caressed her belly, her hips, her legs.

He moved to the end of the chaise longue, looking up at her with questioning eyes as he gently parted her legs. He kissed her ankle, completely healed now, and then continued kissing her, moving up the inside of her calves, stopping to nibble and smiling when she squirmed anxiously underneath him. "I'm going to love you all night," he told her.

His warm hands rubbed circles on the inside of her thighs and Claire closed her eyes against the pleasure. She gripped the edge of the chaise longue, holding on to the furniture because the world was spinning around her. Garrett's mouth was damp and hot against her skin. She could feel the abrasive stubble of his beard, not scratchy, but teasing. When his hand reached the center of her wanting, Claire moaned. Her hands moved to his head, cradling him against her body, wanting more and more of the delicious sensations that were spiraling through her.

While Garrett taunted and teased her with one hand, his other hand moved to the buttons on his trousers. He flicked opened the buttons then pushed the clothing down his hips.

He never stopped touching Claire as he finished undressing. One hand loving her, the other freeing himself to love her more completely. Then he covered her. His hands molding her breasts to fit his mouth while his hips pushed against her, letting her feel the power of his desire, the need that wouldn't be sated no matter how many times he had her.

Claire moaned his name in a whisper of wonderment and slid her arms around his neck. His hands slid under her, arching her body, as his mouth moved over her breasts, touching but never touching enough, until Claire was begging him to stop the torment. When he finally took the tip of one breast into his mouth and began to suckle, Claire dug her fingernails into his shoulders. Garrett groaned at the sensual demand, knowing he could love Claire as fiercely or as gently as he wanted and she'd find pleasure in it. His tongue teased her nipples, licking at them before he suckled her harder.

The moonlight was forgotten as Garrett let himself fall into pure, white fire. Desire burned around him, inside him, and he let the flames consume him. He moved up and down her body, wanting to taste every inch of her, needing to possess her as surely as she possessed him, and obsessed him, every thought, every moment of every day.

He kissed the center of her desire and Claire thought she would die. She cried out in her passion and her hands twisted at the edge of the chaise longue a second time. With each stroke of Garrett's tongue, each caress of his lips, she went higher and higher, until she couldn't climb anymore. Then she fell like a shooting star.

"There's more," Garrett said as he moved to cover her. "More pleasure than you can take. Enough pleasure to make you lose your mind for a brief moment and not care about the insanity. Do you want that kind of pleasure, Claire?"

"Yes," she confessed. Her legs were shaking and her body was on fire. Sweet, hot fire that burned with pleasure, not pain. But it wasn't enough. She wanted more. She wanted Garrett to feel what she was feeling. To burn with her.

His skin was damp, his muscles rigid with control, as he repositioned her. Claire let him control her, sliding onto his lap as he sat up on the longue. He placed her legs on either side of his hips. She sat astride his lap. His hands cupped her bottom as he pulled her close. She could feel his arousal, pressing against her belly. He felt hard and hot and wonderful and she knew he wanted her as badly as she wanted him.

"I want to be inside you," Garrett breathed against her ear. "So deep inside you all you can feel is me." He fisted his hand in her hair and pulled her head back, gently but firmly, until she was looking at him. "I want to love you slow and easy, then hard and fast, then I want to start over again. Give yourself to me, sweetheart. Trust me to keep you safe this time."

"Always," she said.

Claire moved, raising up, then lowering herself, slowly

absorbing his body into hers. Garrett made a low, throaty sound as his eyes closed and his head fell back. Claire moved with him, caressing him with her body, letting him feel her need the way she was feeling his.

"Slow and easy," she said softly. At some deep, instinctive level, she knew she was in control. Garrett wanted her to love him, to make love to him. He was relinquishing control to her, proving that he could receive as well as take.

Claire moved and moved again, each time taking more and more of him, each time giving more and more in return. She kissed the damp skin of his throat and let her hands tease the flat male nipples hidden beneath the dark hair that covered his chest. She whispered words that she'd said only in her dreams, wild exotic words that made Garrett more hungry than he'd ever been in his life. Then when he couldn't take it any longer, when the desire threatened to steal his mind, he let the insanity have its way.

He began to move with her, to thrust hard and deep and strong, reaching for the moment when the world stopped. His mouth kissed her mouth, her throat, the soft, warm skin of her breasts. Claire reached with him, her head tossed back, her body straining for the same magical madness. When it came, she cried out his name and Garrett stole the sound, covering her mouth.

"We should put on our clothes and go upstairs," Claire said lazily.

It was two in the morning by the soft chime of the foyer clock. Garrett moved beside her, pleasantly exhausted from their lovemaking. "Not yet," he said, then kissed her again. The urgency he'd felt earlier had faded, but not the need—or the love. He pulled her head down and rested it on his chest. "You're a delight to love."

Claire blushed, although it shouldn't be possible after some of the things Garrett had taught her. She brushed her hair away from her face and placed a kiss against his bare chest, over his heart. "Do you think Grams heard us?"

"No," Garrett lied. "You were as quiet as a church mouse."

Claire poked him in the ribs. "She'll think I'm a wanton hussy."

Garrett captured her hand and raised it to his lips. "She'll think you love me."

"I do."

Epilogue

Claire repeated the same words on the tenth day of August, 1887. Standing in the small garden at the back of the Nob Hill mansion, wearing a white satin gown and a smile, she gave herself legally to the man who already owned her heart.

Donald, Mae Ling, Dr. Baldwin, and a few close friends watched while the bride and groom stared at each other with love in their eyes. Grams was smiling right along with them. And crying tears of pure joy.

The reception was small and the guests mingled around the garden while a trio of musicians played stringed instruments under the shelter of the portico. Claire had decided against a large wedding and having the reception at the Hotel Landauer. The memories were still too new to ignore and she didn't want her wedding day spoiled by thoughts of the past.

"You did it," Dr. Baldwin whispered, congratulating Grams as he handed her a glass of champagne punch.

"And you owe me one hundred dollars," Grams replied smugly. "I told you. I've always been his weak spot."

Garrett came up behind them. "You shouldn't be drinking," he said, reaching for the glass. He frowned at Dr. Baldwin. "I thought I could depend on you to take care of her while I'm gone. I can't have a good time on my honeymoon if I'm worried about Grams keeling over from too much alcohol."

"I don't need taking care of," Grams scoffed, pretending to be offended. She smiled as Claire joined them. "I'm going to drink champagne and dance until dawn."

Claire laughed at the disgruntled expression on her husband's face. When Dr. Baldwin joined in his grandmother's laughter, his look went from mildly frustrated to confused.

"Go ahead, tell him," Grams prompted, smiling all the while.

"There's nothing wrong with your grandmother's heart," Dr. Baldwin said. "At least nothing that one or two doses of my tonic didn't cure the first time she complained about not feeling well."

"She isn't sick?" Garrett looked from the doctor to his grandmother and then back to the trusted physician. "But you said . . ."

"I lied," Chester Baldwin admitted. "Actually, Grams dared me to lie. She bet me a hundred dollars that if you thought she was on her deathbed and getting married would save her, you'd have a wife before Christmas rolled around again. You know me, Garrett, I've always been a gambling man."

Claire laughed until tears streamed down her face and dripped on the white lace of her wedding dress. She slumped against Garrett's side, using him for support while she dabbed at the tears.

"You fraud," Garrett charged his grandmother. "You mean I married this beautiful, irritating, worrisome woman because you tricked me?"

"No," Claire answered for her. She faced him, draped her arms around his neck, and smiled her best smile. "You married me because you love me. Deny it, if you can."

"I can't," Garrett said. Pulling her close, he kissed her, then whispered. "Grams always was one step ahead of me. Remind me never to play poker with her. I'll lose the bank and then we'll be out in the cold."

"I'll keep you warm," Claire promised.

Discover the Magic of Romance With

Kat Martin

__The Secret
  0-8217-6798-4   **$6.99US/$8.99CAN**

Kat Rollins moved to Montana looking to change her life, not find another man like Chance McLain, with a sexy smile and empty heart. Chance can't ignore the desire he feels for her—or the suspicion that somebody wants her to leave Lost Peak . . .

__Dream
  0-8217-6568-X   **$6.99US/$8.99CAN**

Genny Austin is convinced that her nightmares are visions of another life she lived long ago. Jack Brennan is having nightmares, too, but his are real. In the shadows of dreams lurks a terrible truth, and only by unlocking the past will Genny be free to love at last . . .

__Silent Rose
  0-8217-6281-8   **$6.99US/$8.50CAN**

When best-selling author Devon James checks into a bed-and-breakfast in Connecticut, she only hopes to put the spark back into her relationship with her fiancé. But what she experiences at the Stafford Inn changes her life forever . . .

Call toll free **1-888-345-BOOK** to order by phone or use this coupon to order by mail.

Name_____

Address_____

City _____ State_____ Zip_____

Please send me the books I have checked above.

I am enclosing	$_____
Plus postage and handling*	$_____
Sales tax (in New York and Tennessee only)	$_____
Total amount enclosed	$_____

*Add $2.50 for the first book and $.50 for each additional book.

Send check or money order (no cash or CODs) to: **Kensington Publishing Corp., Dept. C.O., 850 Third Avenue, New York, NY 10022**

Prices and numbers subject to change without notice. All orders subject to availability. Visit our website at **www.kensingtonbooks.com.**

The Queen of
Romance

Cassie Edwards